江西省高等学校重点学科建设项目资助课题
江西省中国语言文学省级重点学科招标课题

The Translation and Study of Chinese Literature in the English-Speaking World

主编 ◎ 曹顺庆

英语世界中国文学的译介与研究丛书

英语世界的《水浒传》研究

谢春平 ◎ 著

中国社会科学出版社

图书在版编目(CIP)数据

英语世界的《水浒传》研究 / 谢春平著. —北京：中国社会科学出版社, 2018.3

（英语世界中国文学的译介与研究丛书）

ISBN 978-7-5161-7904-8

Ⅰ.①英… Ⅱ.①谢… Ⅲ.①《水浒》–英语–翻译–研究 Ⅳ.①H315.9

中国版本图书馆 CIP 数据核字（2016）第 063103 号

出 版 人	赵剑英
责任编辑	任　明
责任校对	李　莉
责任印制	李寡寡

出　　版	中国社会科学出版社
社　　址	北京鼓楼西大街甲 158 号
邮　　编	100720
网　　址	http://www.csspw.cn
发 行 部	010-84083685
门 市 部	010-84029450
经　　销	新华书店及其他书店

印刷装订	北京君升印刷有限公司
版　　次	2018 年 3 月第 1 版
印　　次	2018 年 3 月第 1 次印刷

开　　本	710×1000　1/16
印　　张	22
插　　页	2
字　　数	361 千字
定　　价	95.00 元

凡购买中国社会科学出版社图书，如有质量问题请与本社营销中心联系调换
电话：010-84083683
版权所有　侵权必究

英语世界中国文学的译介与研究丛书　总序

本丛书是我主持的教育部重大招标项目"英语世界中国文学的译介与研究"（12JZD016）的成果。英语是目前世界上使用范围最为广泛的语言，中国文学在英语世界的译介与研究既是中国文学外传的重要代表，也是中国文化在异域被接受的典范。因此，深入系统地研究中国文学在英语世界的译介与研究，既具有重要的学术价值也具有重大的现实意义。

中国正在走向世界，从学术价值层面来看，研究英语世界的中国文学译介与研究，首先，有利于拓展中国文学的研究领域，创新研究方法。考察中国文学在异域的传播，把中国文学研究的范围扩大至英语世界，要求我们研究中国文学不能局限于汉语及中华文化圈内，而应该将英语世界对中国文学的译介与研究也纳入研究范围。同时还需要我们尊重文化差异，在以丰厚的本土资源为依托的前提下充分吸收异质文明的研究成果并与之展开平等对话，跨文明语境下的中国文学研究显然是对汉语圈内的中国文学研究在视野与方法层面的突破。其次，对推进比较文学与世界文学研究具有重要的学术意义。通过对英语世界中国文学的译介与研究情况的考察，不但有助于我们深入认识中外文学关系的实证性与变异性，了解中国文学在英语世界的接受情况及中国文学对英语世界文学与文化的影响，还为我们思考世界文学存在的可能性及如何建立层次更高、辐射范围更广、包容性更强的世界诗学提供参考。

从现实意义层面来看，首先，开展英语世界中国文学研究可为当下中国文学与文化建设的发展方向提供借鉴。通过研究中国文学对"他者"的影响，把握中国文学与文化的国际影响力及世界意义，在文学创作和文化建设方面既重视本土价值也需要考虑世界性维度，可为我国的文学与文化发展提供重要启示。其次，还有助于提升中国文化软实力，推动中国文化"走出去"战略的实施。通过探讨英语世界中国文学的译介及研究，发现中国文学在英语世界的传播特点及接受规律，有利于促进中国文学更好地走向世界，提升我国的文化软实力，扩大中华文化对异质文明的影响，这对于我国正在大力实施的中国文化走出去战略无疑具有十分重大的意义。

正是在这样的认识引导下，我组织一批熟练掌握中英两种语言与文化的比较文学学者撰著了这套"英语世界中国文学的译介与研究"丛书，试图在充分占有一手文献资料的前提下，从总体上对英语世界中国文学的译介和研究进行爬梳，清晰呈现英语世界中国文学译介与研究的大致脉络、主要特征与基本规律，并在跨文明视野中探讨隐藏于其中的理论立场、思想来源、话语权力与意识形态。在研究策略上，采取史论结合、实证性与变异性结合、个案与通论结合的研究方式，在深入考察个案的同时，力图用翔实的资料与深入的剖析为学界提供一个系统而全面的中国文学英译与研究学术史。

当然，对英语世界中国文学的译介与研究进行再研究并非易事，首先，得克服资料收集与整理这一困难。英语世界中国文学的译介与研究资料繁多而零散，且时间跨度大、涉及面广，加之国内藏有量极为有限，必须通过各种渠道进行搜集，尤其要寻求国际学术资源的补充。同时，在研究过程中必须坚守基本的学术立场，即在跨文明对话中既要尊重差异，又要在一定程度上寻求共识。此外，如何有效地将总结的特点与规律运用到当下中国文学、文化建设与文化走出去战略中去，实现理论与实践之间的转换，这无疑是更大的挑战。这套丛书是一个尝试，展示出比较文学学者们知难而进的勇气和闯劲，也体现了他们不畏艰辛、敢于创新的精神。

本套丛书是国内学界较为系统深入探究中国文学在英语世界的传播与接受的实践，包括中国古代文化典籍、古代文学、现当代文学在英语世界的传播与接受。这些研究大多突破了中国文学研究和中外文学关系研究的原有模式，从跨文明角度审视中国文学，是对传统中国文学研究模式的突破，同时也将中国文学在西方的影响纳入了中外文学关系研究的范围，具有创新意义。此外，这些研究综合运用了比较文学、译介学等学科理论，尤其是我最近这些年提出的比较文学变异学理论[①]，将英语世界中国文学

---

① Shunqing Cao, *The Variation Theory of Comparative Literature*, Springer, Heidelberg, 2013.

的译介与研究中存在的文化误读、文化变异、他国化等问题予以呈现，并揭示了其中所存在的文化话语、意识形态等因素。其中一些优秀研究成果还充分体现了理论分析与现实关怀密切结合的特色，即在对英语世界中国文学的译介与研究进行理论分析的同时，还总结规律和经验为中国文化建设及中国文化走出去战略提供借鉴，较好地达成了我们从事本研究的初衷与目标。当然，由于时间仓促与水平所限，本丛书也难免存在不足之处，敬请各位读者批评指正。

曹顺庆

2015 年孟夏于成都

目　录

绪论 ……………………………………………………………… (1)
 第一节　研究目的、意义、范畴及方法 ……………………… (1)
  一、研究目的与意义 ………………………………………… (1)
  二、研究范畴与方法 ………………………………………… (4)
 第二节　英语世界《水浒传》译介、接受与研究述评 ……… (5)
  一、《水浒传》英译述介 …………………………………… (6)
  二、英语世界《水浒传》研究综述 ………………………… (11)
 第三节　国内《水浒传》研究现状 …………………………… (21)
  一、国内学界对英语世界《水浒传》研究的述介与研究 … (21)
  二、国内学界《水浒传》研究述评 ………………………… (24)

第一章　英语世界对《水浒传》的考证探源研究 ………………… (44)
 第一节　《水浒传》的作者问题 ……………………………… (44)
  一、《水浒传》是个人独创抑或多人合著 ………………… (44)
  二、《水浒传》的著作权归属 ……………………………… (47)
  三、小说作者的身份研究 …………………………………… (56)
 第二节　《水浒传》的素材渊源 ……………………………… (60)
 第三节　《水浒传》的成书过程与版本演变 ………………… (71)
  一、《水浒传》的成书过程 ………………………………… (71)
  二、《水浒传》版本研究 …………………………………… (77)

第二章　英语世界对《水浒传》的影响接受研究 ………………… (84)
 第一节　《水浒传》对中国古典文学创作的影响 …………… (85)

一、《水浒传》与明清小说创作 …………………………………… (85)
　　二、《水浒传》与明清水浒戏创作 ………………………………… (102)
　第二节　《水浒传》对中国现代戏剧、影视创作的影响 ………… (107)
　　一、《水浒传》与中国现代戏剧 …………………………………… (108)
　　二、《水浒传》与中国现代影视 …………………………………… (116)
　第三节　《水浒传》对中国社会及对域外文学创作的影响 ……… (123)
　　一、《水浒传》对中国社会的影响 ………………………………… (123)
　　二、《水浒传》的域外传播及对域外文学创作的影响 …………… (129)

第三章　英语世界对《水浒传》的人物形象塑造研究 ……………… (136)
　第一节　《水浒传》人物塑造艺术成就的评价问题 ……………… (136)
　　一、水浒人物塑造的"典型化"论 ………………………………… (136)
　　二、水浒人物塑造的"模式化"论 ………………………………… (140)
　　三、中西小说比较与西方小说观念视域中的水浒人物塑造
　　　　研究 ………………………………………………………………… (143)
　　四、中国文学传统的凸显与水浒人物塑造研究的深化 ………… (148)
　第二节　中国传统社会权力结构中的水浒英雄人物研究 ……… (152)
　　一、英雄的文化含义与特征 ………………………………………… (153)
　　二、帝王型英雄：宋徽宗和宋江 …………………………………… (158)
　　三、书生型英雄：吴用 ……………………………………………… (164)
　　四、武士型英雄：武松、李逵、鲁达和石秀等人 ………………… (165)
　第三节　西方现代反讽观念视域中的水浒英雄人物研究 ……… (171)
　　一、水浒人物研究中反讽要素的确立 …………………………… (171)
　　二、水浒人物描写中反讽意蕴的呈现方式 ……………………… (178)
　　三、水浒英雄中的反面人物 ……………………………………… (181)
　　四、水浒英雄中的正面人物 ……………………………………… (195)
　第四节　水浒女性形象研究 ………………………………………… (202)
　　一、男权社会中的水浒女性形象塑造 …………………………… (202)
　　二、水浒女性形象与淫妇 ………………………………………… (205)

第四章　英语世界对《水浒传》的叙事结构艺术研究 ……………… (210)
　第一节　对《水浒传》叙事结构模型的认识与建构 ……………… (211)

一、韩南论《水浒传》的"联合布局"与"顶层结构" …… (213)
　　二、李培德论《水浒传》的"主题单元"与"环状
　　　　结构" ……………………………………………………… (215)
　　三、浦安迪论《水浒传》的多重结构
　　　　——从"神话框架"、"撞球式"到"聚而复散"的结构
　　　　模式 ……………………………………………………… (220)
  第二节　《水浒传》结构艺术探源 ……………………………… (225)
　　一、对《水浒传》结构形成的"进化论"观点的质疑 ……… (226)
　　二、从《史记》到《水浒传》：《水浒传》的结构艺术
　　　　渊源 ……………………………………………………… (229)
  第三节　《水浒传》的基本结构原则 …………………………… (235)
　　一、通过时间与空间布局来构筑小说的结构模型 ………… (236)
　　二、通过"形象叠用原则"、"人物配对与拆分原则"来构筑
　　　　小说结构模型 …………………………………………… (243)
　　三、通过平衡对称原则来构筑小说结构模型 ……………… (245)
  第四节　梦与酒——《水浒传》文本叙事的黏合剂 ………… (250)
　　一、梦叙事及其结构功能 …………………………………… (250)
　　二、酒——《水浒传》叙事的黏合剂 ……………………… (259)

第五章　英语世界对《水浒传》的主题思想研究 ………………… (266)
  第一节　《水浒传》主题研究中的多种声音 …………………… (266)
　　一、革命、反抗主题及其质疑 ……………………………… (267)
　　二、维护儒家价值理想主题 ………………………………… (271)
　　三、背叛、复仇主题 ………………………………………… (272)
　　四、治乱、空无主题 ………………………………………… (274)
  第二节　水浒世界的道德、价值观念与"义" ………………… (277)
　　一、水浒世界的基本道德规范 ……………………………… (279)
　　二、水浒世界的基本价值观念 ……………………………… (291)
　　三、研究者对"义"的辨识 ………………………………… (294)
  第三节　"厌女症"与水浒世界的女性观 ……………………… (301)
　　一、夏志清与"厌女症"的提出 …………………………… (301)
　　二、孙述宇从"厌女症"到"红颜祸水"论 ……………… (303)

三、吴燕娜论水浒世界的"厌女症"与"恐女症" ………… (308)

结语 ……………………………………………………………… (311)

附录　中英文人名、术语译名对照表（A–Z） ……………… (316)

参考文献 ……………………………………………………… (319)

致谢 …………………………………………………………… (339)

绪　　论

第一节　研究目的、意义、范畴及方法

一、研究目的与意义

作为明代小说四大奇书之一的《水浒传》，在中国叙事文学——长篇白话小说的发展历程中地位独特，具有奠基性的作用；对后世文学发展的影响——尤其是对英雄传奇小说、侠义小说以及公案小说的创作意义重大。三分虚构七分史实的《三国演义》所写内容主要是朝代更替、历史兴衰，所写人物亦是以王侯将相为主。七分虚构三分史实的《水浒传》则把关注的目光转向了"中国游侠"（柳存仁语）、法外流民以及社会底层市井人物平凡琐碎的日常生活。更重要的是，《水浒传》的面世突出强调了一种新的小说理念，那就是对虚构的重视。按金圣叹之论："《水浒传》方法，都从《史记》出来，却有许多胜似《史记》处。"其关键点则是，"《史记》是以文运事，《水浒》是因文生事。以文运事，是先有事生成如此如此，却要算计出一篇文字来。……因文生事即不然，只是顺着笔性去，削高补低都由我"[①]。此"因文生事"，既指出了《水浒传》创作中艺术虚构的作用与意义，同时也孕育着一种新的小说理念。

可以说，没有《水浒传》确立的新的小说艺术理念，就没有《金瓶梅》，就没有中国古代叙事文学史上达到巅峰之作的《红楼梦》。正为此，

[①] （清）金圣叹：《读第五才子书法》，朱一玄、刘毓忱编：《水浒传资料汇编》，南开大学出版社2012年版，第219页。

《水浒传》出现不久就引起人们的关注和研究。鸦片战争的爆发打开了清王朝闭关自守的大门，英语世界的人们很快就发现了《水浒传》这部不朽巨著，并提出"元末明初的小说《水浒传》因以通俗的口语形式出现于历史杰作的行列而获得普遍的喝彩，它被认为是最有意义的一部文学作品"①。此评价可谓切中肯綮。

随着《水浒传》在英语世界流传、接受的越来越广泛，英语世界的汉学家对其展开的研究也越来越深入。古语云："他山之石，可以攻玉。"从他者的眼中来反观自身，对提升、发展自己是一条极有利的途径。在中西文化、文学及学术交流日渐繁荣的今天，如果我们仅仅关注国内的《水浒传》研究，这是非常不明智的。由于研究的历史思维惯性，往往容易束缚研究方法、研究视角的突破、创新，从而容易使研究陷入困境之中。特别是20世纪以来的一百多年中，西方国家文学理论的发展可谓日新月异；在新的理论指导下，他们的文学研究完全可能出现崭新的气象。事实上，英语世界的汉学家在进行《水浒传》研究时的确拥有与国内学者完全不同的方法和视角。英语世界的《水浒传》研究至今已逾百年，是时候对其研究方法、研究范式以及研究中存在的问题展开全面的梳理、分析和研究了。通过研究，发现中英世界《水浒传》研究之异同特质，对于国内的《水浒传》研究来说无疑具有很大的学习、借鉴的意义和价值，同时也具有建构异质文化之间学术上的互识、互证、互补与融汇的作用。而在此基础上去发现异质文化之间学术研究上内在的不同机制与旨趣，则是更深一层的价值所在。这是就学术研究自身来说。

现今，中西文化的交流日益昌盛。研究作为文化载体之一的文学在他国的接受、研究情况，探究英美国家的人们如何看待我们的文学典籍，对促进中外文化交流、逐步达到知己知彼是大有益处的。事实上，从一开始，英语世界的一些学者就是从文化的角度切入研究《水浒传》的。赛珍珠在1933年为英译《水浒传》写的"导言"中就认为《水浒传》是中国大众文化的产物；柳存仁在《中国游侠》中提出《水浒传》是中国游侠精神集大成；浦安迪在《明代小说四大奇书》中则认为《水浒传》等中国文学典籍是文人小说、是士人高雅文化的产物。从此视角来说，探究中国文学典籍在国外的接受、研究情况，对促进中外文化的交流，推动中

---

① 见《大英百科全书·中国文学》"水浒传"词条，2006年版。

国文化、文学进一步走出国门，建设发展中华文化，为实现中华民族的伟大复兴，具有重大的现实意义。

现在，国内对英语世界《水浒传》的译介与研究已有一定的关注，也取得了一定的成绩。其中一类是介绍性的，主要有下列几种：1983年宁夏人民出版社出版的郑公盾所著《〈水浒传〉论文集》一书，有"《水浒传》在欧美的流传"一节；1988年学林出版社出版的王丽娜编著《中国古典小说戏曲名著在国外》一书，在"第一辑·小说部分"辟有"《水浒传》外文论著目录"一节；1994年北京语言学院出版社出版的宋柏年主编《中国古典文学在国外》一书也列有英语世界《水浒传》译介与研究的内容；1997年学林出版社出版的黄鸣奋著《英语世界中国古典文学之传播》一书，其第五章"英语世界中国古典小说之传播"的第三节"明代小说之传播"中有介绍《水浒传》在英语世界的译介、研究状况的相关文字；2011年华东师范大学出版社出版的顾伟列主编《20世纪中国古代文学国外传播与研究》一书，其第五编"神话与小说"部分第五章分两节介绍了《水浒传》在国外的传播与研究的情况。一些期刊论文上也有关于英语世界《水浒传》研究的信息。总体来看，这些期刊论文，除1995年《明清小说研究》第二期刊发的黄卫总撰写的《明清小说研究在美国》一文比较有价值外，其他论文的内容基本上没超越上述著作。另一类是研究文章的选编，主要有1973年香港中文大学出版社出版的海陶伟编《英美学人论中国古代文学》一书，内收有罗伯特·鲁尔曼等人撰写的《水浒传》研究文章。此外，近十年来国内学界出现了一股"《水浒传》英译研究热"。到目前为止，博士论文有孙建成《〈水浒传〉英译的语言与文化：一部中国典籍英译史》、唐艳芳《赛珍珠〈水浒传〉翻译研究：后殖民理论的视角》两部，硕士论文有55篇，期刊论文达近百篇。具体情况留待研究综述再论。

上述种种，要么只是介绍国外《水浒传》译介和研究书目概况，梗概性地介绍相关研究内容，更多地只是具备资料索引的作用；要么只是运用西方的当代理论研究《水浒传》英译的方法、策略、视角、价值取向或者性别取向等，事实上更多地是在描绘《水浒传》的英译史。至于国外学人研究《水浒传》的方法与范式，内容、范畴与价值取向等问题，国内学界尚缺乏综合性的梳理、把握和研究。在这方面，既没有看到有一定分量的论文，更没有出版过专著，这不能不说是一种缺憾。

作为比较文学与世界文学专业出身的高校教师与人文社会科学研究者，选择"英语世界的《水浒传》研究"为课题研究的主题和对象，对其展开全面、系统的梳理、分析和阐释，这不仅与本人的专业知识结构与理论储备相符合，更能弥补当前国内学界《水浒传》研究的一大缺憾。倘若在本书撰写时，笔者能很好地把英语世界汉学家《水浒传》研究的真知灼见带到国内，并能为国内的《水浒传》研究提供可资借鉴的方面，本课题的研究就更有意义和价值了。

上述诸方面正是本课题研究的根本目的所在。

二、研究范畴与方法

（一）研究对象与范畴

在交代研究对象之前，先对"英语世界"一词做个说明。所谓"英语世界"，主要是一个语言范畴而非政治、地域界限的概念，其内涵与外延等同于"英语学术界"。自20世纪90年代以来，"英语世界"一词已为国内学界一致认可，本书就不再改弦更张另用他词。就本书而论，具体来说，"英语世界"指的是人们用英语对《水浒传》进行的译介以及用英语来撰写的关于《水浒传》的研究成果，包括译本、书评、专著、学位论文、期刊论文等学术著作。到目前为止，使用英语来研究《水浒传》的国外汉学家主要集中在英、美两国，所以笔者在本课题的研究过程中将以他们的成果为主体、以其他国家使用英语来研究《水浒传》所取得的成果为补充，以使本课题的研究更充分、更深入。

对"英语世界"一词作此说明后，再来交代本书的研究对象就更清楚更明确了。

以《英语世界的〈水浒传〉研究》为题目，决定了本书的研究对象包括两个方面的内容：一是《水浒传》在英语世界的接受历程，主要是对《水浒传》英译的历史做一个简单的梳理介绍。因为译介是研究的开始，也是构成研究的非常重要的部分；本书的重点则是对英语世界的专家、学者所展开的《水浒传》研究——主要是对其研究方法、范式、机制以及存在的问题，进行系统的考察、分析和论述。二是为了进一步深化本课题的研究，在跨异质文化的视域内对中英世界《水浒传》研究之异同及其互动展开比较分析和阐释，也是一个不可或缺的内容。

(二) 研究方法

本书是在比较文学视域之下，以比较文学的学科理论与研究方法——如流传学、媒介学、文学变异学以及跨异质文化的文学研究等为指导，对英语世界《水浒传》的接受与研究态势展开全面的分析研究。以国内外《水浒传》研究专家、学者既有研究成果为基础，在搜集、整理、研读大量一手资料的基础上，本人将通过文献梳理、文本细读分析、翻译研究、整合描述与比较研究等方法，对英语世界《水浒传》的接受与研究进行多层次、多角度、全方位的分析论述。

第二节　英语世界《水浒传》译介、接受与研究述评

16世纪前后，中国文化、文学典籍开始被译介到西方世界。到十七八世纪，中国文学在欧洲的传播与研究逐渐兴盛起来。中国古典文学作品诸如《好逑传》《玉娇梨》《三言二拍》《赵氏孤儿》等，就已经出现了英、法、德等语种的翻译文本，它们或以片段译文、或以节译本、或以全译本的形式出现在西方读者面前。其中特别是《好逑传》与《赵氏孤儿》两部作品，一出现在西方世界就获得像歌德、伏尔泰这样伟大作家、思想家的高度赞誉，并几乎风靡整个欧洲。只是那时候在欧洲流传的中国文学作品还相当有限，除了上述几部外，很难再找到其他的了。清王朝奉行闭关锁国的政策之后，中国文学的西传就更加屈指可数。

1840年的鸦片战争，使中国逐渐丧失了政治、经济、领土等方面的主权，从而沦为了半殖民地、半封建社会。当时中国的有识之士，为了图强报国、捍卫国家主权与领土的完整，把眼光转向了西方，开始了学习西方的历程。鸦片战争促生的"西学东渐"、"欧风美雨"，为中国带来了西方的现代科技与政治观念以及他们的文化、文学。同时，鸦片战争也加速了中国文学的西传。随着中国大门的打开，西方学人陆续来到中国，这进一步开启了欧美国家了解、研究中国文化和文学的旅程；不管是出于猎奇的心态还是出于促进文化、文学交流的责任感和使命感，这些探索中国的欧美国家的先锋人员逐渐向西方世界翻译、介绍中国古代的文学作品，从叙事文学的小说、戏曲到抒情文学的唐宋诗词都有展开，诸如《三国演义》《西游记》《聊斋志异》《儒林外史》《红楼梦》以及"寒山诗"等就是其中的代表。在这股中国文学西传的大潮中，《水浒传》很快就获得了

西方学者的关注，并被翻译成好几种欧洲国家语言。

到目前为止，《水浒传》在国外的译介与研究，不论是从地域范围还是从语言种类来看，都开展得比较广泛、比较深入了。由于地缘的关系，《水浒传》在亚洲世界的译介与研究要早西方两百余年（17 世纪上半叶已开始在日本展开）。现在，日本、朝鲜（含韩国）、越南、印度尼西亚以及泰国等都已拥有不止一种该国语言的译本。而对《水浒传》的研究，则以日本所取得的成就最高、最具代表性。欧美世界《水浒传》的译介与研究则始于 1850 年前后。目前，法国、意大利、德国、俄罗斯（苏俄）、匈牙利、捷克与斯洛伐克以及波兰等国家，也已有了本国语言的《水浒传》译本。在上述欧美国家中，《水浒传》研究所取得的成绩又以俄罗斯（苏俄）和德国最为突出。

因本书的研究论题是"英语世界的《水浒传》研究"，因此接下来笔者将重点梳理英语世界《水浒传》译介与研究的具体情况。

一、《水浒传》英译述介

《水浒传》的英译总的来说可分为两大类，一是片段译文，二是译本——包括全译本与节译本两种。先来介绍片段选译的情况。

1872—1873 年，香港出版发行的《中国评论》第一期上（China Review, Notes and Queries, Vol. 1, 1872 - 1873），曾刊有署名 H. S. 翻译的《水浒传》前十九回中有关林冲故事的英译文章，译名为 The Adventures of a Chinese Giant，就是现在所说的《中国巨人历险记》一文。这是能找到的、现存最早的《水浒传》英语片段译文文本。

1901 年，纽约 D. 阿普尔顿出版社出版了英国汉学家翟理斯（H. A. Giles）译著的《中国文学史》（A History of Chinese Literature），该书有《水浒传》中"鲁智深大闹五台山"故事的选译文段。

1947 年，美国学者詹姆斯·欧文（James Irving）编译的《〈水浒传〉故事选》（Selections from the Shui-hu Chuan）由耶鲁大学远东出版中心（Far Eastern Publications）出版。

1959 年，美国学人西德尼·夏皮罗（Sidey Shapiro，即沙博理先生）以人民文学出版社整理、出版的《水浒传》为蓝本，翻译了小说第七、八、九、十等四回中林冲被逼上梁山、鲁智深路见不平拔刀相助的故事，取名 Outlaws of Marshes，在北京外文出版社出版的英文版《中国文学》

(Chinese Literature)12月号上刊出。

1963年,已加入中国国籍的西德尼·夏皮罗再次以人民文学出版社整理、出版的《水浒传》为蓝本,翻译了其中第十四、十五、十六等三回中"智取生辰纲"的故事,取名为 Heroes of the Marshes,在英文版《中国文学》10月号上刊载。

1965年,美国学者西里尔·伯奇(白之,Cyril Birch)编著的《中国文学选集》第一卷(Anthology of Chinese Literature,Vol. 1)由纽约格罗夫出版社出版。该书收有《水浒传》第十四回至第十六回"智取生辰纲"故事的英语译文,标题是 The Plot Against the Birthday Convoy。

1982年,我国学人赵继楠(根据 Zhao Ji'nan 音译)根据"花和尚大闹野猪林"故事编译的《营救野猪林》(The Rescue in wild Boar Forest),由北京朝华书屋出版。

上述是《水浒传》英文片段选译的概况。下面再来介绍《水浒传》的英文译本。《水浒传》的英文译本到目前为止有5种。

第一种是英国汉学家杰弗里·邓洛普(Geoffrey Dunlop)根据德国学者埃伦施泰因德文70回节译本转译为英文的,译文书名为 Robbers and Soldiers 即《强盗与士兵》,1929年分别由英国伦敦豪公司和美国纽约A. A. 诺夫公司出版。该译本出版后并未引起多大反响。

第二种是由美国女作家赛珍珠(Pearl S. Buck)以金圣叹评点的贯华堂70回本为底本的节译本,书名为 All Men are Brothers,分成两卷,1933年分别由美国纽约约翰·戴公司和英国伦敦梅休安出版社出版发行。

该译本正文外附有龙墨芗先生(赛珍珠翻译《水浒传》的合作者)所写的"英译《水浒传》序",该序概略性地讨论了水浒故事的来源,《水浒传》的版本、作者等问题。此外,还附有赛珍珠自己撰写的"《水浒传》导言"。在导言里,赛珍珠首先说明其翻译方法是"尽可能地采用直译";其次对《水浒传》作出了非常高的评价:"这部小说所勾勒出的人物画面绝对忠实于生活。其实,它也不应该仅被视为中国过去的一幅图画。它也绝对是当今生活的一个写照。"更重要的是赛珍珠认为《水浒传》"虽经岁月流逝,它仍然畅销不衰,充满人性的意义"。[①] 而且赛珍珠对《水浒传》的题材来源、成书、作者等问题也表达了自己的看法。

[①] 姚君伟编:《赛珍珠论中国小说》,南京大学出版社2012年版,第76—82页。

1937年该译本再版时，赛珍珠加上了"修订版导言"一文，主要是对外界对其翻译文本中的问题提出的意见和建议作出回应。1948年赛珍珠译《水浒传》再版时附有林语堂撰写的导言一篇。

赛珍珠翻译的《水浒传》流传广泛、影响很大，至今已重版近十次。只是研究者发现，赛珍珠翻译的《水浒传》因有删省，对原著不忠实。比如说对书名的翻译改动就很大，根本没能表达出原著的本意；虽然赛珍珠对把《水浒传》译为 All Men Are Brothers 的做法在其译文的《水浒传》导言里作了具体的说明，但此翻译的不确切之处鲁迅在该译本出版的第二年即1934年就指出来了："因为山泊中人，是并不将一切人们都作兄弟看的。"[①] 也有论者以为，赛珍珠把《水浒传》翻译成《四海之内皆兄弟》"是兼容了中西文化的结果"，"公正地说，赛珍珠的译名确实表达了她对《水浒传》有着深刻的理解，表露着她试图进行跨文化沟通的理想"[②]。此外，也有论者以为，因为语言、文化上的隔阂等原因造成的理解上的偏差，导致赛珍珠对《水浒传》中人物的绰号以及那些独具中国语言色彩与意义表达的习语的翻译出现了一些低级错误。（参看钱歌川《翻译的技巧》及张同胜《〈水浒传〉诠释史论》一书的"《水浒传》的海外诠释"部分）对赛珍珠的《水浒传》译本，"西方评论界一般认为，这一译本对原著有所删省，译文流利可读，但在传达原文风格方面却是失败的"[③]。总的看来，对赛译《水浒传》的评价可谓见仁见智。

第三种《水浒传》英译本是英国学人杰克逊（J. N. Jackson）翻译、方乐天编辑的70回节译本，1937年在上海商务印书馆出版。该译本以金圣叹点评本为底本，译名是 The Water Margin，全书分为两卷（第一卷1—30回，第二卷31—70回）。该译本在作品译文外有两个部分是很有特色的，一是在译文主体前列有梁山一百零八将的姓名及与之对应的绰号，二是把"东都施耐庵序"也附上了。此外还附有水浒故事的木刻画。

在《水浒传》的翻译过程中，与赛珍珠不同，杰克逊采用的是意译的方法，因为在该译者看来"逐字逐句的翻译是不可取的"。编辑方乐天在"编者的话"中对该译本评价颇高："正是由于对原文的翻译是恰当的，杰克逊这个译本才是值得出版的。读者在享受《水浒传》的轻松活

[①] 鲁迅：《鲁迅书简》，人民文学出版社1976年版，第431页。
[②] 陈敬：《赛珍珠与中国》，南开大学出版社2006年版，第103页。
[③] 王丽娜编著：《中国古典小说戏曲名著在国外》，学林出版社1988年版，第62页。

泼的译文时,将会感谢杰克逊这个审慎的节译本。"① 西方评论界对杰克逊译本的评价和对赛珍珠译本的评价一样,都认为译文没有很好地传达出原著的风格与精神。

不管人们对赛珍珠译本和杰克逊译本如何评价,他们的努力为最初阶段西方世界了解中国、中国文学与文化所作出的贡献是不可否认的。1955年,《旁观者》(Spectator)杂志刊载的一篇文章如此说道:"我们对中国的理解,很大程度上归因于赛珍珠。既因为她创作的《大地》(The Good Earth),也因为她对中国最伟大的一部小说《水浒传》所作的非常棒的翻译。"②

1980年北京外文出版社出版的、西德尼·夏皮罗(沙博理)翻译的百回全译本《水浒传》是第四种英文译本。此译本,沙博理沿用1959年时的译法把书名译为 Outlaws of the Marsh,全书分为三卷,前两卷各35回,第三卷30回。

据沙博理1979年所写"译者说明",该译本"兼采七十回本与百回本的原文,前七十回是全文翻译,尽力忠实传达原文简捷而优美的风格,后三十回则略去一些次要的韵语和拖沓的文字;原书中的官职名称、政府机构、军事组织、兵器、人物服饰、比喻性描写等,在英语中很难找到相当的词汇,只有尽量选取近似的词汇来表达"③。在此,沙博理先生一方面交代了译本的底本来源,另一方面也说明了自己所采用的翻译策略与方法。正因为沙博理先生采取了"尽力忠实传达原文"的翻译策略与方法,所以该译本的译文总体上来说比较准确。

沙博理先生翻译的《水浒传》几经再版,流传很广。1981年,由美国印第安纳大学出版社和北京外文出版社联合再版,全书改成了两卷。1993年北京外文出版社出版的译本,把原来的三卷分成了四卷;第一卷前加了一篇由中国社会科学院文学研究所的石昌渝教授撰写的有关《水浒

---

① 王丽娜编著:《中国古典小说戏曲名著在国外》,学林出版社1988年版,第63页。

② Our understanding of China owes a great of to Pearl Buck, both for *The Good Earth* and for *All Men Are Brothers*, her admirable translation of the *Shui Hu Chuan*, one of China's greatest novel. Sperenkle, O. B. Vander, *My Several World. By Pearl Buck Mandarin Red. By James Cameron. CHINA PHOENIX*: *THE REVOLUTION IN CHINA. By Peter Townsend* (BookReview), Spectator, 195: 6627 (1955: July 1), p. 21.

③ Sidney Shapiro. Td, *Outlaws of the Marsh*, Beijing: Foreign Language Press Co. Ltd (1993), p. 2146.

传》的介绍文章,内容包括《水浒传》的作者、成书、版本、思想意蕴、艺术特色以及海外翻译出版概况;第四卷末,保存有沙博理先生所撰"译者说明",还附上了译者沙博理先生的生平简介及其在翻译中国文学的道路上所取得的成果。2003年,北京外文出版社还出了该译本的汉英对照本,已分成五卷。

《水浒传》最新的英译本是约翰·登特—扬与阿莱克斯·登特—扬父子(John Dent-Young & Alex Dent-Young)合译的,1994—2002年由香港中文大学出版社陆续出版。该译本,以明万历后期刊行的一百二十回本为底本,书名译为 *The Marshes of Mount Liang*,全书分为五卷。2011年,上海外语教育出版社出版了登氏父子翻译的五卷汉英对照本。登氏父子的《水浒传》翻译极具个性、极具特色,从"译者序"中所作的说明就可见一斑:

> 所有的翻译都有妥协的部分。我们的目的就是要译出一个可读性的英语读本,这决定了我们的一些选择;也就是说,我们……旨在保持英语行文规范的连贯、重心和节奏。①

这个交代,明确了译者、接受者的主体性要求,突出译者语言与文化在翻译过程中的重要性。登氏父子采用的是一种典型的"请作者向读者靠近"的归化翻译法。

从1872年《水浒传》第一个英文选译片段的出版面世至今,《水浒传》的英译已经走过了140余年的旅程,取得了比较丰硕的成果。在这140余年里,源于中西异质的社会历史文化语境,源于不同译者的价值取向以及对《水浒传》的不同理解和接受,也源于不同译者对翻译的不同看法和认识以及在翻译过程中所采用的策略和方法,《水浒传》的英译可谓千人异面、精彩纷呈。② 只是在批评界看来,《水浒传》的英译总是存在这样那样的问题,上文已有所述及。但正如赛珍珠所坦言的:"对《水

---

① 转引自孙建成《〈水浒传〉英译的语言与文化》,复旦大学出版社2008年版,第165—166页。英语原文见 John Dent-Young & Alex Dent-Young T. d, *The Marshes of Mount Liang*. By Shi Nai'an & Luo Guanzhong. HK:Chinese University of HK Press,1994,pp. xii – xiv。

② 关于《水浒传》英译情况的具体研究,可参看2008年复旦大学出版社出版的、孙建成所著《〈水浒传〉英译的语言与文化》一书的第三、四两章。

浒传》这部鸿篇巨制而言,绝不存在完美无缺的翻译。甚至完全屈从于批评家的建议也不能使译作完美无缺,因为还会有其他的批评家对原来的批评家提出批评。"① 确是中肯之言。当然,《水浒传》的英译仍在发展之中,相信将来的译者能够为人们奉献上更加完善的译本。

二、英语世界《水浒传》研究综述

就目前掌握的资料来看,《水浒传》在英语世界的研究始于 1900 年前后,至今已走过 110 多年的历程。根据具体的研究情况,笔者拟将英语世界《水浒传》研究的百年历史大略分成五个阶段,包括拓荒期、拓展期、复苏期、全面发展期以及成熟收获期,详述如下。

20 世纪 30 年代以前的 30 年左右时间是英语世界《水浒传》研究的第一阶段,尚属于拓荒期。因为刚起步,这一时期的研究总体显得比较单一,主要是作文学史的概述,但从研究成果来看,其中并不乏洞见。

1898 年在美国芝加哥出版的乔治·康德林的《中国小说·水浒传》,是此时期的代表性成果。康德林在该文中对《水浒传》的艺术成就给予了相当高的评价,认为它富有力量,"风格惊人,粗犷、直截了当、生动、热烈,每一个字都像雕刻刀可怕的一划","像但丁那样的作家,也不能写得比它更简洁、更生动","它充满画意,是一种尖锐的、粗糙的,大师的笔触"。除对艺术特色作出评价外,该论者还对《水浒传》的思想内容进行了描述,以为《水浒传》"回响着粗暴的威胁性的反叛之声",表现了"愤懑的中国"。② 该文章,就艺术特色的评价来说,可谓一语中的,只是思想内容的描述似乎与金圣叹评点的七十回本的《水浒传》更相符合。更难能可贵的是,对《水浒传》的研究从一开始就有了中西比较的意识。接下来的 20 年,《水浒传》在英语世界的研究稍显沉寂。除 1901 年纽约 D. 阿普尔顿出版社出版了翟理斯编译的《中国文学史》外,很难再找到其他有很高价值的研究文献。

20 世纪 30 年代的 10 年是英语世界《水浒传》研究的拓展期,代表性人物是赛珍珠。1930—1938 年,赛珍珠撰写的与《水浒传》有关或专论《水浒传》的文章主要有《中国早期小说源流》《〈水浒传〉导言》

---

① 姚君伟编:《赛珍珠论中国小说》,南京大学出版社 2012 年版,第 83 页。
② 转引自郑公盾《水浒传论文集》,宁夏人民出版社 1983 年版,第 218 页。

《中国小说》等三篇，论述的主要内容如下：

一是对小说作者问题的关注。关于《水浒传》的作者，国内流行有施耐庵著、罗贯中著以及施、罗合著等说法，但赛珍珠以为："对作者的讨论其实是无足轻重的，因为事实上，无论《水浒传》出自谁的笔下，他都是一个集大成者而非原创者。"① 从《水浒传》成书的历史来看，此观点不无道理。

二是对小说版本的讨论。在《水浒传》版本的讨论中，赛珍珠提到70回、100回、115回、120回以及127回五个版本。只是在赛珍珠看来，后四种版本"添增章节讲述了那些好汉的垮台及他们最终被官府捉拿的经历，其显而易见的目的是为了将该小说从革命文学的领域中排除出去，以迎合统治阶级的道德伦理……这些增补部分无论是内容还是风格都与前70回的精神和活力格格不入"②。从作品主题与风格连贯一致的角度出发，赛珍珠认为70回的《水浒传》是最具有思想和艺术价值的。这与当时胡适提出的观点是很接近的。但很显然赛珍珠的说法有其自身认识的前见，就是西方的个人英雄主义价值观。

三是对作品主题思想的探讨。赛珍珠说《水浒传》"充满人性的意义"，描写了"平民反对腐败官府的斗争"，"绝对忠实于生活"；她之所以用 *All Men are Brothers* 来作该书的英译名就是因为它能"恰如其分地表达书中这群正义的强盗的精神"。此观点与国内流行的"官逼民反"的说法基本一致。

四是对小说艺术风格的分析。在艺术风格上，主要谈论了两个方面。首先是《水浒传》的结构。赛珍珠援引西方评论界的观点指出，像《水浒传》这样的中国小说情节复杂、线索混乱，这使作品"拖沓冗长，毫不协调"。但其次，针对西方学者的此种批评，赛珍珠提出人们应该思考中国古典小说"这种支离破碎本身是否就是对生活的模仿"问题。在她看来："生活中并没有仔细安排或组织好的情节，人们生生死死，根本不知道故事有怎么样的结局，又为何有这样的结局……中国小说缺乏情节连贯性，也许就是一种技巧。这种技巧如果不是精心考虑的，无意中却也是对生活本身的不连贯性的模仿。"③ 正是在此视点观照下，赛珍珠说《水

---

① 姚君伟编：《赛珍珠论中国小说》，南京大学出版社2012年版，第79页。
② 同上书，第80页。
③ 同上书，第31页。

浒传》是一部"结构严密的伟大小说"①。在笔者看来,赛珍珠的观点可谓独具只眼。在人物形象塑造方面,赛珍珠对《水浒传》作了极高的评价:"人物形象塑造常常是一流的。一个词,轻轻一笔,举手投足之间,人物就栩栩如生地出现在我们面前。《水浒传》尤其是这样。在那里,有语言天赋的人只凭人物的用词习惯就能感觉到他要说的内容。"② 在此,赛珍珠对《水浒传》人物形象的个性化特征概括得非常到位。

此外,赛珍珠还讨论了《水浒传》的社会影响以及对中国后世文学发展之影响,还比较了以《水浒传》等为代表的中国小说与西方小说各自不同的特征,等等。

纵观英语世界《水浒传》研究的历史,赛珍珠在研究范畴的拓展上作出的努力和贡献,完全具有奠基性的作用。然而,或许因为第二次世界大战给社会带来的动荡不安,紧接着的20世纪40年代英语世界的《水浒传》研究只能用"荒芜"一词来形容。

进入20世纪50年代,一些汉学家再次把关注的目光投向《水浒传》,英语世界《水浒传》的研究进入复苏期。此阶段的主要研究范畴是作者、作品版本与小说的成书过程考证。不过开篇之作并不是考证《水浒传》的作者、版本等问题,而是在探讨它的主题与作用。1951年春,*Meanjin Quaterly* 杂志刊载菲茨杰拉德(C. P. Fitrgenald)撰写的《表现颠覆力量的中国小说》(*Chinese Novel as a Subversive Force*),作者通过对《三国演义》与《水浒传》的分析,认为这两部作品"都具有社会批评的作用,并且反映了反对权威的一种颠覆力量"③。只是这一时期英语世界的《水浒传》研究根本点主要还是集中在讨论《水浒传》的作者、版本与成书问题。

1953年,理查德·G. 欧文(Richard Gregg Irwin)的《一部中国小说的演变:〈水浒传〉》(*The Evolution of a Chinese Novel: Shui-hu Chuan*)由哈佛大学出版社出版。该书系统考察了自南宋时期起各英雄人物的故事传说到《水浒传》的成书经过,只是书中的说法不尽正确,很快就遭到他人的批评。为此,欧文又撰写了《〈水浒传〉再考察》(*Water Margin Revisited*)的长文发表在《通报》1960年第48卷(*T'ong pao*,48:1960)。该文章首先对《一部中国小说的演变:〈水浒传〉》一书中的错误说法进

---

① 姚君伟编:《赛珍珠论中国小说》,南京大学出版社2012年版,第130页。
② 同上书,第31页。
③ 转引自王丽娜编著《中国古典小说戏曲名著在国外》,学林出版社1988年版,第75页。

行了修订，其次大量引用中国、日本的文献对《水浒传》的版本与成书问题作出新的阐释。除欧文之外，日本学者小川环树也用英文撰写《〈水浒传〉的作者》（The Author of the Shui-hu Chuan）一文来讨论小说作者的问题。该文刊发于《华裔学志》1958年第17卷（Monumenta Serica. 17：1958）。

20世纪六七十年代的20年，对英语世界的《水浒传》研究来说是至关重要的阶段，可称其为全面发展期。因为这一阶段在承续以前研究成果的基础上，很多学者极力拓展、发掘研究主题、研究方法和研究视角，并逐渐在美国的哥伦比亚大学、哈佛大学、普林斯顿大学形成了一定的研究群体，这些因素使《水浒传》研究不仅形成了气候而且收获了不少具有真知灼见的成果。

在众多研究者中，先来谈谈美籍华裔学者夏志清（Hsia C. T.）。1962年，夏志清《〈水浒传〉的比较研究》（Comparative Approaches to Water Margin）刊载于《比较文学与总体文学年鉴》（Yearbook of Comparative and General Literature, Vol. 11）。该文章运用比较研究与新批评的方法，将《水浒传》的中西比较研究推进到完全实践的层面。在论述中，夏志清把《水浒传》与西方传统文学作品、特别是描写北欧"冰岛家族"故事的"萨迦"文学放在一起展开具体的比较研究，指出《水浒传》是一部"伸长的深沉的叙事体"文学作品。1968年，夏志清著《中国古典小说》（The Classic Chinese Novel：A Critical Introduction）由哥伦比亚大学出版社出版，该书有《水浒传》专章。该论著在介绍小说的作者、版本之外，重点之一是分析作品中人物的塑造手法、文本的结构等文学艺术层面的问题，同时也从现代人的视角对梁山好汉信守的道德、价值观念进行了批评阐释。有论者以为"此书的问世（也）标志了美国的中国明清小说研究进入了新阶段——研究的范围不再局限于版本的考据了"。[1] 从《水浒传》的研究来看，情形并不如此。如上文所述，早在20世纪30年代，赛珍珠对《水浒传》所作的研究，就已经在作者、版本、作品主题思想与艺术风格诸方面展开。不过，夏志清在《水浒传》与西方文学作品之间展开的平行比较研究的确是一种很有意义的尝试。在研究中，借用西方浪漫主义的文学观念，夏志清在1974年撰写的题名为《暴力的罗曼史：中国小

---

[1] 黄卫总：《明清小说研究在美国》，《明清小说研究》1995年第2期，第217页。

说的一种文体》(*The Military Romance: A Genre of Chinese Fiction*) 的文章，从文体的角度切入研究《水浒传》一类的作品。

1978年，李培德、茅国权等人 (Winston L. Y. Yang, Nathan K. Mao and Peter li) 发表长文《〈三国演义〉与〈水浒传〉及〈西游记〉与〈镜花缘〉》(*Romance of the Three Kingdoms and The Water Margin, and Journey to the West and Flowers in the Mirror*)。该文指出："《三国演义》和《水浒传》是中国小说史的里程碑。它们流传广泛，代表了中国文学所取得的重大成就。"[①]

除上述诸人外，韩南 (Patric Hanan) 是此阶段英语世界《水浒传》研究中不可或缺的人物。韩南的研究，重在从文学史发展的层面描述《水浒传》的地位、影响、艺术风格及其主题思想等。1963年，韩南的博士学位论文《〈金瓶梅〉探源》刊载于《亚洲专刊》(*Asia Major*) 杂志。该文第一节"长篇小说《水浒传》"分析了"《金瓶梅》借用《水浒传》分两类：一是武松和潘金莲故事的直接引进，二是若干片段被广泛地改编移植于《金瓶梅》"[②] 的事实，指出《水浒传》的素材对中国后世文学发展的影响。1967年，韩南的《早期中国短篇小说》(*The Early Chinese Short Story: A Critical Theory in Outline*) 发表在《哈佛亚洲研究杂志》(*Harvard Jounal of Asiatic-Studies*, 27: 1967)。文章在论述中国早期短篇小说的结构、主题的基础上，通过与《宋四公大闹禁魂张》等短篇故事的比较，作者指出《水浒传》的结构是"联合布局"，而其主题思想则主要为"政治道德"。韩南以为《水浒传》的结构是"联合布局"，这与李培德 (Peter Li) 等人在20世纪70年代提出的《水浒传》的结构模式是"环状链条型"的观点[③]，都富有洞见，都为人们理解《水浒传》的结构提供了新的思路。

普林斯顿大学的浦安迪是20世纪70年代兴起的《水浒传》研究的佼

---

① *Romance of the Three Kingdoms* and *The Water Margin* are important landmarks in the history of Chinese fiction. Popular in China, they represent significant achievements of Chinese literature. Winston L. Y. Yang, Nathan K. Mao and Peter Li. Classical Chinese Fiction: *A Guide to Its Study and Appreciation*. London: George Prior Publishers, 1978, p. 39.

② [美]韩南：《韩南中国小说论集》，王秋桂等译，北京大学出版社2008年版，第225页。

③ 李培德此观点出自 *Narrative Patterns in San-kuo and Shui-hu* 一文，该文章收入 Andrew. H. Plaks, Ed. *Chinese Narrative: Critical and Theoretical Essays*. Princeton, N. J.: Princeton University Press, 1977。

佼者。1974年，在普林斯顿大学召开了美国第一次以中国古典小说研究为主题的学术会议，该会议的重要成果是出版了由浦安迪主编的论文集《中国叙事文学论文集》（Chinese Narrative：Critical and Theorical Essays），其中李培德撰写的《〈三国〉与〈水浒〉的叙事模型》（Narrative Patterns in San-kuo and Shui-hu）一文集中讨论了《水浒传》的叙事模型与叙事结构。有论者以为该文集"反映了当时美国中国古典小说研究的最高水平"[①]。确然。1978年，浦安迪在《新亚学院学报》（New Asia Academic Bulletin）发表了《长篇小说与西方小说：文体上的一个重新评价》（Full-length Hsiao-shuo and Western Novel：A Generic Reappraisal）一文。浦安迪的上述论著，运用叙事学的方法、从文体的角度切入研究包括《水浒传》在内的中国古代叙事文学，借用西方理论家的有关小说理论比较研究中西小说，并提出章回小说与西方小说都具备"反讽"的特征。（浦安迪的这些观点在1987年出版的《明代小说四大奇书》中有更具体的阐释）运用西方现当代的叙事理论来研究《水浒传》，这在英语世界的《水浒传》研究中是一种新的尝试，只是认为中国明代小说"四大奇书"具有"反讽"的特点，却不尽然。

除上述三个代表性人物的研究成果外，这一阶段还有不少值得肯定的《水浒传》研究论著。研究人物形象的有：罗伯特·鲁尔曼（Robert Ruhlmann）的《中国通俗小说戏剧中的传统英雄人物》（Traditional Heroes in Chinese Popular-Fiction and Drama，1960）等；研究思想内容的有：海陶伟（J. R. Hightower）的《中国文学中的个人主义》（Individualism in Chinese Literature，1961），吴杰克（Wu Jack）的《〈水浒传〉的道德问题》（The Morals of All Men are Brothers，1963），黄宗泰（Wong Timothy）的《〈水浒〉中义的价值观念》（The Virtue of yi in Water Margin，1966），孙述宇（Sun Phillip S. Y.）的《〈水浒传〉的煽动性艺术：厌恶女人者或亡命之徒》（The Seditions Art of The Water Margin：Misogynists or Desperados，Renditions Autumn，1973）等；研究《水浒传》的社会影响有：谢诺（Jean-Chesneauz）的《〈水浒传〉与近代的关联》（Modern Relevance of Shui-hu Chuan：Its Influence on the Rebel Movement in 19th-and 20th-century China，1971）等；研究素材及人物渊源的有：松科尔（B. Csongon）的

[①] 黄卫总：《明清小说研究在美国》，《明清小说研究》1995年第2期，第218页。

《论〈水浒传〉前史》（On the Prehistory of Shui-hu Chuan, 1972）等；……此阶段还出现了一篇英语世界《水浒传》研究的综述性文章，是查尔斯·艾尔博（Charles J. Alber）撰写的《英语评论〈水浒传〉纵览》（A Survey of English language Criticism of the Shui-hu Chuan, 1969），该文章广泛地介绍了 1970 年代以前英语世界《水浒传》的研究情况。

纵观 20 世纪六七十年代的 20 年，英语世界的《水浒传》研究开展得越来越广泛、越来越深入。在原有研究方法、研究视角和研究主题的基础上，新批评、叙事学等现代理论一一引入研究领域；影响研究、平行研究、阐发研究（尚局限于单向阐发）等比较文学的研究方法也得到不同程度的运用；形象研究、主题研究、文体研究等研究范畴，或得到深化或得到发掘；研究成果不仅有单篇论文还出现了专著、博士论文等，比如说 1972 年怀特出版社出版了王靖宇（Wang John C. Y.）的《金圣叹》（Chin Sheng-t'an）一书，集中讨论了金圣叹在《水浒传》点评中表现出来的文学思想……总之，这一时期英语世界的《水浒传》研究呈现出一派"百花齐放，百家争鸣"之气象。

20 世纪 80 年代至今，在此前四个研究阶段的基础上，英语世界的《水浒传》研究逐渐走向成熟，并迎来了一次大的收获。此阶段，作者、版本、成书等基础范畴研究进一步深入，艺术风格、人物形象、思想内容的研究获得深化，运用当代文学理论来指导研究的尝试得到发展，从文化的角度切入研究的论著也已出现……整个研究呈现出系统化、理论化的态势。

随着研究走向成熟，研究成果也获得丰收。这一时期，以《水浒传》为研究对象或主要研究对象的博士论文计有 8 部，按发表的时间顺序简介如下：

1981 年，哈佛大学魏爱莲（艾伦·魏德玛，Widmer Ellen）的《十七世纪中国小说批评语境中的〈水浒后传〉》[Shui-hu Hou-chuan in the Context of Seventeenth Century Chinese Fiction Criticism. Thesis (Ph. D.) -Harvard University, 1981]，是《水浒传》续书研究的代表性著作。

1981 年，普林斯顿大学卢庆滨（Andrew Hing-bun Lo）的《史传语境中的〈三国志演义〉和〈水浒传〉研究》[San-kuo-chih yen-i and Shui-hu chuan in the Context of Historiography: an Interpretive Study. Thesis (Ph. D.) -Princeton University, 1981]，从史传文学的传统切入，系统研究了《三国志演义》和《水浒传》的写作体例与特征。

1984 年，伦敦大学龙安妮（Anne Farrer）的《晚明兴起的〈水浒传〉木刻绣像研究》［*The Shui-hu Chuan：a Study in the Development of Late Ming Woodblock Illustration.* Thesis（Ph. D.）-University of London，1984］，为《水浒传》的研究开辟了一个新的领地。

1988 年，芝加哥大学陆大卫（Rolston David Lee）的《理论与实践：小说、小说批评与〈儒林外史〉的创作》［*Theory and Practice：Fiction, Fiction Criticism, and the Writing of the 'Ju-lin wai-shih'*（Volumes I-IV）Thesis（Ph. D.）-The University of Chicago，1988］，其中有一部分内容比较深入地探讨《水浒传》对《儒林外史》创作的影响。

1989 年，普林斯顿大学德波特（Deborah Lynn Porter）的《〈水浒传〉的风格》［*The Style of "Shui-hu chuan".* Thesis（Ph. D.）-Princeton University，1989］，该论者从作者、叙事者、小说的语言模式等角度展开研究，系统论述了《水浒传》的艺术风格、人物形象宋江的塑造与反讽叙事中所蕴藏的文化思想，以及反映出来的小说主题。

1990 年，华盛顿大学邱贵芬（Chiu Kuei-fen）的《空间形式与中国长篇白话小说》［*Spatial form and the Chinese Long Vernacular "hsiao-shuo".* Thesis（Ph. D.）-University of Washington，1990］，该论者运用空间理论观念探讨包括《水浒传》在内的中国长篇白话小说的叙事特质。

1990 年，普林斯顿大学吴德安（Swihart De-an Wu）的《中国小说形式的演变》［*The Evolution of Chinese Novel form.* Thesis（Ph. D.）-Princeton University，1990］，从整个文学发展的轨迹考察中国小说形式、结构的演变历程，其中详细地探讨了《水浒传》的结构特征与结构法则，及其对后世文学创作的影响。

2000 年，俄亥俄州立大学于鸿远（HongyuanYu）的《作为精英文化话语的〈水浒传〉——阅读、创作与赋义》［*Shuihu Zhuan（Water Margin）as Elite Cultural Discourse：Reading, Writing and the Making of Meaning.* Thesis（Ph. D.）-Ohio State University，2000］，该作者从明末清初小说阅读与创作的文化意义开始讨论，详细分析论述《水浒传》文本中存在的多元叙事话语以及其中蕴含的对忠义与造反的叙述，重点是在论述自明末清初至 20 世纪 80 年代之前《水浒传》在中国的接受、批评与研究情况。

该阶段，除博士论文外，还出版了《水浒传》研究专著或以《水浒传》为重要研究对象的论文集，两者合计约有 20 部。下面重点介绍其中的 4 部：

1984 年，杨璐莎（Yang Lo-sa）的《笛福作品与〈水浒传〉之比较》(*The Works of Defoe in Comparison with Shui-hu chuan.* Taibei: *Zhuan xian wen hua shi ye gong si*, 1984) 出版。该书主要从叙事艺术与人物形象塑造两个方面展开研究。

1985 年，王泰珍（据 Wang Tai Jane 音译）出版了《陀思妥耶夫斯基反英雄的中国先例：〈地下室手记〉与中国小说〈水浒传〉之比较》(*The Comparison of Dostoevsky's Notes from Underground and the Chinese Novel Shui-hu Chuan: a Chinese Predecessor of Dostoevsky's Anti-hero.* Monterey, Calif: Monterey Institute of International Studies, 1985)。通过比较，该作者认为《水浒传》是反英雄的经典小说。

1987 年，浦安迪《明代小说四大奇书》(*The Four Masterworks of the Ming Novel: Ssu ta Ch'i-shu.* Princetion: N. J. Princeton University Press, 1987) 付梓。在这部论著中，浦安迪一方面详细考证了《水浒传》等中国明代小说的作者、版本问题；另一方面，通过小说的艺术技巧和文本中体现的文人意识形态的分析，浦安迪提出了"文人小说"的观点，认为包括《水浒传》在内的"四大奇书"都是晚明文人精英文化的产物，并认为"反讽"正是文人创作技巧高超的证明。此说法与国内一直以来盛行的《水浒传》等传统小说是大众通俗文化产物的观点相左。其实，英语世界的不少研究者——如夏志清、何谷理等，也认为《水浒传》等传统白话小说是文人小说而非民间通俗作品。浦安迪等人的说法不无道理。但综合来看，绝大部分中国传统白话小说都具有"雅俗共赏"的特性，要想"一言以蔽之"很难。

1992 年，出版了一部比较有新意的研究著作，这就是王静（Wang Ching）撰写的《石头的故事：互文性与〈红楼梦〉〈水浒传〉〈西游记〉中石头的象征及中国古代的石头爱情》[*The Story of the Stone: Intertextuality, Ancient Chinese Stone Love, and the Stone Symbolism in Dream of the Red Chamber (Hung-lou Meng), Water Margin (Shui-hu Chuan) and The Journey to the West (Hsi-yu Chi)* Durham: Duke University Press, 1992]。该书运用西方当代文学理论中的"互文性"和其他后结构主义的观念来分析上述三部作品中石头的象征义及其关系，显得很新颖。只是有得也有失。有论者曾谈到，该著"有些地方的阐述似乎过于刻意求

新，书出版后专家毁誉参半"。①

2009年，美国宾夕法尼亚大学出版社出版了梅维恒（Victor H. Mair）主编的论文集《女人与男人，爱情与权力：中国小说和戏剧的决定因素》（*Women and Men, Love and Power: Parameters of Chinese Fiction and Drama*），该论文集收录三篇有关《水浒传》的研究文章。其中康磊（Lei Kang）的《大众观点与小说之间的二元对分：〈水浒传〉的道德》（*The Dichotomy between Popular Opinion and the Novel: Morality in Water Margin*），关锦（Jin Guan）的《梁山好汉与现代行帮的价值观》（*The Values of the Mountain Liang Outlaws and of Contemporary Gangs*），此两篇文章集中讨论《水浒传》的道德价值观念问题。康磊从三个层面展开论述《水浒传》的道德内涵，一是梁山好汉内部处理相互之间关系的道德规范，二是水浒英雄处理与朝廷之间关系的道德规范，三是梁山好汉处理与普通百姓之间关系的道德规范。通过比较详细的分析讨论，康磊认为，梁山好汉践行的道德规范会在普通大众与小说之间形成二元对分的结果，这归因于《水浒传》在演变过程中经过明末文人、特别是金圣叹之手的删改与评点。关锦通过对小说文本所作的分析，指出梁山好汉的价值观主要包括荣誉感、慷慨大方、不好女色、正义感以及强健的体魄与超群的本领五个方面。另一篇针对《水浒传》的研究论文是乔什·维托（Josh Vittor）的《松散与醉酒：酒作为〈水浒传〉罕见的黏合剂》（*Incoherence and Intoxication: Alcohol as a Rare Source of Consistency in Outlaws of the Marsh*）。该论者从叙事的角度切入，认为酒这一要素把《水浒传》原本松散的各个故事比较好地链接成为一体。在故事叙述中，围绕酒这个物象，小说作者在对主要人物的描写中形成了喝酒、醉酒、冲突的叙事模式，而且这一模式在《水浒传》前半部分反复出现。

此阶段，在英语世界的《水浒传》研究中，收获的成果还有很多，实难一一详述。但有一个趋势必须提及，那就是随着文学研究泛文化现象的盛行，从文化角度研究《水浒传》亦是一种必然。除前面提到的几部论著外，保尔·史密斯（Paul Jakov Smith）2006年发表在《哈佛亚洲研究杂志》[*Harvard Journal of Asiatic Studies*, Vol. 66, No. 2 (Dec., 2006), pp. 363 – 422]的《〈水浒传〉与北宋军事文化》（*Shuihu Zhuan and the*

---

① 黄卫总：《明清小说研究在美国》，《明清小说研究》1995年第2期，第222页。

Military Subculture of the Northern Song, 960－1127）是一个突出代表。该文章从军事文化的角度切入，非常详细地论述了《水浒传》所描写的北宋时期的军事制度，包括政府体制内各级军事机构（如太尉府、经略府）、管理体制（像地方的保甲制度）与人员职位（如太尉、经略、教头、提辖、都保、保正、保长）的设置，以及地方豪强、庄园主（像晁盖、柴进、祝太公等）组织的军事力量。此外，该作者对作品中写到的刀枪剑戟棍棒等兵器也表现出了浓厚的兴趣。该文章虽然不是从文学艺术的层面展开论述，却是英语世界的批评者对《水浒传》中展现出来的北宋军事文化所作的一次很有意义的探讨。

综上，笔者分五个阶段述介英语世界《水浒传》研究的百年历程，此百年可谓历尽沧桑。鸦片战争加快了《水浒传》西传的步伐，两次世界大战又使其在英语世界的研究备受挫折。然而，历经坎坷后，英语世界的《水浒传》研究还是迎来了"收获的秋天"。

第三节 国内《水浒传》研究现状

根据研究对象和研究性质的不同，笔者把国内《水浒传》研究现状分成两大块来评述，一是国内学人就《水浒传》在英语世界的接受、翻译与研究进行的述介与研究，二是中国学者对《水浒传》这部作品及其相关问题展开的研究。

一、国内学界对英语世界《水浒传》研究的述介与研究

到目前为止，国内学界对英语世界《水浒传》的译介与研究已有一定的关注，也取得了一些成绩。就笔者掌握的资料来看，最早对《水浒传》的英译发表看法的是鲁迅。1934 年在写给朋友的书信中，鲁迅认为赛珍珠把《水浒传》的书名翻译成 All Men Are Brothers 是不确切的，"因为山泊中人，是并不将一切人们都作兄弟看的"。从《水浒传》本身的内容来说，鲁迅的观点是有道理的。在阶级分明的封建社会，梁山英雄与政府官员不可能是地位平等的兄弟；从众好汉对待普通百姓的态度上来看，他们也不可能是地位平等的兄弟。

鲁迅之后，或者因为战争的缘故——1937 年日本发动卢沟桥事变全面抗战爆发，很多国内学者把注意力放在了国家的生死存亡上；或者因为

政治的缘故——1949年中华人民共和国成立后，英美国家对中国采取孤立封锁的政策，中西之间学术交流受到很大的阻碍。在此大环境下，国内学界介绍、研究《水浒传》在英语世界译介、研究的文章非常稀少。直到1980年前后，国内学界重新焕发生机时，英语世界《水浒传》的研究情况才再次得到国人的关注。总体来看，至今为止国内学界的关注焦点基本还是集中在述介的层面。具体情况如下：

1983年，宁夏人民出版社出版郑公盾所著《〈水浒传〉论文集》一书，其中有"《水浒传》在欧美的流传"一节。在英译方面，郑公盾主要介绍了赛珍珠、杰克逊翻译的两种《水浒传》英译本的出版发行概况，其中简略介绍了赛珍珠译本受到的批评问题。此外，该作者还介绍了欧美世界给予《水浒传》正反两面的评价内容。根据郑公盾的介绍，在欧美学界对《水浒传》所作的评价中，正面观点认为《水浒传》是由"像但丁那样的作家"、"大师的笔触"雕刻出来的，负面观点则认为《水浒传》是一部"滑稽小说"、"流氓小说"。

1986年，《安徽教育学院学报》第3期刊载了一篇蔡宇知整理的《爱伦·魏德玛博士谈美国的明、清小说研究》一文。该文是根据魏德玛给学生作的学术报告内容整理而成的，其中简略谈及《水浒传》的版本、金圣叹的《水浒传》研究以及作品中的宋江这一人物，魏德玛博士从西方个人英雄主义思想出发认为宋江"太软弱了"。

1988年，学林出版社出版的王丽娜编著《中国古典小说戏曲名著在国外》一书，在"第一辑·小说部分·水浒传"一节，介绍了《水浒传》的4种片段译文和6种节译本或全译本，介绍了20世纪50—80年代英语世界《水浒传》研究的近30种论文、论著书目。该书出版前、后，王丽娜撰写了《〈水浒传〉外文论著简介》与《〈水浒传〉在国外（上、下）》等文章，前者发表在《湖北大学学报》（哲学社会科学版）1985年第3期上，后者发表在《天津外国语学院学报》1998年第1、2期上，内容与《中国古典小说戏曲名著在国外》一书的相关部分基本一致，不再赘述。

1994年，北京语言学院出版社出版宋柏年主编《中国古典文学在国外》一书，列有英语世界《水浒传》译介与研究章节，总体内容没有超越上两部著作。

1995年，《明清小说研究》第二期刊发了黄卫总撰写的《明清小说研究在美国》一文。该文述介了20世纪60—90年代初期明清小说研究在美国的概况,其中与《水浒传》研究有关的主要提及理查德·欧文1966年出版的《一部中国小说的演变:〈水浒传〉》,夏志清1968年出版的《中国古典小说》,浦安迪主编、1974年出版的《中国叙事文学论文集》,以及浦安迪1987年付梓的《明代小说四大奇书》等论著。该文正如作者黄卫总自己所说,只是对明清小说在美国的研究状况作了"一个极粗略的介绍"。

1997年,学林出版社出版、黄鸣奋著《英语世界中国古典文学之传播》一书,第五章"英语世界中国古典小说之传播"的第三节"明代小说之传播"中用了差不多五页(第197—202页)的文字来介绍《水浒传》在英语世界的译介、研究状况。该著在英文文献的述介上没能超出上述著作,但对英语世界汉学家《水浒传》的研究内容、研究主题等方面作了比较系统的分析,归纳起来有四个方面:一是《水浒传》的作者、成书与素材渊源研究;二是《水浒传》人物形象研究;三是《水浒传》的艺术风格研究,包括语言特色、人物塑造手法、作品结构等;四是《水浒传》的历史作用研究,主要是指对中国近现代社会革命运动的影响方面。黄鸣奋的总结虽然正确但并不全面。

2011年,华东师范大学出版社出版顾伟列主编《20世纪中国古代文学国外传播与研究》一书,其中第五编"神话与小说"部分第五章专述《水浒传》。该书第一节介绍《水浒传》在国外的译介、传播和影响,第二节分"关于小说作者的几种观点"、"小说人物形象分析"、"小说语言风格及结构研究"、"比较方法的运用"以及"小说的禁欲倾向与英雄形象的两重性特点"五个主题介绍国外学界的《水浒传》研究。这与黄鸣奋《英语世界中国古典文学之传播》一书的相关内容很接近,所涉及的英文文献也大体相当。

另外,中国学界(包括台湾、香港、澳门)的一些学者还选编、出版过西方汉学家研究中国古代文学的论文集,笔者已掌握的主要是1973年香港中文大学出版社出版、海陶伟编《英美学人论中国古代文学》一书。内收有罗伯特·鲁尔曼撰写的《中国通俗小说戏剧中的传统英雄人物》(*Traditional Heroes in Chinese Popular-Fiction and Drama*)一文,对水浒人物论述着墨较多。

近十年来国内学界出现了一股"《水浒传》英译研究热"。到目前为止,有2部博士论文、55部硕士论文,期刊论文达近百篇。这些《水浒传》英译研究论著，要么通过中、英文本的比较，要么通过不同英译文本的比较，去发现英译的缺点、不足或差异，如 2011 年上海师范大学李彦昌的硕士论文《〈水浒传〉章回标题的英译研究》，2010 年天津财经大学李桂萍的硕士论文《〈水浒传〉英译的对比研究》等；要么运用西方当代理论研究《水浒传》英译的方法、策略、视角、价值取向或者性别取向等，如 2009 年华东师范大学唐艳芳的博士论文《赛珍珠〈水浒传〉翻译研究：后殖民理论的视角》，2009 年外交学院刘奎娟的硕士论文《接受美学视角下的文学翻译——〈水浒传〉英译本比较研究》等；要么通过考察各阶段英译文本来描绘《水浒传》的英译史，如 2007 年复旦大学孙建成的博士论文《〈水浒传〉英译的语言与文化：一部中国典籍英译史》等。

国内有关《水浒传》英译的研究，主要聚焦于翻译的语言、方法与策略等问题；其次也会关注通过作品的翻译，中国文化、文学在欧美国家的流传以及中西文化的碰撞等问题。但总的来看，基本上没超出翻译研究的范畴。

二、国内学界《水浒传》研究述评

本课题以"英语世界的《水浒传》研究"为对象，研究的主题与重心是《水浒传》在英语世界的研究状况。因此，笔者在梳理国内学界《水浒传》的研究状况时将简单勾勒而不展开详细评述。

从确切可靠的文字记载来看，国内的《水浒传》研究始于明嘉靖年间。嘉靖八子之一的李开先在《词谑》中谈论道："《水浒传》委曲详尽，血脉贯通，《史记》而下，便是此书。"[①] 评价可谓极高。稍后的李贽则开了《水浒传》评点的先河，明末清初的金圣叹则把《水浒传》的评点研究推向了高峰；此两人是国内《水浒传》研究第一阶段的杰出代表。进入清代后，考据之风盛行，《水浒传》的研究主要集中于作者、版本、人物及素材考证方面。事实上，囿于意识形态的缘故，《水浒传》在清代有很长一段时间是受到严禁的，对它的研究未能展开。直到晚清民初，才渐渐兴起研究的热潮。总的说来，明清两代的《水浒传》研究重点还是在主题思想与艺术特色两个方面。至于《水浒传》的作者、版本问题，基

---

① 朱一玄、刘毓忱编：《水浒传资料汇编》，南开大学出版社 2012 年版，第 167 页。

本上只是记述而没有展开考证。正是这种只述不证的态度，为后来学界《水浒传》的作者与版本研究留下了很多不可靠的文字资料，也为后来《水浒传》研究中的争端埋下了引线。

20世纪以来的《水浒传》研究，大概可以分为世纪之初至"五四"运动时期，"五四"运动至新中国成立前，50年代至"文革"前，"文革"时期，以及80年代至今五个阶段。研究主题集中在以下几方面：作者、成书与版本问题，《水浒传》的主题思想，《水浒传》的艺术特色与人物形象研究。研究视角与方法则有下列数种：通史研究，传播学研究，接受美学视域内的研究与诠释，叙事研究，文化、民俗阐释，精神心理学的诠释以及中外文本的对比研究等。"文革"时期的《水浒传》研究，由于受到政党政治意识形态的强大影响，从某一层面来说，它实际上已经偏离了文学研究的轨道。下面，笔者就不对此展开论述。综合起来，国内的《水浒传》研究主要是围绕着下述问题展开的系列论争。

(一) 成书研究之争

《水浒传》成书于何时，这是国内学术界的一个争论焦点。1920年，胡适发表《〈水浒传〉考证》一文。在该文中，胡适认为"元朝文学家的文学技术，程度很幼稚，决不能产生我们现有的《水浒传》"；他指出"明朝有三种《水浒传》：第一种是一百回本，……一百回本的原本是明初人做的，也许是罗贯中做的。罗贯中是元末明初的人"。[①] 这是成书于明初之说。鲁迅的《中国小说史略》把《水浒传》归入"元明传来之讲史"，在《中国小说的历史的变迁》中则明确提出《水浒传》是由"大约生活在元末明初"的罗贯中所作，由此可知该书当完成于元末明初。胡适、鲁迅奠定了《水浒传》成书于元末明初之说。有些学者对《水浒传》成书于元末明初说提出质疑。1956年，陈中凡发表《试论〈水浒传〉的著者及其创作年代》[②] 一文。陈中凡从《水浒传》的体制与语言入手，提出该书当完成于元代中叶，即1350年前后。这不仅驳斥了胡适的《水浒传》不可能成书于元代的说法，更把成书的时间作了一个比较明确的界定。王利器根据《水浒传》的语言以及书中所用之事多是元代，认为该

---

① 胡适：《胡适古典文学研究论集》，上海古籍出版社1988年版，第766、711页。
② 该文刊发在《南京大学学报》1956年1月号。

书当成书于元代①。陈、王二人是持《水浒传》成书于元代的重要代表。

20世纪80年代以来，关于《水浒传》的成书时间出现了更多的说法。戴不凡提出《水浒传》当成书于明中期的嘉靖初年②。在《水浒祖本探考》《再论〈水浒〉成书于嘉靖初年》等文章中，张国光据《水浒传》中所用地名、官制等，对戴的说法表示赞同③。此二人开了《水浒传》成书于嘉靖说的先河。此观点遭到一些学者的反对，李永祜就是其中最有力的一员。李永祜认为，《水浒传》成书于嘉靖一说"存在着舛误和不能自圆其说之处，难以令人信服，还不足以动摇或代替成书于元末明初的观点"④。

同样通过考察历史地理与官制，周维衍则指出成书于元代、元末明初以及嘉靖的说法都不成立。从《水浒传》中"江西信州"、"淮西临淮州"、"代州雁门"、"南京建康府"等的历史沿革情况，周维衍认为"《水浒传》当成书于洪武四年到十年（1371—1377）之间"⑤。

从上文可知，就《水浒传》的成书时间，国内学界主要提出了四种看法。然而，因《水浒传》的成书经历了一个漫长、复杂的过程，同时对小说的成书时间又缺乏确切可靠的文字记载，到目前为止，上述四种说法皆非定论。总体来看，元末明初说因其具有相当依据，弹性又大，成为长期以来流传最广、最为人们所接受的一种观点。

（二）作者研究之争

《水浒传》的成书年代难以确定，作者是谁也仍然是一个谜。20世纪至今，关于《水浒传》的作者问题，国内学界主要形成了下述四种观点。

一种说法认为《水浒传》是罗贯中所著。前期代表性人物是胡适和鲁迅。胡适在《〈水浒传〉考证》中指出："明朝有三种《水浒传》：第一种是一百回本，……一百回本的原本是明初人做的，也许是罗贯中做

---

① 见王利器《〈水浒全传〉是怎样纂修的?》，《文学评论》1982年第3期。
② 见戴不凡《小说见闻录》，浙江人民出版社1980年版，第118—125页。
③ 《水浒祖本探考》刊发于《江汉论坛》1982年第1期，《再论〈水浒〉成书于嘉靖初年》刊发于《武汉师范学院学报》1983年第4期。
④ 见李永祜《〈水浒〉的地名证明了什么?——〈水浒〉成书于"嘉靖说"质疑之一》，《水浒争鸣》第4辑，长江文艺出版社1985年版。
⑤ 见周维衍《〈水浒传〉的成书年代和作者问题——从历史地理方面考证》，《学术月刊》1984年第7期。

的。罗贯中是元末明初的人。"① 只是在行文中胡适对自己的观点并不完全肯定。鲁迅在《中国小说的历史的变迁》中明确提出:"罗贯中名本,钱塘人,大约生活在元末明初。他做的小说很多,可惜现在只剩下四种。……就是:一、《三国演义》;二、《水浒传》;……罗贯中荟萃诸说或小本《水浒》故事,而取舍之,便成了大部的《水浒传》。"② 进入20世纪80年代,王晓家、罗尔纲、周维衍等人在各自的研究中也认为《水浒传》是罗贯中所著。

认为罗贯中是《水浒传》的作者,这种说法在明人的著作中已有相关记述。如郎瑛的《七修类稿》,田汝成的《西湖游览志馀》,王圻的《续文献通考》与《稗史汇编》等,皆明确记述罗贯中是小说的作者。

另一种观点以为施耐庵是《水浒传》的作者。1903年狄平子在《新小说》第一卷发表的《论文学上小说之地位》,1908年天僇生(王钟麒)在《月月小说》第二卷第二期发表《中国三大小说家论赞》,……这些论者都认为《水浒传》是施耐庵所著。同样在《〈水浒传〉考证》一文中,胡适说:"七十回本是明朝中叶的人重做的,也许是施耐庵做的。"在胡适这里,不管是哪种观点,其表达都是不完全肯定的。鲁迅则以为施耐庵是《水浒传》化为繁本的作者(鲁迅认为,《水浒传》的版本经历了由简入繁的演变过程,小说最早的版本即简本的作者是罗贯中)。后来的学者如吴组缃、黄霖等人,通过比较《三国演义》与《水浒传》在主题思想、语言风格等方面的巨大差异,认为施耐庵才是《水浒传》的作者。

而施耐庵是谁,这是又一个争论的焦点。以胡适为代表的一派认为施耐庵"是一个假托的名字";以吴梅、王利器为代表的一派认为,施耐庵就是元杂剧作家施惠;以刘冬、黄清江等为代表的一派认为,施耐庵即元末明初苏北白驹镇人施彦端;以黄霖为代表的一派则认为施耐庵是《靖康稗史》编者"咸淳丁卯耐庵"。然上述观点皆缺乏足够有力的史料文献作为论证的依据。

说施耐庵是《水浒传》的作者,也是有前人记述所依的。明人高儒《百川书志》、郎英《七修类稿》中都有《水浒传》是"钱塘施耐庵的本"的文字,胡应麟《少室山房笔丛》则有"元人武林施某"编著《水

---

① 胡适:《胡适古典文学研究论集》,上海古籍出版社1988年版,第766、711页。
② 鲁迅:《鲁迅全集》第9卷,人民文学出版社2005年版,第322—324页。

浒传》的记述①。而自金圣叹贯华堂本刊行后，施耐庵著《水浒传》成为通行近三百年的说法。

再一种说法认为《水浒传》是施耐庵、罗贯中合著的。1952年《文艺报》第21号刊发刘冬、黄清江合著《施耐庵与〈水浒传〉》一文，初步提出该说法。1981年，刘冬、欧阳健合著的《有关〈水浒〉、施耐庵及罗贯中的几项新发现材料述评》一文认为："施耐庵即繁本《水浒》的完成者，而罗贯中则是施耐庵的助手。两人对于《水浒》的问世有不可分离的关系。在编辑出版方面，罗贯中的贡献可能还要多些。"② 刘世德也持此观点，他说："《水浒传》主要是施耐庵写的，然后罗贯中帮他整理、编辑而成的。所以说，如果是有两个作者的话，那主要的是施耐庵，次要的是罗贯中。我是相信这个说法的。"③ 王利器则认为："《水浒全传》的编纂过程，大概是施、罗二人通力合作的，所以题署为'施耐庵集撰、罗贯中纂修'。"④《水浒传》是施耐庵、罗贯中合著的说法，也有一定的依据。明人高儒《百川书志》有"钱塘施耐庵的本，罗贯中编次"的记述。

上述三种说法虽然都有所依，然其所依据的材料本身往往只是一种可能性叙述，或者同一种文献本身就有多重说法（高儒的《百川书志》就是如此），这就使资料的可靠性存在很大问题。现代学人在论述过程中也往往只是一种推测，难以下定论。事实上，根据本身就存疑的文献进行研究，即使得出肯定的观点，这种观点也是很难令人信服的。

有些学者根据《水浒传》的成书特点，即《水浒传》是一部累积型作品，从而提出《水浒传》是集体创作的观点，他们认为施耐庵和罗贯中只是众多作者中的一部分成员。持此看法的代表人物有何心、聂绀弩等。何心认为："《水浒传》并不是一人一手的创作。最先有一个人把各种梁山泊英雄的故事联缀起来，成为一部长篇小说。后来曾经有过几次增损修改，……所以现在通行的《水浒传》，已经不是原来的真面目了。"⑤ 聂绀弩说："《水浒》不是一人写成，也不是一次写成的；是经过很多人、

---

① 朱一玄、刘毓忱编：《水浒传资料汇编》，南开大学出版社2012年版，第130—131页。
② 江苏省社会科学院文学研究所编：《施耐庵研究》，江苏古籍出版社1984年版，第115页。
③ 刘世德：《〈水浒传〉的作者》，出自《品读〈水浒传〉》，中国人民大学出版社2004年版，第31页。
④ 见王利器《〈水浒全传〉是怎样纂修的?》，《文学评论》1982年第3期。
⑤ 何心：《水浒研究》，上海文艺联合出版社1954年版，第31页。

很长时期、很多次修改才完成的。""假定早期的编者是施耐庵、罗贯中；在他们之后，郭勋、李卓吾、金圣叹，都对《水浒》尽过力，也都是《水浒》的若干程度的作者。"①笔者以为，即便有很多人为《水浒传》以现有模样出现在现代读者面前做出了不少贡献，但小说还是有其最初的写定者。如果《水浒传》不是集体创作的话，其作者就是最初使其以比较完整的面貌出现在读者眼前的那个人。至于其他人，还是把他们放入批评完善者的行列更好些。毕竟在文学史上抑或《水浒传》批评史上，李卓吾、金圣叹等人是以评点家的身份出现的，而这样的事实已为大多数人所接受。

(三) 版本研究之争

在中国古典小说中，《水浒传》的版本可以说是最为复杂的。这就为后来的版本研究带来了很多可争论的因素。比如说各自版本的问世时间，不同版本之间是一种什么样的关系，以及最早的版本（即古本、原本或祖本）是什么样的。

围绕着版本的争论，一个重要的方面就是繁本与简本之间的关系问题。繁本与简本之间的关系大致说来主要有三种观点。一是"由简入繁"论。这种说法是20世纪20年代由鲁迅首先明确提出来的。鲁迅根据当时已知《水浒传》的五种版本并通过比较分析后指出："总上五本观之，知现存之《水浒传》实有两种，其一简略，其一繁缛……若百十五回简本，则成就殆当先于繁本，以期用字造句，与繁本每有差违，倘是删存，无烦改作也。"②后来的郑振铎、何心、聂绀弩等人都支持鲁迅的观点③。此说法的提出与当时进化论思想在国内的盛行是密切相关的。

与"由简入繁"相对的是"删繁为简"论。1929年，胡适在《百二十回本〈忠义水浒传〉序》一文中说："鲁迅先生'删存无需改作'之说不能证明百十五回之近于古本，也不能说明此种简本成于百回繁本之先。"他又提出"百十回本和百二十四回本等等简本大概都是胡应麟所说的坊贾删节本"④。这是"删繁为简"说的最初表述。自20世纪70年代

---

① 聂绀弩：《〈水浒〉四议》，北京大学出版社2010年版，第3、32页。
② 鲁迅：《鲁迅全集》第9卷，人民文学出版社2005年版，第145页。
③ 具体论述可参见郑振铎《中国文学史》、何心《水浒研究》、聂绀弩《水浒五论》的相关部分内容。
④ 胡适：《中国章回小说考证·水浒传考证》，北京师范大学出版社2013年版，第89页。

之后，持此主张的人相对较多，像范宁、张国光、傅隆基、刘世德等就是其中的代表。

上述两种观点之外，有不少学者认为繁本与简本是两个不同的系统。20世纪50年代，严敦易在其论著《水浒传的演变》中首先提出此说法。柳存仁则提出《水浒传》的早期祖本有两部，一是罗贯中所著的简本之祖，二是施耐庵所著的繁本之祖，两个版本之间既平行发展又相互借鉴，其最终成果就是万历四十二年（1614年）刊行的袁无涯刻百二十回本《水浒全传》①。何满子通过追溯研究水浒故事的起源，认为简本出自"讲史"，繁本源于"小说"，"简本形成在前，繁本'集撰'于后。繁本'集撰'之时，必以先出的简本为故事情节发展的轮廓所据；繁本既出，简本也就会吸取繁本的精彩之处加以充实"②。与此观点相近，欧阳健提出"繁简相互递嬗"说。他主张"以辩证的观点把《水浒》不同形态的版本之间的关系看成为一个密切相关而又相互递嬗的进展过程"③。

在《水浒传》的版本论争中，古本（祖本或原本）问题是另一个重要的方面。在此问题上亦是说法各异。胡适以为《水浒传》的祖本应是罗贯中所作"一百回的原本"。鲁迅则在考察当时所知6种版本的基础上提出，《水浒传》的原本是简本，作者是罗贯中。1929年，郑振铎在《〈水浒传〉的演化》一文中提出"《水浒传》的底本在南宋时便已有了"，"罗（贯中）是写定今本《水浒传》的第一个祖本的人"④。至于南宋时的《水浒传》的底本是什么样的，郑振铎并未说明。随后的1931年，郑振铎获得一个五回的繁本残本，断定是郭勋本。

1975年，《京本忠义传》残页由上海图书馆所发掘。顾廷龙、沈津根据所见残页的字体、纸张等特点提出，该书当刊行于明正德、嘉靖间，比郑振铎所获得的本子要早⑤。20世纪80年代初，欧阳健等人据此发现认为，此

---

① 见柳存仁《罗贯中讲史小说之真伪性质》。
② 见何满子《从宋元说话家数探索〈水浒〉繁简本渊源及其作者问题》，《中华文史论丛》1982年第4辑。
③ 具体内容见欧阳健、萧相恺著《水浒新议》中《〈水浒〉简本繁本递嬗过程新证》部分的相关论述，重庆出版社1983年版。
④ 郑振铎：《中国文学论集》，岳麓书社2011年版，第159—160页。
⑤ 见顾廷龙、沈津《关于新发现的〈京本忠义传〉残页》，《学习与批判》1975年第12期。

书的产生年代可以推到更早的元末明初间，可能是现存的最早版本①。

大致与欧阳健等人同时，黄霖、王利器等根据吴从先《小窗自纪》（该书成于万历四十二年，即1614年）中《读水浒传论》一文所记内容推断"吴读本"是一个早期古本，并认为其著者即是元初《靖康稗史》的编者施耐庵②。稍后，侯会提出至迟在嘉靖年间确实流行"吴读本"，并认为该本形成在元初，与《宣和遗事》大约同时产生，是早于今本（百回繁本）的古本③。

金圣叹贯华堂藏七十回本是不是古本，这是《水浒传》版本研究之争中的一个重要问题。据金圣叹所说："吾既喜读《水浒》，十二岁便得贯华堂所藏古本"，"施耐庵《水浒正传》七十卷，又楔子一卷，原序一篇亦作一卷，共七十二卷"④。按金圣叹之说，这就是《水浒传》古本的模样。只是后来人罗贯中好生事端，横加七十回（按金批本回目）后内容，而至出现百回今本。用金之原话说即是："笑杀罗贯中横添狗尾，徒见其丑也。"⑤

对金圣叹之说，现代研究者多表怀疑，普遍认为七十回古本是金圣叹删改所作"伪古本"。如鲁迅，他采用周亮工之说⑥，认为金本是据百回本删改而成，是最晚出的本子⑦。俞平伯亦持此观点⑧。1929年，胡适作《百二十回本〈忠义水浒传〉序》时一改其在1920年所作《〈水浒传〉考证》中提出的"金圣叹没有假托古本的必要"的观点，认为自己"最大的错误是我假定明朝中叶有一部七十回本《水浒传》"⑨。也就是说胡适否

---

① 具体内容见欧阳健、萧相恺著《水浒新议》中《〈水浒〉简本繁本递嬗过程新证》部分相关论述，重庆出版社1983年版。
② 见黄霖《一种值得注目的〈水浒〉古本》，《复旦学报》1980年第4期；王利器《〈水浒全传〉是怎样纂修的?》，《文学评论》1982年第3期，等文章。
③ 见侯会《再论吴读本水浒传》，《文学遗产》1988年第3期；《从南北蓼儿洼看水浒故事与淮南之关系》，《文学遗产增刊》第十八辑，山西人民出版社1989年版；《〈水浒〉源流新证》"关于'吴读本'《水浒传》"部分，华文出版社2002年版。
④ （清）金圣叹：《水浒传序三》，朱一玄、刘毓忱编：《水浒传资料汇编》，南开大学出版社2012年版，第212、214页。
⑤ （明）施耐庵著、（清）金圣叹批评：《水浒传》第七十回回批，凤凰出版社2010年版，第638页。
⑥ 周亮工《书影》中称："近金圣叹自七十回之后，断为罗所续，因极口詆罗，复伪施序于前，此书遂为施所有矣。"
⑦ 鲁迅：《鲁迅全集》第9卷，人民文学出版社2005年版，第146、325页。
⑧ 见俞平伯《论〈水浒传〉七十回古本的有无》一文，《小说月报》十九卷四号。
⑨ 胡适：《中国章回小说考证·水浒传考证》，北京师范大学出版社2013年版，第74页。

定了七十回本是古本的说法。此后几十年，学界普遍认同金圣叹贯华堂藏七十回《水浒传》是"伪古本"的说法。

20世纪80年代，罗尔纲撰写系列文章重新提出七十回本是《水浒传》原本的说法，后以专著《〈水浒传〉原本和著者研究》出版。1981年所撰《水浒真义考》一文中，罗尔纲通过分析百回本《忠义水浒传》存在的诸多矛盾这一"内证"提出："罗贯中《水浒传》原本，只到梁山泊英雄大聚义为止，以惊噩梦结束"，"百回本《忠义水浒传》后二十九回半，却是明朝宣德、正统后，对朱元璋诛杀功臣愤愤不平的人所续加的"。① 1984年，罗尔纲撰写《从罗贯中〈三遂平妖传〉看〈水浒传〉著者和原本问题》，通过《三遂平妖传》与《水浒传》的对勘，进一步论证自己的观点。后来，他还通过《忠义水浒全传》与《忠义水浒传》的对勘，详细探讨了"续加者对罗贯中《水浒传》原本的盗加和删削及盗改"的情况。罗尔纲的研究有一定道理，但论据并不充分，文章刊发不久即遭到张国光、商韬、陈年希、徐朔方等人的质疑与反驳②。

在古本问题上，还必须谈到20世纪刊行的梅寄鹤藏百二十回《古本水浒传》这一版本。该本子后50回1933年由上海中西书局出版，梅寄鹤作序。出版后反响寥寥。后来蒋祖钢重校该版本，并于1985年由河北人民出版社出版。蒋祖钢在"前言"中说："这是我们目前见到的唯一一部署名施耐庵著的长达120回的《水浒传》"古本；该版本"前后的情节结构连贯吻合，布局前后呼应，形成了一个严密的统一体"，而且"前后所反映出来的世界观一致；艺术风格一致；特别是语言的时代特征、地方特征也一致"③。此说法虽获得一些人的响应，只是学界普遍认为《古本水浒传》系伪作而且论证比较有力，到现在，蒋祖钢的声音已基本消失。

就《水浒传》的版本论争，由于上述各家皆缺乏有力的文献资料，谁也无法说服谁。不过，上述各种观点还是为我们提供了研究的不同可能和切入路径。至于真相如何，至今尚无定论。

---

① 罗尔纲：《〈水浒传〉原本和著者研究》，江苏古籍出版社1992年版，第54页。
② 具体见张国光《对罗尔纲先生〈水浒真义考〉一文之商榷》，《武汉师范学院学报》1984年第4期；商韬、陈年希《用〈三遂平妖传〉不能说明〈水浒传〉的著者和原本问题——与罗尔纲先生商榷》，《学术月刊》1986年第1期；徐朔方《〈平妖传〉的版本以及〈水浒传〉原本七十回说辨正》，《浙江学刊》1986年第6期。
③ 见《古本水浒传》前言，河北人民出版社1985年版。

（四）主题研究之争

在20世纪以来国内学界的《水浒传》主题研究中，出现了多种声音，提出了多种观点。1950年之前，情况比较简单，其中鲁迅持"健儿啸聚"之说；陈独秀则认为"赤日炎炎似火烧""这四句诗就是施耐庵作《水浒传》的本旨"①，然"本旨"具体是什么陈并未展开论述。1949年新中国成立之后，《水浒传》的主题问题变得复杂起来。就总体情况来看，在《水浒传》主题的论争过程中主要出现了以下四种观点。

一是"农民起义说"。1950年8月，杨绍萱撰写的《论〈水浒传〉与水浒戏》在《戏剧报》一卷五期刊发，明确提出"农民起义说"。王利器通过分析"赤日炎炎似火烧"一诗以及文本里的其他内容后也认为《水浒传》是写农民革命的作品②。后来，中国作家协会文学讲习所的《水浒传》学习报告则直接提出"《水浒传》是一部描写农民革命战争的小说，它反映了封建社会的主要矛盾"③。冯雪峰等人从现实主义典型环境、典型人物的理论高度出发，指出《水浒传》是一部"以描写北宋末年的一次农民起义为主题，以宋江等英雄人物为主干，全面地描写了中国中世纪时期的社会生活；尤其是深刻地、大胆地描写了农民阶级和地主阶级的矛盾斗争，描写了农民的革命斗争、革命力量和革命思想，反映了封建主义统治下的人民的正义斗争和希望，同时也反映了农民革命思想的不彻底性和革命斗争中所表现的缺点，等等"④。在冯雪峰等人看来，正是因为农民革命思想的不彻底性和革命斗争中存在种种缺点，所以它在经历兴盛之后最终还是遭遇失败。署名"南开大学中文系古典文学教研室"的《〈水浒〉的思想和艺术》一文也认为："《水浒》是我国描写农民战争的著名古典长篇小说"，"它是伟大的农民革命现实的产物，同时也是伟大的农民革命的精神成果"⑤。

到现在为止，在国内学界的《水浒传》主题研究中，"农民起义说"仍然是比较主流的观点。但有些学者对此进行了更加深入的探讨。王俊年等人认为：

---

① 原文见汪元放标点七十回本《水浒》卷首，上海亚东图书馆1928年重排本。
② 见王利器《〈水浒〉与农民革命》，《光明日报》1953年5月27日。
③ 见《文艺报》1954年第3期。
④ 见《回答关于〈水浒〉的几个问题》，《文艺报》1954年第3、5、6、9等期。
⑤ 《四部古典小说评论》，人民文学出版社1973年版，第30—31页。

综观全书，我们认为《水浒传》作者具有当时比较先进的思想，但又未能从几千年来封建统治者所灌输的正统观念中解放出来。因此，思想上充满了矛盾。他一方面不满黑暗现实，不满昏君奸臣，同情、歌颂农民革命，另一方面又有着严重的忠君观念，不赞成推翻当朝皇帝，自立为王；一方面肯定接受招安，另一方面当他面对现实的时候，又清醒地看到此路不通，必将导致起义军的全军覆灭；一方面深被起义军威震朝廷的强大力量所振奋，另一方面又彷徨、苦闷，找不到一条既忠君、又能使农民军扬眉吐气的出路。作者思想上的这些矛盾，构成了作品的矛盾。①

正因为存在此种复杂的情况，王俊年等人进一步指出："《水浒》作者代表的并非历史上最先进的农民思想，而是大多数中间状态的农民的思想。"② 石昌渝先生承认《水浒传》是反映"农民起义"的作品，但他同时也指出：

> 我认为农民起义不能叫作社会革命，过去我们对农民起义这个评价我认为是可以商量的，是可以谈论的。为什么这样说呢？因为农民不代表先进的生产力，这是第一。第二，从事实来看，农民起义它只是改朝换代的工具，并不反对封建制度，只是反对压在头上的那个皇帝，那个政府，然后取而代之。③

"农民起义说"以及对其所作的深入探讨，都有其合理性。但对《水浒传》这样一部思想内容丰富、复杂的作品来说，又不具备完全的统括性。鉴于此，"忠奸斗争说"又重新出炉。

"忠奸斗争"的思想源自李贽。在《〈忠义水浒传〉叙》里，李贽说："《水浒传》者，发愤之所作也。盖自宋室不克，冠履倒施，大贤处下，不肖处上"，"独宋公明者身居水浒之中，心在朝廷之上，一意招安，专

---

① 王俊年、裴效维、金宁芬：《〈水浒传〉是一部什么样的作品》，《文学评论》1978年第4期，第39页。
② 同上书，第45页。
③ 石昌渝：《〈水浒传〉的思想倾向》，《品读〈水浒传〉》，中国人民大学出版社2004年版，第23页。

图报国"①。按此说法，一部《水浒传》写的是忠臣义士如宋公明等与权奸如高俅、蔡京、童贯等之间的斗争。

"文革"结束不久，几位学者接连发文表达此种观点。刘烈茂在文章中指出："贯串《水浒》全书的并不是农民阶级与地主阶级的矛盾和斗争，而是忠与奸的矛盾斗争，它所要表现的主题并不是'官逼民反'而是'替天行道'；它所着力歌颂的理想人物并不是晁盖、方腊那样的农民起义英雄，而是宋江那样的'忠义之士'。"②孙一珍则说："运用历史唯物主义的观点分析《水浒传》，不等于生搬硬套地用阶级斗争和路线斗争的框子要古人就范。""从百回本《水浒传》全书着眼，它所写的是亡国之君宋徽宗统治时期，蔡京、高俅等贪官、奸佞、权势和广大人民群众的矛盾冲突。其中包含着强暴对弱小的欺压，奸佞对忠诚的排挤，邪恶对正直的陷害。"梁山好汉们的行为则"集中地概括了当时广大人民群众所具有的精神如反压迫、反侵略等优秀品质。这些品质当然不是农民所仅有的"。③不过，孙一珍在行文过程中还是承认《水浒传》是反映"农民起义"的作品。与"忠奸斗争说"相近，张锦池提出"乱世忠义"说④。

关于《水浒传》主题的第三种主要观点是"为市井细民写心说"。1954年，冯雪峰在讨论《水浒传》的"农民起义"主题的文章中就曾经说道："《水浒传》有不小篇幅，是描写当时城市人民的生活和正义斗争的。"但他着眼于"农民起义"，并未就此展开讨论。真正对"为市井细民写心说"进行深入研究，是在20世纪70年代中期开始的。1975年，伊永文发表文章质疑"农民起义说"，指出"《水浒传》是反映市民阶层利益的小说"，"《水浒传》漫长的成书过程，是和当时社会上阶级斗争的发展、商品经济的增长、城市市民阶层的壮大等分不开的"⑤。他还运用阶级观点和阶级分析方法，对《水浒传》中的主要人物、社会基础和政

---

① 李贽：《忠义水浒传》叙，朱一玄、刘毓忱编：《水浒传资料汇编》，南开大学出版社2012年版，第171—172页。

② 刘烈茂：《评〈水浒〉应该怎样一分为二?》，《中山大学学报》1979年第1期，第34页。

③ 孙一珍：《〈水浒传〉主题辨》，《文艺研究》1979年第3期，第118—119页。

④ 见张锦池《中国四大古典小说论稿》，华艺出版社1993年版；《"乱世忠义"的颂歌——论〈水浒〉故事的思想倾向》，《社会科学战线》1983年第4期。

⑤ 伊永文：《〈水浒传〉是反映市民阶层利益的作品》，《天津师院学报》1975年第4期，第74页。

治路线进行具体的分析,以证明自己的观点。在另一篇文章中,伊永文指出作品中大批的非农民化人物成了主人公,而"这些一直被某些研究者推崇为'农民起义的英雄'们,生活场所经常交换,根本没有对土地的热爱之情,更缺乏农民的那种劳动的逻辑和劳动的道德"。因此他认为:"《水浒传》这部小说,以宋江等三十六人横行河朔的事件为原始素材,根据市民阶层的理想,着重地表现了市民阶层的反抗思想和行为","《水浒传》是市民阶层用来反映自己对现实、历史的认识的文学作品"①。

欧阳健、萧相恺二人是持"为市井细民写心说"的又一中坚力量。20世纪80年代,他们连续发表《〈水浒〉"梁山泊聚义"性质辨》、《〈水浒〉"为市井细民写心"说》、《〈水浒〉"为市井细民写心"二说》、《〈水浒〉作者代表什么阶级的思想》等系列文章,比较系统地论述了《水浒传》"为市井细民写心说"的主题。其理由主要有两点:(1)由于小说创作中的虚构以及文学叙述与历史事实之间的差异,作品中的"梁山泊聚义"并不是指历史上的宋江起义;(2)作品所说的"官逼民反"中的"民"主要不是指农民,梁山好汉宣扬的"替天行道"之"道"主要也不是农民之道②。

"为市井细民写心说"的提出,丰富了理解《水浒传》主题的路径,同时也遭到一些学者的批评。有人认为,在中国历史上并不存在"市民阶级";宋元时期发展起来的"城市居民"情况复杂,不能一概地称为"市民阶级";所谓的"为市井细民写心说"实际上犯了主次颠倒的错误,以"市民社会"取代封建社会,以"市民思想"取代封建思想,这与作品所写实际情况并不相符。还有人认为,不能因为作品中存在大批的非农民化主人公就否定《水浒传》反映农民起义的事实③。就既存文本来说,这些批评的声音,听起来也不无道理。

在《水浒传》主题研究中,"反映游民意识说"的明确提出是相对较

---

① 伊永文:《再论〈水浒传〉是反映市民阶层利益的作品》,《河北大学学报》1980年第4期,第68、72页。
② 具体内容见《〈水浒〉"梁山泊聚义"性质辨》,《钟山文艺论集》,江苏人民出版社1980年版;《〈水浒〉"为市井细民写心"说》《〈水浒〉"为市井细民写心"二说》,《水浒新议》,重庆出版社1983年版;《〈水浒〉作者代表什么阶级的思想》,《社会科学研究》1980年第4期;等等。
③ 见黄霖、陈荣《论〈水浒〉研究中的"市民说"》等文章,《水浒争鸣》第2辑,长江文艺出版社1983年版。

晚的事。王开富在1980年发表的一篇文章中提出这么一个看法,他认为《水浒传》所写宋江起义原型其实是"封建社会的无业游民的武装斗争"①。这一说法已触及《水浒传》中的游民问题,只是王开富并未就此展开论述。

真正对"反映游民意识说"进行系统、深入研究的是王学泰。在1989年中华书局(香港)出版的《中国流民》一书(该书2012年上海远东出版社出版时题名为《中国游民》,本文所引以远东版为准),王学泰用了一整节讨论作为"流民意识载体"的通俗小说,经典作品之一就是《水浒传》。他提出,《水浒传》这样的表现、反映游民情绪和游民意识的典范之作形象地为我们描绘出了有关游民文化的下列问题:

首先是游民性格。王学泰认为:"游民是脱离了社会正常秩序的一群,他们在社会中的特殊地位及其独特的经历,造成了他们群体性格的独特性。这独特的一面突出地表现在他们对自己的观念、性格很少掩饰。"②具体说来就是"强烈的帮派意识"、"赤裸的野蛮残暴"与"垂涎于财货金银"。这种性格特征,也决定了游民对社会的破坏性作用。在《水浒传》中,突出的表现就是像李逵的无理性的血腥嗜杀行为,以及梁山好汉为了自己团体的利益对平民百姓的践踏,为营救卢俊义而火烧大名府就是典型。

其次是游民的人格楷模。在王学泰看来,"侠客是游民的人格楷模",像不顾一切利害、路见不平拔刀相助的鲁智深这样的"武侠",像急人之困、救人危难的宋江这样的"义侠",就是让江湖好汉钦慕的典范。

再次是游民的道德。游民道德中,首先也是最重要的就是"义","讲义气"。但这种"义"不同于儒家之义,儒家强调义、利两分,所谓"君子喻于义,小人喻于利"。而在游民文化中,以《水浒传》来说,王学泰认为其中所讲的"义"和"义气","是指金钱和其他物质上的援助";所谓"讲义气","不是单方面的施与,它是以平等为基础的,有施有报的。施者之初也是以回报为期望的"。③ 正因此,梁山好汉所讲的"忠"也和儒家的"忠"不一样。儒家所讲的"忠"强调臣子对君王的绝对服从,而梁山好汉所讲的"忠"不过是"义"的陪衬。

---

① 具体见王开富《〈水浒传〉是写农民起义的吗?》,《重庆师院学报》1980年第3期。
② 王学泰:《中国游民》,上海远东出版社2012年版,第33、34页。
③ 同上书,第45—46页。

最后就是游民的理想问题。王学泰认为,基于结义形成的"四海之内皆兄弟"的世界是游民理想的人际关系,《水浒传》中描绘的"八方共域,异姓一家"、"不分贵贱"、"不问亲疏"的梁山泊,是游民的理想之所在,它"反映了游民对于平等的追求"①。

王学泰在1999年出版的《游民文化与中国社会》一书中,对《水浒传》的"反映游民意识"主题作了进一步的论述。他提出,如果我们用传统的、占主流地位的儒家思想观念来分析《水浒传》的话,有很多现象很多问题是无法解释的通的。而如果用盛行于社会底层、游民世界的上述有关游民的性格、道德、理想追求等观念来研究《水浒传》,原来在儒家思想观照之下的梁山好汉各种显得矛盾、不可理喻的行为,就能得到比较圆满的解答。基于此种认识,王学泰对"农民起义说"、"忠奸斗争说"等观点都进行了批驳。

在《水浒传》的主题研究中,上述四种主要观点之外,王齐洲提出《水浒传》写的是"地主阶级内部革新派与守旧派的斗争"②;倪长康等人认为《水浒传》写的是封建时代人们美好理想的幻灭③;宋克夫、佘树声等则认为《水浒传》表达出的是悲剧主题④;还有一些学者认为,《水浒传》因其内容的丰富、成书过程的复杂以及作者世界观的内在矛盾,其主题思想是多元的⑤;等等。然而,不管是哪种观点,都在一定程度上受到质疑和批驳。

在《水浒传》主题研究过程中,研究者会得出这样多元性的认识、提出多样的见解,笔者认为,一方面是与《水浒传》文本自身叙述的复杂性,以及情节发展中主要人物言行的内在矛盾性密切相关的;另一方面,漫长的成书过程以及作者自身思想的复杂性,也决定了《水浒传》主题呈现的多样性;同时,这种理解的多元性也与研究者所处时代的意识

---

① 王学泰:《中国游民》,上海远东出版社2012年版,第53—54页。
② 见王齐洲《〈水浒传〉是描写农民起义的作品吗?》,《水浒争鸣》第1辑,长江文艺出版社1982年版。
③ 见倪长康《封建长夜中的一个理想国梦——〈水浒〉主题之我见》,《明清小说研究》1991年第1期;韩晓谅《〈水浒〉主题新解》,《明清小说研究》1994年第2期。
④ 见宋克夫《乱世忠义的悲歌——论〈水浒传〉的主题及思维方式》,《湖北大学学报》1993年第6期;佘树声《论〈水浒传〉的悲剧意义》,《齐鲁学刊》1999年第3期。
⑤ 见郭振勤《从生成史略论〈水浒传〉的主题》,《汕头大学学报》1993年第3期;殷恢章《〈水浒传〉主题的多元与主元》,《重庆师范学院学报》1997年第4期。

形态脱不了干系。从某一时间段来说，意识形态完全起着主导性的作用，如"文革"期间"评《水浒》运动"中批判的所谓"宋江的投降主义"就是一个典型，当然这是非常特殊的。

（五）结构艺术之争

《水浒传》的结构是"有机的"还是"非有机的"，这是其艺术研究中长久以来争论的一个中心问题。明李开先在《词谑》里说："《水浒传》委曲详尽，血脉贯通。"按此说，《水浒传》在结构上当然是一部"有机的"的经典之作。现代学者郑振铎进一步发展了此种观点。他在1929年撰写的《〈水浒传〉的演化》一文中指出，罗贯中《水浒传》"这个原本的结构原是一个很严密的组织。就全部观之，确是一部很伟大的很完美的悲剧"。① "因为全书的布局是这样严密，每位英雄的身世结果都已安排好了，完全不能更动，作续书的人要插增几段故事进去，便觉非常困难，如要使这种'插增'成为'无缝的天衣'，却更为难中之难。所以那几位做'插增'《水浒》的人都感到左支右绌，无往而不露出大裂缝来。"② 郑氏图文并茂，按情节发展的"起点"、"顶点"到"终点"的过程来说明《水浒传》结构的严密性，的确有可取之处。

然而，就《水浒传》这样一部复杂的作品来说，郑振铎之观点也不是"天衣无缝"的。1950年，茅盾发表《谈〈水浒〉的人物和结构》一文，其中提出："从全书来看，《水浒》的结构不是有机的结构。我们可以把若干主要人物的故事分别编为各自独立的短篇或中篇而无割裂之感。但是，从一个人的故事看来，《水浒》的结构是严密的，甚至是有机的。"③ 茅盾的说法可以这样来解读，从《水浒传》的大结构方面来说那是"非有机的"，但具体到某一主人公的故事则是"有机的"。笔者以为，茅盾的观点兼顾小说的大、小情节，分析的还是很有道理的。和茅盾的看法不同，李希凡认为"《水浒》的长篇章回结构，尽管还残留着说话时朴素的章回形式，若干章节还有着个别英雄传奇的特色，但是，就长篇结构

---

① 笔者在此要做以下说明：一是郑振铎认为罗贯中著《水浒传》是小说原本，其中不包括我们现在所见的"征田虎"、"征王庆"两个故事；二是郑氏《水浒传》结构布局图为：误走妖魔（起点）—史进鲁智深等出现—劫生辰纲—杀阎婆惜—闹江州—三打祝家庄—打曾头市—梁山泊英雄排座次（顶点）—闹东京—二败童贯—三败高俅—全伙受招安—征方腊—功成遭害—魂聚蓼儿洼（终点）。

② 郑振铎：《〈水浒传〉的演化》，《中国文学论集》，岳麓书社2011年版，第119页。

③ 茅盾：《谈〈水浒〉的人物和结构》，《文艺报》二卷二期，1950年。

来说，它仍然是有机结构的统一体"。①

进入 20 世纪 80 年代，针对茅盾"从全书来看，《水浒传》的结构不是有机的结构"的观点，王齐洲撰文说，"《水浒传》的长篇结构乃是有机的，作者根据表达主题的需要，巧妙地组织和安排了作品的人物、环境和情节，形成独特的结构艺术，并对后世的长篇小说创作产生了深远的影响"；从人物性格发展对作品结构的作用上，王齐洲进一步谈道，"细读《水浒传》，我们发现：《水浒传》人物和情节的安排，是作者按照自己对生活的理解，为表现作品主题而精心设计的，贯串这些人物事件的重要线索是作品的中心人物宋江的性格发展。有人认为《水浒》是'由几个主要人物的传记缀合而成'，这并不符合《水浒》的实际"。据此，王齐洲的结论是："从宋江的性格发展来看，从中心人物形象的塑造与主题表达来看，《水浒》的长篇结构是紧凑的、严密的，因而是有机的。如果我们忽视宋江性格发展这条贯串全书的线索，就只能看到《水浒传》是无数个短片的缀合，甚至是杂乱无章的拼凑；而一旦我们抓住了这条线索，我们就能发现《水浒》长篇结构是有着内在逻辑的不可分割和颠倒的艺术整体。"②

后来，欧阳健、萧相恺二人从"梁山泊农民起义的全过程"这个大情节与"单个的英雄的故事"的小情节的关系入手，他们提出：就《水浒传》全书来看，大情节"只不过是一种极为粗糙的故事梗概而已"，"《水浒》中真正的情节，只能是那些单个的英雄人物故事的'小情节'"；结果，如果以大情节为基本情节，小说的整体结构似乎是"有机的统一体"，而如果以小情节为基本情节，则会得出"不是有机结构"的结论。正是大情节与小情节之间这种难以调和的矛盾和冲突，造成了《水浒》整体结构"非有机"的弊病③。

上述争论中，不管认为《水浒传》的结构艺术是"有机的"还是"非有机的"，其实在具体的论述过程中，他们都看到了《水浒》结构中内在的统一性与矛盾性。就是说，他们都发现了《水浒》结构中"有机

---

① 李希凡：《〈水浒〉的作者和〈水浒〉的长篇结构》，《文艺月报》1956 年第 1 期。
② 王齐洲：《〈水浒传〉的结构"不是有机的"吗?》，《水浒争鸣》第 4 辑，长江文艺出版社 1985 年版，第 257、258、264 页。
③ 具体论述见欧阳健、萧相恺著《水浒新议》一书《〈水浒〉情节结构刍议》部分，重庆出版社 1983 年版，第 208—215 页。

的"一面和"非有机的"另一面。总的来说,《水浒传》的艺术结构,有其成功的地方,也有其不足的地方。

(六) 人物形象研究

在《水浒传》的接受、研究史上,水浒人物一直以来是人们关注的重点。有明一代,自《水浒传》刊行始,批评者就着力对水浒人物进行品评。在《批评〈水浒传〉述语》中,怀林曰:"和尚读《水浒传》,第一当意黑旋风李逵,谓为梁山泊第一尊活佛"[1],将李逵形象推到极高的地位。无名氏《梁山泊一百单八人优劣》文章,虽寥寥数百字,但对梁山好汉中的李逵、宋江、吴用等主要人物都作了相当精到的评价。评李逵则曰:"李逵者,梁山泊第一尊活佛也,为善为恶,彼具无意。宋江用之,便知有宋江而已,无诚心也,无执念也。"品宋江则曰:"若夫宋江者,逢人便拜,见人便哭,自称曰:'小吏,小吏',或招曰:'罪人,罪人'的是假道学,真强盗也。然能以此收拾人心,亦非无用人也。当时若使之为相,虽不敢曰休休一个臣,亦必能以人事君,有可观者也。"至于说吴用则是"一味权谋,全身奸诈,佛性到此,澌灭殆尽。倘能置之帷幄之中,似亦可与陈平诸人对垒"。[2] 署名李贽评点的容与堂本《水浒传》里面,对人物的评价时有精妙之语。如第六十七回评李逵:"李大哥妙处,只在一言一动都不算计,只在任天而行,率性而动。"在《〈忠义水浒传〉序》里,李贽评价宋江则誉其为"忠义之烈"。[3] 凡此种种,不多赘述。上述评论虽不能说完全正确,但对人物性格特征的概括还是很到位的。

明末清初的金圣叹,在《读第五才子书法》中沿袭人物品评之风气,将水浒人物分为三六九等。在上上人物中,武松被誉为"天神";鲁达则"心地厚实,体格阔大","已是人中绝顶";李逵则是"一片天真烂漫到底",金圣叹并以为"《孟子》'富贵不能淫,贫贱不能移,威武不能屈',正是他好批语"。至于林冲,"只是太狠。看他算得到,熬得住,把得牢,做得彻,都使人怕"。……凡此种种,不一而足。与李贽相反,在金圣叹

---

[1] (明) 怀林:《批评〈水浒传〉述语》,朱一玄、刘毓忱编:《水浒传资料汇编》,南开大学出版社2012年版,第185页。

[2] (明) 无名氏:《梁山泊一百单八人优劣》,朱一玄、刘毓忱编:《水浒传资料汇编》,南开大学出版社2012年版,第185页。

[3] 本书所引容与堂本《水浒传》内容以上海古籍出版社1988年版为据。

看来，宋江与时迁"是一流人，定考下下"，玩弄权术，表里不一，为人虚伪；虽与吴用一样"奸猾"，却心地不如吴端正①。金圣叹之品读水浒人物，内容甚多，不一一赘述。在继承前人研究成果的基础上，现代学人对水浒人物也发表了很多很精到的看法。笔者就以人们对宋江的评价为例略述如下。

20 世纪 60 年代，李希凡在研究中指出，宋江性格的复杂性和矛盾性是封建社会不同矛盾作用的反映。他还说："宋江的矛盾性格，也在一定程度上反映了水浒义军的反抗斗争的局限性，宋江的忠义观念，实际上也在一定程度上反映了水浒义军反抗精神的悲剧矛盾。"②

80 年代，宋江形象的研究进一步深化。唐富龄在《宋江形象的分裂性、统一性及其他》一文指出，宋江的一生经历了"由不革命到走向革命以致最后叛变革命的三部曲"，他的性格经过了一个矛盾冲突的发展过程，在"忠"与"义"之间产生了分裂，最后又在"忠"上面获得统一。唐富龄认为，《水浒传》的作者对宋江虽有微词，基本上还是把他当作正面形象来塑造的③。与此观点相近，李永祜也认为《水浒传》的作者是从肯定的方面来塑造宋江这个人物的。他说："显然，认为《水浒》的作者是'完全反对'招安的，就是要'拿宋江当反面教员'这种看法，一是割裂了作品塑造的完整、统一的宋江的艺术形象，二是抹煞了作者的主观意图和艺术形象的客观意义的区别，三是以今人的看法代替了古人的认识。"④ 从作者创作动机与读者阅读接受效果之间的差异来谈论人们在宋江形象评论中存在的问题，这是很有意义的，也是值得每一个做古典文学研究的现代学者加以反思的。与上述诸人同时，欧阳健、萧相恺从"为市井细民写心说"出发，认为"宋江是市民阶级心目中最最完美的人物"⑤。

---

① 金圣叹评论水浒人物之文字，具体请参见其《读第五才子书法》，朱一玄、刘毓忱编：《水浒传资料汇编》，南开大学出版社 2012 年版，第 218—225 页。

② 具体论述见李希凡《〈水浒传〉中宋江的悲剧形象和义军的悲剧结尾》，《论中国古典小说的艺术形象》，上海文艺出版社 1961 年版。

③ 唐富龄：《宋江形象的分裂性、统一性及其他》，《水浒争鸣》第 1 辑，长江文艺出版社 1982 年版，第 65—82 页。

④ 李永祜：《评〈水浒〉招安结局的思想倾向》，《水浒争鸣》第 2 辑，长江文艺出版社 1983 年版，第 202 页。

⑤ 具体见欧阳健、萧相恺著《水浒新议》一书的"柴进·晁盖·宋江论"部分，重庆出版社 1983 年版，第 109 页。

进入21世纪，郭英德在研究中指出，宋江形象是中国传统社会儒家文化与民间江湖文化相互作用的产物，这决定了其"左右为难的性格特征"；宋江的"人格内蕴"及其悲剧，说到底是两种不同价值观的文化碰撞、冲突的结果[①]。笔者对此论深表赞同。宋江研究，在此仅拣起具有代表性的观点陈述如上。至于研究其他水浒人物的情况，恕不再展开。

　　上述六个方面之外，国内还有不少学者对明清时期的《水浒传》评点进行了深入的研究。李贽《水浒传》评点的真伪问题是争论的一个焦点；金圣叹评改《水浒传》的功过也是个争论不休的话题，特别是对金圣叹评改中的思想倾向问题，褒贬之间差异甚大。但限于本课题的研究对象，在此就不再讨论。

　　总体看来，国内四百多年的《水浒传》研究，经历了一个由最初的"散点式"批评走向现在的系统化、理论化研究的过程，经历了立足国内资源到现在不断借鉴国外理论、方法来指导研究的过程。人们的研究越来越深入、越来越广泛，所取得的成果也越来越丰硕。但存在的问题也不容忽视，比如：在人物评价、主题研究中存在的以今人之看法代替古人之认识的情况，以及抓住某一点不及其余的片面性现象；在作者、版本研究中，在缺少充足资料的情况下，不少论者以猜测、臆断作为结论的不严谨性；……所有这些都是需要我们反思、反省的地方。

---

① 具体见郭英德著《四大名著讲演录》一书的《左右为难的人生困境——说宋江》部分，广西师范大学出版社2006年版。

第一章

英语世界对《水浒传》的考证探源研究

在英语世界，对《水浒传》的作者、素材来源、成书历史等问题的考证，是研究者关注的最基本的课题。这与中国学术界的现状是基本相似的。然而，英语世界的专家、学者对这些问题的研究并没能形成定论，这也与中国学术界一样。只是英语世界对这些问题的研究具体呈现出怎样的状况呢？本章就来讨论这些问题。

第一节 《水浒传》的作者问题

《水浒传》的作者是谁？这部小说是一个人独立创作的还是经多人之手编撰而成的？小说作者是一个什么身份的人？这些问题是英语世界的批评者在《水浒传》作者研究中的基本关注点。下面，笔者就分类来讨论这几个问题。

一、《水浒传》是个人独创抑或多人合著

在《水浒传》是个人独立创作还是多人合著这个问题上，李培德（Peter Li）等人坚持"多位作者"（multiple authors）论。他们说：

> 《水浒传》的文本历史很复杂，著作权更是一个谜团。曾经把它归到多位作家名下，包括罗贯中和施耐庵。把著作权归于罗贯中，这从未形成定论，施耐庵的身份则存在严重问题。因为这部作品实质上是经过不同时代、不同人之手编撰而成的。作者是谁并不是评价这部

小说的关键。①

在此，李培德等明确指出《水浒传》是经多人之手编撰而成的。他们还指出："正确评价《水浒传》，需要考虑到它漫长的演变过程，多位作者以及民间口头渊源。"②

德波特（Deborah L. Porter）对此持不同意见。在1989年的博士论文《〈水浒传〉的风格》，以及在此基础上发表的论文《一个形象的构成：宋江形象形成的语言模型分析》中，德波特通过对《水浒传》文本中宋江形象形成的几个关键片段所作的修辞学和语言学分析，认为小说文本前后之间在语言、修辞层面存在明显的一致性。由此他提出《水浒传》这部作品是由一个人完成的。他说：

> 即使《水浒传》的作者明显采用了先前存在的素材，但作品中众多值得注意的修辞策略的一致性，说明这部作品是由一个人完成的。③

德波特所说构成宋江形象的几个关键片段，指的是如下几处：

第一处是小说第18回，宋江刚出场时作者对他的介绍。作者通过何

---

① The textual history of *The Water Margin* is complex and its authorship especially puzzling. It has been attributed to various writers, including Lo Kuan-chung and Shih Nai-an. The attribution to Lo has never been firmly established, and the identity of Shih has been seriously questioned. Since the book is essentially a compilation of different hands at different times, a knowledge of its authorship is not crucial to its appreciation. Winston L. Y. Yang, Nathan K. Mao and Peter Li, "Romance of the Three Kingdoms and The Water Margin," and "Journey to the West and Flowers in the Mirror." Classical Chinese Fiction: A Guide to Its Study and Appreciation. London: George Prior Publishers, 1978, pp. 39 – 51. *Literature Criticism from 1400 to 1800*. Ed. Lynn M. Zott. Vol. 76. Detroit: Gale, 2002. From Literature Resource Center.

② A proper appreciation of *The Water Margin* requires the consideration of its long evolutionary process, its multiple authors, and its folk and oral origins. Winston L. Y. Yang, Nathan K. Mao and Peter Li, *Romance of the Three Kingdoms* and *The Water Margin*, and *Journey to the West* and *Flowers in the Mirror*. Classical Chinese Fiction: A Guide to Its Study and Appreciation. London: George Prior Publishers, 1978, pp. 39 – 51. *Literature Criticism from 1400 to 1800*. Ed. Lynn M. Zott. Vol. 76. Detroit: Gale, 2002. From Literature Resource Center.

③ The remarkable consistency with which many of the rhetorical devices are employed suggests that the work is the product of one man, despite his obvious approriation of preexisting source materials. Deborah L. Porter, The Formation of an Image: An Analysis of the Linguistic Patterns That Form the Character of Sung Chiang, Journal of the American Oriental Society, Vol. 112, No, 2 (Apr.-Jun., 1992), pp. 233 – 234.

涛来描绘宋江的长相模样与志向才干，以及其仗义疏财的品行。原文是这样的：

> 何涛看时，只见县里走出一个吏员来。看那人时，怎生模样，但见：
>
> 眼如丹凤，眉似卧蚕。滴溜溜两耳悬珠，明皎皎双睛点漆。唇方口正，髭须地阁轻盈；额阔顶平，皮肉天仓饱满。坐定时浑如虎相，走动时有若狼形。年及三旬，有养济万人之度量；身躯六尺，怀扫除四海之心机。志气轩昂，胸襟秀丽。刀笔敢欺萧相国，声名不让孟尝君。①

德波特认为，宋江刚出场时，作者为了展现其仗义疏财的品行，小说中与此相似的语言修辞策略尚有：

> 平生只好结识江湖上好汉，但有来投他的，若高若低，无有不纳。……时常散施棺材药饵，济人贫苦，赒人之急，扶人之困，以此山东、河北闻名，都称他做及时雨，却把他比做天上下的及时雨一般，能救万物。②

以及一首《临江仙》词赞其好处：

> 起自花村刀笔吏，英灵上应天星，疏财仗义更多能。事亲行孝敬，待士有声名。济弱扶倾心慷慨，高名水月双清。及时甘雨四方称，山东呼保义，豪杰宋公明。③

德波特指出，小说作者对宋江的这些介绍，让他拥有"孝义黑三郎"、"及时雨"的好名声。

---

① 见施耐庵、罗贯中著，李卓吾批评本《水浒传》（上），上海古籍出版社1988年版，第二四五页。另：本论文在引述《水浒传》相关内容时，以上海古籍出版社1988年版百回李卓吾批评本《水浒传》为据。如有特殊，另作说明。
② 同上书，第245页。
③ 同上书，第246页。

第二处同样在第18回,是描写宋江应对何涛给晁盖通风报信"私放晁天王"事件。德波特此处所引对宋江的描写有下面几处:

> 宋江应答何涛的话,一是"休说太师处着落,便是观察自费公文来要,敢不捕送。只是不知道白胜供那七人名字"。二是"理之当然,休这等说话。小吏略到寒舍,分拨了些家务便到,观察少坐一坐"。三是"只是这一件,这实封公文,须是观察自己当厅投下,本官看了便好施行发落,差人去捉,小吏如何敢私下擅开?这件公事,非是小可,勿当轻泄于人"。①

描写宋江应答何涛后的反应则是:

> 离了茶坊,飞也似跑到下处。先分付伴当去叫直司在茶坊门前伺候:"若知县坐衙时,便可去茶坊里安抚那公人道:'押司稳便',叫他略待一待。"②

德波特对构成宋江形象的其他方面的分析,尚有:"宋江的政治野心:铤而走险的必然结果","魔幻和权威:成为领袖",以及"法定权威:石碣天文"等三部分。内容琐碎繁杂,不详论。

对李培德等人的"多位作者"论与德波特的"一人创作"说,笔者以为此两者并不矛盾。李培德等人着眼的是在《水浒传》的漫长成书过程中,有多人为此作品的完成做出了贡献;而德波特关注的则是小说的最后写定者,或者说是编撰者。事实上,《水浒传》的最后写定工作,应该是一个人完成的,只不过他是以前人的材料为基础。

二、《水浒传》的著作权归属

《水浒传》的著作权应归于谁,这在英语世界的研究中存在很大分歧。在一般的描述层面,有一些学者认为是施耐庵所作,像赖明(Ming Lai)等在介绍中国文学时就持此观点;有一些人则坚持施耐庵与罗贯中

---

① (明)施耐庵、罗贯中:《水浒传》(上),李卓吾批评本,上海古籍出版社1988年版,第247页。
② 同上。

合著说,像赛珍珠、沙博理等人英译《水浒传》时,就把施耐庵和罗贯中同署为小说作者。而进入研究层面,情况则大不一样。主要观点有如下几种:

以赛珍珠为代表的批评者认为,不管《水浒传》最终由谁写成,他都只是一个"集大成者"而非"原创者"。赛珍珠说:

> 《水浒传》的发展(形成现在的形式),是一个有趣的故事。像许多其他中国小说一样,它是逐渐完善而非一步写成的。直到今天,小说的最后写定者是谁仍不得而知。据说是施耐庵所著,但除了据说他祖籍江苏淮安,在元代,进士及第后在浙江钱塘担任过官职之外,其他方面对他一无所知。很多中国学者相信《三国演义》的作者罗贯中也创作了《水浒传》。似乎可以相当肯定地认为,不论罗贯中是否只用笔名施耐庵写成《水浒传》一书,至少他修订过这部作品,并可能做过大量的改动与增补。至少有一位中国学者坚信《水浒传》一定出自罗贯中之手。他依据的事实是,《水浒传》是一部如此邪恶的书,其作者必然遭受诅咒——他的后人三代聋哑。既然罗贯中子孙三代聋哑,因此,他一定是小说的作者。
>
> 但这里对作者的讨论无足轻重。因为现存的事实说明,不管《水浒传》是谁写成的,他都只是一个集大成者而非完全的原创者。这本书近似于现在的形式,大概写成于14世纪或15世纪,也就是明中前期。只是在此前两个多世纪里,《水浒传》中的一些故事已基本形成。①

---

① The story of the growth of *Shui Hu Chuan* into its present form is an interesting one. Like many of the Chinese novels it developed rather than was written, and to this day its final author is unknown. It is said to be written by one Shih Nai-an, but little is known of him exception that it is said he was a native of Huai-an in Kiangsu province, and became an official in Ch'ien-tang in Chekiang province, after graduating as *chin shih* in the Yüan Dynasty. Many Chinese scholars believe Lo Kuan Chung, the author of *The Three Kingdoms*, wrote *Shui Hu Chuan* also, and it seems fairly sure that at least he revised it and perhaps made substantial changes and additions, whether or not it be true that he wrote the whole, using Shih Nai-an merely as a pen name. One Chinese scholar at least gives as authority for Lo Kuan Chung's authorship the fact that *Shui Hu Chuan* is so evil a book that the curse was laid upon the author that for three generations his descendants were to be deaf and dumb and since for three generations Lo Kuan Chung's descendants were deaf and dumb therefore he must be the author.

如果我们确信《水浒传》的成书经历了如赛珍珠所说的两三百年的历史，那么，这部小说的最终写定者确实可以称其为"集大成者"。但问题是，如果在这位"集大成者"写定之前并没有出现一部比较完整的《水浒传》，该"集大成者"只是把先前那些在社会流传的、零散的水浒人物故事收集起来作为自己创作的素材的话，笔者以为还是具有原创的性质。创作一部像《水浒传》这样庞大的写实性文学作品，如果没有丰富的材料积累，那是完全不可想象的。像闻名世界的现实主义文学巨匠巴尔扎克、左拉、托尔斯泰等，有哪位没有经历大量素材的积累就写出了传世杰作呢？因此，在这个问题上，笔者认为无论《水浒传》的最后写定者是谁，他都是一位伟大的"创造者"。因为如果没有他个人独特的思想与创作动机的指引，是绝不可能把那些流传至今或者已经亡佚的水浒人物故事材料，组织成我们现在所能看到的"这一"《水浒传》的文本形式的。

欧文（Richard Gregg Irwin）在1953年出版的论著《一部中国小说的演变：〈水浒传〉》中，对小说的作者问题也作了讨论。该论者指出，根据《水浒传》的最早记述文献资料，施耐庵和罗贯中两人经常与该作品联系在一起；传统的看法加上对罗贯中的了解，又倾向于认为罗是小说的作者；而如果《施氏族谱》的记述真实的话，这部作品则是两人合著的。对此，欧文说：

> 我并不接受对作者身份所作的那种更多是尝试性的鉴定。但墓志铭描写的某些细节，和其他文献来源所记述的情形很契合。像施的生平时间，居住钱塘的时期，他对颓败官场的不平，罗在福建的出现（这可以解释他和贾仲明失去联系的原因），以及施、罗两人

But the discussion is scarcely of general importance here, since the fact remains that whoever wrote *Shui Hu Chuan* performed an eclectic rather than a wholly creative role. The book in approximately its present form was probably written in the early or middle part of the Ming Dynasty in the fourteenth or fifteenth century, but more than two centuries before there were already the stories of which *Shui Hu Chuan* was later to be made, stories not only in prose and told by the professional story tellers, but in poems and plays.

I am not prepared to accept the identification as more than tentative. But certain details of the tomb inscription fit well into the pattern constructed from other sources: Shih's date, the period of residence in Ch'ien-t'ang, and his indignation with decadent government, as well as Lo's appearence in Fukien (which might explain his loss of contact with Chia Chung-ming), and Lo's relation to Nai-an. Pearl S. Buck, *Introduction of Shui Hu Chuan*, *All Men Are Brothers*, NewYork: The John Day Company, 1933, p. vii.

的关系。①

根据此论述，很明显，欧文倾向于"施、罗合著"说。基于这样的认识，欧文设想了下面的系列事情：

> 由于对官场失望，施辞官归隐，甚至放弃了为其谋得官职的古典文学研究。他继续待在浙江，转向白话创作。与这种新的兴趣一致，他很自然地在某个书会找到了相似的精神寄托。在书会成员中，他遇到了罗贯中，而且他们加入了一项很有吸引力的事情，那就是对《水浒传词话》进行扩展、提炼。他们天才的合作造就了一部杰作，超越了罗的独自写作。②

很显然，欧文的看法建立在设想、推断的基础之上，并无确凿的文献资料可据，自然就缺乏足够的说服力。而且根据欧文的论述，施、罗两人合著的是祖本《水浒传》（The original *Shui-hu-chuan*），自然他们就只是小说祖本的作者。

以夏志清为代表的批评者坚持认为《水浒传》的著作权应归于罗贯中。对此问题，夏志清是这样论述的：

> 从留下来的文人对小说的即兴评点和现存所有版本中的书名页来判断，明代对于《水浒》的作者问题有两种观点：一种认为《水浒》是罗贯中一个人的作品，另一种则认为《水浒》系施耐庵和罗贯中的合作。但那些承认施耐庵功劳的版本只说他是小说基本材料的作者，是罗贯中根据这些材料编写了他的小说。这么说，很可能像是用陈寿的材料写成《三国》那样，用施的材料写成了《水浒》。既然我

---

① Richard Gregg Irwin, The evolution of a Chinese novel: *Shui-hu-chuan*, Cambridge Massachusetts: Harvard University Press, 1953, p. 50.
② Let us postulate the following sequence of events leading to their collaboration in the writing of a novel. Disappointed with office, Shih renounced even the classical studies which paved the way to his appointment, and remaining in Chekiang, turned instead to vernacular writing. In accordance with this new interest he naturally sought for kindred spirits in one of the shu-hui. Among its members he met Lo, and they joined forces in an intriguing project, the expansion and refinement of a Shui-hu-chuan tz'u-hua. The combination of their talents resulted in a masterpiece which surpassed anything Lo ever wrote alone. Richard Gregg Irwin, The evolution of a Chinese novel: Shui-hu-chuan, Cambridge Massachusetts: Harvard University Press, 1953, p. 50.

第一章 英语世界对《水浒传》的考证探源研究

们实际上对施耐庵一无所知,既然他的《水浒》(假如它确实存在过的话)早已被溶进了罗贯中的本子,那么,如果要把《水浒》归于某个特定的作者的话,首先把它归于罗贯中,是完全公平合理的。①

夏志清根据有关文献对施耐庵、罗贯中二人信息记载的可考性与可靠性来判断《水浒传》的作者问题,提出"如果要把《水浒》归于某个特定的作者的话,首先把它归于罗贯中,是完全公平合理的"的观点。但实际上,目前所能看到的记述罗贯中的文献资料也并不完全翔实可信,尤其在他是否真正写作过《水浒传》上更是如此。

不论是欧文还是夏志清,他们的观点都没有如山铁证的支持,更多的是停留在推断、猜想的层面。基于这样的研究现状,浦安迪在论著《明代小说四大奇书》中提出②,无论是罗贯中还是施耐庵,都不能确定就是小说的作者。对此,浦安迪如此说道:

我们所能想到的那些记述繁本《水浒传》到嘉靖朝就已通行的同一批文献书目,几乎无疑义地认定小说早就已经写成,并署名其主要编撰者或者是罗贯中抑或是施耐庵。而从16世纪至今,每一个版本的封面实际上都清楚地把该作品最初的编著权归于这两人或是其中之一。这就更加强了这个事实。③

面对这些文献的记载情况,浦安迪认为:

这些说法无助于解决小说的著作权问题,事实上只是使这个问题更加扑朔迷离。首先,罗贯中早已认定是14世纪的剧作家,至少他的一部剧作仍然保存下来了。关于其背景信息的确切记载,在包括贾

---

① [美]夏志清:《中国古典小说》,胡益民等译,江苏文艺出版社2008年版,第73页。
② 该论著已由我国学者沈亨寿翻译成中文《明代小说四大奇书》,中国和平出版社1983年版。
③ Most immediately, we can recall that the very same bibliographical evidence used to document the circulation of the fan-pen recension by the Chia-ching period nearly unanimously asserts that the novel had been composed much earlier, naming as its principal compiler either Lo Kuan-chung 罗贯中 or Shih Nai-an. To this is added the fact that virtually every edition from the sixteencentury down to the present day clearly states on its title page that one or both of these men were responsible for its original compilation. Andrew H. Plaks, The Four Masterworks of the Ming Novel, Princeton University Press, 1987, p. 293。

仲明的《录鬼簿续编》等文献来源中皆可查到。但这种材料并没有像后来嘉靖时期的文献书目中所记载的那样，为我们提供他作为一位小说家、进行小说创作的证据。柳存仁提出，在小说某一简本中，一个名叫许贯中的神秘人物的出现，可能是罗的自我点名之处。这种说法纵然新奇有趣，却缺乏说服力。近来，王利器发掘出他认为小说著作权一定属于罗贯中的完整确切的证据：第27回塑造了小说中唯一正直、贤明的清官——东平府府尹陈文昭，而这恰好就是深受罗贯中敬重的友人、同僚的名字。但是，除了这些令人好奇的迹象，我们没有可靠的证据把罗和小说联系在一起。①

至于施耐庵，浦安迪认为情况也是如此。他说：

> 施耐庵的情形也一样，因为除了一部参考文献（恰好是我们手头最早的资料，即是高儒的《百川书志》）外，施只是作为一个次要角色被提及。直到金圣叹把伪托的施序插入其删节本时，在后来的数个世纪，小说的著作权才归入施耐庵名下。如果说罗贯中是何许人并不能确定，其生平历史还是有据可查，而施耐庵的身份则更加模糊不清。②

---

① These attributions, rather than solving the question of authorship of the novel, in fact only pose further puzzles. First, Lo Kuan-chung has been readily identified as a fourteenth-century dramatist, at least one of whose plays is still extant. A certain amount of background information about him is available, Including a biographical note in the *Hsü Lu-kuei pu* 续鬼簿 of Chia Chung-ming 贾仲明 and other sources. But nowhere in this material do we find any documentary evidence of his alleged activity as a novelist, such as we get later in the Chia-ching bibliographical sources. Liu Ts'un-yan's suggestion that the apperaence of an oracular figure with the name Hsü Kuan-chung 许贯中 in a *chien-pen* text of the novel may constitute a signature on Lo's part is intriguing but inconclusive. More recently, Wang Li-ch'i has uncovered what he believes to be complete proof of Lo's authorship in the giving of the name Ch'en Wen-chao 陈文昭, the same as that of a highly respected friend and colleague of Lo Kuan-chung, to a noble-minded official who provides a unique xeample og judicial integrity in chapter 27. But aside from these tantalizing hints, we have no solid evidence linking Lo to the novel. Andrew H. Plaks, The Four Masterworks of the Ming Novel, Princeton University Press, 1987, p. 294.

② The same situation holds true for Shih Nai-an, since with the exception of one reference (which does, however, happen to be the earliest in hand: Kao Ju's *Pai-ch'uan shu-chih*), Shih was as a rule mentioned only in a subsidiary capacity, until Chin Sheng-t'an inclusion in his edition of a pretended preface by Shih established the claim of Shih's authorship for succeeding cunteries. If Lo Kuan-chung is a somewhat shadowy figure despite the proof of his historicity, Shih Nai-an's identity is even more obscure. Andrew H. Plaks, The Four Masterworks of the Ming Novel, Princeton University Press, 1987, pp. 294-295.

第一章　英语世界对《水浒传》的考证探源研究　　53

针对施、罗两人是《水浒传》作者的文献资料，浦安迪还指出：

虽然缺乏确凿的证据解决这个问题，但普遍认为此两人是小说作者的证词积累的多了，这种观点就很难被驳倒。事实上，那些冗繁的关于施、罗二人是小说作者的材料，甚至连出版发表的价值都没有，因为所有这些都存在抄袭的问题。因此，它们的正确性都有赖于最早出处可靠与否。①

而且浦安迪还提到这样一个事实，他说：

使事情更为混乱不清的是，我们应该注意到这样的情况，即使那些署名罗贯中或施耐庵的版本，似乎也没有指出是他们的原作，而是冠以"编次"、"集撰"、"纂修"等字眼来标明他们在成书过程中所做的贡献。只有高儒的那个早期文献确信施耐庵是小说底本的作者。②

基于上述几方面的理由，浦安迪提出，如果一定要把《水浒传》的著作权归于罗贯中或施耐庵，或者认为小说某一较简底本的作者是罗贯中或施耐庵，那么，他对"这种固执的看法只能屈从"③。

总之，在《水浒传》作者问题的考证、研究上，浦安迪认为，目前所能找到的文献资料并没有确凿有力的证据说明，罗贯中或者施耐庵抑或其他某人就是《水浒传》的作者。在他看来，至今为止大多数

---

① Despite this lack of positive evidence to settle the question, the cumulative weight of testimony makes the nearly universal attribution of the novel to these names difficult to dismiss. Actually, the value of the voluminous evidence regarding to Lo-Shih authorship is even less than it appears, since all of the sources in question copy each other, and thus depend on the correctness of the earliest attribution. Andrew H. Plaks, The Four Masterworks of the Ming Novel, Princeton University Press, 1987, p. 295.

② To add to the confusion, we should note that even the attribution to Lo Kuan-chung or Shih Nai-an seems to indicate not an original composition, but instead a form of contribution labeled with such terms as "editing", or "compiling" (pien-tz'u 编次, chi-chuan 集撰, tsuan-hsiu 纂修). Only Kao Ju's early reference credits Shih Nai-an with authorship of a basic text (ti-pen) of the novel. Andrew H. Plaks, The Four Masterworks of the Ming Novel, Princeton University Press, 1987, p. 296。

③ I would bow to the persistent attribution to Lo Kuan-chung or Shih Nai-an of a simpler prototype. Andrew H. Plaks, The Four Masterworks of the Ming Novel, Princeton University Press, 1987, p. 301.

文学专家坚持认为罗贯中或者施耐庵是小说作者的看法，是缺乏具有足够说服力的资料的。因为如上文谈到的，很多关于罗贯中或施耐庵是小说作者的文献，本身就缺乏确凿的可靠性，以之为依据得出的结论自然缺少正确性。所以，到目前为止，《水浒传》的作者是谁尚无法确定。

石昌渝在为沙博理英译《水浒传》撰写的导论中，表达了与浦安迪相似的观点。他说："《水浒传》第一次以书的形式出现是在什么时间？这部作品是谁写成的？这些问题仍然在学者之间争论不休。"[①] 按石昌渝之论，学界根据郎瑛的《七修类稿》、高儒的《百川书志》、贾仲明的《录鬼簿续编》等文献资料的记载，一般认为这部小说是元末明初的罗贯中和施耐庵所著。但石昌渝同时也指出，即使高儒、郎瑛等人的记述是可靠的，在罗贯中、施耐庵是《水浒传》作者的讨论上仍然存在三大问题。对此，该论者指出：

  首先，古代作家经常使用笔名或别名。清初的周亮工就表达过对《水浒传》著作权的质疑。他说："予为世安有为此等书人，当时敢露其姓名者，阙疑可也。定为耐庵作，不知何据？"因此，我们需要更多有力的证据来论证作者问题。第二个问题是，假设施耐庵与罗贯中是小说作者的真名，而此罗贯中就是《录鬼簿续编》提到的那位杂剧、乐府、隐语作家罗贯中，可是为什么该书没有提到《三国演义》《水浒传》或者《三遂平妖传》呢？这些长篇小说也归于罗贯中名下，而且比其杂剧作品更具影响力。此外，在古代，人们有相同的名字并不罕见。第三个问题是，最早提到《水浒传》一书的文献全都始于嘉靖年间，小说现存最早版本也是嘉靖时期刊印的。该作品题为《忠义水浒传》的版本仍然存留至今（仅有第10卷的第17和36页），所有其他版本的刊印始于万历年间（1573—1620）或稍后。因而，说《水浒传》第一次以作品的形式出现是在元末明初，我们没有权威版本可考。因此，关于"《水浒传》是元末明初的施耐庵所著"的论争仍然有问题；在我们得出这

[①] Shi Changyu, Introduction, *Outlaws of the Marsh*, translated by Sidney Shapiro, Beijing: Foreign Language Press, 1993, Vol. I, p. 4.

样的结论之前，需要进行更深入的研究。①

　　石昌渝的分析、论述，环环相扣，逻辑严密，很有说服力。事实上，从目前可考的文献资料来看，施耐庵的生平我们一无所知，对罗贯中我们也所知无几。因此，在没找到有足够说服力的文献资料之前，在研究尚不够深入时，我们与其匆忙断定罗贯中或者施耐庵，抑或是其他某人是《水浒传》的作者，不如先把此问题搁置起来，等到某一天发现了确凿的文献资料时，再来下结论。

　　在英语学术界，对《水浒传》的作者问题进行过研究的尚有：翟楚（Chuchai）与翟文伯（Wingberg Chai）在《中国文学瑰宝》中推断施耐庵是小说作者，罗贯中是一百二十回本的编者，金圣叹则是七十回本的加工者；古德里奇（L. C. Goodrich，亦译为富路特）在《明代传记辞典》中认为施耐庵是水浒故事、传说、话本及戏剧等素材的第一收集者；张心沧在其编写的《中国文学》里坚持《水浒传》是施、罗二人合著的杰作，不过施是撰写者，罗是编者；等等。这些说法的相同之处是，他们都只是推论，而且大都是只言片语的讨论。

---

① The accounts by Gao Ru and Lang Ying are reliable. However, three problems remain. The first is the fact that ancient writers often used pen names and aliases. Zhou Lianggong, who lived in the early part of Qing Dynasty, expressed his doubt about the authorship of *Outlaws of the Marsh* thus: "As it is doubtful that any writer in those days would have dared to put his real name to such a book, I do not know upon what grounds we can attribute *Outlaws of the Marsh* to Shi Nai'an." Therefor, we need more solid evidence for the authorship. The second problem is that, supposing Luo Guanzhong and Shi Nai'an are the real names of the authors of the book, and that Luo Guanzhong is the person named Luo Guanzhong mentioned in *the Sequel to the Record of Ghosts* as a writer of *zaju* plays, ballads and esoteric language, why is there no mention of *The Three kingdom*, *Outlaws of the Marsh* or *The Sorcerer's Revolt and Its Suppression by the Three Suis*, full-length novels also attributed to Luo Guanzhong and which had a far greater impact than his *zaju*? Besides, it was not uncommon for people to bear identical names in olden times. The third problem is that the earliest documents that mention the book of *Outlaws of the Marsh* all date from the Jiajing reign period, and the earlist extant version of the book was published during the Jiajing reign period. This version is titled *The Loyal and Righteous Outlaws of the Marsh*, and only two pages-pages 17 and 36 of Volume 10-of the book are still extant. All other versions of the book date from the Wanli reign period (1573 – 1620) or later. So, to say that *Outlaws of the Marsh* first appeared in book form in the late Yuan or early Ming dynasty, we have no definitive edition to examine. Therefor, the argument that "*Outlaws of the Marsh* was written by Shi Nai'an of the period from the end of Yuan Dynasty to the beginning of the Ming Dynasty" is still questionable and further research is needed before we can draw such a conclusion. Shi Changyu, Introduction, *Outlaws of the Marsh*, translated by Sidney Shapiro, Beijing: Foreign Language Press, 1993, Vol. I, pp. 6 – 7.

三、小说作者的身份研究

《水浒传》的作者具体是谁，尚无定论，但这并不妨碍人们对小说作者的身份展开研究。在此问题上，小川环树（Ogawa Tamaki）和浦安迪有过比较经典的论述。

1958年，日本汉学家小川环树撰写并发表了一篇题为《〈水浒传〉的作者》的英文文章。在文章中，小川环树说："据我猜测，小说作者是一个处于官僚阶层最底层的胥吏。"[①] 通过对《水浒传》的历史，小说的故事梗概，小说描绘的社会背景，作品所展现出来的江湖道德，梁山好汉的两个阶层归属，小说所呈现出来的中下层阶级的心理状态，以及作品所塑造的人物形象七个层面的分析讨论，小川环树进一步指出：

> 这部传世经典的作者，表现出对普通百姓的极大理解和同情。一个写书的人不可能目不识丁，而他对底层人物有如此的洞察，说明他和这些人很接近。
>
> 《水浒传》展现出的上述特点，说明其作者处于社会的中间阶层——在普通百姓与统治阶级之间。像故事的编者一样，他理解普通百姓的感情，欣赏梁山好汉那未经驯化的粗犷、正直，也懂得文人士大夫阶层的思想观点。否则，他可能既设计不出接受招安的故事结局让这些反叛者进行自我救赎，并以完美的忠义观念让文人士大夫得到满足，也不能创造出像宋江这样的首领，他既与最野蛮、最狂放不羁的暴徒为伍，又能约束他们不越过彻底反叛的界限。
>
> 胥吏处于这样的位置，一边接触普通百姓，一边接触上流社会。作为最底层的官吏，他与百姓联系密切，能最好地观察他们的生活与思想方式。同时，他仍是传统文化培养出来的统治阶级管理系统的一部分，受到忠君观念的影响。
>
> 胥吏的其他方面与故事的总体大意也非常契合。他属于上流社会，但不被他们接受。作为官吏，他又没有通过科举考试得到官职，因而被那些通过考试金榜题名者轻视。他受过最低限度的教育，文学

[①] It is my guess that the author was a *hsü-li* 胥吏, a clerk of the lowest rank of the official hierarchy. Ogawa Tamaki, The Author of the *Shui-hu Chuan*, Monumenta Serica, Vol. 17 (1958), p. 316.

才能贫弱，没有升迁希望。在科举考试的等级中，秀才只是藐视的对象。胥吏所遭受上级的轻视与挫败的怨念，在近代小说《官场现形记》中描写得鲜明生动，这种情形在 14 世纪可能并不比 19 世纪轻。出自元杂剧的一句谚语说："秀才人情纸半张"，总体上表达了这种社会情绪，特别是胥吏的辛酸。

一个促使胥吏胆敢冒险在小说中宣泄自己感情的因素是，在蒙古人统治之下暂时取消了科举考试。中国文人士大夫所遭受的这种史无前例的打击，在谢翱和其他人的诗歌中得到了回应。学识得不到赏识，结果在清闲自在的中国平民中间，为某个社会底层的博学者创作《水浒传》提供了称心的氛围。

至少小说人物漠视法律（它们束缚高级官员使其为难）的行为，表达了胥吏自身的感受。像推翻第一任首领的故事，也是对"秀才不当"说法的一种满足的轻微掩饰。第一任首领王伦，参加举人考试失败了。起码的事实是，如果他中了举人，就可以不与胥吏为伍，但他没成。因为缺乏侠义和容人肚量，他不适合做草寇英雄的领导，结果在晁盖一伙的火并中被杀害。

而且在这些英雄里没有秀才。第一位英雄宋江是个胥吏。可能有人认为这些事实并没有什么意义，首先因为不只是最底层的官吏才会成为强盗，其次因为宋江的社会地位已是这个世代流传的故事的一部分而非作者的发明创作。即使他们证明这些毫无意义，但这些事实至少增加了作者是个胥吏的可能性。

彻底造反、叫嚣让晁盖或宋江做皇帝的激烈言辞，也可能具有特殊的意义。它总是出自像李逵这种愚昧无知的村夫之口，而不会出自有教养的强人之口。毕竟，在政府公职和忠君的传统中，胥吏有他自己的根，他所有的诋毁只是针对高官。因此，一个胥吏不会毫不犹豫就轻率地造同属自己阶级的人的反。

来自作品之外的不止一个因素支持我的论点。在元代最后的数年中，戏剧的作者由显著人物转向无名官吏。小说的作者也极可能如此。

因此，我提出这样的结论：此人最大可能是一个处于官僚阶梯最末端的胥吏。他既能创作小说，又能在造反与忠君之间保持微妙的关系；他既欣赏血性汉子的冲动，也赞美有教养之人的谨慎。①

在论述中，小川环树始终突出作者身份与胥吏之间的关系。尤其是小说展现出来的对普通百姓生活、思想的熟悉程度，对他们的同情与理

---

① The author of this timeless masterpiece shows a great sympathy with and understanding of the common people. A man who writes a book can hardly be one of the unlettered himself; but to have such insight into the character of the lower classes he was perhaps not far removed from them.
The features of the *Shui-hu chuan* loulined above suggest that its author stands on the social scale halfway between the common people and the ruling class. Like the editors of his story he shares the feelings of the common people and enjoys the rugged integrity of the rough diamonds of Liang-shan. But he understands the viewpoints of the cultured classes also -otherwise he could neither have devised the end of the story which redeems the rebels and satisfied their concept of loyalty and justice, nor have created side by side with the wildest and most uninhibited ruffians leaders like Sung Chiang whose restraints keeps the gang within bounds and stops them short of outright rebellion.
The *hsü-li* 胥吏 was in a position to side with either common people or gentry. Being the lowest of all officials he was the one who had most contact with the people and could best observe their life and way of thinking. At the same time he was still a part of the administrative system of the ruling class brought up in the traditional culture and imbued with a sense loyalty to the ruler.
Something else about the *hsü-li* fits in well with the general tenor of the story. He was an official clerk; but he had not passed civil service examinations to get his job, and he was despised by those who had. He had a minimum of education, a meagre literary ability, and no hope of advancement. As an official he may have commanded the respect of the people; but to holders of degrees, the *hsiu-ts'ai*, he was an object of scorn. The contempt of their superiors and the rankled frustrations of the *hsü-li* so vividly described in the modern novel *Kuan-ch'ang hsien-hsing chi* 官场现形记 were probably no less in the 14th century than in the 19th. A proverb which appears in Yüan dramas: "A *hsiu-ta'ai*'s favor is only half a sheet of paper," expresses the sentiments of society in general, but especially the bitterness of the *hsü-li*。
One factor which may well have encouraged a*hsü-li* to give vent to his feelings in a novel was the temporary withdrawal under the Mongols of the civil service examinations. The shock felt by the Chinese intellgentsia at this unprecedented move echoes in the poems of Hsien Ao 谢翱（1249 – 1295）and others; and the depreciation os learing which resulted among the Chinese populace at large would provide a congenia atmosphere for one of the lowest of the lettered to produce a *Shui-hu chuan*。
At any rate the characters of the novel, whose reckless disregard for law embarrassed the senior officials, express what the *hsü-li* homself must have felt. Episodes like the overthrow of the first chieftain also are thin disguise for a satisfaction in the inadequency of a *hsiu-ts'ai*. The first chief, Wang Lun 王伦, had been a candidate in the *chü-jen* examination. He had failed; but the mere fact that he qualified for the examination was enough to make him unpopular with the *hsü-li* who did not. Wang Lun was found unfit for leadership of the brigand because of lack of chivalry and toleration. He was killed in a *coup d'etat* by Ch'ao Kai and company.
Further, among the heroes there were no "*hsiu-ts'ai*", and the number one hero, Sung Chiang, was a *hsü-li*. It may be argued that these facts are of little significance, the first because one could hardly except any but the lowest of the officials to become robbers, and the second because Sung Chiang's social position was already a part of the tradition and not an invention of the writer. But the facts are there, and even if they prove nothing thay at least add weight to the possibility that the author was a *hsü-li*.

解，以及根深蒂固的忠君思想所带来的招安救赎的情节转折，这极大地说明了作者所受到的传统儒家思想文化与植根于普通百姓的市井文化（王学泰称之为"游民文化"）中侠义思想的影响与冲击之深。而这两种思想文化在作者身上的交织、碰撞和冲突，正好说明他是穿行在上流社会与市井细民之间的。按小川环树之论，这种人最大可能是胥吏。而根据小川环树的讨论，笔者以为，胥吏之外，他还极可能是混迹官场多年、深谙其中黑幕，后因某种缘故辞官归隐，常年游走在市井、游民之中的地方官员。

在日本汉学界，宫崎市定对《水浒传》作者的身份也持"胥吏"说。通过对小说文本故事情节叙述中呈现出来的情感倾向的分析，该论者指出：

> 据《水浒传》作者的说明，在宋代为官容易做吏难。朝廷任命的官员倚仗权势，诈得百姓钱财复做贿赂朝廷命官之用，以求能得升迁机会。而因官高权大，即便有罪也免于处罚，想来这世上再也没有比当官更美的差事了。而胥吏却不一样，一辈子只能在地方衙门耗着，没伺候好上司便被棍棒伺候，要犯了罪那就只有发配远恶军州孤岛荒漠的分（份）儿了。作者慨叹世道的不公，很明显这是基于胥吏立场的社会观和人生观。①

宫崎市定对"宋江施舍银子给阎婆"（《水浒传》金本第19回）这一情节稍作分析之后进一步说："《水浒传》有部分情节与元曲相似，所以

It is perhaps significant also that the wild mords of outright rebellion, the shouts that Ch'ao Kai or Sung Chiang become emperor, should always come from the mouths og ignorant riffraff like Li K'uei and not from cultured brigands. For all his disparagement of higher officials, the *hsü-li* had his roots, after all, in the tradition of government service and loyalty to emperor. A *hsü-li* would no doubt hestitate to make thoughtless rebels of men of his own class.

One more factor from an outside source supports my convention. In the last years of the Yüan the authorship of dramas shifted notables to obscure officials. It is quite probable that the authorship of novcls did too.

I submit then that the man who was able both to write a novel, and to maintain a tension between rebellion and loyalty, and to admire both boorish impulsiveness and cultered circumspection was most probably a man on the lowest rung of the official ladder, a *hsü-li*. Ogawa Tamaki, The Author of the *Shui-hu chuan*, Monumenta Serica, Vol. 17（1958），pp. 327 – 330.

① ［日］宫崎市定：《宫崎市定说〈水浒〉——虚构的好汉与掩藏的历史》，赵翻、杨晓钟译，陕西人民出版社2008年版，第113页。

原作者可能有过为吏经验。"①

与小川环树诸人的"胥吏"说不完全相同,浦安迪认为《水浒传》与《三国演义》《西游记》《金瓶梅》一样,都是16世纪的文人小说。对此,他指出:

> 我对这些"奇书"的认识基于这样的信念,即它们承载着最富有意义的阐释。因为它们不只是通常所认为的通俗叙事材料的纲要,而是反映了晚明时期那些资深练达的文人士大夫的文化价值与思想观念。我相信这几部小说最完善的修订本,是由创作了明代"文人画"与"文人剧"精品的同一群人编撰的,并在他们之间传阅。这就是我为什么有些自负并令人困惑地称其为"文人小说"的缘故。②

在此,浦安迪认为《水浒传》最完善修订本的编撰者与创作明代"文人画"、"文人剧"的作者是同一群人。笔者以为这与小川环树等人的看法并不冲突,因为他们所谈论的不完全是同一个问题。小川环树一直关注的是"作者"(author),浦安迪说的则是最完善修订本的"编撰者"(compiler)。

第二节 《水浒传》的素材渊源

《水浒传》在正式成书之前,小说中的一些主要人物、故事就已经以书面文字或口头说唱的形式在社会上广为流传。据目前可考的文献来看,当《水浒传》正式成书时,那些早先流传的水浒人物故事有不少已被小说作者吸收、采纳,成为《水浒传》创作的重要素材来源。那么,《水浒

---

① [日]宫崎市定:《宫崎市定说〈水浒〉——虚构的好汉与掩藏的历史》,赵翻、杨晓钟译,陕西人民出版社2008年版,第115页。
② First, my readings of these "amazing books" are based on the conviction that they yield the most meaningful interpretations when viewed not simply as compendia of popular narrative materials, but as reflections of the cultural values and intelectual concerns of the sophisticated literary circles of the late Ming period. I believe that the fullest recensions of each these novels were composed by and for the same sort of people who gave us the startlingly original achievements of Ming "literati painting" and the gems of the contemporary "literati stage", which is why I speak of them with the somewhat pretentious, and perhaps misleading term "literati novels". Andrew H. Plaks, The Four Masterworks of the Ming Novel, Princeton University Press, 1987, p. ix.

传》的素材渊源主要有哪些呢？在英语世界批评者中，又有哪些进入了他们的研究视域呢？本节，笔者就来梳理英语世界的批评者对《水浒传》素材渊源的研究情况。

在英语世界的批评者中，赛珍珠很早就谈论过《水浒传》的素材来源问题。在1933年为其英译《水浒传》撰写的"导言"中，赛珍珠说："确信这个故事源于历史，主要的36位首领生活在北宋末年，他们横行中原，并和政府军队相抗衡。"① 此外，赛珍珠还指出：

> 这本书近似于现在的形式大概写成于14世纪或15世纪，也就是明中前期。只是在此前两个多世纪里，《水浒传》中的一些故事已基本形成。这些故事不仅见于散文之中由专业说书人讲述，也能在诗歌和戏剧中看到。②

赛珍珠的论述至少点明了《水浒传》创作素材的四个方面来源：史书、说书、戏剧与诗（词）。当然，这个史书有正史、野史之分，戏剧则主要是元杂剧。至于说书，因为资料亡佚太多，现在已无确切的文献可考。赛珍珠还提到诗歌，她特地引用了高文秀写黑旋风李逵的诗。很遗憾的是，对上述《水浒传》素材来源，赛珍珠只是粗略点过，并未详细展开。

欧文在论著《一部中国小说的演变：〈水浒传〉》中，对小说的素材来源作了更进一步的考证。与赛珍珠的意见不完全相同，欧文认为《水浒传》的创作主要并不是"按史演义"（romanticized history）而是"原创"（original creation），不过也有历史作为创作的基础。

欧文指出《水浒传》的创作有其历史基础，具体来说是指作品中的主要人物宋江、杨志和史进三人是有历史记载的。对此他说：

---

① There is good authority for believing that the tale is based on history, and that the thirty-six chief robbers were men who lived at the very end of the north Sung Dynasty and who ravaged central China and defied the state soldiery. Pearl S. Buck, *Introduction of Shui Hu Chuan*, *All Men Are Brothers*, NewYork: The John Day Company, 1933, p. vi.

② The book in approximately its present form was probably written in the early or middle part of the Ming Dynasty in the fourteenth or fifteenth century, but more than two centuries before there were already the stories of which *Shui Hu Chuan* was later to be made, stories not only in prose and told by the professional story tellers, but in poems and plays. Pearl S. Buck, *Introduction of Shui Hu Chuan*, *All Men Are Brothers*, NewYork: The John Day Company, 1933, p. vii.

中国小说有两种主要类型，包括按史演义与原创，《水浒传》毫无疑问属于第二种。因为这个故事（除了方腊起义）是从通俗传奇中发展而来的，并未受到历史事实的影响。只是这些故事传说是以历史人物宋江——梁山集团的首领——为核心的。①

为了证实历史上确有宋江其人，欧文援引《宋史·徽宗纪》的记载如下：

宣和三年，二月甲戌，降诏招抚方腊。……是月，方腊陷楚州。淮南盗宋江等犯淮阳军，遣将讨捕。又犯京东、江北，入楚、海州，明知州张叔夜招降之。②

欧文还引《宋史·侯蒙传》说：

宋江寇京东，蒙上书言："江以三十六人横行齐、魏，官军数万无敢抗者，其才必过人。今青溪盗起，不若赦江，是讨方腊以自赎。"帝曰："蒙居外不忘君，忠臣也。"命知东平府，未赴而卒。③

根据这两处记载，欧文指出，很显然，这36人是当时造反运动中一支武装力量的分支。再根据《宋史·张叔夜传》的相关记载，欧文认为历史上的宋江造反不过持续了四年多时间，其最后结局是被张叔夜招降。他还结合《宋会要稿》、《国朝续会要》以及《宋史》中其他人如童贯、刘光世等的传记指出，宋江等36人归降之后参加了平定方腊起义的军事

---

① There are two main types of Chinese fiction, romanticized history and original creation. Shui-hu-chuan unquestionably belongs in the second category, for the story, with the exception of the Fang La campaign, has developed from popular legend uninfluenced by historical fact. But the tales on which it is based do center about an historical figure, Sung Chiang, the leader of an outlaw band. Richard Gregg Irwin, The evolution of a Chinese novel: Shui-hu-chuan, Cambridge Massachusetts: Harvard University Press, 1953, p. 9.
② Richard Gregg Irwin, The Evolution of a Chinese Novel: Shui-hu-chuan, Cambridge Massachusetts: Harvard University Press, 1953, p. 9.
③ Ibid., p. 9.

行动。①

在这36人中，欧文认为，除宋江之外，杨志、史进在历史上也应确有其人。对杨志这个人物，该论者说：

> 宋江本人曾淡出人们的视界，而据龚圣与和《宣和遗事》的记述，三十六人中的杨志在此前一年（1121）征方腊的行动中跟随童贯一同前往。因此，作为"彪悍的强人，他曾经接受过招降"，这似乎有理由认为他是宋江的后继者。而杨志和付先锋赵明的关系，更有力地证明了这个事实。②

至于史进这个人物，欧文认为可能就是史斌。他说："参考这一时期历史学家的记载，宋江集团中只有一个成员是具体可考的：史斌可能就是小说里的史进。"③

根据上述，在欧文对《水浒传》人物故事历史渊源的考证中，宋江是确切无疑的，至于杨志和史进，主要还是停留在推测的层面。在小说人物故事的历史来源考证上，英语世界的批评者乔治·海德（George Hayden）也做过研究④。只是他的看法和主张并没有超越欧文，也没有发现什么新的、更有力的文献。故不论。

欧文认为，《水浒传》的创作，其人物故事除了有历史的渊源外，还有其他方面的来源，比如说宋元"词话"（tz'u-hua）、元代"杂剧"（tsa-chü）等文学作品。欧文指出，词话虽然被当时流行的戏剧淹没，也并没

---

① Richard Gregg Irwin, The Evolution of a Chinese Novel: Shui-hu-chuan, Cambridge Massachusetts: Harvard University Press, 1953, pp. 11–14.

② Sung himself had dropped out of sight, but Yang Chih, includeed among the thirty-six bu Kung Sheng-yü and *Hsüan-ho i-shih*, was one of a group of subcommanders, half of whom had seen action the preceding year against Fang La, who accompanied T'ung Kuan at this time. Since he is characterized as a "powerful bandit who had accepted the invitation to surrender", it seems justifiable to regard him as Sung's successor. The case is further strengthened by his association with Chao Ming as co-leader of a picked vanguard. Richard Gregg Irwin, The Evolution of a Chinese Novel: Shui-hu-chuan, Cambridge Massachusetts: Harvard University Press, 1953, p. 15.

③ Only one member of Sung's band is specifically reffered to as such by historians of the period: Shih Pin 史斌, who may be the Shih Chin 史进 of the novel. Richard Gregg Irwin, The evolution of a Chinese novel: Shui-hu-chuan, Cambridge Massachusetts: Harvard University Press, 1953, p. 15.

④ 见 George Hayden, A Skeptical Notes on the Early History of the *Shui-hu Chuan*, Monumenta Serica, 32, 1976, pp. 374–399.

有一部专门的《水浒传词话》保存下来，但他坚持认为："有充分的证据说明《水浒传》与大约同时出现的其他小说一样，源于早前的词话。"①在欧文看来，通过分析《水浒传》的文本可以发现，小说中以下几处很明显是来自先前的词话作品的。对此，该论者指出：

> 第一处，一首词幸免被删除的命运（在后来所有的小说中这是它们通常的命运）仍然在第48回中找到。第一次攻打祝家庄被击退之后，宋江亲自率领第二次袭击。当他的军队到达时，通过"有篇诗赞"，他们看见了祝家庄：
> 独龙山前独龙冈，独龙冈上祝家庄。
> 绕冈一带长流水，周遭环匝皆垂杨。
> 墙内森森罗剑戟，门前密密排刀枪。
> 飘扬旗帜惊鸟雀，纷纭矛盾生光芒。
> 强弩硬弓当要路，灰瓶炮石护垣墙。
> 对敌尽皆雄壮士，当锋都是少年郎。
> 祝龙出阵真难敌，祝虎交锋莫可当。
> 更有祝彪多武艺，咤叱喑呜比霸王。
> 朝奉祝公谋略广，金银罗绮有千箱。
> 樽酒常时延好客，山林镇日会豪强。
> 久共三村盟誓约，扫清强寇保村坊。
> 白旗一对门前立，上面明书字两行：
> 填平水泊擒晁盖，踏破梁山捉宋江。
>
> 因为这支先锋的这一叙述而不是代之以类似的叙述，因此可以肯定它一定来自某一部词话。……像这样的词在修订的70回本中被删掉了，但在100回及120回本里，这首词如最初宋代时一样保存着。……毫无疑问，最初它是由说书人引用的，而且是众多诗词中的

---

① There is ample evidence that Shui-hu-chuan, like other novels which appeared at about the same time, derives from earlier *tz'u-hua*. Richard Gregg Irwin, The evolution of a Chinese novel：Shui-hu-chuan, Cambridge Massachusetts：Harvard University Press, 1953, p. 15.

第一章　英语世界对《水浒传》的考证探源研究

一首而已。只是长久以来,其他的作品以散文的形式作了意译。①

欧文紧接着分析道:

> 小说中其他地方也有词话留下的印记。……在《水浒传》文本中,至少有两个这样的标题嵌入其中。一个在第16回:"那计较都是吴用主张,这个唤做智取生辰纲。"另一个在第40回:"这个唤做白龙庙小聚会。"②

欧文的分析在理,论述有据。上面他提到的这几个地方,的确有从说书人底本或者词话中援引删改的印记。这在中国学界的研究中也是普遍认同的。

而说到《水浒传》人物故事的"词话"来源,最重要的就是大约成书于元代的《大宋宣和遗事》。欧文不仅把《大宋宣和遗事》中和《水浒传》人物故事情节相关的部分翻译成了英文③,他还比较详细地分析了《水浒传》作者在创作时对《宣和遗事》中人物故事情节的采用情况。欧文指出:

> 在《宣和遗事》中,至少能区分出六个单独的故事:杨志卖刀杀人与最终获救上太行山落草为寇,智取生辰纲,杀阎婆惜,宋江得天

---

① In the first place, one of the *tz'u* escaped the deletion which was their common fate in later editions of all the early novels and is still found in Chapter 48. After an initial attack on the Chu Family Village had been repulsed, Sung Chiang himself led a second assault. When his force approached it, they saw, in the words of the *tz'u*, ... Since this forwards the narrative instead of paralleling it, it must come from directly from a *tz'u-hua*. Such was the case with this *tz'u* in the revision which cut the novel to seventy chapters, but in the 100- and 120-chapter versions it was retained as originally sung.... Unquestionably, it was originally employed by a storyteller and was but one of many, though the others have long since been paraphrased in prose. Richard G. Irwin, The evolution of a Chinese novel: Shui-hu-chuan, Cambridge Massachusetts: Harvard University Press, 1953, pp. 39 – 40.

② Elsewhere, too, the *tz'u-hua* have left their inprint on the novel.... At least two such titles are still imbedded in the text of *Shui-hu-chuan*, one in Chapter 16: "This is known as staeling the borthday gifts by a ruse," and the other in Chapter 40: "This is known as the small assembly at White Dragon Temple." Richard Gregg Irwin, The evolution of a Chinese novel: Shui-hu-chuan, Cambridge Massachusetts: Harvard University Press, 1953, p. 40.

③ Richard Gregg Irwin, The evolution of a Chinese novel: Shui-hu-chuan, Cambridge Massachusetts: Harvard University Press, 1953, pp. 26 – 31.

书上梁山,宋江三十六人横行掠夺遭到政府围剿,远游泰山。①

通过分析水浒故事中地理方位的明显差别,以及根据李玄伯的观点,欧文把水浒故事分为三个独立的系统,第一个以梁山泊为中心,第二个以太行山为中心,第三个以浙江(征方腊事件)为中心。该论者还指出,在写定之前,这三个不同系统的水浒人物故事在人们之间口头流传,这些故事描绘了各自特别的英雄人物,后来它们全部汇集在《水浒传》中。②不管水浒故事在写定之前可以分成几个单独的系统,《宣和遗事》记载的水浒人物故事很明显就能在小说《水浒传》中找到。对此,欧文指出:

> 智取生辰纲出现在小说第16回,宋江报信私放晁天王出现在第18回,宋江杀阎婆惜出现在第21回,毫无疑问这些都源自梁山泊系列。小说第1—4回,故事发生在陕西和山西,很可能来自太行山系统,只是我们缺少确实的证据。史进和鲁智深是这一部分的主要角色,他们都不是《宣和遗事》故事中上太行山落草为寇十二人中的一员。③

欧文的这个分析是很到位的,与小说文本的实际情况基本相符。

关于《水浒传》人物故事素材的《大宋宣和遗事》来源,欧文之后,

---

① At least six separate episodes can be distinguished in this account: Yang Chih's crime and uitimate rescue, the theft of the birthday gifts, the mueder of Yen P'o-hsi, Sung's receipt of the Heavenly Writ and arrival at Liang-shan-po, pillaging which led to punitive measures on the part of the government, and the pilgrimage to Mount T'ai. Richard Gregg Irwin, The evolution of a Chinese novel: Shui-hu-chuan, Cambridge Massachusetts: Harvard University Press, 1953, p. 31.

② During the period before such incidents were first written down, that is, while the legends simple circulated orally among the people, Li Hsüan-po believes there were three separate story-cycles, each with its partical heroes, all subsequently combined in *Shui-hu-chuan*. They were geographically distinct, one centering on Liang-shan-po, east of the capital, the second, on the T'ai-hang Mountains to the northwest, and the third on the campaign against Fang La in Chejiang. Richard Gregg Irwin, The evolution of a Chinese novel: Shui-hu-chuan, Cambridge Massachusetts: Harvard University Press, 1953, p. 31.

③ Undoubtedly the theft of the birthday gifts (Chapter 16), Sung's waring which enabled Ch'ao to escape (Chapter 18), and his murder of Yen P'o-hsi (Chapter 21) derive directly from the Liang-shan-po series. Chapter 1-4, laid in Shenxi and Shanxi, amy well come from the T'ai-hang cycle, but we lack any positive froof. Neither Shih Chin nor Lu Chih-shen, who play the principal roles in this section, was one of the twelve who, in the *Hsüan-ho i-shih* story, made off to the T'ai-hang Mountains to become bandits. Richard Gregg Irwin, The evolution of a Chinese novel: Shui-hu-chuan, Cambridge Massachusetts: Harvard University Press, 1953, p. 32.

夏志清在论著《中国古典小说》第三章《水浒传》部分有过简单讨论①，亨尼塞（Willian O. Hennessey）在文章中也曾谈论过②，吴德安也在其博士论文中提及（后文将论及），只是他们并未展开具体讨论。

在欧文的讨论中，元杂剧是小说素材的一个重要源泉。的确，元代演绎水浒主题的杂剧不少。根据欧文的统计约有 23 部。（事实上不止 23 部，英语世界的批评者吴德安后来对此作了进一步的研究。下文将会论及）对这 23 部元杂剧，欧文作了一个分类，他说：

> 这 23 部杂剧可分成四类：第一类是现已亡佚、但它们的标题显示没有内容并入《水浒传》；第二类是在亡佚的部分杂剧中，它们描写的故事包括在《水浒传》中；第三类是现存的、在情节上和小说不同的五部杂剧；第四类是唯一的一部其故事完整地保存在小说中的杂剧。③

根据欧文之论，这些已经亡佚的、其故事被小说采纳的元杂剧包括以下这些：

高文秀的《双献头武松大报仇》，其故事大体相当于小说第 26 回的"供人头武二郎设祭"；

高文秀的《黑旋风乔教学》，其故事大致是小说第 74 回；

高文秀的《黑旋风斗鸡会》，其故事大致是小说第 99 回；

杨显之的《黑旋风乔断案》，其故事大体相当于小说第 74 回的"李

---

① 见夏志清《中国古典小说》，胡益民等译，江苏文艺出版社 2008 年版，第 71—72 页。
② 见 *Xuanhe yishi* 宣和遗事 is the longest single work of Chinese vernacular narrative extant from the period prior to the beginning of the Ming dynasty. 2 Traditional Chinese bibliographers tended to treat the work as a piece of unreliable history. Other Chinese critics, owing to the fact that the hero of *Shuihu zhuan* 水浒传, Song Jiang, and some thirty-six of his comrades also appear in a brief section of the work, have devoted their attentions to the relationship between it and the much more famous Ming novel. William O. Hennessey, Classical Sources and Vernacular Resources in *Xuanhe Yishi*：The Presence of Priority and the Priority of Presence. Chinese Literature：Essays, Articles, Reviews（CLEAR）, Vol. 6, No. 1/2 （Jul., 1984）, p. 33。
③ These twenty-three *tsa-chü* fall into four categories：those now lost whose titles reflect no material incorporated in Shui-hu-chuan; lost dramas which portrayed episodes it includes; five whc＝ich though extant differ in their plot from anything the novel contains; and one only which enacts a story largely identical to one of its episodes. Richard Gregg Irwin, The evolution of a Chinese novel：Shui-hu-chuan, Cambridge Massachusetts：Harvard University Press, 1953, p. 35。

逯寿张乔坐衙";

红字李二的《折担儿武松打虎》，内容大致是小说第23回的"景阳冈武松打虎";

李文蔚的《燕青射雁》，讲述的故事是小说第110回的"燕青秋林渡射雁"。

就欧文上述六部已亡佚的元杂剧与小说《水浒传》之间的关系，笔者以为高文秀后两部作品从它们的标题来看，很难在欧文所说的《水浒传》的相应章回找到类似的内容。其他基本没有什么疑问。而在现存的水浒杂剧中，康进之的《梁山泊李逵负荆》，其情节被吸收、采纳，成为小说里的一个完整的故事。这是很多专家学者认同的。①

在英语世界，就《水浒传》素材渊源这一问题的研究，美国普林斯顿大学出身的汉学家吴德安可以说是一位集大成者。吴德安在其1990年撰写的博士论文《中国小说形式的变迁》中，专列一小节对《水浒传》的素材来源进行了比较全面的梳理。根据该论者的研究，《水浒传》的人物故事主要有7个源头。具体情况如下：

第一就是《宋史》中的相关记载。吴德安指出，在《宋史》侯蒙、张叔夜等人的传记中，就已简略提及宋江与其同伴36人的事情。②

第二则是《大宋宣和遗事》记述的水浒人物事件。该论者说，《大宋宣和遗事》中保存的好几则宋江36人的故事片段，也在后来的小说中出现了。③

第三是描写水浒人物故事的元曲作品，事实上主要是元杂剧。对这一点，吴德安指出：

> 共有31部水浒主题的杂剧，只是保存下来的只有七部。因为杂

---

① Richard Gregg Irwin, The evolution of a Chinese novel: Shui-hu-chuan, Cambridge Massachusetts: Harvard University Press, 1953, p. 35, 36.

② *Song shi* (*The History of the Song Dynasty*). Song Jiang and his band of thirty-six were brifly mentioned (in the biographies of Hou Meng and Zhang Shuye, etc.). De-an Wu Swihart, The Evolution of Chinese Novel form, Thesis Ph. D. The Department of East Asian Studies of Princeton University, 1990, p. 25.

③ *Da Song xuanhe yishi* (*Tales of the Xuanhe Reign of the Great Song Dynasty*). This contained several episodes which also appeared in the later novel as well as some of the figures of Song Jiang and his band of thiety-six. De-an Wu Swihart, The Evolution of Chinese Novel form, Thesis Ph. D. The Department of East Asian Studies of Princeton University, 1990, p. 26.

剧的很多人物故事和《水浒传》的相关人物故事大相径庭,甚至名字都不一样,郑振铎认为杂剧取材于小说并经过大幅度的改动,而王利器则主张小说和戏剧有不同的来源。①

面对郑振铎、王利器二人不同的看法,在元代水浒杂剧是不是小说素材的来源问题上,吴德安并未给出自己的意见。

在《水浒传》第四个方面的素材来源上,吴德安提到的是周密《癸辛杂识续集》中记载的龚开创作的《宋江三十六人赞》。② 不过,就《宋江三十六人赞》中的人名、故事及人物活动的地点来看,也和小说《水浒传》存在很大的不同。

第五是宋代以降的文人笔记。对此,吴德安说宋、明、清诸朝私人笔记中记述的一些人物、故事、诗词也出现在小说《水浒传》里。在这些笔记中,该论者认为最重要的有下面这些:宋代王明清的《挥麈后录》(记载了高俅发迹的经历),明代郎瑛的《七修类稿》,清代俞樾的《小浮梅闲话》与《茶香室丛钞》,以及《佣余漫墨》《娱萱室随笔》等。③ 对这一点,笔者要指出的是,既然《水浒传》成书于元末明初或是明代中叶(关于《水浒传》的成书时间,说法众多,具体参见本书绪论部分"国内学界《水浒传》研究述评"之"成书研究之争"),那么,很显然的是,清代私人笔记里的记述就不可能影响小说的创作。

---

① Yuan drama. There were altogether thirty-one on the *Shuihu* theme, but only seven pieces are extant. Since many characters and episodes in the dramas are quite different from those of The Men of the Marsh, and even the names are not the same, Zheng Zhenduo claimed that the dramas had drawn on the novel and undergone drastic revisions, while Wang Liqi maintained that the novel and the drama came from different origins. De-an Wu Swihart, The Evolution of Chinese Novel form, Thesis Ph. D. The Department of East Asian Studies of Princeton University, 1990, p. 26.

② "Eulogy" of Song Jiang and his band of thirty-six composed by Gong Kai (in Zhon Mi's *Guixin zazhi xuji*). De-an Wu Swihart, The Evolution of Chinese Novel form, Thesis Ph. D. The Department of East Asian Studies of Princeton University, 1990, p. 26.

③ Biji (literary sketches). The most salient among them were *Hui chen houlu* (*A Collection of Sundry Notes and Comments*, Vol. Ⅱ) by Wang Mingqing of the Song dynasty, which includeed an account of the ancestry of Gao Qiu, and *Qixiu leigao* (Sundry Notes and Comments in Seven Categories), *Xiao fumei xianhua* (Miscellaneous Talks of Xiao Fumei), *Yongyu manmo* (Random Thoughts in Idle Hours), *Chaxiang shi congchao* (Comments Written in the Hall of Tea Fragrance), *Wuyuai shi suibi* (Casual Notes Made in the Yuai Chamber), etc. Of the Ming dynasty, which possessed some characters, episodes and poems or ci-poems also found in the nivel. De-an Wu Swihart, The Evolution of Chinese Novel form, Thesis Ph. D. The Department of East Asian Studies of Princeton University, 1990, p. 26.

第六则是来自讲述水浒英雄故事的口头流传的南宋说书。根据罗烨《醉翁谈录》的记载,吴德安指出,《水浒传》中的人物故事有一些来自南宋说书的内容,像"公案类"中的"石头孙立","朴刀类"的"青面兽杨志","杆棒类"的"花和尚"鲁达和"行者"武松,等等。只是这些文本并未保存下来。①

第七是按吴德安之论,《水浒传》的创作有现实原型。他说:"曾经盛传'强盗结伙造反提高声望而后成为高级军官'的故事。"② 在该论者看来,这个故事就是《水浒传》的叙事原型。对此,吴德安进一步论述道:

> 李宗侗指出,口头流传有三个这样的故事,一个在山东,一个在太行山地区,一个在浙江。王利器坚持认为,《水浒传》是以三个最初的版本为基础创作而成的:一个集中于讲述梁山的故事,另一个主要讲述太行山的故事,第三个即施耐庵的版本则是讲述方腊的故事。③

水浒故事存在三个单独系统的说法,目前的文献资料很难证实。但从小说《水浒传》文本中对地理方位处理上存在的问题来看,又的确存在这样的可能性。从现存各个不同版本的《水浒传》来说,确实有把水浒故事的北方太行山系统、梁山泊系统与南方浙江系统融合为一的痕迹。

综合上述英语世界批评者对《水浒传》素材渊源问题的研究,我们大致可以把小说的素材来源分成两大类:一是历史事实,二是文学艺术。

---

① Storytelling of the SouthernSong dynasty. According to Luo Ye's Zuiweng tanlu (Talks of a Drunken Old Man), storytelling of the Southern Song dynasty included the story of Sun Li, in the section of the "Stone Head" entiled "Famed Culprits", the story of Yang Zhi, the "Blue-faced Beast", in the section "Bravos with the Po-knife" (pudao lei) and the stories of Lu Da, the "Tattooed Monk" and Wu Song the "Hairy Priest" in the section "Bravos wwith the Club" (gunbang lei). But all such texts are no longer extant. De-an Wu Swihart, The Evolution of Chinese Novel form, Thesis Ph. D. The Department of East Asian Studies of Princeton University, 1990, p. 26, 27.

② The once popular stories of "outlaws who with knives and clubs rise to fame and become high-ranking officers". De-an Wu Swihart, The Evolution of Chinese Novel form, Thesis Ph. D. The Department of East Asian Studies of Princeton University, 1990, p. 27.

③ Li Zongtong pointed out that there were in oral circulation: one such story in Shandong, the second in the Taihang Mountain region, and the third in Zhejiang. Wang Liqi maintained that *The Men of the Marsh* was based on three oriognal version: one that centered on stories of the Liangshan, another that centered on stories of the Taihang Mountain and the thied, Shi Naian's version, that centered on stories of Fang La. De-an Wu Swihart, The Evolution of Chinese Novel form, Thesis Ph. D. The Department of East Asian Studies of Princeton University, 1990, p. 27.

前者如《宋史》《宋会要稿》《国朝续会要》《皇宋十朝纲要》等。后者又可分成两类，一是书面形式的文学作品。如元杂剧诸种作品，私人笔记，以及可能是说书人底本的《大宋宣和遗事》；二是民间口头流传的水浒人物故事。只是这些只在私人著作中有一定的记载，像罗烨《醉翁谈录》中提及的"公案类"的"石头孙立"，"朴刀类"的"青面兽杨志"，"杆棒类"的"花和尚"鲁达和"行者"武松等，然具体内容已无可考。

第三节 《水浒传》的成书过程与版本演变

《水浒传》的成书究竟经历了一个怎样的过程，《水浒传》现存的各种版本究竟经历过怎样的演变，这些和小说作者问题一样也仍是一个谜。特别是对假设曾经存在的"原本"（或称为"底本""祖本"等）到现存的各个版本之间是一种怎样的演变情况，以及繁本与简本之间又是一种什么样的关系等问题的认识方面，更是众说纷纭、令人困惑。本节，笔者就来讨论英语世界的专家、学者对这些问题的研究情况。

一、《水浒传》的成书过程

综合目前的研究可知，与其他中国古典小说相比，《水浒传》的成书历史比较漫长，过程比较复杂。但与小说的作者和版本问题不一样的是，人们对小说成书过程的认识大体上还是取得了比较一致的意见。

在英语世界的研究中，批评者一般认为《水浒传》的创作有其历史根据，像上文提到的赛珍珠、欧文、吴德安、夏志清诸人皆持此观点。但与《三国演义》等不同的是，《水浒传》不完全是"按史演义"的成果，而是如人们常说的是"三分史实，七分虚构"。毕竟该作品的人物故事确凿可据的历史文献实在不多，而且语焉不详。而从历史到小说的最后成书，也就是大约从北宋末年到明嘉靖、万历朝的数百年间，人们根据现存各种相关文献书目的记载提出，《水浒传》经历了从口头形式（包括说书和民间传说）到书面形式（包括词话、杂剧等）的发展、演变。

对《水浒传》的成书过程，英语世界的批评者李培德等人作过非常简略的概括。原文不长，引述如下：

《水浒传》经历一个漫长的演变过程。《宋史》有对宋江三十六人的记载,他们屡败官军,后投降朝廷,1121年参与镇压方腊起义。宋江一伙的英雄业绩莫名其妙就捕获了大众的头脑,并最终成为南宋职业说书人极受欢迎的说书主题。已知最早的对宋江一伙的虚构记述是在《宣和遗事》中。该书可能是元初的一部作品,它部分基于说书人底本、部分基于其他文学资源而写成。一般认为《宣和遗事》是《水浒传》的原型,它激发了各种各样的关于宋江一伙的传说、口头故事、书面故事以及元杂剧的创作。这些作品为元末明初小说的第一部书面版本的出现奠定了基础。明代,大量的故事添加到小说里面,很多版本也在这一时期刊行。现存最早的本子始于16世纪中叶。1614年出现的120回本是最完整的本子,该本子一直通行到1641年。之后,著名小说评点家、白话文学的拥趸金圣叹(1610?—1661),推出了一部70回本。该刻本仅保留1614年本的前71回,金圣叹把小说第一回改为楔子,加上了评点。金本使小说结构更严谨,并最终成为最流行的版本。赛珍珠、杰克逊两人的英译本都是以金本为底本。[1]

---

[1] The *Water Margin* came about through a slow process of evolution. The *History of the Sung* (*Sung shih*) contains a note on a band of thirty-six outlaws led by Sung Chiang, their repeated victories over government troops, their subsequent surrender to the government, and their participation in the successful government campaign of 1121 against the rebel Fang La and Fang's followers. The exploits of this band somehow captured the popular imagination and eventually became popular subjects for Southern Sung professional storytellers. The earliest known fictional account of the Sung Chiang band is found in the Historical Anecdotes of the Hsüan-ho Period (Hsüan-ho i-shih), probably an early Yüan work based partly on storytellers' prompt-books and partly on other literary sources. Generally considered the prototype of The Water Margin, the Historical Anecdotes inspired the creation of countless legends, oral tales, written stories, and Yüan plays about the band, leading up to the novel's first written version toward the end of the Yüan or at the beginning of the Ming. But this version is no longer extant. During the Ming a number of episodes were added to the novel, and many editions are believed to have been published during that period. The earliest surviving edition dates from the middle of the sixteenth centuries. In 1614 a 120-chapter edition, which is the most complete version, appeared. It had remained popular until 1641 when a famous fiction commentator and champion of vernacular literature, Chin Sheng-t'an (1610 – 1661), prepared a 70-chapter version. Retaining only the first seventy-one chapters of the 1614 edition and using Chapter 1 as the prologue, he added a commentary to the novel. His version tightened the novel's loose structure and eventually became the most popular edition. The two available English translations (by Pearl Buck and J. H. Jackson respectively) were both based on Chin's version. Winston L. Y. Yang, Nathan K. Mao and Peter Li, "Romance of the Three Kingdoms and The Water Margin," and "Journey to the West and Flowers in the Mirror." Classical Chinese Fiction: A Guide to Its Study and Appreciation. London: George Prior Publishers, 1978, pp. 39 – 51. *Literature Criticism from 1400 to 1800*. Ed. Lynn M. Zott. Vol. 76. Detroit: Gale, 2002. From Literature Resource Center.

这种概括虽然缺乏实质性的学术价值，但对小说演变线索的描述还是很清楚的。

在英语世界，欧文是到目前为止唯一一位比较系统、翔实研究《水浒传》成书历史与版本演变的批评家，上文提到的论著《一部中国小说的演变：〈水浒传〉》就是其研究成果。根据欧文的研究，《水浒传》的发展、演变经历了如下几个阶段：

第一阶段是"历史基础"。对水浒人物故事的历史记载，首先要提到的是《宋史》。欧文在研究中所引《宋史》内容是我们比较熟悉的，主要是《徽宗纪》《高宗纪》《曾孝蕴传》《蒲宗孟传》《侯蒙传》《张叔夜传》等人物传记。《宋史》之外，欧文还提到《宋会要稿》《国朝续会要》《皇宋十朝纲要》等历史性著作对宋江等36人的记述。①

第二阶段是"初步发展"。按欧文之论，《水浒传》的初步发展首先就是南宋时期的书会说书。根据洪迈《夷坚志乙志》、陆游诗歌《小舟游近村舍舟步归》（"斜阳古柳赵家庄，负鼓盲翁正作场。身后是非谁管得？满村听说蔡中郎。"）等的记述，欧文说南宋时期书会已经非常兴盛，艺人说书几乎遍布各重要城镇。同时，欧文还提出：

> 然而，说书人即席讲故事，尤其是描写或对话的段落，要是没有引人注目、激动人心的感觉，他是不可能成功的。每个故事的梗概在早期的话本（一种台词类的书）中都能找到。这些是由书会成员——包括说书艺人和受过较好教育的人——编纂的。他们可能是科举落第者。在公开演出之前，他们帮助把这些故事编写好。②

保存下来的宋元话本故事的确不少，但有关水浒人物故事的却几乎没

---

① Richard Gregg Irwin, The evolution of a Chinese novel: Shui-hu-chuan, Cambridge Massachusetts: Harvard University Press, 1953, pp. 9 – 18.

② While telling his tale the raconteur omprovised, especially in passages of description or conversation, for without a lively sense of the dramatic he could never have succeeded. But the main outlines of each story were to be found very early in a *hua-pen* 话本, a sort of prompt-book. These were compiled by members of the *shu-hui* 书会, or storyteller's guild, which included raconteurs and bettered-educated men, possibly unsuccessful candidates for degrees, who helped compose the stories before their public presentation. Richard Gregg Irwin, The evolution of a Chinese novel: Shui-hu-chuan, Cambridge Massachusetts: Harvard University Press, 1953, p. 24.

有。然根据《宣和遗事》及明代钱曾《戏瑕》的记述,欧文确信宋元时期曾经存在《水浒传词话》这么一部作品,其中可能包括大部分水浒故事传说。对此,该论者指出:

> 李玄伯推断,在口头传统的初创阶段,宋江三十六人的短篇故事在人们之间流传。不久移入话本中,并在"街头巷尾"流行。它们甚至影响到文人的创作,像龚圣与受说书人创作的影响而写的"宋江三十六人赞"就是很好的证明。这些故事大部分已经亡佚很久了。很幸运的是,《水浒传》创作初期的一些核心故事,在16世纪的一部词话《宣和遗事》(该书源自著名藏书家钱曾的藏书)中保存了下来。①

按欧文之论,从说书到词话的形之于口向形之于文的转变,这就完成了《水浒传》的初步发展。特别是说书人的"底本"(prompt-book),在欧文看来,更是为施、罗二人天才的合作——传世巨著《水浒传》的创作,奠定了坚实的基础。(这在著作权归属部分已有交代)

《水浒传》初步发展的第二方面是元代的杂剧和词话创作。对此,欧文说:"到《宣和遗事》编成时,词话的受欢迎度已被另一种典型的白话文学形式杂剧所超越。"② 而水浒题材的杂剧创作在当时是非常兴盛的。但即使如此,该论者相信在水浒杂剧创作的同时,水浒词话的创作也仍在继续。就此问题,他说:

---

① Li Hsüan-po postulates an initial period of oral tradition during which such short stories circulated among the people. It was but a short remove to the hua-pen, and a popularity "in street and lane" not without effect even upon men of letters, as demonstrated by the "Encomium to Sung Chiang and His Thirty-six" written by Kung Sheng-yü under the spell created by raconteurs. Many, perhaps the majority, of these tales have long since disappeared. But a few, combined in a unfied account which embodies the embryonic nucieus of Shui-hu-chuan, have fortunately been preserved in a portion of Hsüan-ho i-shih, one of sixteen tz'u-hua 词话 originally in the collection of the distinguished bibliophile, Ch'in Tseng 钱曾(1629-99). Richard Gregg Irwin, The evolution of a Chinese novel: Shui-hu-chuan, Cambridge Massachusetts: Harvard University Press, 1953, p. 25。

② By the time Hsüan-ho i-shih was actually compiled, the tz'u-hua, of which it is typical, had been surpassed in popularity by a different form og vernacular literature, the tsa-chü 杂剧. Richard Gregg Irwin, The evolution of a Chinese novel: Shui-hu-chuan, Cambridge Massachusetts: Harvard University Press, 1953, p. 33。

第一章　英语世界对《水浒传》的考证探源研究　　75

虽然词话的受欢迎度被时行的杂剧掩盖，但其创作仍在继续。因为元末出现的最早的一批长篇小说都是这种形式。长篇小说从宋代词话的单个故事发展而来，这代表了一种完整的传统。虽然《水浒传词话》没有保存下来，但仍然可能发掘出两种分属不同系统的水浒词话。①

对此，欧文指出，从大量水浒戏剧描写的人物、事件来看，其中一种水浒词话在由金入元时期的北方流传，另一种则在元末的南方地区流传。而且，欧文认为后一种水浒词话在元末已经写定。② 事实上，欧文猜测的所谓两种水浒词话系统，更像上文该论者援引李玄伯的观点所提出的，水浒故事存在包括以梁山泊与太行山为核心的北方系统和以浙江为核心的南方系统。遗憾的是，欧文这些观点的提出虽然已经过去60余年了，却仍然无法证实。或许历史上从来就没有过所谓的《水浒传词话》这样的作品。元代的水浒杂剧创作的大致情形在《水浒传》的素材渊源部分已经作了比较详细的讨论，此处就不再赘述。

词话、杂剧等各种不同形式的讲述水浒英雄故事的文学作品的大量涌现，推动了《水浒传》发展、演变第三阶段的到来。这就是欧文所说的祖本《水浒传》（The original Shu-hu-chuan）的创作完成阶段。欧文认为，小说祖本的创作是在元末明初时完成的。作为书会成员的施耐庵、罗贯中，两人意气相投。他们对说书底本《水浒传词话》进行扩展、提炼，一方面对作品的故事情节、人物形象等加以充实，另一方面对小说的艺术形式、手法技巧加以提升。结果，他们天才地合作创作出传世经典——小说《水浒传》。③

按欧文之论，祖本《水浒传》创作的完成并不是《水浒传》成书历

---

① Although overshadowed by the current popularity of the drama, tz'u-hua continued to be written. For the earlist full-length novels, which made their appearance late in the Yüan period, were all in this form, and must represent an unbroken tradition stemming from the single-episode tz'u-hua of Sung times. No *Shui-hu-chuan tz'u-hua* has been preserved, but it is still possible to discover what two or possibly two groupes of them included. Richard Gregg Irwin, The evolution of a Chinese novel: Shui-hu-chuan, Cambridge Massachusetts: Harvard University Press, 1953, p. 34.

② Richard Gregg Irwin, The evolution of a Chinese novel: Shui-hu-chuan, Cambridge Massachusetts: Harvard University Press, 1953, p. 34.

③ Ibid., p. 50, 51.

史的终结。根据现存文献记载以及现存《水浒传》刻本残页给我们提供的信息,再结合欧文的《水浒传》祖本创作于元末明初的假设可知,从小说祖本写作的完成到高儒《百川书志》(该书于明嘉靖1540年出版)首次记录施、罗合著100卷《水浒传》本子,其间相隔近两百年。就现存《水浒传》不同版本之间的差异可知,后来出现的各种《水浒传》刻本在故事情节上有不小变动,就是同时出现的不同小说文本,相互之间也差异甚大。这个过程即是欧文所说的《水浒传》的删改与现今所见小说繁简系统中各版本的写定形成阶段。欧文对这个阶段的论述主要涉及的是版本问题,笔者把它放在下一部分"版本研究"中来讨论。

综合欧文的分析、论述,《水浒传》故事的演变过程可以概括如下:

金、南宋时期:宋江等三十六人的传说诞生,并以梁山泊、太行山、浙江为核心地域形成了三个不同的水浒故事系统,它们的融合、发展形成了《水浒传词话》;

金、元时期:北方地区水浒故事的发展以杂剧为主,南方地区则集中在《宣和遗事》;

元末:水浒杂剧与《宣和遗事》中的水浒人物故事逐渐融合进后来的南方水浒词话,也就是欧文坚信存在的作为施、罗二人创作基础的书会说书底本《水浒传词话》;

元明之际:施、罗二人合作把作为说书底本的《水浒传词话》改造成祖本《水浒传》;

明16世纪50年代:插入征辽故事;

明16世纪90年代:书商删削小说文本,插入征田虎、王庆故事;

1596—1602年:最后的插入修订,小说原本的恢复;

1641—1644年:金圣叹腰斩《水浒传》,删去招安后所有故事。[①]

这个概括,时间线索比较清楚。从金、南宋到明末清初,《水浒传》一步步由历史、民间传说、书会说书、词话、杂剧,终至慢慢形成我们现在所看见的各种小说定本。只是对此过程不同阶段所作的各种假设、推想,有一些是缺乏确凿的文献资料支撑的:像对以梁山泊、太行山、浙江为核心地域形成三个不同水浒故事系统的推断,像对存在《水浒传词话》

---

① Richard Gregg Irwin, The evolution of a Chinese novel: Shui-hu-chuan, Cambridge Massachusetts: Harvard University Press, 1953, p. 206.

的设想，都是如此。

二、《水浒传》版本研究

根据上述事实，欧文提出，施、罗二人合著的祖本《水浒传》写成后，该小说历经多人之手发生了很大的变化，形成了后世名目繁多的不同小说刊本。欧文说，文献资料记录的《水浒传》早期刻本，除郭本外，尚有其他三个版本值得一提。一是《也是园书目》所记罗贯中古本20卷《水浒传》，欧文认为在此三种版本中这可能是最早的本子。二是《百川书志》记录的"《忠义水浒传》100卷，钱塘施耐庵的本，罗贯中编次"。该论者说此本也早于郭本。三是《古今书刻》记录的"都察院《水浒传》"。欧文认为这是1559年以后出现的。该论者说，这三个本子之间的关系，以及它们与郭本之间的关系，已不可知。但在对后世《水浒传》各版本的最后写定上，郭本的影响是最大的。因为欧文认为，据目前可考的文献来看，《水浒传》后来的所有刊本都是以郭本为据[1]。对郭本在《水浒传》版本演变过程中的重要性，欧文如此谈道："郭本的重要性不可低估，即使有一定的变化，但与现存任何本子相比，它是最接近施、罗原本的。"欧文说，很明显，120回修订本《水浒传》第83—90回的征辽故事是后来插入的，施、罗原本并无此内容[2]。该论者也指出，就是征田虎、王庆的故事也是后来插入的。

---

[1] Befor examining the Kuo edition from which all later versions stem, three others deserve mention. These versions of the novel are either contemporary with or earlier than the Kuo edition, and their relationship to it and each other is unknow. One is described in *Yeh-shih-yüan shu-mu* as an "ancient edition of Lo Kuan-chung, *Shui-hu-chuan*, in twenty *chüan*." This catalogue was not compiled until the end of the seventeen century, but it lists a collection os almost unparalleled rarity. Since this edition of the novel retains the division by *chüan* rather than by chapter, it is probably the earliest of the three, though not the first to be recorded. Next comes "*Chung-i shui-hu-chuan* in one hundred chapters, the work of Shih Nai-an, native of Ch'ien-t'ang, arranged by Lo Kuan-chung," listed in *Po-ch'uan shu-chih*, which also antedated the Kuo edition. The third edition, "*Shui-hu-chuan* printed by the Censorate," is catalogued in *Ku-chin shu-k'e*, a work which did not appear until after 1559. Richard Gregg Irwin, The evolution of a Chinese novel: Shui-hu-chuan, Cambridge Massachusetts: Harvard University Press, 1953, pp. 61 – 62.

[2] In major features they were identical but for one important change, the interpolation of the campaign against the Liao which comprises Chapters 83 – 90 of the 120-chapter recension. That this section was not a portion of the Shih-Lo work is obvious from its position in relation to the expedition against Fang La. Historically, such campaigns did not take place until after the subdual of Fang... Richard Gregg Irwin, The evolution of a Chinese novel: Shui-hu-chuan, Cambridge Massachusetts: Harvard University Press, 1953, p. 63.

如上文所说，以郭本为基础形成的后世《水浒传》诸版本，故事情节、文本叙述方面的增删改动还是很大的。这种变化，一方面是"文本的删改"。按欧文之论，这种删改是"删繁就简"，这主要是指文字表达上的简化。另一方面随着"文本的删改"发生的则是"故事的扩充"。根据胡应麟等人的记述，欧文指出："16世纪末，书商对小说作了改动，变得比郭本更简单。出于商业考虑，出版了两个新的版本，它们删节文本，但保留了原著的基本叙事框架。"① 欧文认为，余象斗双峰堂刊印的《新刊京本绣像插增田虎、王庆忠义水浒全传》，雄飞馆刊印的《英雄谱》，就是这种商业操作的产物②。该论者说，这些书商在郭本的基础上，一方面删削文字，另一方面插入征辽、征田虎、王庆故事，结果就形成了新的小说版本。根据欧文的论述，《水浒传》的这些新本子正是学界所说的"文简事繁"本，也就是统称的简本。

在论著《一部中国小说的演变：〈水浒传〉》中，欧文虽然没有明确点出小说繁本与简本之间的关系，但他在论述过程中提出的《水浒传》版本"删繁就简"的演变过程，其实已非常清楚地阐明了他的观点，即在小说版本的演变上，简本是从繁本而来的。这和胡适等人的观点一样（见绪论第三节"版本研究之争"部分）。因为一个明显的事实是，他提到的余象斗双峰堂刻本《新刊京本绣像插增田虎、王庆忠义水浒全传》与雄飞馆刻本《英雄谱》等新版本是简本系统的经典本子，而其依据的郭本则是繁本，源、流之间线索分明。

在《水浒传》诸版本中，欧文还讨论了容与堂刻百回本《李卓吾先生批评忠义水浒传》、袁无涯刻百二十回本《忠义水浒传全书》以及李玄伯本、天都外臣序本、芥子园刻本、贯华堂刻金圣叹删节批点《水浒传》等各版本的大概情况。这些主要是繁本。对小说简本，除双峰堂《新刊京本绣像插增田虎、王庆忠义水浒全传》与雄飞馆《英雄谱》两种外，欧文还提到宝翰楼刊本《李卓吾原评忠义水浒全传》，及题署"清源姚宗镇国藩父编"的藜光堂《新刻全像忠义水浒传》115回本。欧文指出，藜光

---

① Near the close of the sixteen century booksellers made changes in the novel which were more drastic than those of the Kuo edition. Motivated solely by business considerations, two of them brought out new editions which abridged the text while preserving its basic narrative. Richard Gregg Irwin, The evolution of a Chinese novel: Shui-hu-chuan, Cambridge Massachusetts: Harvard University Press, 1953, p. 66.

② Richard Gregg Irwin, The evolution of a Chinese novel: Shui-hu-chuan, Cambridge Massachusetts: Harvard University Press, 1953, pp. 63 – 75.

堂本题署"清源姚宗镇国藩父编",这显然是时人对小说原本的冒名篡改之作。

在该论著中,欧文还对小说各版本之间的关系作了一个推断,具体见下表:

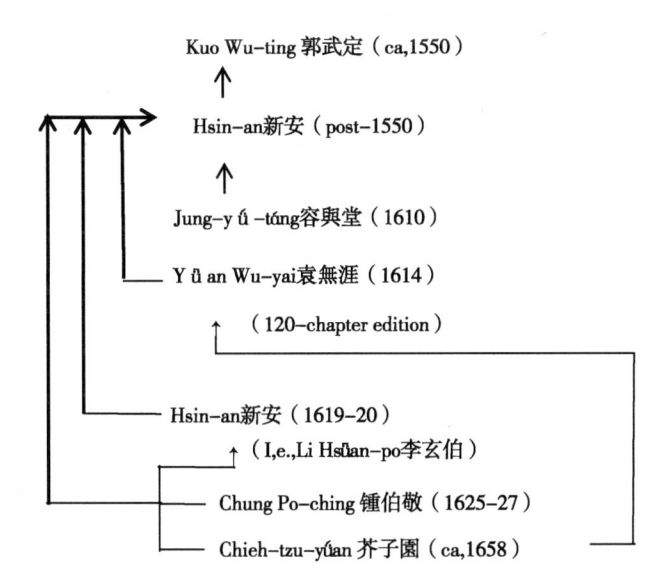

```
                    Kuo Wu-ting 郭武定 (ca,1550)
                         ↑
                    Hsin-an 新安 (post-1550)
                         ↑
                    Jung-yü-táng 容與堂 (1610)
              ┌──── Yüan Wu-yai 袁無涯 (1614)
              │        ↑  (120-chapter edition)
              │
         ┌──── Hsin-an 新安 (1619-20)
         │        ↑  (I,e.,Li Hsüan-po 李玄伯)
         ├──── Chung Po-ching 锺伯敬 (1625-27)
         └──── Chieh-tzu-yüan 芥子園 (ca,1658)
```

1950 年,欧文推断出的《水浒传》版本源流结构图表①

根据此表可知,欧文认为郭本是后来所有小说版本的"源",在郭本基础上出现的"新安"刻本又是后来各版本的"标杆"。根据沈德符《野获编》的记载,新安刻本即是天都外臣序本,欧文并未弄清楚它们之间的关系。此外,欧文在该图表中提到的新安(1619—1620)刻本其实只是原新安刻本(post-1550)的重刻本,而非出现的某一新本子,并不具有版本学的意义。

1960 年,根据学界对《一部中国小说的演变:〈水浒传〉》一书的批评,欧文又撰写、发表了《〈水浒传〉再考察》一文,专门研究《水浒传》不同版本之间的关系。在该文中,欧文对中国、日本、欧美等各地图书馆所藏《水浒传》版本进行比较详细的考察后,对其 1950 年的推断作了修订,具体见下表:

这次修订,以"天都外臣"替代"新安"字样,凸显天都外臣序本

---

① Richard Gregg Irwin, *Water Margin Revisited*, Toung pao, 48 (1960), p. 415.

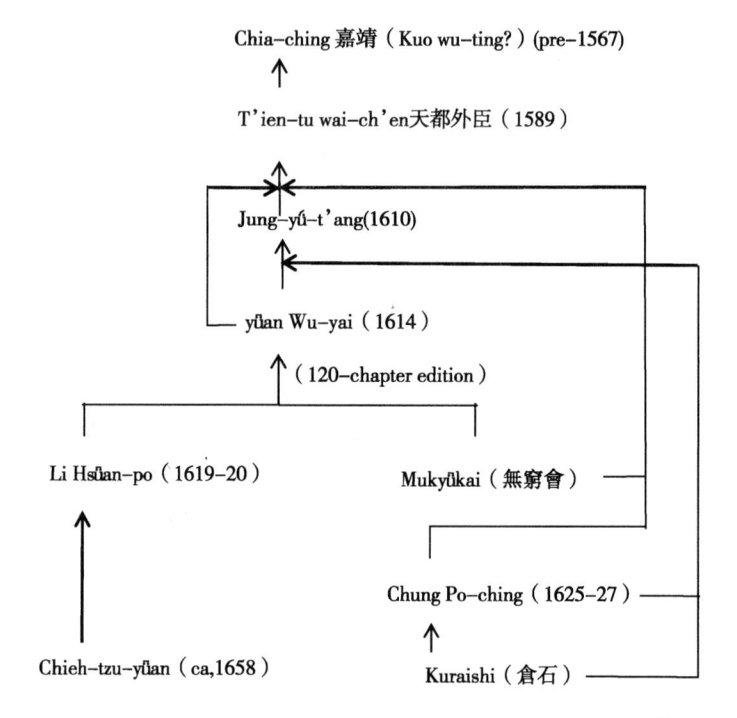

```
                    Chia-ching 嘉靖（Kuo wu-ting?）(pre-1567)
                              ↑
                    T'ien-tu wai-ch'en 天都外臣（1589）
                              ↑
                    Jung-yü-t'ang(1610)
                              ↑
                 ┌── yüan Wu-yai（1614）
                 │           ↑
                 │   （120-chapter edition）
        ┌────────┴────────┐
   Li Hsüan-po（1619-20）   Mukyūkai（無窮會）
        ↑
        │                Chung Po-ching（1625-27）──┘
        │                        ↑
   Chieh-tzu-yüan（ca,1658）  Kuraishi（倉石）
```

1960年，欧文重新推断的《水浒传》版本源流结构图表①

的重要性。从本文来说，天都外臣序本在小说繁本的发展中非常重要。就目前学术界比较一致的认识来看，后世所有繁本的形成都与其脱不了关系。必须明确的是，欧文对《水浒传》版本关系的推断基本上都没有提到现存的各种简本。

浦安迪对《水浒传》的版本演变与繁、简本之间的关系也进行过研究。在综合各种文献资料的记载与结合后来人们对小说版本发展的认识的基础上，浦安迪对小说繁本的发展提出如下观点：

> 基于所有这些证据，我们可以描绘出一幅晚明时期繁本《水浒传》发展的全景图：嘉靖年间一种百回本首次出现；此后，和郭勋有关的刻本刊行，在万历朝中期（1589后）及万历朝的最后几年（1610和1614），该本重新刊印；最后，明末时期，小说遭到删节，

---

① Richard Gregg Irwin, *Water Margin Revisited*, Toung pao, 48（1960）, p.415.

重新编定。①

而在这些繁本中,浦安迪根据学界的普遍认识认为,容与堂刻本是上承假设的嘉靖本、郭本与天都外臣本、下接后来版本系统的代表性本子,而其中最有影响的则是袁无涯1614年刻印的120回本《李卓吾原评忠义水浒全传》。② 其实,浦安迪所作的《水浒传》繁本的发展世系与欧文的推断是基本一致的。

浦安迪对《水浒传》繁本与简本之间关系的认识与欧文的"删繁就简"论不同。浦氏一方面接受了鲁迅等人的简本先于繁本的观点,另一方面也接受了柳存仁提出的繁本与简本两个系统平行发展、后来相互借鉴补充的假设。在此两种观点的基础上,浦氏主张,在早期两者是平行发展的系统,后来到了某一阶段才开始相互影响,现存某个特定简本可能是16世纪繁本的删节本。而他又提出简本系统先于繁本系统出现,但他又坚持认为繁本有其独立的演变过程,它们对现存简本的影响是有限的。对此,浦安迪的理由是:

> 正如我在评论《西游记》世德堂本与朱鼎臣文简本究竟谁在先的类似论争时说过的,这种拉锯式的论争肯定没有结果。因为对版本先后问题的决定,依赖于偶然存留至今的那些本子的校勘。我们有各种理由怀疑,实际上这些本子没有一种是各自世系的源出范本,甚至可能根本不具代表性。而另一方面,如果我们发现我们对待的是平行发展的两个版本支系,它们只是在后来的某个时间点才开始相互影响,那么,总体上看,我们把简本看作是一个更早发展的证据,同时承认我们手头拥有的某些特定的简本是十六世纪繁本删节而成的,这两者

---

① On the basis of all these pieces of evidence, we can put together a fairly complete picture of the process of textual developement of the *fan-pen Shui-hu chuan* during the late Ming period: from the first appearance of a hundred-chapter text in the Chia-ching period, its subsequent printing with some sort of connection to the house of Kuo Hsün, its reprinting in the Wan-li period after 1589 and again toward the end of the Wan-li period in 1610 and 1614, and finally its truncation and reediting at the very end of the dynasty. Andrew H. Plaks, The Four Masterworks of the Ming Novel, Princeton University Press, 1987, p. 293.

② Andrew H. Plaks, The Four Masterworks of the Ming Novel, Princeton University Press, 1987, p. 289.

之间根本就不矛盾。从另一方面来看，我们可以接受繁本一定有过更早范本的看法，而无须落入此种假设的圈套，即认为任何现存的简本就是这种祖本的样本。

　　事实上我自己的推测大致如下：我对坚持认为罗贯中或施耐庵（所作的本子）是较简原本的看法只能屈从，这可能使我最终进入简本在先的行列；但我坚持认为繁本有其独立的发展历史，繁本后来对现存的简本给予过有限的影响。①

浦安迪提出的观点有一定的道理，他的推测也存在可能性。因为从目前来看，不论是鲁迅等人的"由简入繁"论，还是胡适等人提出的"删繁就简"论，都没有足够的说服力，因为我们无法找到权威性的刻本来证明这些论点。同时，从本书来说，"由简入繁"的进化过程是可能的，但社会学的进化论是否就完全适合文学创作的规律也是个问题；而"删繁就简"的做法也并不就没有可行性。只是《水浒传》的成书与版本演变问题实在过于复杂，笔者只能就此打住话头。

英语世界尚有其他批评者对《水浒传》的成书和版本问题进行过讨论，像赛珍珠在《〈水浒传〉导言》中就曾谈到小说的四个版本（包括70回本、115回本、120回本与100回本），但只是停留在介绍的层面而缺少学术性，故不论。

---

　　① As I have said in my review of the comparable controversy over the prioty of the Shih-te t'ang 世德堂 Hsi-yu chi versus the shorter Chu Ting-ch'en text 朱鼎臣, this seesaw debate is necessarily inconclusive, since it relies on comparing those extant texts that have by chance come down to us to determine historical priority, when we have every reson to suspect that none of these are in fact original exemplars of their respective systems, and may not even be particularly representative. If, on the other hand, we find that we are derling with two parallel strains, which only after a certain point enter into a relationship of mutual influence, then there is no contradiction in viewing the *chien-pen* line in general as evidence of an earlier stage of development, while still recognizing that the particular *chien-pen* examples we have in hand may be the result of a later process of abridgment of the sixteen-century *fan-pen* texts. O r, to look at it from another direction, we can accept that the *fan-pen* must have had earlier prototype, without falling into the trap of assuming that the *fan-pen* as we have them must provide models of this "original" form。

　　My own speculation would in fact run along something like these lines: I would bow to the persistent attribution to Lo Kuan-chung or Shih Nai-an of a simpler prototype, which may have eventually fed into the chien-pen system; yet I would also insist on the notion of a separate development of the *fan-pen* recension, with this later excersing a conditioning influence on the *chien-pen* exemplars mow extant.

　　Andrew H. Plaks, The Four Masterworks of the Ming Novel, Princeton University Press, 1987, p. 301.

附　欧文《水浒传》版本源流结构图表原页[1]

```
WATER MARGIN REVISITED                    415

T'ien Hu and Wang Ch'ing, but that he revised this interpolation
by an unknown author taken over from the Paris text.
University of California, Berkeley.

              FILIATION OF SHUI-HU-CHUAN TEXTS
Table A (1950 postulation):

              Kuo Wu-ting 郭武定 (ca. 1550)
                    ↑
    ┌──→Hsin-an 新安 (post-1550)
    │        ↑
    │   Jung-yü-t'ang 容與堂 (1610)
    │        ↑
    ├──→Yüan Wu-yai 袁無涯 (1614)
    │        ↑
    │   (120-chapter edition)
    ├──→Hsin-an 新安 (1619-20)
    │        ↑
    │   (i.e., Li Hsüan-po 李玄伯)
    ├──←Chung Po-ching 鍾伯敬 (1625-27)
    └──→Chieh-tzu-yüan 芥子園 (ca. 1658)

Table B (1960 reappraisal):

         Chia-ching 嘉靖 (Kuo Wu-ting?) (pre-1567)
              ↑
         T'ien-tu wai-ch'en 天都外臣 (1589)
              ↑
         Jung-yü-t'ang (1610)
              ↑
         Yüan Wu-yai (1614)
         (120-chapter edition)

    Li Hsüan-po (1619-20)   Mukyūkai 無窮會
                            Chung Po-ching (1625-27)
                            Kuraishi 倉石
    Chieh-tzu-yüan (ca. 1658)
```

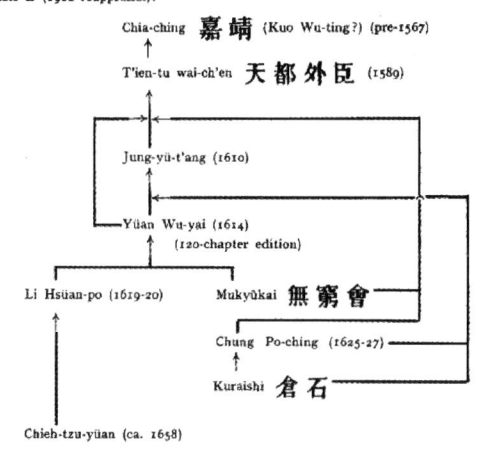

---

[1] Richard Gregg Irwin, *Water Margin Revisited*, Toung pao, 48（1960）, p. 415.

第二章

英语世界对《水浒传》的影响接受研究

英语世界的学者李培德等人在研究中指出:"《三国演义》和《水浒传》是中国小说史上重要的里程碑","两部作品的作者开创了不同的通俗叙事类型,……两者都是中国散文小说发展的标志"[①]。正因为在中国文学发展史上具有如此重要的地位,《水浒传》自其诞生之日起就对中国文学产生了非常大的影响。不管是对小说创作还是戏剧创作,不管是在故事题材、人物形象还是在思想主题方面,不管在古代还是现代,其影响绵延不断。而当其被译介到中国之外的其他国家、被当地的文人墨客接受时,对他们的创作也形成了一定的影响。这些都是英语世界的批评者在研究时关注的问题。

当然,《水浒传》的影响不只在文学创作一隅。它对中国社会国民思想与民族心态的构成,特别是对中国革命运动的发生、发展,都具有不可估量的影响力。这些也是英语世界的批评者在研究时关注的内容。

英语世界的学者在研究《水浒传》所产生的影响时,既有文学的维度也有社会学、历史学的维度,既有对中国自身的影响也有跨国传播的影响。因此,本章所用的"影响研究"一词并不是特指完全比较文学法国学派倡导的"国际文学关系史"意义上的"影响研究",而是指英语世界的批评家对《水浒传》发生的影响所作的研究。

---

① *Romance of the Three Kingdoms* and *The Water Margin* are important landmarks in the history of Chinese fiction... The authors of the two books created different types of popular narrative, ... both landmarks in the developement of Chinese prose fiction. Winston L. Y. Yang, Nathan K. Mao and Peter Li. Classical Chinese Fiction: *A Guide to Its Study and Appreciation*. London: George Prior Publishers, 1978, p.39, 45.

第一节 《水浒传》对中国古典文学创作的影响

在明清文人作家的书信、日记及论述文章里面，有很多关于《水浒传》的记述与评论文字。这一现象说明《水浒传》在当时文人中引起了很大的反响。同时，在有形或无形之中，自然也会对他们的创作产生一定的影响。

在英语世界学者的研究中，《水浒传》对中国古典文学的影响可以分成两个方面，一是对小说创作的影响，如兰陵笑笑生的《金瓶梅》、陈忱的《水浒后传》、青莲室主人的《后水浒传》及俞万春的《荡寇志》等；二是对戏剧创作的影响，这基本集中在明代水浒戏上，如李开先的《宝剑记》、陈与郊的《灵宝刀》、沈璟的《义侠记》等。细究之则可发现，这种影响，有故事素材、人物形象、主题思想方面的直接引进或改编，有艺术风格、创作手法、文体类型的继承和发展等。

一、《水浒传》与明清小说创作

就《水浒传》对明清小说创作的影响，中国学者石昌渝在为沙博理英译本撰写的导论中曾作过简洁的描述。他指出：

> 《水浒传》的影响相当深远。它为后世的小说创作提供了丰富的艺术经验，同样为后来的文学家提供了大量的素材来源。除众多的戏曲作品从《水浒传》截取主题材料之外，许多小说也追踪这部作品的线索而展开创作。比如说，《金瓶梅》就源于《水浒传》的第23—26回；沿袭《水浒传》的故事，清初出现了一部续书。此外，《说岳全传》里的一些人物被认为是梁山英雄的后代转化而来；从坚持抗金的角度来说，这部作品是梁山故事的继续。[1]

---

[1] The influence of Outlaws of the Marsh has been extremely far-reaching. It provideed a wealth of artistic experience for the creation of novels by later generations as well as material sources for later literary scholars. Apart from a host of dramas which drew their subject matter from Outlaws of the Marsh, many novels trace their line of descent back to it. For instance, the Jin Ping Mei springs from chapters 23 to 26 of Outlaws of the Marsh; and a sequel to it appeared in the early Qing Dynasty, carrying on the story. In addition, some of the characters in the novel The Complete Tale of the Yue Family are supposed to be alater generation of the Liangshan heroes, and this wor can be viewed as a continuation of the Liangshan story from the point of view of the anti-Jin resistance. Shi Changyu, Introduction, *Outlaws of the Marsh*, translated by Sidney Shapiro, Beijing: Foreign Language Press, 1993, Vol. I, pp. 13 – 14.

由此可知，《水浒传》与其后的多部明清小说之间的关系是很密切的。它和《金瓶梅》及"水浒续书"之间的影响关系是很显然的，至于对其他明清小说创作存在的或隐或显的影响细究之也能发现。下面，笔者就分类来论述英语世界对这个问题的研究。

（一）《水浒传》与《金瓶梅》

在英语世界的研究中，《水浒传》对《金瓶梅》的创作，最大的影响就在其为后者直接提供了故事素材和人物形象。吕立亭（Tina Lu）在撰写《剑桥中国文学史》的相关章节中指出，《金瓶梅》是从《水浒传》里的几个人物开始写起的，然后围绕这些人物及其家庭为读者描绘了一个错综复杂的"儒家的反乌托邦"世界①。而且吕立亭以为："和公安三袁、李贽一样，该小说作者肯定很推崇《水浒传》，因为《金瓶梅》第一回就重述了《水浒传》里的一段故事。"不过，吕立亭指出，这种重述不是完全的转述，而是借用、移植和改写的有机结合。他说：

> 淫荡的潘金莲是《水浒传》中英雄武松的嫂子，她谋杀自己那长相丑陋、五短身材的丈夫而与情人西门庆私奔。《水浒传》中，武松不久即为兄长之死报了仇；与之相反，《金瓶梅》的大部分故事情节则发生在武松抓住潘金莲之前的那几年里。换句话说，整部小说已将自我意识植入到先前的小说主体之中。②

就《金瓶梅》文本的实际情形看，小说作者在创作时的确具有非

---

① Beginning with just a few characters from *Water Margin*, *The Plum in the Golden Vase* draws in their families and then follows those characters to draw in their families and acquaintances, and so on, building up a cast of hundreds to create a simulacrum of a society in its entirety···The Cambridge History of Chinese Literature, Edited by Kang-I Sun Chang, Stephen Owen, Cambridge University Press, 2010, Vol. 2, p. 110.

② Like the Yuan brothers and Li Zhi, the novel's author must have admired *Water Margin*, because the first chapters of *The Plum in the Golden Vase* retell a portion of the earlier novel. The licentious Golden Lotus is the sister-in-law of Wu Song, one of the heroes of *Water Margin*; she murders her crippled husband to run off with her lover Ximen Qing. In *Water Margin*, Wu Song avenges his brother's death shortly thereafter; in contrast, most of *The Plum in the Golden Vase* takes place in the years it takes Wu Song to catch up with Golden Lotus. The whole novel is, in other words, a self-aware insertion into an earlier body of work. The Cambridge History of Chinese Literature, Edited by Kang-I Sun Chang, Stephen Owen, Cambridge University Press, 2010, Vol. 2, p. 107.

强烈的自我意识，他只是借用《水浒传》的相关故事与人物来开始自己的创作，在构架文本世界——"儒家的反乌托邦"世界时，创作者独立的主体意识是彰显的。

在英语世界，就《金瓶梅》引入、改写《水浒传》的故事与人物形象的研究，韩南的功课相对来说做得细而扎实，同时他也是最早着手研究该问题的学者之一。1960年，韩南在伦敦大学撰写的博士论文《〈金瓶梅〉成书及其来源的研究》就对该问题作了比较深入的探讨。1963年，在博士论文的基础上他又发表《〈金瓶梅〉探源》一文，其中第一小节专论《金瓶梅》借用、改编《水浒传》故事与人物的具体情形。

通过仔细研读、校对《水浒传》与《金瓶梅》两个小说文本，韩南提出："《金瓶梅》作者所用的《水浒传》版本已经亡佚。在现存版本里面，与之最接近的是署1589年（明万历十七年）天都外臣序100回本（真正1589年的刻本也已不存，那是清代重刻的）。"[①] 在故事与人物的借用、改编方面，韩南进一步指出："《金瓶梅》借用《水浒传》分两类情形，一是武松与潘金莲故事的直接引入，再就是其他片段故事被大量改编、移植到《金瓶梅》中。"[②]

就武松、潘金莲故事引入《金瓶梅》的具体情形，韩南作了比较详细的分析考辨。他指出：

> 《水浒传》第23—27回叙述的武松故事分三处引入《金瓶梅》。其中1—6回，从武松打虎讲到武大被谋杀；9—10回，写武松出差回家以及他意欲为兄报仇；第87回，叙述他杀死金莲。[③]

---

① The edition of the *Shui-hu chuan* which the author of the *Chin P'ing Mei* used is no longer extant. Among the surviving editions, the closest to it is the 100-chapter edition which has a preface by T'ien-tu wai-ch'en 天都外臣 dated 1589. (The actual 1589 edition does not exist; this is a Ch'ing reprint.). Hanan Patrick, Sources of The Chin P'ing Mei, Asia Major N. S. （10：1），1963，p. 25。

② Borrowing from the *Shui-hu chuan* are of two kinds-the story of Wu Sung 武松 and P'an Chin-lien 潘金莲, which has been borrowed directly, and other passages, which have been extensively adapted to fit into the *Chin P'ing Mei*. Hanan Patrick, Sources of The Chin P'ing Mei, Asia Major N. S. （10：1），1963，p. 25。

③ The adventures of Wu Sung as narrated in Chapters 23–7 of the *Shui-hu chuan* are copied into the *Chin P'ing Mei* in three different places. Chapters 1 to 6 tell his story from the fight with the tiger as far as his brother's murder; Chapters 9 and 10 tell of his return and attempted vengeance; Chapter 87 tells of his murder of Chin-lien. Hanan Patrick, Sources of The Chin P'ing Mei, Asia Major N. S. （10：1），1963，p. 26。

上文已经说过，《金瓶梅》对水浒故事、人物的借用经过不小的改编，所以两个文本之间的差异还是很明显的。对这种差异性，韩南也作了仔细的分析。在韩南看来，两部小说之间差异的形成，主要是因为《金瓶梅》的作者在故事情节上作了如下处理：

> 与《水浒传》情节之间的主要差别来自《金瓶梅》第9回。武松出差回来时，金莲已不在其力所能及范围，她已嫁入西门庆家。武松试图杀西门庆报仇，结果误杀了他的同伴。为此，他被发配远方，很久之后才回来。因而就推迟了武松的复仇。在原本简单的《水浒传》事件的框架里面，《金瓶梅》的作者设计了很多情节，并将之嵌入其中。①

在韩南的讨论中，《金瓶梅》作者出于某种难以猜测的动机，把《水浒传》中故事情节发生的地点由阳谷县变成了清河县。这个改动是很明显的。对武松、潘金莲故事在这两部作品之间的差异性，韩南进一步指出：

> 在这些借用的章节里，虽然《金瓶梅》非常接近《水浒传》的原文，但作者始终让它们服从自己的创作目的。存在明显的删节和大量的压缩以突出主题。也有大量的增加片段，其中大部分显示了作者的态度。有时，作者对来自《水浒传》的人物重新作了构思。两者之间叙述技巧有不同，小说家处理作品中故事素材的手法更是存在重大的差异。②

---

① The main divergence from the plot of the *Shui-hu chuan* comes in Chapter 9; by the time Wu Sung returns from the mission on which he has been sent, Chin-lien is already out of his reach, installed in Hsi-men Ch'ing's 西门庆 household. In an attempt to kill Hsi-men, Wu Sung kills his companion by mistake; for this deed he is sent into an exiile from which he does not return until much later. By thus postponing Wu Sung's vengeance, the author of the *Chin P'ing Mei* has contrived to fit most of the action of his novel within the framework of a brief *Shui-hu chuan* incident. Hanan Patrick, Sources of The Chin P'ing Mei, Asia Major N. S. (10: 1), 1963, p. 26。

② Within these borrowed chapters, although the *Chin P'ing Mei* follows the text of the *Shui-hu chuan* fairly closely, the author has constantly subordinated it to his purpose. There are some notable excisions and a good deal of fore-shortening. There numerous added passages, some of them most revealing of the author's attitude. The characters taken over from the *Shui-hu chuan* have sometimes been differently conceived. There are difference in narrative technique, and more fundamental in the novelist's approach to his work. Hanan Patrick, Sources of The Chin P'ing Mei, Asia Major N. S. (10: 1), 1963, p. 26.

第二章 英语世界对《水浒传》的影响接受研究

按韩南的分析、推测,《金瓶梅》作者对《水浒传》中武松、潘金莲故事所作的删节——主要是删去了仅仅涉及武松个人的那些情节,其目的在"尽快让金莲成为《金瓶梅》中受人关注的中心"①。《金瓶梅》在情节进展、人物描写的处理上的确如此。在增补方面,韩南说:"出于需要,在《水浒传》文本基础上《金瓶梅》增添了很多重要的细节。"据韩南的论述,这种增添具体说来主要有:首先增添了几个人物形象,一是西门庆的家人,二是武植那可怜的小女儿迎儿,三是西门庆家的丫头婢女如秋菊等;再就是新增了对武松、潘金莲的描写,从而在一定程度上改变了他们的形象。比如说潘金莲,在《水浒传》里只是一个目不识丁的使女,在《金瓶梅》中则是一个能拉会唱的女子。对武松,在表现其刚强正直的同时更加渲染突出他"残酷的复仇者的形象"。②

在韩南的讨论中,《金瓶梅》作者对《水浒传》中武松、潘金莲故事所作的删、改、增还有不少。不再赘述。《金瓶梅》中出自《水浒传》其他方面的引文,韩南认为主要有如下几处:

首先,《金瓶梅》主角之一的李瓶儿极可能借自《水浒传》里的角色——大名府梁世杰的姬妾。从《金瓶梅》第 10 回对该人物的身世经历所作的交代来看,李瓶儿很明显来自《水浒传》第 66 回《吴用智取大名府》。对此,韩南认为"李瓶儿这个人物的构思一定程度上可能受到《水浒传》相应部分的不太准确的记忆的影响"③。

其次,韩南提出:"第 84 回,周密地把《水浒传》的几个故事整合成一。月娘上泰山岳庙进香,至少借用了《水浒传》的四个片段。"④ 具

---

① Most of the excisions are designed to bring the *Chin P'ing Mei* as quickly as possible to the point at which Chin-lien becomes the centre of interest. Incident which concern Wu Sung alone have been omitted of abridged. Hanan Patrick, Sources of The Chin P'ing Mei, Asia Major N. S. (10: 1), 1963, p. 26.

② Many of the additions to the text of the *Shui-hu chuan* are examples of the greater detail demanded by the later novel. One character is added, besides the members of Hsi-men's household, in these early chapters. She is the pitiful little daughter of Wu Chih 武植, Ying-erh.... Other additions indicate a difference in the author's conception of the chacters which he has derived from the *Shui-hu chuan*, notably Chin-lien and Wu Sung. Hanan Patrick, Sources of The Chin P'ing Mei, Asia Major N. S. (10: 1), 1963, p. 27.

③ It is therefore just barely possible that the conception of Li P'ing-erh's character was influenced by somewhat inaccurate memory-witness the mistake about Li K'uei-of this part of the *Shui-hu chuan*. Hanan Patrick, Sources of The Chin P'ing Mei, Asia Major N. S. (10: 1), 1963, p. 29.

④ In chapter 84, there is a deliberate attempt to combine several *Shui-hu chuan* stories into one adventure. The occasion is the visit of Yüeh-niang to the temple on T'ai Shan; at least four parts of the *Shui-hu chuan* are drawn on. Hanan Patrick, Sources of The Chin P'ing Mei, Asia Major N. S. (10: 1), 1963, p. 29.

体说来即是：

一是"月娘所见的对碧霞宫娘娘的描写来自《水浒传》第42回宋江梦中所见的玄女娘娘。"①

二是"月娘逃出碧霞宫事件来自《水浒传》两个不同的故事。"② 其中，"殷天锡的形象及其事迹来自《水浒传》第52回。他是当地恶霸，觊觎柴进叔父的住宅，就尽力想据为己有"。③ "碧霞宫诱奸以及其他大量故事则来自《水浒传》第7回。这一片段写高俅的义子调戏林冲娘子。"在韩南看来，高衙内两次调戏林娘子的情节都被《金瓶梅》所采用④。

三是在人物形象塑造上，《金瓶梅》中的殷天锡是《水浒传》里的高衙内与殷天锡两个恶棍的合体，他用了其中一人的名字，用了另一人的绰号。⑤

四是韩南说："月娘逃出碧霞宫后再次遇险。在回清河途中，她被好色的强人首领王英所劫持，经宋江的干预才被释放。这整个插曲来自《水浒传》第32回，在那里被俘的女人是当地清风寨文官刘知寨的夫人。"⑥

---

① The description of the goddess as seen by Yüeh-niang comes from Sung Chiang's dream in Chapter 42. Hanan Patrick, Sources of The Chin P'ing Mei, Asia Major N. S. (10: 1), 1963, p. 29.

② The account of Yüeh-niang's escape from danger in the temple is derived from two separate stories of the *Shui-hu chuan*. Hanan Patrick, Sources of The Chin P'ing Mei, Asia Major N. S. (10: 1), 1963, p. 29.

③ The figure of Yin T'ien-hsi, together with some of the incident, is drawn from Chapter 52 of the *Shui-hu chuan*. He is a local bully, who, coveting the land of Ch'ai Chin's uncle, is endeavouring to make him give it up. Hanan Patrick, Sources of The Chin P'ing Mei, Asia Major N. S. (10: 1), 1963, p. 30.

④ The attempted seduction in the temple, together with a good deal more incident, is, however, drawn from Chapter 7 of the *Shui-hu chuan*. The passage deals with the attempt of the adopted son of Kao Ch'iu 高俅 to seduce Lin Ch'ung's 林冲 wife. Hanan Patrick, Sources of The Chin P'ing Mei, Asia Major N. S. (10: 1), 1963, p. 30。

⑤ Thus the figures of two villains from the *Shui-hu chuan* have been amalgamated; the composite *Chin P'ing Mei* villain even has the name of one and the nickname of the other. Hanan Patrick, Sources of The Chin P'ing Mei, Asia Major N. S. (10: 1), 1963, p. 30.

⑥ After her escape in the temple, Yüeh-niang survived yet another danger. On her way to Ch'ing-ho, she was captured by the lascivious bandit chief Wang Ying 王英, and was freed only on the intercession of Sung Chiang himself. This whole episode is drawn from Chapter32 of the Shui-hu chuan, where the captured woman is the wife of the local magistrate. Hanan Patrick, Sources of The Chin P'ing Mei, Asia Major N. S. (10: 1), 1963, p. 30。

再次，《水浒传》中不少形象化的、对仗工整的文言韵语被引入《金瓶梅》，这些韵语在两部作品里表情达意大有不同。韩南举例说，《水浒传》第21回描写宋江和阎婆惜"两个在灯下坐着，对面都不做声"，有一首韵语引进《金瓶梅》第59回，用来描写李瓶儿夜深时坐着守护重病的儿子①。

最后，韩南指出，《水浒传》第16回白胜所唱"赤日炎炎似火烧"抗议社会贫富不均的主题，在《金瓶梅》第27回中通过"那三等人怕热"与"那三等人不怕热"的议论获得进一步的发挥。而且韩南说，《金瓶梅》里的"词和绝句都是来自《水浒传》第16回"。②

就《水浒传》对《金瓶梅》创作在人物形象、故事情节上产生的影响，韩南以为由于后者对前者强烈的依赖性，除上面谈到的这些外可能还有更多不留痕迹的借用，只是一时很难考证。

综合上述可知，韩南对《金瓶梅》借用《水浒传》中的人物故事以及小说作者在创作时进行的改编所作的考证是非常详细的。他对两部小说文本所作的阅读、对照，条分缕析，证据确凿，细微之处亦悉心考证，其治学之认真严谨可见一斑。

对《金瓶梅》的《水浒传》来源，吴德安在1990年的博士论文《中国小说形式的变迁》中也作过讨论。他说："《水浒传》里武松打虎和关于西门庆与潘金莲的故事，在《金瓶梅》第1—9回以及第87回中重现。"此外，他还指出："《水浒传》中清风寨的故事，在《金瓶梅》第

---

① Hanan Patrick, Sources of The Chin P'ing Mei, Asia Major N. S. (10：1), 1963, p. 30. 韩南所说的韵文，在《水浒传》中是："银河耿耿，玉漏迢迢。穿窗斜月映寒光，透户凉风吹夜气。谯楼禁鼓，一更未尽一更催；别院寒砧，千捣将残千捣起。画檐间叮当铁马，敲碎旅客孤怀；银台上闪烁清灯，偏照闺人长叹。贪淫妓女心如火，仗义英雄气似虹。"《金瓶梅》中则是："银河耿耿，玉漏迢迢。穿窗皓月耿寒光，透户凉风吹夜气。雁声嘹亮，孤眠才子梦魂惊；蛩韵凄凉，独宿佳人情绪苦。谯楼禁鼓，一更未尽一更敲；别院寒砧，千捣将残千捣起。画檐前叮当铁马，敲碎仕女情怀；银台上闪烁灯光，偏照佳人长叹。一心只想孩儿好，谁料愁来在梦多。"两者之间，除了个别词句几乎完全相同。

② Hanan Patrick, Sources of The Chin P'ing Mei, Asia Major N. S. (10：1), 1963, p. 31, 32. 《金瓶梅》中出现的韩南所说的"词"是："祝融南来鞭火龙，火云焰焰烧天红。日轮当午凝不去，方国如在红炉中。五岳翠干云彩灭，阳侯海底愁波竭。何当一夕金风发，为我扫除天下热。"该诗在《水浒传》容与堂本与袁无涯刻本第16回都出现了。这首诗最早见于《全唐诗》卷二十四，题《苦热行》，王毂作。用词稍有出入。另一首在《水浒传》中是："赤日炎炎似火烧，野田禾稻半枯焦。农夫心内如汤煮，公子王孙把扇摇。"在《金瓶梅》中则是："赤日炎炎似火烧，野田禾黍半枯焦。农夫心内如汤煮，楼上王孙把扇摇。"个别词略有不同。

84回里也重现了。"① 和韩南相比,吴德安的论述显得非常简略。

在上文的讨论中我们知道,韩南曾指出,在叙事技巧、处理素材的艺术手法上,《金瓶梅》与《水浒传》之间存在重大的差别。即便如此,《水浒传》对《金瓶梅》之影响绝不仅在故事情节、人物形象等的借用、移植和改写。事实上,在文学风格、叙事传统与叙事技巧等方面,后者对前者的继承也是很明显的。毕晓普(John L. Bishop)指出:"明代后来的小说与短篇故事,其作者接受了《三言》和《水浒传》的叙事传统。"②具体到《金瓶梅》,毕晓普进一步指出:"另一方面,在风格和叙事技巧上,《金瓶梅》和之前的小说很难区分得开。它很自然地继承了《水浒传》的故事并构成其关键的部分,在风格上亦无明显的变化。"据毕晓普的论述,《金瓶梅》对《水浒传》等小说奠定的文学风格与叙事传统的继承和运用主要有三个方面:一是白话文学风格的传承;二是行文过程中叙述者的明显干预;三是作者把大量松散而又相关的事件缀合在一起,并通过内在的主题单元赋予这些事件某种程度的一致性。不过,在该论者看来,后两者属于"拙劣的叙事传统"。③ 评价不论,单就上述三点,笔者以为毕晓普是抓住了问题的核心和关键要素的。

以上内容是英语世界的批评者就《水浒传》影响《金瓶梅》创作所作的研究。当然,笔者只是讨论了其中具有代表性的批评者的研究成果。至于那些零散的、甚至是重复性的观点,就不再一一述及。

---

① Certain stories in The Men of the Marsh-Wu Song Killing the tiger, and a story about Ximen Qing and Pan Jinlian-appear again in Jing Ping Mei (chapter 1 – 9 and 87). The episode about the Camp of Clear Winds (Qing feng zhai 清风寨) in The Men of the Marsh appears again in Jing Ping Mei, chapter 84. De-an Wu Swihart, The Evolution of Chinese Novel form, Thesis Ph. D. -The Department of East Asian Studies of Princeton University, 1990, p. 35。

② In the subsequent fiction of the Ming period, writers of novels and short stories accepted the narrative conventions of the San-yen collections and Shui-hu-chuan. John L. Bishop, Some Limitations of Chinese Fiction, Far Eastern Quarterly, 15: 2 (1956: Feb.), p. 242.

③ In style and narrative technique, on the other hand, Chin p'ing mei indistinguishable feom the fiction which precedes it. It continues quite naturally and without noticeable variation in style from the Shui-hu-chuan incident which is its point of departure. Furthermore, a colloquial short story embedded in one of its later chapters is stylistically indistinguishable from the context in which it appears. In other words, Chin p'ing mei employs most of the inept narrative conventions of earlier fiction, except obvious inteusions by the narrator, and binds together a wealth of loosely related episodes, giving these a degree of homogeneity by its implicit unity of theme. John L. Bishop, Some Limitations of Chinese Fiction, Far Eastern Quarterly, 15: 2 (1956: Feb.), p. 243.

（二）《水浒传》与"水浒续书"及其他

清代的《水浒传》续书，代表性作品有清初陈忱的《水浒后传》和署名"青莲室主人"的《后水浒传》，以及晚清俞万春的《荡寇志》——又名《结水浒传》。《水浒传》对这三部小说创作的影响是显而易见的。陈忱在《水浒后传·序》中就指出，小说作者"古宋遗民"（实则是陈忱自己）是借《水浒传》的残局而著成该书的；在《水浒后传·论略》里，陈忱明确指出"《水浒》愤书也"，"《后传》为泄愤之书"[1]。可见《后传》继承了《水浒》"发愤"的创作思想。俞万春在《荡寇志·缘起》中则直接说明："偶见东都施耐庵先生《水浒传》，甚惊其才，雒诵回环，追寻其旨，觉其命意深厚而过曲，曰：是可借为题矣。"[2] 在《荡寇志》卷一中，俞万春还指出："看官须知这部书乃是结耐庵之《前水浒传》，与《后水浒》绝无交涉也。"[3] 这些文字足可见出《水浒传》对水浒续书创作的影响是证据确凿的。不过，英语世界的批评者在研究时，对上面这些极具说服力的材料很少提及，更多的是作文本的分析、比较。这实在是一个大缺憾。

在研究过程中，英语世界的批评者重点关注的对象主要有两点，一是人物故事的沿袭或改写，二是主题思想、创作态度的继承或反叛。事实上，从更细、更深的角度来看，续书对原作的接受和利用方式是多种多样的。对此，李惠仪（Wai-yee Li）指出："纵贯清初的明代小说续书，是以模仿、延续、扩展、重写、反驳种种形式繁荣起来的。"[4] 水浒续书和《水浒传》之间的关系大体就是这样。

而在明末清初这个特殊的社会时代会出现上述两部具有重大影响力的水浒续书，李惠仪认为是有其特定原因的。她说："《水浒传》和《金瓶梅》这两部小说反映出的北宋末年政局动荡的时代背景，与明王朝即将覆亡之间有着明显的相似。"[5] 这样的历史事实与时代环境很自然在一定程

---

[1] 朱一玄、刘毓忱编：《水浒传资料汇编》，南开大学出版社2012年版，第488—489页。
[2] 同上书，第509—510页。
[3] 同上书，第510页。
[4] Sequels of Ming novels in the form of imitations, continuations, extensions, reworkings, and rebuttals flourished throughout the early Qing. The Cambridge History of Chinese Literature, Edited by Kang-I Sun Chang, Stephen Owen, Cambridge University Press, 2010, Vol. 2, p. 213.
[5] Political disorder in *Water Margin* and *The Plum in the Golden Vase*, both set in the last years of the Northern Song, provides obvious analogies with the fall of the Ming. The Cambridge History of Chinese Literature, Edited by Kang-I Sun Chang, Stephen Owen, Cambridge University Press, 2010, Vol. 2, p. 213.

度上影响到《水浒后传》与《后水浒传》这两部水浒续书的基本样貌。

在水浒续书的形成问题上，李惠仪认为它们不仅受到《水浒传》原书与社会时代背景的影响，同时也受到小说评点家的思想观念的影响。她说：

> 和评点一样，续书决定对明代小说接受和借用的范围。有时评点塑造续书；金圣叹《水浒传》的评点尤其影响《水浒传》的续书。当"母小说"不只作为续书延续或挑战的典范与模型，而且还以描写或叙述对象出现在续书中时，内化于续书当中的评点意识就成了"原小说"。比如……陈忱的《水浒后传》里，幸存的梁山英雄观赏《水浒记》的演出。在这个层面上，评点和续书标志着小说自觉新的高峰。①

李惠仪以李贽的《水浒传》评点提倡"忠义"，及其在《忠义水浒传·序》里提出的施耐庵和罗贯中"虽生元日，实愤宋事"为例，说明其观点的可行性。

总体来看，英语世界的研究者更为关注的是主题思想层面的影响。当然，这种影响不只是接受，还有发展和背离。下面，笔者就进一步具体展开英语世界对《水浒传》和水浒续书关系的讨论。

在《水浒传》与《水浒后传》之间，李惠仪说：

> 清初的《水浒传》续书，吸收了造反的思想，并将之具体表现为忠义与保家卫国的主题。一个显著的例子就是《水浒后传》。陈忱在雁宕山樵的笔名下，采用评点修辞为政治伪装，特意在序中把纪年提前到1608年，声称发现了佚名"古宋遗民"元初所著《水

---

① Along with commentaries, sequels define the reception and appropriation of Ming fiction. Commentaries shaped sequels; Jin Shengtan's commentary was especially influential in sequels to *Water Margin*. The built-in commentarial consciousness of sequels becomes metafictional when the parent novels are not only held up as models to be continued or challenged but also enacted as representation, as... or when the surviving heroes of Liangshan watch a play entitled *Water Margin* (*Shuihu ji*) in Chen Chen's (1614-after 1660) *Water Margin: Later Traditions* (*Shuihu houzhuan*, 1664). In this sense, commentaries and sequels mark a new high point in fictional self-consciousness. The Cambridge History of Chinese Literature, Edited by Kang-I Sun Chang, Stephen Owen, Cambridge University Press, 2010, Vol. 2, p. 213.

浒后传》。①

李惠仪认为，作为坚贞、忠诚的遗民，陈忱这样做具有深层的政治原因。她说："陈忱通过幸存的梁山英雄的英勇事迹，包括抗击金人入侵保卫宋王朝、远赴暹罗建立乌托邦王国，实则表达了明朝遗民的希望、忧虑与哀痛。"② 这些是《水浒后传》对《水浒传》忠义思想的继承。

同时，李惠仪也指出，《水浒后传》所虚构的暹罗乌托邦和《水浒传》描绘的梁山是大相径庭的。《水浒后传》具有比较浓厚的浪漫色彩，其中减少了暴力，具有更多的人性温暖和对普通人的天伦之乐的描写，在对待女性的态度上肯定赞扬之处很明显。更为重要的是，在暹罗乌托邦中，儒家倡导的文官政体和文人文化得到延续。③

对《水浒传》与《后水浒传》之间的关系，李惠仪这样指出：

> 在另一部续书，佚名"青莲室主人"的《后水浒传》中，梁山好汉转世的英雄们继续与对金人屈膝称臣的腐败的南宋政权展开斗争。这部小说的反抗意识更加坚决，严厉批评昏君与乱臣贼子，竭力反对招安。另一方面，宋江转生的杨幺坚持忠于高宗皇帝，竭力进谏。只是在最后，这群草莽英雄被岳飞打败，并化作一团黑气。因此，《后水浒传》可以说具体展现了《水浒传》原作及其阐释传统中

---

① The idea that rebellion may embody loyalty and express nationalist strivings is taken up in early Qing sequels to Water Margin. One notable example is Water Margin: Later Traditions. Adopting the rhetoric of commentary as political camouflage in the preface (deliberately backdated to 1608), Chen Chen, under his usual penname of Woodcutter of Mount Yandang (Yandang shan qiao), claims to have discovered the book, authored by the anonymous Loyalist of the Ancient Song (Gu Song yimin) during the early Yuan. The Cambridge History of Chinese Literature, Edited by Kang-I Sun Chang, Stephen Owen, Cambridge University Press, 2010, Vol. 2, p. 214.

② A staunch loyalist and a member of the Poetry Society of Vigilant Withdrawal mentioned earlier, Chen used the valiant exploits of the surviving bandit heroes in fighting Jurchen invaders, defending the Song dynasty, and escaping to the distant utopia of Siam to express the hopes, fears, and woes of Ming loyalists. The Cambridge History of Chinese Literature, Edited by Kang-I Sun Chang, Stephen Owen, Cambridge University Press, 2010, Vol. 2, p. 214.

③ The bandit heroes' ideal polity in Siam is very different from Liangshan: there is less violence and lawlessness, more appreciation for women and domestic happiness, and greater promotion of civil bureaucracy and literati culture. The Cambridge History of Chinese Literature, Edited by Kang-I Sun Chang, Stephen Owen, Cambridge University Press, 2010, Vol. 2, p. 214.

对梁山好汉明显的模棱两可的态度。①

同时,该论者也说,《后水浒传》中岳飞虽然与这些造反英雄对立,但当后者同样以保家卫国的身份出现在战场上时,两者的界限便变得很模糊②。从这一点来说,《后水浒传》的作者是吸收、发挥了原作中"忠义"主题的。

根据李惠仪的论述,以上两部水浒续书对《水浒传》原作的接受和借用,不论是故事情节、人物形象还是主题思想,主要呈现的是"模仿、继续、扩展"的关系。具体到《后水浒传》还增加了"重写"这一层,在对梁山好汉的态度上则出现了一定的"反驳性"元素,如上文提及的这群英雄被岳飞打败的情节。

到晚清俞万春的《荡寇志》即《结水浒传》,小说作者对《水浒传》原作的"反驳"态度就完全彰显。当然,这种"反驳"态度是有其根源的,最重要的就是金圣叹在《水浒传》评点中提出的系列观点,如极力诋毁宋江这个人物形象、坚决否定小说的"忠义"思想,以及金氏对原作进行的改写、删节。事实上,俞万春《荡寇志》的故事情节就是紧接着金圣叹腰斩的 70 回本《水浒传》的。对《荡寇志》与《水浒传》之间

---

① In another sequel, *Water Margin Continued* (*Hou Shuihu zhuan*) by the anonymous Master of the Blue Lotus Chamber (Qinglian shi zhuren), the reincarnated heroes continue their struggle against a corrupt Southern Song government capitulating to the demands of Jurchen invaders. The counter-government ideology is more uncompromising in this novel, with its virulent critique of the emperors and not just of their evil ministers, and of the idea of accepting "pacification." On the other hand, Yang Yao, Song Jiang's reincarnation, protests his loyalty and remonstrates with Emperor Gao zong. In the end, the bandit heroes are defeated by Yue Fei and "turned into black ether." The novel thus embodies the ambivalence toward the bandit heroes evident in both *Water Margin* itself and its interpretive traditions. The line between Yue Fei and the bandit heroes becomes more blurred when the latter are recast as defenders of the realm in Qian Cai's (ca 1662-ca 1721) *The Complete Story of Yue Fei* (*Shuo Yue quanzhuan*). In this novel, Yue Fei-who shares a teacher with the Liangshan rebels - encourages the bandits to join the common cause against the Jurchens, and descendants of the bandit heroes become leaders in Yue Fei's army. The Cambridge History of Chinese Literature, Edited by Kang-I Sun Chang, Stephen Owen, Cambridge University Press, 2010, Vol. 2, p. 214, 215.

② The line between Yue Fei and the bandit heroes becomes more blurred when the latter are recast as defenders of the realm in Qian Cai's (ca 1662-ca 1721) *The Complete Story of Yue Fei* (*Shuo Yue quanzhuan*). In this novel, Yue Fei-who shares a teacher with the Liangshan rebels - encourages the bandits to join the common cause against the Jurchens, and descendants of the bandit heroes become leaders in Yue Fei's army. The Cambridge History of Chinese Literature, Edited by Kang-I Sun Chang, Stephen Owen, Cambridge University Press, 2010, Vol. 2, p. 215.

的此种关系,王德威(David Der-wei Wang)指出:

> 晚清侠义公案小说源出于俞万春(1794—1849)的《荡寇志》(1853)。俞的《荡寇志》是金圣叹(1608—1661)70回本的续书,该书改写了梁山好汉向宋王朝投诚的故事。在此小说中,梁山反贼是公然作乱的强盗,甚至威胁到王朝的生死存亡。正如小说标题所暗示的,这些反叛者最终被镇压;他们的失败和死亡,并非如惯常的阅读所感受到的是悲剧结局,而是罪有应得。①

由此可知,《荡寇志》在思想观念与创作态度上是对《水浒传》的一次全面彻底的反叛,也就是李惠仪说的它是以"反驳"的形式完成的续书。小说作者以压倒一切的忠君思想,淹没了原作所颂扬的社会底层百姓身上爆发出来的强烈的反叛精神,因而基本否定了原作的主题、宗旨。按王德威之论即是:

> 《荡寇志》不只是一部有关武力平叛的小说,还意味着一场文学运动。它"终结"了由《水浒传》倡导并由其蔓延开来的"官逼民反"思想的小说传统。虽然写作时具有维护皇权政体的目的,小说创作的灵感却是从散播颠覆性主题的作品中获得的。②

---

① Late Qing chivalric and court case romance originated with Yu Wanchun's (1794 - 1849) *Quell the Bandits* (*Dangkouzhi*, 1853). Written as a sequel to Jin Shengtan's (1608 - 1661) seventy-chapter edition of the *Water Margin*, Yu's *Quell the Bandits* rewrites the story of the reconciliation between the Liangshan band and the Song government. The Liangshan rebels become outright bandits, ever threatening the dynasty's well-being. As the novel's title suggests, the rebels are all eventually put down; their defeat and death represent not tragic downfall, as the conventional reading would have it, but well-earned retribution. The Cambridge History of Chinese Literature, Edited by Kang-I Sun Chang, Stephen Owen, Cambridge University Press, 2010, Vol. 2, p. 432.

② *Quell the Bandits* is more than a novel about a military crackdown on rebellious uprisings, however. It is also meant to be a literary campaign to "terminate" a novelistic tradition-that of the *Water Margin*-that had allegedly been responsible for propagating or disseminating thoughts of banditry and treason. Although written with the avowed purpose of honoring the institution of imperial power, the novel nevertheless took its inspiration from a narrative cycle known for its subversive themes. The Cambridge History of Chinese Literature, Edited by Kang-I Sun Chang, Stephen Owen, Cambridge University Press, 2010, Vol. 2, p. 432, 433.

王德威此论中肯切实。事实上，笔者以为，《水浒传》不仅为《荡寇志》提供了创作的灵感源泉，对《水浒后传》与《后水浒传》同样如此。

以上内容是就英语世界的学者们对《水浒传》对水浒续书影响的研究成果所作的一个讨论。依据他们的论述，从整体上看，《水浒传》对上述三部水浒续书所产生的影响，或者说水浒续书对《水浒传》原作的接受和利用，基本上是以李惠仪所说的"模仿、延续、扩展、重写、反驳"诸种形式实现的。具体到不同作品，又有各自不同的侧重点，对《水浒后传》而言，重在模仿、延续与扩展；对于《后水浒传》，在前四者的基础上增添了一定的"反驳"色彩；至于《荡寇志》，则突出了"反驳"这一层，并在主题思想上进行了完全相反的诠释。

(三)《水浒传》的叙事手法、结构艺术对后世白话章回小说创作的影响

上面几位英语世界的学者就《水浒传》对《金瓶梅》与"水浒续书"等中国文学创作的影响，虽然有对叙事艺术手法方面影响的论述，但主要还是从人物故事、思想主题方面展开的。在《水浒传》的叙事手法、结构艺术对后世小说创作的影响上，英语世界的批评者浦安迪、吴德安、吴燕娜等也展开过专门的研究。只是据笔者掌握的资料来看，这方面的成果并不多。

浦安迪在1980年发表的《〈水浒传〉与十六世纪的小说形式：阐释的再思考》一文以及论著《明代小说四大奇书》中，就《水浒传》的形式、结构艺术对后世白话小说创作的影响也有一定的讨论。他说，《水浒传》开头"误走妖魔"的神话结构——早期繁本如杨定见本的"引首"及后来金圣叹删节本中的"楔子"，成为后世中国白话小说的普遍特征。[1]此其一。其二，《水浒传》与其后16世纪小说惯常形式的另一个相似之处就是小说开篇上场诗与每一章开头入回诗的运用；特别是《水浒传》第一回托名邵雍的入回诗被引录在《西游记》的首页，其中可见它们之

---

[1] The fact that this opening chapter presents the outline of a minimal supernatural framework of sorts for the novel, what was eventually to become a common feature of later examples of colloquial Chinese fiction. Andrew H. Plaks, The Four Masterworks of the Ming Novel, Princeton University Press, 1987, p. 308.

间存在紧密的关系①。

沿着浦安迪开创的思路,同样是普林斯顿大学出身的吴德安在其1990年的博士论文《中国小说形式的演变》中,专列"《水浒传》结构对后世章回小说的影响"一节。他认为,作为章回小说的开拓性作品,《水浒传》的结构虽然并不成熟,但其结构原则极大地影响了章回小说的发展。直到《儒林外史》的出现,《水浒传》的某些结构原则才提升到一个更精致的阶段。②根据他的论述,这种影响主要表现在以下几个方面:

第一,吴德安认为,后世章回小说家有时在他们小说开篇写一个楔子,是受到金圣叹删改《水浒传》设立楔子,及其关于楔子的作用的理论的影响。而且他说:"这些楔子的功能也是源自《水浒传》,或者是为小说建立一个主题象征框架,或者是创设一个事件以贯穿小说主要故事并起揭示作用。"③

第二,吴德安说:"在《水浒传》的影响之下,后世章回小说家有时偏爱运用人物群像或是'集体传记',而非采用一个核心情节或单个的人物作为基本结构。"④

第三,吴德安提出:"像《水浒传》一样,很多章回小说都有精心的

---

① One more interesting point in chapter 1 that seems to link *Shui-hu chuan* with the formal cinventions of the later sixteenth-century novels may be seen in the opening verse, which functions much like the introductory piece later inserted on the fiest page of the Mao Tsung-kang edition of *San-kuo*. in *Shui-hu*, this poem is attributed to none other than ShaoYung, whose corresponding citation on page one of *Hsi-yu chi* clearly betrays a self-conscious linkage on the part of at least one of th two authors. Andrew H. Plaks, The Four Masterworks of the Ming Novel, Princeton University Press, 1987, p. 309, 310.

② These structural principles of *Shuihu zhuan* strongly influenced the development of the zhanghui novel. By the time *Rulin waishi* (*The Scholars*) appeared in the middle of the 18th century, some of these structural principles had already developed to a more sophisticated stage, as we will see in the next chapter. De-an Wu Swihart, The Evolution of Chinese Novel form, Thesis Ph. D. -The Department of East Asian Studies of Princeton University, 1990, p. 35.

③ Under the influence of Jin Shengtan's prologue design and his theory of th function of the prologue section, later zhanghui novel writers sometimes included a prologue chapter at the beginning of their novels. The function of these prologue, also derived from *Shuihu zhuan*, is to either set up a symbolic and thematic framework for the novel, or to initiate an incident which is later revcealed through the main story in the novel. De-an Wu Swihart, The Evolution of Chinese Novel form, Thesis Ph. D. The Department of East Asian Studies of Princeton University, 1990, p. 94.

④ Under the influence of *Shuihu zhuan*, later zhanghui novelists sometimes favors the use of a large number of characters or the "collective biography", instead of ueing a centralized plot or single character as the basic structure. De-an Wu Swihart, The Evolution of Chinese Novel form, Thesis Ph. D. The Department of East Asian Studies of Princeton University, 1990, p. 94.

结构设计。其中有两个很常见的基本方法，一是人物映衬原则，另一则是运用象征寓意事件与主题的重现来建立结构密度。"①

第四是小说创作时对称原则使用上的影响。在吴德安看来，对称原则有以下三点：

  a. 小说的高潮一般出现在叙事的中间，从而使文本中高潮的两端形成平衡。

  b. 小说的结尾一般通过各种各样的方法返回到开篇。

  c. 成组的或相似或相反相成的人物形象形成并置的方面。②

第五是小说叙述中的空间构思方面的影响。吴德安说："空间构思有时形成两个平行的世界。比如说《金瓶梅》中西门庆家那个围墙内的小世界与围墙外的帝国大世界，以及《红楼梦》里宝玉与众女子所在的大观园的纯净世界与大观园外的肮脏世界。"③

第六则是小说叙述的时间编排上的影响。吴德安说："集体传记形式的时间编排，往往以日月的推移而展开，季节的轮回则对应于人物的描写。在整体叙事中也是按时间的年代顺序排列，这是历史撰写的典型模式。"④

在吴德安的讨论中，《水浒传》的结构艺术对后世章回小说的创作，

---

① Like Shuihu zhuan, many zhanghui novels are illustrations of carefully planned textural design. Two basic methods are usually evident: one is the principle of refraction of character, and the other is the use of recurrent symbolic events and motifs to establish structural density. De-an Wu Swihart, The Evolution of Chinese Novel form, Thesis Ph. D. The Department of East Asian Studies of Princeton University, 1990, p. 95.

② The principle of symmetry including the following points: a. The climax of the novel usually occurs in the middle of the narrative, and the textt on each side of the climax forms a balance. b. The end of the novel usually harks back to the beginning in various ways. c. Paired characters form parallel aspects of similarity or complementary opposites. De-an Wu Swihart, The Evolution of Chinese Novel form, Thesis Ph. D. The Department of East Asian Studies of Princeton University, 1990, p. 95.

③ The spatial design sometimes forms two parallel worlds, such as the compound of Ximen Ching's household and the macrocosm of the imperial world outside in *Jing Ping Mei*, and the pure world of Baoyu and the girls in the garden and the dirty world outside the garden in the *The Dream of the Red Chamber*. De-an Wu Swihart, The Evolution of Chinese Novel form, Thesis Ph. D. The Department of East Asian Studies of Princeton University, 1990, p. 95.

④ The temporal design in the collective biographical form is usually a procession of months and days, and seasonal cycles which correspond with the despictions of the characters. There is also a chronological arrangement of time within the overall narrative, which is modelled on historical writing. De-an Wu Swihart, The Evolution of Chinese Novel form, Thesis Ph. D. The Department of East Asian Studies of Princeton University, 1990, p. 95.

既有文本结构、叙事手法上的影响，也有人物塑造方面的影响。这种影响用吴德安自己的话来说就是："《水浒传》的结构原则强有力地影响了章回小说的发展。"①

就《水浒传》叙事艺术手法对后世小说创作的影响，吴燕娜（Yenna Wu）在《〈水浒传〉中法外强徒的权力与地位之梦》一文也有相应论述，主要是讨论了《水浒传》中的"梦叙事"这一艺术手法对清代几部小说创作的影响。吴燕娜通过梳理中国古代文化与文学传统中对梦的描写与理解，再结合《水浒传》里对宋江、李逵、宋徽宗等人的梦的叙述，认为《水浒传》运用梦进行叙事的艺术手段对明清好几部小说的创作都产生了影响。她说：

> 《水浒》是自觉运用大量的梦事件作为文学审美手段而出现的第一部主要的中国小说；在这方面，为后世文学树立了典范。它直接影响陈忱《水浒后传》的书写，该小说利用梦来预言一个乌托邦；它还间接影响《西游记》和《红楼梦》的写作。在这两部小说中，梦扮演着重要的角色。②

不过，在唐传奇中，利用梦展开叙事已不罕见。沈既济的《枕中记》，李公佐的《南柯太守传》，这两部流传广泛的作品就是"梦叙事"的经典之作。吴燕娜在论述中也提到，《南柯太守传》中就使用梦来表达世俗性成功转瞬即逝的寓言③。既然如此，笔者以为，在"梦叙事"上《水浒传》对上述几部小说的创作影响应是很有限的。

---

① De-an Wu Swihart, The Evolution of Chinese Novel form, Thesis Ph. D. The Department of East Asian Studies of Princeton University, 1990, p. 96.

② *Shuihu* emerges as the first major Chinese novel that consciously uses extensive dream episodes as a literary and aesthetic device; in this regard it serves as a paradigm for later literature. It directly influenced the composition of Chen Chen's *Shuihuhouzhuan* 水浒后传（*The Water Margin: A Sequel*, 1664）, a novel utilizing dreams to predict a utopia, and indirectly influenced the writing of *Xiyou bu* 西游记（*A Tower of Myriad Morrors*, 1641）and *Honglou meng* 红楼梦（*The Dream of Red Chambe*r, also known as *Shitou ji* 石头记, or The *Story of the stone*, c. 1760）, two novels in which dreams figure prominently. Yenna Wu, Outlaw's Dreams of Power and Position in *Shuihu zhuan*, Chinese Literature：Essays, Articals, Reviews（CLEAR）, Vol. 18（Dec., 1996）, p. 46。

③ Yenna Wu, Outlaw's Dreams of Power and Position in *Shuihu zhuan*, Chinese Literature：Essays, Articals, Reviews（CLEAR）, Vol. 18（Dec., 1996）, p. 47。

二、《水浒传》与明清水浒戏创作

传世的明清水浒戏，包括六部明代水浒传奇，分别是李开先的《宝剑记》、陈与郊的《灵宝刀》、沈璟的《义侠记》、许自昌的《水浒记》、李素甫的《元宵闹》以及范希哲的《偷甲记》；七部明代水浒杂剧，分别是朱有燉的《黑旋风仗义疏财》与《豹子和尚自还俗》，无名氏的《梁山五虎大劫牢》《梁山七虎闹铜台》《王矮虎大闹东平府》与《宋公明排九宫八卦阵》，凌濛初的《宋公明闹元宵》；两部清代水浒杂剧，一是张韬的《戴院长神行苏州道》，二是唐英的《十字坡》。①

《水浒传》对明清水浒戏创作的影响是相当显然的，但并非所有的创作都受其影响。因为就目前所能看到的文献，我们无法证实亡佚的元代水浒杂剧就没有对明清水浒戏创作产生过影响。据笔者掌握的资料，上述作者里面，至少有两位有确切的记述《水浒传》的文字流传至今。（因笔者不敢肯定撰写《梁山泊一百单八人优劣》《水浒传一百回文字优劣》和《又论水浒传文字》的无名氏与明代水浒杂剧作者的无名氏为同一个人）在这两位作者中，其中一个是《宝剑记》的作者李开先。他在《一笑散·时调》中援引唐荆川等人的观点说"《水浒传》委曲详尽，血脉贯通，《史记》而下，便是此书"②，对《水浒传》的叙事艺术给予了非常高的评价。另一位是《水浒记》的作者许自昌。在《樗斋漫录》里，许氏对《水浒传》的人物故事来源、成书时间、作者与流传情况，小说记事系年、人物活动地点与《宋史》之间的出入等问题都有讨论③。

上述材料说明，明清水浒戏的作者对小说《水浒传》是非常熟悉的。基于此，他们从《水浒传》中掘取题材进行戏曲创作自是水到渠成之事。很遗憾的是，英语世界的研究者在讨论《水浒传》对明清水浒戏创作的影响时，对上述材料基本上未提及。而要论证文学作品之间的影响关系，不查找出这样确凿的材料并以之为凭据展开论述，始终还是缺乏足够的说服力。而在中国，在《水浒传》，情况尤为特殊。《水浒传》成书之前的宋元两朝，已有大量的水浒故事在社会上流传；在元代，水浒杂剧创作非

---

① 见傅惜华编《水浒戏曲集》，上海古籍出版社1985年版。
② 朱一玄、刘毓忱编：《水浒传资料汇编》，南开大学出版社2012年版，第167页。
③ 具体内容见朱一玄、刘毓忱编《水浒传资料汇编》，南开大学出版社2012年版，第191—192页。

常兴盛,亡佚之外,流传到现在的尚有六部。《水浒传》的创作,本身就是在宋元史传、说书的基础上进行的,并且吸收了很多元代水浒杂剧中的内容。而且《水浒传》的成书时间又存在很大争议。倘若真如有些学者(如戴不凡等,见绪论"国内学界《水浒传》研究述评"之"成书研究之争"部分)所提出的成书于明嘉靖(1507—1567)年间,不少明代的水浒戏创作显然不可能受其影响。

在这样的背景下,只是根据文本的相似就判定《水浒传》对某部明清水浒戏的创作存在影响,显然是不够的。此问题暂告段落,下面就来讨论英语世界的批评者就《水浒传》对明清水浒戏创作的影响所作的具体研究。

2007 年,沈静(Jing Shen)发表《中国戏剧、影视里水浒女性的改写》一文。在文章中,她说:

> 现存明代(1368—1644)水浒传奇,都是来自小说《水浒传》。像李开先(1502—1568)的《宝剑记》(1547)、陈与郊(1544—1611)的《灵宝刀》、沈璟(1553—1610)的《义侠记》、许自昌(1578—1623)的《水浒记》以及李素甫的《元宵闹》,都是如此。①

她还指出:

> 大部分传奇剧作家都受过精英教育,他们把士大夫关注的问题写进了剧作里面。虽然他们聚焦于个体英雄人物,但和文人小说《水浒传》相似,这些传奇剧强调时代的政治斗争主题。它们可能表达了作者政治雄心的挫败。晚明官场是一个危险的舞台,出现了严重的党争与虐政。人们能够发现,像李开先、沈璟等剧作家在辞官归隐之后,

---

① The existing Ming (1368 - 1644) *chuanqi* (romance) plays about the Water Margin legend are all based on the novel *The Water Margin*: Li Kaixian's (1502 - 1568) *Baojian ji* (The Double-Edge Sword, 1547), Chen Yujiao's (1544 - 1611) *Lingbao dao* (The Precious Sword), Shen Jing's (1553 - 1610) *Yixia ji* (The Altruistic Knight-Errant), Xu Zichang's (1578 - 1623) *Shuihu ji* (The Water Margin) and Li Sufu's *Yuanxiao nao* (The Clamor of the Lantern Festival). Jing Shen, Re-Visions of Shuihu Women in Chinese Theater and Cinema, China Reciew, Vol. 7, No. 1 (Spring 2007), p. 105, 106.

都专心于传奇剧创作。这种复杂微妙的文学形式,为文人士大夫阶层提供了一个宣泄他们政治挫败的途径。①

中晚明文坛,"缘情泄愤"的创作思想比较盛行。李贽在《忠义水浒传序》里就说:"《水浒传》者,发愤之所作也。"取材于《水浒传》的剧作,再加上作者的阅历,承继"缘情泄愤"的创作动机是完全可能的。事实上,明代文人创作的水浒戏,的确是在表达剧作者的政治思想与社会意识。

出于此种认识,沈静认为李开先辞官归田后创作的《宝剑记》有影射当时政局的意味。她说:"这部戏剧表现了李开先对结束官场生涯愤恨之情的影射;由于抵触内阁元首严嵩和他的儿子,他丢了官。"② 在研究过程中,沈静也指出,《宝剑记》虽然取材于《水浒传》,作者李开先对故事情节、人物形象等还是进行了大幅度的再创造,并且突出了政治性主题。她指出:

> 小说中高衙内调戏林娘子后,林冲被高太尉诬陷,被逼变成了无家可归之人。在《宝剑记》里则不同,林冲一开始是以忠臣与爱国者的形象出现的。由于弹劾高俅和宦官童贯勾结贪腐的事实触怒了高俅从而落草。小说中,直到杀了梁山第一任首领王伦,林冲才最终落草。相比而言,李开先笔下的林冲,始终是一个敢于和奸臣贼子作斗争的人。对险恶的宗派斗争的戏剧性描写,揭示了明代官僚体制的黑

---

① Many *chuanqi* writers were members of the educated elite, and they wrote literati concerns into *chuanqi* drama. The *chuanqi* plays resemble the literati novel The *Water Margin* in underscoring the political strife of their times, although they focus on individual heroes. They may be expressions of frustrated political ambitions. There were serious factional conflicts and despotic powers in late Ming officialdom, which was a perilous arena. One can observe in the authors of these works a pattern of engagement in *chuanqi* after leaving office, as in the case of Li Kaixian and Shen Jing. This sophisticated literary form allowed the class of scholar-officials a way to vent their frustrations. Jing Shen, Re-Visions of Shuihu Women in Chinese Theater and Cinema, China Reciew, Vol. 7, No. 1 (Spring 2007), p. 106.

② The play voices Li Kaixian's resentment of the innuendo that ended his official career; he was dismissed from office after having offended the Senior Grand Secretary Yan Song and his son. Jing Shen, Re-Visions of Shuihu Women in Chinese Theater and Cinema, China Reciew, Vol. 7, No. 1 (Spring 2007), p. 106.

暗现实。①

沈静还指出，《宝剑记》中，不仅林冲这个人物形象发生了很大变化，其他人物如鲁智深和林娘子等也是如此；故事情节上，也成了大团圆结局。这些都是李开先再创造的成果。沈静认为，戏剧创作中的这些改写有助于突出政治主题。她说："这部剧作，突出政治斗争，形成戏剧张力。林冲被改写成高级军官的后裔，具有崇高的理想。这有助于提升该剧的政治高度，也符合文人传奇剧创作的传统。"②

对李开先的《宝剑记》，孙康宜（Kang-i Sun Chang）说："在李开先的传奇作品中，最著名的就是《宝剑记》。这部剧作源自《水浒传》，但经过作者的再创造。"③ 在孙康宜的论述中，《宝剑记》的主要情节来自《水浒传》第7—12回，但作者的再创造亦是非常显著的。这种再创造，正如沈静所指出的，一是人物形象的改写，如把原本是属于底层军官的林冲变成了高级军官的后裔，并把他变成了忠心耿耿的大臣；二是故事情节的改写，如在剧末，林冲和忠贞的娘子团圆，奸臣父子则被处死。在主题上，孙康宜也认为《宝剑记》继承了《水浒传》"泄愤"的政治思想。他说：

> 《宝剑记》完成于作者罢官后的两三年，即1547年（嘉靖二十六年）。这部剧作在很多方面有意表达了作者对当时政局的批评。从

---

① According to the novel, Instructor of Imperial Guards Lin Chong is framed by Marshal Gao and forced to become an outcast after Gao's son takes a fancy to Lin's wife. In *The Double-Edged Sword*, however, Lin Chong as a loyal and patriotic subject first offends Marshal Gao by submitting a memo to impeach Gao for his collusion with the eunuch Tong Guan in corrupt practices. Lin Chong in the novel submits to humiliation till he kills Wang Lun, the first bandit chief entrenched on Mount Liang. By contrast, Li Kaixian's Lin Chong is always a forthright speaker against trencherous official. This theatrical depiction of treacherous faction discloses the darkness of the Ming bureaucrracy. Jing Shen, Re-Visions of Shuihu Women in Chinese Theater and Cinema, China Reciew, Vol. 7, No. 1 (Spring 2007), p. 106, 107.

② This, however, highlights the political conflict that engenders the tension. Lin Chong is rewritten as a descendant of a high-ranking general, with lofty aspirations to fulfil, which helps expand the political dimension of the play. This also conforms to the convention of literati *chuanqi* drama. Jing Shen, Re-Visions of Shuihu Women in Chinese Theater and Cinema, China Reciew, Vol. 7, No. 1 (Spring 2007), p. 107.

③ His most famous play in the southern style is the *Story of the Sword* (Baojian ji), a re-creation of an episode from the *Water Margin*. The Cambridge History of Chinese Literature, Edited by Kang-I Sun Chang, Stephen Owen, Cambridge University Press, 2010, Vol. 2, p. 57.

当时的文化与政治背景来看，很容易理解为什么李氏会从《水浒传》获得灵感并从中取材，因为《水浒传》的一个重要主题就是揭示本分守法的老百姓是如何被逼上梁山、成为强人的。①

就《水浒传》对明清水浒戏创作的影响，英语世界的研究者尚有下列成果：

沈静在研究中指出，沈璟的《义侠记》改编自小说《水浒传》第22—30回的武松传。不过，两者在主题上有很大差别。该论者援引吕天成为《义侠记》所作的序说，沈璟是想把武松的故事变成社会道德剧。②服务于这样的主题思想，沈璟在改写、创作时，对武松进行了很大的改动。和小说中的形象相比，剧作里的武松变得温和、宽厚、理智，多了一份人性的美好与光辉。而且作品还添加了一位正面女性形象，那就是武松忠贞的妻子贾氏。

商伟（Shang Wei）在论述清中期（1723—1840）中国"戏曲写作的新方向"时，对唐英的作品《十字坡》作过简单讨论。他说：

> 独幕剧《十字坡》是一部阴暗的身体喜剧（physical comedy），是以《水浒传》的一个片段故事为基础润色而成的。它描写母夜叉孙二娘色诱旅客，然后残忍地把他们肢解，直到遇上好汉武松才被暴力征服。③

---

① Finished in 1547, a few years after he resigned from office, the play represents in many ways Li's self-conscious critique of the contemporary political situation. Viewed from the perspective of the cultural and political milieu of the time, it is easy to understand why Li's imagination should have been fired by the Water Margin, one of whose main themes explores the process by which law-abiding men are forced to join a band of outlaws. The Cambridge History of Chinese Literature, Edited by Kang-I Sun Chang, Stephen Owen, Cambridge University Press, 2010, Vol. 2, p. 57.

② The Altruistic Knight-Errant is adapted from the Wu Song cluster of chapters 22 to 30 in the novel. Lü Tiancheng in his preface to The Altruistic Knight-Errant points out Shen Jing's intent to transform social morals through the play. Jing Shen, Re-Visions of Shuihu Women in Chinese Theater and Cinema, China Reciew, Vol. 7, No. 1 (Spring 2007), p. 109.

③ Crossroad on a Slope (Shizi po), a single-act play that embellishes an episode from Water Margin, is a dark physical comedy figuring Sun Er-niang as a tigress who brutally dismembers her tenants after seducing them, until she encounters the knight-errant Wu Song and is herself subjected to violent conquest. The Cambridge History of Chinese Literature, Edited by Kang-I Sun Chang, Stephen Owen, Cambridge University Press, 2010, Vol. 2, p. 314.

综合上述可知,《水浒传》对明清水浒戏创作的影响,与对水浒续书的影响是大体相当的。一是故事情节、人物形象的借用,二是思想主题的沿袭或背离。但后者——不论是水浒续书的创作还是水浒戏的创作,在故事情节、人物形象以及主题思想方面都进行了很大的改动。可以说,水浒续书也好,水浒戏也罢,它们的创作都是对《水浒传》的借用和改写的结合。只是在不同的作品中,两者的分量有不同而已。

英语世界的批评者就《水浒传》对中国明清小说、戏剧创作的影响所作的研究,整体来看水平参差不齐。有的很简略,有的只是现象描述。其中韩南、吴德安两人的分析论述,相对来说是比较细、比较深入的。

第二节 《水浒传》对中国现代戏剧、影视创作的影响

《水浒传》对20世纪以来中国现代戏剧（不包括各种数量繁多的民间创作的地方戏）、影视创作的影响,是非常大的。1949年新中国成立之前已出现多部根据《水浒传》人物故事改编、创作的现代戏剧作品,新中国成立后《水浒传》的戏剧化、影视化事业更加兴盛。其中代表性戏剧类作品主要有：1927年欧阳予倩创作的京剧（后改写成话剧）《潘金莲》,1944年刘芝明、齐燕铭等根据杨绍萱初稿集体加工修改、编剧的京剧《逼上梁山》（后来也制作成了电影）,1945年任桂林、魏晨旭、李伦编写的京剧《三打祝家庄》（以上两部新编水浒京剧是延安时期的作品）,1985年魏明伦创作的川剧《潘金莲》,等等。根据《水浒传》改编、创作的电影,早期的有1962年崔嵬（合作）导演、制作的《野猪林》,1963年应云卫导演、制作的《武松》。80年代以来,中国（包括内地与香港）制作的水浒英雄系列电影作品更加繁荣多样。香港制作水浒电影代表性的有陈会毅导演,王祖贤、梁家辉等主演,于1992年上映的《英雄本色》。在内地,其他的不论,仅韩三平、刘信义任总制片人,张建亚导演、巩向东编剧、中国电影集团出品,于2006年开机拍摄的《水浒英雄谱》系列电影,已上映的就达27部之多。戏剧、电影之外,80年代初曾经拍摄过8集电视连续剧《武松》。1998年至今,已上映的根据《水浒传》改编、制作的大型电视连续剧就出现了两部。一是张绍林导演,李雪健等领衔主演,于1998年开播的43集《水浒传》;二是鞠觉亮、邹集成联合导演,宁财神制作,张涵予等领衔主演,于2011年开播的86集《水

浒传》。

在100年左右的时间里,《水浒传》对中国现代戏剧、影视的创作形成了如此巨大的影响。难怪英语世界的批评者沈静在研究时会说:"中国电影自其诞生之日起就与传统戏曲交织在一起,观看源自《水浒传》的戏曲、电影是一项重要的事情。"[①]

实际上,《水浒传》对中国现代小说创作也影响不小。1930年8月至9月间,在《小说月报》第21卷第8、9号上,茅盾以蒲牢的笔名连续发表两篇取材于《水浒传》的短篇小说,一是《豹子头林冲》,二是《石碣》。茅盾的这两篇小说与同时发表的《大泽乡》,其创作主旨都在运用马克思主义阶级矛盾和阶级斗争的观念来重新阐释经典故事。1940年至1943年初,张恨水创作了取材于《水浒传》的长篇小说《水浒新传》。根据张恨水在《自序》中的交代,这部小说的创作动机是出于爱国主义的情怀为抗日战争做宣传鼓动。由此可见,《水浒传》对他们创作的影响主要在意识形态方面。只是英语世界的批评者并未关注《水浒传》对这些小说创作的影响。

一、《水浒传》与中国现代戏剧

在英语世界的批评视域中,欧阳予倩的《潘金莲》、杨绍萱等人的《逼上梁山》、魏明伦的《潘金莲》等中国现代水浒戏是比较受关注的。这一方面是因为其中涉及的潘金莲是一个备受争议的人物形象,而在这个人物形象之下带来的是一个很敏感的女性话题,不管是在"五四"运动前后还是在20世纪80年代都是如此;另一方面是它们的创作与中国当时的政治形势关系密切,具有很强的社会、政治主题。特别是《逼上梁山》这部剧作,更是社会政治形势的产物。

(一)《水浒传》与欧阳予倩的《潘金莲》

《水浒传》给予欧阳予倩创作《潘金莲》的影响是证据确凿的。英语世界的批评者沈静指出:"在自序中,欧阳予倩描述了小说《水浒传》如何给予他创作《潘金莲》的思想灵感。该剧以杀嫂为中心,兼及其他相

[①] As Chinese cinema has interwoven with traditional theatre since its birth, it is important to look at filmed operas based on *The Water Margin*. Jing Shen, Re-Visions of Shuihu Women in Chinese Theater and Cinema, China Reciew, Vol. 7, No. 1 (Spring 2007), p. 112.

关故事情节。"① 沈静所说欧阳予倩在自序里所作的描述是这样的：

> 民国十四年春末夏初，我别了奉天小河沿上挣扎着不肯化的雪，往看北平等着要开的丁香。看花的路上，有朋友买得一部旧版子《水浒》，无意中提起潘金莲；回来在津浦车上遇见傅彦长先生，彼此谈一些有关历史和小说的话。正谈着马可罗，一扯就又说到潘金莲身上。我当时就想拿潘金莲来作题材，编出独幕剧，及至回家来一想，无论如何一幕不够；便改变计划，编成三幕。不久我拿杀嫂一幕大致编好，……②

在沈静看来，欧阳予倩会从《水浒传》中汲取题材创作《潘金莲》，这是与其所受教育密切相关的。欧阳予倩是中国传统教育与西方现代教育合璧培养出来的中国现代戏剧、影视的先驱者。沈静认为这样的教育背景决定了他的戏剧创作无论在审美形式还是在主题思想上，都具有中西文化、文学的双重元素。对此，她说：

> 欧阳予倩既接受中国传统教育又接受西方现代教育，这影响了他的戏剧生涯。他既从事中国传统戏剧创作，又从事现代话剧实践，还喜欢从古典小说中寻找剧本创作素材。他开始以京剧的形式创作《潘金莲》，而后把它改写成现代话剧并出版发行，后来又以京剧的版本演出。③

的确，经历"五四"新义化运动洗礼的欧阳予倩，在吸收西方话剧文体要素基础上创作的《潘金莲》，虽然创作灵感与素材是来自中国古典

---

① In his preface to *Pan Jinlian*, Ouyang Yuqian describes how the novel *The Water Margin* gave him the idea of creating a play about Pan Jinlian. The play centreing on the episode of *Sha sao*（Killing the Sister-in-Law）and other related ones. Jing Shen, Re-Visions of Shuihu Women in Chinese Theater and Cinema, China Reciew, Vol. 7, No. 1（Spring 2007），p. 117.
② 欧阳予倩：《欧阳予倩全集》第1卷，上海文艺出版社1990年版，第92页。
③ He had received both traditional Chinese and modern Western education, which influenced his career in theatre. He practised both traditional Chinese opera and modern spoken drama and liked to draw materials from classical fiction for his plays. He first created *Pan Jinlian* as a Beijing opera play, then rewrote and published it as a modern spoken play, and later performed its opera version. Jing Shen, Re-Visions of Shuihu Women in Chinese Theater and Cinema, China Reciew, Vol. 7, No. 1（Spring 2007），p. 116.

小说《水浒传》，实则是中西方文学与文化合璧的产物。对此，沈静说作者在创作时"借中国传统戏剧的暗示性风格打破西方戏剧的现实性传统"，"《潘金莲》融合了中西方戏剧元素"①。

沈静认为，欧阳予倩的《潘金莲》，创作灵感与素材虽然来自小说《水浒传》中的人物故事，却实实在在是"五四"新文化运动带来的中国现代社会思潮的产物。作者打破了中国传统社会的男尊女卑的思想观念，对一直以来被视为淫妇的潘金莲的命运遭遇表达了深深的同情。她说："虽然欧阳予倩宣称该剧并不是对传统观念的颠覆，但他确实表达了对潘金莲所处困境的同情。这是与小说的视角不一样的。"②事实上，欧阳予倩在自序中所作的交代亦如此：

> 不过一个女子，当了奴婢，既不能拒绝主人的强奸，又不能反抗主人的逼嫁，尽管有姿色有聪明有志气有理性，只好隐藏起来，尽量的让人蹂躏。除掉忍气吞声把青春断送，没有办法。这种境遇，又何以异于活埋？在软弱的女子呢，她只好听天由命；若遇着个性很强像潘金莲一流的人，她必定要想她的出路。潘金莲被张大户强迫收房，她立意不从；那张大户恼羞成怒，故意拿她嫁给丑陋不堪没有出息的武大。她起先还是勉强忍耐，后来见着武松一表人才，她那希望的火燃烧起来，无论如何不能扑灭。倘若是她能改嫁武松，或者是能够像现时这样自由离婚，便决没有以后的犯罪。偏偏武松是个旧伦理观念极深的人，硬教武大拿夫权把她闭起来，她又如何肯便甘心？所以，她私通西门庆已经是一种变态的行为。况且旧时的习惯，男人尽管奸

---

① In the process of adopting Western theatre genres such as modern spoken drama, the literati of the New Culture Movement (around the time of the May Fourth Movement in 1919) began to see the renewable value of traditional Chinese theatre, which was appreciated by Western dramatists who borrowed the suggestive style of Chinese theatre to break the realistic conventions of Western theatre. In response to that, such as *Pan Jinlian* blended Chinese and Western theatrical elements... Jing Shen, Re-Visions of Shuihu Women in Chinese Theater and Cinema, China Reciew, Vol. 7, No. 1 (Spring 2007), p. 112.

② In his preface to *Pan Jinlian*, Ouyang Yuqian describes how the novel *The Water Margin* gave him the idea of creating a play about Pan Jinlian. The play centreing on the episode of *Sha sao* (Killing the Sister-in-Law) and other related ones.... Although Ouyang Yuqian claims that the play is not meant to be a reversl of the verdict, he does express his sympathy for Pan Jinlian's predicament, which is not the perspective of the novel. Jing Shen, Re-Visions of Shuihu Women in Chinese Theater and Cinema, China Reciew, Vol. 7, No. 1 (Spring 2007), p. 117.

女人，姘外妇，妻子丝毫不能过问；女人有奸，丈夫可以任意将妻子杀死，不算犯法。所以潘金莲时时刻刻有被杀的恐怖，结果激而至于杀人。平心而论，我们对于她的犯罪，应加惋惜，而她的最后被杀，更是当然的收场。①

欧阳予倩自序中的这段话，对传统伦理观念、特别是夫权对女性自由的束缚进行的批判，对弱女子悲惨处境的同情，是溢于言表的。

基于剧作者这样的创作观念与文本事实，沈静进一步指出："该剧围绕潘金莲事件的道德主题不再那么黑白分明。武松之外（他的刚性最后变得柔和了），没有哪个角色是无辜的。"② 与主题思想相适应，欧阳予倩对戏剧的故事情节也作了大幅改动。对此，沈静指出：

> 这部戏剧以武大之死开始，集中于"杀嫂"部分。它跳过潘金莲引诱武松和西门庆勾引潘金莲的情节。色情不是这部剧作的主题，它是与淫妇潘金莲联系在一起的。强大的个性与自由之精神贯穿戏剧对话和动作。③

随着作品主题思想的改变，剧本对女主角潘金莲的描写也发生了很大变化。沈静分析道：

> 剧本中的潘金莲和小说里的角色不一样。小说中，潘金莲只是需要一个比武大更强的男人以满足她的欲望，不管是武松还是西门庆都

---

① 欧阳予倩：《欧阳予倩全集》第1卷，上海文艺出版社1990年版，第92—93页。
② In this play, the moral issue centring on Pan Jinlian's affair is made less black and white, None of the characters except for Wo Sonf is innocent, but even his masculinity is softened in the end. Jing Shen, Re-Visions of Shuihu Women in Chinese Theater and Cinema, China Reciew, Vol. 7, No. 1 (Spring 2007), p. 118.
③ This play opens with the aftermath of Wu Da's death and centres on the episode "Killing His Sister-in -law"; it skips Pan Jinlian's seduction of Wu Song and Ximen Qing's seduction of her. Sexuality, usually associated with the seductress Pan Jinlian, is not a main issue in the play; rather, strong character and free spirit underlie the dramatic conversation and action. Jing Shen, Re-Visions of Shuihu Women in Chinese Theater and Cinema, China Reciew, Vol. 7, No. 1 (Spring 2007), p. 119.

行。剧本里的潘金莲则不同,她对武松有真情,即使武松要杀她也一样。①

在研究中,沈静进一步指出:"欧阳予倩笔下的潘金莲是'五四'运动时期攻击儒家妇女道德标准的激进的女代言人。她是一个意志坚强的女性,一个敢于向强加于她身上的错误婚姻发起挑战的女性。"②

就欧阳予倩对潘金莲的改写,沈静认为这是当时社会思潮影响的结果。一方面,她说:"潘金莲献身于武松的理由是他体格和精神的力量。强或弱是区分所有人物形象的根本要素。这或许是'五四'时期社会达尔文主义影响的折射。"另一方面,沈静引用欧阳予倩自己的说法,认为《潘金莲》的创作在细节处理上也受到当时流行于日本的唯美主义的影响。③

(二)《水浒传》与杨绍萱等的《逼上梁山》

杨绍萱、刘芝明、齐燕铭等人于1943年集体编剧、创作的京剧《逼上梁山》,也是取材于《水浒传》的经典剧作。不过这也是一部具有很强时代色彩的作品。

对这部戏剧创作的时代背景和内容,沈静说:"响应毛泽东《在延安文艺座谈会的讲话》,1943年,根据《水浒传》创作了京剧《逼上梁

---

① Pan Jinlian is shown to have real passion for Wu Song even when he kills her, unlike her counterpart in the novel who just a man better than Wu Da to fulfil her desire, whether ti is Wu Song or Ximen Qing. Jing Shen, Re-Visions of Shuihu Women in Chinese Theater and Cinema, China Reciew, Vol. 7, No. 1 (Spring 2007), p. 118.

② His Pan Jinlian is a radical spokenswoman of the May Fourth movement attacking the Confucian standard of a virtuous woman. She is portrayed as a strong-willed woman who defies the mismatch imposed her. Jing Shen, Re-Visions of Shuihu Women in Chinese Theater and Cinema, China Reciew, Vol. 7, No. 1 (Spring 2007), p. 118, 119.

③ What justifies her devotion to Wu Song is his physical and mental strength. Being strong or weak is the promenent quality that classifies allthe characters, which ma reflect the influence of Social Darwinism duringthe May Fourth era. Ouyang Yuqian also reflected that he had been influenced by aestheticism-popular in Japan then-so his Pan Jinlian "displays an undisciplined worship of strength and beauty" and "those parts such as in the end when she is willing to die under the sword of her beloved fuether embodied a masochist". Jing Shen, Re-Visions of Shuihu Women in Chinese Theater and Cinema, China Reciew, Vol. 7, No. 1 (Spring 2007), p. 118.

山》。像《野猪林》一样，这部剧作描写了林冲是如何落草为寇的。"① 通过与《野猪林》的进一步比较，沈静指出：

> 相比于《野猪林》，《逼上梁山》通过增加代表农民的人物形象，把林冲改写成爱国主义者，并写他不赞同高太尉与女真侵略者妥协的政策，更加突出阶级斗争主题。政治分歧而非关于女人的争端，是高太尉阴谋排挤林冲的导火索。在这一点上，《逼上梁山》与李开先的《宝剑记》相似。②

在论述中沈静还指出："林冲娘子的表现，与要求人民毫不妥协地反抗统治阶级压迫的意识形态是相一致的。她忠贞，不妥协，强烈反抗高衙内的迫害。"③

出于这样的创作背景、创作思想与文本事实，沈静认为《逼上梁山》一剧与毛泽东的"延安讲话"和《论持久战》的精神是非常接近的。也正因为这样，该剧能获得毛泽东的好评，说它"展现了人民对统治阶级压迫的反抗"④。

（三）《水浒传》与魏明伦的《潘金莲》

20世纪80年代是中国改革开放政策实施不久的特殊年代，文坛也迎来了一股新风。先锋文学、实验戏剧就是在这时期兴盛起来的。按沈静之

---

① In response to Mao Zedong's "talks at the Yan'an Forum on Literature and Art", the Beijing opera's production of *Forced Up Mount Liang*（based on *The Water Margin*）was created in 1943. Like *Wild Boar Wood*, this tale describes how Lin Chong becomes an outlaw. Jing Shen, Re-Visions of Shuihu Women in Chinese Theater and Cinema, China Reciew, Vol. 7, No. 1（Spring 2007）, p. 113.

② Compared with *Wild Boare Wood*, *Forced Up Mount Liang* places greater stress on class struggle by adding characters who represent peasants and reinscribing Lin Chong as a patriot who disagrees with Marshal Gao's policy of compromise with the Jurchen invaders. This political difference, not the dispute over a woman, is the primary trigger og Gao's scheme to remove Lin Chong, similar to Li Kaixian's *The Double-Edged Sword*. Jing Shen, Re-Visions of Shuihu Women in Chinese Theater and Cinema, China Reciew, Vol. 7, No. 1（Spring 2007）, p. 113.

③ The representation of Lin Chong's wife coincides with the ideology that demands the people's uncompromising resistance against ruling-class opression. She looks faithful and unyielding, vehemently fighting against her oppressor, Marshal Gao's son. Jing Shen, Re-Visions of Shuihu Women in Chinese Theater and Cinema, China Reciew, Vol. 7, No. 1（Spring 2007）, p. 114.

④ Jing Shen, Re-Visions of Shuihu Women in Chinese Theater and Cinema, China Reciew, Vol. 7, No. 1（Spring 2007）, p. 113, 114.

论，这一时期中国戏剧创作复苏了"五四"的精神，毛泽东年代革命文学、艺术一统天下的局面已经解冻[①]。魏明伦的《潘金莲》创作于80年代中期。这样的时代背景，再加上魏明伦"新编历史剧"作家的身份，必然在这部剧作上留下特殊的烙印。

根据沈静的论述，该剧的特殊性，首先表现在通过特殊的叙述视角来描写女主角潘金莲这一形象。她说：

> 这部戏剧，主要是通过来自现代小说中的一位离异女性（吕莎莎）阅读古典名著《水浒传》的方式展开描写的。该剧的潘金莲是一个高傲、热情、有见识的角色，她超越财富来评判爱情。她努力改变张大户给她安排的错误婚姻，运用文学和历史的案例鼓励武大成为真正的男人（即使长相丑陋不堪）。[②]

根据此论，魏明伦笔下的潘金莲，刚毅不屈，完全拥有和男英雄同等的精神力量。更为重要的是，潘金莲不仅具有完全的女性意识，还拥有完整的个体意识。从这一点来看，的确是对"五四"精神的回应，和欧阳予倩的潘金莲具有很大的相似性。

作为一部先锋实验剧作，魏明伦的《潘金莲》在艺术风格上亦别具特色。沈静说："这部荒诞川剧，把西方现代主义戏剧元素融入中国地方戏的实验是成功的。"更为重要的是，沈静认为这部剧作的独特之处不仅在其中西戏剧元素的融合，更在其叙述话语与叙述视角的与众不同。该论者指出："这部戏剧与其他改编自《水浒传》的剧作的区别，不在其对封建伦理的简单的现代批评，而在其通过'荒诞'的方式把混杂的话语、

[①] The May Fourth ethos revived in contemporary Chinese theatre of the 1980s when revolutionary stereotypes which had dominated literature and arts during the Mao period were dissolving. Jing Shen, Re-Visions of Shuihu Women in Chinese Theater and Cinema, China Reciew, Vol. 7, No. 1 (Spring 2007), p. 119.

[②] This play is primarily presented as a reading of the classical masterwork *The Water Margin* by a female divorcee from a contmporary novel, in which Pan Jinlian figures as a woman of pride, spirit and learing who values love above weath. Pan Jinlian tries to make the most of the mismatch arranged bu Zhang Dahua and uses literary and historical examples to encourage Wu Da to be a real man despite his repulsive appearance. Jing Shen, Re-Visions of Shuihu Women in Chinese Theater and Cinema, China Reciew, Vol. 7, No. 1 (Spring 2007), p. 119.

多元的视角组合在一起。"① 这表现为魏明伦在创作时把不同的表演风格、表演形式融入川剧,如把昆曲、绍兴戏、河南戏、西方戏以及摇滚舞等和川剧混杂在一起。

作为一部前卫派实验剧作,魏明伦的《潘金莲》也以其在独特的艺术形式之下对内容所作的大胆处理而在文艺圈引起轰动。对此,沈静指出:

> 魏明伦1986年创作的川剧《潘金莲:一个堕落女人的历史》,因其实验艺术观,以及围绕潘金莲故事对色情关系的新阐释,在文艺圈引起了全国性轰动。超过40家刊物发表了约100篇关于该剧的评论文章。②

沈静所说的"实验艺术观",具体来说即是,魏明伦的《潘金莲》让传统的浪漫文本《红楼梦》《西厢记》与《水浒传》之间形成争辩,让西方文学和中国文学相遭遇,从而进一步把现代价值观念与传统伦理道德交织在一起,让非道德视野与家长制度产生冲突③。实际上,引起轰动的关键要素是剧作家对色情所作的处理。而根据上述统计数据,魏明伦《潘金莲》的演出,在圈内的确发生了很大的影响。

上面的讨论,是英语世界的批评者沈静对中国现代水浒戏创作中三部代表性作品的基本状况所作的研究。在讨论时,沈静把三部剧作放置在各

---

① This Sichuan opera of the absurd was a successful experiment integrating Western modernist theatrical elements into Chinese local opera. What distinguishes this play from other adaptations of The Water Margin does not lie simply in its modern critique of feudal ethica but in its hybrid discoures and multiple perspectives arrayed in an "absurd" way. Jing Shen, Re-Visions of Shuihu Women in Chinese Theater and Cinema, China Reciew, Vol. 7, No. 1 (Spring 2007), p. 120.

② His 1986 Sichuan opera *Pan Jinlian*: *The history of a Fallen Woman* caused a nationwide sensation among literary and art circles with its experimental artistic conception and new interpretation of sexual relationship centring on the story of Pan Jinlian: over 40 periodicals published about 100 reviews of this play. Jing Shen, Re-Visions of Shuihu Women in Chinese Theater and Cinema, China Reciew, Vol. 7, No. 1 (Spring 2007), p. 119.

③ It allows the traditional romantic texts *Honglou meng* (Dream of the Red Chamber) and *Xixiang ji* (The Story of the Western Wing) to contest The Water Margin, Western literature to meet Chinese literature, modern values to correlate with traditional ethics, and unorthodox views to clash with the patriarchal system. Jing Shen, Re-Visions of Shuihu Women in Chinese Theater and Cinema, China Reciew, Vol. 7, No. 1 (Spring 2007), p. 120.

自不同的创作时代背景与社会思潮之中，具有很强的历史感，也很深入。在结论中，沈静也对欧阳予倩的《潘金莲》与魏明伦的《潘金莲》不同的创作动机进行了比较。她说：

> 欧阳予倩对《水浒传》的重新阐释，批判了旧的封建家长制度，并通过富有争议的人物潘金莲强烈的反叛声音为充满活力的民族精神辩护。其目的在塑造一种现代政治观念。……魏明伦则把潘金莲放置在不同的话语之中，以激起人们对女性主题与自由恋爱的争论。①

事实上，不同创作动机的形成是与当时特定的社会时代背景密切相关的。不管是欧阳予倩还是魏明伦，抑或杨绍萱等人，以及下文即将讨论的崔嵬（合作）导演的《野猪林》与应云卫导演的《武松》，他们对《水浒传》人物故事的借用和改写，都继承了中国文学创作中"古为今用"的传统，而意识形态元素在其中起着相当重要的作用。

二、《水浒传》与中国现代影视

与欧美国家相比，中国的影视发展相对滞后。1905年，中国出现第一部无声电影《定军山》——改编自四大名著之一的《三国演义》。根据上文的统计，《水浒传》的影视化改编要比这更迟很多，而在20世纪90年代之后则展现出后来居上的势头。

（一）《水浒传》与电影《野猪林》《武松》

根据沈静的研究，《水浒传》最初的影视化改编出现在新中国成立之后的20世纪60年代。这一时期的水浒电影，不管在背景设置还是在人物对话上，都具有很浓厚的传统戏剧（京剧）的因素。而且这一时期《水浒传》的影视改编与当时中国政府行为密切相关。她说：

> 自20世纪50年代起，在中华人民共和国，传统戏曲电影的产量

---

① Ouyang Yuqian's reinterpretation of the novel *The Water Margin* attacks the old patriarchal system and argues for vital national spirit through the strong rebellious voice of the controversial Pan Jinlian. It aimed to shape a modern political view. ... Wei Minglun places Pan Jinlian in diverse discourses to evoke a debate on women's issues and freedom of love. Jing Shen, Re-Visions of Shuihu Women in Chinese Theater and Cinema, China Reciew, Vol. 7, No. 1 (Spring 2007), p. 121.

盛况空前,歌剧传统被彻底淹没。新政府号召改造旧歌剧。在此期间,改编自《水浒传》的两部影片运用电影装置为歌剧表演服务,并试图在电影中使暗示性的传统戏剧与现实情境相协调。①

由此可知,这一阶段的水浒电影主要还是以戏剧化的形式在表演,尚不具备完全现代意义上的电影形态。

沈静这里所说改编自《水浒传》的两部影片,一是1962年崔嵬(合作)导演的《野猪林》,二是1963年应云卫导演的《武松》。对这两部电影,沈静指出:

> 两部电影皆展现出舞台布景与现实情境的结合,融合戏剧与电影空间于一体。现实外景与电影媒介相兼容,让场景切换迅速跟上对戏剧唱腔的描绘。电影媒介也使戏剧表演更简洁。②

在这方面,上面谈到的《逼上梁山》也与此相似。而之所以形成这样的艺术特点,是和电影制作人的出身密不可分的。沈静说:"60年代初制作的、关于水浒人物的故事片,是戏剧演员的作品。"③像《野猪林》,京剧大师李少春既是林冲的扮演者,同时又是编剧;电影《武松》的男主角盖叫天,也是京剧名角。

对这两部电影的内容,沈静也作了介绍。崔嵬导演的《野猪林》叙述的是我们耳熟能详的林冲被逼上梁山的故事。沈静说:

---

① Since the 1950s, traditional opera films in the People's Republic of China received an unprecedented number of productions, and opera traditions were thoroughly covered. The new government had called for reform of the old opera. The two adaptations of *The Water Margin* during this period used cinematic devices to serve the operatic presentation and tried to harmonize the suggestive traditional theatre with the realistic setting in the film. Jing Shen, Re-Visions of Shuihu Women in Chinese Theater and Cinema, China Reciew, Vol. 7, No. 1 (Spring 2007), p. 112.

② Both of the films show the combination of stage sets and real settings, blending theatrical and cinematic spaces. The real locations are compatible with the film medium, which allows quick changes of scenery following the description of arias. The cinematic mdium also makes the operatic presentation concise. Jing Shen, Re-Visions of Shuihu Women in Chinese Theater and Cinema, China Reciew, Vol. 7, No. 1 (Spring 2007), p. 112.

③ The feature films about the characters from *The Water Margin* made in the early 1960s are products of the opera stars. Jing Shen, Re-Visions of Shuihu Women in Chinese Theater and Cinema, China Reciew, Vol. 7, No. 1 (Spring 2007), p. 113.

1962年制作的《野猪林》，描述了禁军教头林冲与花和尚鲁智深是如何被逼上梁山的。迷恋于林娘子的美貌，高衙内怂恿太尉高俅陷害林冲并把他流放到沧州。当高太尉派遣的解差在野猪林企图谋害林冲时，林的结义兄弟鲁智深救了他的命。[1]

沈静认为，应云卫导演的电影《武松》，是为主角盖叫天的武生特长量身定做的。她说："电影《武松》，应云卫的目的是重温京剧名角盖叫天的特殊风格。"[2] 根据沈静的论述，这部电影包括景阳冈打虎、狮子桥酒楼、十字坡、快活林、飞云浦、鸳鸯楼等故事；在小说原著中，这些情节有很多潜在的浪漫感情纠葛，只是电影并不探讨、表现这些内容。对此，该论者说："情感的表达并不是这部电影的主要关注点，电影里的大部分时间都是打斗表演。"[3] 该论者进一步指出，由于这样的艺术设计，电影中，从开篇的景阳冈打虎到最后的血溅鸳鸯楼，一个一个的演出高潮都是由打斗表演构成的；像杀嫂这个在原著中很重要的情节，因其并不是打斗的片段则隐入幕后。对武松故事的改编与小说原著之间的差异性，沈静也作了比较研究。她指出：

> 在飞云浦和鸳鸯楼事件中，武松杀敌报仇构成另一个演出高潮。杀死无辜的人，这在小说里开始展现武松强人的一面。飞云浦报仇打破浩劫标志着一个转折：武松并不是一个正义的护卫者，而成了残忍的复仇者。后来为了宣泄自己的愤怒，他杀死了张家所有的人。……自我控制的缺失，为这些强人悲惨的未来投下了可见的阴影。同时，

---

[1] *Wild Boar Wood*, made in 1962, describes how the instructor of imperial guards Lin Chong is forced to join the bandits with monk Lu Zhishen at the marshes of Mount Liang. Infatuated with the beauty of Lin Chong's wife Zhenniang, Marshal Gao's son induces Gao to frame Lin Chong and exile him to Cangzhou. Lin Chong's sworn brother Lu Zhishen rescues him in Wild Boar Wood where the guards sent by Gao attempt to mueder him. Jing Shen, Re-Visions of Shuihu Women in Chinese Theater and Cinema, China Reciew, Vol. 7, No. 1 (Spring 2007), p. 113.

[2] Likewise, the film *Wu Song* (made in 1963) looks like a series of highlights tailored to Gai Jiaotian's expertise as the military male lead. Ying Yunwei's purpose in *Wu Song* is to recapture the distinctive style of the Beijing opera star Gai Jiaotian. Jing Shen, Re-Visions of Shuihu Women in Chinese Theater and Cinema, China Reciew, Vol. 7, No. 1 (Spring 2007), p. 114.

[3] Still, it indicates that expression of feelings is not a main concern of this film, in which much time is allocated to martial arts presentation. Jing Shen, Re-Visions of Shuihu Women in Chinese Theater and Cinema, China Reciew, Vol. 7, No. 1 (Spring 2007), p. 114.

这种过度的行为也使这些形象少了一份英雄的崇高而多了一份人的本性。这种精微的细节揭示出文人小说比表演艺术高明的地方。电影中的特技表演总是会抹去复仇的过度。而且这样的处理把武松的反抗和英雄气概放置在积极的处境之中。这种传统的程式化角色，也使武松的形象比生活更高大。①

而且电影的改动不只在此。沈静指出：

> 电影的结局武松加入梁山泊的反抗者行列，这与纯粹的英雄形象相符合。而在小说中并不如此直接。他打算先加入二龙山的强人团伙，并一直希望未来能得到招安，让自己拯救自己。这样类似的简单化的结局也出现在电影《野猪林》里。这样的结局设计，与电影制作时代人民起义、参加革命的意识形态是相符合的。②

按沈静之论，20世纪60年代《水浒传》的影视化改编，极大地受到意识形态的影响。这种影响有时甚至起决定性的作用。实际情形的确如此。1949年新中国成立后一直到80年代实行改革开放之际，革命与阶级斗争始终是当时中国人生活的一大主题。这样的时代背景必然影响到《水

---

① The episodes of *Flying Clouds Quay* and *Ducks and Drakes Tower* in which Wu Song kills enemies in revenge constitute another climax of acrobatics. In the novel, this begins to show Wu Song's bandit side; he kills innocent people unnecessarily. The havoc Wu Song wreaks at Flying Clouds Quay marks a turning point: Wu Song becomes not a defender of justice but a rethless avenger who later kills all the members of the Zhang household to appease his rage... This lack of self-controle that grows more visible among the outlaws foreshadows a bleak future for them; at the same time, such excessiveness makes the characters less heroic and more human. This subtly reveals the literati novel behind the performance. The acrobatic display in the film totally srases this sence of excessiveness in revenge. Instead, it foregrounds Wu Song's rebellious and heroic quality in a positive light. The traditionally stylised role also contributes to the image of Wu Song being larger than life. Jing Shen, Re-Visions of Shuihu Women in Chinese Theater and Cinema, China Reciew, Vol. 7, No. 1 (Spring 2007), p. 115.

② The pure heroic image of Wu Song does conform to the ending of the film: Wu Song goes to the marshes of Mount Liang to join the rebellious bandits. In the novel, it is not this clear-cut; he plans to join a group of outlaws at Twin Dragon Peak temporarily and still hopes for a future amnesty that would allow him to redeem himself. A similarily simplified ending is also seen in the film *Wild Boar Wood*. These endings conform to the ideology of the times when the films were made: the people rebel and join the revolution. Jing Shen, Re-Visions of Shuihu Women in Chinese Theater and Cinema, China Reciew, Vol. 7, No. 1 (Spring 2007), p. 115.

浒传》的影视化改编。何况正如论者沈静所指出的，中国这一阶段的电影制作乃是政府行为的产物。

(二)《水浒传》的电视剧改编

本节伊始，笔者就已交代，自1998年至2011年间，根据《水浒传》改编、制作、播放的大型电视剧出现了两部。其中张绍林导演的第一部在英语世界获得不小的关注。1998年1月19日，张绍林导演的第一部《水浒传》电视剧刚在中国中央电视台开播不久，纽约《中国日报》就刊发了题为《中国草莽英雄跨上电视荧屏》的专题报道文章。该文章对《水浒传》的此次电视剧改编、制作及其在观众中引起的反响等情况，进行了简明扼要的介绍。在此，笔者择其要点简述如下。

首先是对小说《水浒传》原著的简介。该文章指出：

> 《水浒传》的故事之于中国人，就像侠盗罗宾汉及其伙伴的传奇故事之于英国人，都是非常受大众欢迎的。罗贯中（1330—1400）与施耐庵（1296—1370）创作的文学杰作《水浒传》，故事主要发生在宋代（960—1279）的1101—1125年间。这部小说叙述了108位好汉如何一起走上梁山（在今山东省内），并与腐败的政府军队和地方贪官污吏抗争的。[1]

其次是关于《水浒传》的电视剧改编、制作情况。对此问题，通过对电视剧总导演张绍林的采访，该文章告诉我们：

> 为了确保《水浒传》电视剧改编的成功，编剧和导演吸取了《西游记》《红楼梦》和《三国演义》等其他三部名著在电视剧改编过程中的经验教训，广泛咨询、听取相关专家、学者的意见和建议，采用了观众和影

---

[1] The popular stories of the "Outlaws of the Marsh" (*Shuihu Zhuan*), to the Chinese, are like the legendary tales of Robin Hood and his men to the British people.... The original novel *Outlaws of the Marsh*, a literary tour de force authored by Luo Guanzhong (1330 – 1400) and Shi Nai'an (1296 – 1370), is set mainly between the year of 1101 and 1125 in the Song Dynasty (960 – 1279). It is about why and how 108 men and women banded together on a mountain surrounded by marshes in what today is Shandong Province, and fought against troops of a corrupt government and local despots. China: Marsh heroes stride onto TV screen. China Daily, North American ed. [New York, N.Y] 19 Jan, 1998: 1.

评者对它们的批评意见,以避免犯同样的错误。① 此其一。

其二,为了电视剧制作的成功,对扮演男女主角演员的挑选非常精细,可谓千里挑一,即使他们不一定是知名的电影明星。剧务组成员全都是顶级的专业人士。为了使这部电视剧更有趣,特地邀请了两位香港导演负责功夫镜头的设计和制作。为了保证拍摄质量,使用了新的先进的设备,如数码摄像机和多媒体等。而且为了使电视剧尽量精美,制作组到7个省及自治区对拍摄场地进行实地考察。该文章对电视剧中人物的语言运用也作了说明:"对话是简单的口语,绝大部分采用现代汉语。"②

再次是有关电视剧改编、制作过程中对小说原著的接受与改动问题。该文章援引张绍林导演的话说:

这部电视剧采用现实主义方法和小说作者的叙述方式来拍摄制作。通过这种方式,我们能如实地描绘农民起义从开始到失败的全过程;充实英雄们的生活细节,从而把故事发生的社会环境全景式地搬上荧屏。③

不过,即便如此,电视剧对小说原著还是存在一定的改动。该文章援引张绍林的话进一步指出:"因为《水浒》故事已是家喻户晓,为了增加

---

① To ensure a successful adaptation, the script writers and directors have sought advice from senior artists, historians and scholars on the studies of ancient Chinese literature. . . . Zhang said he and his staff also took into consideration viewers' criticisms of the previous three adaptations so that they would not make the same kinds of mistakes during the shooting of the "Outlaws." China: Marsh heroes stride onto TV screen. China Daily, North American ed. [New York, N.Y] 19 Jan, 1998: 1.

② Actors and actresses who play the leading roles were carefully chosen from thousands of candidates. "But they are not necessarily famous movie stars," Zhang said. He said that the crew members, such as cameramen, makeup designers and music writers, are all top-flight professionals. The dialogues are spoken in simple, mostly modern language. Two Hong Kong directors were invited to take charge of designing the kungfu scenes to make the TV serial more interesting than those in other historical TV serials. The production team have been to seven provinces and municipalities for location shootings to make the TV serial as exquisite as possible. New advanced equipment, such as digital cameras and multi-media, were used to insure the shooting quality. China: Marsh heroes stride onto TV screen. China Daily, North American ed. [New York, N.Y] 19 Jan, 1998: 1.

③ The TV serial was made in a realistic approach and in the way the novel was narrated by the authors, according to Zhang. In this way, "We can honestly depict the whole process of the uprising, from its start to its defeat, to flesh out the heroes and heroines and to reproduce on the screen a panoramic picture of the social circumstances where the story took place," he said. China: Marsh heroes stride onto TV screen. China Daily, North American ed. [New York, N.Y] 19 Jan, 1998: 1.

一些悬念,电视剧在情节上做了细微改动。"①

最后,该文章对《水浒传》电视剧在社会上引起的反响、批评也作了介绍。要成功地把像《水浒传》这样大部头的著作搬上荧屏,并不是一件容易的事,而要使其符合众多观众的口味和审美需要则更是一件难上加难的事情。1998年初,张绍林导演的《水浒传》电视剧在中国中央电视台一开播,就在观众与影评者中间激起了强烈反响。根据该文章的报道,观众的反应大部分是积极、正面的。其援引一位有影响力的影评家邵木军的观点说,这部电视剧结构紧凑,电视剧把至少30位主角以及小说中一些配角的故事情节紧密地交织在一起而不混淆。他还说:"观众很容易就能感受到,故事中英雄人物性格的发展是很自然的。"不过该论者也指出,功夫镜头的拍摄太过华丽、不真实,这与整个故事的现实主义风格是相违背的。②

该文章指出,在年轻观众之间,批评的声音更为强烈。主要在于他们习惯了动作影视剧的快节奏,从而对《水浒传》电视剧的慢节奏表示失望。其中一人说:"故事进展如此缓慢,我已失去了等待看完所有43集的耐心。"③还有观众提及电视剧在人物塑造上存在不足。有一些人指出,不同主角的性格发展不平衡,"如军官,林冲和杨志从良民到草寇的转变叙述清晰,其他人的转变则显得相当粗糙、仓促"④。

---

① As the story is well-known to every household, the TV serial makes slight modifications in plots to add some suspense, Zhang said. China: Marsh heroes stride onto TV screen. China Daily, North American ed. [New York, N.Y] 19 Jan, 1998: 1.

② Shao Mujun, an influential film critic, praised the TV serial for its tight organization. Despite the fact that the story consists of a lot of intriguing plots and at least 30 major figures whose characters are well developed, this TV serial has the plots so closely interwoven that even those who are unfamiliar with the novel will not get confused, he said. "The audience can easily perceive how the development of the heroes' characters happen naturally in the story." But he criticized the kungfu scenes as being too showy and untrue, which goes against the realistic style of the whole story. China: Marsh heroes stride onto TV screen. China Daily, North American ed. [New York, N.Y] 19 Jan, 1998: 1.

③ Some young viewers, who are accustomed to the quick rhythm of imported action movies and TV serials, are disappointed by the slow rhythm of the TV serial. One of them said that "the story develops so slowly that I have lost patience and wait watch all the 43 parts." China: Marsh heroes stride onto TV screen. China Daily, North American ed. [New York, N.Y] 19 Jan, 1998: 1.

④ Fault in the characterization is also mentioned by the audience. Some pointed out that the character development of different leading figures is not well balanced. "For army officers, the change of Lin Chong and Yang Zhi from law-abiding persons to outlaws is narrated clearly while the other's change is shown in a rather rough and hasty manner," one viewer said. China: Marsh heroes stride onto TV screen. China Daily, North American ed. [New York, N.Y] 19 Jan, 1998: 1.

在不少观众看来，电视剧《水浒传》的确存在上述缺陷和不足。但即便如此，这部电视剧播放之后仍然吸引了非常多的观众。而且正如上文所说，绝大多数观众的反馈还是积极、正面的。

第三节 《水浒传》对中国社会及对域外文学创作的影响

本章开篇，在综合梳理英语世界的批评者对《水浒传》的影响所作的研究时，笔者就已说过，《水浒传》的影响不只在文学创作一隅。它对中国社会国民思想与民族心态的构成，特别是对中国革命运动的发生、发展，都具有不可估量的影响力。而且英语世界的学者在研究《水浒传》所产生的影响时，不只局限在中国范围，还对其跨国传播的影响给予了一定程度的关注。

一、《水浒传》对中国社会的影响

在中国，《水浒传》的影响不只在文学艺术范围。它对中国民众思想的影响是有目共睹的，尤其是在动荡的年代，它对农民起义、社会革命运动的影响更加强烈。

在上文谈论《水浒传》对中国现代戏剧、影视创作的影响时，研究者沈静就曾指出，不管是欧阳予倩的《潘金莲》还是杨绍萱等人的《逼上梁山》，都具有浓厚的社会政治意识形态色彩。特别是《逼上梁山》，更是当时中国共产党在延安领导之下的革命运动的产物。该论者说："这部剧目紧跟毛泽东的延安讲话精神，也和中国抗日战争（1937—1945）的发展保持着一致步调。"[①] 根据沈静的研究，就是 20 世纪 60 年代拍摄的两部水浒电影《野猪林》和《武松》，也与当时人民起义、参加革命的意识形态紧密结合在一起。当然，这只是以文学艺术的形式折射出来的冰山一角。

与沈静的研究视角相一致，20 世纪 30 年代初，赛珍珠就注意到《水浒传》在社会政治意识形态方面的影响。她在《中国早期小说源流》一文中这样说："现在，处于革命时期，共产党影响着中国青年的思想，

---

① The opera programme followed closely Mao Zedong's Yan'an talk and kept abreast of the War of Resistance Against Japan (1937–1945). Jing Shen, Re-Visions of Shuihu Women in Chinese Theater and Cinema, China Reciew, Vol. 7, No. 1 (Spring 2007), p. 115.

《水浒传》又有了意义。"在该文中,赛珍珠还对当时中国学术界利用《水浒传》进行政治宣传作过描述。她说:"(《水浒传》)新版序言由一个激进分子用笔名写出,他一本正经地认为这本书是一篇声讨帝国主义和资本主义的檄文。"① 随后,赛珍珠在其英译"《水浒传》导言"中也有类似的交代。她说:

> 而今,中国最新、最激进的政党——中国共产党——非常看重《水浒传》,他们发行了一个本子,内附有一位中国共产党领导人所作的序言。该领导人以为此书是中国第一部共产党的文学作品,它适用于现在,正如适用于它创作的时代。②

从上面这些文字可见《水浒传》对当时中国社会拥有非常大的影响,尤其是在政治意识形态宣传方面,更是为政党政治所充分利用。

对《水浒传》产生的社会性影响,孙康宜也作过简略的论述。他说:

> 《水浒传》对中国民众影响之大,正如奥斯卡·王尔德所言:"生活之模仿艺术远胜于艺术对生活的模仿。"自1586年(万历十四年)之后,造反者的领袖引用《水浒传》的话——如"替天行道"等作为他们的口号,是非常通行的做法;某些造反首领甚至使用《水浒传》中人物的名号,如宋江、李逵等。正因为此,《水浒传》屡屡被政府禁止。③

从这简短的论述中,我们可以看到《水浒传》对中国民众的生活与

---

① 姚君伟编:《赛珍珠论中国小说》,南京大学出版社2012年版,第30页。
② Today the newest and most extreme party in China, the Communist, has taken the *Shui Hu Chuan* and issued an edition with a preface by a leading Communist, who calls it the first Communist literature of China, as suitable to this day as to the day it was written. Pearl S. Buck, *Introduction of Shui Hu Chuan*, *All Men Are Brothers*, NewYork: The John Day Company, 1933, p. ix.
③ The effect of *the Water Margin* on the Chinese imagination can aptly be described by Oscar Wilde's aphorism, "Life imitates art." Since 1586, it has been fashionable for leaders of rebellions in China to use quotations from *the Water Margin* (e.g. "to implement the Way on behalf of Heaven") as their slogans; some have even adopted the names of individual characters, such as Song Jiang and Li Kui. For this reason *the Water Margin* has been periodically banned by the government. The Cambridge History of Chinese Literature, Edited by Kang-I Sun Chang, Stephen Owen, Cambridge University Press, 2010, Vol. 2, p. 54.

思想，特别是对中国社会革命运动（其中尤以农民起义为最）之影响，是相当巨大的。不过，无论是赛珍珠还是孙康宜，他们的论述都只是片言只语。与这两位批评者相比，下文即将讨论的马克林（Colin Patrick Mackerras）的研究要略显具体些，只是其研究对象也仅局限在一个小范围就是。

马克林在1976年曾经发表《戏剧与太平天国》（Theatre and the Taipings）的长文，其中有一节内容专门讨论"通俗文学对太平天国思维方式的影响"（The influence of popular literature on Taiping ideology）。马克林说：

> 这些不幸的人们虽然遭到社会的蔑视，但他们却积极地从他们的艺术中获得乐趣。更重要的是，他们注意从舞台演出的剧目中吸取教训、总结经验。在反对儒家秩序的起义团体中，很多都接受过戏剧的影响，太平天国尤其如此。①

马克林援引施友忠（Vincent Shih）的观点进一步指出：

> 根据施友忠（1967：285—296）的观点，在太平天国革命运动思维方式（意识形态）的来源中，一个非中国传统权威元素是小说。只是在这种语境中，很难区分究竟是来自小说还是来自通俗戏剧，因为这两种文学形式的故事内容都是一样的。因而，传达给太平天国革命者的思想，或是武装他们头脑的力量，一般可能是通过小说或者是戏剧的媒介而获得。②

---

① Society despised these unfortunate people but did not hesitate to derive enjoyment from their art. More important, it paid attention to the lessons played out on the stage. Among the many groups influenced by the theatre have been rebels against the Confucian order and, in particular, the Taipings. Colin Patrick Mackerras, Theatre and the Taipings, Modern China, Vol. 2, No. 4 (Oct., 1976), p. 476.

② According to Vincent Shih (1967: 285 - 296), one of the sources of the traditional Chinese nonestablishment element in Taiping ideology was the novel, but it is difficult to distinguish between novels and popular dramas in this context because the stories and content of both forms of literature were the same. Thus ideas conveyed to the Taipings or strengthened in their minds could usually have come through the medium of either novels or dramas. Colin Patrick Mackerras, Theatre and the Taipings, Modern China, Vol. 2, No. 4 (Oct., 1976), p. 476.

根据马克林的论述，在这些通俗小说中，对太平天国革命发生重大影响的尤以《三国演义》和《水浒传》为最。他说：

> 对太平天国革命影响最重要的，是《三国演义》与《水浒传》的故事和人物。基本可以肯定，太平天国革命从这两部小说学到了大量的战争策略。①

马克林的这一说法是有据可依的。他援引曾国藩的高级幕僚张德坚的记述来证实自己的观点。张德坚在《贼情汇纂》卷五《诡计》中这样写道：

> 而贼无定法……（其懈我、诱我、图我、误我）无非诡计。兵法战策，草野罕有。贼之诡计，果何所依据？盖由二三黠贼，采稗官野史中军情，仿而行之，往往有效，遂宝为不传之秘诀。其取裁《三国演义》《水浒传》为尤多。②

作为曾国藩镇压太平天国革命运动的重要智囊，以及那段历史的亲历者与见证者，张德坚的记述是完全可信的。

马克林认为，《三国演义》《水浒传》等中国小说、戏剧对太平天国革命运动的影响，不只表现在行军打仗的策略上，更在精神层面激励着这些革命者。他说："太平天国革命者视这些小说、戏剧中的英雄人物为自

---

① Of course the most important stories and characters to influence the Taipings were *The Romance of the Three Kingdoms* and *Water Margin*. The Taipings almost certainly learned a great deal about strategy from them. Colin Patrick Mackerras, Theatre and the Taipings, Modern China, Vol. 2, No. 4 (Oct., 1976), p. 476.

② Zhang De-jian, who was chief of the intelligence Bureau in Zeng Guo-fan's headquarters, wrote (1855: 154): The bandits have no set methods... everything they do is trickery. Their military tactics and strategy are lowly and very meagre. What then is the basis of the bandits' tri-cks? Military intelligence is selected by two or three shrewd bandits from historical novels, they then imitate it in practice Frequently this is effective, so they regard it as precious and a secret not to be divulged. *The Rorance of the Three Kingdoms* and *Water Margin* are particularly important sources (for their tricks). Colin Patrick Mackerras, Theatre and the Taipings, Modern China, Vol. 2, No. 4 (Oct., 1976), p. 476. 笔者所引原文见张德坚撰《贼情汇纂》卷五《诡计》，中华文史丛书之六十四，民初刻本影印（壬申十一月盈山精舍印），王有立主编，（台湾）华文书局有限公司印行，1968—1969 年，第 481 页。

己的榜样，并颂扬他们身上展现出来的英勇、忠诚、坚贞的道德品质。"①

不过，马克林说，在《三国演义》与《水浒传》等通俗文学中，《水浒传》对中国革命运动的重要性要胜过其他作品。他说："从确信无疑的方面来看，通俗文学、尤其是《水浒传》的影响更为重要。这在太平天国革命的整个社会、道德理想层面都获得了践行。"② 他援引法国学者、近现代中国历史研究的创始人谢诺（Chesneaux）的观点进一步指出：

> "《水浒》是造反者的政治文学教科书。"（谢诺，1971.4）可以肯定来自小说、特别是《水浒传》的"忠义"观念，更为太平天国革命所强调。事实上，水浒英雄聚义的地方就叫忠义堂。按施友忠之论，"太平天国的政治使命，他们宣称要建立的天朝的一个鲜明特征，正是《水浒传》描绘的造反者社会所展现出来的"。③

说到法国学者谢诺，他曾经用法文写过一篇《〈水浒传〉的近代关联：对中国19、20世纪起义运动的影响》文章。该文系统讨论《水浒传》对中国19、20世纪农民起义、革命运动、秘密会社在政治、军事等方面产生的影响，发表后在美国学界获得好评。但其不在英语世界的范围，故不论。

就《水浒传》的社会影响，石昌渝在为沙博理英译本撰写的导论中也有过一番简明扼要的阐述。他说：

> 《水浒传》的影响并不局限于文学领域，它也影响到农民起义和秘密会社。明末农民起义的领袖李自成，太平天国的缔造者洪秀全，

---

① The Taipings regarded the heroes of these novels and dramas as models and praised them for such virtues as courage, loyalty, and persistence. Colin Patrick Mackerras, Theatre and the Taipings, Modern China, Vol. 2, No. 4 (Oct., 1976), p. 476.

② More important is the influence which certain items in popular literature, especially *Water Margin*, exercised on the overall social and moral ideals of the Taipings. Colin Patrick Mackerras, Theatre and the Taipings, Modern China, Vol. 2, No. 4 (Oct., 1976), p. 477.

③ *Shuihu* was "the politico-literary 'model' of rebellion". (Chesneaux, 1971.4) The concepts of "loyalty and fraternity" (zhongyi), much stressed by the Taipings, certainly derive from novels, in particular *Shuihu*. Indeed, the hall where the heroes of *Water Margin* foregathered to swear eternal ties to one another was called Zhongyi. In Shih's words (1967 293–294), "The political mission of the Taipings in acting for heaven to make the heavenly way prevail was a distinct feature of the rebel society as described in *Shui-hu chuan* (*Shuihu zhuan*)." Colin Patrick Mackerras, Theatre and the Taipings, Modern China, Vol. 2, No. 4 (Oct., 1976), p. 477.

黑旗军（清末的一支农民起义队伍）的首领之一宋景诗等，都标举"替天行道"的口号。密谋反清的秘密会社，把他们聚义的地方叫作"忠义堂"。所有这些很明显是从《水浒传》得到启发的。众所周知的还有，一些农民起义的首领研究梁山好汉行军打仗的战略、策略。小说在这方面的影响，既有积极的意义也有消极的含义。主宰《水浒传》的路见不平拔刀相助、快意恩仇的侠义精神与根深蒂固的歧视女性的思想观念，已深入中国社会，其程度之深难以轻易抹去。①

根据上述，《水浒传》对中国民众思想、社会革命运动以及秘密会社的影响是非常大的。不过在影响方式上，英语世界的研究者持有不同的看法。施友忠认为，以《水浒传》为代表的通俗小说对中国革命运动产生的是直接的影响。柯文（C. A. Curwen）对此表示怀疑。他提出：

> 和秘密会社一样，太平天国受到通俗小说的影响。但似乎并没有充足的理由证实（如施友忠所认为的那样）这是直接影响的结果。因为像《水浒传》《三国演义》与《封神演义》等小说，也只是中国"小传统"的一部分。作为思想启示的资源，甚至是军事指导手册，它们长久以来就在为造反者服务。②

---

① But the influence of *Outlaws of the Marsh* is not confined to the sphere of literature; it also influenced peasent rebels and secret societies. Li Zicheng, who led the peasent uprising at the end of the Ming Dunasty, Hong Xiuquan, who set up the Taiping Heavenly Kingdom, and Song Jingshi, who was one of the leaders of the Black Banner Army (an uprising force at the end of the Qing Dynasty), all raised the slogan of "defending justice on behalf of Heaven." Secret societies plitting against the Qing Dynasty called their meeting places "Halls of Loyalty." All these obviously drew their inspiration from *Outlaws of the Marsh*. It is also known that some leaders of peasent rebellions studied the strategies and tactics of the Liangshan outlaws. So the influence of the novel in this respect had both positive and negative connotations. Besides, the chivalric spirit and sence that injustice must be avenged which are prominent on *Outlaws of the Marsh*, as well as its deep-seated prejustice against women, have permeated Chinese society to an extent that cannot be lightly passed over. Shi Changyu, Introduction, *Outlaws of the Marsh*, translated by Sidney Shapiro, Beijing: Foreign Language Press, 1993, Vol. I, pp. 14 – 15.

② In a recent study, C. A. Curwen (1972. 66) comments: Like the secret societies, the Taipings were influenced by popular novels, but there seems to be little reason to suppose (as V Y C Shih does) that this was the result of direct influence, since novels like *Shui-hu chuan* (Shuihu zhuan), *San-kuo yen-i* (Sanguo yanyi), and *Feng-shen yen-i* (Fengshen yanyi) were also part of the Chinese "little tradition" and had long served rebels as sources of inspiration and even as military handbooks. Colin Patrick Mackerras, Theatre and the Taipings, Modern China, Vol. 2, No. 4 (Oct., 1976), p. 477.

按柯文的意思,这种影响更可能是在中国民众、特别是造反者之间一代一代传递的。马克林也觉得此观点可能是对的,应该更切合实际。不过马克林也提出,戏剧演出更加形象生动,而它们的内容也与《水浒传》等通俗小说一样。因此,通过戏剧表演的方式来传达小说中的思想内容,从而影响到农民起义、革命运动,这样的可能性更大。但据笔者掌握的相关中国明清历史文献来看,有不少是直接阅读《水浒传》等而受其影响的[①]。

在中国明清历史文献里面,记载《水浒传》社会影响的内容相当丰富。不仅有上文谈到的对农民起义、社会革命的影响,《水浒传》也是很多秘密会社如"天地会"的思想来源[②]。此外,《水浒传》也为当时中国社会中下层普通百姓的日常生活带来很大的影响,如玩水浒叶子戏,以水浒人名行酒令,以水浒人物故事作酒筹取乐,等等。

英语世界的批评者在研究时,更为关注的是《水浒传》在社会意识形态与革命运动层面的影响,而对其在日常生活中形成的影响则研究的很少。

二、《水浒传》的域外传播及对域外文学创作的影响

《水浒传》的域外影响是与其在域外的传播、译介、接受密切相关的。从现存的资料来看,中国古代小说中,《水浒传》是最早在域外传播、接受并发生影响的作品之一。《水浒传》的域外传播、接受,首先是在中国周边的东亚国家开始的,如日本、朝鲜、越南、泰国等国家,时间约在17世纪初期。在上述国家中,尤以在日本传播、接受最为兴盛。1840年之后,《水浒传》逐渐被西方世界接受。《水浒传》在西方的译介,最早是由法国著名汉学家巴赞(A. P. L. Bazin)完成的。巴赞的《水浒传摘译》分别发表在巴黎出版的《亚洲杂志》1850年第57期(第449—495页)和1851年第58期(第5—51页)上。此后,《水浒传》的拉丁文、英文、德文、意大利文、俄文、匈牙利文、捷克及斯洛伐克文、波兰文等西文译本陆续出版发行。在《水浒传》的西译过程中,有不少是从人物故事的摘译、编译而过渡到小说文本全译的,像《水浒传》的英译就是典型(在绪论"《水浒传》英译述介"部分已有说明)。这与学术发展的规律是相符合的。

[①] 这方面的文献资料很多,具体请参看朱一玄、刘毓忱编《水浒传资料汇编》"六影响编"之"(一)对社会的影响"部分。

[②] 具体可见罗尔纲撰写《〈水浒传〉与天地会》及其他相关研究文章。

据确切可靠的文献记载，《水浒传》在域外的传播及对接受国文学创作的影响，以日本为最。而这也是目前《水浒传》域外传播、影响研究的核心课题。

中国学者严绍璗在研究中指出，日本江户时代（1603—1867）初期——具体来说是1624年、后水尾天皇宽永元年，《京本增补校正全像忠义水浒志传评林》（明万历年间，余象斗双峰堂刊本）就已入藏当时政僧天海的私人藏书库"天海藏"①。《水浒传》传入日本的时间显然要早于此。

根据王丽娜的梳理、统计，自1757年冈岛冠山根据李贽评点的百回本《水浒传》编译的《通俗忠义水浒传》刊行至1987年，日本学界、出版界已经以各种形式（包括翻译、编译、编著等）出版了20种《水浒传》，其中纯翻译是11种②。香港中文大学谭汝谦博士的统计数据则远超过此。根据后者的统计，截至1978年，《水浒传》的日文译本就已达33种之多，在所有日译中国古典文学作品中居首位③。从这可见的数据中，我们就能感受到《水浒传》在日本的接受之广与影响之大。

随着《水浒传》在日本的传播、接受越来越广泛，它对日本文学创作的影响力也逐渐呈现出来。王丽娜指出：

> 《水浒传》对一些国家的文学产生了巨大的影响，它对日本文学创作的影响尤为巨大，正如日本杉本达夫所说："《水浒传》在江户时代已传入日本，在日本广为流传。日本受《水浒传》影响而创作的小说有许多种，其中最长的一部是泷泽马琴的《南总里见八犬传》，这部著作为广大日本读者所熟知。"泷泽马琴在1814—1842年用28年时间写成的《八犬传》，共98卷，106册，是传奇式的长篇小说。作者在写八犬士的母亲伏姬生八犬时采取《水浒》中"洪太尉误走妖魔"式的神奇写法，这部小说的惩恶扬善精神也和《水浒传》相一致。在《八犬传》之前，日本还有建部绫足写的《本朝水浒传》、仇鼎山写入（此"入"疑为多出字）的《日本水浒传》、伊丹椿园写的《女水浒传》、振鹭亭写的《伊吕波水浒传》以及山东京

---

① 严绍璗：《日藏汉籍善本书录·集部·话本小说类》，中华书局2007年版，第1992页。
② 见王丽娜《〈水浒传〉在国外》（下），《天津外国语学院学报》1998年第1期，第78—80页。
③ 谭汝谦：《中日之间翻译事业的几个问题》，《日本研究》1985年第3期。

传写的《忠臣水浒传》等，它们都取材于日本历史，模仿《水浒传》的形式而创作的。泷泽马琴写《八犬传》就是受到了建部绫足等作者的启发。①

王丽娜的统计、分析虽然简略，却能抓住《水浒传》在艺术手法与精神主旨上对《八犬传》等日本文学作品创作的影响这一核心问题。在讨论《水浒传》人物塑造问题时，日本"京都学派"巨匠宫崎市定就《水浒传》对泷泽马琴《八犬传》创作的影响也作过简单论述。他说："据说日本的泷泽马琴在写《八犬传》的时候就从《水浒传》中得到启示，将主人公的人数限定为八人。"②

就《水浒传》对日本学界及文学创作的影响，中国学者赵苗也曾指出：

> 从江户时代中期开始，日本文坛陆续出现大量的翻改水浒之作，大多数翻改作品是借鉴《水浒传》的题材及表现技巧，结合日本本国的历史事件和历史人物进行再创作，如《本朝水浒传》《湘中八雄传》《日本水浒传》《忠臣水浒传》《南总里见八犬传》《倾城水浒传》等，这类作品的出现进一步扩大了《水浒传》在日本的影响，并对日本后期"读本小说"产生了直接影响。此外，为便于阅读和理解《水浒传》，日本还出现了《水浒传解》《水浒传钞译》《水浒传译解》《语解》《字汇外集》等解释《水浒传》白话词汇的工具书。为阅读一部外国小说而编纂如此多的语言工具书，这在日本文学史上也是十分罕见的。③

江户时代日本文坛出现的翻改水浒之作与中国明末之后出现的系列《水浒传》续书，在创作方式上是极为接近的，不管是续写、改写、重写还是反写，都是从《水浒传》获得创作的启示。

就《水浒传》在日本的传播与影响这个课题，出现了系列研究成果。

---

① 王丽娜：《〈水浒传〉在国外》（下），《天津外国语学院学报》1998年第1期，第63—64页。
② ［日］宫崎市定：《宫崎市定说〈水浒〉——虚构的好汉与掩藏的历史》，赵翻、杨晓钟译，陕西人民出版社2008年版，第4页。
③ 赵苗：《〈水浒传〉与江户日本》，《文史知识》2010年第4期，第92—93页。

日本学界的代表性论文、论著主要有：青木正儿的《〈水浒传〉对日本文学的影响》，长泽规矩的《江户时代〈水浒传〉的流行情况》，村上芳郎的《杂记〈水浒〉嗜好者马琴》，白木直也的《〈水浒传〉的渡来与文简本》，木村淳哉的《中国明代四大小说在日本的传播》，等等。其中木村淳哉 2009 年在中国复旦大学撰写的博士学位论文《中国明代四大小说在日本的传播》"第五章《水浒传》研究"讨论《水浒传》对日本文学的影响，分"思想方面"与"在日本的衍生作品"两块，在"在日本的衍生作品"之下又列出"小说"、"漫画"、"连续剧"与"游戏"四类，对《水浒传》在日本文坛的影响进行了全面、系统的梳理研究。中国学界的代表性研究成果主要有：严绍璗的《明代俗语文学的东渐和日本江户时代小说的繁荣》，李时人、杨彬的《中国古代小说在日本的传播与影响》，赵苗的《〈水浒传〉与江户日本》，马兴国的《〈水浒传〉在日本的流传及影响》，高日晖的《〈水浒传〉的跨文化接受》，汪俊文的《日本江户时代读本小说与中国古代小说》，等等。凡此种种，不胜枚举。

不过，对《水浒传》在日本的传播与影响问题的研究，主要还是在中、日学界展开。英语世界的批评者如何谷理（Hegel E. Robert）等，虽也研究中日文学关系，但集中研究《水浒传》在日本的传播与影响的却几乎没有。

就笔者目前掌握的资料来看，丹尼斯·沃什本（Dennis Washburn）在《代笔者的文学纠缠：〈雨月物语〉中伦理道德对艺术的臣服》一文里面对此问题有一定的讨论[①]。沃什本在文章开篇指出：

> 上田秋成（1734—1809）的《雨月物语》几乎从 1776 年初版刊行开始就被认为是日本文学的经典。这部作品，因其优美的散文风格——把伦理道德或审美论争交织进故事的细腻方式与精致的叙述方法——而受到称赞。在显而易见的艺术控制意识与灵异的主题材料之间，贯穿着令人愉悦的张力。事实上，《雨月物语》所取得的成就不在该作品任何单一的方面，而在张力——一种奇异之美，故事中不同要素的综合创作出来的危险的平衡。更重要的是，这种平衡不是纯粹的偶然，而是某一引导上田秋成出于自己的目的，对早期中国与日本

[①] Dennis Washburn, Ghostwriters and Literary Haunts. Subordinating Ethics to Art in *Ugetsu Monogatari*, Monumenta Nipponica, Vol. 45, No. 1 (Spring, 1990), pp. 39–74.

的灵异故事进行改编的意识形态假定的结果。①

这段文字为我们提供了一些很重要的信息,最明显的是上田秋成在创作《雨月物语》时借用了中国素材;其次是该作品在人物故事叙述与社会伦理道德之间,即在审美与道德关系的处理上,有类似于《水浒传》的地方。而根据沃什本后来的论述,上田秋成在创作思想、创作观念上的确受到《水浒传》的影响。沃什本说:

> 《雨月物语》表达的关于艺术和艺术家的思想,对传奇故事结构与语言的形成具有重大意义。其中两个观念尤为重要。首先是文学艺术家是传统的翻译员的思想,就像音乐家阐释曲谱,在既定的主题之上生发出各种变化。……其次是艺术家总是与超自然现象有某种关系的思想。……这些思想的根本来源是中国文人的理想以及俳谐诗人对这些思想的移植、归化。②

---

① The collection of tales *Ugetsu Monogatari* 雨月物语 ("Tales of Rain and Moon"), written by Ueda Akinari 上田秋成, 1734 – 1809, has been an acknowledged classic of Japanese literature almost from the time of its publication in 1776. The work has been praised for the beauty of its prose style, the careful way in which ethical or aesthetic arguments are woven into the stories, and the sophistication of the narrative perspectives. There is throughout a pleasing tension between the apparent controlling artistic consciousness and the supernatural subject matter. Indeed, the achievement of *Ugetsu Monogatari* rests not on any single aspect of the work, but rather on that tension-the strangely beautiful, precarious balance created by the synthesis of diverse elements in the stories. That balance, moreover, is not merely fortuitous, but is the result of certain ideological assumptions that led Akinari to adapt earlier Chinese and Japanese tales of the supernatural to his own purposes. Dennis Washburn, Ghostwriters and Literary Haunts. Subordinating Ethics to Art in *Ugetsu Monogatari*, Monumenta Nipponica, Vol. 45, No. 1 (Spring, 1990), p. 39。

② The ideas about art and the artist presented in Ugetsu Monogatari play a significant role in shaping both the structure and language of the tales. Two notions are especially important. The first is the idea of the literary artist as an interpreter of tradition who, like a musician interpreting a composition, plays out variations on established themes. Since his material was already known, the interest of any new story lay in the degree and quality of its variation. Thus the idea of the artist as an interpreter of his tradition not only justified the rewriting of earlier ghost stories, but also provided the narrative mechanism by which to achieve these variations. The second is the notion of the artist as having some connection with the supernatural. Often supernatural encounters in the stories are the result of an act of artistic creativity, so that the notion of a deep connection between art and the supernatural is embedded in the text. The primary sources for these ideas were the Chinese ideal of the literatus, and the naturalization of that ideal by the practitioners of haikai poetry. Dennis Washburn, Ghostwriters and Literary Haunts. Subordinating Ethics to Art in *Ugetsu Monogatari*, Monumenta Nipponica, Vol. 45, No. 1 (Spring, 1990), p. 50, 51.

沃什本进一步指出：

> 在作品中，上田秋成有意识地提及自己和传统之间的关系。因为，他认为自己对其他作品的借用、改编、吸收是非常明显的。而在《世间妾气》(*Seken Tekake Katagi*)的序言中，他承认自己对中国与日本文学传统所欠下的债。①

根据沃什本的论述，上田秋成在《雨月物语·序》中详细阐述了自己的艺术观，并直接点明了自己的创作与《水浒传》之关系。其序如下：

> 罗子撰《水浒》，而三世生哑儿；紫媛著《源语》，而一旦堕恶趣者，盖为业所逼耳。然而观其文，各奋奇态，哗哗逼真。低昂宛转。令读者心气洞越也。可见鉴事实于千古焉。余适有鼓腹之闲话，冲口吐出，雉雏龙战，自以为杜撰，则摘读之者，固当不谓信也。岂可求丑唇平鼻之报哉。明和戊子晚春。雨霁月朦胧之夜。窗下编成。以畀梓氏。题曰《雨月物语》云。剪枝畸人书。②

---

① Akinari consciously invoked his relationship with his tradition throughout his work. That he believed he was following accepted practice in borrowing or adapting other works is apparent in his willingness to acknowledge his debts to both the Chinese and Japanese literary traditions in comments he made in the preface to *Seken Tekake Katagi* 世间妾气, his second ukiyo-zoshi, written shortly before he began composing *Ugetsu Monogatari*. Dennis Washburn, Ghostwriters and Literary Haunts. Subordinating Ethics to Art in Ugetsu Monogatari, Monumenta Nipponica, Vol. 45, No. 1 (Spring, 1990), p. 52, 53。

② Lo Kuan-chung wrote Shui hu chuan, and subsequently monstrous children were born to three generations of his descendants. Murasaki Shikibu wrote Genji Monogatari and subsequently she descended into hell. It is thought that the reason for their suffering was punishment for having led people astray with their fiction. Yet when we look at their works we see in them an abundance of strange and wondrous things. The force of their words draws near the truth; the rhythm of their sentences is mellifluous and lovely, touching the heart of the reader like the reverberations of a koto. They make us see the reality of the distant past. As for myself, I have a few stories that are nothing more than the products of idleness in an age of peace and prosperity. But when the words come tumbling from my lips, they sound as strange and inauspicious as the raucous crying of pheasants, or the roar of dragons. My tales are slipshod and full of errors. Accordingly, those who thumb through this volume are not expected to mistake my jottings for the truth. On the other hand, I shall avoid the retribution of descendants with three lips or noseless faces. Dennis Washburn, Ghostwriters and Literary Haunts. Subordinating Ethics to Art in Ugetsu Monogatari, Monumenta Nipponica, Vol. 45, No. 1 (Spring, 1990), p. 53. 中文引文见曹顺庆主编《东方文论选》，四川人民出版社1996年版，第790页。

从这序中可知，上田秋成在创作思想与创作态度上对《水浒传》的借鉴似乎并非是正面的、直接的。沃什本也认为，上田秋成在序中使用"剪枝畸人"的名字暗示他对这些作品采取的是反讽的态度。不过事实并非如此。沃什本同时也指出，上田秋成嘲弄了儒、释两家从狭隘的现实主义角度来阐释《水浒传》与《源氏物语》的做法；那些人把虚构的描写当作真实，以为这些作品使人误入歧途。该论者还指出，"剪枝畸人"名字的使用是一种狡猾的手段，上田秋成是想避开道学家的攻击，同时显示文学的价值，并声明自己是罗贯中的残疾后裔[1]。而事实上，上田秋成热衷于描写灵异事件，正如泷泽马琴采用神奇的手法创作《八犬传》一样，都受到《水浒传》的影响。

---

[1] Akinari then ridicules Confucianist and Buddhist interpretations that, in reading only a narrow realism in *Shui hu chuan* and *Genji Monogatari*, conclude that these works threatened to lead people astray by presenting fictional experience as true. Out of the tradition of this type of moralistic reading legends arose about how both Lo and Murasaki were punished for writing so well. That Akinari took an ironic view of these legends is suggested by the name he used for the preface-Senshi Kijin 剪枝畸人, the eccentric with clipped fingers. When Akinari was five years old he contracte smallpox, and an infection caused two of his fingers, one on each hand, to atrophy, leaving him noticeably deformed. Like another of his pseudonyms, Mucho ("the crab"), Senshi Kijin is a self-mocking reference to his crippled hands. In all his surviving works, "Senshi Kijin" is used only once. This choice of names was a sly way for Akinari to reject the moralists and proclaim the value of literature and of his own position as one of the deformed descendants of Lo. Dennis Washburn, Ghostwriters and Literary Haunts. Subordinating Ethics to Art in Ugetsu Monogatari, Monumenta Nipponica, Vol. 45, No. 1 (Spring, 1990), p. 54, 55。

第三章

英语世界对《水浒传》的人物形象塑造研究

研究《水浒传》，缺不了对其人物形象进行研究，缺不了对其人物形象塑造所取得的成就作出评价。在中国学界如此，在英语世界的学者中亦然。不过，源于独特的文化传统、知识谱系与观念结构，源于研究者特定的学术素养背景与理论修养水平，英语世界的水浒人物研究呈现出自身独特的一面。

第一节 《水浒传》人物塑造艺术成就的评价问题

在水浒人物塑造艺术成就的研究上，英语世界的学者中存在多种不同的声音。其一认为，水浒人物的塑造达到了高度的"典型化"、"个性化"水准；另一则认为，除少数人物外，其他大部分角色都是"模式化"（stereotyped）、"类型化"的。有一部分学者运用比较的方法，来分析、思考中西小说之间在人物塑造方面的差异性，以及中国小说中人物描写的艺术特征。这使研究进入一个更深的层面。但因其是以西方文学批评理论、观念作为衡量中国小说人物描写艺术的标准，导致所提出的看法、观点存在很大的偏见。有少数研究者意识到此种偏见，他们试图从中西文学不同传统的宏观层面出发，考察中国小说在人物描写艺术上不同于西方小说的特性。这则把研究推进到了一个更高的层面。

一、水浒人物塑造的"典型化"论

我国学人，由明入清的金圣叹，在评价《水浒传》人物形象塑造方面所取得的艺术成就时说："别一部书，看过一遍即休。独有《水浒传》，只是看不厌，无非为他把一百八个人性格，都写出来。《水浒传》写一百八个人性格，真是一百八样。"① 金圣叹之论虽有不少夸张、失实的成分在里面，但因其对水浒人物描绘把握上的独具只眼，还是获得不少后来者的肯定。300 年后，英语世界学者中也有其知音。笔者首先要谈到的是美国作家赛珍珠。

赛珍珠在中国生活数十年，深谙中国文化与文学。她不仅以金圣叹贯华堂 70 回本为底本把《水浒传》翻译成英文，把它推向了世界，她还在 20 世纪 30 年代撰写的谈论中国小说的系列文章中多次讨论《水浒传》的诸种问题②，人物塑造是其中的核心话题。

1931 年，赛珍珠发表《早期中国小说源流》一文。赛珍珠在该文中指出，在中国早期的长篇小说中，"人物形象塑造常常是一流的。一个词，轻轻一笔，举手投足之间，人物就栩栩如生地出现在我们面前。《水浒传》尤其是这样。在那里，有语言天赋的人只凭人物的用语习惯就能感觉到他要说的内容"③。

1933 年，赛珍珠在其撰写的英译《水浒传》"导言"中进一步赞扬《水浒传》在人物形象描写上所取得的艺术成就。她说："这部小说所描绘出的人物画面是绝对忠实于生活的。它不仅是过去中国的一幅画像，更是现今中国的真实写照。至今，各界人士仍然热情洋溢地在阅读该作品。"④ 这不仅说明了《水浒传》对读者的巨大吸引力，更是指出了在中国这个"典型环境"中塑造出来的"典型形象"——水浒人物所具有的强大的生命力。

1938 年，赛珍珠在诺贝尔文学奖颁奖典礼上作了《中国小说》的演讲，更加深化了此种论点。她指出：

---

① （清）金圣叹：《读第五才子书法》，朱一玄、刘毓忱编：《水浒传资料汇编》，南开大学出版社 2012 年版，第 220 页。

② 赛珍珠研究中国小说的 12 篇文章已由国内学人翻译成中文，收入姚君伟主编《赛珍珠论中国小说》一书，并由南京大学出版社 2012 年出版。本书所引赛珍珠文章内容，主要参考该书的翻译，其中不同之处系笔者斟酌之后的重译。

③ Pearl S. Buck, *The Early Chinese Novel*, The Satueday Review of Literature, No. 46, Vol, 7, 1931. 见姚君伟主编《赛珍珠论中国小说》第 31 页，张丹丽译。

④ Pearl S. Buck, *Introduction of Shui Hu Chuan*, *All Men Are Brothers*, NewYork: The John Day Company, 1933, p. vi.

《水浒传》被认为是他们最伟大的三部小说之一,并不是因为它充满了刀光剑影的情节,而是因为它生动地描绘了 108 个人物。这些人物各不相同,每个都有其独特的地方。我曾常常听到人们津津乐道地谈论那部小说:"在 108 人当中,不论是谁说话,不用告诉我们他的名字,只凭他说话的方式我们就知道他是谁。"因此,人物描绘的生动逼真,是中国人对小说质量的第一要求,但这种描绘是由人物自身的行为(acts)和语言(speech)来实现的,而不是靠作者的解释。①

抓住"行为"和"语言"这两个关键要素来分析《水浒传》的人物塑造艺术,可以说是成功把握住了水浒人物描绘的要诀与精髓;同时也可以说是成功把握住了中国古典小说中人物塑造的核心元素。因为在不少欧美学者看来,与西方小说的发展及其特征相比,中国古典小说是不善于描写环境与人物心理的。赛珍珠就说在中国"早期长篇小说中,没有特别好的描写,尤其是自然描写"。事实上,在习惯于用西方小说理论观念来衡量、评价中国古典小说的中国学者眼中,亦然。

赛珍珠的水浒人物塑造达到了高度"典型化"、"个性化"水准的论点,在菲茨杰拉德那里获得进一步的发展。在菲茨杰拉德看来,不仅梁山 108 人,就是那些次要的人物(minor characters),也是非"模式化"(stereotyped)的。他说:

> 和 108 强人以及他们的敌人、那些政府官僚一样,大量的次要人物也绝非因袭传统的模式化形象。每一个人物都有其鲜明的个性,他的行为(acts)和语言(speech)与他的性格是一致的。而且这种性格是唯一的、独特的。②

赛珍珠与菲茨杰拉德等人对《水浒传》在人物形象塑造的"典型化"、"个性化"上所取得的艺术成就作出如此高的评价,这是值得商榷的。笔者以为,就是把水浒人物完全置于西方小说理论"典型环境中的典

---

① Pearl S. Buck, *The Chinese Novel*: *Nobel Lecture Delivered before the Swedish Academy at Stockholm*, December 12, 1938 (New York: The John Day Company), pp. 24 – 25. 该文已由王逢振译为中文,见姚君伟主编《赛珍珠论中国小说》第 114—139 页。本书所引部分出自第 121 页。

② C. P. Fitzgerald, *China*, *A Short Cultural History*, New York: Praeger, Inc, 1950, p. 501.

型形象"的视域之中来评价,不管是梁山108人还是其他大量的次要人物,其实并不是所有的人物形象都达到他们所说的"这些人物各不相同,每个都有其独特的地方","每一个人物都有其鲜明的个性,他的行为(acts)和语言(speech)与他的性格是一致的"这样高的艺术水准。就以扈三娘来说,她在梁山众好汉里功夫是相当了得的,但在《水浒传》中这个人物形象却描写得非常模糊,基本上没什么个性可言。从第48回"一丈青单捉王矮虎,宋公明两打祝家庄"正式出场到第97回"睦州城箭射邓元觉,乌龙岭神助宋公明"阵亡,自始至终扈三娘只留给读者"这厮无理"①一句四个字的台词,此外小说作者再没有对她做过正面的语言描写。至于其他,不再赘述。

鉴于此,笔者以为,此两人对水浒人物描写的评价是有悖文本事实的,一定程度上拔高了《水浒传》在人物塑造上所取得的成就。

在《水浒传》人物描写艺术成就的评价上,我国学者冯沅君的观点和上述两人很接近。她说:

> (《水浒传》)这部史诗性的小说描写了一百零八位好汉。……他们都是体格强健、拥有强烈的正义感和巨大的勇气的人物。他们可以战斗到死;他们能明辨是非,区分敌友。在描写所有这些强人时,小说作者赋予每一个人物鲜明的个性。宋江、吴用和其他梁山领袖性格迥异。宋江精明,阅历丰富,慷慨仗义。他的声誉是如此之高,因而人们都乐意为他效力。最初,他维护、支持封建秩序,但是他的想法逐渐发生了变化,最终决定反抗。……吴用是这支农民军的军师,一位狡猾的战略家,他的精明、远见使他赢得一系列的胜利。……这部书中,还有其他很多像李逵、武松和鲁智深这样的显著的角色。李逵是一位真正的农民。他单纯、鲁莽、慷慨、忠诚,是一位彻底的造反者。他完全忠实于自己的同伴,对敌人则是彻骨的憎恨。只是他的单纯中混杂着粗鲁。武松是一位铁骨铮铮的汉子,具有惊人的力量和勇气;一旦对统治阶级的幻觉破灭,他就会燃起复仇的火焰。鲁智深是

---

① 扈三娘此话出现的具体情境见一百回李卓吾评本《水浒传》第48回一丈青迎战王矮虎情节,"原来王矮虎初见一丈青,恨不得便捉过来,谁想斗到十合之上,看看的手颤脚麻,枪法便都乱了。不是两个性命相扑时,王矮虎却要做光火起来。那一丈青是个乖觉的人,心中道:'这厮无理'!"

另一位不可比拟的战士。他鲁莽性急，诚实可靠，维护弱小，在不断的追逐中加入了农民军队。小说作者的人物描写是如此卓越，直到今天，宋江、李逵和其他英雄仍然活在千百万读者的心中。①

冯沅君通过对几位梁山英雄的分析来研究、批评水浒人物的描写，其关注的还是为数不多的"点"而没有达到比较完全的"面"的高度。她说小说作者的人物描写艺术卓越，这没错；但与菲茨杰拉德一样认为"小说作者赋予每一个人物鲜明的个性"，这就过了。

英语世界的学者认为《水浒传》的人物塑造艺术达到了高度的"典型化"、"个性化"的水准，这在一定程度上来说是对的。但我们也要看到小说作者在人物描写中存在的问题，并对之作出辩证的分析、思考。如果只是一味地肯定，得出的看法、观点就难免片面、失实。

二、水浒人物塑造的"模式化"论

与赛珍珠、菲茨杰拉德等人完全充分肯定《水浒传》人物描写的艺术成就不同，英语世界的另外一些批评者认为，《水浒传》中除少数人物外大部分都是"模式化"（stereotyped）的形象。这种论点基本上是在20世纪50年代之后兴起的。据其原因，这可能与西方学者对《水浒传》的进一步了解、研究是密切相关的。如詹姆斯·克伦普（James I. Crump）所说，在50年代之前，西方学界真正看过《水浒传》这部小说的人还是很少的（"few had seen it at work"）②。当西方学界的研究者对《水浒传》的真实情形了解得更多、更全面之后，在具体的批评过程中他们也就不再以他人马首是瞻。发生这种变化，更主要的原因或许还在批评者自身的学术观念结构与知识背景方面。当然，这只是论者的推测，事实是否如此并不确然。

英语世界对《水浒传》的人物塑造持"模式化"、"类型化"论的批评者中，赖明是一个典型。1964年，赖明所著《中国文学史》在纽约出版。该论著在讨论《水浒传》中梁山108人的描写问题时，赖明指出：

---

① Feng Yuanjun, An Outline History of Classical Chinese Literature, translated by Yang Xianyi and Gladys Yang, HongKong: Joint Publishing Co., 1983, pp. 82 - 83.

② James I. Crump, A Sherwood in Kiangsu (Book Review), Chicago Review, 12: 1 (1958: Spring), p. 62.

第三章 英语世界对《水浒传》的人物形象塑造研究

除李逵、鲁智深和武松，其他人物描写得并不好。很明显，他们之中的大部分人都是用来凑足三十六"天罡星"与七十二"地煞星"之数的。其他人像吴用、公孙胜等，是模式化的形象（stereotyped characters）。这帮人的领袖，晁盖这个形象，从来没有活现过。即使是深受这个团伙的每一个强人欢迎的宋江，也从没有全面地展现出来。①

赖明的批评与菲茨杰拉德的观点可谓截然相反。如果说这是对菲茨杰拉德等人看法的纠正，又不免矫枉过正，走向了另一个极端。梁山108人中，的确有一些描写得相当模糊。公孙胜可以说是一个模式化的人物，严格说晁盖也可以归入其中。但说宋江这个形象"从没有全面地展现出来"，笔者实不敢苟同。在《水浒传》这部小说中，作者着墨最多的一个人物毫无疑问就是宋江。自第18回"宋公明私放晁天王"到第100回"宋公明神聚蓼儿洼"，宋江形象的丰富性、复杂性与人格的内在矛盾性是一步一步展现在读者眼前的。从黑白两道通吃的刀笔小吏到远走他乡的逃犯，从誓死不愿落草的孝子到流放江州的罪犯，从渴盼刑满回归正常生活的常人到逼上梁山的英雄（强人）首领，从接受招安、征战四方到封疆一域的忠臣，直至最后被毒死的结局，宋江这一形象在作者笔下如剥茧抽丝一般层层展现在读者眼前；其性格的发展、内心的矛盾，其在儒家思想与侠义精神两种不同文化之间纠缠、挣扎的灵魂，最终导致他必然走向悲剧的命运。所有这一切在《水浒传》里显得是那么的自然，完全是循着宋江内在的心理发展轨迹在书写，其命运结局可谓水到渠成。

海陶伟（James R. Hightower）虽然没有直接批评说《水浒传》的人物描写是"模式化"、"类型化"的，其观点却和赖明很接近。他说：

这班强人循着他们成员各自不同的历史汇聚到一起，但他们反抗社会却不是个人性的主张。社会的腐败，对老实人权利的剥夺，迫使他们开始以更接近于理想的模式来组织自己的社会。真正个性主义者的唯一范例是拥有金子般内心的暴徒，喜剧式的人物鲁达。[The only example of a real individualist is the comic ruffian-with-a-heart-of-gold (Lu-

---

① Lai Ming, *A History of Chinese Literature*, NewYork: John Day & Co., 1964, p.294.

Ta)]。只因太过天真无邪，意识不到自己行为的后果，因而无论身处何地，他总是按照自己的内心冲动行事。空拳攻击一个屠户后，他略显不安地站在那人旁边，假旁观者的身份说"别诈死"，并寻思道："谁曾想三拳竟打死了他！"即使完全无拘无束，他还是难得这样把个体的不安情绪具体化。①

在海陶伟看来，梁山众人的反抗社会只是一种集体的、无意识的被动行为，缺乏真正意义上的个性。即使像鲁达这样的"真正个性主义者的唯一范例"，《水浒传》这部小说也不是总能够把他的个性具体展现出来。其他人物就更加没有个性可言了。或许可以这样说，在海陶伟的批评视域中，梁山英雄人物在人格方面基本上是被动型、集体型的。相比于西方文学传统中描写出来的那种个性张扬的人物，《水浒传》所塑造出来的形象就只能是一种"模式化"、"类型化"的形象。

在《水浒传》人物塑造艺术成就的评价上，相比于赛珍珠、菲茨杰拉德等人的高度肯定态度和赖明、海陶伟等的基本否定态度，毕晓普的批评算是比较客观、公正的，与《水浒传》这部小说总体呈现出来的人物描写的基本情况相符合。毕晓普说："《水浒传》这部小说，期待他（指西方读者，笔者注）跟随一百零八位英雄的故事前行。在这些英雄中，超过三分之一的人物是主要角色。"②

对水浒英雄，李培德等人也认为："他（《水浒传》的作者，笔者注）可能受困于作品中大量的人物形象，描写的人物大部分是缺乏发展或是类型化的。"同时，他们又提出，"虽然大部分英雄人物是类型化的，但有一些还是有很好的个性发展。"③ 相对来说，这种观点是经过比较全面、理性的分析得出来的，也是与作品本身比较契合的。

---

① James R. Hightower, *Individualism in Chinese Literature*, Journal of the History of Ideas, Vol. 22, No. 2 (Apr. - Jun., 1961), pp. 167 – 168.

② John L. Bishop, *Some Limitations of Chinese Fiction*, Far Eastern Quarterly, 15: 2 (1956: Feb.), p. 242.

③ He may also be distuebed by its large cast of characters, many of whom are undeveloped or stereotyped.... although most heroes are stereotypes, some are well developed individuals. Winston L. Y. Yang, Nathan K. Mao and Peter Li, "Romance of the Three Kingdoms and The Water Margin," and "Journey to the West and Flowers in the Mirror.", Classical Chinese Fiction: A Guide to Its Study and Appreciation. London: George Prior Publishers, 1978. p. 43. Rpt. in Literature Criticism from 1400 to 1800. Ed. Lynn M. Zott. Vol. 76. Detroit: Gale, 2002. Literature Resource Center. Web. 11 Sep., 2012.

然而，上述诸人的评价，是客观公正的也好，是夸张失实的也罢，在跨异质文化圈的《水浒传》人物塑造研究中，印象式的批评是解决不了任何问题的。如果不抓住关键要素、找定适合的标准来分析水浒人物形象的特征，并在此基础上评价《水浒传》在人物形象描写艺术上所取得的成就，结果往往只会带来更大的混乱。因为作为中国文学传统的产物，《水浒传》的人物描写有其自身别具一格的手法，水浒人物形象有其特殊的民族品质，自然也会形成其独有的文本表现特征与审美形式规律。

三、中西小说比较与西方小说观念视域中的水浒人物塑造研究

中西文学传统，在理论观念与创作手法等方面的差别甚大，这是一个客观事实。相比于西方小说，中国古典长篇小说的人物描写可谓大异其趣。赛珍珠在"中国小说"[①] 研究文章中就曾指出下述两个重要的方面：

首先，中国古典长篇小说"人物众多"，千头万绪，不同人物之间往往存在千丝万缕的关系。按赛珍珠的说法就是，"这些中国小说"，"人物也过于拥挤"[②]。就《水浒传》来说，的确如此。梁山108人外，像高俅、蔡京、童贯、宿元景、梁世杰、慕容知府、蔡九、黄文炳等大大小小的政府官僚就数以十计，而像郓哥、唐牛儿、金氏父女、郑屠、牛二、潘金莲、西门庆、王婆、白秀英、潘巧云、裴如海等有名无名的次要人物就更加多。这些人物，通过偶然或必然的事件又走在一起。

其次，在中国古典长篇小说这种"枝节过多""情节特别复杂"的叙事文体中，不仅"人物众多"，有时候还出现这样的情况，那就是：有些人物"出现了一会儿，却在接下来的几章中消失，一直到小说结尾处才又不经意地露面，或者干脆就不再出现，有关线索就断在那里"[③]。其结果，不仅使小说情节缺乏连贯性，人物形象也显得很模糊不清。《水浒传》里，"私走延安府"的禁军教头王进，"三打祝家庄"时走失的栾廷玉，就是此种现象的典型。

---

① 赛珍珠所说的"中国小说"是一个特定的范畴。按其在诺贝尔文学奖授奖仪式上的演讲内容就是："我说中国小说时指的是地道的中国小说，不是指那些杂牌的产品，即现代中国作家所写的那些小说。"

② Pearl S. Buck, *The Chinese Novel: Nobel Lecture Delivered before the Swedish Academy at Stockholm*, December 12, 1938 (NewYork: The John Day Company), p. 32.

③ Pearl S. Buck, *The Early Chinese Novel*, The Satueday Review of Literature, No. 46, Vol. 7, 1931.

以《水浒传》等为代表的中国古典长篇小说在人物描写中存在的上述现象,按赛珍珠之论,"对西方评论界来说"则是明显的缺点。赛珍珠也提出,中国小说中"这种支离破碎本身是否就是对生活的模仿"这一问题值得深入思考;她还认为,"中国小说缺乏情节连贯性,也许就是一种技巧"①。即使如此,对那些习惯了西方小说人物描写艺术手法的欧美读者,甚至是那些研究中国文学的西方专家们,要他们来鉴赏中国小说描写的人物形象,或者对中国小说人物描写的艺术性问题作出符合文本实际的评价,就会比较艰难。艾尔博(Charles J. Alber)就指出,海陶伟和赖明之所以认为水浒人物绝大部分是"模式化"的,就是因为他们被《水浒传》人物描写的中国文学传统特征所"困惑"②。很遗憾的是,这几位批评者并没有意识到自己在研究中存在的这个问题。

正因为英语世界的学者们在《水浒传》等中国小说人物研究时遇到了这样的困惑,他们中的一些批评者就试图通过中西小说人物描写的比较,来探讨中西小说各自在人物描写中的不同特征,以更好地认识、把握中国小说在人物塑造方面的艺术特色。

1956年,毕晓普发表《中国小说的某些局限》一文。其中,他专门讨论了以《水浒传》等为代表的中国古典小说与西方小说在人物描写方面的差异。他指出:

> 在人物的描写问题上,中国小说和西方小说之间的差异是明显的。两种文学都试图以现实主义的方法来描写社会典型,但它们之间的差别是有程度之分的。两者皆利用对话作为区别人物个性与社会地位的手段。然而,西方小说更加彻底地探索人物的心理,而且长期以来精通此道,这使整部小说只限于表现个人心理活动变得可能,像维吉尼亚·伍尔芙与詹姆斯·乔伊斯的创作就是这样。但对中国小说家而言,只是在必要时,他才会对笔下人物的心理过程作探讨,而且探讨时还那样小心翼翼。由于这个原因,他运用现实小说的主要关注点之一(表象与现实之间的差异)的能力就受到很大的限制;因为他

---

① Pearl S. Buck, *The Early Chinese Novel*, The Satueday Review of Literature, No. 46, Vol. 7, 1931.

② Charles J. Alber, A Survey of English language Criticism of the Shui-hu Chuan. Tsing Hua Journal of Chinese Studies. Vol. 2 (1969), p. 107.

极少向我们展示他笔下人物所说与所想之间的巨大差异。①

在研究中,罗伯特·鲁尔曼(Robert Ruhlmann)表达了与毕晓普相似的观点。他指出,在《水浒传》《三国演义》等中国传统小说中,英雄的"个性总是为英雄特征的强调作出牺牲。英雄一出场,其形象是相当的淳朴、鲜明、心思专一,毫不犹豫就作出决定。只是在作品里面,极少展现英雄的心理发生、发展过程"②。在具体讨论宋江这一"帝王型英雄"(prince)时,鲁尔曼说,虽然这是一种比较特殊的英雄人物,他们出身奇特,经历丰富多彩。只是由于这些英雄人物身上的共性太明显,小说、戏剧在描写他们时又往往呈现出公式化的特点。按鲁尔曼之说即是:

> 小说、戏剧虽然描写这种人的个性特征,但在叙述他们登上权力宝座的关键阶段常常是采用一种固定的方式:开始时,他必定是一个强人(strong man),在一个兵荒马乱的年代担负起保护一方百姓的重任;他那寥寥无几的追随者逐渐滚雪球般发展壮大成一支军队,最终占居各省乃至全国。其成功,一半是通过战争与协商的方式所取得,一半也因为个人的神奇魅力,使他赢得所有他所遇见的人的自发的支持。③

毕晓普、鲁尔曼虽然以西方小说的观念与创作手法为参照系,来批评中国小说在人物描写方面的局限,但相对于印象式的评价来说,这种研究已经深入了很多。事实上,中国古典小说确实很少像西方小说那样对人物的心理活动展开描写。这可以说是中国古典小说的一个特征。至于这是优点或是缺点,并不是三言两语所能说得清楚的。就接受效果来讲,中西小说中描写成功的人物形象在各自文化圈里都拥有良好的读者群体;即使在异质文化圈中,不少人物形象也能获得众多读者的欢迎。拿梁山英雄中的鲁智深(鲁达)来说,在中国他可谓家喻户晓的人物;在英语世界,鲁

---

① John L. Bishop, *Some Limitations of Chinese Fiction*, Far Eastern Quarterly, 15: 2 (1956: Feb.), p. 245.
② Robert Ruhlmann, Traditional Heroes in Chinese Popular Fiction, The Confucian Persuasion, ed. by Arthur F. Wright (California: Stanford University Press, 1960), pp. 149–150.
③ Robert Ruhlmann, Traditional Heroes in Chinese Popular Fiction, The Confucian Persuasion, ed. by Arthur F. Wright (California: Stanford University Press, 1960), p. 157.

智深同样受到广大读者的喜爱。1872—1873年,鲁智深"倒拔垂杨柳"、"大闹野猪林"的故事就以《中国巨人历险记》为标题翻译成了英文,被介绍到了西方世界;20世纪20年代,翟理思在论著《中国文学史》中,特地把"鲁智深大闹五台山"的故事介绍给西方读者。在英语世界的批评者那里,鲁智深也获得广泛关注。上述诸人外,刘若愚(James J. Y. Liu)把鲁智深看作"侠客精神的最杰出典范"[1],此评价可谓相当高。当然,英语世界里也不免有批评者以一种"猎奇"的心态来研究中国小说中的人物形象,前面提到的海陶伟就是一例。他就以为鲁智深只是一个"意识不到自己行为后果"的"天真无邪"的人,而没有认识到他身上所具有的那种疾恶如仇、行侠仗义的高贵品质。

笔者承认,与印象式的批评相比,毕晓普等人的研究是深入了很多。但以"形象塑造的心里成熟度"为标准,来研究《水浒传》的人物描写,来评价中国古典小说在人物描写上所取得的艺术成就,这明显是西方中心主义氛围中的一种学术偏见,是一种很不可取的学术态度。艾尔博在回顾、总结20世纪70年代之前的英语批评《水浒传》的历史时就指出:

> 在他们(指赖明、海陶伟等,笔者注)对中国小说"人物心理不成熟"的观察上,这些批评者的观点几乎是一致的。很明显,他们并不认为《水浒传》是个例外。他们迫使我们去接受一个这样的理论——如贝克(Baker)所提出的,那就是在故事与小说之间存在区别。故事里,个性之外人物形象必须拥有更多的东西。[2]

中国古代,"白话小说作者"的确是"把他热情的眼睛放在'动作'(movement)上,把他灵敏的耳朵放在'日常生活语言'(the speech of daily life)上",并以此作为"区分他所虚构人物形象"的描写方式与手段[3],但就可以说这是中国古典小说人物描写艺术上的一种"缺陷"(lack)吗?笔者在上文已经说过,中国古典小说确实很少像西方小说那

---

[1] James J. Y. Liu, The Chinese Knight-Errant, (Chicago: University of Chicago Press, 1967), p. 113.

[2] Charles J. Alber, A Survey of English language Criticism of the Shui-hu Chuan. Tsing Hua Journal of Chinese studies. Vol. 2 (1969), p. 108.

[3] John L. Bishop, *Some Limitations of Chinese Fiction*, Far Eastern Quarterly, 15: 2 (1956: Feb.), pp. 245 – 246.

样对人物的心理活动展开描写。至于这是优点或是缺点,并不是三言两语所能说得清楚的。就接受效果来讲,中西小说中描写成功的人物形象在各自文化圈里都拥有良好的读者群体;即使在异质文化圈中,不少人物形象也能获得众多读者的欢迎。

西方小说的发展——不管是毕晓普欣赏的"法国小说"还是"英国小说",的确在人物心理的发掘上具有比较悠久而成功的历史。至于他提出,"心理分析的局限似乎是影响中国小说发展的一种社会因素";中国文学中,"贵族气派的、女性的传统这一支的缺失",或者"在文学语言或白话小说文体中女性作家的缺乏",等等,是造成中国小说"人物心理不成熟"的因素[①],所有这些问题都需要进一步深入探讨。

上述事实告诉我们,运用比较的方法来寻找、探究中西文学传统中各自小说人物描写的特征,并不能解决研究过程存在的问题。因为如果英语世界的研究者仅以西方文学批评的理论、观念作为研究中国小说的标准,只作一种单向度的阐发,而不从中国文学传统中进行纵向的考察,这样的研究极可能存在很大的偏见,甚至会提出错误的看法与观点。因为此种削足适履的研究方法与批评行为,根本无法比较客观、真实、全面地展现出中国小说人物描写的原貌。

上述现象同时也揭示出这样一个本质性问题,那就是在英语世界的不少批评者眼中,中国小说是无法与西方小说相媲美的。因为在他们看来,中国小说的发展远落后于西方小说。就如毕晓普所说,中国小说与西方小说,"它们之间的差别是有程度之分的"。此话虽然说得有些含糊,但该论者内心所隐藏的西方小说优越论还是相当明显的。按这些论者的看法,如果说西方小说已进化到现代意义的水平,其人物描写已进化到充分的心理探索的高度;那么,中国小说尚处于讲故事的初级阶段,中国小说作者仍然需要通过"行为"和"语言"的描写来塑造人物。总之,西方小说是优越于中国小说的。也正是由于这样的心态,英语世界的不少批评者虽然在谈"中国小说的特征"(the characteristic of Chinese fiction),但他们在中国小说人物描写的具体研究过程中却并未真正进入"中国文学传统"(the tradition of Chinese novel)之中。而他

[①] John L. Bishop, *Some Limitations of Chinese Fiction*, Far Eastern Quarterly, 15:2 (1956: Feb.), p. 246.

们所说的"中国小说的特征",也只不过是西方文学批评理论、概念映照下的一个副产品。

四、中国文学传统的凸显与水浒人物塑造研究的深化

前面讨论的英语世界的水浒人物描写研究,不管是"典型化"论抑或是"模式化"论,不管是以西方小说的批评标准来谈论中国小说人物描写的特征与缺陷,在笔者看来,都只是游离于中国文学传统之外的中国文学研究。因为他们对《水浒传》这样的中国小说在人物描写方面的特殊性,根本没有给予关注。艾尔博在批评他们的研究时就指出:

> 上面提到的对《水浒传》的批评(指以赛珍珠、菲茨杰拉德为代表的"典型化"论,以赖明为代表的"模式化"论,及毕晓普等以西方小说的批评标准来谈论中国小说人物描写的特征与缺陷的研究行为。笔者注),几乎没有为我们理解他们所批评的作品带来任何帮助。他们,不是以模式化来界定人物,就是强调人物描写技巧的局限。只是,他们根本没有专门关注过中国小说人物描写的特殊性。[1]

艾尔博的批评可谓一针见血。任何民族、国家的文学都有其独特的发展历史,也有其自身别具一格的创作技法与审美形式。研究中国小说的人物描写艺术及其所取得的成就,需要外部的标的作为参照,这是无可厚非的。但不能仅仅以外部的参照系作为品评好坏、优劣的标准,更应该进入该文学自身的传统与历史发展进程来考量、研究,然后作出评价。也就是说,在研究中,我们既需要横向的比较,也需要纵向的审视。且在横向的比较中,也必须有历史的概念,而不能仅仅以现代的标准去批评、指责古人,要求他们的创作达到今人的认识水平。只有这样,才可能获得比较客观公正的认识。我国学者徐顺生在中西小说人物形象的研究中就曾指出,与《水浒传》等中国古代小说基本处于同一发展阶段的西方小说,如塞万提斯的《堂吉诃德》、笛福的《鲁滨孙漂流记》,基本上都是"通过人

---

[1] Charles J. Alber, A Survey of English Language Criticism of the Shui-hu Chuan. Tsing Hua Journal of Chinese Studies. Vol. 2 (1969), p. 108.

物的语言和行动表现人物的性格特征","它们都体现出在行动中刻画人物的鲜明特点"①。

英语世界的某些批评者,也认识到从中国文学传统与中国小说发展历史进程来研究《水浒传》人物描写的重要性。欧文是其中的一个重要人物。在论著《一部中国小说的演变:〈水浒传〉》里,通过对林冲、鲁智深、柴进、雷横等人"逼上梁山"故事的分析,欧文指出:

> 在人物命运的描写上(他们的任务,是充当人民大众与奴役他们的那些滥用职权的少数派之间斗争的先锋),这部小说远远超越了它之前的作品。从文学技巧的角度来看,这部小说所取得的最大成就源自人物描写,最突出的表现就是宋江与李逵之间关系的处理。……从初次相逢开始,由于性格上的不同,他们就性情相投、相互吸引。他们之间关系的发展,贯穿小说过程。这是心理洞察力的一个证据,应该得到最高的赞扬。②

欧文之分析虽然不够具体详尽,但他已明确认识到《水浒传》的作者对人物心理把握的内在洞察力,并对其给予充分肯定。而不是像赖明那样,认为"对中国小说家而言,只是在必要时,他才会对笔下人物的心理过程作探讨,而且探讨时还那样小心翼翼"。事实上,《水浒传》中,在人物心理上,作者把握的最准确、描写的最精彩、最令人印象深刻的,笔者以为还是"武十回"里的潘金莲。而且在小说作者笔下,潘金莲也并非天生荡妇。她的性格是一步一步得到发展的,她的悲剧命运是社会大环境一手造成的。

海陶伟虽然说《水浒传》描写的反抗社会并不是个人性的主张,梁山108人中只有鲁达是"真正个性主义的典范";在研究中,他还是认为:"中国大部分的虚构作品,特别是小说,属于另一个文学传统。"而且他还对毕晓普的观点进行了批评。他说:"如约翰·毕晓普所评论的,'细节繁多,努力于复制社会大宇宙而不是去探索人类的微观世界,这似

---

① 徐顺生:《中西小说人物形象与表现方法比较》,见饶芃子等《中西小说比较》,安徽教育出版社1994年版,第105—113页。
② Richard Gregg Irwin, The Evolution of A Chinese Novel: *Shui-hu-chuan*, Cambridge, Mass.: Harvard University Press, 1953, pp. 45–46.

乎是中国小说的一个特征'。这种看法对短篇虚构小说是切实的。"① 此批评不管正确与否，该论者已明确认识到英语世界的学者在中国小说研究中存在的问题。海陶伟在研究中进一步指出："《水浒传》里，一帮法外强人在'忠义'的旗帜下，做出破坏性行为，却并没有反讽的意味。"② 与浦安迪从"反讽"理论出发来研究《水浒传》的人物描写相比，笔者以为，海陶伟的观点是和小说文本实际比较一致的，是与小说作者的创作动机比较契合的。(在1987年出版的专著《明代小说四大奇书》中，浦安迪以"反讽"理论作为研究的立足点，把水浒英雄分成反面人物与正面人物两大类。具体内容笔者将在本章相应部分进行论述)

汉斯·弗兰克（Hans H. Frankle），另一位英语世界的学者，他在考察中国小说与西方小说在批评方法上的冲突时指出：

> 运用于现代文学批评中的观念、标准，并不适用于中国小说的研究。因为中国小说的运行有一套完全不同于我们的关于个性的理论。简要来说即是，传统中国理论并不把人物个性看作是一个发生、发展的过程，而这恰好是现代西方小说的首要关注点。在中国人的观念里，一种人格（个性）有一种既定的模型，它只在人们的生活过程中逐渐展现出来。一种人格（个性）模型能够被行家里手所识别。而且个性的逐渐展现，在早期阶段就能为他们预料到。③

在讨论中，弗兰克不仅指出跨异质文化圈之间文学批评观念、标准的适用性问题，他还从中国文学传统的个性理论出发，指出中国小说人物描写特征的形成原因，以及批评观念、标准适用性问题产生的根源。这已经进入中国文化比较核心的范畴。

笔者认为，中国文化中，在认识人的性格、命运方面，有两个因素发挥了极大的影响。一是宗教世界里的因果报应思想，二是俗世社会中的身份等级观念。此两者的结合，形成了对中国人影响极大的命定观。所谓

---

① James R. Hightower, *Individualism in Chinese Literature*, Journal of the History of Ideas, Vol. 22, No. 2 (Apr.-Jun., 1961), p. 167.
② Ibid.
③ Hans H. Frankel, The Chinese Novel: a Confrontation of Critical Approaches to Chinese and Western Novels, Literature East and West, Vol. 8, 1964, p. 2.

"龙生龙凤生凤",是此观念的最世俗化表述。而这种既定的、因果的命运观,对中国小说的创作、对人物形象的描写,影响是非常大的。《水浒传》里的108好汉,不管他们在上梁山之前是干什么的,因为合着三十六天罡、七十二地煞之数,最终他们都走上反抗之路。因为这就是他们的命运,而他们终其一生就是把这种性格、命运逐渐展现出来。其实,在"洪太尉误走妖魔"的神话叙述中,梁山好汉的反抗型人格及其命运就已经安排好了。《水浒传》的这种人物描写,按弗兰克所说就是:"在中国人的观念里,一种人格(个性)有一种既定的模型,它只在人们的生活过程中逐渐展现出来。"此看法拿来分析鲁智深、林冲、武松、李逵等人物形象,是相当契合的。

在研究中,弗兰克进一步把《水浒传》等中国古代小说界定为"人物型小说"(The Figurenroman)。他指出,"这种小说围绕着单一人格(性格)(a single personality)的发展而展开";而西方学者解决对"人物型小说认识的不足的办法",就得抓住人物描写的这种"围绕着单一人格(性格)的发展而展开"的特点①。按此说,笔者以为,在西方小说发展的早期阶段,像拉伯雷的《巨人传》、塞万提斯的《堂吉诃德》等就是典型的"人物型小说"。庞大固埃也好、堂吉诃德也罢,他们都属于弗兰克所说的"单一人格(性格)"的人物形象。

本节,笔者从总体上梳理了英语世界对《水浒传》(以及中国古典小说)人物描写艺术的评价态度。赞扬者称其在人物描写上达到了高度的"个性化"、"典型化"的水准,即使是次要角色也写得活灵活现、个性鲜明。批评者则认为,除了少数几个角色,其他绝大部分都是"模式化"的人物形象。批评者还指出,中国古典小说的作者在人物心理的挖掘上缺乏技巧,导致小说中的人物都是"心理未成熟的形象",而这种缺陷也成了"影响中国小说发展一种社会因素"。有少数几位研究者则从历史的视域出发,通过对中国小说发展的纵向审视与中西小说特征的横向比较,充分肯定了《水浒传》人物描写艺术在中国小说发展史上的地位;同时,他们也认识到中国文学传统中个性(人格)理论的独特性,该理论形成的社会历史文化根源,以及对中国小说创作与中国小说审美特征的影响。

---

① Hans H. Frankel, The Chinese Novel: a Confrontation of Critical Approaches to Chinese and Western Novels, Literature East and West, Vol. 8, 1964, p. 5.

总的来说，英语世界的批评者对水浒人物描写的研究有一个逐渐深入的过程；同时，有的批评者提出的观点也存在相互矛盾的地方。出现这种现象，一方面与该论者对《水浒传》认识的逐渐深入有关，另一方面也和《水浒传》这部作品内容的丰富、复杂以及思想的内在矛盾有关。

当然，《水浒传》在人物形象的塑造上的确存在不足，这是毋庸讳言的。美籍华裔学者夏志清在研究水浒英雄人物形象时指出：

> 一百零八将中有较完整的故事的依次有鲁智深、林冲、杨志、宋江、武松、李逵、石秀和燕青。真正堪称大手笔的当推鲁智深、武松、李逵以及林冲的故事。除了宋江、李逵是例外，大部分好汉最令人难忘的经历都发生在上梁山前。一旦上山聚义，大家就都成了区别不大的带兵头领，其形象就不再那么分明。没羽箭张清的形象倒颇有点浪漫的色彩，但却是一成不变的，没有什么发展。在小说家未把英雄们陷入臆造历史的泥潭之前，英雄们基本上生活在一个充满传奇式冒险的世界里。他们或当军官，或充衙吏，或为商贩、店主，或做窃贼、娼优，或是僧人、道士。他们组成了一个比《三国》写的天地丰富得多，也生动得多的人间世界。正是这个熙熙攘攘并且常常是野蛮的世界，使《水浒》迸发出不同凡响的包含人生真谛的气息。①

笔者认为，从《水浒传》这部小说呈现出的总体情况来看，夏志清对该作品在人物描写上所取得成就及存在的问题进行的评价是比较中肯的。水浒英雄人物，个性鲜明者有，形象类同者也有；上梁山之前不少人物是个性化的，上梁山之后绝大部分都类型化了。作者把这些人物当作传奇性的江湖英雄来描写时，他们是栩栩如生的；当作者把他们放进历史的框架之中、作为皇帝之臣属时，梁山好汉则失去了其有血有肉的一面，也就失去了其作为个体存在的生活气息，而成为征战四方厮杀疆场的工具。

第二节 中国传统社会权力结构中的水浒英雄人物研究

上一节，笔者从总体上梳理、分析了英语世界对《水浒传》人物描

---

① [美]夏志清：《中国古典小说》，胡益民等译，江苏文艺出版社2008年版，第83—84页。

写艺的评价,并对各种观点发表了自己的看法。笔者以为,在这些评价之中,可取之处固然不少,可商榷的地方也存在。这在上文已讨论过,不再赘述。

从本节始到第三节,笔者将从研究视角切入,分析英语世界《水浒传》人物形象的分类研究情况。水浒人物,按其社会身份地位之不同,按作者情感倾向之差异,按读者阅读、接受效果之区别,可以分为多种类型。通过考察英语世界水浒人物类型研究的实际状况,笔者发现,其划分人物类型的依据主要有两种:一是水浒人物在社会权力结构中的地位归属,这是罗伯特·鲁尔曼、李培德等人的研究视角;二是现代小说反讽理论观照之下水浒人物的品行差异与角色身份,这是浦安迪、夏志清等人的研究视角。本节,笔者将就中国传统社会权力结构中的水浒英雄人物研究展开论述。至于反讽理论观照下的水浒人物研究则留待本章第三节讨论。

然而,不管从哪一视角来研究水浒英雄,有一个问题是无法逃避的,那就是他们身上充满矛盾。孙康宜在研究中指出:

> 作者采用不同的视角来描写这些英雄人物,因而在他们身上矛盾的品质特征常常可见。他们大多反抗贪官,信守兄弟结义,相信"四海之内皆兄弟"。他们几乎都武艺高强,路见不平拔刀相助。但同时,他们又是冷酷的杀手,施行暴力毫不犹豫。[①]

《水浒传》在英雄人物描写时出现的这种复杂性和矛盾性,为批评者从不同的视角切入研究这些人物形象提供了一定的空间。然而,也正是这种复杂性和矛盾性,又使人们不管从哪一角度展开研究都不尽然。笔者将在下文指出此现象。

一、英雄的文化含义与特征

从总体来看,中国古典小说绝大部分是以处于社会权力结构中的帝王

[①] The author adopts widely divergent perspectives on heroism, so that contradictory qualities are often found in the same person. Rebels against corrupt government, the out-laws are nevertheless totally committed to brotherhood, believing that "all men are brothers." Nearly all are experts in the martial arts and are dedicated to righting the wrongs of those who are unjustly treated. At the same time, they are merciless killers who will not hesitate to commit acts of extreme violence. The Cambridge History of Chinese Literature, Edited by Kang-I Sun Chang, Stephen Owen, Cambridge University Press, 2010, Vol. 2, p. 54.

将相以及他们的事迹为描写对象。这不仅因为中国古典小说的发展深受高度发达的史传传统的影响,而且在大部分中国人的思想中,小说往往是普通百姓对历史的一种叙述与认识,是民间观念的一种呈现方式。正因此,小说这种"街谈巷语"的东西也就成了与官方正史相对的"稗官野史"。中国历史的撰写,除司马迁在《史记》中以相对平民精神为侠客立传外,其他史书基本上都是为处于社会权力结构中的高层人物立传的。因而,人们也就往往从社会权力结构这一视角来谈论小说里的人物形象,谈论他们的社会身份、地位和他们的性格特征。

《水浒传》描写的宋江等36人虽然有史迹可考,但他们主要还是一群生活在社会中下层的草莽英雄;小说作者虽然花费很多笔墨来描写他们异于常人的人生事迹,但水泊梁山却是一个与封建社会体制存在巨大差别的江湖世界;《水浒传》里所描写的人物,除宋徽宗、蔡京、高俅、童贯等外,绝大部分也并非严格意义上的社会权力结构中的帝王将相。但在此种大环境之下,从历史的、社会权力结构的视角来研究《水浒传》里的英雄人物类型也就成为很正常的现象。这不仅是国人的讨论视角,英语世界的批评家罗伯特·鲁尔曼、李培德等人也是从这一角度切入研究《水浒传》等中国古典小说的英雄形象的。

1960年,鲁尔曼撰写的长文《中国通俗小说中的传统英雄人物》(*Traditional Heroes in Chinese Popular Fiction*)出版①。该文主要分析、研究宋元以降至清代——尤其集中在元明两朝我国通俗叙事文学中的传统英雄人物形象。而其中,作者又用了很大部分的笔墨来讨论《水浒传》里的英雄人物。

在分析研究《水浒传》等中国通俗小说里的英雄人物之前,鲁尔曼先对英雄的文化含义与特征展开了讨论。鲁尔曼认为,文学艺术对英雄形象的描写、塑造具有很特别的意蕴。他指出:

> 文学艺术中的英雄人物,不仅表达了独特的作者们个人的主张和梦想,他们还把时行的价值观念与理想具体化了。而且作品中英雄人

---

① 罗伯特·鲁尔曼文章标题为 *Traditional Heroes in Chinese Popular Fiction*,收入 Arther F. Wright 所编 *The Confucioan Persuasion* 一书。该文20世纪70年代由中国香港学者朱志泰翻译成中文,标题为《中国通俗小说戏剧中的传统英雄人物》,收入《英美学人论中国古典文学》一书,1973年由香港中文大学出版社出版。本书借鉴了朱志泰的翻译,特此说明。

物的描写也把当时社会中不同势力之间的冲突有力地刻画了出来。这些声名显赫的人物，既是超人又有人性；他们的人格激励、鼓舞人们仿效，创造或是复兴各种行为风尚，因而在历史的形成中担当着重要的角色。①

鲁尔曼的论述，特别强调英雄人物在社会上的影响力，以及他们对历史发展的作用。这是英雄崇拜的体现。笔者以为，在文明史以前，人类的英雄崇拜是纯粹的对原始的自然力量的向往与追求；而在文明社会里，人们的英雄崇拜则在对原始自然力量向往与追求的基础上，把重心转向了对社会权力的渴望和追逐。因而，英雄总是与力量和权力纠缠在一起。这也就决定了英雄不同于常人的独特之处。对此，鲁尔曼说：

> 普通人做事谨小慎微，总是避免与人发生正面冲突，惧怕权贵，往往接受各种妥协建议。英雄则是铮铮铁骨。他们鄙视寻常的成功之道，超越种种挫败那些谨慎胆小、犹豫不决的人们的困境。他们满足了我们内心最深处对自我超越的、意义非凡的生存的想象和期盼。②

这是鲁尔曼对世界文学艺术中英雄人物总体特征的概略描述。具体到中国文化、中国通俗小说与戏剧，鲁尔曼指出，"hero"这个词在中文里相当于"英雄"（ying-hsing，"male," "outstanding man"），古汉语里则是"大丈夫"（ta-chang-fu，"great man"），民间则称作"好汉"（hao-han，"good fellow"）；在小说文本中，"非常人"（fei-ch'ang-jen，"extraordinary man"）一词也广泛使用。③

鲁尔曼在论述中进一步指出，在中国文化与文学里，上述词汇是有特定含义的。他说：

> 这些词，往往意味着不同寻常的体格或道德力量，旺盛的精力与坚强的意志；或是指为或好或坏的伟大目标而献身，以及不符常规的

---

① Robert Ruhlmann, Traditional Heroes in Chinese Popular Fiction, The Confucian Persuasion, ed. by Arthur F. Wright (California: Stanford University Press, 1960), p.141.
② Ibid., p.150.
③ Ibid..

行为；有时还指异乎寻常的相貌和体型。①

而在鲁尔曼眼里，这些奇异的体貌特征又是极具象征意味的。对此，他指出：

> 在见证于言行事迹之前，它们就显示出英雄内在的伟大之处。英雄们为人热情、感觉敏锐，人格高尚、才华横溢，行事果断高于贤人和智者。他们仁慈、慷慨，不计回报；为了责任与理想，不惜牺牲自己所拥有的最珍贵、最亲近的一切。总之英雄是"超道德的"（supramoral）。②

正是英雄的此种特点，这就决定了中国"通俗叙事文学中英雄故事体裁与'凡尘'（sublunary）故事体裁之间的基本区别"。在鲁尔曼看来，中国文学中的"凡尘"故事，描写的只是现实世界本身，描写的不过是现世中庸常人甚至是"坏人"（evil people）的声色犬马的生活；其中主角即使是具有儒家美德的人物，他们也不过是一些谨小慎微、折中妥协的形象。因此，"凡尘"故事缺乏起码的理想化色彩。③ 英雄故事则不同。"真正的英雄是超越生活中的'真人'（life-size）的"，"他意志坚强，能做成自己想做的事情，克服种种困难和障碍，反对一切的妥协和让步。因此，英雄行为比非英雄行为更能真实地展现出人类的本性和欲望"。④

在鲁尔曼看来，《水浒传》里的武松就是典型的英雄人物。与赫拉克勒斯、诸葛亮等人一样，武松"完成了超人的任务"。"武松轻松把玩三五百斤重的石墩，令旁观者惊叹喝彩：'非凡人也！真天神！'"纵观武松一生所经历的种种遭遇，在他身上，英雄与魔幻已没有明确的界限；而在普通人眼里，通俗小说中的英雄人物如武松，"是神（gods），是魔（genii），或只是超群的人（superior men），并没有一个简单、明

---

① Robert Ruhlmann, Traditional Heroes in Chinese Popular Fiction, The Confucian Persuasion, ed. by Arthur F. Wright（California：Stanford University Press, 1960），p. 150.
② Ibid., p. 151.
③ Ibid..
④ Ibid..

了的答案"。① 人、神、魔的三位一体，这是世界各国文学艺术中英雄人物的共同特点。英雄人物身上的这一特点，也在世界各国、各民族中形成了一种普遍的心理认同意识。按鲁尔曼所说即是："中国与其他地方一样，人们往往把英雄以及他所经历、克服的磨难，视为对人类精神严峻考验的一种象征。"②

总之，在鲁尔曼看来，不管在西方还是在中国，人们对英雄特征、对英雄文化含义的认识与把握其实是相通的。而这种认识和把握，反映在社会意识与民族心理上就是强烈的英雄崇拜。鲁尔曼就是根据中国人的英雄崇拜心理，来划分中国通俗小说中的传统英雄人物类型的。他说：

> 所有阶层的中国人，从孩提时起就习惯于把英雄当作榜样来看。需要的时候，他们之间就援引历史上或是传说中的先例相互勉励。这一事实，为我们研究帝王（the prince）、书生（the scholar）与武士（the swordman）三种英雄典型增添了兴趣。③

如上文所说，在文明社会里，人们的英雄崇拜重心由对原始自然力量的向往与追求转向了对社会权力的渴望和追逐，而英雄则总是与力量和权力纠缠在一起。鲁尔曼将《水浒传》等中国古典小说中的英雄人物划分为帝王、书生和武士，实际上就是把这些人物放置在社会权力结构之中来考察的。

在中国古代社会中，帝王处于权力结构金字塔的顶端，文臣与武将则是其中两大重要支柱。对此，鲁尔曼指出，谋士和武将是统治集团的重要组成部分，两者只是扮演着不同的角色、担当着不同的任务而已。他说：

> 在统治者的下属中，谋士与武将之间的一个重要区别是，前者用智，后者用力。
> 他们是使用不同武器的战士，一者用剑尖杀敌，一者用舌尖、更厉害的则用笔尖杀敌。两者同样大胆勇敢，只是武士是在战场上，书

---

① Robert Ruhlmann, Traditional Heroes in Chinese Popular Fiction, The Confucian Persuasion, ed. by Arthur F. Wright（California：Stanford University Press, 1960），p. 151, 153.
② Ibid., p. 151.
③ Ibid., p. 155.

生一般则在朝廷或是会议中。

在治国平天下的过程中，此两者也担当着不可或缺的、相辅相成的作用。谋士分析形势，制定策略，为君王提供建议；他最终要完成的任务就是让一个安定有序的国家与社会得以建立。而当必须使用暴力，或迫于某种紧急形势的压力而暂时放弃常规方式时，武将则得到君王的召唤。他们一旦放出便发挥所能，自由驰骋沙场，率领军队冲锋陷阵，杀敌不倦。①

鲁尔曼在论述中还指出，在中国通俗叙事文学中，谋士和武将"这两种人物形象形成了一对相反相成的心理模型"，"一者急躁、鲁莽、直爽、坦率，另一则温和、神秘、行为谨慎"②。总之，从行事方式上来看，书生是深思熟虑型的英雄，武士则是"先斩后奏"（"kill first and talk later"）型的英雄。

基于以上认识，鲁尔曼在具体讨论《水浒传》里的人物时，把宋徽宗、宋江二人归入帝王型英雄一类；军师吴用则是书生型英雄的代表；在武士型英雄中，鲁尔曼特别推崇武松、李逵、鲁达、石秀诸人。详细论述如下。

二、帝王型英雄：宋徽宗和宋江

对于帝王这一类型的英雄人物，鲁尔曼指出：

小说中的国王与皇帝，透露出很多人民大众对中国封建专制政体以及对以前的统治者个人的爱憎感情。他们的声望，他们专权为善或是作恶，他们在金宫玉苑中度过的雍容奢华的生活，这些都刺激着民众的想象。③

这段话告诉我们，帝王型英雄存在正面形象和反面形象之分。在他们之中，有"为善"的英明皇帝，也有"作恶"的"昏君"（hun jun,

---

① Robert Ruhlmann, Traditional Heroes in Chinese Popular Fiction, The Confucian Persuasion, ed. by Arthur F. Wright (California: Stanford University Press, 1960), pp. 161 – 162.
② Ibid., pp. 161 – 162.
③ Ibid., p. 155.

"muddle-headed")或"末代昏君"("bad last ruler")。前者获得人们的爱戴,后者则被人诟病斥责。

(一)宋徽宗

《水浒传》里的宋徽宗是典型的昏君形象。鲁尔曼说,在通俗叙事文学中,宋徽宗和唐玄宗一样,都被视为"昏君",是"两个'很坏的'统治者"(two "rather bad" rulers)。"他们虽然没有把江山毁掉,却极大地削弱了国家的实力。此两人都是浪漫型人物(romantic figures),他们的艺术天赋引人瞩目,却缺乏道德操守。"[①] 援引西方心理学家亚瑟·赖特(Arthur Wright)的性格学说理论,鲁尔曼进一步指出,宋徽宗这样的皇帝表现出来的主要是"消极特性"(passive features),例如他"忽视正直官员,袒护贪官污吏,酗酒,懒惰,个人品行不修"等[②]。对宋徽宗做这样的评价,基本上是客观的。

鲁尔曼又提出,宋徽宗这样的统治者"貌似消极,其实超脱"[③]。而这种"貌似消极,其实超脱"的帝王其实只是懦弱无能、不负责任的统治者。因为他沉溺酒色,不理朝政,用人不明,甚至任由奸臣贼子把持朝纲,因而他给国家和百姓带来的往往是灾难性的后果。这一点鲁尔曼在论述中也曾谈到。他说:

> 《水浒传》描写的宋徽宗,酷爱奇石和艺术品,具有字画天赋,喜爱足球(蹴鞠)。但因选人不当、用人不明,这位审美学家并不能维持帝国的太平安定,也不能守卫边疆。朝政腐败,导致宋江、方腊反叛,也刺激金人入侵。这些都是这位艺术家皇帝昏庸无能造成的后果。[④]

根据鲁尔曼的论述,可以这样来评价宋徽宗:他是一位极具天赋的艺术家,却并不是一个称职的皇帝。由于自身的消极特性,他只是奸相(bad minister)手中的玩偶,一个典型的昏君。

[①] Robert Ruhlmann, Traditional Heroes in Chinese Popular Fiction, The Confucian Persuasion, ed. by Arthur F. Wright (California: Stanford University Press, 1960), p. 156.
[②] Ibid., p. 156.
[③] Ibid., p. 157.
[④] Ibid., pp. 156-157.

（二） 宋江

《水浒传》中的另一位帝王型英雄宋江，鲁尔曼给予他非常高的评价，称其为"梁山的'无冕之王'（the "uncrowned king" of Mount Liang）"。同时，鲁尔曼视梁山为一个实质性的新兴独立政权，把宋江当作"王朝奠基者"（founders of dynasties）或者说是"开国皇帝"这一类英雄人物来看待。其实，鲁尔曼把宋江的身份定位得这么高，是受到了司马迁的影响的。司马迁以一种比较平民的精神撰写《史记》，他不仅把秦末农民起义的领袖陈涉归入"世家"一列，还开辟"游侠列传"为国家权力结构之外的英雄立传。司马迁的撰史精神在后来的史官中未获得发扬。对此，鲁尔曼感叹道："自司马迁后，官方正史不再为'侠'（hsia）立传。"① 但这种精神却在民间、在通俗叙事文学中得到继承。

基于上述研究视点，鲁尔曼认为，宋江身上具有刘邦（Liu Pang）、刘备（Liu Pei）、李世民（Li Shih-min）、赵匡胤（Chao K'uang-yin）、朱元璋（Chu Yüan-chang）等王朝奠基者的共同特征。

首先，鲁尔曼认为王朝奠基者基本上都是一些比较特殊的人物。他们的出身奇特，经历丰富多彩。按鲁尔曼之说即是：

> 王朝的奠基者是更为引人瞩目的人物，他们更加接近欧洲英雄国王（hero-king）的典型。一位从乡村或是绿林之中崛起的新人（outsider），经历连续不断的挑战与时常发生的危险，最终登上帝国的宝座。相比于娇生惯养的皇室贵胄所过的单调乏味的生活，他们的经历自然拥有更为丰富多彩的事迹和更加生动传奇的背景。②

因而，当作家们把他们的故事写入通俗文学作品的时候，就显得格外吸引读者。只是由于这些英雄人物身上的共性太明显，小说、戏剧在描写他们时又往往呈现出公式化的特点。对此，鲁尔曼指出：

> 小说、戏剧虽然描写这种人的个性特征，但在叙述他们登上权力

---

① Robert Ruhlmann, Traditional Heroes in Chinese Popular Fiction, The Confucian Persuasion, ed. by Arthur F. Wright (California: Stanford University Press, 1960), p. 172.
② Ibid., p. 157.

宝座的关键阶段常常是采用一种固定的方式：开始时，他必定是一个强人（strong man），在一个兵荒马乱的年代担负起保护一方百姓的重任；他那寥寥无几的追随者逐渐滚雪球般发展壮大成一支军队，最终占据各省乃至全国。其成功，一半是通过战争与协商的方式所取得，一半也因为个人的神奇魅力，使他赢得所有他所遇见的人的自发的支持。①

就《水浒传》所写的宋江来看，该论者所说的这一特征是比较准确的。宋江之身份、经历的确丰富多彩，特别是其个人魅力——那种仗义疏财的义气给他带来的社会威望，更是让江湖人士——不论谋面与否都异常钦佩。

其次，鲁尔曼认为宋江具有绝大部分帝王身上的"消极特性"。这种"消极特性"的形成，与"道家的'无为'（"no intervention against Nature"）理想有关；也和儒家倡导的理念相关，即君王通过昭示其美德以使国家安定和谐，而无须步出宫廷甚至把手伸出衣袖之外"②。

在鲁尔曼的讨论中，昏君之外，帝王身上的"消极特性"并不是一种弱点，而是一种处理人和事的特殊能力。他说：

> 如果不把这种消极无为当作一种弱点而是视其为一种狡猾的计谋，（君王的）能力就能获得部分解释。"哭刘备"（"Cry-baby Liu Pei"，"Ku Liu Pei"）和梁山的"无冕之王"宋江，就经常使用微妙的手段，使部下之间相互牵制以保持平衡；面对强大的人物，他们也是间接地抑制而非公开反对。③

由于王朝奠基者奇特的出身和丰富的经历，按常理来描写、解释他们的生平事迹就显得很不够。因而，作家们在以这些英雄人物及其故事为题材进行创作时，自然或不自然地就在他们身上添加了一些神秘的因素，或者说一种超自然的色彩。在鲁尔曼看来，这是中国通俗文学中王朝奠基者

---

① Robert Ruhlmann, Traditional Heroes in Chinese Popular Fiction, The Confucian Persuasion, ed. by Arthur F. Wright (California: Stanford University Press, 1960), p. 157.
② Ibid., p. 157.
③ Ibid., p. 159.

一类英雄人物的另一特征。对此，他说：

> （对帝王）这种理性的解释显然是不够的。在中国通俗叙事文学中，王朝奠基者往往为一种超自然的神秘氛围所笼罩。出生时，他们的母亲就有梦兆。帝王的高贵命运通常由各种征兆昭示出来，如火球或者飞龙出现在他（们）头顶上空，或是熟睡时一条赤蛇在他（们）的嘴巴、耳朵、鼻子里爬来爬去。年幼时，他（们）就已有成为领袖的先兆。……宋江被差人追捕时，得到九天玄女的庇佑而度过劫难。玄女娘娘授予他三卷论兵法谋略的天书（heavenly book），后来还通过梦对其加以指点。①

总之，鲁尔曼认为，中国通俗叙事文学中的帝王型英雄"基本上是懦弱的人物，放荡、伪善，只是名义上的领袖"。②

为什么在中国通俗叙事文学中，宋徽宗、宋江等帝王型英雄人物会呈现出上述特征呢？此问题鲁尔曼从三个方面进行了阐述：

首先，"叙事文学的作者和演员把典型的统治者塑造成懦弱无能的形象是为了凸显其超凡的个性，说明在人类能力之外统治者尚需要神奇魅力的辅助。"③

其次，"无须明显的努力或壮烈的行动，英雄就能获得他人的效劳拥戴，这种能力是对其威望的最好衡量。"④

最后，"通俗叙事文学常常把典型的统治者塑造成基本上是懦弱的人物，放荡、伪善，只是名义上的领袖。有时，这种描写是夸张的，但作者的意图或许是好的。他欲借此提高大臣和将士的声望，并使人想到帝王必然拥有神奇的魅力。"⑤

对帝王型英雄的讨论，鲁尔曼的研究视角及其观点，总体上比较符合中国社会历史文化传统观念。只是，笔者有一个困惑，那就是我们如何界定"英雄"这一概念。虽然说对"英雄"的认识、评价与界定是很主观

---

① Robert Ruhlmann, Traditional Heroes in Chinese Popular Fiction, The Confucian Persuasion, ed. by Arthur F. Wright (California: Stanford University Press, 1960), p. 160.
② Ibid., p. 161.
③ Ibid., p. 160.
④ Ibid..
⑤ Ibid., p. 161.

的,对文学作品中的人物尤其如此,但不论在西方还是在中国,还是存在一些基本的衡量准则。在英语文化传统中,人们一般对"hero"作如下界定:

> 英雄是指"一个人,尤其是一个男人,因做事勇敢、或做出了有益的事而受到很多人的崇拜"。或者是指"一个人,尤其是一个男人,因具有特殊的品质或技能而受人崇拜"。①

在中国文化传统里,人们是这样来界定"英雄"一词的:

> 英雄是指"本领高强、勇武过人的人",或者指"不怕困难,不顾自己,为人民利益而英勇斗争,令人钦敬的人"。②

根据英语文化传统与中国文化传统中人们对"英雄"所作的界定可知,"英雄"首先是具有特殊的品质或本领的人,最重要的是他们利用自己的本领作出了对大多数人有益的事,因而得到很多人的尊敬和崇拜。综合这两点,笔者以为,就《水浒传》中的宋徽宗和宋江这两个帝王型人物来说,我们可以认为宋江是英雄。无论作品反映的是什么主题,宋江仗义疏财的侠义精神获得很多江湖人士的崇拜,后来他带领梁山众人建立了一个"八方共域,异姓一家"的乌托邦式政权。这些都说明了他特殊的本领,以及他为社会中的某一为数众多的人群所作的有益的事。宋江称得上"梁山的'无冕之王'"。

宋徽宗则不然。鲁尔曼就曾指出,《水浒传》描写的宋徽宗虽然具有字画天赋,但他并没有给自己的国家和百姓带来好处。"因选人不当、用人不明,这位审美学家并不能维持帝国的太平安定,也不能守卫边疆。朝政腐败,导致宋江、方腊反叛,也刺激金人入侵。这些都是这位艺术家皇

---

① "A person, especially a man, who is admired by many people for doing sth brave or good." or "A person, especially a man, that you admire because of a particular quality or skill that they have." Oxford Advanced Learner's English-Chinese Dictionary, ed. By Sally Wehmeir, Oxford University Press, 2000, p. 826.
② 《现代汉语词典》(第6版),中国社会科学院语言研究所词典编辑室编,商务印书馆2012年版,第1559页。《汉语大词典》亦如此界定。

帝昏庸无能造成的后果。"① 所以，在皇帝的位置上，宋徽宗只是一位"昏君"，他并不受人尊敬、崇拜。

综合上述，笔者以为，在帝王型英雄的讨论中，鲁尔曼对《水浒传》中的宋徽宗、宋江两人所作的评价，对他们的性格特征进行的概括，总体上是比较客观准确的。这些人身处社会权力结构的顶端，当小说家以他们的故事为题材进行创作时，自然而然就增添了很多超自然的、神秘的想象。只是该论者把"昏君"宋徽宗归入英雄行列，笔者以为并不妥当。

三、书生型英雄：吴用

在帝王型英雄的讨论中，鲁尔曼指出，消极性是他们身上的一个重要特征。正是最高统治者的这种消极特性，为他们的下属留下了更多、更大的展现自我的空间。同时，也为文学描写、表现这些人物的各个方面提供了更宽广的舞台。鲁尔曼说：

> 统治者身上明显的消极性，把（表演的）前台留给了他的下属。在帝国的宫廷里，文学不仅发现了那些最伟大的英雄以及最可恶的坏蛋，也找到了一面映照普通人类心理的镜子。在那里，野心、嫉妒与怨憎的狂热情绪横行高涨，且因常处于成功与毁灭之边缘而更加强烈紧张。②

在统治者的下属里面，书生（在中国文化与文学中常称为谋士）扮演着非常重要的角色。相对于武士的孔武有力以及"'激烈的'行动分子"（the "violent" man of action）的特征，鲁尔曼把书生称作"'温和的'知识分子"（the "soft" of intellectual）。在他看来，这一类型的英雄人物是通过大脑运用智慧，使用"舌尖"甚至是"笔尖"杀敌作战的。而且通过比较，鲁尔曼说："中国的书生型英雄（the scholar-heroes），相当于西方足智多谋的奥德修斯（polytropos Odysseus）。"③

在论述中，鲁尔曼认为《水浒传》里的军师吴用和春秋战国时期的

---

① Robert Ruhlmann, Traditional Heroes in Chinese Popular Fiction, The Confucian Persuasion, ed. by Arthur F. Wright (California: Stanford University Press, 1960), pp. 156 – 157.
② Ibid., p. 161.
③ Ibid., p. 162.

蔺相如、苏秦、晏子等人物一样，都是书生型英雄的典型形象。他说：

> 《水浒传》里最重要的人物之一军师吴用，绰号"智多星"，也是位书生。他从未因困难的局面而灰心沮丧，他总是有简单、漂亮、有效的对策，乃至在必要时采取阴险的计谋。①

《水浒传》里，吴用设计"智取生辰纲"，"双用连环计"攻打祝家庄，"使时迁盗甲"大破连环马，"赚金铃吊挂"大闹西岳华山，"智赚玉麒麟"壮大梁山声威，"雪天擒索超"降服猛将，派"时迁火烧翠云楼"、"智取大名府"救出卢俊义等故事情节，都给鲁尔曼留下了深刻的印象。该论者也给予吴用高度评价，称其是"使用战术、间谍和第五纵队的大师"②。

《水浒传》所描写的人物，书生型英雄极少。吴用外，梁山好汉中尚有一位诨名"神机军师"的朱武算是此类形象。但在小说中，其地位不高、作用不大，作者对他的描写也很有限。自然也就没有引起研究者的关注。

四、武士型英雄：武松、李逵、鲁达和石秀等人

《水浒传》里的英雄，有头有脸的人物以武士占绝大多数。以梁山108英雄而论，除却宋江、吴用，剩下的106人基本上都是以一身的武术或者说是功夫行走江湖。当然，在西方人眼里，入云龙公孙胜更像他们文学中的巫师，鼓上蚤时迁则更近乎间谍③。在《水浒传》的武士型英雄中，鲁尔曼最关注的人物是武松，其次则是李逵、鲁达、石秀等人。

对于武士型英雄（the swordsman hero），鲁尔曼认为他们的主要特征在其本身强壮的筋肉和天生神力。对此，鲁尔曼说：

---

① Robert Ruhlmann, Traditional Heroes in Chinese Popular Fiction, The Confucian Persuasion, ed. by Arthur F. Wright (California: Stanford University Press, 1960), p. 162.

② He traps enemies in snow-covered pits, tricks all kinds of useful people into joining his band, and is a master in tactics and the use of spies and fifth columnists. One of his lesser triumphs is maneuvering a caravan of pseudo-merchants, ostensibly laden with dates but actually with drugged wine, through a mountain pass to meet escorted wheelbarrows en route to the capital with the prime minister's birthday presents. The day is hot and the escorters happily drink themselves; when they wake, the presents are gone. Robert Ruhlmann, Traditional Heroes in Chinese Popular Fiction, The Confucian Persuasion, ed. by Arthur F. Wright (California: Stanford University Press, 1960), p. 162.

③ 鲁尔曼认为吴用是使用间谍的高手，而其所派遣的间谍中，时迁是首当其冲的那位。

武士型英雄的主要特征是孔武有力（great bodily strength）。危急时刻需要使用武力，战争中如果官兵不能战胜敌人，纵使有再高明的谋略也一无是处。但武士不只是帝王与书生英雄的得力助手。他们强健有力的肌肉本身就能吸引关注并获得尊重。[1]

谈到武士的孔武有力，在中国文学中除关羽、张飞等人物形象外，给鲁尔曼留下深刻印象的则是水浒英雄武松。《水浒传》中"景阳冈武松打虎"一节，对武松打虎过程惊险迭出而又酣畅淋漓的描写，是最让人感受到英雄的力量之美的，也是获得最多研究者关注的。鲁尔曼说："武松在棍棒一断为二之后，仍然赤手空拳和老虎进行激烈的打斗而将其击毙；在虎头上击打六七十拳才让它断气。"[2] 在前文的论述中，笔者也曾谈到，鲁尔曼对武松在孟州牢城营时轻松挪动、举起天王堂前数百斤重的石礅是赞赏有加的。而像武松这样武艺高强的英雄人物，在鲁尔曼看来那是数年接受武术训练的结果。[3] 对武松打虎，李培德等人也说："在小说的众多精彩事件中，武松赤手空拳打死老虎的描写是最杰出的。"[4]

鲁尔曼认为，在孔武有力之外，武士型英雄尚具有以下几方面特征：
首先，鲁尔曼指出："真正的武士型英雄并不满足于英勇善战，而

---

[1] Robert Ruhlmann, Traditional Heroes in Chinese Popular Fiction, The Confucian Persuasion, ed. by Arthur F. Wright (California: Stanford University Press, 1960), p. 166.

[2] Kuan Yü, Chang Fei, and the heroes of the Water Margin and of more modern novels of adventure, such as Chi's Hsia Wu I and Er Nü Ying-hsiung Chuan, are able to lift stones weighing several hundred pounds. They are not flushed or out of breath after these exertions, and their hearts do not beat faster. Little Hsüeh Chiao is only twelve but he can hoist the stone lions standing outside his house, each weighing half a ton. Wu Sung, when his stick breaks in two, kills a tiger with his bare hands after a fierce struggle; it takes sixty or seventy punches on the head to knock the beast out. Robert Ruhlmann, Traditional Heroes in Chinese Popular Fiction, The Confucian Persuasion, ed. by Arthur F. Wright (California: Stanford University Press, 1960), p. 166.

[3] Good fighters have trained for years in "military arts" (wu-shu). Robert Ruhlmann, Traditional Heroes in Chinese Popular Fiction, The Confucian Persuasion, ed. by Arthur F. Wright (California: Stanford University Press, 1960), p. 166.

[4] Among the many exciting episodes in the novel, the description of Wu Sung's bare-hand killing a tiger is outstanding. Winston L. Y. Yang, Nathan K. Mao and Peter Li, "Romance of the Three Kingdoms and The Water Margin," and "Journey to the West and Flowers in the Mirror.", Classical Chinese Fiction: A Guide to Its Study and Appreciation. London: George Prior Publishers, 1978. p. 43. Rpt. in Literature Criticism from 1400 to 1800. Ed. Lynn M. Zott. Vol. 76. Detroit: Gale, 2002. Literature Resource Center. Web. 11 Sep., 2012.

是常常以幽默的表现（humorous bravura）为他们自身的勇敢添加一份乐趣，从而使严肃的行为掺夹进戏剧性的气氛。"该论者以为，江州城劫法场救宋江时，李逵的行为就属于这种情形。他说："12世纪极像张飞的李逵，为了营救首领宋江的性命，在江州城宋江公开斩首行刑的那天，赤身露体从屋顶跳入刑场，挥舞两把板斧，向藏在人群中的同伴发出信号。"①

营救宋江的确是严肃的行动，李逵的表现也似乎有那么一点乐趣。而且李贽在评点《水浒传》的过程中，对李逵的行为也反复以"趣"来形容②。但就江州城劫法场一回对李逵的描写来看，笔者以为并不有趣，也谈不上幽默。且看原文：

> 又见十字路口茶坊楼上，一个虎形黑大汉，脱得赤条条的，两只手握两把板斧，大吼一声，却似半天起一个霹雳，从半空中跳将下来。手起斧落，早砍翻两个行刑刽子，便往监斩官马前砍将来。③
> 李卓吾对这段文字所作的眉批是："真忠义，真好汉。只消这一个，也自干得事来。"可见，就是一直推崇李逵为"趣人"的李卓吾，对此处李逵的行为也不觉得有"趣"。

在此，笔者提出一个问题，那就是，中国古典小说评点中的"趣"与西方文学批评中的"幽默"这两个范畴，存在多大的共通性，又在什么层面上是相通的呢？像李逵这样的英雄，能否运用西方文学传统中的"幽默"范畴对其进行批评研究呢？这些都值得思考。

---

① Not content to fight well and bravely, the true swordsman-heroes add to their prowess the spice of an often humorous bravura, crowning serious action with an aura playful art.... Chang's twelfth-century counterpart Li K'uei, to save the life of his chieftain Sung Chang, on the very day set for his public beheading in Chiang-chou city, gives the signal to his companions hidden in the crowds by leaping, stark naked, from a roof into the execution square, brandishing two battle axes. Robert Ruhlmann, Traditional Heroes in Chinese Popular Fiction, The Confucian Persuasion, ed. by Arthur F. Wright (California: Stanford University Press, 1960), p. 167.
② 在李卓吾批评《水浒传》百回本的第72回"李逵元夜闹东京"，第73回"黑旋风乔捉鬼"，第74回"李逵寿张乔坐衙"等回目里，李贽一直强调李逵行为的有"趣"。尤其是第74回"李逵寿张乔坐衙"，李贽连用数十个"趣"字来描述李逵的行为。
③ （明）施耐庵、罗贯中：《水浒传》，（明）李卓吾评本，上海古籍出版社1988年版，第587页。

其次,"这些英雄在忍受痛苦方面,表现出和战场上一样的勇气。"①鲁尔曼说,《三国演义》中有关羽刮骨疗伤的美谈,《水浒传》里则有武松不畏惧杀威棒的豪气。对此,该论者如此写道:"武松入狱时,照例要受一百杀威棒。但他拒绝绑住行刑,并夸口说绝不会吼一声。他甚至挑衅狱卒要打得更狠毒些。"②

再次,鲁尔曼指出:"心直口快、真诚坦率、脾气火爆,是通俗小说中绝大多数武士型英雄的特点。他们迟钝、坦诚、天真、好斗、狂暴、易怒、无礼,并且完全无所顾忌。他们以夸口、争吵为消遣,偶尔误伤人命。"③ 而且对这些武士型英雄来说,"随性而动的慷慨宽大是他们最讨人喜欢的特性"④。在这一点上,该论者说,和张飞一样,李逵也是一个容易相信他人谤言的人。在第73回"梁山泊双献头"故事中,李逵一听刘太公说宋江抢了他女儿,不经思考奔回梁山后就差点要了宋江性命。鲁达也是粗俗无礼、无所顾忌的人物。第四回"大闹五台山"时,他不仅自己喝酒吃肉,还迫使两个和尚犯了荤戒。武松亦是如此。第32回"武行者醉打孔亮",为了口舌之利,武松痛打孔亮,醉酒后竟然和一只吠叫的狗过不去。⑤

---

① These heroes show the same courage in resisting pain as in fighting battles. Robert Ruhlmann, Traditional Heroes in Chinese Popular Fiction, The Confucian Persuasion, ed. by Arthur F. Wright (California: Stanford University Press, 1960), p. 167.

② And Wu Sung, when he is to receive the "customary" hundred blows on entering prison, refuses to be held down during the punishment and boasts that he will not utter one cry. He even challenges the jailers to strike harder. Robert Ruhlmann, Traditional Heroes in Chinese Popular Fiction, The Confucian Persuasion, ed. by Arthur F. Wright (California: Stanford University Press, 1960), p. 167.

③ Outspoken biuntness and a volcanic temper characterize most swordsman-heroes in popular fiction. They are obtuse, guileness, childish, belligerent, tempestuous, irascible, devoid of manners, and completely uninihibited. They boast and quarrel as a pastime, and occasionally kill by mistake. Robert Ruhlmann, Traditional Heroes in Chinese Popular Fiction, The Confucian Persuasion, ed. by Arthur F. Wright (California: Stanford University Press, 1960), p. 167.

④ Impulsive generosity is their most likable trait. Robert Ruhlmann, Traditional Heroes in Chinese Popular Fiction, The Confucian Persuasion, ed. by Arthur F. Wright (California: Stanford University Press, 1960), p. 168.

⑤ Li K'uei too readily believes slanderous reports against his chieftain Sung Chiang and rushes to kill him forthwith.... Lu Ta bullies monks into eating meat against their vows. Drunk one winter night, Wu Sung takes a dislike to a dog and pursues it, knife in hand, along a brook, stumbling and falling twice into the icy water, where he is canght by some men he has previously insulted and beaten. Robert Ruhlmann, Traditional Heroes in Chinese Popular Fiction, The Confucian Persuasion, ed. by Arthur F. Wright (California: Stanford University Press, 1960), pp. 167 - 168.

第三章　英语世界对《水浒传》的人物形象塑造研究

最后，谈到梁山好汉，不好女色自然是他们身上的一大特点。鲁尔曼说：

> 如众人所料想的，好汉对女色没什么兴趣。"他们不在儿女私情上浪费时间，只为了修炼武艺而养精蓄锐打熬筋骨。"他们遵循传统的阴阳养生之道，认为要练拳就不能把精力耗费在其他方面。①

夏志清也认为不好女色是梁山英雄的一个重要特点。他同时也提出：

> 在大多数社会里，禁欲是与节食忌酒并重的。但是《水浒》中的好汉虽然不贪女色，却酷爱大碗喝酒，大块吃肉，以此作为补偿。像武松、鲁智深、李逵这些对女色毫不动心的最了得的英雄，却是最能吃喝最爱酒的……关于莽汉纵情于口腹（即使有性禁欲之类的上下文）的描写，堪称为中国小说中一个可爱的特色。②

然而，鲁尔曼指出，好汉的不好女色又带来了另一个问题，那就是造成家庭、特别是夫妻之间关系的不和谐：妻子因难以忍受独守空房的苦楚而出轨。他以杨雄、潘巧云两人为例说："《水浒传》中，一个不贞的妻子和一个和尚有染。只因为她的丈夫醉心于武艺，甚至晚上都在衙门营房留宿，而让其独守空闱。"③ 在《水浒传》中，类似杨雄、潘巧云的事例还有卢俊义和其妻子贾氏。卢俊义也是醉心于武艺而忽视了妻子的存在，从而使贾氏与管家李固勾搭在一起。只是鲁尔曼并未注意到这一案例。

总之，在鲁尔曼的论述中可以看到，梁山好汉中的武士型英雄，优点

---

① As might be expected, the hao-han are little interested in women. "They waste no time in amorous dalliance, but conserve their energies for feats of valor." Following traditional theories on yin-yang and on cultivating one's vitality (yang-sheng), they believe their training in boxing to be incompatible with other claims on their energy. Robert Ruhlmann, Traditional Heroes in Chinese Popular Fiction, The Confucian Persuasion, ed. by Arthur F. Wright (California: Stanford University Press, 1960), p. 168.

② C. T. Hsia, Chinese Classical novel, Newyork: Columbia University Press, 1968, pp. 89 - 90.

③ One of the unfaithful wives in *the Water Margin* starts an affair with a monk because her husband, too interested in gymnastics, spends his nights at the yamen barracks and leaves her alone. Robert Ruhlmann, Traditional Heroes in Chinese Popular Fiction, The Confucian Persuasion, ed. by Arthur F. Wright (California: Stanford University Press, 1960), pp. 168 - 169.

明显，缺点同样突出。他们既有超自然的色彩，却也有常人的血肉之躯。他们嬉笑怒骂、吃喝玩乐、爱憎分明，甚至给人粗俗无礼莽汉的印象。但即便如此，"这些鲁莽的汉子仍然得到同伴和小说读者的喜爱"。之所以这样，鲁尔曼认为：

首先，"因为他们诚实、正直、坦率"，和他们在一起不用担心与官僚相处那样阳奉阴违；而且"他们之间的友谊，在街头、酒店、或是其他低下的地方结成，并无利害存在，都是自发的、性情相投的关系"。其次，"他们不奉承、谄媚，没有什么能够改变他们的忠诚"。而且"他们是意志坚定的人，随时准备为了朋友而牺牲自己的生命；他们绝不会投降，也不会受制于人或受人羞辱"。鲁尔曼说，《水浒传》中石秀"拼命三郎"的绰号（the nickname "Do-or-die"）是所有武士型英雄当之无愧的，他们拥有"好汉"这一词语包含的所有品质。①

谈到梁山好汉的英雄品质，笔者以为就《水浒传》对他们的描写来看，李培德、茅国权等人对武松的评论是最具典型性的。他们说：

> 作为一百零八位英雄中的一员，他对兄弟武大和自己的同伴非常忠诚。武松是一个有原则和强烈正义感的人。认为正确的事情他就去做，宁愿进监牢或去死也不屈服。即使粗犷的外表与如猛兽般的力量似乎显示他是一个缺乏智慧的人，但他却有足够的道德毅力抵制嫂子的诱惑。武松，对敌人残暴无情，对朋友慷慨忠诚。在中国，他是最

---

① Why are these raving bullies still so loved by their and by the devotees of fiction? First, because they are honest and straight-forward in a world in which persons officially vested with authority prefer the devious approach. With them one knows where one stands. Their friendship, born in the street, in wineshops, or in other humble places, are disinterested, spontaneous alliances of congenial souls. They are totally indifferent to money and will not take a penny of what is not theirs. They do not fawn and flatter, and nothing can make them shift their loyalty. All deserve the nickname "Do-or-die" bestowed to Shih Hsiu, one of their nember. They are resolute men, always ready to lay down their lives for their friends, never will surrender or to let themselves be cuebed or humiliated. Muscle play brings them a natural sxhilaration, their strength and courage lead to a careless self-confidence, their crude jokes reveal a robust sense of hunor, and their whole manner excudes *joie de vivre*. They have all the companionable qualities that are subsumed in the phrase *hao-han*, "good fellow". Robert Ruhlmann, Traditional Heroes in Chinese Popular Fiction, The Confucian Persuasion, ed. by Arthur F. Wright (California: Stanford University Press, 1960), p. 168.

受欢迎的一位虚构英雄。[1]

他们从武松身上的"忠诚"（loyalty）、"原则"（principle）与"正义感"（sence of justice）三个方面展开论述，可谓抓住了问题的核心。

从上文的讨论中可以发现，鲁尔曼、李培德等人对水浒英雄人物的评论、研究，与中国传统主流观念看法是比较接近的。虽然因思想、文化以及文学批评概念的不同而在某些具体的观点上存在一定的差异，但上述论者对梁山好汉的特征、品质，以及对他们身上的优缺点的把握还是相当到位的。因此，笔者把这些论者的研究视角归入传统观念的框架之中。

第三节　西方现代反讽观念视域中的水浒英雄人物研究

与鲁尔曼等人从中国传统社会权力结构切入来研究水浒英雄人物类型不同，浦安迪等人以西方现代反讽观念为理论基础展开研究。在《明代小说四大奇书》这部论著的第四章"《水浒传》——英雄主义的幻灭"中，浦安迪在反讽理论的指导下把水浒英雄人物分为反面英雄人物（negative character or anti-heroes）和正面英雄人物（positive heroes）两大类[2]。

一、水浒人物研究中反讽要素的确立

英语世界中，以浦安迪为代表的批评者为什么会坚持从反讽的视角来研究《水浒传》等中国小说"四大奇书"（Ssu ta ch'i-shu）？且看浦安迪的夫子自道：

---

[1] One of the one hundred and eight heroes of the band, he is intensely loyal to his brother Wu Ta and to his comrades. A man of principle and imbued with a strong sense of justice, he does what he considers to be right and he would rather go to jail or die than to yield. Even though his rough appearance and brute strength may suggest a lack of intelligence, he has enough moral fiber to resist the temptations of his seductive sister-in-law. Violent toward his enemies but generous and loyal to his friends, he is one of the most popular fictional heroes in China. Winston L. Y. Yang, Nathan K. Mao and Peter Li, "Romance of the Three Kingdoms and The Water Margin," and "Journey to the West and Flowers in the Mirror.", Classical Chinese Fiction: A Guide to Its Study and Appreciation. London: George Prior Publishers, 1978, p. 44. Rpt. in Literature Criticism from 1400 to 1800. Ed. Lynn M. Zott. Vol. 76. Detroit: Gale, 2002. Literature Resource Center. Web. 11 Sep., 2012.

[2] 浦安迪对水浒人物的研究集中在其《明代小说四大奇书》（*The Four Masterworks of the Ming Novel*）这部专著里。该书第四章"《水浒传》——英雄主义的幻灭"（*Shui-hu chuan*: Deflation of Herosim）对《水浒传》这部小说展开了比较全面的论述。

我坚持对这些小说做反讽的研究，是想揭示这样一个事实，即我是以比较文学的方法论，尤其是从西方文学批评中新近的小说理论来分析阐释这些作品的。①

　　这告诉我们，该论者是应用阐释研究的方法，运用西方小说批评理论——具体来说就是反讽理论，来研究《水浒传》等中国小说"四大奇书"的。那么，为什么他会运用反讽理论来阐释《水浒传》呢？因为在他看来《水浒传》这部作品和《三国演义》《西游记》《金瓶梅》一样，都是"富有反讽色彩的杰作"，这些小说的作者对"以前的故事来源和流行形象"等素材"主要是作了彻底的反讽处理"。而且他说："在我的理解中，反讽修辞在明代小说发展中所起的决定性作用，正如稍后欧洲小说文体形式情况一样，是一把双刃剑。"②

　　其实，运用西方理论来阐释中国作品，这是很常见的研究方式。只是，浦安迪提出的《水浒传》等"四大奇书"都是"富有反讽色彩的杰作"，"反讽修辞在明代小说的发展中"起着"决定性的作用"。这些观点是否妥当、是否符合中国明代小说的发展事实，仍是个问题。而且就浦安迪以反讽理论来分析、研究水浒英雄人物的具体论述来看，笔者认为，在很多时候是很难解释得通的。特别是站在中国文化、文学传统的立场来看时，更是显示出其非常牵强的一面。这一点在下文的相关讨论中将进一步展开。

　　事实上，浦安迪等人对水浒英雄人物进行反讽研究，近代以来的西方小说批评理论不是其唯一的理论来源。浦安迪会把梁山一百零八人分为正

---

① My consistence on an ironic reading of these books betrays the fact that I come to them from the perspective of comparative literature methodoly, and in particular from recent thoeries of the novel in Western criticism. Andrew H. Plaks, The Four Masterworks of the Ming Novel, Princeton University Press, 1987, p. x.

② To put it another way, I wish to suggest that each of the major texts under study here represents not just the most elaborate reworking of the respective narrative traditions, but actually a thoroughgoing process of revision of these materials, one governed primarily by ironic treatment of the prior sources and popular images. In my understanding, the crucial role of ironic rhetoric in the development of the Ming novel, as in the case of the slightly later European novel form, is a doubie-edged tool. …In my very tentative gropings toward the range of meanings thus projected in these four ironic masterpieces, I try as far as possible to locate the odeas I see replected in them on the map of Ming intellectual history. Andrew H. Plaks, The Four Masterworks of the Ming Novel, Princeton University Press, 1987, p. x.

面英雄人物与反面英雄人物两大类,特别是把梁山好汉的领袖宋江放入反面人物的行列,并作为反面的典型形象展开讨论,是直接受到中国古代《水浒传》评点家们的影响,其中尤以受明末清初金圣叹评点之影响为最深。这在其论述过程中反复引用《水浒传》评点家们的相关看法和观点就可发现。对此,浦安迪在《明代小说四大奇书》这部论著的"序"里也作了明确的交代。他说:

> 此外,另一个原因使我相信,在这里作出的阐释并不会如它看起来那样陌生。这是因为我获得的主要的启发和指导,都来自中国的传统小说评点家。他们的批注,附在这些小说明末清初的很多精刻本里。①

根据笔者的统计,为浦安迪对水浒英雄进行反讽研究提供启发和指导的中国传统评点家们的学术资源,主要有下面这些:

首先是署名袁无涯(据明人袁中道《游居杮录》)的《忠义水浒全书发凡》。该"发凡"有语云:"昔贤比于班、马,余谓近于丘明,殆有《春秋》之遗意焉,故允宜称传。"②浦安迪从中深受启发,认为理解《水浒传》的主题不能只看文本的外在叙述,而应该挖掘言外之意、文外之旨,以领会作者的用心。所谓言外之意、文外之旨,亦即"春秋笔法",实则暗含着讽刺的深意。而这则与浦安迪的反讽研究具有了契合点。

其次是金圣叹为贯华堂本《水浒传》撰写的系列批评文章,以及为全书所作的评点文字。其中,《读第五才子书法》与金圣叹在各章回中所作的人物评点,最为浦安迪所看重。金圣叹在《读第五才子书法》中提出的"弄引法"、"獭尾法"、"欲合故纵法"、"横云断山法"、"草蛇灰线法"、"绵针泥刺法"等15条"文法"("compositional devices",wen-fa)——浦安迪称其为

---

① Beyond this, there is an other reason I believe the ieterpretations offered here are less alien than they may appear. This is because I draw my principal inspiration and guidance from the traditional Chinese commentators, whose critical readings accompanied many of the best late Ming and early Ch'ing editions of these novels. Andrew H. Plaks, The Four Masterworks of the Ming Novel, Princeton University Press, 1987, p. xi.

② 转引自朱一玄、刘毓忱编《水浒传资料汇编》,南开大学出版社2012年版,第132页。

"形象叠用原则"（the principle of figural recurrence）①，以及金圣叹对水浒人物形象展开的具体评点、尤其是对宋江的评价，为浦安迪从反讽角度切入研究水浒人物形象提供了有力的理论资源。

浦安迪非常看重金圣叹视宋江、李逵为相反相成的一组人物的观点。像金圣叹在《读第五才子书法》中提出的：

> 只如写李逵，岂不段段都是妙绝文字？却不知正为段段都在宋江事后，故便妙不可言。盖作者只是痛恨宋江奸诈，故处处紧接着一段李逵朴诚来，做个形击。其意思自在显宋江之恶，却不料反成李逵之妙。

以及金圣叹在小说第42回的回评中所说："此书处处以宋江、李逵相形对写，意在显暴宋江之恶，固无论矣。"浦安迪视金圣叹的这些评论为自己重要的理论依据，在研究过程多次加以引用。也正是以金氏的这些观点为依据，浦安迪认为宋江与李逵二人之间的微妙关系正暗含着反讽的意味。②

此外，署名怀林的《梁山泊一百单八人优劣》文章，把石秀与杨雄、鲁达与林冲、武松与施恩作为成对的人物放在一起加以讨论，这样的批评方法也为浦安迪进行反讽研究提供了重要的启发③。

总之，上述所有这些中国古代小说评点家的研究成果，都给浦安迪坚

---

① 浦安迪说，"最有意义的是，金圣叹使用广泛的批评术语可以归结到一个核心点上，就是本文所运用的'形象叠用原则'。"... it is most significant than Chin Sheng-t'an's wide-ranging critical vocabulary can be reduced to a central focus on the ways in which the principle of figural recurrence operates in this text. Andrew H. Plaks, The Four Masterworks of the Ming Novel, Princeton University Press, 1987, p. 314.

② This range of treatment, from light humor to bitter irony, must be kept in mind when we come to consider the complex image of Sung Chiang as developed in the *fan-ben* novel, since in a number of Li K'uei and Sung Chiang comprize the most crucial pair of linked opposites in the book. Andrew H. Plaks, The Four Masterworks of the Ming Novel, Princeton University Press, 1987, pp. 327 – 328。

③ Chin Sheng-t'an discourses at length on the significance of the Sung Chiang -Li K'uei pair in a chapter-commentary to chapter 43 (42: 7a – 8b). See also the "Huai-lin" prefatory essay "A Comparative Ranking of the 108 Liang-shan Heroes 梁山泊一百单八人优劣," which puts this pair on an equal level with the more positive comradeship of Shin Hsiu and Yang Hiung. Andrew H. Plaks, The Four Masterworks of the Ming Novel, Princeton University Press, 1987, p. 328。

持认为《水浒传》是一部具有反讽意蕴的作品奠定了坚实的基础①。而在此基础上，浦安迪提出，《水浒传》里"形象叠用原则"的运用塑造出了"重现类型的系列人物"，如鲁达、武松、李逵等英雄好汉，如先后成为山寨之主的王伦、晁盖、宋江。他认为："在这些重现类型的系列人物中，作者的主要目的是通过控制角色与类型并置中异同的冲突方面，从而为所有相关人物的最终阐释投下反讽的映象。"②

事实上，浦安迪在反讽理论观照之下把水浒人物分成正面英雄形象和反面英雄形象，这是与《水浒传》这部作品在人物描写以及小说作者在思想认识上暴露出来的问题和缺陷密切相关的。这些暴露出来的问题和缺陷，最突出的一点就是《水浒传》太多地展现出中国人传统心理的阴暗面，而其中最为突出的就是水浒人物身上表现出来的血腥嗜杀残暴与阴谋权诈虚伪。前者以武松、李逵等人为代表，后者则以宋江、吴用两人为典型。而正是对人物阴暗心理过多的展现，与同样是描写英雄好汉"侠盗罗宾汉"的西方作品相比，《水浒传》就给人少了一份田园牧歌式的美好理想和温暖的感受。而血腥嗜杀残暴与阴谋权诈虚伪，是否是英雄好汉所应该有的品质呢？这在浦安迪等西方批评者看来是很值得怀疑的，也为他们进行反讽研究提供了启发。浦安迪在论述中就说："在这点上，夏志清、孙述宇及其他现代批评者对《水浒传》描写的传统中国人心里阴暗面所

---

① At the very least, a reading of the novel as some sort of indirect statement is suggested by the Yüan Wu-yai *fa-fan* preface, which speaks of the "lingering meaning in the spirit of the Ch'un-ch'iu classic" 有春秋之遗意焉. I also take this as the implication of the last line in the opening verse of chapter 71 in the Yien-tu wai-ch'en edition (moved to the end of the inauguration scene in the Yüan Wu-yai and Chieh-tzu yüan editions, omitted in the most others): "This I present to my readers for their careful perusal" 付与诸公仔细看. For that matter, one may say that the repeated advice of Jung-yü t'ang and Yüan Wu-yai commentaries to "pay attention" (cho-yen 着眼) to a given passage often implies that there is a hidden meaning involved. Chin Sheng-t'an provides a fairly enplicit discussion of the ironic dimension of the text in his chapter-commentary to chapter 19. Andrew H. Plaks, The Four Masterworks of the Ming Novel, Princeton University Press, 1987, p. 319. 浦安迪认为金圣叹《读第五才子书法》中提出的"草蛇灰线法"、"绵针泥刺法"是反讽修辞，详情请见 The Four Masterworks of the Ming Novel, pp. 315 – 318。

② I will attempt to show below that in each of these chains of recurrent types the author's chief aim is to manipulate the conflicting aspects of similarity and difference involved in the juxtapositions of roles and types in order to cast an ironic reflection on the final interpretation of all figures involved. Andrew H. Plaks, The Four Masterworks of the Ming Novel, Princeton University Press, 1987, p. 316.

作的使人大开眼界的评论，让我们受到很大启发。"①

说到夏志清对《水浒传》描写的传统中国人心理阴暗面所作的批评，笔者在此作一个简略论述。夏志清认为，《水浒传》对传统中国人心理阴暗面的描写主要表现在以下几个方面：

第一，为了罗致英雄，梁山好汉往往不惜采取残酷的手段。比如说，为了拉秦明、朱仝、卢俊义等人入伙，宋江等人残忍地火烧瓦砾场并使秦明全家遇害，吴用设计使卢俊义家破人亡，为绝朱仝后路李逵斧劈小衙内，这些都是血淋淋的事实。

第二，在复仇的主题下，滥杀无辜的武松是"被恶魔驱使的代表"，李逵活割黄文炳则有过之而无不及。这完全是背离人类文明的行为，而《水浒传》的作者却对好汉们的野蛮复仇行为大加赞赏、表示肯定。

第三，梁山好汉对待女性的态度暴露出的厌恶、敌对心理完全是非理性的。武松之于潘金莲，杨雄之于潘巧云，可谓残忍至极。

第四，梁山好汉是勇敢的造反者，却"不是觉悟了的革命势力"。他们虽然看重忠义，树立"替天行道"的大旗，却整体耽于杀戮，"应被视为创造混乱的工具"，是文明社会必须防范的力量。夏志清说"李逵堪称这种凶险力量的象征"，如果说"宋江是文雅体面、开明的造反者，李逵则是淳朴却凶残的无法无天的造反者"。②

浦安迪正是抓住小说人物描写中暴露出来的这些问题，认为《水浒传》的作者在创作时是具有明确的反讽目的的。当然，这是西方思想文化观照之下得出的结论。就《水浒传》对人物的描写来看，笔者以为就是最血腥的"血溅鸳鸯楼"，小说作者也并未表现出对武松这一人物的批判态度。此点，笔者将在后文述及。

而且非常重要的一点是，在不少批评者看来，《水浒传》的作者在描写梁山好汉时，往往会出现模棱两可、态度暧昧的地方。这就给读者、研究者留下了理解的多种可能空间，从而得出相对甚至截然相反的观点。这是与反讽理论相当契合的。而所谓反讽，按玛格丽特·A. 罗斯之论，它

---

① Here we are indebted to the eye-opening discussions of C. T. Hsia, Sun Shu-yü, and other recent critics on the tendency of the *Shui-hu chuan* to dwell on the darker side of the traditional Chinese mentality. Andrew H. Plaks, The Four Masterworks of the Ming Novel, Princeton University Press, 1987, p. 320.

② C. T. Hsia, Chinese Classical novel, Newyork：Columbia University Press, 1968, pp. 93 – 107.

具有这样的特征:"反讽和戏仿可以说都提供不止一种信息供读者解码,从而混淆了正常的沟通过程。"① 具体来说即是:

> 术语反讽一般而言描述的是对一位模棱两可的人物的陈述,这种陈述包括一个代码,其中至少又包含两个信息,一个是反讽者对"入门的"读者隐藏起来的信息,另一个更容易被理解,但是(笔者疑应译成"就是",因未见原文只是推测)"含义反讽"的编码信息。②

德波特(Deborah L. Poter)在研究中就认为,宋江这一形象具有相当浓厚的反讽特性。他说:

> 在《水浒传》一百回的叙事中,心理因素对宋江行为的影响,使他成为中国文学中最复杂、最让人好奇的文学形象之一。事实上,正是这种复杂性,导致在宋江的道德评价上出现截然相反的意见:有一些人称赞他是忠义行为的典范,其他人则斥责他是阴险狡诈的伪君子。③

而为什么会出现此种情形呢?德波特说:

> 我认为,这些明显相互矛盾的观点,是源于构成宋江这个形象的众多语言模型中暗含着矛盾、冲突。这不是宣称每一个确定的语言模型自然就蕴含着矛盾、冲突,而是在构成宋江形象的语言中——通过他自己的语言或是叙述者的语言,而这些词语传达出潜在的张力——

---

① [英]玛格丽特·A. 罗斯:《戏仿:古代、现代与后现代》,王海萌译,南京大学出版社2013年版,第87页。

② 同上。

③ Despite the relative paucity of antecedent materials concerning this figure, the extensive attention paid to psychological factors influencing his behavior in the one-hundred-chapter narrative transformed Sung into one of the most complex and intriguing literary personalities in Chinese literature. Indeed, it is this complexity that has elicited the extensive range of dissenting opinions regarding Sung Chiang's virtue: there are those who laud him as an exemplar of loyal and righteous behavior, while others deplore him as cunning and hypocritical. Deborah L. Porter, The Formation of an Image: An Analysis of the Linguistic Patterns That Form the Character of Sung Chiang, Journal of the American Oriental Society, Vol. 112, No. 2 (Apr. - Jun., 1992), pp. 233 – 234.

有一个贯穿小说始终的、一贯的预示。①

循此思路分析,《水浒传》这部小说中,不仅对宋江的描写如此,对武松、李逵等人的描写也出现了这样的情况。正是小说文本中存在这种与反讽理论的契合之处,这就为西方批评者进行反讽阐释留下了空间。

以上诸方面,是浦安迪等英语世界的批评者在《水浒传》的研究中确立反讽研究视角的主要因素。

二、水浒人物描写中反讽意蕴的呈现方式

那么,《水浒传》对梁山一百零八人的描写,哪些方面让英语世界的研究者觉得具有嘲笑、调侃的意蕴与反讽的色彩呢?

浦安迪认为,小说作者对水浒英雄的反讽映射(the ironic reflection),与《金瓶梅》《西游记》一样呈现出递进的两个层面:较轻松的层面与较严肃的层面②。根据浦安迪的论述,"较轻松的层面"是指小说作者在人物描写以及给人物取名时,夸张、双关等修辞手法的运用。该论者说:

> 有时候,小说章节段落中的反讽笔法似乎只是轻松的嘲笑。如我们所看到的描写王英王矮虎时那近乎荒诞的夸张,或在第45回里描写一位和尚的虔诚热情时猥亵的双关语的使用③。在另一些情形中,这种调侃的意味则表现在用双关语取名的古老惯例上。这本是中国叙事文学中的一个传统特色。《水浒传》里由于关键人物的绰号、星辰名号特别多,

---

① These apparently contradictory views derive, I believe, from the linguistic patterns that form the literary image of Sung Chiang a contradiction is implicit in many of them. This is not to claim that every occurrence of a certain pattern automatically implies conflict, but there is throughout the novel a consistent projection of the image of Sung Chiang (be it through his own words or the words of the narrator) in terms that convey an underlying tension. Deborah L. Porter, The Formation of an Image: An Analysis of the Linguistic Patterns That Form the Character of Sung Chiang, Journal of the American Oriental Society, Vol. 112, No. 2 (Apr.-Jun., 1992), p. 234.

② In my earlier discussions of the ironic dimensions of *Chin P'ing Mei* and *Hsi-yu chi*, it was helpful to proceed from the lighter to the heavier side of the ironic reflection perceived in those two books. In *Shui-hu chuan* as well, we see similar graduations of seriousness. Andrew H. Plaks, The Four Masterworks of the Ming Novel, Princeton University Press, 1987, p. 320.

③ 浦安迪原注第113条,具体内容是:SHCC, 2: 738. Chin Sheng-t'an (chapter 44: 20b) adds to the fun by changing "sharing a pillow, they took their pleasure" 共枕欢愉 to "they fulfilled their heartfelt vows" 了其心愿. Andrew H. Plaks, The Four Masterworks of the Ming Novel, Princeton University Press, 1987, p. 320。

因而运用这种方法进行嘲讽的可能性就自然增大了。①

在这一点上，浦安迪以为，梁山好汉绰号前标的"小"字或"病"字②，虽然有说他们酷似前辈英雄的意思，却也似乎在嘲笑他们和前辈比起来相差太远。他还以为，梁山泊的军师"吴用"这个名字也可读作"无用"，就是"吴加亮或吴学究这两个名字也可能具有反讽含义"。③ 这是就"较轻松的层面"而论。

但"这类轻松的笔法"并不是浦安迪要着重论述的。他讨论的重点在"较严肃的层面"。在浦安迪看来，《水浒传》人物描写中反讽色彩呈现的"较严肃的层面"主要有两点：一是作者对核心人物所作的特定的细节描写；二是作者设置一系列相关的人物形象，并使他们的角色与行动相互映衬，从而产生反讽效果。④ 这也就是上文谈到的"重复出现的类型

---

① Sometimes the ironic touch in passages in the novel seems to amount to nothing more than light mockey, as in the grotesque exaggeration we see in the depiction of Wang Ying 王英（Wang Ai-hu 王矮虎），or in the use of ribald double-entendre in chapter 45 to describe one Buddhist monk's devotional fervor. In another cases, the playful tone comes out in the timeworn practice of using punning personal names, a conventional feature of Chinese narrative that enjoys increased possibilities in *Shui-hu* due to the unusual abundance of nick-names, star-names, and the like for its various key figures. Andrew H. Plaks, The Four Masterworks of the Ming Novel, Princeton University Press, 1987, p. 320。

② 浦安迪原注第 114 条如下：These characters include Hua Jung（Little Li Kuang 小李广），Yang Hsiung（Sick Kuan So 病关索），Sun Li 孙立（Sick Yü-ch'ih 病尉迟），Lü Fang（Little Marquis Wen 小温侯），Chou T'ung 周通（Little Hegemon 小霸王），Hsüeh Shui 薛水（Sick Man-eater 病大虫）（应为病大虫薛永——笔者注），Sun Hsin 孙新（Little Yü-ch'ih 小尉迟），and possibly Kuo Sheng 郭盛（Rival Jen-kuei 赛仁贵）. On the identification of the elusive figure Kuan So, see below, chapter 5, n. 410. Wang Li-ch'i argues that the epithet "sick"（ping）is simply a descriptive tag for a sallow complexion（see "Shui-hu ying-hsiung ti ch'o-hao," p. 282）. Andrew H. Plaks, The Four Masterworks of the Ming Novel, Princeton University Press, 1987, p. 320。

③ For example, the frequent labeling of warriors as a "junior"（hsiao 小）or "sick", i. e. deficient（ping 病）copy of an earlier hero seems to poke fun at the small-time status of some of the *Shui-hu* warriors... The name given in the novel to Sung Chiang's principal adviser is particularly noteworthy in this context. As far as I can tell, the use of the name Wu Yung, with its very obvious stock pun（for 吴用 read 无用，"good-for-nothing"），is not to be found in the earlier sources, where this figure is known by the designations Wu Chia-liang 吴加亮 or Wu Hsüeh-chiu 吴学究（both of which, by the way, also provide possibilities for ironic interpretation. Andrew H. Plaks, The Four Masterworks of the Ming Novel, Princeton University Press, 1987, pp. 320 – 321。

④ However, this sort of light ironic is far less significant for my purpose than the manner in which the author generates ironies regarding some of the central figures in the text by means of the manipulation of specific details in their presentation, and by setting up a network of cross-reflections between figurallly linked characters and actions. Andrew H. Plaks, The Four Masterworks of the Ming Novel, Princeton University Press, 1987, p. 321.

人物"和"角色与类型的并置"问题。

此外,浦安迪认为,小说在叙述秦明、李应、朱仝、徐宁、卢俊义等人被迫入伙梁山的再现模式,也是水浒人物形象描绘中反讽含义呈现的重要方式。在这过程中,反讽矛头主要是针对宋江及其党羽亲信如吴用等人的。他说:

> 对宋江及其主要谋士的怀疑,没有什么比他们在迫使英雄们入伙的再现模式中表现出来的奸诈行为更令人不安的了。在梁山势力发展壮大的过程中,这不仅是把众多分散叙事单元连接起来的一种重要的结构要素,而且也是对通俗材料中梁山好汉形象进行反讽改写的一项至关重要的例证。①

在论述中浦安迪进一步指出,作品中此一叙事模式的反复出现,"不仅表明其招贤纳士方式本身的不可取,还严重损害了梁山好汉宣称的崇高理想"。而且浦氏以为在迫使英雄入伙的再现模式中,"从残酷无情强迫的总体方案到表达此用意时特定词语的斟酌使用,作者构设这些特殊场景的用意是显而易见的"。②

总之,从一般意义的层面来说,所有这些主要还是源于德波特提出的构成人物形象的"语言模型中暗含着矛盾、冲突"。也就是《水浒传》的作者在描写人物时运用的语言,为读者、批评者提供了至少两个信息编码,从而导致人们在阐释、研究时完全可以朝相反的路径展开。正如德波特谈到的:"正是这种复杂性,导致在宋江的道德评价上出现截然相反的意见:有一些人称赞他是忠义行为的典范,其他人则斥责他是阴险狡诈的

---

① Suspicions regarding the duplicity of Sung Chiang and his principal adviser are nowhere more troubling than in the recurrent pattern of the forced recruitment of warriors. This is not only an important structral element linking many of the separate narrative units within the larger framework of the gathering of forces, but it also provides a central illustration of the ironic revision of the image of the Liang-shan bandits in popular materials. Andrew H. Plaks, The Four Masterworks of the Ming Novel, Princeton University Press, 1987, p. 343.

② ... seriously undermines both the method of recruitment itself and the broder claims regarding the noble puepsoses of the band. The care with which the author has framed these particular scenes is evident, from the overall pattern of merciless coercion down to the level of specific langeage with which this is presented. Andrew H. Plaks, The Four Masterworks of the Ming Novel, Princeton University Press, 1987, p. 343.

伪君子。"

三、水浒英雄中的反面人物

在传统主流批评者那里——不论是中国还是外国，梁山一百八人因各自不同的缺点并不能称为完美的英雄。但他们身上具有的疾恶如仇、行侠仗义、锄强扶弱的品质，也就是李培德等人谈到的"忠诚"（loyalty）、"原则"（principle）与"正义感"，却也让他们算得上顶天立地的汉子，是令人称颂的人物，基本上都属于正面的文学形象。像鲁达、武松、李逵为朋友两肋插刀，像宋江、柴进资助朋友豪气干云。凡此种种不胜枚举。

但在反讽理论的观照之下，英语世界的批评者浦安迪，通过分析考察小说作者对武松、李逵、鲁达、宋江等核心人物所作的特定的细节描写，通过比较研究小说文本中出现的如武松、李逵与鲁达及王伦、晁盖与宋江这样的"重现类型的系列人物"，通过斟酌审视小说中塑造的如宋江、李逵这样的并置组合型人物之间的正反关系，认为小说作者在这些梁山好汉的身上涂上了一层微妙的反讽色彩，从而把他们归入反面英雄的行列。

（一）武松、李逵与鲁达

作为"重复出现的类型人物"，武松、李逵、鲁达是浦安迪讨论的头三位反面英雄。通过分析考察小说作者对这三位人物形象所作的描写，浦安迪提出：

> 在某种意义上，我们能够看到，贯穿这三位人物的叙述进展中有一个共同的法则在起支配作用，那就是在对每一位个体英雄的刻划中，反讽含义逐渐得到加强加深。①

在浦安迪的论述中，这种反讽含义不断强化、深化的叙述法则体现在武松身上，主要有下面几点。

首先也是最重要的是，从打虎英雄到残暴的复仇者的转变，武松形象中阴暗的一面不断暴露。浦安迪认为，在这个过程中，"作者开始触及英

---

① In a certain sence, we can see in the narrative progression through these three figures the same principle of rising intensity or seriousness that governs the gradual deepening of ironic implications in the portrayal of each of the individual heroes. Andrew H. Plaks, The Four Masterworks of the Ming Novel, Princeton University Press, 1987, p. 327.

雄行为与暴力行为之间微妙的界线，这构成作品一个核心主题的层面"。①而在向潘金莲讨还血债、斗杀西门庆到血溅鸳鸯楼的叙述进程中，"作者所作的就是把复仇的主题放置在前后不同的两种环境之下，目的是使读者去体会、思考其中更深层的含义"。尤其是对血溅鸳鸯楼的描写，"正是作者的高妙笔法，描写出无辜的奴婢们绝望乞怜、武松卷走金银器皿以及令我们回顾的武松也曾为玉兰的姿色动心的微妙揭示等细节。所有这些合在一起，最终加深了我们对武松血腥残暴、滥杀无辜的印象"。②

小说对武松身上这种血腥残暴、滥杀无辜的描写的确是毫不掩饰的，但同时，作者也并没有表现出批评指责的意思。从血溅鸳鸯楼后的"证诗"——"都监贪婪甚可羞，谩施奸计结深仇。岂知天道能昭鉴，渍血横尸满画楼。"③可知，作者批判的矛头是指向张都监的。而且作者对武松出逃路上月夜的描写也是充满着诗情画意的。据此，在这个问题上，笔者对浦安迪提出的小说作者的笔触之中具有反讽含义一说表示怀疑。

其次，浦安迪认为，自血溅鸳鸯楼后，武松的命运际遇明显变坏，尤以随后发生的蜈蚣岭事件最能说明问题。该论者提出，蜈蚣岭事件中，武松发怒的动机、对被救姑娘的态度，与后世口头流传的武松故事之间是形成尖锐对比的。他说：

> 这里，武松愤怒的动机完全被含混不清的原因所遮蔽。在看见道士和一位似乎是自愿的女伴调情时，武松怒火的爆发其原因并不清楚。而且他自己对被救姑娘的态度也显得很矛盾。这与后世口头流传

---

① But by the time we come to the replay of Wu Sung's vengeful wrath in subsequent chapters, the author begins to approach the fine line between heroics and havoc that comprises one of the central thematic dimensions of his work. Andrew H. Plaks, The Four Masterworks of the Ming Novel, Princeton University Press, 1987, p. 322.

② So it is only the author's fine brushwork details—the hopeless pleas of the innocent servants, the theft of the gold and silver dishes, and, in retrospect, Wu Sung's subtly disclosed vulnerability to the attractions of the girl Yü-lan 玉兰—that, taken together, add up to the final impression of excessive, even wanton bloodletting. In other words, what our author does is take the theme of merciless revenge and present it first in one set of circumstances, then in another, in order to force the reader to consider some of the deeper implications involved. Andrew H. Plaks, The Four Masterworks of the Ming Novel, Princeton University Press, 1987, p. 322。

③ （明）施耐庵、罗贯中：《水浒传》，（明）李卓吾评本，上海古籍出版社1988年版，第441页。

的把这一故事描写成武松路见不平勇救少女是形成尖锐对比的。①

血溅鸳鸯楼事件后，武松的命运确实发生了很大的变化。出逃路上被菜园子张青、母夜叉孙二娘手下喽啰绑住，差点被当作"好行货"开剥掉；自扮成行者离开十字坡，便一路躲逃最终上了二龙山，武松的确成了落魄的英雄。但就蜈蚣岭事件武松发怒的原因，作者通过人物的心理已作了明确的交代。且看原文：

> 走过林子那边去，打一看，只见松树林中，傍山一座坟庵，约有十数间草屋，推开着两扇小窗，一个先生搂着一个妇人，在那窗前看月嬉笑。武行者见了，怒从心上起，恶向胆边生，便想道："这是山间林下出家人，却做这等勾当！"②

从上文可知，武松之怒全在他认为道士与妇人之间的调情嬉笑是不合伦理道德的行为，此外并无他念。至于说对该妇人的态度，武松在杀死飞天蜈蚣王道人后，自叫她收拾金银财帛快走下岭去投靠亲戚。而后一把火烧了坟庵，自望青州地面去，并无其他枝节。武松之行为正如李贽之眉批所说，一面是"管闲事"，另一面则是"既不贪财，又不好色"③。

最后，浦安迪说，在作品"武十回"中，武松从打虎英雄、打抱不平的救星到无力自救的可怜虫这一角色的转变，不禁让人想起他由刚出场时身患疟疾的乞丐形象到小说最后成了独臂"废人"的过程。在浦安迪

---

① From this point on, the treatment of the fortunes of Wu Sung turns perceptibly sour. Most telling, I believe, is the incident at Wu-kung ling 蜈蚣岭 immediately following. Here the motivation for Wu's fury is shrouded in the thickest of ambiguities. The cause of his explosive indignation at the Taoist priest's dalliance with an apparently willing partner is not made very clear; and his own attitude toward the girl he has saved remains suggestively ambivalent, in sharp contrast with the unquivocal sense of a damsel in distress in the treatment of the sense in the more recent oral cycle. Andrew H. Plaks, The Four Masterworks of the Ming Novel, Princeton University Press, 1987, p. 322。

② （明）施耐庵、罗贯中：《水浒传》，（明）李卓吾评本，上海古籍出版社1988年版，第448页。

③ 同上书，第448、452页。

看来，这正是作者的反讽笔触逐渐加强、加深的表现。①

浦安迪指出，同属《水浒传》里的反面英雄人物，在性格、处事方面，李逵和武松之间有很多相通的地方。不过，浦氏同时指出，小说作者在叙事过程中对不同人物的处理还是存在区别的。该论者认为：

> 李逵这个人物身上的反面特性暴露得更早一些，它们最终也带来了令人不安的结局。
>
> 在早期的很多场景中读者就见识到了李逵身上的破坏性行为。只是作者一般是以轻松的笔调写出，让人感觉那只是非常幽默滑稽的事件而已。②

当然，浦安迪也说，在第 38 回大闹江州渔场、第 74 回寿张县乔坐衙，以及第 53 回斧劈罗真人未遂而后请罪等故事中，"黑旋风"李逵还是以性情豪放、心地基本善良的正面形象出现的③。只是浦安迪认为在李逵身上终是"瑜不掩瑕"。他说："然而，在繁本小说的文本中，李逵反政府主义倾向中的某些阴暗面的暗示，很快就暴露得让人无法忽视。"④浦安迪以为，第 43 回李逵强行取母，以十分轻松的戏仿笔调开始，却以闹剧、悲剧结束。取母途中所遇冒名人物李鬼，其名字和性格正反映出李

---

① Finally, the section of the novel devoted to the Wu Sung hero-cycle closes with this invincible slayer of beasts and avenging angel rendered nearly powerless. By the end, we have seen him beaten to the point of making a false confession in chapter 30, bound for slaughter in chapter 31, and, most graphically, floundering heipless in a river in chapter 32. At this point, one recalls the introduction of the figure as a sullen beggar wracked with sickness in chapter 22, and we look ahead to his ultimate fate when he is described as a one-armed cripple, a "wreck of his former self" (fei-jen 废人), by the close of the work. Andrew H. Plaks, The Four Masterworks of the Ming Novel, Princeton University Press, 1987, pp. 322 – 323。

② In this case, however, the negative implications in the character surface sooner, and they are subsequently carried to more deeply troubling conclusions. In a number of early scenes, the reader is introduced to examples of Li K'uei's disruptive behavior, but in a manner that is governed by a generally light tone of presentation, which ensures that the incidents will be taken in good humor. Andrew H. Plaks, The Four Masterworks of the Ming Novel, Princeton University Press, 1987, p. 323.

③ This more or less positive image of the "Black Whirlwind" 黑旋风 as an uninhibited free spirit with basically good intentions is predominant in the disturbance among the fishermen at Chiang-chou in chapter 38, in his antics in official robes in chapter 74, and even in the abortive ax murder of the Taoist master Lo Chen-jen and Li's subsequent penance in chapter 53. Andrew H. Plaks, The Four Masterworks of the Ming Novel, Princeton University Press, 1987, p. 323。

④ In the text of the *fan-pen* novel, however, some of the darker implications of Li k'uei's anarchitic tendencies soon become too insistent to be ignored. Andrew H. Plaks, The Four Masterworks of the Ming Novel, Princeton University Press, 1987, p. 323.

逵形象中野蛮、凶残的一面；其中描写虽然带有幽默色彩，情节发展却开始出现更多深层的暗示，令人深思。而当这个小闹剧最终导致李母被老虎咬死、吃掉时，幽默就开始朝另一个方向转变。其中写李逵杀虎与武松打虎形成鲜明的对比，武松赤手空拳打死老虎，李逵却把利刃捅入那畜生的尾巴底下。浦安迪说："这里的不可言说的细节描写，正展现出作者的辛辣机智。"浦氏在该条注释（第122条）中还提出："（李逵杀虎）这一场景的反讽意味，在后来第93回的李逵梦境里再一次得到强调。"①

李逵取母，其鲁莽处确实可恨；因鲁莽而导致悲剧，亦的确可叹。但从中华孝道文化传统来说，笔者以为，李逵感触于宋江取父、公孙胜取母而回家取母，实乃出于一片孝心。正如李逵自己所言："我只有一个老娘在家里，我的哥哥又在别人家做长工，如何养得我娘快乐？我要去取他来这里，快乐几时也好。"②此话说得可谓一片天真烂漫，一片赤诚无瑕。至于李逵把腰刀捅入母大虫粪门而置其于死地的行为，从"证诗"的最后两句"立诛四虎威神力，千古传名李铁牛"来看，作者似乎并无讽刺的意思。

浦安迪以为，在对李逵的描写中，第73回的四柳村事件有着和取母事件相似的反讽意味。他说：

> 李逵自愿进入闺房驱赶折磨少女的妖魔（这使人想起鲁达在第5回中的相同处境。而这和《西游记》第22回孙悟空与猪八戒初次见

---

① For example, Li's forced abduction of his own mother in chapter 43 begins with a light enough tone at the outset, when his grotesquely distorted feelings of filial piety present a parody of similar sentiments expressed by Kung-sun Sheng 公孙胜 and Sung Chiang 宋江 himself immediately before. The encounter with his own double, Li Kuei 李鬼, whose name and attributes mark him as a reflection of the savage side of Li's character, begins to become more suggestive, although this is still essentially a humorous touch. But when this little escapade is shown to result in the mauling of his mother by a tiger, the humor begins to take a different turn. This is another excellent example of the complexity of figural recurrence at work in the novel. Not only is Li K'uei's escape with his mother on his back modeled on Wang Chin's Aeneas-like flight from the capital at the start of the narrative, but the encounter with the four tigers also forces a comparison with the tiger-slaying episode of Wu Sung. Only in this case, Li K'uei's reckless is shown to have fatal consequences. Here the author's acid wit comes out in the fine details. Where Wu Sung conquers his beastly foe in face-to-face combat, the author has one of Li K'uei's thrusts find its mark, to put it nicely, under the tail of the animal. 在122条注释中，浦氏说，The ironic import of this scene is later reemphsized in Li K'uei's dream vision in chapter 93. Andrew H. Plaks, The Four Masterworks of the Ming Novel, Princeton University Press, 1987, pp. 323 – 324。

② （明）施耐庵、罗贯中：《水浒传》，（明）李卓吾评本，上海古籍出版社1988年版，第621页。

面相似），却引出小说中最冷血残暴屠杀的一幕。这是又一个以轻松笔调开始上演的俗套故事的极好例子。但当作者强烈的同情心倾注在那对绝望的小鸳鸯和姑娘那无助的父母身上时，他的处理方式立刻变得严肃起来。这使我们读后感觉到在这个简单的正义故事里蕴藏着更为深刻的含义。①

的确，李逵的残暴行为是让人无法接受的，也是令现代读者难以理解的。只是作者在描写这血腥的屠杀时，似乎是抱着一种冷观、甚至是欣赏的心态，或许我们可以说那是一种完全超乎常人可以理解的变态心理。小说作者不仅对李逵的屠杀过程描写得津津有味，他还抓住"偷汉子"这一议题通过李逵之口来指责可怜的狄太公，并说"除却奸淫，有诗为证：恶性掀腾不自由，房中剁却两人头。痴翁犹自伤情切，独立西风哭未休"。② 当然，在此事件上，小说作者一定程度上确实也表现出了对"姑娘那无助的父母"的同情，也在一定程度上流露出对李逵的责备③。要说其中蕴含深意，似乎也可以。只是这种情感倾向并不明显。而且就文本的总体情况来看，小说作者极少在人物描写时表现出此处所流露出的情感倾向。

说到李逵这一人物的阴暗面，他身上表现出来的冷血凶残，浦安迪以为"在刻画李逵形象阴暗面时，最不可饶恕的就是第51回中残忍地劈死朱全监护下的那个小孩"。在浦安迪看来，如果把这解释成为了凑足梁山好汉的

---

① A similar case may be seen in the incident at Ssu-liu ts'un 四柳村 in chapter 73, where Li K'uei offer to enter a maiden's chamber to exorcise a demon assumed to be tormenting her, figurally reminiscent of Lu Ta's comparable position in chapter 5 (itself similar to the first encounter of Sun Wu-k'ung 孙悟空 and Chu Pa-chieh 猪八戒 in chapter 22 of *Hsi-yu chi*), leads to one of the most coldblooded killings in th book. Once again, we have a good example of a scene that begins lightly enough, with the reenactment of a stereptyped popular story. But the author's treatment soon become more serious as he injects a strong measure of pathos for the desperate young couple and the helpless parents of the girl's, and we are left with a sence that there is more at stake here than a simple case of frontier justice. Andrew H. Plaks, The Four Masterworks of the Ming Novel, Princeton University Press, 1987, p. 323。

② （明）施耐庵、罗贯中：《水浒传》，（明）李卓吾评本，上海古籍出版社1988年版，第1074页。

③ 关于这个问题，且看小说第1073、1074页中一段原文："太公却引人点着灯烛，入房里去看时，照见两个没头尸首，剁做十来段，丢在地下。太公、太婆烦恼啼哭，便叫人扛出后面去烧化。李逵睡到天明，跳将起来，对太公道：'昨夜与你捉了鬼，你如何不谢将？'太公只得收拾酒食相待，李逵、燕青吃了便行。"笔者以为，其中"烦恼啼哭"一词足见两位老人之可怜，"只得"一词亦可见人们对李逵凶残一面的畏惧及指责。只是在总体的行文过程中，小说作者极少有这样的描写。

天罡地煞之数的无奈之举，可作者又精心描写出朱仝与其上司之间相互尊重的关系，以及朱仝对小衙内真诚的疼爱，这种解释就完全是无力的。① 换句话说，在浦氏的研究中，文本前后之间的描写存在着如此大的矛盾冲突之处应是作者的有意之举，而这就为反讽阐释留下了足够的空间。笔者以为，就第 51 回"美髯公误失小衙内"这个故事来看，单从凑足天罡地煞之数来解释该事件的确不是很合情理。然而，联系到作者在小说开篇第一章"洪太尉误走妖魔"中所作的交代，又确实为该解释伏下了合理的叙事线索和行文逻辑。虽然这种神话结构在现代读者看来实在虚幻，但它却是统领整部作品的纲要，也是让一百零八人最终走到一起的内在叙事动力。

在浦安迪的研究中，小说作者对李逵作的下述描写也是具有反讽含义的。

首先，李逵不近女色或者说是厌女症的态度与实际对待女性行为之间的关系，以及这种行为所产生的叙事效果。就《水浒传》第 38 回对李逵因歌女宋玉莲打断自己夸夸其谈的讲话而暴跳如雷的场景的描写和他在结义兄弟之中作为最标榜不近女色之间的对比所作的描写，第 72 回李逵在李师师寓所门口因暴躁闹事而使梁山好汉错失尽早受招安机会的描写，以及作者在第 93 回对李逵那富有暗示性的梦境所作的描写，等等，浦安迪认为，"这些情节之中的反讽笔调是不言而喻的"②。

其次，李逵在梁山一伙中的地位和角色，李逵身上那打破一切的造反

---

① The most unforgivable example of the problematic side of the portrait of Li K'uei, however, is surely the brutal killing of the small child in Chu T'ung's protection in chapter 51. I suppose that it would not be entirely impossible to interpret this act as a necessary evil in the cause of fulfillin the preordanained numerical strength of the Liang-shan band. But the author invalidates this interpretation by carefully portraying Chu T'ung's relationship with his superior as one based on mutual respect, and by pressing the point of sincere affection between Chu and the child. Andrew H. Plaks, The Four Masterworks of the Ming Novel, Princeton University Press, 1987, p. 325.

② In fact, there are a number of scenes in the novel in which it is specifically a female figure who unwittingly provokes Li K'uei rage, as for example at the end of chapter 38, when the singer Sung Yü-lien's 宋玉莲 unwise interruption of Li's manly boasting triggers a disproportionately violent reaction. The ironic tone of these scenes is unmistakable, given the fact that among the members of the brotherhood it is most often Li K'uei who voices the hao-han 好汉 code of sexual pride. This is perhaps most noticable in chapter 72, when it is Li's nervous impatience outside the apartment of Li Shih-shih 李师师 that undermines the chance for an early amnesty for the band. Many of these associations are brought together in Li K'uei's very suggestive dream in chapter 93, in which he first rescues a damsel in distress and refuses to take her as his wife, later wipes out all the evil minister at the imperial court, and finally sees his own mother back in the woods, threatened by another tiger. Andrew H. Plaks, The Four Masterworks of the Ming Novel, Princeton University Press, 1987, pp. 324 – 325。

天性不仅针对皇权还针对梁山内部,李逵"天煞星"的星辰名号,小说描写李逵走上战场时反复出现的"见一个杀一个,见两个杀一双"的俗语映照之下的滥杀无辜,李逵在比武时经常失败的事实,李逵在第68回的一场恶仗中恰好大腿根部受伤,以及李逵在征方腊的最后一仗中败得一塌糊涂……浦氏以为,所有这些细节都证实了他提出的作者在描写李逵这一形象时是具有反讽含义的观点,是有据可依的[①]。

在浦安迪的讨论中,鲁达和武松、李逵一样都属于"重现类型的系列人物",都是具有反讽色彩的反面英雄。浦安迪说,这三个人物不仅形体相像,性格特征也非常接近。尤其是鲁达和武松,自二龙山始就以"二行者"而命运相连。不过,浦氏对鲁达的论述很简略。遵循讨论武松、李逵两人的思路,他说:

> 在第3至第7回对鲁达系列冒险行动的叙述中,作者保持了一种相对轻松的笔调。从打死郑屠,大闹五台山,在东京大相国寺管理菜园,到处身野猪林营救林冲,在这叙述过程中,作者并未刻意左右读者享受这位自由不羁的英雄的冒险行为所带来的乐趣。[②]

浦安迪认为,鲁达的命运转变——强及必弱的主题的揭示,是在第6回灵异的瓦罐寺事件中开始发生的。不过,这位赤条条的和尚在小说第119回圆寂时,还是实现了初愿、修成了正果。[③]

按上述之论,既然浦氏把鲁达放入反面英雄行列,在论述中却根本没有涉及负面话题,更没有提及作者描写该形象时蕴含的反讽含义,这是很难理解的。据此,笔者以为,浦氏的研究理论与研究视角根本无力把鲁达这一形象囊括在其中。换句话说,浦氏的研究存在以理论来框文本的问题。这一点

[①] Andrew H. Plaks, The Four Masterworks of the Ming Novel, Princeton University Press, 1987, pp. 325, 326, 327.

[②] In the early recounting of the adventures of Lu Ta in chapter 3–7, the author maintains a relatively light touch. In the episodes of killing of Cheng the Butcher, Lu's naked riot in the monastery at Wu-t'ai shan 五台山, and his stint as a gardener in the capital that positions him to rescue Lin Ch'ung, the author does little to qualify the reader's delight in the adventures of an irrepressible hero. Andrew H. Plaks, The Four Masterworks of the Ming Novel, Princeton University Press, 1987, p. 327。

[③] Andrew H. Plaks, The Four Masterworks of the Ming Novel, Princeton University Press, 1987, p. 327.

在浦氏对鲁达、武松与李逵这组人物形象所作的比较中露出了端倪。

浦安迪认为,小说作者在描写鲁达时,总体上给人的是痛快愉悦的感受。不过,这种阅读中的情感体验在武松、李逵身上则发生了变化。他说:

> 当这种人物性格类型在第22—31回重现于武松身上时,特定场景中痛快愉悦的阅读体会则让位给了敬畏、甚至是某种令人烦恼不安的模棱两可的感觉。只是武松这个形象总体上仍然能获得读者的同情。然而,李逵这一形象则使系列人物中前两个范例所蕴含的深意得以彻底暴露,而形成必然的结论。因此,至少从第51回无故杀害小衙内始,小说描写的暴行就不再好笑或是令人敬畏。这些暴力行为,往好里说是荒唐可笑的,往坏里说则是完全一无是处。[①]

小说对武松、李逵的描写,确实暴露出中国传统人物心理的阴暗面。在此,笔者的疑惑是,既然浦安迪在前面的讨论中根本没有谈到鲁达身上的负面问题,也没有提到作者在描写这一人物形象时所蕴藏的反讽含义,为什么在此处又说其身上蕴含深意呢?既然说作者对鲁达的描写总体上给人痛快愉悦之感,那反面意义又是如何产生的呢?据此,笔者以为,浦氏在反讽理论的观照下把鲁达放入反面人物的行列是缺乏充足的说服力的。

(二) 宋江

在水浒英雄的反面人物里面,宋江是浦安迪的重点讨论对象。这不仅因为宋江是《水浒传》中最复杂的形象,而且受怀林、金圣叹等人观点的影响,浦氏认为宋江和李逵构成了小说中至关重要的相反相成的一对人物。事实上,浦安迪以反讽理论研究水浒人物,只是以西方小说观念为表而以金圣叹等中国古代小说评点家的观点为里。这表现在其所使用的批评术语和具体的论点上。不止如此,在浦安迪看来,繁本小说对宋江的描写,也有一个由轻松幽默到辛辣反讽的发展变化。对此,浦安迪说:

[①] When this character type is recast in the person of Wu Sung in chapter 22 – 31, delight gives away to awe and troubling ambiguity in certain scenes, but the portrait still generally continues to command the reader's sympathies. In the figure of Li K'uei, however, the implications that are present in the earlier two instances of the chain reach ultimate conclusions, so, at least from the point of the gratuitous killing of the child in chapter 51, the violent actions portrayed are no longer very funny or awe-inspiring. They are at best grotesque, and at worst profoundly negative. Andrew H. Plaks, The Four Masterworks of the Ming Novel, Princeton University Press, 1987, p. 327.

> 当我们讨论繁本小说中塑造的宋江这个复杂的人物形象时，必须记住有一个由轻松幽默到辛辣反讽的层层深入的发展过程。因为在多种意义上，李逵和宋江构成了作品中一对至关重要的相反关系的人物。①

由此可知，浦安迪认为小说作者对宋江的描写和武松、李逵、鲁达三人一样，也有一个由轻松幽默到辛辣嘲讽的层层深入的过程。而这一过程是通过对人物的精妙的细节刻画得以实现的。在浦氏眼里，小说对宋江的描绘，处处都有反讽含义。

首先，宋江的肖像与体型特征含有反讽意蕴。浦安迪说：

> 从体型特征开始，我们首先注意到宋江并非长得仪表堂堂。从一开始，他就被描绘成是一位皮肤黝黑的矮子。而且在某些地方作者还告诉我们他有点胖。第33回，当描写他踮起脚尖、穿过人群观看元宵花灯时，作者还对其短小身材加以渲染嘲讽。他脸色黝黑，因而绰号"黑三郎"、"黑宋江"。这些皆非无故之笔，这使宋江和那些高贵的君王之理想的仪表显得迥然有别。而且更为重要的是，它使我们联想到小说中与之相关的另外几个可疑的人物形象。这些人物包括好色的侏儒王英王矮虎，相貌粗陋、戴绿帽子的（三寸丁谷树皮活乌龟）武大，以及一系列上起刘唐、终至李逵的黑脸暴徒。在第38回，李逵本人在他们初次相遇时就注意到宋江的黝黑肤色。②

---

① This range of treatment, from light humor to bitter irony, must be kept in mind when we come to consider the complex image of Sung Chiang as developed in he *fan-pen* novel, since in anumber of senses Li K'uei and Sung Chiang comprise the most crucial pair of linked opposites in the book. Andrew H. Plaks, The Four Masterworks of the Ming Novel, Princeton University Press, 1987, pp. 327 – 328.

② Beginning at the level of physical attributes, the first thing we notice is that Sung Chiang does not cut a very imposing figure. He is described from the very outset as the heavy side. His diminutive stature is played up for ironic effect in chapter 33, when he is forced to stand on his tiptoes and peer through a crowd to get a look at Yüan-hsiao Festival lanterns. His dark complexion, as indicated by his nicknames Black Third Son（Hei san-lang 黑三郎）and Black Sung Chiang（Hei Sung Chiang 黑宋江）, is not simply an idle detail, as it sets him apart from the ideal physiognomic qualities of a nobel ruler, and more to the point, also gives the first suggestion of a figural link to several other problematic individuals in the novel. These include the lustful dwarf Wang Ying-the "dwarf tiger"（Ai-hu）-the gnarled cuckold Wu Ta, and a series of swarthy outlaws beginning with Liu T'ang and culminating in Li K'uei, who himself calls attention to Sung's dark color at their first meeting in chapter 38. Andrew H. Plaks, The Four Masterworks of the Ming Novel, Princeton University Press, 1987, p. 328。

据浦安迪之论，宋江长相的确其貌不扬，并因此长相而沦落到武大的地步。但我们能否仅抓住作者描写宋江"面黑身矮"这一点就说其中含有深意呢？要知道，浦安迪论述所依的繁本《水浒传》第 18 回宋江初出场时，作者对他的描写可并非如此。且看原文如下：

> 看那人时，怎生模样，但见：眼如丹凤，眉似卧蚕。滴溜溜两耳垂珠，明皎皎双睛点漆。唇方口正，髭须地阁轻盈；额阔顶平，皮肉天仓饱满。坐定时浑如虎相，走动时有若狼型。年及三旬，有养济万人之度量；身躯六尺，怀扫除四海之心机。上应星魁，感乾坤之秀气；下临凡世，聚山岳之降灵。志气轩昂，胸襟秀丽。刀笔敢欺萧相国，声名不让孟尝君。①

由此观之，宋江哪里无君王之仪表呢？李卓吾在眉批中尚且说"太诶，强盗安得如此好相"。就此处所写，在小说作者眼中，宋江不仅仪表非凡，而且胸怀大志，既具才学又有品行。

其次，宋江的诨名绰号具有反讽含义。浦安迪指出：

> 在小说中，宋江的诨名绰号比其他任何人物都多。除了指他皮肤黝黑的那些绰号，他还以"呼保义"、"及时雨"和"孝义黑三郎"为我们所熟知。在一定程度上，这样众多的名号只是反映了有关宋江的历史资料来源之多及其传奇故事流传之广。但在文人小说的媒介中，这为作者展现其反讽智慧提供了非常肥沃的土壤。②

以"孝义黑三郎"这个江湖诨名来说，浦氏认为"作品中，宋江身

---

① （明）施耐庵、罗贯中：《水浒传》，（明）李卓吾评本，上海古籍出版社 1988 年版，第 245 页。

② Sung Chiang is endowed with more nicknames and descriptive tags than any other character in the book. In addition to the references to his swarthiness, he is also known variously as Guardian of Valor (Hu pao-i 呼保义), Timely Rain (Chi-shih yü 及时雨), and the Filial and Noble (Hsiao-i hei san-lang 孝义黑三郎). At one level, this multiplicity of names simply reflects the various kinds of historical sources and popular legends regarding Sung. But in the medium of the literati novel, this provides very fertile ground for the author to plant some of his ironic wit. Andrew H. Plaks, The Four Masterworks of the Ming Novel, Princeton University Press, 1987, pp. 328 – 329.

上'孝'的方面是大成问题的"。他说：

> 一开始作者使我们相信"孝"是宋江最美好的品质之一。第22回，正是他父亲控告其忤逆行为的诡计，而在假意否定中给予强有力的肯定。但是，随着小说的发展，人物对话中反复出现的论题就把梁山强人无法无天和有辱父母家庭的观念明确地联系在一起。这个思想观念在第36回那场至关重要的争议中特别得到强调。①

至于"及时雨"这个绰号，浦安迪认为也同样具有反讽意蕴。他以为该绰号虽然有慷慨大方的意思，也指宋江解囊相助、周济好汉的美好声誉，但在"雨水丰沛"的比喻中却暗含着对宋江动不动就流眼泪这个习性的一丝嘲讽。浦氏还认为，在这一点上宋江与《三国演义》里的刘备是相似的，在行军作战方面的描写中根本没有"及时"的行动。②并且浦氏以为小说对宋江为人"仗义疏财"这一品性的描写蕴藏我们通常所理解之外的另一种含义。他说，宋江因为武艺平平，所以只能依靠其仗义疏财的江湖声望来救自己的性命。而宋江对待江湖人士"若高若低无有不纳"的不辨清白不明是非的态度却给他带来了灾难性的后果，不仅危及家庭幸福还威胁到帝国的安危。③

---

① For example, the issue of Sung Chiang's filiatily comes up for quite a bit of questioning in the text. At first we are led tobelieve that this is indeed one of Sung's finest attributes. This is strongly affirmed precised by its pretended negation in the ruse by which his father denounces him for unfilial behavior in chapter 22. But as the novel progresses, repeated points in the dialogues draw a clear link between the lawlessness of the band and the concept of dishonor to parents and family. This idea is particularly emphasized in the pivotal debates in chapter 36. Andrew H. Plaks, The Four Masterworks of the Ming Novel, Princeton University Press, 1987, p. 329.

② The same sort of ironic undercurrents may easily be percived in Sung's nickname Timely Rain, an expression usually glossed in the sense of beneficent generosity, as an indication of his reputation as an unsynting patron of *hao-han* fellows. In this metaphor of bounteous rain we may perhaps note a hint of ironic reference to Sung Chiang's very noticeable propensity to tears, a reading that may appear less far-fetched if one considers the parallel to Liu Pei in San-huo on this same point. At any rate, in many scenes in the novel Sung's actions are depicted as anything but timely, and this is especially true with regard to his planning and execution of military strategy. Andrew H. Plaks, The Four Masterworks of the Ming Novel, Princeton University Press, 1987, pp. 329 – 330.

③ Andrew H. Plaks, The Four Masterworks of the Ming Novel, Princeton University Press, 1987, p. 330.

在浦安迪看来，对宋江的描写最构成反讽意蕴的是下面几个事件。一是阎婆惜事件。通过仔细研读这一事件的相关细节，浦氏提出：

> 随着故事情节的发展，作者通过人物并置和关键细节，揭示出蕴藏在宋江和阎婆惜关系之下更为深刻的反讽含义。如此，《宣和遗事》所写因通奸而复仇杀人的简单行为，在小说里就变成了更为复杂的对人性动机的探索。①

而且浦安迪认为通过细读阎婆惜事件中的不少场景可以发现，"有许多其他点缀笔墨似乎都在抹黑宋江这个英雄形象"。他以阎婆惜听到娘叫"你亲爱的三郎"竟误以为宋江是其真正的情人张三郎这一细节为例，说那是"绝妙的笔触"。②

二是将一丈青许配给王矮虎事件。浦安迪说：

> 小说中，宋江对一丈青态度的处理更是蕴含着反讽的弦外之音。第48回，繁本作者通过微妙的细节告诉我们，宋江为那位女将的本领"暗暗的喝彩"。当她最后被林冲生擒，宋江把她送回梁山泊其父亲处听候发落时，所有在场的人自然以为他要把她据为己有。正在此时，繁本小说作者不失时机增添有力的一笔：宋江彻夜未眠。后来，当宋江把她交给声名狼藉的王英时，人们会把这看作是宋江慷慨大度品性的证据。但鉴于此种把本领高强的女将嫁给侏儒的不相匹配的可笑做法，以及上文我们讨论过的宋江和王英体型上的相似，很难不让

---

① As the section develops, the author brings out deeper ironies in the relationship between Sung Chiang and Yen P'o-hsi through a variety of figural juxtapositions and pointed details; thus, what was presented in *Hsü-ho i-shih* as a simple act of revenge for adultery becomes in the novel a far more complex exploration of human motivations. Andrew H. Plaks, The Four Masterworks of the Ming Novel, Princeton University Press, 1987, p. 330.

② When the Yen P'o-hsi scene is read in this way, numerous additional details seem to chip away at thee foundations of the heroic image of Sung Chiang, as for example in the clever touch of having Sung miataken for Yen P'o-hsi's real lover, Chang San-lang 张三郎, when he is announced as "your darling San-lang" 你亲爱的三郎. Andrew H. Plaks, The Four Masterworks of the Ming Novel, Princeton University Press, 1987, p. 331。

人发现其中相当深刻的嘲讽意味。①

浦氏以为,宋江的这些行为是梁山好汉在不近女色的口号之下蕴藏着的"情欲反讽含义",实则揭示出宋江等人表里不一的内在品质,以及那种对野心、权力、肉欲(口腹之欲、性欲、色欲)既想抑制又想攫取的矛盾心理和深层的精神状态。在讨论中,浦安迪列举第39回宋江因贪食而患病、后在浔阳楼题反诗,第72回宋江在李师师酒色诱使下咏诗抒怀等场景,认为正暴露了宋江的此种心理,这些细节则为作品增添了一层反讽色彩。而繁本《水浒传》中的这种思想内容,最主要的是通过贯穿作品的宋江与李逵这对相反人物之间相互影射的关系形成的主旋律展现出来的。②

上面谈到权力欲问题,浦安迪认为权力欲驱使下梁山发生的系列"争权"事件是最具反讽色彩的,又最能揭示出宋江的虚伪、野心与权力欲的膨胀。浦安迪说:"描写宋江在等级森严的梁山爬上头把交椅过程中那些暗示其虚伪的事件,是最具嘲讽意味的。"③浦安迪以为在宋江和晁盖之间,从三打祝家庄到攻打曾头市是一种富有讽刺意味的争夺梁山领导权的拉锯战,而这一拉锯战在第60回晁盖宣称"不是我要夺你的功劳"中完全明朗化。对晁盖之死,浦氏指出,金圣叹《水浒传》批评中使用"弑"这个意指篡夺王位的词告诉我们,宋江在此事件中有共谋的嫌疑。"而在

---

① The treatment of Sung's attitude toward this last female figure is even more pregnant with ironic undertones. Through his subtle control of fine details, the author of the *fan-pen* version informs us of Sung Chiang's "secret sighs of admiration" 暗暗喝彩 for the female knight's prowess in chapter 48. When she is finally captured (by the mighty arms of Lin Ch'ung) and Sung has her sent back to the custody of his father on Liang-shan-po to be disposed later, all those present naturally assume that he intends to take the girl for himself. At this point, the author of the *fan-pen* text takes the time to add a telling touch: Sung spends that entire night sleeoless. Thereafter, when he delivers her into the unsavory hands of Wang Ying, one might take this as futher evidence of Sung's generosity of spirit, but in view of the ludicrous mismatch of valiant maid-in-arms to dwarf, on top of the figural linkage we have noted between Sung and Wang, it is hard to avoid seeing in this resolution a rather sardonic note. Andrew H. Plaks, The Four Masterworks of the Ming Novel, Princeton University Press, 1987, p. 332。

② Andrew H. Plaks, The Four Masterworks of the Ming Novel, Princeton University Press, 1987, pp. 333 – 337.

③ These intimations of hypocrisy are most sardonic in the treatment of the process by which Sung Chiang rises to the top position in the outlaw hierarchy. Andrew H. Plaks, The Four Masterworks of the Ming Novel, Princeton University Press, 1987, p. 340.

此事件之后，对宋江争夺梁山领导权的嘲讽变得越来越辛辣尖刻。"①

总之，在浦安迪眼里，小说作者对宋江的描写处处都有深意，其一言一行一举一动都蕴藏着反讽色彩。而在浦氏反讽论的观照下，宋江是一个虚伪、奸诈、欲望膨胀的人物形象。

四、水浒英雄中的正面人物

在浦安迪的反讽研究中，《水浒传》不仅描写了上面谈到的武松、李逵、鲁达、宋江等典型的反面英雄人物，也塑造了为数不少的正面人物形象。他说：

> 在反讽叙事的另一面，我想强调一个事实，那就是小说在描绘人物阴暗面的同时，也尽力刻画出一大批正面的人物形象和思想观念。其目的在使读者尽可能对所描写的事件保持一种更均衡的理解。②

在开始研究水浒英雄中的正面人物形象之前，他进一步指出：

> 在把反讽界定为一种叙事修辞原则的同时，我也坚持认为它是一个具有某种肯定含义的概念。因此，必须重点强调指出，小说作者通过塑造一系列体现中国传统英雄观念的正面人物，以平衡对这些人物（指宋江等反面形象，笔者）的阴暗面所作的各种描写。③

---

① This ironic tug-of war becomes all but exciplicit in chapter 60, when in finally winning his point Ch'ao protests, "It is not that Twant to steal your glory" 不是我要夺你的功劳, thus dispelling any remaining pretense of innocence on his part.... In this light, Chin Sheng-t'an seems to hit the mark when he goes as far as to denounce Sung's passive complicity in Ch'ao's death with the starkest Confucian term of opprobrium: *shih* 弑, normally reserved for instances of patricide or regicide. From this point on, the iriniies in Sung Chiang's takeover of the band become more and more bitter. Andrew H. Plaks, The Four Masterworks of the Ming Novel, Princeton University Press, 1987, p. 341。

② On this other side of the coin, I will emphasize the fact that the novel also takes pains to present a certain number of positive figures and ideals, alongside its more somber portraits, in order to keep before the reader's eyes the possibility of a more balanced understanding of the meaning of the events portrayed. Andrew H. Plaks, The Four Masterworks of the Ming Novel, Princeton University Press, 1987, p. 320.

③ In definiing irony as a principle of narrative rhetoric, however, I have also insisted on the notion of some kind of projection of a positive ground of meaning. It is extremely important, therefore, to point out that the author of the novel also provides a counterweight to the darker aspects of his treatment of these figures, through a string of characters who present a more upright embodiment of the traditional Chinese conception of the hero. Andrew H. Plaks, The Four Masterworks of the Ming Novel, Princeton University Press, 1987, pp. 343 – 344.

根据浦安迪的论述，作者描写正面英雄形象是为了起一种平衡作用。这不仅能削弱作品对人物阴暗面的揭示所带来的负面效果，同时也在一定层面上肯定了小说文本中塑造的大部分梁山好汉及呈现出来的思想观念。

（一）林冲、杨志与卢俊义等人

在浦安迪看来，水浒英雄中正面类型的人物主要包括林冲、杨志、秦明、朱仝、关胜、呼延灼、卢俊义和燕青等人。浦氏指出，这些人物虽然经历遭遇各不相同，却拥有不少相通的地方。他说：

> 这些人虽然因环境迥异而经历各自不同的人生遭遇，但在体形特征与心理素质方面却拥有相通的地方。其中最重要的是他们都非常看重江湖"义气"。在这一点上恰与前面论述的梁山英雄中几个关键人物那有失体面的行为形成尖锐的对比。①

说到心理素质上的相通性，燕青之外，浦安迪认为：

> 这些孔武的勇士脆弱的一面，最为生动地表现在他们总体上呈现出一种孤僻的心态。这通常用几乎成为套语的"闷闷不乐"一词来形容。这些近乎史诗般的英雄人物画像上也笼罩着美中不足的过分骄傲的阴影。②

而正是这种孤僻的、过分骄傲的心态，导致他们在处事时总是那么固执、自信，其结果就使这些人物的命运朝悲剧的方向发展。浦安迪说：

---

① Among the stories of each of these men differentiated by varying circumstances, they are share a fairly compact set of physical and psychological qualities. Most important among these is a very strong sence of personal honor (i-ch'i 义气), an element that provides a pointed contrast to the sort of compromising behavior I have traced above in the case of the principle Liang-shan heroes. Andrew H. Plaks, The Four Masterworks of the Ming Novel, Princeton University Press, 1987, p. 344。

② The weaker side of these mighty warriors is most movinglymanifested in their common tendency to exhibit a kind of loner mentality, so often expressed in the nearly formulaic epithet "sunk in hopeless depression" (men-men pu-le 闷闷不乐). The portraits of these potentially epic figures are also clouded by a common flaw of excessive pride. Andrew H. Plaks, The Four Masterworks of the Ming Novel, Princeton University Press, 1987, p. 345。

第三章 英语世界对《水浒传》的人物形象塑造研究

这类形象中的每一个人，正是此种固执、骄傲、自信使他们处于孤立无援的境地，最终沦陷到"有家难奔有国难投"的绝境。①

以卢俊义、杨志为例，浦氏指出：

最为明显的事实是，第61回中，卢俊义因过分自信而导致其第一次被梁山好汉所擒。第16回对杨志刚愎自用行为的处理，我们也能看到一种相似的情形，虽然在那种特定的环境中杨志蛮横地对待下属可能实在是无奈之举。②

浦安迪认为，小说第一回描绘的王进就已为《水浒传》里正面英雄人物类型的塑造张本。对此，他说：

出现在小说开篇部分的林冲，是这类人物中第一个获得充分发展的形象。事实上，早在作品第一回中描写的王进，就已为此类人物的刻画奠定了基调。在职业、性格特征乃至遭受高俅迫害方面，他和林冲具有非常明显的关系。林冲自然有其成问题的方面，但明显继承了这类人物的特点，并将其传到小说中一长串个体人物的身上。他们包括杨志、秦明、杨雄、朱仝、关胜、呼延灼和卢俊义，其中大部分是职业军官，后在梁山号称"骁将"。③

---

① In each case, it is this unbending attachment to proud self-image that places such men in a position of total isolation, "with neither home nor country to turn to for refuge" 有家难奔有国难投. Andrew H. Plaks, The Four Masterworks of the Ming Novel, Princeton University Press, 1987, p. 345。

② This is obviously true of the treatment of Lu Chün-i's overblown self-assurance, which leads to his first capture by the Liang-shan men in chapter 61. And we can see a similar sence, in the treatmen of Yang Chih's arrogant behavior in chapter 16, although here his uncompromising harshness to his men is probably justified under the circumstances. Andrew H. Plaks, The Four Masterworks of the Ming Novel, Princeton University Press, 1987, p. 345.

③ The first fully developed example of this type of figure materializes early in the book, in the case of Lin Ch'ung. In fact, the model for this character type was already set up in th very first chapter of the book in treatment of Wang Chin, who is clearly linked to Lin Ch'ung by profession, character traits, and even parallel clashes with the power of Kao Ch'iu 高俅. Lin Ch'ung is not without his problematic side, but he clearly continues this model, and passes it on to a long list of individuals, including Yang Ch'ih, Ch'in Ming, Yang Hsiung, Chu T'ung/ Kuan Sheng 关胜, Hu-yen Cho, and Lu Chün-i, most of whom are also professional military men of the sort later labeled "crack general" (hsiao-chiang 骁将). Andrew H. Plaks, The Four Masterworks of the Ming Novel, Princeton University Press, 1987, p. 344。

在该论者看来,林冲与杨志之关系正如王进与林冲一样,都是并置共构的人物形象。他说:

> 林冲与杨志之间相似之处相当明显,因为这两位勇士不仅拥有相同的性格与相似的命运,他们各自不同的人生遭遇也因"宝刀"这个共同的母题而形成某种类型的并置结构。①

按此论,其实梁山好汉中的绝大多数人物都属于这种并置共构的形象。上述反面人物中的武松、李逵、鲁达如此,本小节提到的正面人物林冲、杨志、秦明、朱仝、关胜、呼延灼、卢俊义和燕青等人亦然,浦氏在讨论时未提及的三阮、张横、张顺、李俊、童威、童猛、解珍、解宝等人亦莫不如此。

虽然视杨志、朱仝、关胜、呼延灼、卢俊义等人为正面英雄人物,但在描写他们"逼上梁山"的方式上,浦安迪认为其中仍具有反讽意味。浦氏说:

> 这些出身名门的真正的勇士被"逼上梁山"的方式,往往并非如该词语的通俗观念所揭示的是一种无奈之举而是将其曲解成劫持与谋害的事实,不能不使小说在这一特殊方面增添强烈的反讽色彩。②

只是在这里,反讽的矛头是指向这些人物本身呢?还是指向那些迫使他们上梁山的梁山好汉呢?抑或是指向小说的思想意蕴呢?浦安迪并未阐明。

(二) 燕青

在水浒英雄的正面人物中,浦安迪讨论最力、评价最高的是燕青。

---

① The contrived link between Lin Ch'ung and Yang Chih is especially obvious, since these two warriors not only share a variety of attributes and similar fates, but their seperate stories are also set into a kind of parallel construction through the common motif of the treasure sword (pao-tao 宝刀). Andrew H. Plaks, The Four Masterworks of the Ming Novel, Princeton University Press, 1987, p. 344。

② In this light, the fact that these true warriors of nobel stock are so often "forced to climb Liangshan" 逼上梁山 in a manner that distorts this popular notion from valiant desperation into the area of kidnapping and murder cannot but intensify the ironic light in this particular aspect of the novel. Andrew H. Plaks, The Four Masterworks of the Ming Novel, Princeton University Press, 1987, p. 345。

林冲、杨志、卢俊义等虽同属于正面英雄人物，但如上文所述，他们身上还是存在很明显的缺陷。与这些人相比，燕青则全然不同。浦安迪指出：

> 《水浒传》描绘的另一个人物也属于这些正面英雄之列，而又避免了那潜在的残酷无情的反讽针砭。他不是上文论及的那些职业军官中的一员，而只是一位身份低下的人物——卢俊义家的仆人燕青。初次出场他并未给人留下特别深刻的印象，他看起来似乎是我们在早先见识过的浪子辈中的成员之一而已。然而，在小说的后半部分，我们逐渐知晓并欣赏此人特别的品质（在此，声名倒在其次，人物是实在的）。①

而所谓"特别的品质"，在浦安迪看来，一是本领超群、勇敢无畏、赤胆忠心；二是理智冷静，在情感上具有超强的自我控制能力；三是有远见、识时务。

在第一个方面，浦安迪以为燕青不仅具有强健的体魄、堪与张顺相媲美的洁白肌肤以及一身漂亮的文身，作者还赋予他众多特殊技能。对此，浦安迪说："他是一位相扑高手，一位出色的歌者，一位百发百中的神箭手，甚至还精通各地方言，此项本领在很多场合都起着重要作用。"当然，这些对燕青来说还在其次。浦氏进一步指出：

> 此外他是一位具有勇敢无畏战斗精神的人，正如我们在第74回看到的，在相扑比赛开始之前他就在心理上震慑住了对手。而且他还有一颗赤胆忠心，就如在第62回里他对主人卢俊义所展现的义不容

---

① There is one character presented in the *Shui-hu chuan* who, while loosely falling into the category these positive heroes, still manages to escape from the inexorable process of ironic undercutting. This is not one of the professional military men considered just now but rather the less pretentious figure of Lu Chün-i's retainer, Yen Ch'ing. In his initial appearence, Yen is not particularly impressive__ he appears to be yet another member of the class of idlers (*lang-tsu* 浪子) we saw burlesqued earlier. Throughout the second half of the book, however, we gradually come to know and appreciate some of the exceptional attributes of the man (in this case it is the reputation that is petty and the man who is subatantial). Andrew H. Plaks, The Four Masterworks of the Ming Novel, Princeton University Press, 1987, p. 346。

辞的强烈情感。①

不过，在浦氏的论述中，这些对燕青的优秀品质来说并不是最重要的。浦安迪认为，勇力再强也不如在处理大事上所展现出来的那种理智冷静与自我控制的精神品质。他说：

> 展现燕青英雄豪情最有意义的事例，不在其勇力或本领较量上的获胜，而在其对情感的自我控制。这在第81回中得到充分的完善。在那里，正是燕青的自我控制才抵挡住李师师的轻浮挑逗撩拨，并最终使宋江招安的愿望得以实现。燕青在这儿的行为举止，反过来正映衬出宋江这个意志薄弱的人物在第72回相似情境中的表现。而那第一次会面，也全是凭借燕青的本领周旋才得以实现。②

在此，浦安迪通过燕青与宋江之比较，对燕青的品行与智慧极尽赞美之情，对宋江则尽情指责鞭笞。而且浦氏还认为，"当作者紧接着断定'若是第二个在酒色之中的，也坏了大事'时，其矛头所向已是相当清楚"。③ 按浦安迪之意，小说作者这句话是嘲笑讽刺宋江的。为了凸显燕青的完美品行，浦安迪自然也没有忽略小说中燕青设计与李师师结拜"拜住那妇人一点邪心"的细节。

---

① He is an accomplished wrestler, a fine singer, an unfailing archer, and even proficient in a variety of local dialects, a skill that has an important use in a number of scenes. In addition, he is a man of intrepid fighting spirit, as we see in the psychological manipulation that crushes his opponent even before the start of the wrestling match in chapter74. He also possesses an admirable sense of personal loyalty, as he demonstrates in his intense emotional commitment to his lord Lu Chün-i in chapter 62. Andrew H. Plaks, The Four Masterworks of the Ming Novel, Princeton University Press, 1987, p. 346.

② The most significant example of Yen Ch'ing's heroism, however, surfaces not in feats of strength or skill, but rather in his emotional self-mastery. This is fully developed in chapter 81, where it is Yen's self-control in resisting the careless flirtations of Li Shih-shih that finally enables Sung Chiang to legitimize his ambitions. Yen's behavior here reflects back to the weak-kneed figure of Sung Chiang in a similar situation in chapter 72 where, significantly, it was the dash and skill of Yen that brought about that meeting in the first place. Andrew H. Plaks, The Four Masterworks of the Ming Novel, Princeton University Press, 1987, p. 346.

③ When the author goes on to pointedly state, "If this had been another man subject to the attractions of wlne and sex, the grand undertaking would have been undermined" 若是第二个在酒色之中的，也坏了大事, the object of his barb is fairly obvious. Andrew H. Plaks, The Four Masterworks of the Ming Novel, Princeton University Press, 1987, p. 347。

在有远见、识时务方面，浦安迪说：

> 作品结尾处燕青在美梦将逝之际及时全身而退，足见其具有超凡的洞察世事的能力与智慧。这就是作者为何说他"知进退存亡之机"的原因。①

在浦安迪看来，和其他水浒英雄中的正面人物相比，燕青是一个"近乎完美无瑕的形象"。这个引人注目的形象从肉体到精神方面的美德可用小说中多次形容他的"风流"一词来概括，而所谓"风流"更多是一种正面的含义，即是"既注重感情又洒脱不羁"之意。②

浦安迪反讽理论观照下的水浒人物研究，视角的确比较新颖，某些观点也具有一定的借鉴意义。但从整体上来看，或许是源于文化差异与文化隔阂，不少论述还是显得很牵强，缺乏足够的说服力。有时，浦氏往往只抓住人物描写上的片言只语就得出其中具有反讽含义的结论。如在讨论宋江这个人物时，浦安迪抓住其"面黑身矮"这一点大做文章，说其具有反讽意蕴，而对宋江出场时作者所写赞诗却视而不见。这种做法显然是很不可取的。这在上文相关部分已有讨论，不再赘述。而且笔者在考察浦氏的研究时发现，其所依据的是袁无涯刻120回繁本《水浒传》，但他却经常引用金圣叹在贯华堂本中提出的观点。既然贯华堂70回本《水浒传》是金圣叹删改过的，不要说排座次后的内容完全删去，单就金圣叹对入回诗、行文中的韵文以及人物赞诗所作的删削，就使其在细节描写、词语表达方面和袁无涯刻本存在很大的差别。那么，以金圣叹贯华堂本中的观点来评价袁无涯刻本里的水浒人物形象，其间会出现多大的误差呢？这是一个问题。还有就是，以西方反讽理论来研究中国古典小说里的人物形象，

---

① In the end, Yen's timely withdrawal from the faded dream of glory is credited to a kind of insight or experimental wisdom, whereby he "understood the secret hinge of commentment and withdrawal, life and death" 知进退存亡之机. Andrew H. Plaks, The Four Masterworks of the Ming Novel, Princeton University Press, 1987, p. 347。

② ... the author has expended on drawing a nearly unbiemished portrait of Yen Ch'ing... This wide range of physical and spiritual qualities in the very appealing image of Yen Ch'ing may be summed up in the ambivalent term *feng-liu* 风流, applied to him at several points in the text. In Yen's case, the sencse conveyed by this term falls more on the positive side of its semantic range, so that it means something like "affectionate and dashing". Andrew H. Plaks, The Four Masterworks of the Ming Novel, Princeton University Press, 1987, p. 347。

其可行性有多大，也是一个必须反思的问题。

第四节 水浒女性形象研究

《水浒传》所写人物虽然以男性为主，但也描绘了一些让人印象深刻的女性形象。潘金莲自不必说，阎婆惜、孙二娘、顾大嫂、扈三娘等也是有名号可循的；就是金氏女（翠莲）、林娘子、刘高妻，在片言只语中也有自己的性格。只是相对于男性人物的描写，水浒世界的女性形象就要逊色不少，不论是作者所用笔墨还是她们在小说中的地位都是如此。就笔者掌握的资料来看，英语世界专论水浒女性形象的文章（或论著）寥寥可数，其他散论的文字也非常少。相对来说，他们更多把精力放在讨论《水浒传》的作者与作品里的男性人物是以什么样的态度对待女性的，以及为什么会形成此种态度等问题。

一、男权社会中的水浒女性形象塑造

在现代批评者看来，《水浒传》里的女性人物形象是很不可思议的。在结义兄弟基础之上描写的屈指可数的那么几个女性人物，要么本领高强勇猛凶悍，要么淫荡不贞满身罪恶，要么严守妇道坚贞不屈，反正没有一个具有现代意义上完整鲜活的人性。

《水浒传》在女性形象的塑造上为什么会出现这样的情形呢？夏志清认为，首先也是最根本的是这部小说被"突出的厌恶女性的倾向"所主宰[①]，而在厌恶与仇视女性这种非理性心理的左右之下塑造出来的女性人物自然是异化的、非正常的形象。

对这个问题，孙述宇有更详细的论述。在他看来，《水浒传》里的这些女性人物，不管是女英雄还是淫娃荡妇抑或贞节娘子，她们都只是男性的附属物，都只是旧中国男权社会男性自由意志支配之下塑造出来的人物形象。他说：

> 《水浒传》这部非常特殊的作品烙上了显著的阳性创作印痕。这不仅是以男性为中心的所谓"男性沙文主义"，更是对女性极端的残

[①] C. T. Hsia, Chinese Classical novel, Newyork: Columbia University Press, 1968, p. 104.

忍。其他著作可能集中描写男人的事务，只关注男性美德，或者描绘一系列没有女人的男性形象，却极少表现出如此极端的敌视女性的态度。①

基于这样的认识，孙述宇进一步指出："由于旧中国是一个男权中心社会，《水浒传》反映这样的现实，自然就把女性降格到次要的位置。"②忠义堂排座次，梁山108好汉中的3位女英雄全都不在天罡星之列就是很好的证明。而在该论者看来，扈三娘的本领是胜过霹雳火秦明的。不过，孙述宇也指出：

<blockquote>
仔细考察，水浒世界并不久完全憎恶女色，作品中也有个别获得赞美的女子。……小说里被杀的女性，要么犯有不贞的罪名，要么协助或唆使使其发生。被杀的也有男性触犯者，如西门庆和裴如海。③
</blockquote>

总体来说，对于《水浒传》所描绘的女性形象，孙述宇认为："小说虽然降低她们的社会地位，却让她们享受到很好的艺术待遇。"他说：

<blockquote>
小说纵然没有女性主角，但它设计的几个反面女性人物却是推进情节发展的枢轴。如果有谁认为《水浒传》的作者不擅于描绘女性形象，那他可就大错特错。作品中不少女性人物描写得相当娴熟到位，比那些普通的跑龙套的男性人物出色得多。有些读者或许会忘记王婆和阎婆两位老太婆，但她们生动鲜活远比朱丽叶的乳母更具艺术
</blockquote>

---

① *Shui Hu Chuan* (*The Water Margin*) strikes one as a very peculiar book of masculine creation. It not only is centered about men and may deservedly be called "male-chauvinistic", but also is exceedingly cruel to women. Other books may focus on men's business, take note of only manly virtues, or present a cast of men without women, yet few appear to be so hostile to the other sex. Phillip S. Y. Sun, The Sedtitious Art of The Water Margin-Misogynists or Desperadoes?, Renditions Autumn (1973), p. 99.

② Since the old Chinese society was man-centered, *The Water Margin*, reflecting this reality, naturally relegates women to an inferior position. Phillip S. Y. Sun, The Sedtitious Art of The Water Margin-Misogynists or Desperadoes?, Renditions Autumn (1973), p. 99.

③ To be accurate, the world of *The Water Margin* does not hate the female sex as a whole. There are individual good women commended in the book. ... Women slain in the book have either committed adultery, or aided and abetted it. Slain too are the male offenders, e. g., Hsi-men Ch'ing and P'ei Ju-hai; Phillip S. Y. Sun, The Sedtitious Art of The Water Margin-Misogynists or Desperadoes?, Renditions Autumn (1973), p. 102.

生命力。从她们这边来说,西门庆、宋江这些男人看起来就显得黯然失色。①

《水浒传》对女性人物的描绘的确有非常精彩之处,但由于敌视、憎恶女性的心理与思想观念在其中作梗,小说作者描写、塑造女性形象时往往作一种极端的处理。对这种情况,孙述宇指出:

> 然而,由于对肉欲的厌恶,小说中的女性在人格上很少集美貌与美德于一身。娼妓和淫妇全都很漂亮,梁山上的好女人的典型如顾大嫂则长得"眉粗眼大,胖脸腰肥"。②

孙氏还说:

> 《水浒传》对女性敌视得很,书中的女人除了几位梁山女英雄不算,其余全是道德败坏的,她们年少的纵欲(书里叫她们作"淫妇"),年老的贪财(叫作"虔婆"),而两者之忘恩负义则如出一辙。③

上述是《水浒传》在女性人物形象塑造时出现的一种极端倾向。水浒作者在描写女性形象时的另一做法则是让她们异化为男性。对此,孙述宇指出:"从忠义堂三姐妹的情形看,似乎女子亦可与男子平等;不过这

---

① Besides, women enjoy good artistic positions in the novel, however low their social position. The novel, albeit without female protagonists, has several negative roles assigned to women that are pivotal to the development of its plot. And one cannot be more mistaken than to think that the authors of *The Water Margin* were not good at portraying women. Quite a few of them in the book are expertly delineated, much better than the common run of its men. Few readers willforget the two crones Grandma Wang and Grandma Yen, who have more vividness and vitality than Juliet's nerse; by their side, men like Hsi-men Ch'ing or Sung Chiang look dull. Phillip S. Y. Sun, The Sedtitious Art of The Water Margin-Misogynists or Desperadoes?, Renditions Autumn (1973), pp. 99 – 100.

② However, owing to the distaste for carnality, women in the novel seldom combine beauty and virtue in their persons. The whores and lewd women all look pretty, but the good woman of Liangshan, as tupified by Ku Ta-sao (Elder Sister Ku), may well have "thick eye-brows, big eyes, fat face, and broad waist". Phillip S. Y. Sun, The Sedtitious Art of The Water Margin-Misogynists or Desperadoes?, Renditions Autumn (1973), p. 102.

③ 孙述宇:《水浒传:怎样的强盗书》,上海古籍出版社2011年版,第237页。

时她们做的是男人的事，在样貌各方面也渐趋男性化，失却原来的女性了。"① 从作品对她们的描写来看，尤其是孙二娘和顾大嫂，的确如此。

对此问题，在夏志清、孙述宇等人研究的基础上，吴燕娜则认为《水浒传》在女性形象的塑造上会出现上述问题，一方面与对女性的恐惧有关，另一方面则是由小说的主题所决定的②。

以上是英语世界学者对水浒女性形象描写特征及其形成原因的大致观点。

二、水浒女性形象与淫妇

由上文可知，《水浒传》所塑造的女性形象皆非完全正常意义上的人物，她们身上展现出来的只是人性之中某一端的特征、某一方面的特点。正因为《水浒传》在女性形象的描绘上出现这样特别的情形，批评者沈静在研究时援引中国学者徐江的观点说，我们可以把有代表性的水浒女性人物形象分为三大类：第一类是上应天罡地煞之数加入梁山好汉队伍的三位女英雄，包括扈三娘、孙二娘和顾大嫂；第二类是淫妇潘金莲、潘巧云、阎婆惜和卢俊义的夫人贾氏；第三类则是贞节娘子张贞娘，也就是林冲娘子。③

第一类中的三位女英雄也就是小说里的"好女人"，则几乎完全男性化了。如上文孙述宇指出的，小说在描写顾大嫂时就说她有一副"眉粗眼大，胖脸腰肥"的样貌。对孙二娘，孙氏说"'母夜叉'就是她的外貌"；而"母夜叉"原是佛教中的邪恶女性形象，可知长得肯定不漂亮，但该论者以为，"以梁山标准衡量不算太恐怖"。至于扈三娘，该论者告诉我

---

① 孙述宇：《水浒传：怎样的强盗书》，上海古籍出版社2011年版，第246页。

② Among them, two contrasting types, the physically strong, martial women and the seductive adulteresses, offer an interesting comparison. The novel's theme tends to exclude the claims of family, especially those of women, and so it shows martial women (who fight for the interest of the group) prospering, and seductresses (who act for self-interest) meeting ghastly deaths. Yenna Wu, Condemnation: Other Fiction, The Chinese Virago: A Literary Theme. Literature Criticism from 1400 to 1800. Ed. Lynn M. Zott. Vol. 76. Cambridge: Harvard University Press, 1995, pp. 106 – 123.

③ As Xu Jiang observes, the young women characters who stand out in The Water Margin can be classified in the following three categories: 1) woman warriors who later join the bandits at the Marshes of Mount Liang-Miss Hu (Steelbright), Sister Sun (the Ogress) and Auntie Gu; 2) adulteresses-Pan Jinlian, Pan Qiaoyun, Yan Poxi and Nee Jia; 3) virtuous wife-Zhang Zhenniang. Jing Shen, Re-Visions of Shuihu Women in Chinese Theater and Cinema, China Reciew, Vol. 7, No. 1 (Spring 2007), p. 105, 123.

们:"扈三娘是美人,但是她出场时的赞诗(797页)除了很笼统的一句'天然美貌海棠花'之外,只描述她在马上的英风豪气。"由此可知,作者在描写这类女性人物时并没有什么特别的地方。其结果就是,批评者在研究她们时自然也就没有给予太多的关注。第三类的张贞娘,也就是林冲娘子,出场不久即便消失,根本没给研究者留下什么空间。对于此种现象,孙述宇猜测小说作者"大概是不希望读者听众太注意不邪恶的美色"①。

在水浒女性形象中,以潘金莲为代表的所谓"罪恶女性"、"淫妇"这类人物,相对来说是描绘得最出彩、最成功、最让人印象深刻的,自然也是最受研究者关注的。而在这类女性人物里面,潘金莲又是备受关注的焦点。

从现代思想观念出发,研究者对这类女性总体抱以同情的态度。夏志清如此论述道:"《水浒》中的妇女并不仅仅是因为心毒和不贞而遭严惩,归根到底,她们受难受罚就因为她们是女人,是供人泄欲的冤屈无告的生灵。"② 这话显然是针对潘金莲、阎婆惜、潘巧云、贾氏以及娼妓李瑞兰、李巧奴等人而说的,其同情、怜悯之情溢于言表。该论者接着说:

> 小说所写的四个罪恶女性——讹诈贪婪的阎婆惜、毒杀亲夫的潘金莲、谗言害人的潘巧云以及卢俊义的前妻——不管她们的其他罪行如何,除各自所犯的罪行外,都是对婚姻不满或不甘受约束的偷夫养汉的女人。③

而她们之所以会出现此行为并最终遭到好汉们的报复虐杀,其原因与责任却应归咎在好汉们的头上。夏志清指出:

> 心理上的隔阂使严于律己的好汉们与她们格格不入。正是由于他们的禁欲主义,这些英雄下意识地仇视女性,视女性为大敌,是对他们那违反自然的英雄式自我满足的嘲笑。④

---

① 孙述宇:《水浒传:怎样的强盗书》,上海古籍出版社2011年版,第246页。
② [美]夏志清:《中国古典小说》,胡益民等译,江苏文艺出版社2008年版,第101页。
③ 同上。
④ 同上。

和夏志清相似，沈静在研究时对所谓的"淫妇"这类水浒女性人物是表示理解并同情其遭遇的。在讨论潘金莲这个人物时，该论者说：

> 小说中，潘金莲是一个淫妇和谋杀亲夫武大的凶手，但她并非一开始就是个淫荡的女人。因她拒绝、反抗主人张大户的色诱（她是一个婢女），作为惩罚，把她嫁给了侏儒武大。后来，由王婆促使，她才与西门庆通奸并杀害武大。①

从这论述中可知，沈静认为潘金莲的悲剧人生是由其生活的社会环境造成的，而非其本性使然。她只是以张大户为代表的男权世界的牺牲品，其婢女的身份告诉人们，她只是一个弱者。综合夏志清之论，这类人整个就是一弱势群体。伊爱莲（Irene Eber）在研究时也表达了相同的观点，她认为《水浒传》中的女性属于弱势群体②。

在孙述宇眼里，《水浒传》描绘的潘金莲是一个非常成功的文学形象。他说：

> 事实上，金莲这个被称作狐媚邪恶的女子是一个完美的艺术创造。第24回描写她设计勾引叔叔武松，一直不断用那妩媚诱人、令人骨头发酥的语调喊着"叔叔"，就是很好的证明。③

对此，孙述宇论述道：

---

① In the novel, she is an adulteress and murders her husband WuDa, but she is not a wanton woman from the beginning. Because Pan Jinlian resisted her master's sexual advances (she is a maidservant), he marries her off to the dwarf Wu Da as a publishment. She later commits adultery with Ximen Qing and murders Wu Da, instigated by Wang Po. Jing Shen, Re-Visions of Shuihu Women in Chinese Theater and Cinema, China Reciew, Vol. 7, No. 1 (Spring 2007), pp. 109 – 110.

② Irene Eber, Weakness and Power: Women in the *Water Margin*, in Anna Gerstalacher, R. Keen, et al., eds., *Women and literature in China*, Bochum: Studienverlag Brockmeyer, 1985, pp. 3 – 28.

③ And Golden Lottus, called the arch wicked woman, is in fact superb as an artistic creation. Witness how, in chapter 24, scheming to seduce her brother-in-law Wu Sung, she chirps and chirps, and sprinkles her alluring words with the siren address "*Shu-shu*". Phillip S. Y. Sun, The Sedtitious Art of The Water Margin-Misogynista or Desperadoes?, Renditions Autumn (1973), p. 100.

这是她头一场小小的戏，但演到这里，已给读者留下印象。《水浒》写人物容貌的方法与一般长篇旧小说无异，算不上高明，但作者在这里改用声音来制造效果。潘金莲的话一句句有不同的声调与表情，清晰得很，她的妖娆，她那些由情欲而生的气力与黠慧，都表现出来了。说起来，梁山的大英雄说话之时倒很少给人这样深刻的印象。①

同一回里，武松拜辞其兄武大时小说作者对武松与潘金莲之间所作的那番语言描写（原文见脚注）②，孙氏对之更是赞誉有加。他说：

何时何地，民间口头文学能达到如此高的艺术水准呢？小说经常尝试描写人物的激烈情绪，但难得描写得如此之棒。上面这段，词语的运用与金莲曾经做过大户人家的婢女和对丈夫长期管制的经历之间保持着高度的一致性，也把她因羞愧而生的怒火以戏剧化的方式鲜活地表现出来了。任何没有精心观察过女性的作家都不可能写出如此的文字。③

小说中，潘金莲的塑造的确非常成功。作者通过语言描写、"用声音来制造效果"，把潘金莲的心理变化、情感流动，特别是把她因引诱不成

---

① 孙述宇：《水浒传：怎样的强盗书》，上海古籍出版社2011年版，第234—235页。
② 那妇人被武松说了这一篇，一点红从耳朵边起，紫涨了面皮；指着武大，便骂道："你这个腌臜混沌！有甚么言语在外人处说来，欺负老娘！我是一个不戴头巾男子汉，叮叮当当响的婆娘！拳头上立得人，胳膊上走得马，人面上行得人！不是那等搠不出的鳖老婆！自从嫁了武大，真个蝼蚁也不敢入屋里来！有甚么篱笆不牢，犬儿钻得入来？你胡言乱语，一句句都要下落！丢下砖头瓦儿，一个个要着地！"武松笑道："若得嫂嫂这般做主，最好；只要心口相应，却不要'心头不似口头'。既然如此，武二都记得嫂嫂说的话了，请饮过此杯。"那妇人推开酒盏，一直跑下楼来；走到半扶梯上，发话道："你既是聪明伶俐，却不道'长嫂为母'？我当初嫁武大时，不曾听说有甚么阿叔！那里走得来'是亲不是亲，便要做乔家公'！自是老娘晦气了，鸟撞着许多事！"哭下楼去了。那妇人自妆许多奸伪张致。——第二十四回"王婆贪贿说风情 郓哥不忿闹茶肆"。
③ When and where has oral folk literature attainted such levels of artistic accomplishment? Violent emotion is often attempted in fiction but rarely well presented. The above passage, using words in keeping with Lotus' background of having been a maidservant in an affluent household and having long henpecked her husband, vividly dramatises her ire that comes from shame and guilty conscience. It cannot have been authored by anyone not observant of women. Phillip S. Y. Sun, The Sedtitious Art of The Water Margin-Misogynista or Desperadoes?, Renditions Autumn (1973), p. 100.

反受武松奚落从而恼羞成怒的一面活灵活现地展现给了读者，确实是精彩非凡。

只是，《水浒传》毕竟是一部以男性为绝对主体的作品，留给女人的空间是相当有限的。作者在女性人物的描绘上即使有如此成功的地方，但那实在少得可怜。到此，笔者对英语世界水浒女性形象研究的讨论暂告结束。

第四章

英语世界对《水浒传》的叙事结构艺术研究

作为中国古代长篇叙事文学——白话章回小说发展史上的奠基之作，《水浒传》和《三国演义》一样，因其一出现就达到了很高的艺术水准，两者皆成为中国古代白话小说发展历程中具有非常大影响的、里程碑式的杰作。而所谓里程碑式的杰作，最根本的就在其开创了一种新的文学样式，在创作手法、叙事方式、结构艺术诸方面都具有文体学的开拓性意义。按中国学界的基本共识，"七分史实、三分虚构"的《三国演义》是根据史书记载的人物事件为本创作而成的文学作品，它的成书开创了"按史演义"的长篇章回小说文体形式。与《三国演义》不同的是，"三分史实、七分虚构"的《水浒传》充分发挥小说家的想象能力，把草莽英雄、市井细民的日常生活作为书写的对象，它的成书则开创了"英雄传奇"的白话章回小说文体形式。

而在英语世界的批评者李培德看来，在中国文学发展的历史上，《三国演义》和《水浒传》的出现意义非常重大。该论者认为，它们一方面标志着新的文学时代——中国叙事文学、小说时代的到来，另一方面则为后来的小说创作开创了不同的叙事类型。对此，李培德说：

> 《三国演义》和《水浒传》在风格、情节和主题上存在显著的差异，这两部作品标志着中国小说时代的来临。……《三国演义》和《水浒传》的作者开创了颇受大众欢迎的、不同的叙事类型，后来的模仿之作几乎没有哪部作品达到了它们的艺术水准，此两者是中国散

文小说发展的里程碑。[1]

作为这种具有里程碑意义的著作,《水浒传》一进入英语世界的读者与批评者的阅读、接受视野,他们就对小说的创作手法、叙事艺术与文本结构等文体方面的独特之处感到非常新奇。而当他们以西方小说的标准来衡量《水浒传》的情节叙述手法与文本结构形式时,则感到从未有过的困惑与不解。因为《水浒传》这个传统中国文化、文学环境的产物,具有迥异于西方文化、文学的创作模子。这对于英语世界的读者与批评者来说,是一种完全陌生的文学模式,它打破了他们固有的阅读习惯。

那么,英语世界的批评者是如何看待《水浒传》这样一部新奇、陌生的文学作品的叙事、结构艺术特征的呢?本章,笔者就来讨论他们对上述问题的相关研究情况。

第一节 对《水浒传》叙事结构模型的认识与建构

作为中国古代"英雄传奇"长篇白话章回小说文体的扛鼎之作,自成书至今,《水浒传》的结构艺术在中国学术界引起很大的争议。肯定者说其结构严密、是个有机的整体,如李开先称其"委曲详尽,血脉贯通",郑振铎则认为小说"结构原是一个很严密的组织。就全部观之,确是一部很伟大的很完美的悲剧"。批评者则认为《水浒传》的结构正如鲁迅评价《儒林外史》时所说的那样,"虽云长篇,颇同短制"[2],实在算不上结构完美的长篇小说。对此,茅盾就曾指出,小说中不同的人物故事完全可以拆分开来,因而"从全书来看,《水浒》的结构不是有机的结构"[3]。而从整体来看,批评者中的主流观点还是认为《水浒传》是一部

---

[1] Notwithstanding differences in style, plot and theme, the Romance and The Water Margin marked the coming of age of the Chinese novel.... The authors of the two works created different types of popular narrative, but very few later works patterned after them achieved the level of artistry as found in either the Romance or The Water Margin, both landmarks in the development of Chinese prose fiction. Winston L. Y. Yang, Nathan K. Mao and Peter Li, "Romance of the Three Kingdoms and The Water Margin," and "Journey to the West and Flowers in the Mirror." Classical Chinese Fiction: A Guide to Its Study and Appreciation. London: George Prior Publishers, 1978, pp. 39 – 51. Literature Criticism from 1400 to 1800. Ed. Lynn M. Zott. Vol. 76. Detroit: Gale, 2002. From Literature Resource Center.

[2] 鲁迅:《中国小说史略》,岳麓书社2010年版,第150页。

[3] 茅盾:《谈〈水浒〉的人物和结构》,《文艺报》二卷二期,1950年。

结构比较松散的长篇小说。

与中国学术界的情形大体相同，英语世界的批评者从开始关注、评价《水浒传》的叙事结构一直到现在，绝大部分人都认为这是一部结构松散的小说。如赛珍珠所指出的，对西方的读者与批评者来说，《水浒传》等中国小说的主要弱点就在情节结构方面。该论者说：

> 对西方评论界来说，这三部（指《水浒传》《三国演义》与《西游记》，笔者注）长篇的缺点和优点同样明显。主要的弱点在情节方面。情节特别复杂，还有很多次要的情节处理得很糟糕。人物众多，出现了一会，就从接下来的几章中消失，一直到小说结尾处才又不经意地露面，或者干脆都不再露面，有关线索就断在那里。结果，小说变得拖沓冗长，毫不协调，有时是一片混乱。①

此观点的提出，既有小说文本自身的原因，也是以西方文学标准为参照的结果。赛珍珠在1938年诺贝尔文学奖颁奖仪式上所作的《中国小说》的演讲中就说：

> 按照西方的标准，这些中国小说并不完美。它们总是没有自始至终的计划，也不严密，就像生活本身没有计划性和严密性一样。它们往往太长，事件太多，人物太拥挤，材料中事实和虚构混杂，方法上浪漫传奇与现实主义交融，结果，一种不可能出现的魔幻或梦幻的事件可以被描绘得酷肖逼真，以至使人违背一切理性去相信它。②

用所谓现实主义的或浪漫主义的理论观念来批评、衡量《水浒传》等中国小说的叙事艺术，这是英语学术界中国文学研究中"以西释中"

---

① 姚君伟编：《赛珍珠论中国小说》，南京大学出版社2012年版，第30—31页。
② These Chinese novels are not perfect according to western standards. They are not always planned from beginning to end, nor are they compact, any more than life is planned or compact. They are often too long, too full of incident, too crowded with character, a medley of fact and fiction as to material, and a medley of romance and realism as to method, so that an impossible event of magic or dream may be described with such exact semblance of detail that one is compelled to belief against all reason. Pearl S. Buck, The Chinese novel: Lecture Delivered before the Swedish Academy at Stockholm, December 12, 1938 (New York: John Day Co., 1939), p. 32.

的典型案例，也是所谓的"文化帝国主义"的具体表现。

不过，即使英语学术界的主流声音认为《水浒传》是一部结构松散的长篇叙事文学作品，但随着对中国文化与文学传统研究的不断发展、深化，不少批评者逐渐认识到中国小说在叙事结构艺术上的民族特质。因而把研究的视角逐渐转向中国文学本身，并从中国文学的历史发展来寻找阐释的依据。正是从"以西释中"到"融合中西以释中"这一学术理路的转变，英语学术界的批评者在《水浒传》叙事结构艺术的研究上逐渐找到了新的阐释起点，从而抛却简单的"不严密"、"拖沓冗长"与"松散"的认识，把研究重心转向探索《水浒传》的叙事结构模型与基本结构原则上。

就《水浒传》的结构模型，英语世界的批评者自韩南到浦安迪，前后之间大致提出了四种不同的看法。不过，仔细研究可以发现，它们之间的相通性还是很大的；甚至可以说，在最根本的层面上它们具有基本的一致性。这将在下文作具体的讨论。其中，夏志清的论述非常简略，他认为"《水浒传》的结构是综合型的"，而且在该论者看来"它的艺术性比直叙史实的《三国演义》要略逊一筹"[①]。夏志清对此问题未作更深入的探讨，就不再展开。其他三种观点依次是由韩南、李培德、浦安迪与吴德安提出的。下面，笔者就按此顺序论述之。

一、韩南论《水浒传》的"联合布局"与"顶层结构"

1967年，韩南在《早期中国短篇小说》一文中曾就中国早期短篇小说与《水浒传》《三国演义》等长篇章回小说展开过比较研究，并对中国小说布局的发展作过一个简略的论述。在分析论述过程中韩南提出，像《水浒传》这一类型的小说，在情节结构上属于"联合布局作品"（linked works）[②]。所谓"联合布局"小说，是与"单一布局小说"（unitary fiction）相对而言的。韩南认为，此两种小说结构布局之区分，主要表现在

[①] [美]夏志清：《中国古典小说》，胡益民等译，江苏文艺出版社2008年版，第71页。

[②] The rise of a new kind of thematic story provides further evidence. This is the kind of story that treats some historical or pseudo-historical event as a matter of moral concern. Of course, concern with political morality is evident in linked works such as the *Shui-hu chuan* and the *San-kuoyen-i*, but it is not found among the early short stories. Patrick Hanan, The Early Chinese Short Story: A Critical Theory in Outline. Harvard Journal of Asiatic Studies, Vol. 27 (1967), p. 203.

文体形式与情节方面①。

按韩南之论，所谓"单一布局"是这样的一种情形：

> 情节无论如何复杂、曲折，结构布局仍是完整一体的；如果从中抽出具有实质性的内容，就会破坏故事情节的完整性。②

而"联合布局"则不同，韩南说：

> 情节只是一系列松散地联合在一起的故事片段的框架，其中的某些内容移除之后，对故事的整体布局不会造成不可弥补的破坏；这些不同的部分本身皆可成为独立的小布局。③

这就是韩南所说的中国古代小说中的"单一布局与联合布局"（the unitary plot and the system of linked plots）的各自特征及区别。

在韩南看来，《水浒传》不仅具有"联合布局"的结构模型，还具有把不同部分的"联合布局"的人物故事情节统一起来的"顶层结构"（superstructure）。韩南以小说中的武松故事为例说，武松的每一段历险故事差不多都构成一个几乎完美的单一布局，对文本中的某些内容进行删节、剪裁，并不妨碍情节的完整。而且虽然讲述武松故事的若干章回是自成一体的联合布局，但它们又与其他联合布局，如讲述宋江故事的那些章回相互环扣在一起。而贯通这两个不同的联合布局之间的纽带则是此两主

---

① The main differences between linked and unitary fiction were found to be, on the formal level, a difference in plot, and on the non-formal level, a difference in mimetic scale. Patrick Hanan, The Early Chinese Short Story: A Critical Theory in Outline. Harvard Journal of Asiatic Studies, Vol. 27 (1967), p. 200.

② At one extreme, we have the plot which, no matter how intricate it may be, is all of one piece; nothing substantial can be subtracted from it without destroying it as a plot. Patrick Hanan, The Early Chinese Short Story: A Critical Theory in Outline. Harvard Journal of Asiatic Studies, Vol. 27 (1967), p. 183.

③ At the other extreme, we have the plot which is a framework for a series of loosely linked segments, some of which could be removed without doing irreparable damage to the whole; potentially, these segments are minor plots in their own right. Let us call these polar types the unitary plot and the system of linked plots. Patrick Hanan, The Early Chinese Short Story: A Critical Theory in Outline. Harvard Journal of Asiatic Studies, Vol. 27 (1967), p. 183.

角的偶然相遇。① 根据《水浒传》中反复出现的这种情节结构布局方式，韩南提出：

> 因此，在《水浒传》及其他相似的作品中，有一个我们称之为结构之上的"顶层结构"，它把各个联合布局组织在一起。《水浒传》中，英雄们的聚合，从开始造反到结束，所有这些都是操控不同联合布局系统并把它们组合成一体的"顶层结构"。②

根据韩南的论述，笔者以为我们其实可以把联合布局看作《水浒传》的小结构，而顶层结构则是统管整部作品、把各个不同的联合布局组织成一体的大结构。在小结构里面，作者不断把梁山好汉个体演绎在读者眼前；在大结构里面，作者则把所有这些英雄们聚合在一起，也就是作品中多次描写的、规模逐渐发展壮大的"聚义"。像第15回"公孙胜应七星聚义"，第40回"白龙庙英雄小聚义"，第58回"三山聚义打青州"，这些回目中的叙事，作者就是把分散各地的英雄们不断地聚合在一起，最终达到第71回"梁山泊英雄排座次"的鼎盛局面。换句话说，英雄们的由散而聚，再由聚而散，也就是韩南所说的英雄主角的偶遇，以及他们从开始造反到结束，这就是韩南提出的贯串整部作品的顶层结构。

二、李培德论《水浒传》的"主题单元"与"环状结构"

1977—1978年，李培德连续在两篇文章中讨论了《水浒传》的叙事

---

① As an example of the latter, the system of linked plots, we could take the Wu Sung chapters of the *Shui-hu chuan*. Each of Wu Sung's adventures consists of an almost perfect unitary plot in itself, and some of them could, with a little bridging of the gap, be removed from the text without great loss. But although the Wu Sung chapters form a system of linked plots, they are themselves linked to other systems, for example the chapters that deal with Sung Chiang. There is a master-link between the two systems, in this case the recurring motif of the chance confrontation that ends in firm friendship. Patrick Hanan, The Early Chinese Short Story: A Critical Theory in Outline. Harvard Journal of Asiatic Studies, Vol. 27 (1967), pp. 183 – 184.

② Therefore, in the *Shui-hu chuan* and in certain other works, there is a level of organization above the kind we have been speaktig of, a superstructure – in this work the assembling of the heroes, the birth and death of the rebellion-which controls the various systems of linked plots. Patrick Hanan, The Early Chinese Short Story: A Critical Theory in Outline. Harvard Journal of Asiatic Studies, Vol. 27 (1967), p. 184.

结构模型问题①。在此两篇文章中,该论者吸收了韩南的"联合布局"的看法,并在此基础上提出《水浒传》的基本叙事结构模型是"联合布局"(linked-plot)的"环状结构"(a cyclical chain or, more accurately, a sequence of cycles,亦译为"环状链"或"环状序列"结构)的观点②。该论者指出:

> 《水浒传》是由一系列叙事环构成的,每一个叙事环由不同的英雄为主角。《水浒传》前七十回由八个故事环所主宰,这八个故事环以鲁智深、林冲、武松、宋江等八位重要英雄为核心。③

按李培德之论,小说前七十回中的八个联合布局的故事环分别是这样的:第三至七回,以鲁智深为核心进行叙事;第七至十二回,以林冲为核心展开叙述;第十二至十三回、十六至十七回,以杨志为叙事中心;第十四至十五回、十八至二十回,以晁盖为叙事中心;第二十一至二十二回、三十二至四十二回,宋江是故事的主角;第二十三至三十二回,武松是故事的主角;第五十四至五十八回,小说围绕着呼延灼展开叙述;第六十至七十回,则围绕着卢俊义展开叙述。④ 李培德所说的这些以某一英雄为核心的故事环,按中国学界的认识其实就是小说作者从史书借用来的"人物

---

① 前一篇文章是《〈三国〉和〈水浒〉的叙事模型》,Peiter Li, Narrative patterns in *San-Kuo* and *Shui-hu*, Plaks, Andrew. Ed. Chinese narrative: critical and theoretical essays. Princeton, N. J.: Princeton University Press, 1977. 后一篇文章是《〈三国演义〉和〈水浒传〉与〈西游记〉与〈镜花缘〉》,Winston L. Y. Yang, Nathan K. Mao and Peter Li, "*Romance of the Three Kingdoms* and *The Water Margin*", and "*Journey to the West* and *Flowers in the Mirror*". Classical Chinese Fiction: A Guide to Its Study and Appreciation. London: George Prior Publishers, 1978, pp. 39 - 51. *Literature Criticism from 1400 to 1800*. Ed. Lynn M. Zott. Vol. 76. Detroit: Gale, 2002. From Literature Resource Center。

② Peiter Li, Narrative patterns in *San-Kuo* and *Shui-hu*, Plaks, Andrew. Ed. Chinese narrative: critical and theoretical essays. Princeton, N. J.: Princeton University Press, 1977, p. 80.

③ *The Water Margin* is composed of a sequence of cycles, each of which features a different hero. The first seventy chapters of *The Water Margin* are dominated by eight story cycles centering around eight important heroes, such as Lu Chih-shen, Lin Ch'ung, Wu Sung, and Sung Chiang. Winston L. Y. Yang, Nathan K. Mao and Peter Li, "Romance of the Three Kingdoms and The Water Margin," and "Journey to the West and Flowers in the Mirror." Classical Chinese Fiction: A Guide to Its Study and Appreciation. London: George Prior Publishers, 1978, pp. 39 - 51. *Literature Criticism from 1400 to 1800*. Ed. Lynn M. Zott. Vol. 76. Detroit: Gale, 2002. From Literature Resource Center.

④ Peiter Li, Narrative patterns in *San-Kuo* and *Shui-hu*, Plaks, Andrew. Ed. Chinese narrative: critical and theoretical essays. Princeton, N. J.: Princeton University Press, 1977, pp. 80 - 81.

列传"书写体例。

谈到《水浒传》前70回里的叙事"环状链",李培德认为:"这个环状链是由劫持、营救与对抗朝廷等行动元素联缀而成的。"该论者同时也指出:"我们必须承认,与相互交织的叙事线索相比,这种联合布局的叙事体系,从根本上来说还是一种比较松散的结构形式。"[1] 但即便如此,李培德仍然指出:

> 即使小说的内部结构存在这样的缺点,但《水浒传》里矛盾冲突与解决的总体方式还是给人留下深刻的印象。矛盾冲突的双方,一个是法律意义上的"正义的"逃犯,一个是腐败、专制的朝廷。在第1—70回中,冲突的模式形成;随着众多好汉的出现,以及他们的组织势力变得越来越强大,矛盾冲突的张力也随之增大。当一百零八好汉全部汇聚在一起时,梁山势力达到了顶峰。不久之后,在75—80回中,朝廷先后派出童贯和高俅去镇压这帮英雄。但梁山的力量实在太强大,他们两败童贯,三败高俅。然而,在第八十二回里,当宋江接受朝廷的招安时,就找到了解决双方对抗、冲突的办法。此时,情节继续展开。诗性正义(poetic justice)需要这帮好汉获得更大、令人印象更加深刻的胜利。因此,他们展开征四寇行动,并取得成功。冲突的最后解决就是宋江死于高俅与童贯的阴谋。[2]

基于这样的认识,李培德进一步指出:

---

[1] This cyclical chain is interspersed with descriptions of raids, rescue missions, and campaigns against the givernment. But it must be recognized that the system of linked plots is fundamentally a looser form of organization than that of the interweaving of narrative strands. Winston L. Y. Yang, Nathan K. Mao and Peter Li, "*Romance of the Three Kingdoms* and *The Water Margin*," and "*Journey to the West* and *Flowers in the Mirror*." Classical Chinese Fiction: A Guide to Its Study and Appreciation. London: George Prior Publishers, 1978, pp. 39 – 51. *Literature Criticism from 1400 to 1800*. Ed. Lynn M. Zott. Vol. 76. Detroit: Gale, 2002. From Literature Resource Center.

[2] In spite of this weakness in internal structure, the overall pattern of conflict and resolution in *The Water Margin* seems impressive. The opposing groups in the conflict are the "righteous" fugitives from the law on the one hand and the corrupt, despotic government on the other. In Chapters 1 – 70, a pattern of confrontation emerges; tensions increase as the number of outlaws grows and their organization strengthens. The group reaches its full strength when the number hits 108. Shortly afterwards, in Chapters 75 – 80, the government sends T'ung Kuan and Kao Ch'iu on separate occasions to suppress the band, but the band is too strong. It defeats T'ung Kuan twice and Kao Ch'iu thrice. However, in Chapter 82, a resolution of the

虽然联合布局体系让《水浒传》的内部结构存在这样的不足，但通过主题单元、矛盾冲突与解决的总体方式、地理聚焦以及好汉们的总体目标诸因素的结合，小说却拥有一个强大的外部结构模型。①

根据李培德的论述，我们可以把"环状结构"分为两层，一是主宰整部小说的大的"外部结构模型"（external pattern），或者说是"整体结构模型"（overall pattern）；二是以不同英雄人物为主角形成的小的"故事环"（story cycles），也就是"内部结构"（internal structure）。而以不同英雄为主角形成的各个"故事环"又构成了叙事过程中一个个相对独立的"主题单元"（unity of theme）。然而，由于联合布局之上的"顶层结构"的支配、协调作用，这些看起来相对独立的叙事"主题单元"实际上又有一条强大的线索把它们相互扣合在一起。

从总体上来说，《水浒传》是在"顶层结构"的主宰之下，由不同的"故事环"扣合在一起而形成了一部完整的作品。不过，李培德提出，小说前七十回的八个联合布局是以八个重要的英雄为叙事核心，后四十回的四个"故事环"则是以英雄们的群体行动——征四寇为叙述的关键要素。第八十三至九十回叙述接受招安后的梁山好汉征辽，第九十一至一百回写他们征田虎，第一百零一至一百一十回写征王庆，第一百一十一至一百一十九回则讲述征方腊。对后四个叙事环，李培德说："这种叙事模型没有遵循特别的逻辑，只是重复而已。除了最后征方腊时一百零八好汉十死七

---

confrontation is reached, when Sung Chiang surrenders to the government. Meanwhile, the plot continues to unfold. Poetic justice demands that the outlaws score greater and more impressive triumphs. They wage four successful campaigns against various rebel groups. And the final resolution takes places when Sung Chiang himself succumbs to the machinations of Kao Ch'iu and T'ung Kuan. Winston L. Y. Yang, Nathan K. Mao and Peter Li, "Romance of the Three Kingdoms and The Water Margin," and "Journey to the West and Flowers in the Mirror." Classical Chinese Fiction: A Guide to Its Study and Appreciation. London: George Prior Publishers, 1978, pp. 39 – 51. *Literature Criticism from 1400 to 1800*. Ed. Lynn M. Zott. Vol. 76. Detroit: Gale, 2002. From Literature Resource Center.

① On the other hand, while the system of linked-plots gives *The Water Margin* a relatively weak internal structure, the novel has a strong external pattern achieved through the combination of the following factors: unity of theme, an overall conflict and resolution situation, a geographic focus, and the band's common goals. Winston L. Y. Yang, Nathan K. Mao and Peter Li, "Romance of the Three Kingdoms and The Water Margin," and "Journey to the West and Flowers in the Mirror." Classical Chinese Fiction: A Guide to Its Study and Appreciation. London: George Prior Publishers, 1978, pp. 39 – 51. *Literature Criticism from 1400 to 1800*. Ed. Lynn M. Zott. Vol. 76. Detroit: Gale, 2002. From Literature Resource Center.

八之外，每次出征基本没什么区别。"① 从《水浒传》后四十回的内容来看，李培德之论不虚。

在讨论中，李培德还指出，小说的第七十一至八十回并不属于环状结构叙事模型。他说："在第七十一回作品的高潮部分，这种环状模型结束了。"② 该论者以为，小说作者在这一部分写"忠义堂石碣受天文，梁山泊英雄排座次"，是为了点明这些英雄作为一个群体的关系以及他们的共同目标，而最根本的是要揭示出他们的聚义并非偶然而是天意使然。这就与小说开篇的楔子相呼应。而这样写显然是强大的外部结构在起作用。同时，这也是"顶层结构"把原本分散的、相对独立的各个故事环凝聚成一部意义完整的作品的内在需要。

至于两败童贯、三败高俅的那些章回，李培德说："第七十五至八十的中间六回有一个不同的结构；在这里，叙事的环状链变成了对五场相连战役的快速描写。"③ 该论者以为，在这几个章回中，梁山好汉先后与童贯、高俅带领的朝廷军队展开正面较量，一方面使矛盾双方的问题和大规模冲突爆发出来，另一方面则展现出好汉集体的本领和才能。这些章回的叙述，特别是写"宋公明排九宫八卦阵"，李培德说："如果作品里有第二个高潮的话，这肯定就是那个高潮了。"④ 在李培德看来，小说中这些内容的叙述其实就是要推进对立双方矛盾、冲突的解决。如上文引用的李培德的论述那样，"在第八十二回里，当宋江接受朝廷的招安时，就找到了解决双方对抗、冲突的办法"。很显然，《水浒传》故事情节的发展正是以梁山好汉的接受招安作为一个大的转折的。按李培德之论，正是这个

---

① The pattern follows no particular logic other than that of repetition. One more or one less campaign does not make much difference, except for the last one in which 81 of the 108 heroes die. Peiter Li, Narrative patterns in *San-Kuo* and *Shui-hu*, Plaks, Andrew. Ed. Chinese narrative: critical and theoretical essays. Princeton, N. J: Princeton University Press, 1977, p. 82.

② Peiter Li, Narrative patterns in *San-Kuo* and *Shui-hu*, Plaks, Andrew. Ed. Chinese narrative: critical and theoretical essays. Princeton, N. J: Princeton University Press, 1977, p. 81.

③ The six middle chapters (75 – 80) have a different structure; the cyclical chain dissolves into a quick succession of five battles. Peiter Li, Narrative patterns in *San-Kuo* and *Shui-hu*, Plaks, Andrew. Ed. Chinese narrative: critical and theoretical essays. Princeton, N. J: Princeton University Press, 1977, p. 81.

④ If there exists a second high point in the work, this must be it. Peiter Li, Narrative patterns in *San-Kuo* and *Shui-hu*, Plaks, Andrew. Ed. Chinese narrative: critical and theoretical essays. Princeton, N. J: Princeton University Press, 1977, p. 81.

招安，小说后四十回的叙事又返回到环状结构的轨道①。不过，小说叙述征四寇时的叙事单元的主题，已不再是前七十回里演绎的英雄们的不断相遇、聚义的兄弟之"义"，而变成了对"忠"的描写。

综合李培德之论，笔者以为，我们可以这样来理解《水浒传》的情节结构：

首先，作者以重要的英雄人物或事件为叙事的核心，形成一个个不同的故事环，而这些不同的故事环又形成一个个不同的叙事主题单元。这是李培德提出的小说叙事环状结构中的一个层面，也就是作品的内部结构。不过，《水浒传》的内部结构是比较脆弱的。因为不同的故事环是相对独立的，正如韩南提出的联合布局那样，就是把其中的重要内容抽调，也几乎不会影响作品的完整性。这个时候，小说就需要一个强大的外部结构来控制全局。

其次，在李培德看来，《水浒传》强大的外在结构模型是由主题单元、矛盾冲突与解决的总体方式、地理聚焦以及好汉们的总体目标等多个要素综合作用形成的。而其中的关键要素则是解决矛盾冲突的方式，先是梁山好汉集体接受招安，再就是好汉们的不断亡散，终至于宋江的被毒杀。此时，对抗双方——忠义英雄与奸臣贼子——的势力就完全失衡，矛盾也就意味着基本解决。换句话说，《水浒传》强大的外部结构，最根本的就是由对抗双方矛盾、冲突的产生到不断解决的过程所主宰的。而这也为我们理解阮小五的"酷吏赃官都杀尽，忠心报答赵官家"提供了一个路径。因为从根本上来说，《水浒传》中矛盾冲突的双方并非所谓的农民阶级与地主阶级，而是作者赞颂的像宋江这样比较接近儒家人格理想的忠义之士与"酷吏赃官"的代表蔡京、童贯、高俅、杨戬等。

三、浦安迪论《水浒传》的多重结构
——从"神话框架"、"撞球式"到"聚而复散"的结构模式

就《水浒传》的结构，浦安迪认为虽然情节曲折，但总体布局是比较松散的。因此，浦氏指出，像李开先称赞该作品"委曲详尽，血脉贯通"，天都外臣称赞它"……浓淡远近，点染尽工，又如百尺之锦，玄黄

---

① The forty odd chapters that follow Sung Chiang's surrender revert to a cyclical pattern. Peiter Li, Narrative patterns in *San-Kuo* and *Shui-hu*, Plaks, Andrew. Ed. Chinese narrative: critical and theoretical essays. Princeton, N. J: Princeton University Press, 1977, pp. 81 - 82.

经纬,一丝不纰",金圣叹赞美它"……其二千余纸,只是一篇文字",所有这些"盛赞作者在结构操纵上得心应手"的赞誉之词,不知其根据何在①。即使浦安迪对认为《水浒传》是一部结构完整、精美的作品的观点进行质疑,但他同时也指出,通过对小说文本的总体框架以及在此文本总体框架之内较大的结构划分的仔细观察,可以发现,那些源自民间的叙事素材貌似是杂乱、随意拼凑的,但最终却会让我们强烈感受到编撰者对这些故事片段所作的精心安排②。由此可知,虽然像韩南、李培德所提到的那样,小说里面不少联合布局的叙事单元具有相对的独立性,但《水浒传》的情节结构编排还是很有讲究的;在创作过程中,小说作者是经过深思熟虑的,并采取多种结构技巧来处理人物故事素材。

首先,浦安迪提醒我们必须注意小说开头的结构作用。浦氏指出,《水浒传》作者在小说开篇的"引首"与第一回"洪太尉误走妖魔"里面,就为整部作品铺设好了一个非常简单的"神话框架"(supernatural framework)的叙事纲要③。在浦氏看来,小说开头的这个神话框架具有很重要的结构作用,虽然这部分内容与作品主体是截然分开的,但它却照应后面的故事,并为推动情节的发展提供某种超自然、超因果的叙事逻辑。而且,在反讽理论的指导之下,浦氏说:

> 作为小说主体的补充,楔子对后来故事情节的发展具有反讽影射的作用:它预先就提醒读者,这部小说对民间传统英雄的处理未必就

---

① Andrew H. Plaks, The Four Masterworks of the Ming Novel, Princeton University Press, 1987, p. 304.

② A similar situation may be observed with regard to the larger structural divisions within the overall shape of the text. Once again, the initial impression here of a random linking of narrative materials derived from popular sources ultimately gives way to a strong sence of the careful ordering of constituent segments. Andrew H. Plaks, The Four Masterworks of the Ming Novel, Princeton University Press, 1987, p. 306.

③ Looking at the structural significance of the opening of the novel, one immediately notices once again the presence of an initial narrative section (the release of the star-spirits) that is set clearly apart from the spatial-temporal frame of the main body of the work. This justifies setting off the separate "prologue" chapter in the Chin text, itself on the separation of a small portion of this material as an "introduction" (yin-shou 引首) in the earlier fan-pen editions. The fact that this opening chapter presents the outline of a minimal supernatural framework of sorts of the novel…Andrew H. Plaks, The Four Masterworks of the Ming Novel, Princeton University Press, 1987, p. 306。

与人们极其简单化的期待相符合。①

按浦氏之论,《水浒传》开头的这个"神话框架"正是统领小说叙事的宏大结构。撇开浦氏的反讽论,以笔者之见则是,在此框架之下,作品前70回叙述梁山一百零八好汉的不断聚合就具有内在的叙事动力。即使在现代人眼中,梁山好汉招募秦明、朱仝、卢俊义等人时太过残酷,完全违反了英雄信条,但在作者的创作中,英雄们的相聚是契合上界星辰的行为,是天意使然,不管通过什么样的方式上梁山,上梁山都是这一百零八好汉的必然命运。事实上,在笔者看来,《水浒传》中的这个"神话框架"是把韩南所说的小说文本中各个联合布局扣合在一起的最根本、最内在的"顶层结构"。正是在这个"神话框架"的叙事纲要之中,分散各地的英雄才能不断相遇,梁山的势力才能不断发展壮大、并在一百零八好汉聚齐时达到鼎盛,也才能最终竖起"替天行道"的大旗与北宋王朝分庭抗礼。而正是在此叙事的基础上,才可能出现后面的受招安、征四寇,也才可能在众好汉不断亡散的过程中演绎浦安迪提出的"聚散兴亡"的"空无"主题。而作品里演绎的"万事皆空"主题,显然是通过浦安迪所说的"聚而复散"的结构模式展现出来的。下面就来讨论小说的"聚而复散"叙事结构。

浦安迪认为,明代小说具有"一般美学"(the general aesthetics)特征,那就是在叙事结构与故事情节长度的处理上,保持着某种"显著的数字平衡感与对称性"②。在浦安迪看来,《水浒传》不管是100回本还是由其衍生出来的120回本,抑或是金圣叹腰斩的70回本,都保持了结构上的这种平衡与对称。而小说结构上的平衡与对称是与故事叙述、主题揭示紧密相关的。按浦氏之论,根据明代小说的一般美学特征,《水浒传》前半部分既然叙述了英雄们由散而聚、梁山势力不断发展壮大的过程,后半部分必然要叙述众好汉的零落衰败。对此,浦安迪说:

---

① If anything, what the prologue chapter does add to the novel is what can only be called an ironic reflection on what is to come: an advance warning that the treatment of the heroes of the popular tradition in this novel will not necessarily conform to simplistic expectations. Andrew H. Plaks, The Four Masterworks of the Ming Novel, Princeton University Press, 1987, p. 306.

② Andrew H. Plaks, The Four Masterworks of the Ming Novel, Princeton University Press, 1987, p. 306.

第四章　英语世界对《水浒传》的叙事结构艺术研究

虽然在梁山好汉的势力发展到鼎盛时，小说叙述戛然而止似乎很轻易就把作品结尾几部分删削了，但实际上，根据明代小说的一般美学，它仍隐含着这帮结义兄弟必然分散凋零的后续叙事。①

根据浦安迪提出的《水浒传》结构上的平衡与对称特点，再结合浦氏的上述讨论，可知，梁山好汉的"由散而聚"到"聚而复散"，这是贯穿整部作品的重要结构模式。这种"聚而复散"的结构模式与作品开篇设立的"神话框架"的叙事纲要相结合，就构成了《水浒传》的总体叙事结构模型，也就是上文李培德所说的作品强大的外部结构。

在浦安迪的研究中，《水浒传》既有宏大的总体结构模型，同时也有构成总体结构模型的具体的结构形式。根据浦氏的研究，小说的具体结构形式主要有两种，一是"撞球式"的结构模型（structural pattern of the "billiard ball"），二是以十回为节奏的基本叙事单元（ten chapters each, ten-chapter rythms）。

浦安迪认为，《水浒传》最初数回讲述王进、史进、鲁智深和林冲等人种种惊险曲折的经历时，小说作者就建立了他喜爱的"撞球式"结构模型。那什么是"撞球式"结构模型呢？它又有什么叙述功能呢？对此，浦氏指出：

（所谓"撞球式"结构模型是这样的，）叙述焦点依次变动，按照叙述焦点的变化，先沿着一个主人公的经历发展叙述下去，直到他遇上了另一个主人公，于是就跟随后者冒险事迹的新路线进行叙述，而把前者撇下，或许在后来的某个时刻又提到他。②

---

① This is to say, although the effect of bringing the development of the Liang-shan band to a sudden halt at the apogee of its power seems to dispense quite readily with the final sections of the book, in fact it still carries the implication, within the general aesthetics of the Ming novel, of the xeistence of additional narrative sequences outlining the inevitable dispersal of the brotherhood. Andrew H. Plaks, The Four Masterworks of the Ming Novel, Princeton University Press, 1987, p. 306.

②　... the favored structural pattern of the "billiard ball" shift in narrative focus, according to which we follow the course of one figure until he runs into another, whereupon the narrative then follows the new trajectory of the latter's adventures, leaving the former in his tracks, perhaps to be reiintroduced at a later juncture. Andrew H. Plaks, The Four Masterworks of the Ming Novel, Princeton University Press, 1987, p. 309.

对这一结构模型的叙述功能，浦安迪如此说：

> 这种不连贯的情节发展有时显得混乱无序，但事实上它隐藏着一种非常重要的叙述功能，因为在很大程度上，它为主宰小说文本意蕴的形象再现方式奠定了基础。①

这里提到的形象再现方式，在浦安迪的反讽研究中主要是人物塑造的一种方法，这在前面相关部分已经讨论过。

浦安迪提出的《水浒传》中以十回为节奏的基本叙事单元，类似于韩南提出的"联合布局"结构模型，与李培德提出的叙事"主题单元"则基本一致。按浦氏之论，这种叙事单元具有相对的独立性，前七十回以几位重要英雄人物为核心，后五十回则以梁山好汉的集体行动为中心②。这和李培德的论述几乎一样，不再展开。

在研究《水浒传》的结构时，与浦安迪的看法比较接近，吴德安认为这部小说的整体结构是由多种叙事要素紧密结合在一起构成的。首先就是"开放性部分"（the opening section）。在吴德安看来，《水浒传》中具有结构功能的开放性部分，不仅包括浦安迪提到的"楔子"或是"引首"。该论者认为，现存的接近小说原本的一些小说版本，每回开头保留的类似于"楔子"的"入回诗"（a poetic opening section），也具有构建小说文本结构的作用③。从保留有"入回诗"的容与堂百回本《水浒传》来说，每回开头的这种开放性部分，在小说文本结构布局上，的确有衔接过渡的作用。

事实上，不仅"入回诗"具有衔接过渡的结构功能，小说作者在每一回结尾的"有分教"部分所作的交代，其实也具有类似的结构功能。对《水浒传》每一回结尾部分小说作者所作的这种具有指引性功能的交

---

① This discontinuous movement may appear disturbingly erratic at times, but in fact it conceals a very significant narrative function, as it lays the groundwork dor the pattern of figural recurrence that governs the meaning of the text to such a great extent. Andrew H. Plaks, The Four Masterworks of the Ming Novel, Princeton University Press, 1987, p. 309.

② Andrew H. Plaks, The Four Masterworks of the Ming Novel, Princeton University Press, 1987, pp. 306 – 307.

③ De-an Wu Swihart, The Evolution of Chinese Novel form, Thesis Ph. D. -The Department of East Asian Studies of Princeton University, 1990, pp. 73 – 74.

代，乔什·维托（Josh Vittor）指出："这种回末问题担当着重要的叙事手段，提供了把各回连接起来的艺术凝聚力，从而使各回之间不会显得毫无关联。"① 只不过，作者抛出的这些"回末问题"，它们构建小说文本叙事结构的功能与作用主要体现在局部而已。

在吴德安的论述中，《水浒传》里构筑小说整体结构的要素除上述"开放性部分"之外，还包括"集体列传形式"、"人物配对原则"与"人物拆分原则"等人物描写手法的运用，以及平衡对称原则与时空布局方法的应用等。不过，这些属于构筑小说总体结构模型的具体的方法和技巧，留待下文"《水浒传》的基本结构原则"部分讨论。

综合韩南、李培德、浦安迪与吴德安等人的论述，笔者认为，《水浒传》的结构模型是多重的。简单说来可分为统领整部作品的宏大的外部结构与构成相对独立的故事环的具体的内部结构，前者包括韩南提出的"顶层结构"、李培德提出的"总体结构模型"与浦安迪提出的"神话框架"和"聚而复散"的结构模型，后者则包括这三位批评者提出的"联合布局"、"环状链"与"主题单元"以及"撞球式"等叙事结构模型。

第二节 《水浒传》结构艺术探源

英语世界的批评者比较一致地认为，从整体来看《水浒传》是一部结构松散的作品。但其中像韩南、夏志清、李培德与浦安迪等人又提出，事实上如上文所讨论的那样，《水浒传》又有其自身作为一部完整的长篇小说的结构模型。这样的事实说明，小说作者或编撰者在把那些具有相对独立性的"联合布局"的"故事环"组织成《水浒传》这部完整的作品时，是经过深思熟虑的，是采用了各种不同的叙事结构方式与结构技巧的。

根据浦安迪、吴德安等人的研究，作为中国古代具有里程碑意义的、影响巨大的一部叙事性文学作品，虽然《水浒传》的整体比较松散，但

---

① ... the chapter-ending questions serve as a narratological ploy, providing artificial cohesion to consecutive chapters that may not have anything to do with each other. Josh Vittor, Incoherence and Intoxication: Alcohol as s Rare Source of Consistency in *Outlaws of the Marsh*. "Women and Men, Love and Power: Parameters of Chinese Fiction and Drama" Sino-Platonic Paper, edited by Victor H. Mair, 193 (Novermber, 2009), p. 160.

小说作者或编撰者在撰写过程中仍然采取了多种结构方式与结构技巧。不过，这些结构方式、结构技巧，从大的方面来说是有本可循的。下面，笔者就先来讨论英语世界的批评者对《水浒传》结构艺术渊源所作的研究。

一、对《水浒传》结构形成的"进化论"观点的质疑

就《水浒传》叙事结构模式的形成与结构艺术的渊源问题，吴德安首先对20世纪以来学界提出的"进化论"观点作了一个简略的梳理。在此基础上，该论者指出，在达尔文"进化论"的影响之下，一些学者认为"《水浒传》的'片段式'结构，并不被认为一个创作的问题，而被视为小说不同的素材来源进化的结果"。[①] 该论者以为，像胡适的《〈水浒传〉考证》与《〈水浒传〉后考》，郑振铎的《〈水浒传〉的演化》，就是这种思想影响的产物。因为胡适坚持认为，《水浒传》有早期的文学来源；郑振铎则相信"《水浒传》的不同章回是由多位作者编撰而成的，只是在后来才汇聚在一起"[②]。根据他们的研究，就形成了如下认识：

> 这样的创作特性，造成《水浒传》的结构如欧文描绘的那样，"几乎是一个故事集……像串珠子那样是由一长串的片段插曲构成的"。或如严敦易认为的那样，《水浒传》是由短篇故事组成的一部小说。[③]

在综合考察胡适、郑振铎、严敦易、韩南、李培德、宫崎市定[④]等中外学者对《水浒传》结构的研究成果之后，吴德安进一步指出：

[①] The "episodic" structure of Shuihu zhuan however, has not been regarded as a compositional problem, but as a result of the evolution of the novel out of various source materials. De-an Wu Swihart, The Evolution of Chinese Novel form, Thesis Ph. D. -The Department of East Asian Studies of Princeton University, 1990, p. 49.

[②] De-an Wu Swihart, The Evolution of Chinese Novel form, Thesis Ph. D. -The Department of East Asian Studies of Princeton University, 1990, p. 49.

[③] This composite nature caused the structure of Shuihu zhuan to be described by R. Irin as "merely a collection of tales... consisting of a long chain of episodes strung together like beads." Yan Dunyi 严敦易, suggested that it was a novel made up of short stories. De-an Wu Swihart, The Evolution of Chinese Novel form, Thesis Ph. D. -The Department of East Asian Studies of Princeton University, 1990, pp. 49 - 50.

[④] 宫崎市定的观点见《宫崎市定说水浒——虚构的好汉与掩藏的历史》，赵翻、杨晓钟译，陕西人民出版社2008年版。韩南的观点见收入《韩南中国小说论集》中的《早期的中国短篇小说》与《〈金瓶梅〉探源》两文，王秋桂等译，北京大学出版社2008年版。

很明显，《水浒传》结构进化观点的提出，是受小说进化理论所支配的。按照《水浒传》演变的研究，有关宋江集团的许多"水浒"故事都有其历史来源。这些故事经历了一个长时期的、具有重大影响的发展阶段，在此阶段，它们以诸如说书、戏曲的文学形式出现，最后在明中叶才全部汇聚在一起以长篇小说的形式刊行。①

不过，吴德安并不赞同胡适、郑振铎等人提出的《水浒传》的结构是由小说漫长的成书演变过程形成的观点。该论者说："然而，纵观本人对这些素材来源的研究，发现很难证明从简单、独立的故事到复杂、统一的小说，《水浒传》与其假定的素材之间具有某种一致性。"② 因此，该论者提出，贴在历史与小说、杂剧与小说之间的，曾经广为接受的"进化论的标签"是值得怀疑的。吴德安认为："事实上，《宋史》只是简单提到宋江三十六人起义。很明显，不可能在如此贫乏的历史文献与人物姓名的基础上创作出《水浒传》这样的长篇小说。"③ 至于《水浒传》与《宣和遗事》及元代水浒杂剧之间的关系，吴德安结合严敦易的研究成果指出，现存的水浒杂剧，除唯一的《梁山泊李逵负荆》外，其他剧作的情节几乎与小说没什么关系；就是《宣和遗事》，与小说《水浒传》之间也是如此④。

---

① It is clear that the evolution of the structure of Shuihu zhuan has been dominated by the evolutionary theory of the novel. According to the studies on the evolution of Shuihu zhuan, many "shuihu" stories about Song Jiang's group have their origin in history. These stories underwent a long formative period during which they were developed in many literary forms such as in storytelling and drama and finally converged in printed form in the length novel around the middle of Ming dynasty. De-an Wu Swihart, The Evolution of Chinese Novel form, Thesis Ph. D. -The Department of East Asian Studies of Princeton University, 1990, pp. 50 - 51.

② However, through my study of these source materials, I find it is difficult to prove that the novel and its supposed source materials together fall into a continuum from simpler, separated stories to a complex, unified novel. De-an Wu Swihart, The Evolution of Chinese Novel form, Thesis Ph. D. -The Department of East Asian Studies of Princeton University, 1990, p. 51.

③ In fact, the Song history inly briefly mentions the uprising of Song Jiang and his thirty-six outlaws. It is obvious that Shuihu zhuan could not have developed into a length novel based on this meager historical reference and the character's names. De-an Wu Swihart, The Evolution of Chinese Novel form, Thesis Ph. D. -The Department of East Asian Studies of Princeton University, 1990, p. 51.

④ The evolutionary tie between drama and the novel is also challenged by modern scholars. Based on his study of Yuan dramas containing "Shuihu" themes, Yan Dunyi observed that five of the six extant plots bear no relation to either the novel or The Lost Tales of Xuanhe Reign. Only one of them, "Liangshanpo Li Kuie fujing" (Li Kuie shoulders thorns at Liangshanbo) presents a story identical to one of the novel's episodes (chapter 73). De-an Wu Swihart, The Evolution of Chinese Novel form, Thesis Ph. D. -The Department of East Asian Studies of Princeton University, 1990, p. 53.

为了论证自己对《水浒传》的结构是由漫长的成书过程形成的观点的质疑是有理可据的,吴德安系统分析了《水浒传》与其素材来源之间的关系,并对人们加在它们之间的所谓的"进化的线索"进行了批驳。据此,该论者得出的结论是:

> 基于上面的分析,我认为,并不存在强有力的证据支持《水浒传》进化的看法。就目前拥有的证据,我们最多能断定,《水浒传》在小说形式上是一部原创的作品。这部小说有它自己的结构设置,而非一部故事集。这个结论能够获得这一事实的支撑,那就是在小说里面,是根据结构的需要而使用相关素材的。[①]

吴德安以小说第14—16回"智取生辰纲"的故事为例说,这个故事与《宣和遗事》相比就大不一样。在《宣和遗事》里面,杨志与这个事件没有关系,他的故事是生辰纲故事之后的一个独立的叙事单元。而且在《宣和遗事》中,押解生辰纲进京的是马安国,而非小说里说的是杨志。为了结构设置的需要,小说中,这两个故事融合在了一起;杨志是押解生辰纲的头领。因为他武艺高强、阅历丰富,任何个人都无法盗取他们押解的生辰纲。因此,晁盖一帮人"七星聚义"就成为必须,而这次聚义也成为梁山108好汉聚义的一次预演。事实上,"聚义"是小说前半部分的一个重要的结构方式。此七位英雄的首次聚义直接引导小说的叙事节奏。据此,吴德安再次强调:"这个睿智的结构设置,说明这是一部原创的作品,而非仅仅是早先故事的一个集合。"[②]

对吴德安的这个观点,笔者表示赞同。在讨论《水浒传》的著作权归属时,笔者就说过,《水浒传》是一部具有原创性质的作品。在如何把

[①] Based on the above analysis, I believe that there is no evidence which strongly supports the Shuihu zhuan evolution theory. From the evidence we have now, at best we can judge Shuihu zhuan to be a work originally created in novel form, and the novel has its own structural design, rather than being a mere collection of tales. This conclusion can be supported by the fact that the source materials were utilized in the novel according to the demands of its structure. De-an Wu Swihart, The Evolution of Chinese Novel form, Thesis Ph. D. -The Department of East Asian Studies of Princeton University, 1990, p. 57.

[②] The intelligent structural desige shows that the novel is a creative work, and not just a collection of preexisting stories. De-an Wu Swihart, The Evolution of Chinese Novel form, Thesis Ph. D. -The Department of East Asian Studies of Princeton University, 1990, p. 57.

先前那些在社会上流传的、零散的水浒人物故事组织成一部完整的小说的过程中，在如何让那些原本并无内在关联的素材成为一体的过程中，小说的作者是进行过一番比较缜密的构思的；虽然以现代小说的观念和标准来衡量，《水浒传》的结构形式并不完美。

二、从《史记》到《水浒传》：《水浒传》的结构艺术渊源

即使吴德安强调《水浒传》在结构设置上是原创的，但他并没有否认小说的结构艺术是有本可循的事实。在综合前人如李开先、天都外臣、金圣叹，特别是现代学者余嘉锡、王利器等人的研究成果的基础上，吴德安认为《史记》为《水浒传》提供了结构模型。对此，该论者说：

> 以贫乏的历史文献为基础，为什么《水浒传》以长篇叙事形式写成，而其他所有水浒主题的文本都是短篇呢？我认为，在结构设置问题上能够找到可能的解释。与《宣和遗事》不一样，《水浒传》的原初材料是取自真实人物的生活事迹的。按余嘉锡、王利器之论，小说作者积累了大量的历史人物素材。根据余和王提供的资料，看起来《水浒传》的作者运用了许多真实的人物故事来创作小说。如此，这些人物故事就有助于《水浒传》结构的形成。使用人物群像（collection of characters）的方法来构建叙事，这是在模仿《史记》。[1]

按吴德安之论，《水浒传》对《史记》结构艺术的模仿，主要不在具体的叙述方法与技巧，而在"列传形式"（biographical form）的借用。吴德安说，一部《史记》可分为五部分，而其中三部分都是以人物传记的形式创作的；作为"纪传体"（"Annals-biographies form"）史书的典范，

---

[1] Based on these meager historical references, why is it that *Shuihu zhuan* is written in a long narrative form while all of the other genres of the Shuihu theme are short? I think the possible explanation can be found in the problem of structural desige. Unlike *The Lost Tales of the Xuanhe Reign*, the creative matarials of *Shuihu zhuan* were drawn from the lives of actual persons. According to Yu Jiaxi 余嘉锡 and Wang Liqi 王利器, the author of *Shuihu zhuan* accumulated a large amount of data about historical figures. Based on Yu and Wang's sources, it appears that the author of *Shuihu zhuan* employed many actual persons' stories to conpose the novel. Thus the characters' stories contribute to the formation of the structure os *Shuihu zhuan*. The method of using a collection of characters to construct the narrative is modeled on *Shi ji*. De-an Wu Swihart, The Evolution of Chinese Novel form, Thesis Ph. D. -The Department of East Asian Studies of Princeton University, 1990, p. 59。

《史记》不仅有记述单个人物的"本传"("the basic biography of this person"),还存在多种形式的"集体传记单元"("collective biographies units"),也就是"合传"("joined biographies")。在吴德安看来,"集体列传"的传记形式对中国长篇小说发展的影响尤为重大。对此,该论者说:"《史记》中的集体列传形式肯定影响到了中国章回小说的发展。《水浒传》就是一个鲜明的例子。"① 对此问题,该论者进一步分析道:

> 《史记》里面大量的集体性质的列传形式,为中国长篇小说的发展提供了叙事模型。与最早的小说《水浒传》一样,中国小说家喜爱使用众多的人物形象来构筑他们的小说,而不是运用某一核心情节或单个的人物。比如说,《水浒传》中把108好汉刻在石碣上,据统计,这部小说(有名有姓)的人物就有787个。②

据此,吴德安认为,集体列传形式不仅对小说叙事非常重要,同时也为我们理解小说的结构提供了重要的路径③。

从列传与集体列传的角度切入来理解《水浒传》的结构形式,这是一条比较好的路径。吴德安指出,在《水浒传》的阐释历史中,袁无涯、金圣叹诸人就曾拿它与《春秋左氏传》和《史记》相提并论。他们所作的比较,既有思想意蕴方面的,更有结构形式方面的。前者,如袁无涯认为"《水浒传》有《春秋》之遗意焉";后者,如金圣叹所指出的那样,小说作者在叙述人物故事时,就采用了类似于司马迁的人物传记形式。④

---

① The collective biography form of *Shi ji* certainly influenced the development of the Chinese zhanghui novel. Shuihu zhuan is a viable example. De-an Wu Swihart, The Evolution of Chinese Novel form, Thesis Ph. D. -The Department of East Asian Studies of Princeton University, 1990, p. 64.

② The largely collective nature of the biographical form of *Shi ji* has provided a narrativ model for the development of the Chinese full-length novel. As early as the novel *Shuihu zhuan*, Chinese novelists favored the use of large numbers of characters to construct their novels instead of using a centralized plot or single character. For instance, there are 108 bandits listed on a stone tablet in the novel, and by one counting there are 787 characters in *Shuihu zhuan*. De-an Wu Swihart, The Evolution of Chinese Novel form, Thesis Ph. D. -The Department of East Asian Studies of Princeton University, 1990, p. 63.

③ In any case, the collective biography in the novel is important for us to understand the structure of the novel. De-an Wu Swihart, The Evolution of Chinese Novel form, Thesis Ph. D. -The Department of East Asian Studies of Princeton University, 1990, p. 63.

④ De-an Wu Swihart, The Evolution of Chinese Novel form, Thesis Ph. D. -The Department of East Asian Studies of Princeton University, 1990, p. 64.

在此基础上，吴德安进一步指出：

> 《水浒传》的标题可以翻译为"The Biography of Shuihu"。这个标题揭示出，小说是以"地理实体"（the geographical entity）为中心的，在那里108好汉将聚集成一个团体。因此，"水浒"（the marsh or shuihu）只是108好汉这个团体的一个象征。列传更多是基于好汉整体而非任何个别人物。①

在笔者看来，吴德安的这个观点能比较好地帮助我们理解《水浒传》的叙事结构。因为如前面讨论过的那样，小说的整个叙事节奏是在作品开篇"引首"设立的"神话框架"的主宰之下一步步发展起来的，而小说叙事的最终任务就是要把这108好汉汇聚成一个集体；而他们奔向的目的地就是水泊梁山，也就是小说标题中的"水浒"。事实上，就《水浒传》来说，小说作者也只有这样才能把分散各地的梁山好汉最终捏合在一起。这也就形成了《水浒传》模仿《史记》而不同于《史记》的地方。

说到《水浒传》对《史记》结构艺术方法的模仿，笔者必须对浦安迪提出的"人物配对原则"（the principle of paired characters）与吴德安提出的"人物拆分原则"（the principle of "refraction of characters"）作一交代。根据浦安迪的研究，《水浒传》不仅广泛采用"人物配对原则"来塑造人物形象，更是反复使用这一原则来构筑小说文本结构。而"人物配对原则"显而易见是从《史记》的"人物合传"模仿、演变而来的。对此，吴德安说：

> 运用配对人物来构成一个列传，是《史记》的另一个重要结构原则。这个技巧一般在两个人的"合传"中使用。《史记》中，并置的

---

① The title *Shuihu zhuan* may be rendered *The Biography of Shuihu*. This title reveals that the novel centers on the geographical entity in which the 108 heroes will assemble as one group. Thus, the marsh (shuihu) is a symbol of the group of 108 heroes. The biography is based more on the group as a whole than on any individual character. De-an Wu Swihart, The Evolution of Chinese Novel form, Thesis Ph. D. -The Department of East Asian Studies of Princeton University, 1990, pp. 64-65.

人物要么相似，要么相反。①

　　对此种情形，吴德安举例说，《史记》里的《孙武、吴起列传》叙述的是两个相似的杰出将军，《张耳、陈馀列传》讲述的则是两个相反的人物形象。对"人物配对原则"在《水浒传》结构布局中的运用，吴德安指出："叙述中，相似的或互补、相反关系的两个并置人物，也反映在《水浒传》的结构安排上。"② 该论者认为，金圣叹提出的"背面敷粉法"指的就是此种用一个人物作为另一个人物的陪衬的叙事方法，小说对宋江与李逵、杨雄与石秀、雷横与朱仝等配对人物的描写都属于这种方法。据此，吴德安说："配对人物原则的应用，是小说的一个重要结构原则。"③ 而且在该论者看来，"配对人物原则"对后世章回小说创作也具有深远的影响。至于什么是"人物配对原则"以及作者如何运用它来构筑小说结构，将在下文"《水浒传》的基本结构法则"部分展开讨论。

　　根据吴德安的论述，"人物拆分原则"也是《水浒传》的一个重要结构方法，这个方法也是从《史记》发展来的。对此，吴德安指出：

> 《史记》主要是由集体列传构成的。为了把这些列传捏合成一个整体，司马迁创造了一个我称之为"人物拆分"的方法，这个方法把一个人物的故事分成许多部分，并让它在叙事过程中出现。④

---

① Using paired characters to construct a biography is another important structural principle of *Shi ji*. This technique is usually found in the two person "joint biography". In *Shi ji*, the juxtaposed characters are either similar or contrasting. De-an Wu Swihart, The Evolution of Chinese Novel form, Thesis Ph. D. -The Department of East Asian Studies of Princeton University, 1990, p. 71.

② The parallel aspect of similarity of complementary opposites involved in the juxtaposed of two characters in the narrative is also reflected in the structural arrangement of *Shuihu zhuan*. De-an Wu Swihart, The Evolution of Chinese Novel form, Thesis Ph. D. -The Department of East Asian Studies of Princeton University, 1990, p. 71.

③ Using the "paired characters" device becomes an important sttuctural principle in the novel. De-an Wu Swihart, The Evolution of Chinese Novel form, Thesis Ph. D. -The Department of East Asian Studies of Princeton University, 1990, p. 72.

④ *Shi ji* is primarily composed of collective biographies. In order to integrate these biographies into a whole, Sima Qian created a method which I call "refraction of character," which means a character's story is broken up into many pieces and appears in different places in the narrative process. De-an Wu Swihart, The Evolution of Chinese Novel form, Thesis Ph. D. -The Department of East Asian Studies of Princeton University, 1990, pp. 68 – 69.

吴德安说，《史记》中"人物拆分原则"有两种使用方式：一是一个人物的传记和某一群体的其他人联系在一起，而且还在其他部分再现，这时会使用"人物拆分原则"，像《仲尼弟子列传》《儒林列传》与《货殖列传》就是如此。再就是，某个重要人物，在他自己的本传中突出其主要的方面，而把他次要的或负面的事迹放到他人的传记中来写。像刘邦，在其"本纪"中描写了他的功成名就和对汉王朝发展的巨大影响，而对其真实心理、人格的揭露则放在《项羽本纪》来讲述。

就"人物拆分原则"，吴德安指出，在《水浒传》里，我们能够发现小说作者对这一结构布局方法的频繁应用①。就小说中"人物拆分原则"的应用情形，该论者说：

> 表面上，《水浒传》有许多列传单元，数回集中叙述一个人物。一个人物消失，紧接着另一个人物出现，这使小说的结构成为一系列人物传记的形式。事实上，小说作者通过"人物重现原则"把单个的人物列传单元编织在一起。在此原则之下，当一个主要人物退到行动的边沿、他的重点章回已经结束时，他并没有从叙事场景中彻底消失，而是频繁出现在以后的章节中。②

吴德安以史进的故事为例说，小说前两回他是主角，第3回遇到鲁达时，他就从舞台上撤下。但他仍然在叙述过程中出现。第6回，他又遇上了鲁达，告诉鲁达别后发生的事情，他们两人还在瓦罐寺共同打败丘小乙、崔道成两个流氓。事后，史进再次走下舞台。第57回，已加入梁山好汉集团的鲁达想起史进，并把他招入梁山，史进再次出现，而且在接下来的数回中成为故事聚焦的主角。总结上述分析，吴德安指出：

---

① De-an Wu Swihart, The Evolution of Chinese Novel form, Thesis Ph. D. -The Department of East Asian Studies of Princeton University, 1990, p. 69.

② On the surface, *Shuihu zhuan* has many biographical units, several chapters concentrating on one character. The characters appear and vanish one after another and this make the structure of *Shuihu zhuan* a series of biographies. In fact, the author of *Shuihu zhuan* weaves toghther the individual biographical "buits" through the principle of the "recurrent character." Under this principle, when a main character, his major chapters finished, retreats into the periphery of action, he does not disappear entirely from the scene, but frequently reemerges in a later section. De-an Wu Swihart, The Evolution of Chinese Novel form, Thesis Ph. D. -The Department of East Asian Studies of Princeton University, 1990, p. 70.

人物的反复出现，以及人物之间故事的叠合，这种方法构成《水浒传》的叙事结构。源自《史记》的"人物拆分"技巧，成为后来章回小说的一个主要结构原则。①

的确，《水浒传》前半部分，很大程度上就是通过"人物配对原则"与"人物拆分原则"来构筑小说的文本结构的。然而，它们只是《水浒传》结构原则中的其中两种。在下文《水浒传》的基本结构原则部分，我们将看到这部小说还有多种其他结构原则。

在研究中，吴德安也意识到，在中国文化、文学传统中，"传"是一个含义很广泛的词，而在历史书写与小说书写中，"列传形式"也是一个很容易混淆的词。但即便如此，该论者认为，我们还是可以使用"列传"一词来分析《水浒传》的叙事结构。对此，他说：

> 使用"列传形式"来分析《水浒传》是意义含糊的，因为这个词很容易混淆历史书写与小说书写；但我们仍然可以使用"传"这个词来分析《水浒传》及其他章回小说，因为一些主要人物的故事是以列传单元的片段形式描写的。它们可以视为是人物的"列传"，但它们与历史书写的"列传形式"并无相似之处。某些人物的"列传"长些，有的短些，有的则比其他的更详细。如金圣叹评论的："《水浒传》一个人出来，分明便是一篇列传。至于中间事迹，又逐段逐段自成文字，亦有两三卷成一篇者，亦有五六句成一篇者。"②

---

① The device of the frequent reemergence of one character and his story's overlapping with others constitutes *Shuihu zhuan*'s narrative texture. This technique of "refraction of character" was derived from *Shi ji* and became a major structural principle of later "zhanghui" novel. De-an Wu Swihart, The Evolution of Chinese Novel form, Thesis Ph. D. -The Department of East Asian Studies of Princeton University, 1990, p. 65.

② The use of the term "biographical form" in analyzing *Shuihu zhuan* is ambiguous because it is easy to confuse historical and novel writing, but we can still use the term "zhuan" or biography to analyze the form of *Shuihu zhuan* and some other zhanghui novels, because the stories of some major characters are presented in segments as biographical units. They can be seen as "biographies" of characters, but they do not bear resemblance to the biographical form in historical writing. Some of the "biographies" of characters are long, some short, some are more than detailed than others. As Jin Shengtan observed: "For every character who appears in the *Shuihu zhuan*, a clear-cut biography is provided. As for the events contained within them, each successive unit further forms an independent one in itself. Sometimes two or three chapters will form such a unit. Sometimes it takes just five or six sentences." De-an Wu Swihart, The Evolution of Chinese Novel form, Thesis Ph. D. -The Department of East Asian Studies of Princeton University, 1990, p. 65.

就小说书写中的"传"（zhuan），吴德安认为，可以把它理解成我们熟悉的"故事"（story）。而《水浒传》所叙述的那些事件是为人物描写服务的，作者如何安排那些素材，是根据展现人物道德品质的需要而定的。对此，该论者说：

> 《水浒传》里所谓的"传"，在一定程度上相当于"故事"。只是小说中的人物"列传"事迹是并置的，缺乏因果关联。事件的顺序选择，是根据界定主题人物的特定的道德品质而安排的。①

根据金圣叹对《水浒传》与《史记》在叙事方式及人物列传中所写事件的叙事功能所作的比较，吴德安进一步指出："《水浒传》里的事件与《史记》所写的那些相似，它们在叙事中的功能是介绍、说明人物，揭示作者的情感和思想。"②而且该论者还认为："虽然《水浒传》里的事件不是按照因果链安排的，但作为一个整体，这部小说仍然是由紧密交织在一起的要素构成的。"③仔细研读《水浒传》故事情节的发展，小说每一章回之间（楔子除外）的确存在紧密相扣的结构要素。说到把不同人物的故事组织称一个整体，就必须对《水浒传》作者所使用的各种结构方法、结构技巧展开分析论述。下面，笔者就来讨论浦安迪、吴德安等人对《水浒传》的基本结构原则所作的研究。

第三节 《水浒传》的基本结构原则

在英语世界的批评者中，浦安迪、吴德安等人先后对《水浒传》的

---

① The so-called "biography" in *Shuihu zhuan* is in a way equal to "story". However, the events in *Shuihu zhuan*'s "biographies" are juxtaposed without causal linkage, the order chosen to substantially define the subject's character according to certain moral values. De-an Wu Swihart, The Evolution of Chinese Novel form, Thesis Ph. D. -The Department of East Asian Studies of Princeton University, 1990, p. 66.

② The events in *Shuihu zhuan* are similar to those of *Shi ji*. The function of these events in the narrativr is to illustrate character, and reveal the author's feelings and thoughts. De-an Wu Swihart, The Evolution of Chinese Novel form, Thesis Ph. D. -The Department of East Asian Studies of Princeton University, 1990, p. 66.

③ Although the events in *Shuihu zhuan* are not arranged in a causal chain, the novel as a whole is still composed of slosely interwoven elements. De-an Wu Swihart, The Evolution of Chinese Novel form, Thesis Ph. D. -The Department of East Asian Studies of Princeton University, 1990, p. 66.

结构方法进行过比较全面的探讨和研究。尤其是后者，在前者的研究基础上，更是对小说的基本结构原则进行了比较全面系统的分析论述。综合他们的研究成果，可以发现，《水浒传》的结构方法与结构技巧主要有如下几个方面。

一、通过时间与空间布局来构筑小说的结构模型

对《水浒传》里作者在叙述过程中对时间与空间发展模式的安排，浦安迪认为，在时间图式上，最明显的是运用"季节循环"（seasonal cycle）来构筑小说情节设置的关键点[①]。对这一点，浦安迪说，和《金瓶梅》《西游记》一样，《水浒传》作者喜欢把时令季节与叙述内容结合在一起。尤其是元宵节和中秋节，小说中的许多关键情节、场景恰好就被安排在这样的日子里。像第33回宋江在清风寨被捕获捆绑，第66回从大名府死囚牢救出卢俊义和石秀，第72回李逵大闹东京，等等，这些事件都发生在元宵节；第51回写李逵残杀小衙内则发生在盂兰盆节；第119回写鲁达的弃世，圆寂，则是在月满之时的中秋节。浦氏以为，这样的情节安排应该不是偶然为之。[②]

对《水浒传》结构安排上的时间布局，吴德安作了更细的研究。他认为，在小说前半部分的集体列传里，时间图式以日月演进（the progression of months and days）与季节循环为根本，年则没有提到[③]。在此两者中，虽然频繁提及日月演进，事实上，作者是以季节顺序的运用作为主要的叙事策略，从而为英雄们的不同历险事迹提供背景[④]。为了更加直接明了地说明小说作者在时间图式安排上的别有匠心，吴德安比较详细地统计

[①] Andrew H. Plaks, The Four Masterworks of the Ming Novel, Princeton University Press, 1987, p. 311.

[②] Ibid., p. 311, 312.

[③] However, the temporal design within the collective biographical form of the first half of the novel is based on the progression of months and days and seasonal cycles, and the years are not mentioned. De-an Wu Swihart, The Evolution of Chinese Novel form, Thesis Ph. D. -The Department of East Asian Studies of Princeton University, 1990, p. 90.

[④] The progression of months and days is mentioned fairly trequently in this way to lend a strong seasonal sequence to the first 70 chapters. The seasonal sequence is used as a narrative device primarily to provide settings for the various adventures of the heroes. De-an Wu Swihart, The Evolution of Chinese Novel form, Thesis Ph. D. -The Department of East Asian Studies of Princeton University, 1990, p. 91.

了《水浒传》前70回里日月、季节的变化，并制作成表格，具体如下①：

回目/CHAPTER	时间/TIME	回目/CHAPTER	时间/TIME
1	秋季/autumn	46	11月中/middle of the 11th month
2—6	夏季/summer	50	本月15/15th of the month
7—11	冬季/winter	51	8月/the 8th month
12—13	2月/the 2nd month	52—53	初冬/early winter
14—16	5月/the 5th month	54	冬季/winter
16—17	夏季/summer	58	2月中/middle of the 2nd month
18—20	8月/the 8th month	60	春季/spring
24—26	11—12月/11th—12th months	61	秋7月/7th to autumn
27—29	6月/the 6th month	62	初冬/early winter
30—31	秋季（10月）/autumn（10th）	63	冬季/winter
32	11月/the 11th month	65—66	初春/early spring
32	元宵节/Lantern Festival	67	元宵节/Lantern Festival
35	初春/early spring	68	春季/spring
36	4月/the 4th month	70	4月15/15th of 4th month
38	6月/the 6th month	70	4月22/22nd of 4th month
40	夏季/summer	70	4月23/23rd of 4th month
44	秋季/autumn	70	元宵节/Lantern Festival

而且根据金圣叹针对第9回（金本回目）林冲故事的叙述安排所作的评点："耐庵此篇，独能于一幅之中，寒暑间作，写雪便其寒彻骨，写火便其热照面。"再结合小说对其他英雄人物描写的具体的时令背景，吴德安认为："各个人物的故事有自己的季节背景，这是与揭示其性格或事件的意蕴直接相关的。"②

与吴德安提出的小说作者运用特定的季节背景来揭示人物的性格或事件的意蕴的观点相似，浦安迪认为，和《金瓶梅》一样，《水浒传》作者

---

① De-an Wu Swihart, The Evolution of Chinese Novel form, Thesis Ph. D. -The Department of East Asian Studies of Princeton University, 1990, pp. 90 - 91.

② Each character's story has its own seasonal setting (e. g. Lin Chong's story) and this is directly related to the need for revealing his character or the meaning of events. De-an Wu Swihart, The Evolution of Chinese Novel form, Thesis Ph. D. -The Department of East Asian Studies of Princeton University, 1990, p. 91.

也有意识地运用冷热意象作为小说的结构策略。浦氏举例说,第10回描写林冲的命运、性格变化时,就把火与雪的意象交织在一起。①

根据上述,《水浒传》结构布局中时间图式的安排,前70回是以日月演进与季节循环为主,从第71回开始则发生了变化。对此,吴德安指出:"当108好汉全部在梁山聚齐时,时间图式就回到了历史编年的模式。"②该论者说,在小说第71回降下石碣天文之后发现了第二个确切的日期[第一个确切的日期出现在楔子部分,是嘉祐三年(1058)三月三日];而在第82回"梁山泊分金大买市"之后,具体日期的频繁使用则凸显出《水浒传》是一部历史类型的小说③。对第71回开始的历史编年,吴德安也进行了详细的统计,具体见下表④:

回目/CHAPTER	时间/TIME
第71回	宣和二年四月(1120);排座次,宋江颁布号令
第75回	宣和三年四月(1121);皇帝第一次招安
第81回	宣和四年一月(1122);闻焕章为梁山好汉申辩致宿太尉书信
第82回	宣和四年二月;皇帝最后招安;三月三日梁山宣布大买市告示
第83回	宣和四年五月;接受诏封,征辽
第85回	宣和四年七月;众好汉占领幽州
第89回	宣和四年冬;辽王受降称臣
第90回	宣和五年新年(1123);开始征田虎
第100回	宣和五年四月,征田虎结束
第101回	宣和六年春(1124);开始征王庆
第110回	征王庆结束
第111回	宣和六年冬;开始征方腊
第119回	宣和七年八月(1125);征方腊结束

---

① Andrew H. Plaks, The Four Masterworks of the Ming Novel, Princeton University Press, 1987, p. 312.

② De-an Wu Swihart, The Evolution of Chinese Novel form, Thesis Ph. D. -The Department of East Asian Studies of Princeton University, 1990, p. 92.

③ After the destruction of the band's lair in chapter 82, dates are frequently uesd to emphasize that *Shuihu zhuan* is a historical novel of sorts. De-an Wu Swihart, The Evolution of Chinese Novel form, Thesis Ph. D. -The Department of East Asian Studies of Princeton University, 1990, p. 92.

④ De-an Wu Swihart, The Evolution of Chinese Novel form, Thesis Ph. D. -The Department of East Asian Studies of Princeton University, 1990, pp. 92 – 93.

第四章　英语世界对《水浒传》的叙事结构艺术研究　　239

综合上述分析、论述，吴德安的结论是：

　　第一部分与第二部分的时间图式把小说分成两部分，这是很清晰的。小说第一部分中季节循环的布局，具有强烈的象征功能。因为季节布局提供的或热或冷的背景，有助于展现人物的情感及其所处的形势，这个布局与集体列传布局相呼应。小说第二部分放弃了季节布局的象征功能，转而采用历史编年顺序。然而，在楔子中建立的最后的时间暗示，又恢复了时间布局的象征功能。这是在"徽宗帝梦游梁山"的一首描绘蓼儿洼美景的诗（词）中发现的①。该诗最后一行"凉风冷露九秋天"，在此，"九"字意味着"深"（deep），同时也是数字"九"的意思，这就和小说开篇的"阳尽于九"之间形成回应。②

从《水浒传》文本来看，吴德安提出的小说前半部分以季节布局为主形成叙事结构、后半部分则采用历史编年的方式来构筑叙事结构的观点，总体来说是有一定说服力的。上面两个表格，非常清晰地展现了该论者提出的小说结构布局中的这种时间图式。至于说楔子里的"阳尽于九"与小说最后一回里的诗句"凉风冷露九秋天"之间前后呼应，具有构筑小说整体结构的功能与作用，笔者对此持保留意见。

至于《水浒传》结构上的空间安排模式（patterns of spatial arrangement），浦安迪是这样看待的，他说：

---

①　吴德安所说的诗原文如下：漫漫烟水，隐隐云山。不观日月光明，只见水天一色。红瑟瑟满目蓼花，绿依依一洲芦叶。双双鸿雁，哀鸣在沙渚矶头；对对鹁鸪，倦宿在败荷汀畔。霜枫簇簇，似离人点染泪波；风柳疏疏，如怨妇蹙颦眉黛。淡月寒星长夜景，凉风冷露九秋天。

②　The temporal designs of the first and second halves of the novel are quite distinct. The design of the seasonal cycle in the first half of the novel carries a strong symbolic function. SInce the seasonal design provides settings (hot ot cold) to show the feeling and the situation of the character, this design corresponds to the design of the collective biographies. The symbolic function of the seasonal function is given up in the second half of the novel, and the use of chronicle order is adopted. However, the last time indicator, found in the epilogue, brings back the symbolic function of the temporal design. It is found in a poem describing the beauty of Liaoerwa in the emperor's dream journey to Liangshan. The last line of the poem reads: " The wind cool, the dew icy, it was deep autumn." The word "jiu" here means "deep", but it is also means the number nine which resonates with the "uymost point of yang" at the beginning of the novel. De-an Wu Swihart, The Evolution of Chinese Novel form, Thesis Ph. D. -The Department of East Asian Studies of Princeton University, 1990, pp. 92 – 93.

在小说前面部分的叙述中，描写梁山地区与其他权力中心之间的往返移动似乎是强调山寨的偏远。但随着这帮好汉军事力量的发展壮大，梁山这个综合山寨控制的范围也随之扩大，直至它成为一个较大的政权中心。①

而且浦氏以为，梁山不断发展成为一个强大的势力中心，是可以从其自身的空间格局反映出来的。浦氏说，梁山这个堡垒由崇山峻岭所环抱，四周是汪洋水域，这就形成了一个坚固的同心环堡垒。②浦安迪还指出，根据小说的描绘，作为位于河北与山东西部这个特定地理位置的好汉们聚义的大本营，梁山的势力具有向四面八方辐射的特征：以梁山为中心，东至青州，北至沧州和大名府，西至京畿地区和孟州，南至江州等地。③

根据浦安迪的论述，笔者以为我们可以这样来理解《水浒传》前半部分的空间布局，那就是在地理方位上，梁山经历了由边缘到中央的发展过程；而随着梁山泊成为小说叙事的绝对地理中心，同时也就意味着众好汉大聚义的最终形成。换句话说，在《水浒传》前半部分，小说的空间布局具有强烈的中国传统思维观念的"中央—四方"模式。不过，从好汉们的活动轨迹来看，小说前半部分是一个从四方不断聚集到中央的过程，也就是"由散而聚"的叙事过程。

对《水浒传》后半部分的空间布局，浦安迪认为也具有这种"中央—四方"的结构模式。对此，浦氏说：

> 这种模式在全传本后半部分的结构框架设计中再次被采用，结果，征四寇可视作是根据逆时针方向所作的安排：北方征辽，西北征田虎，西南征王庆，南方征方腊，而在声势浩大的围攻江南名城时达

---

① Early in the narrative, the alternating movement between the Liang-shan region and other centers of power seems to underscore the remoteness of the mountain lair. But as the military potential of the band grows, the sphere of control of the Liang–shan complex gradually swells, until it becomes a major center of the power in its own right. Andrew H. Plaks, The Four Masterworks of the Ming Novel, Princeton University Press, 1987, p. 312.

② Andrew H. Plaks, The Four Masterworks of the Ming Novel, Princeton University Press, 1987, p. 312.

③ Ibid., pp. 312–313.

到顶峰。①

只是在小说的后半部分，叙事的地理中心不再是梁山，而是帝都汴京。征四寇都是由汴京出发又回到汴京。当然，就梁山好汉自身来说，在叙事中心由梁山转移到汴京的过程中，他们的势力则分崩离析了。而这也和前面讨论的浦安迪提出的"聚而复散"的结构模型相呼应。

总之，按浦安迪之论，《水浒传》结构布局上的空间图式，是由中国传统的"中央—四方"观念所构成的。前半部分由东、南、西、北四方不断汇聚到梁山这一中央，后半部分则由汴京这个中央辐射向四方。

在《水浒传》结构安排的空间布局问题上，吴德安的观点与浦安迪比较一致。首先，吴德安认为小说中存在叙事的中心地理实体；其次，小说前后部分的地理背景发生了变化；最后，小说叙事空间关系的转移和英雄们的聚散兴衰相对应。吴德安的具体论述如下：

> 《水浒传》里有两个平行的世界：108好汉的小世界与儒家的世界秩序。从地理上来说，前者描写的是梁山泊，后者则是梁山之外的世界。作为好汉团体的象征，梁山泊形成结构布局的基础。如杨明琅所言："夫《水浒》、《三国》，何以均谓之英雄也？曰：《水浒》以其地见，《三国》以其时见也。"小说前半部分的地理背景，以好汉们聚义的、几乎人格化的梁山泊为中心。小说第二部分的空间背景则从中转移出来。这些空间关系，对应于108好汉的聚和散。
>
> 小说前半部分（第2—70回）的主要行动，是好汉们的聚义与英雄世界梁山泊的缔造。因此，最频繁反复的主题是来自不同地方的英雄加入梁山行列，或是为了营救他们的"兄弟"而离开梁山去攻打城市与村镇。在这部分，梁山构成地理背景的轴心。第72—83回，因为处在接受朝廷招安的过程中，好汉们往来于梁山与作为儒家世界秩序中心的东京（开封）之间。其中七回集中在梁山，因而梁山仍

---

① This pattern is then taken up once again in the framing of the concluding portions of the complete editions, so that the four campaigns can be viewed in terms of a counterclockwise sweep: against the Liao in the north, T'ien Hu to the northwest, Wang Ch'ing to the southwest, and Fang La in the south, culminating in the monumental sieges of the great cities of the Chiang-nan region. Andrew H. Plaks, The Four Masterworks of the Ming Novel, Princeton University Press, 1987, p. 313.

然是空间结构的核心背景。第83回,当这帮好汉接受朝廷的招安,放弃自己的世界而听命于儒家世界秩序的权威时,好汉们的根据地梁山被毁掉了。从此,东京开始成为小说的空间轴心。在《水浒传》的不同版本中,虽然征战次数有变化(一次、两次或是四次),但每次征战之后英雄们还是返回东京。但开封并非他们真正的家园,因为皇帝从未真正信任过他们。因此,返回后他们只能驻扎在城外。小说结尾,好汉们回到一个叫蓼儿洼的地方。作为水浒的一部分,蓼儿洼在小说开篇数回被反复提及。在这最后的故事中,虽然背景已经变化,但对蓼儿洼的描绘却与梁山泊相似。我认为,这揭示了小说作者把蓼儿洼当作梁山象征的良苦用心。因此,在某种意义上,这部小说的开始与结束都在梁山泊。[1]

---

[1] There are two worlds in *Shuihu zhuan*: the microcosm of the 108 heroes and the Confucian world order. Geographically, the former is represented by the marsh, and the latter is the world outside the bandits' lair. The marsh as the symbol of the bandit group forms the basis of the structure design. As Yang Minglang 杨明琅 said: "How can one call the characters in *Shuihu* and *Sanguo* heroes? I say, in *Shuihu* the heroes are represented by a space (the marsh) and in *Sanguo* they are represented by time." The geographical setting of the first half of the novel centers on this almost personified marsh where the bandits gather. The spatial setting of the second half of the novel shifts away from the marsh. These spatial relationships correspond to the gathering and attrition of the 108 heroes。

The main action in the first half of the novel (chapter 2 – 70) is the assembling and creation of the bandit world -the Liangshan Marsh. Thus, the most frequently repeated motif is that in which the heroes come to Liangshanto join the band from various reigns or leave Liangshan to attack city or village to save their "brothers". Liangshan constitutes the central geographical setting in this part. From chapter 72 to 83, because of the process of accepting the imperial amnesty, the characters move between Liangshan and the eastern capital of the Song dynasty, Kaifeng, the center of the Confucian world order. Seven of these chapters concentrate on Liangshan, thus it is still the central setting of the spatial structure. Liangshan, the bandits' lair, is destroyed in chapter 83 when the band accepts the imperial amnesty and submits to the authority of the Confucian world order by giving up its own microcosm. Then the Eastern capital starts to become the spatial center of the novel. Although there are varying numbers of campaigns (one, two, or four) in the different editions of *Shuihu zhuan*, the heroes return to the capital after each campaign. But Kaifeng is not their real home because they are never really trusted by the emperor and thus can live outside the city after their return. In the end, they goback to a place called Liaoerwa 蓼儿洼. Early chapters repeatedly mention it as one sector of the marsh, but in this final episode though the setting is changed the description of it is similar to that of the marsh. I believe this reveal the desire of the novelist to use Liaoerwa as a symbolic Liangshan. Thus in a sense the story hegins and ends at the marsh。

De-an Wu Swihart, The Evolution of Chinese Novel form, Thesis Ph. D. -The Department of East Asian Studies of Princeton University, 1990, pp. 88 – 90.

按吴德安之论，《水浒传》的空间布局不仅具有结构上的功能，还具有揭示小说作者创作意图以及揭示作品主题的作用。

综合浦安迪、吴德安的上述看法和观点，在叙述过程中，小说作者对时间布局与空间布局的精心安排，是构筑《水浒传》情节结构的重要方法和手段。而这些叙述方法与手段，不仅具有结构形式上的意义，同时也与小说主题的呈现紧密相关。小说作者通过空间背景轴心的转换——从梁山到开封，展现出梁山好汉"由散而聚"到"聚而复散"的全过程，并由此揭示出如浦安迪所提出的"万事俱空"的主题。

二、通过"形象叠用原则"、"人物配对与拆分原则"来构筑小说结构模型

通过时间和空间布局来构筑小说结构，这是《水浒传》叙事结构形成的重要方法。根据金圣叹《读第五才子书法》的相关论述，浦安迪与吴德安提出，通过形象描绘方式来构筑小说结构，也是《水浒传》作者采用的非常重要的文本结构技巧。根据浦安迪与吴德安两人的分析、研究，在小说的形象描绘方式中，具有构筑小说文本的叙事结构功能的主要是"形象叠用原则"（the principle of figural recurrence），或者叫"形象重现"方式。不过，必须先说明的一点是，在金圣叹的论述中，"形象叠用"里的形象，不仅指"人物形象"，在小说某些特定的故事片段中也指具有构筑情节结构功能的"物象"。与之相应，浦安迪指出，《水浒传》中，像武松打虎情节中一再提到的武松的"哨棒"，潘金莲偶识西门庆段落里一再提及的具有象征作用的"帘子"，就属于具有构筑小说结构功能的这类"物象"[1]。当然，这些只是小说局部结构安排的问题。

按浦安迪之论，"形象叠用原则"具有重要的叙事结构功能。浦氏指出，从表面来看，"形象叠用"的创作方法，似乎只是把早先存在的故事素材随意地拼缀在一起，但仔细推敲就能发现，在组成小说文本的这些重复叙述模式的显而易见的相似之中，在各种各样的形象叠用的表现形式之内，其实存在某种非常微妙的差异以及情节结构上

---

[1] Andrew H. Plaks, The Four Masterworks of the Ming Novel, Princeton University Press, 1987, p. 315.

的前后呼应①。浦安迪援引金圣叹提出的"正犯"与"略犯"的文法为例说，像武松打虎与李逵杀虎，林冲买宝刀与杨志卖宝刀，鲁达拳打郑屠与武松醉打蒋门神，甚至于潘金莲、阎婆惜与潘巧云等人如出一辙的通奸行为，在这些故事情节中，相同或相似的形象（意象）连续使用，但具体的场景描写却存在微妙的差别，在结构上则具有形成前后之间相互对照、呼应的作用。

就"形象复现"的描写方法，吴德安说那也是一种重要的小说结构方法②。根据金圣叹对《水浒传》第9回"林教头风雪山神庙，陆虞侯火烧草料场"中关于"火"的形象的如下评点：

> 此文通篇以"火"字发奇，乃又于大火之前，先写许多火字；于大火之后，再写许多火字。我读之，因悟同时火也，而前乎陆谦，则有老军借盆，恩情朴至；后乎陆谦，则有庄客借烘，又复恩情朴至；而中间一火，独成大冤深祸……

吴德安指出，在此叙事发展进程中，"火"的形象根本不存在前因后果的关系（cause-and-effect relationship），但小说作者却在对"火"的描写中一步步推动故事情节的发展。据此，吴德安说："这些反复出现的紧密交织在一起的'火'，形成了林冲故事的特殊文本。"而且吴德安还提出："许多这种类型的具有象征意义的细节的运用，构建起《水浒传》的文本结构。"③

以上是对浦安迪、吴德安就"物象叠用"的结构功能进行的分析。笔者以为，《水浒传》中小说作者对这些物象的使用，其实是很典型的

---

① Although this method of composition is partly responsible for the impression of a haphazard stiching together of preexisting source materials, a closer examination reveals that, beneath the very noticeable similarity in repeating narrative patterns that make up much of the text, there lies a level of careful differentiation and cross-reflection within the various manifestation of recurrent figures. Andrew H. Plaks, The Four Masterworks of the Ming Novel, Princeton University Press, 1987, p. 315.

② De-an Wu Swihart, The Evolution of Chinese Novel form, Thesis Ph. D. -The Department of East Asian Studies of Princeton University, 1990, p. 66.

③ Hence, these repeated fires are closely interwoven so as to give a particular texture to Lin Chong's story. Many of these kinds of symbolic details are uesd to construct the textual fabric of *Shuihu zhuan*. De-an Wu Swihart, The Evolution of Chinese Novel form, Thesis Ph. D. -The Department of East Asian Studies of Princeton University, 1990, p. 67.

"物态叙事"。像上文提到的哨棒、帘子、火，以及小说中随处可见的酒，都具有把原本并无因果关系的松散的人物故事凝聚在一起、捏合为一体的作用。不过，这不是笔者在此处要论述的问题，不展开。下面，我们就来讨论"形象叠用原则"中的人物形象塑造的结构作用。

具体到人物形象描写层面，浦安迪与吴德安把小说文本中出现的人物形象的重现现象称作"人物配对原则"与"人物拆分原则"。按浦安迪之论，所谓"人物配对原则"，是指小说作者在创作过程中把相同或相似类型或者是互补、对立类型的人物结合在一起，并深入比较、探索他们的异同，从而展现出相互之间的重大差异[①]。浦安迪指出，《水浒传》中，小说作者反复使用"人物配对原则"来塑造人物形象，并通过这种方式来构筑文本结构。如人物形象研究部分提到的，浦安迪认为，宋江和李逵、鲁达和武松、杨雄和石秀、卢俊义和燕青以及解、曹、孙、孔等小说中出现的不同的兄弟组合描写，都运用了人物配对原则。而在这些重现类型的系列人物中，浦安迪认为，宋江和李逵这一对人物对小说结构的构筑以及文本意蕴的揭示，意义最为重大。浦氏说："宋江和李逵是最显著的例子，他们之间复杂的异同关系建立起小说意蕴的核心轴。"[②] 事实上，《水浒传》前半部分的叙事结构就是由这种配对人物的不断出场构成的。而一次次规模不断壮大的好汉聚义，正是不同的配对人物持续不断汇聚到一起的结果。

关于吴德安提出的"人物拆分原则"，在上文的讨论中我们已经知道它是源自《史记》的一种结构方式，对该论者的相关看法和观点，上文也已论述过，在此就不再展开。以上内容，就是英语世界批评者对小说作者运用人物描写方法来构筑《水浒传》文本结构的研究情况。

三、通过平衡对称原则来构筑小说结构模型

平衡对称原则也是《水浒传》结构布局的一种重要手段。根据浦安

---

① ... the author very quickly moves beyond a simplitic joining of similar types (or complementary opposites) to a deeper exploration of the serious differences brought out in the respective comparisons. Andrew H. Plaks, The Four Masterworks of the Ming Novel, Princeton University Press, 1987, p. 316.

② This is most obvious in the case of Sung Chiang and Li K'uei, whose complex relationship of similarity and difference sets up a central axis of meaning for the novel. Andrew H. Plaks, The Four Masterworks of the Ming Novel, Princeton University Press, 1987, p. 316.

迪的研究，明代小说像《水浒传》《三国演义》《西游记》与《金瓶梅》等，在叙事结构与故事情节的安排上具有明显的平衡对称的"一般美学"特征。文本形式上的这种美学追求，必然影响到小说的结构布局。按照浦安迪说的这种平衡对称原则，《水浒传》前半部分写了梁山好汉的"由散而聚"与不断发展壮大，后半部分则必然描写他们的"聚而复散"与衰败凋零。在浦安迪的研究中，小说"聚而复散"结构模型也的确是这么形成的。

对《水浒传》结构布局中平衡对称原则的运用，吴德安的着眼点与浦安迪不同，前者是从"忠义"的观念模式来讨论小说结构布局中这一原则的应用情况的。吴德安指出：

> 在更大的范围内，小说前半部分的叙事结构由"义"的观念所主宰，招安之后，叙事结构发生了改变，转而由"忠"的观念所支配。第 72 回，梁山好汉全部聚集，聚义达到巅峰。帝国招安的达成，在梁山好汉之间注入了一个分裂的要素，从而改变了叙事的方向。因此，招安是梁山好汉与皇帝之间的基本纽带，接受招安反映了儒家"忠"的观念。然而，考虑到好汉们所代表的基本原则，这是一个四海之内皆兄弟的、独立于更大的社会环境的自给自足的团体，忠于朝廷实在是一个反讽曲笔。然而，好汉们一旦接受帝国的招安，他们就必须放弃自己的世界。于是，接受招安、忠于朝廷与反对招安、保持结义兄弟之情两者之间的分歧与冲突，成为接下来 10 回（72—82）情节发展的动力。
>
> 忠（忠于朝廷）和义（忠于结义兄弟）是两个相对又密切相关的道德价值观念。这种内在于小说文本中的相反相成的二元对立，是最具有统一性的元素，并拥有强烈的主题暗示作用。与这一结构原则一致，小说前半部分 108 好汉的不断聚义就与后半部分英雄们的逐渐亡散相对应，并形成平行的叙事结构。然而，随着征辽、平田虎、平王庆三个结构单元不断插入《水浒传》后半部分的叙事之中，使这部分显得不协调，叙事也显得拙劣。取而代之的是描写 108 好汉在征战过程中的不断伤亡，当故事戛然而止时，梁山 108 好汉实际上也在最后的征方腊中遭受毁灭性的打击。因此，小说前后两部分显得截然不同。这种结果，可能是由主宰小说两部分的忠、义观念之间的矛盾

造成的。①

根据上述分析,再结合《水浒传》文本结构的发展历史,吴德安认为,小说编撰者追求的就是平行的叙事结构。而且该论者还指出:"后来的编撰者把越来越多的故事插入小说后半部分,这样的事实揭示出他们意欲平衡小说前半部分叙事的目的。"②该论者说,小说编撰者追求在情节发展高潮两边形成对称的叙事结构,这明确反映在郑振铎详解《水浒传》结构演化的图表中③。郑振铎的《水浒传》结构演化图表具体如下:

---

① On a larger scale, where the concept of justice (yi) governs the narrative structure of the first of the novel, after the "amnesty" episode the narrative is redirected and governed by the concope of "loyalty" (zhong). When the band reaches its full complement in chapter 72, the gathering process reaches its climax. The obtaining of an imperial amnesty injects a constant element of division into the band and redirects the narrative. Since the amnesty is the fundamental tie between the band and the emperor, accepting the imperial amnesty reflects a certain Confucian concept of loyalty (zhong). However, loyalty to the dynasty is an ironic twist, considering the basic principles that the band represents: a self-contained group in which all men are brothers, independent from the larger social context. Yet, once the band accepts the imperial amnesty, they bave to give up their own microcosm. Therefore, the conflict between accepting the imperial amnesty and working wholeheartedly for the dynasty and opposing the imperial to retain the unified britherhood creats divisions within the band, and forms the plot motivation for the following 10 chapters (72 – 82). Loyalty to the dynasty (zhong) and loyaoty to the band (yi) are certainly two contrasting but inseparable moral values. This contrasting duality is the most unified element underlying the somposition of the novel, and has strong thematic implications. Consistent with this structural principle, a gradual gathering of the 108 heroes (ju 聚) in the first half of the novel should be matched by a gradual dispersal (san 散) in the second half to form a parallel structure in the narrative. However, the three structural units of the campaigns against the Liao, Tian Hu, and Wang Qing in the second half, gradually incorporated into the narrative of *Shuihu zhuan*, produce the inconsistency and inferiority of this part. Instead of depicting the 108 heroes gradually dwindling in the service of the state during these campaigns, the 108 heroes are virtually wiped out in the last campaign against Fang La as the story comes to its abrupt end. Thus, the two parts of the novel appear to be quite distinct. This result might be caused by the contradiction between the zhong and yi concepts governing the two parts of the novel。
De-an Wu Swihart, The Evolution of Chinese Novel form, Thesis Ph. D. -The Department of East Asian Studies of Princeton University, 1990, pp. 85 – 86.

② The fact that the later compilers added more and more episodes to the later section of the novel reveals a tendency toward attempting to balance the narrative of the first part of the novel. De-an Wu Swihart, The Evolution of Chinese Novel form, Thesis Ph. D. -The Department of East Asian Studies of Princeton University, 1990, p. 86.

③ 郑振铎:《中国文学论集》,岳麓书社2011年版,第119、125、146页。

1. 郭本，So-called Kuo Edition.

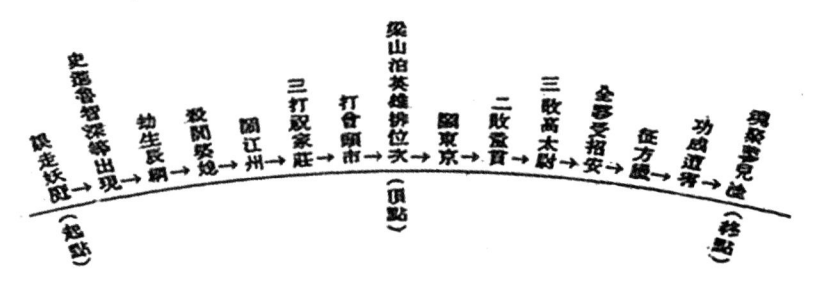

2. 100 回本（1589 年），100 Chapter Edition.

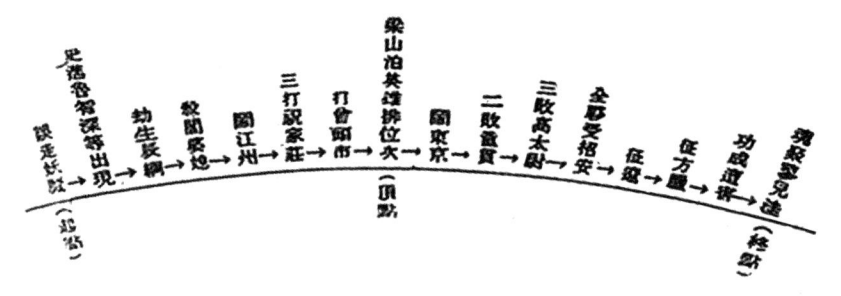

3. 120 回本（1614 年），120 Chapter Edition.

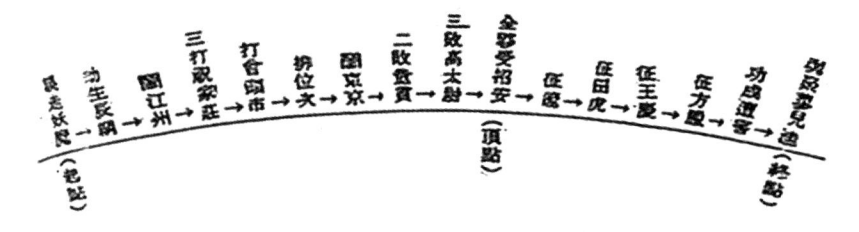

就《水浒传》结构布局上的这种平衡对称的美学追求，浦安迪认为，不仅上述郑振铎提到的三种小说版本如此，就是后来出现的金圣叹删节本同样具有此种特征。对此，浦氏指出，金本前后两部分之间结构上的分界，恰好就在小说叙事的正中间，第 35 回宋江遭刺配路过梁山时与晁盖等人的小型聚义正是故事发展的分水岭；之后的第 40 回 "白龙庙英雄小聚义"（章回标题在第 39 回，具体内容在后一回中）是整体叙事的一个重大升级，结束了小说前半部分对好汉们地方性打家劫舍的描写，标志着在小说后半部分梁山好汉的发展崛起与壮大，并成为中央政权的一个重大

第四章　英语世界对《水浒传》的叙事结构艺术研究

威胁①。

吴德安则从更大的范围指出，平衡对称的结构原则不只是明代小说的"一般美学"特征，它更是强烈地影响着后世章回小说的创作。对此，吴德安说：

> 《水浒传》的结构演化，反映出编撰者这样的意图：把故事情节的高潮放置在叙事的中间部分，并在高潮的两边形成某种平衡。这强烈地影响到后世章回小说的叙事结构。而且《水浒传》结构中显而易见的运用主题模式来支配小说结构的原则，对后世章回小说亦影响深远。②

按照吴德安的这种思路来分析，的确有不少中国明清小说呈现出这样的结构特征。明代的《三国演义》《西游记》《金瓶梅》不说，清代具有代表性的《儒林外史》与《红楼梦》，故事情节的发展都经历了从不断发展兴盛到盛极而衰的过程。

综合上述，在叙述过程中，小说作者或编撰者通过时间与空间布局，通过"形象叠用原则"、"人物配对原则"与"人物拆分原则"，通过"平衡对称原则"与"主题模式原则"，等等，来构筑《水浒传》的整体文本结构。按吴德安之论，这些属于构建《水浒传》结构的基本原则。而在这些基本的结构原则之外，英语世界的其他批评者如吴燕娜、乔什·维托等人发现，小说作者或编撰者还运用了其他方式来构建《水浒传》的叙事结构。下面，笔者就来讨论这些研究者的观点和看法。

---

① Curiously, however, Chin's own artificially obtained seventy-chapter length seems at some points to carry a certain structural login of its own. For example, we can observe the structural division that falls around the middle of Chin's text, punctuated by the miniature ceremony of dedication in chapter 35, and then the major escalation in chapter 40, which brings to close the localized banditry of his first "half" and marks the emergence of the band as a serious threat to centralized power in the second. Andrew H. Plaks, The Four Masterworks of the Ming Novel, Princeton University Press, 1987, p. 306.

② The textual evolution of *Shuihu zhuan* reflects the intention of the compilers to place the climax in the middle if the narrative and form a parallel balance on each side of the climax. This strongly influenced the narrative structure of later zhanghui novels. Moreover, the principle of using a thematic pattern to govern the structure of the novel, as is evident in the structure of *Shuihu zhuan*, also deeply influenced later zhanghui novels. De-an Wu Swihart, The Evolution of Chinese Novel form, Thesis Ph. D. -The Department of East Asian Studies of Princeton University, 1990, p. 88.

第四节　梦与酒——《水浒传》文本叙事的黏合剂

如果说上一节论述的时间与空间布局、形象叠用、人物配对与人物拆分以及平衡对称等基本结构原则是构筑《水浒传》总体叙事结构的岩石和砖块，那么，小说中反复出现的梦与酒则是把那这些岩石、砖块紧密地凝聚在一起的强有力的黏合剂。

一、梦叙事及其结构功能

中国没有古希腊那样发达的神话故事传说，也没有形成那么成熟的神话谱系，但在中国古典文学的书写中，以及作为历史书写典范的《左传》《史记》等典籍里面，却完全不缺乏类似于神话因素的叙述要素。魔幻神异的因子，充斥着中国一切形式的文学书写，不论书面形式还是口头形式，无论按史演义还是虚构创作。而在这魔幻神异的诸因子里面，梦是其中最为常见的一种。对中国文学、文化传统中出现的梦叙述现象，吴燕娜指出：

> 长久以来，梦使中国作家为之着迷。在非文学性的文献资料中，无论是官方历史还是非官方历史，都记载着人们渴望成为皇帝或皇后的梦想。在儒家经典与《左传》里，人们发现，梦涉及预言与精神。早期的道家哲学著作，诸如《列子》、《庄子》，使用梦的寓言来质疑梦与现实经验之间习以为常的差异，并把本体论与认识论合并在一起。从六朝到明代，在志怪作品、经典传奇以及轶事趣闻的汇编中，充满梦的记述和梦的故事，虽然绝大部分非常简短。[①]

[①] Dreams have long fascinated Chinese writers. Among non-literary sources, both official and unofficial histories record dreams related to emperors- and empresses- to-be as well as men of destiny. Dreams involving prediction and spirits are found in Confucian classics and the *Zuo zhuan* 左传. Early Taoist philosophical texts such as *Liezi* 列子 and *Zhuangzi* 庄子 use dream parables to question the conventional distinction between the dream and waking experience and to conflate ontology and epistemology. Accounts and stories of dreams, though mostly brief, abound in anecdotal writings, classical tales, and encyclopedic compilations from the Six Dynasties through the Ming. Yenna Wu, Outlaw's Dreams of Power and Position in *Shuihu zhuan*, Chinese Literature: Essays, Articals, Reviews (CLEAR), Vol. 18 (Dec., 1996), p. 45。

在此基础上，从中国社会思想文化的层面切入，吴燕娜进一步分析了中国作家笔下梦的成因，以及人们对梦所作的哲学性的理解。吴燕娜说，中国作家习惯于从心理过程（包括思想、情感、记忆）到生理过程（包括身体、感觉器官）和外在环境之间的失衡的角度来理解梦的形成原因；而且在许多早期的文献资源中，很多则把梦归因于超自然的因素。而在宗教哲学的角度，人们的理解又有不同。该论者说，道教哲学家与佛教徒，用梦来论证现象世界的无常；某些佛家思想家则认为，梦可以成为宗教拯救的方法和途径，能够揭示出一个人的往世与来生。[1]

正是中国文学与文化传统中，存在如此浓厚的对于梦的理解与书写的悠久历史，从而无形中影响着一代又一代的中国文学创作。作为中国古代叙事文学发展历史上具有里程碑意义的经典，《水浒传》的创作自然也深受其影响。根据朱迪思·T. 蔡特林（Judith T. Zeitlin）的分析统计，《水浒传》中，小说作者描写的梦，大大小小加起来超过 12 个[2]。对小说作者描写的这些梦，吴燕娜认为，它们一方面有助于把原本松散的故事片段组织成连贯的整体，另一方面也有助于人们对作品思想意蕴展开比较深入的理解。对后者，该论者说：

> 这些文学性的梦想，为《水浒传》增添了整体的象征与神话意蕴，同时为重估儒家的忠、义、孝观念提供了线索，有时也向人们展现出一丝矛盾的、甚至是反讽的色彩。[3]

---

[1] Traditionally Chinese writers have categorized dreams on the basis of causes ranging from psychological processes-thoughts, emotions, or memories-to physiological processes-imbalances within the body or sensory stimulation from the environment. In addition, many early sources ascribe supernatural causes to certain dreams which serve as the meeting ground between humans and immortals and bring messages from the spirit world. 6 Like the Taoist philosophers, Buddhist teachers used dreams to illustrate the ephemerality of the phenomenal world. More importantly, certain Buddhist thinkers believed that dreams might be a means to achieve religious salvation and may reveal one's past lives (karma) and possible reincarnations (prophecy). Yenna Wu, Outlaw's Dreams of Power and Position in Shuihu zhuan, Chinese Literature: Essays, Articals, Reviews (CLEAR), Vol. 18 (Dec., 1996), pp. 45 – 46.

[2] Judith T. Zeitlin, Historian of the Strange: Pu Songling and the Chinese Classical Tale (Stanford: Stanford University Press, 1993), pp. 135 – 140.

[3] These literary dreams add to the overall symbolic and mythical meanings of the novel, while providing clues for re-evaluating such Confucian values as loyalty (zhong 忠), righteousness (yi 义), and filial piety (xiao 孝), showing them sometimes in an ambivalent and even ironic light. Yenna Wu, Outlaw's Dreams of Power and Position in Shuihu zhuan, Chinese Literature: Essays, Articals, Reviews (CLEAR), Vol. 18 (Dec., 1996), p. 46。

对这些梦的叙事结构功能，吴燕娜这样指出：

> 这些梦（其中一些很简短），只是预知未来，泄露真情，或是带来神助。这些梦里面，篇幅比较长的四个——宋江两次，他后来成为造反者的首领，宋江的结义兄弟李逵一次，徽宗皇帝一次，它们是综合、多义的。这些梦具有几个方面的作用：它们有助于描写形象与解释心理；在段落之间构成重要的结构和主题线索，并为这部似乎片段式的、组织结构松散的小说提供必要的一致性的叙事线索；营造一个和谐的氛围，创造柔和的张力，使叙事活动变化多样。作为神话框架的组成部分，这些梦与平淡的叙事主体形成鲜明的对比。①

在此论述中，吴燕娜明确指出，《水浒传》里描写的梦，具有"在段落之间构成重要的结构和主题线索，并为这部似乎片段式的、组织结构松散的小说提供必要的一致性的叙事线索"的功能和作用；而且梦叙事也使得小说叙事有变化，从而在一定程度上改变了小说单调、重复的叙事模式。

在此论述的基础上，吴燕娜对《水浒传》中描写的四个篇幅较长的梦的叙事功能展开了具体的分析论述。就《水浒传》第42回"还道村受三卷天书，宋公明遇九天玄女"所写宋江遇九天玄女摆脱追捕的厄运并得到天书的第一个梦，吴燕娜说："对现代读者来说，这个梦只是一个幻觉，因为很难相信宋江在遭遇惊恐的经历过后能进入梦乡。"② 但作者正是通过这个梦，通过玄女娘娘的言语的预示，使小说的整体叙事发生了巨

---

① Some of these dreams are brief and bring only prophecy, revelation of truth, or divine assistance. But four of the dreams-two by Song Jiang 宋江 who later becomes the rebel leader, one by his sworn brother Li Kui 李逵, and one by Emperor Huizong 徽宗-are polysemous "complex dreams" of greater length. These dreams serve several purposes: They contribute to characterization and allow for psychological interpretation; constitute important structural and thematic links among episodes, providing essential coherence to this seemingly episodic and loosely-organized novel; and supply a peaceful atmosphere and feminine strain, thereby varying the narrative movement. As part of the supernatural framework, they contrast with the mundane major portion of the narrative. Yenna Wu, Outlaw's Dreams of Power and Position in Shuihu zhuan, Chinese Literature: Essays, Articals, Reviews (CLEAR), Vol. 18 (Dec., 1996), p. 46。

② The "dream" may strike the modern readers as a hallicination, since it is difficult to believe that Song Jiang cold fall asleep immediately after a frightening experience. Yenna Wu, Outlaw's Dreams of Power and Position in Shuihu zhuan, Chinese Literature: Essays, Articals, Reviews (CLEAR), Vol. 18 (Dec., 1996), p. 46。

大的转折。对此转折,吴燕娜指出:

> 第42回写宋江的梦,使宋江的生涯与小说叙事发生了一个关键的转折。在此梦之前,宋江并不愿意加入梁山;即使加入之后,他仍然不清楚自己的使命。玄女娘娘的指示因而提醒了宋江,并给予他一个新的生活目标。此梦之后,宋江意识到自己的特殊使命,以及注定担当梁山首领的角色,并对此充满信心。从这一回起,小说增加了玄女不时的预示和天书,在解释英雄聚义时,小说叙事开始提到星宿天命。宋江明显受到自己对玄女所作承诺的约束,坚信应该努力达成招安,为皇帝而征战。虽然梁山的力量壮大到足以推翻朝廷、建立自己的政权,他的手下也反复催促他这样做,但宋江保持着自己对朝廷坚贞不变的忠诚。①

按吴燕娜之论,小说作者对宋江此梦的描写,已经预设了《水浒传》后半部分梁山好汉必然接受招安,以及四处征战效忠皇帝的所有故事情节。而事实上,小说后来的情节发展的确是遵循着这一轨迹前进的。

宋江的第二个梦,出现在《水浒传》第88回"颜统军阵列混天象,宋公明梦授玄女法"中。此回写梁山好汉接受招安之后受命征辽,被辽军打败。其时宋江百般寻思、无计可施,沉吟闷坐寨中,到的夜里二鼓时"神思困倦,和衣隐几而卧",恍惚之间进入梦中。经青衣童子引导,宋江面见九天玄女娘娘,并于梦中得玄女娘娘兵法天书。而得到玄女娘娘这个神灵的帮助,并借助梦中所得玄女娘娘的兵法天书,宋江等人最终大败辽军。对宋江的这个梦,吴燕娜说:

---

① A crucial turning point both in Song's career and in the narrative occurs in Song's dream in chapter 42. Before this dream, Song was unwilling to join the band; even after being forced to join, he is still unclear about his destiny. The goddess's instruction thus empowers Song and gives him a new focus in life. After the dream, he becomes aware of, and feels confident about, his special mission and his destined role as leader and begins consciously to recruit comrades. From this chapter on, in addition to its occasional mention of the goddess and the Divine Books, the narrative begins referring to the star spirits more often in explaining the gathering of the heroes. Song obviously feels contractually bound by his promise to the goddess, believing that he should try to obtain amnesty and fight for the emperor. Although the band becomes powerful enough to take over the state and his comrades repeatedly urge him to do so, he remains steadfast in his loyalty to the imperial court. Yenna Wu, Outlaw's Dreams of Power and Position in Shuihu zhuan, Chinese Literature: Essays, Articals, Reviews (CLEAR), Vol. 18 (Dec., 1996), pp. 51 – 52.

宋江的第二个梦,是又一个特殊时刻。此时,因为得到神的力量的帮助而非天书本身的帮助,宋江赢得了战斗。实际上,在与辽军的作战中,宋江最初的挫败,只是作者创造出需要玄女重现以及制造出另一个转折的策略之一。[1]

对宋江的第二个梦,该论者还指出:

从结构、主题以及审美的层面,第二个梦为小说文本提供了内在的凝聚力。像《水浒传》中许多其他类似的故事一样,在变化之中,这个梦重复着第一个梦的结构、主题甚至是措辞。[2]

从这一角度来说,小说对梦的反复描写是"形象叠用原则"的另一种具体运用而已。而根据吴燕娜的分析论述,小说作者描写的宋江的这两个梦,的确为《水浒传》的叙事结构提供了内在的凝聚力,为看似无逻辑关系的故事情节带来了超自然的、具有魔幻性质的叙事线索。

李逵的梦出现在小说第93回,该回标题直书"李逵梦闹天池"。其时李逵饮酒贪杯,在众人谈说之中悠悠入睡。李逵的这个梦,包括多个故事,概括起来是这样的:李逵走出盖州州城,路遇一秀士,经其指点来到天池岭;天池岭上,李逵打杀强人,救下一女子,后拒绝其父母的许配请求跑出门来;在门外,李逵遇到先前那伙逃走的一个强人,与之打斗、追赶,来到文德殿;文德殿上,李逵看见蔡京、童贯、高俅、杨戬四贼臣,因愤怒他们欺诳皇帝、诬蔑梁山众好汉,李逵斧劈四贼臣;而后李逵返回,再遇前秀士,告知李逵"要夷田虎族,须谐琼矢镞"暗语。李逵梦中最后所得"要夷田虎族,须谐琼矢镞"的暗语,又与没羽箭张清、琼

---

[1] Song's second dream is one of the occasions on which he wins the battle because of the help from some supernatural force, rather than from the Divine Books. Indeed, Song's initial defeat in fighting the Liao army is one of the authors' devices in creating a need for the goddess's reappearance and for another turning point. Yenna Wu, Outlaw's Dreams of Power and Position in Shuihu zhuan, Chinese Literature: Essays, Articals, Reviews (CLEAR), Vol. 18 (Dec., 1996), p. 53.
[2] Structurally, thematically, and aesthetically, the second dream provides cohesion within the text. Like many other analogous episodes in *Shuihu*, it repeats with variations the structure, the motifs, and even the diction of the first dream. Yenna Wu, Outlaw's Dreams of Power and Position in Shuihu zhuan, Chinese Literature: Essays, Articals, Reviews (CLEAR), Vol. 18 (Dec., 1996), p. 53.

英两人之间具有心灵感应色彩的梦的具体内容相呼应。对小说作者描写的李逵的这个梦，吴燕娜如此分析道：

> 通过直接或间接映射先前的故事，这些故事同时展现了人物的矛盾心理，李逵的梦构成了小说的结构单元。李逵英勇救助被强抢的女子，是在重复第73回那个类似的故事。李逵在文德殿上受到皇帝的褒奖，使人想起第82回宋江等梁山好汉在朝廷受到皇帝召见。①

根据吴燕娜的论述，作者把李逵过去以及最近的一些记忆，通过乔装改扮融入了他的梦里面。这个梦，一部分是在照应以前发生的故事，并展现出人物的性格，以及当时李逵的真实心理动态。这在叙事上是承前。而小说作者写李逵得到秀士那"要夷田虎族，须谐琼矢镞"的暗语，这一片段则有预示未来的叙事功能。《水浒传》接下来的情节发展，写没羽箭张清与琼英的结合，并借机平定田虎，正是照应了这十个字的预设。因而，李逵的这个梦，梦中所得这个预示性的言语，既是在创造悬念、调动读者，又是在揭示下文、设下伏笔。对此问题，吴燕娜说：

> 在宋江和李逵的梦里，通过鬼神传达的预言，让做梦的人和读者感到晦涩难懂。秀士告诉李逵的言语中隐藏的信息（困扰着宋江和吴用，但并未困扰没羽箭张清和神医安道全），包含将来情节发展的线索。这种情形，为读者创造了悬念，因为不知道为什么这两人先就理解了这个预言，因而焦急地等待谜底的揭开。②

---

① Li Kui's dream contributes to the novel's structural unity by directly or indirectly mirroring previous episodes while it displays the ambivalences of the character. Li's heroic rescue of the girl echoes a similar episode in chapter 73 (73.900 – 906). Li's recognition of the palaces harks back to chapter 82 when Song Jiang and his outlaw band receive an audience at court. Yenna Wu, Outlaw's Dreams of Power and Position in Shuihu zhuan, Chinese Literature: Essays, Articals, Reviews (CLEAR), Vol. 18 (Dec., 1996), p. 57.

② The prophecies conveyed by supernatural beings in both Song Jiang's and Li Kui's dreams remain opaque to the dreamers and to the reader. The cryptic message given by the mysterious scholar to Li Kui contains clues for future development which baffle Song Jiang and Wu Yong, but not Zhang Qing 张清, the general skilled in stone-throwing, and the physician An Daoquan 安道全 (93.1125). This situation creates suspense for the reader who, not knowing why these two have privileged understanding, anxiously awaits the solution to the enigma. Yenna Wu, Outlaw's Dreams of Power and Position in Shuihu zhuan, Chinese Literature: Essays, Articals, Reviews (CLEAR), Vol. 18 (Dec., 1996), p. 58。

吴燕娜提出的这种情形,在中国古代小说中是很常见的。如上文提到的,在中国文学的书写中,这种魔幻、神异的因素是非常多的。

根据吴燕娜的论述,李逵的梦,颠倒了大量事实,如现实中根本没机会接近蔡京等奸臣,却写李逵斧劈四贼臣;宋徽宗昏庸误国、被奸臣蒙蔽,却写他聪明智慧、是一个慈父形象;李逵的母亲被老虎咬死吃掉了,却写她复活了。吴燕娜认为,所有这些描写,都具有对现实的补偿的功能和作用。通过这个补偿性的梦,李逵得到权力去纠正错误、赢得荣誉,而在现实生活中,李逵是经常缺少这种权力的。

按吴燕娜之论,《水浒传》里描写的宋江与李逵的这三个梦,它们除了具有衔接过渡、预示情节发展的叙事功能和作用,还揭示出小说的内在意蕴。对此,该论者指出:

> 在梦里,李逵和宋江退化到幼稚的状态。表面看来不可征服的英雄,他们却只能通过梦幻的方式实现自己的目标。因此,通过对比他们清醒时与睡梦中的状况,读者能够感受到他们的性格是复杂多样的。因为他们没有自主权,必须在梦中通过鬼神或者皇帝才能得到权力,读者因而视他们为无助、无能的人物。这样的分析让我们更深入地发现,他们的梦,除了把各个叙事部分连接在一起之外,还有助于挖掘出两种不同类型的英雄。[①]

按照吴燕娜的分析论述,《水浒传》中描写的宋江和李逵的这些梦,一方面有助于塑造人物形象、揭示作品思想内涵,另一方面则有助于把各个不同的叙事部分连接在一起构建小说的情节结构。

至于小说最后一回"徽宗帝梦游梁山泊"所写宋徽宗的那场梦,吴燕娜说:"与宋江、李逵经历的预示性的梦不一样,就其本质而言,

---

① In their dreams, Li Kui and Song Jiang regress to infantile states. Ostensibly invincible heroes, they can only achieve their goals through fantasy. The reader is therefore able to derive a sense of the complexity of their characters by contrasting their waking and dreaming states. The reader sees them as truly helpless and impotent, without adult autonomy, because they must be empowered in dreams by either the goddess or the emperor. Such analysis thus enables us to see further how, in addition to linking the various parts of the narrative together, their dreams serve to undercut both as heroic types. Yenna Wu, Outlaw's Dreams of Power and Position in Shuihu zhuan, Chinese Literature: Essays, Articals, Reviews (CLEAR), Vol. 18 (Dec., 1996), p. 58.

最后一回徽宗皇帝的梦是揭示性与补偿性的。"① 只是这个梦并不是宋徽宗思绪的结束，也没有解决问题。该论者指出，自从赐酒与宋江之后，宋徽宗就被对宋江的思念所困扰，但又不能从臣子们那里得到实情。对宋江的这种连续不断的想念之情，触发宋徽宗的这个梦。而在这个梦里，宋徽宗游览梁山泊，知晓了奸臣们的阴谋诡计，知道了宋江等英雄坚定不移的忠诚与冤屈而死的实情。吴燕娜认为，这个梦表现了皇帝的不安与内疚，表面上表达了对梁山好汉忠诚的补偿②。而在笔者看来，这是小说作者通过文学的形式，对英雄们所作的一种"诗性正义"的补偿。

从叙事的层面来说，吴燕娜认为，宋徽宗通过梦的方式得知英雄的屈死，是叙事的需要。因为宋徽宗经常受奸臣欺骗、蒙蔽，即使那些奸臣如此险恶行事，他们并没有被处死。因此，该论者说："梦是死去的英雄向皇帝揭露真实情形的唯一手段，并因此为自己沉冤昭雪。"③ 也就是说，这场梦的描写，是小说作者展现梁山好汉忠诚的一个必需的叙事手段。在吴燕娜看来，宋徽宗的这场梦，地点从皇宫禁苑转移到梁山泊，小说作者通过梁山好汉的"忠义"把这两个原本对立的"他者"联系在一起，从而把小说统一起来。对此，该论者说："作者们使用不同的具有象征意义的平行对立的梦的场所，把小说统一在一起。"④ 而且"纵观徽宗帝的梦的背景，通过把梁山泊与蓼儿洼合并成一体，作者们努力把小说的开篇和

---

① Unlike the prophetic dreams experienced bu Song Jiang and Li Kuei, the emperor's dream in the last chapter is both revelatory and compensatory. Yenna Wu, Outlaw's Dreams of Power and Position in Shuihu zhuan, Chinese Literature: Essays, Articals, Reviews (CLEAR), Vol. 18 (Dec., 1996), p. 58.

② In the dream the emperor is transported to Liangshanbo, where Song and the other heroes inform him of their unshaken loyalty despite their wrongful deaths. This dream compensates for the emperor's uneasiness and sense of guilt, as well as his desire for the outlaws' loyalty. Yenna Wu, Outlaw's Dreams of Power and Position in Shuihu zhuan, Chinese Literature: Essays, Articals, Reviews (CLEAR), Vol. 18 (Dec., 1996), p. 58.

③ the dream is the only instrument the dead heroes have to reveal the truth to the emperor, thus vindicating themselves passively. Yenna Wu, Outlaw's Dreams of Power and Position in Shuihu zhuan, Chinese Literature: Essays, Articals, Reviews (CLEAR), Vol. 18 (Dec., 1996), p. 59.

④ The authors use symbolic parallels and contrasts in the various dream-loci to unify the novel. Yenna Wu, Outlaw's Dreams of Power and Position in Shuihu zhuan, Chinese Literature: Essays, Articals, Reviews (CLEAR), Vol. 18 (Dec., 1996), p. 59.

结尾衔接起来。"① 吴燕娜的这个看法,与上文浦安迪、吴德安等人提出的,《水浒传》的作者通过空间布局来构筑小说叙事结构的观点是一致的。

除了上文讨论的这四个梦,《水浒传》作者还描写了不少其他的梦,其中一些在一定程度上也具有组织、建构小说文本结构的功能,像与李逵的梦相呼应的没羽箭张清与琼英那具有心灵感应的梦就是如此。综合自己对《水浒传》中描写的几个重要的梦的叙事功能的分析论述,吴燕娜的结论是:

> 作为一种结构方法,梦具有衔接功能。特别是那些主要的梦,把叙事紧密交织在一起。它们把不同的叙事部分,如开篇的误走妖魔、梁山好汉的历险、与其他造反者的战斗以及忠义主题等,连接起来。宋江的两个梦,不仅为他提供神灵的信息和援助,还告诉读者他作为"星主"(Star Lord)的独特身份及其既定的命运。这些梦和其他神秘的事件,尤其是星宿的神话起源、他们作为英雄的化身、他们接受上天的制裁以及他们的死亡与重回天国等,联系在一起,构成小说的环状顶层结构。②

综合吴燕娜的研究可知,在《水浒传》的叙事过程中,梦担当着非常重要的角色。如上文所说,这些梦把各种各样的叙事成分、叙事要素紧密地衔接、凝聚在一起,从而构成韩南提出的统领整部小说的顶层结构。

---

① Through the setting of the emperor's dream, the authors try to connect the beginning and the end of the novel by conflating both Liangshanbo and Liaoerwa 蓼儿洼. Yenna Wu, Outlaw's Dreams of Power and Position in Shuihu zhuan, Chinese Literature: Essays, Articals, Reviews (CLEAR), Vol. 18 (Dec., 1996), p. 59.

② As a structural device, dreams serve a cohesive function. The major dreams, in particular, are organically interwoven with the narrative. They link the various parts of the narrative together, e. g., the introductory release of demons, the Liangshanbo adventures, battles with other rebels, and the theme of loyalty and righteousness. Song Jiang's two dreams not only provide him with divine messages and aid, but also inform the reader of his unique status as Star Lord and his preordained fate. These dreams tie in with other mythical events which constitute the circular superstructure, in particular the supernatural origins of the star spirits, their incarnation as heroes, the divine sanction they receive, and their deaths and return to Heaven. Yenna Wu, Outlaw's Dreams of Power and Position in Shuihu zhuan, Chinese Literature: Essays, Articals, Reviews (CLEAR), Vol. 18 (Dec., 1996), pp. 66 – 67.

二、酒——《水浒传》叙事的黏合剂

上文在讨论《水浒传》作者运用"形象叠用原则"来构建小说的叙事结构时，我们知道，浦安迪非常重视具体的物象在构成小说结构中的作用。在浦氏眼里，像武松打虎里的哨棒，潘金莲与西门庆通奸里的帘子，林冲买宝刀与杨志卖宝刀里的宝刀，等等，都是具有非常重要的结构意义的实物。对小说作者运用具体物象来构建小说文本的叙事现象，笔者称其为"物态叙事"。在《水浒传》的"物态叙事"里面，浦安迪忽视了一个非常重要的元素，那就是在小说叙事中反复出现的、与梁山好汉几乎形影不离的"酒"。

事实上，对酒的描写是贯穿小说始终的，不仅大碗喝酒是梁山好汉的一个重要外在特征，就是对《水浒传》的整体叙述，酒这个形象也具有重要的意义和作用。要知道，就《水浒传》前半部分的叙事，直接和酒有关的章回就有十来回，像第四回"赵员外重修文殊院，鲁智深大闹五台山"，第五回"小霸王醉入销金帐，花和尚大闹桃花村"，第十四回"赤发鬼醉卧灵官殿，晁天王认义东西村"，第十六回"杨志押送金银担，吴用智取生辰纲"，第二十一回"虔婆醉打唐牛儿，宋江怒杀阎婆惜"，第二十三回"横海郡柴进留宾，景阳冈武松打虎"，第二十七回"母夜叉孟州道卖人肉，武都头十字坡遇张青"，第二十九回"施恩重霸孟州道，武松醉打蒋门神"，第三十二回"武行者醉打孔亮，锦毛虎义释宋江"，第四十五回"杨雄醉骂潘巧云，石秀智杀裴如海"，等等，所有这些章回的叙事都与酒紧密相关。①

《水浒传》后半部分故事情节的发展、转折，更是和酒息息相关。小说作者所写第一次招安的失败，虽然朝廷方面有不可推卸的责任——主要包括诏书的措辞、语气，以及蔡京派遣的张干办、高俅派遣的李虞侯对待梁山好汉的颐指气使的恶劣态度，但"活阎罗倒船偷御酒"的结果却有过之而无不及。御酒变村酿白酒，这虽然是梁山内部人干的，却极大地激怒了不明内情的一众水浒英雄，并直接导致鲁智深、刘唐、武松、穆弘、史进等重要头领抄起家伙"一齐发作"。此消息传出之后，梁山更是"四

---

① 本处所说小说回目，以2009年上海古籍出版社出版《水浒传》120回本为据。

下大小头领,一大半闹将起来"。① 其结果就是宣告第一次招安的彻底失败。正是这次招安的失败,才有后来的两败童贯、三败高俅的五回精彩叙事,也才有后来更为曲折的第二次招安的描写。

在《水浒传》后半部分的叙事中,除上述章回之外,和酒直接相关的重要叙事则是小说结尾第120回的"宋公明神聚蓼儿洼,徽宗帝梦游梁山泊"。此回中,且不说蔡京、童贯、高俅、杨戬四贼臣如何设计暗害卢俊义,致其"因醉"坠落淮河而死。单就此四奸臣假宋徽宗赐御酒之名下药毒杀宋江,以及宋江以此毒酒毒杀李逵的情节叙述,笔者以为,这正是小说作者展现宋江之"忠义"以及营造浓厚的悲剧气氛的神来之笔;而借毒酒写宋江之死,又是必要的艺术使命,也是小说叙事的终极任务。

总之,对上述提到的这些小说章回,酒在其叙事过程中具有重要的"关目"作用。有的事件是因酒而起,或者说酒具有导火索的作用,像"武行者醉打孔亮"就是一个典型;有的事件因酒而写得一波三折、精彩非凡,像"景阳冈武松打虎"正是如此;有的事件,酒在其叙述过程扮演着重要的"道具"角色,"吴用智取生辰纲"那一回,要是没有白日鼠白胜挑来的那两桶酒,故事情节的发展就难以出现大转折。凡此种种,不再展开。

对《水浒传》中反复出现的"酒"这一形象在小说文本叙事中的意义与作用,英语世界的批评者如夏志清、乔什·维托(Josh Vittor)等人也进行过相应的研究。特别是乔什·维托,在夏志清研究的基础之上,写了一篇题为《松散与醉酒:酒作为〈水浒传〉罕见的黏合剂》的文章②,对此问题进行了专门的分析讨论。根据西方读者阅读《水浒传》的体验和感受,维托指出:

> 如果一个读者打算逐页阅读中国古典小说《水浒传》,他可能会作出这部小说是描写各个好汉的历险事迹的推断,而所有这些好汉都喜欢暴力。他可能会惊讶,为什么每回结尾都有引导性的指示语——它们意欲把各回连接起来,各回之间在人物与情节的发展上却几乎没什么连贯性。事实上,初次阅读的人可能会惊奇地发现小说中存在丰富的对酒的

---

① 具体内容见120回本《水浒传》第七十五回"活阎罗倒船偷御酒,黑旋风扯诏骂钦差",上海古籍出版社2009年版,第675—680页。

② Josh Vittor, Incoherence and Intoxication: Alcohol as s Rare Source of Consistency in *Outlaws of the Marsh.* "Women and Men, Love and Power: Parameters of Chinese Fiction and Drama" Sino-Platonic Paper, edited by Victor H. Mair, 193 (Novermber, 2009), pp. 159 – 168.

描写，仅仅因为酒似乎是唯一连续出现的具有主题意义的物体。[1]

在此论述中，维托指出了酒对《水浒传》叙事的重要意义。在他看来，在《水浒传》这部结构松散、情节支离破碎的中国古典小说里面，酒似乎是唯一的把小说的各个叙事部分连接起来的具有主题性作用的物体。基于这样的认识，该论者进一步论述道：

> 对在中国被视为最伟大的一部小说来说，认为酒及其对主要人物的影响在其中可能担当着重要的作用，这样的看法似乎是愚蠢的。当精读《水浒传》最初的百来页时，人们会发现，对酒与醉酒的描写远远超过对任何一个形象的描写，因而仍然难以否定酒的重要性。我们的读者很快就会发现，这部皇皇巨著经常不连贯、无法预料；这种变化多样的特性，一方面使其成为一部令人兴奋的、受大众欢迎的小说，但另一方面这也可能使人感到些许的疏离和混乱。事实证明，反复消费的酒，是小说中读者能够清点出来的极少的几个要素之一，它为作品提供了一个罕见的黏合剂，从一开始它就有助于人们了解这部小说更加崇高的主题诉求。[2]

---

[1] If a reader were to turn through the pages of the classic Chinese novel *Shuihu Zhuan* (Outlaws of the Marsh), the might gather that the novel depicted the adventures of various outlaws or bandits, all of whom had a penchant for violence. He might wonder why there seems to be so little coherence in terms of plot or character development from chapter to chapter, despite leading directivess at the end of each chapter that seem to connect them. In fact, a tirst-time reader might be surprised to find him-or herself tracking the presence of copious amounts of alcohol in the novel, simply because it seems to be the only thematic entity that consistently appears. Josh Vittor, Incoherence and Intoxication: Alcohol as s Rare Source of Consistency in *Outlaws of the Marsh*. "Women and Men, Love and Power: Parameters of Chinese Fiction and Drama" Sino-Platonic Paper, edited by Victor H. Mair, 193 (Novermber, 2009), p. 159.

[2] The notion that alcohol, and its complications for the main characters, could play a central role in what is considered one of the greatest novels in Chinese might seem a bit silly. Still, it is difficult to deny its prominence when a perusal of the first hundred pages of *Outlaws of the Marsh* yields far mor mentions of alcohol and drunkness than it dies of any one character! Our reader would soon discover that this massive tome is often disjointed and unpredictable; this variability is part of what makes it such an exciting and popular novel, but it also can be somewhat alienating and confusing. As it turns out, the repeated consumption of alcohol is one of the few elements on which our reader can count, providing a rare source of consistency in the novel and a starting point from which to discern the novel's more lofty thematic aspirations. Josh Vittor, Incoherence and Intoxication: Alcohol as s Rare Source of Consistency in *Outlaws of the Marsh*. "Women and Men, Love and Power: Parameters of Chinese Fiction and Drama" Sino-Platonic Paper, edited by Victor H. Mair, 193 (Novermber, 2009), p. 159.

从物态叙事的层面来说，认为酒是《水浒传》里一个"罕见的黏合剂"，这是有一定道理的。因为从小说文本的叙事情形来看，在《水浒传》中，确实找不出比酒的出现频率更高的物象，更找不出像酒这样使小说叙事如此腾挪辗转、曲折生花、节外生枝的形象。而且从笔者上文讨论的"活阎罗倒船偷御酒"故事来看，酒的确在《水浒传》的叙事中扮演着重要的"黏合剂"的角色。

在此总体认识的基础上，就酒作为《水浒传》文本叙事的"黏合剂"这一功能和作用的表现，乔什·维托展开了具体的分析和研究。通过统计《水浒传》前32回的标题，该论者指出："在小说前三十二回的标题中，有四回包含'醉'（drunk）这个字眼，以描绘该回的主角。"① 乔什·维托所说的这四回，具体是指：第五回"小霸王醉入销金帐，花和尚大闹桃花村"，第二十一回"虔婆醉打唐牛儿，宋江怒杀阎婆惜"，第二十九回"施恩重霸孟州道，武松醉打蒋门神"，第三十二回"武行者醉打孔亮，锦毛虎义释宋江"。事实上，在小说前32回里面，标题中出现了"醉"这一字眼的还有第十四回"赤发鬼醉卧灵官殿，晁天王认义东西村"。通过对第五回小说作者所写鲁智深豪饮、痛打小霸王周通的情景的分析，乔什·维托指出：

> 在整部小说中，喝酒偏重于直接导致身体冲突，喝酒直接与肉体、经常是野蛮残忍联系在一起。在我们对这部冗长又复杂的小说的一致性的研究中，酒是冲突来临的一个可靠的信号。②

再结合对第21回、29回及32回的分析，该论者进一步指出：

---

① Of the first thirty-two chapter titles, four contain the word "drunk," used to describe the protagonist of the chapter. Josh Vittor, Incoherence and Intoxication: Alcohol as s Rare Source of Consistency in *Outlaws of the Marsh*. "Women and Men, Love and Power: Parameters of Chinese Fiction and Drama" Sino-Platonic Paper, edited by Victor H. Mair, 193（Novermber, 2009）, p. 162.

② Throughout the novel, the consumption of alcohol tends to lead directly to physical altercation, linking drinking directly to physicality and, often, brutality. In our search for consistency, therefore, in this long and complicated novel, aocohol serves as a reliable signal that conflict is becoming. Josh Vittor, Incoherence and Intoxication: Alcohol as s Rare Source of Consistency in *Outlaws of the Marsh*. "Women and Men, Love and Power: Parameters of Chinese Fiction and Drama" Sino-Platonic Paper, edited by Victor H. Mair, 193（Novermber, 2009）, p. 162.

  至关重要的是，如上文描述的那样，这些章回每一次都遵循相同的蓝本——主角喝了大量的酒，而后陷入某种形式的身体冲突结果几乎总是我们的英雄获胜。这种模式经常在同一回里发生两次，以第二十一回为例说，宋江在被其外室阎婆惜激怒并随后把她杀死之前，先就和婆惜的母亲一起喝酒。而且这种醉怒的主题，并不仅仅局限于标题中附有"醉"字形容的那些章回。至少，小说前半部分，酒几乎在每一回都扮演关键的角色，几乎总是导致流血、死亡。[1]

  根据乔什·维托的论述，在《水浒传》中，因为酒这个物象，围绕小说主角形成了喝酒、醉酒、冲突的叙事模式。而且随着酒在小说中的反复出现，这一叙事模式也反复上演。从上文的该论者的分析来看，的确如此。

  至于《水浒传》后半部分的情况，乔什·维托说，虽然碰巧第32回之后没有哪一回的标题带有"醉"的字眼，但仍然存在大量的对喝酒的描写，喝酒同样导致冲突、战斗[2]。不过，在该论者看来，由于小说后半部分的主题已发生了微妙的变化，小说作者虽然仍然在描写醉酒、暴力，叙事的焦点却不再是英雄个人，而转向了梁山好汉群体[3]。由于作品主题发生了变化，小说的叙述重心也随之发生了变化，对此情形，该论者说："因此，即使这些主角继续喝酒，即使他们的醉酒继续导致暴力，但因为

---

[1] Crucially, each of these chapters follow the same blueprint as described above-the protagonist drinks copious amounts of wine and ubesuently gets into some form of physical battle, almost always resulting in victory for our hero. Often, the pattern will occur twice in one chapter-in chapter 21, for example, Song Jiang drinks with Poxi's mother before becoming enraged with his wife, subsequently killing her (more on this later). Furthermore, this drunken rage motif is not simply restricted to the chapters with the adjective "drunk" in the title. For at least the first half of the novel, alcohol plays a crucial role in nearly every chapter, almost always leading to bloodshed and death. Josh Vittor, Incoherence and Intoxication: Alcohol as s Rare Source of Consistency in *Outlaws of the Marsh*. "Women and Men, Love and Power: Parameters of Chinese Fiction and Drama" Sino-Platonic Paper, edited by Victor H. Mair, 193 (Novermber, 2009), p. 163.

[2] Josh Vittor, Incoherence and Intoxication: Alcohol as s Rare Source of Consistency in *Outlaws of the Marsh*. "Women and Men, Love and Power: Parameters of Chinese Fiction and Drama" Sino-Platonic Paper, edited by Victor H. Mair, 193 (Novermber, 2009), p. 163.

[3] Josh Vittor, Incoherence and Intoxication: Alcohol as s Rare Source of Consistency in *Outlaws of the Marsh*. "Women and Men, Love and Power: Parameters of Chinese Fiction and Drama" Sino-Platonic Paper, edited by Victor H. Mair, 193 (Novermber, 2009), p. 163, 164.

他们这样做是作为结义兄弟的组成部分,因而对他们醉酒的突出就可能减少。"① 对酒在《水浒传》后半部分叙事上的重要性,乔什·维托没有进行具有实质性的讨论。这实在令人遗憾。事实上,如笔者在上文所讨论的,酒对《水浒传》后半部分故事情节的发展、转折,实在至关重要。第一次招安时写"活阎罗倒船偷御酒",使小说叙事变得跌宕起伏,荡漾出层层的波澜。这些已在上文论述过,就此打住。

综合乔什·维托等人的论述,在《水浒传》里,酒的广泛存在,具有几个重要的主题的与象征的影响与意义。具体来说,酒这个形象在小说里的功能和作用主要有如下五点:

首先,在小说中,酒这一要素确实为《水浒传》支离破碎的叙事状态"提供某种一致性和连贯性"。

其次,《水浒传》对酒的大量描写,酒在梁山好汉生活中的盛行和普遍,"有助于界定、区分梁山好汉主角"。

再次,在小说中,酒扮演着非常重要的角色,"经常作为一场迫在眉睫的战斗或冲突的导火索",从而推动故事情节的进一步发展。

复次,小说写英雄们大碗喝酒、嗜酒如命,这"成为英雄豪情的一个重要组成部分"。②

最后,夏志清把酒与色联系在一起,他提出:"作为对英雄们不好女

---

① Therefore, while the protagonists continue to drink, and their drunkenness continues to lead to violence, the emphasis on their inebriation is perhaps diminished because they are doing so as part of the Gallant Fraternity. Josh Vittor, Incoherence and Intoxication: Alcohol as s Rare Source of Consistency in *Outlaws of the Marsh*. "Women and Men, Love and Power: Parameters of Chinese Fiction and Drama" Sino-Platonic Paper, edited by Victor H. Mair, 193 (Novermber, 2009), p. 164.

② In ligthe of the inconsistent nature of *Outlaws of the Marsh*, as evidented by Hsia's thesisless essay, I shall try, in the follwing pages, to illluminata just one element of the novel that actually does offer some consistency and goherence. I will focus on the role of alcohol in *Outlaws of the Marsh*, its prevalence, and the way in which it helps to define and distinguish the bandit protagonists. I will show how (or what) alcohol plays a remarkably important role in the novel, often serving as a signal for a looming fight or conflict. The heroes consume vast quantities of "wine," such as Hsia suggests in his essay and will be discussed below, becomes an extension of their masculinity. Josh Vittor, Incoherence and Intoxication: Alcohol as s Rare Source of Consistency in *Outlaws of the Marsh*. "Women and Men, Love and Power: Parameters of Chinese Fiction and Drama" Sino-Platonic Paper, edited by Victor H. Mair, 193 (Novermber, 2009), p. 161.

色的补偿,因而他们大块吃肉、大碗喝酒"①。

上述前三个方面是乔什·维托个人的观点,后两个方面则是该论者援引夏志清在《水浒传》研究时提出来的相关看法。基于上述认识,乔什·维托说:"从小说一开始,酒就是一个显而易见的、活跃的主题,它凌驾在其他那些松散的情节主线与众多的人物形象之上。"② 而根据上文乔什·维托对酒在《水浒传》里所担当的几个方面的功能与作用的论述,很显然,其中像为《水浒传》支离破碎的叙事状态"提供某种一致性和连贯性",以及"经常作为一场迫在眉睫的战斗或冲突的导火索",这两个方面是与小说叙事直接相关的。事实上,即便把酒看成是小说描写的"一个显而易见的、活跃的主题",酒仍然能够以主题的形式来构建《水浒传》的叙事结构。如上文浦安迪提出的那样,在万事皆空主题的统领之下,小说形成了"聚而复散"的结构模式。

总之,酒的形象,酒在《水浒传》里的反复出现,酒对梁山好汉的重大影响,使小说叙事跌宕生姿、一波三折,让那些原本平淡无奇的故事顿起波澜。作为《水浒传》具有一致性和连贯性的"黏合剂",酒在把那些略显疏离的小说叙事成分连接起来的同时,更为读者的阅读带来许多趣味。

---

① The heroes compensate for their sexual abstinence by their gross delight in meat and wine. C. T. Hsia, "The Water Margin," from *The Classic Chinese Novel*: Acritical Introduction (New York: Columbia Press, 1968), p. 89.

② From the very beginning of the novel, alcohol is a visible and active motif, which transcends the otherwise divergent plotlines and myriad characters. Josh Vittor, Incoherence and Intoxication: Alcohol as s Rare Source of Consistency in *Outlaws of the Marsh*. "Women and Men, Love and Power: Parameters of Chinese Fiction and Drama" Sino-Platonic Paper, edited by Victor H. Mair, 193 (Novermber, 2009), p. 161.

第五章

英语世界对《水浒传》的主题思想研究

作为一部史诗性的经典之作,《水浒传》全景式地描绘了北宋末年的社会生活画卷:下到乡村市井上到帝都皇宫,从贩夫走卒到帝王将相,各个阶层的思想观念几乎都囊括其中。而对梁山好汉的价值观、人生观、女性观及伦理道德等的突出描写,则为我们呈现出完全独树一帜的社会人文景观——水浒世界,一个英雄的国度。

数百年来,水浒世界这个英雄的国度令人困惑、让人深思。赞扬者如古人李贽,称其忠义贤孝,说天下英雄尽在草莽;批判者如今人刘再复,说其是"地狱之门"、"黑暗王国",作品对"抢劫有理"的肯定,对"屠杀快感"的审美化描写,所有这些皆是"非人文化"[1]。

那么,《水浒传》的主题究竟是什么?小说反映出来的社会历史文化与思想观念究竟是怎么样的呢?水浒世界究竟是一个怎样的社会人文景观呢?本章,笔者就来探讨英语世界的批评者对这些问题的研究。

第一节 《水浒传》主题研究中的多种声音

《水浒传》内容庞杂,思想驳杂,冲突、矛盾之处亦不少。此种情形的存在,为批评者的阐释、研究提供了巨大的空间,也为研究者从不同视角切入、展开论述提供了可能性。正是因为小说文本的这种可供多元阐释的特性,学界在《水浒传》主题的研究中自然就出现了多重声音。此种

---

[1] 具体见刘再复《双典批判——对〈水浒传〉和〈三国演义〉的文化批判》,生活·读书·新知三联书店 2010 年版。

情形在英语世界的研究中亦不例外。综合英语世界批评者对《水浒传》主题的研究,我们大体上可以把他们的观点分成如下几类:革命、反抗主题,维护儒家价值理想主题,背叛、复仇主题,治乱、空无主题。下面,我们就来展开具体探讨。

一、革命、反抗主题及其质疑

在《水浒传》的研究中,绝大部分批评者都会关注到作品对梁山好汉反抗行为的描写,以及好汉们在反抗中所表现出来的坚贞不屈的精神品质。

到1898年时,《水浒传》在欧美国家的传播、接受为时并不长。而乔治·康德林在当年出版的《中国小说》的《水浒传》研究部分就已指出,《水浒传》中"回响着粗暴的威胁性的反叛之声",表现了"愤懑的中国"[①]。根据康德林的论述,所谓"愤懑的中国",指的就是小说所写时代中国底层平民百姓对贪污腐败、民不聊生的社会现实的不满和反抗。而"粗暴的威胁性的反叛之声",自然就是受压迫的底层民众对中国封建统治者所发出的。

20世纪30年代,赛珍珠对小说的反抗性主题作了进一步的阐释。在为其英译《水浒传》撰写的导言中,赛珍珠说:"这些好汉,由于各种原因——或是贪官污吏、或是无法忍受的政府压迫、或是邪恶的社会环境,被迫逃离社会,走上梁山寻求避难之所。"[②] 因此,赛珍珠认为,梁山好汉代表的是正义的力量;即使把他们称作强盗,他们也是一群"正义的强盗",他们的反抗行为是"平民反对腐败官府的斗争"[③]。赛珍珠还指出,她之所以选择孔子的名言"四海之内,皆兄弟也"(All Men are Brothers)作为小说英译的标题,就是因为"这个标题恰如其分地表达了作品中这群

[①] 转引自郑公盾《水浒传论文集》,宁夏人民出版社1983年版,第218页。

[②] These men are compelled for the various reasons of unjust officials, or an oppressive government and evil social conditions, to flee from society and to take refuge on a great mountain set in a lake and surrounded by a reedy marsh. Pearl S. Buck, *Introduction of Shui Hu Chuan*, *All Men Are Brothers*, NewYork: The John Day Company, 1933, p. vi.

[③] Pearl S. Buck, *Introduction of Shui Hu Chuan*, *All Men Are Brothers*, NewYork: The John Day Company, 1933, p. vi.

正义的强盗的精神"①。

菲茨杰拉德在研究时指出，《水浒传》和《三国演义》一样，都具有社会批评的作用，而且都表现出反对权威的思想②。鲁尔曼则认为《水浒传》是中国革命的教科书，梁山好汉"替天行道"的口号，反映了他们对邪恶、腐败社会的抗议及对皇帝权威的挑战③。只是鲁尔曼认为梁山好汉的行为是为维护儒家的价值理想，笔者特留待下一部分讨论。

沙博理则认为，小说讲述一百零八好汉如何被逼上梁山、成为数以千计的绿林英雄的首领，他们英勇善战，并一次又一次地发起反对自负、残忍的专制统治者的战斗④。与之相应，石昌渝在为沙译本撰写的导论中这样说：

> 《水浒传》里的英雄们，并非如元代文献中所描写的那样，是一群打家劫舍的凶残暴徒；也不是如元杂剧里所刻画的那样，是一伙除恶务尽、维护太平的复仇者。事实上，《水浒传》是对人民反抗封建社会政治统治与官僚压迫的一次生动、敏锐的记录。⑤

根据上述诸人的论述可知，《水浒传》展现了人民对浮华堕落、贪污腐败、残暴不公的封建统治者的强烈的反抗精神，具有阶级斗争的性质。只是人们很早就对这种革命反抗、阶级斗争的观点表示了质疑。像克伦普、夏志清、李惠仪就是其中的代表。

1958年，克伦普（Crump, James I）在针对赛珍珠英译《水浒

---

① I have chosen arbitrarily, therefore, a famous saying of Confucius to be the title in English, a title which in amplitude and in implication expresses the spirit of this band of righteous robbers. Pearl S. Buck, *Introduction of Shui Hu Chuan*, *All Men Are Brothers*, NewYork: The John Day Company, 1933, pp. v – vi.

② C. P. Fitrgerald, "Chinese Novel as a Subversive Force," Meanjin, X (Spring, 1951), pp. 259 – 266.

③ Robert Ruhlmann, Traditional Heroes in Chinese Popular Fiction, The Confucian Persuasion, ed. by Arthur F. Wright (California: Stanford University Press, 1960), p. 170.

④ Sidney Shapiro, Translator's Note, *Outlaws of the Marsh*, translated by Sidney Shapiro, Beijing: Foreign Language Press, 1993, Vol. IV, p. 2145.

⑤ What *Outlaws of the Marsh* is all about is not a group of muederous and plundering wilderness loutlaws, as Yuan Dynasty records describe them; nor is it about a band of avengers xetirpating evil and restoring order, as depicted in the Yuan *zaju*. It is in fact a lively and acute critique of the people's revolt against official oppression in the social and political conditions of feudalism. Shi Changyu, Introduction, *Outlaws of the Marsh*, translated by Sidney Shapiro, Beijing: Foreign Language Press, 1993, Vol. I, pp. 13 – 14.

第五章　英语世界对《水浒传》的主题思想研究　　269

撰写的一篇书评中,就对当时中国学术界甚嚣尘上的"阶级斗争"说表达了明确的质疑态度①。他认为,去证明施耐庵是出于"阶级立场"的情感而创作《水浒传》,就如让一个英国人从众议院跑到诺丁汉郡去证实《罗宾汉谣曲》是由14世纪诺丁汉当地的一个小职员出于对现代保守党宗旨的支持而收集整理成书一样,很明显是一种愚蠢的做法②。克伦普认为,像《水浒传》这样一部百科全书式的作品,内容非常丰富,主题是多元的。他说:

  在逐渐流行起来的那几个世纪,《水浒传》对个体的中国人来说是包含着多方面内容的,是能够雅俗共赏的,他们也不用为小说中那些方面的内容具体是什么而倍感折磨。我们却被告知,通过多棱镜的辩证透视,有充足的理由相信,这些故事是指向社会经济、阶级斗争的。③

夏志清对我们熟悉的阶级斗争、反抗政府主题的驳斥,主要是出于两方面的理由,一是梁山好汉的行动意愿,二是英雄们的身份阶级属性。就第一方面,夏志清指出,我们要区分反贪官与反政府之间的不同,不能把梁山好汉的反贪官行为上升到社会革命的高度。对此,他说:

  任何稍微熟悉《水浒》的读者也许还希望提一提好汉们的反政府

---

① 根据克伦普的论述,该书评的撰写有一个现实缘由,主要是针对1953年初春中华人民共和国文化部的一个学术委员会在江苏兴化县的一次学术活动。在那次学术活动中有这么几个主题,一是证明施耐庵是《水浒传》的作者,二是论证施是下层民众的一员,再就是证实施是出于"阶级立场"的情感创作《水浒传》的。具体见 Crump, James I., A Sherwood in Kiangsu (Book Review), Chicago Review, 12: 1 (1958: Spring), p. 61。

② ...to verify...that he wrote the work with a feeling for "class standpoint". The idiocy of this journey can be made more clear to the Westerner if he will picture a delegation from the House of Commons travelling to Nottingham to establish that the ballads of Robin Hood had been collected by a local functionary in the fourteen century out of a feeling he held for the doctrines of the modern Conservative party. Crump, James I., A Sherwood in Kiangsu (Book Review), Chicago Review, 12: 1 (1958: Spring), pp. 61 – 62.

③ Those who felt that centuries of waxing popularity might indicate *Shui-hu chuan* contained many facets appealing to the individual Chinese need no longer fret over what these facets were because, we are told, the stories appealed to a socio-economic *class* and did so for reasons which are quite clear when seen through the dialectical diminishing-lens. Crump, James I., A Sherwood in Kiangsu (Book Review), Chicago Review, 12: 1 (1958: Spring), p. 62.

立场和干革命的雄心。实际上，虽说有几位暴烈的英雄表达了反政府的思想，但这一态度并不是好汉们所必须具备的。屡挫官军之后，梁山好汉坚持招安，接着又去为国家南征北战。……他们的主要雄心是报国扬名，光宗耀祖，只有那些平民英雄，最突出的是阮氏三雄，才呼出了饱受官府压迫的广大民众的不平。评论家常常引用他们的言论和歌谣，武断地把它们看作是对《水浒》主题的表现。不过，一般来讲，好汉们都反贪官，正如他们仇恨一切邪恶和不义之徒一样。但是他们的仇恨不可能上升到要发动一场革命的理论高度。①

在夏志清看来，梁山一百零八人中，除一直被高俅迫害的林冲之外，其他人很难说是被"逼上梁山"的，也谈不上真正要闹革命。因为大部分头领都是自愿入伙的，有一些原政府军官则是被迫加入梁山好汉行列的。说到梁山好汉的出身和身份的阶级归属，夏志清指出：

中国大陆评论家们一致赞扬《水浒》是一部伟大的革命小说。他们误把梁山好汉看作是具有阶级觉悟的农民力量的先锋队，是在为开明的政治经济革命而努力奋斗。实际上，梁山主要头领称得上农民的只有李逵一人。而他也早就离开乡土，成了游民。②

基于上述认识，夏志清认为，与其把小说中表达的对官府的普遍的不满情绪和对贪官污吏的仇恨看成好汉们的革命热情，不如把它们看作英雄们身上表现出来的那种阴暗的狂热的复仇心理的另一种反映③。

李惠仪对《水浒传》研究中提出的革命、反抗主题的质疑，其理由和夏志清比较接近。该论者认为，小说的关注点主要不在表现统治者对平民百姓的迫害，而重在表现英雄们在复仇或愤怒的暴力行为的驱使之下走上梁山的过程。李惠仪说：

现代批评倾向于认为《水浒传》是反抗压迫势力、反对专制统治的英雄颂歌。确实，某些反叛者（最典型的林冲）是被贪官污吏滥

---

① ［美］夏志清：《中国古典小说》，胡益民等译，江苏文艺出版社2008年版，第90页。
② 同上书，第102页。
③ 同上。

用权力"逼上梁山"的。只是这部作品最感兴趣的并不是此类社会牺牲品。小说中,往往是复仇行动或愤怒的暴力行为,迫使这些人走上梁山。在许多事件里面,被迫上梁山的原因不在政府,而在反叛者自己。一些有本事的成员则是被坑害后被迫加入梁山组织的。①

李惠仪指出,像武松、杨雄是因复仇而走上梁山的代表,宋江、雷横则因自己愤怒的暴力行为而付出了相应的代价,最悲惨、最不公的则是被梁山好汉坑害之后上梁山的扈三娘、秦明与朱仝等人。

二、维护儒家价值理想主题

《水浒传》展现了维护儒家价值观念与社会理想的主题,这是罗伯特·鲁尔曼在《中国通俗小说中的传统英雄人物》一文中提出来的。鲁尔曼认为,根据作品的描写,"八方共域,异姓一家"的梁山,显然比当时的现实社会更符合儒家的社会理想和道德价值观念。而且在鲁尔曼看来,儒家倡导的理想人物"君子"的唯一的容身之地,也只有水浒世界了。他说:

> 《水浒传》将当时盛行的腐败归咎于官僚机构而非皇帝,这可能看起来是懦弱的,但这部小说认为梁山好汉的社会远比正统社会更合乎真正的儒家社会理想,确是非常极端的。的确,在当时恶劣的环境

---

① Modern criticism tends to eulogize *Water Margin* as an antiauthoritarian saga protesting against the repressive forces in Chinese civilization. It is true that some rebels (most notably Lin Ch'ung) are "forced to go up Liang-shan" by corrupt officials abusing their power. But the book is not deeply interested in victimhood. More often than not, acts of vengeance (e.g., Wu Sung kills P'an Chin-lien and Hsi-men Ch'ing, his adulterous sister-in-law and her lover, who murdered his brother; Yang Hsiung disembowels his adulterous wife, P'an Ch'iao-yün) or violent outbursts of anger (e.g., Sung Chiang kills his "kept woman," Yen P'o-hsi, when she threatens to expose his association with Liang-shan outlaws; Lei Heng kills the singing girl Pai Hsiu-ying with his cangue – which he is wearing for having injured Pai's father – when she curses his mother) drive the characters toward Liang-shan. In many cases, coercion "to go up Liang-shan" comes not from the government but from the rebels themselves. Capable potential members are duped or forced into complicity with the Liang-shan establishment – among the most chilling examples are Hu San-niang, sole survivor of her clan after gory battles with Liang-shan; Ch'in Ming, whose family is executed by the governor when the Liang-shan outlaws stage his rebellion; and Chu T'ung, whose charge, his master's young child, is murdered by Li K'uei. The Columbia History of Chinese Literature, Victor H. Mair editor. New York: Columbia University Press, 2001, p. 629.

中，强人的山寨是儒家"君子"的唯一容身之所。①

基于这样的认识，鲁尔曼认为，梁山好汉的反抗是为了维护儒家的基本价值观念，而他们反抗的对象——朝廷与贪官污吏，则是背叛儒家基本价值观念的。在鲁尔曼看来，好汉们"替天行道"的口号，其实质与儒家倡导的"君权神授"、"王者受命于天"是相通的。梁山好汉反抗贪官污吏、社会不公，就是在诠释天意，而好汉们行事的依据和标准就是儒家思想。换句话说，儒家的思想观念就是梁山好汉反抗的理论根源。正因此，鲁尔曼说："在反抗他们认为背叛了儒家基本价值观念的社会制度时，梁山好汉就拥有一种内在的真理和对上天的忠诚做自己行动的后盾。"②

如果我们把"替天行道"这一口号的性质与内涵，理解成是属于儒家思想范畴的话，鲁尔曼的观点是站得住脚的。但正如下文讨论梁山好汉的基本道德规范及其核心观念"义"时，批评者提出的那样，梁山好汉的很多行为其实是和儒家思想观念背道而驰的。从这个角度来说，鲁尔曼认为《水浒传》的主题是维护儒家的价值观念与社会理想，这个观点又是值得商榷的。

三、背叛、复仇主题

就《水浒传》的主题，持背叛复仇论的代表人物是吴杰克与夏志清。当然，讨论小说中的复仇问题的批评者有很多，但绝大多数人都是在探讨作品的道德规范的层面展开的，真正明确提出背叛复仇是小说《水浒传》主题的主要还是上述两人。

1963年，吴杰克（Wu Jack）发表《〈水浒传〉的道德》一文。在该文章中，吴杰克指出，"小说作者描绘的是一个腐败的社会"，在那个社会里，充斥着"背叛"、"通奸"、"欺骗"和"不忠"；而"在背叛、通

---

① Robert Ruhlmann, Traditional Heroes in Chinese Popular Fiction, The Confucian Persuasion, ed. by Arthur F. Wright (California: Stanford University Press, 1960), pp. 169–170.

② Against a system that is looked upon as betraying the fundamental "Confucian" values, the outlaws of Mount Liang have recourse to an inner truth and a higher allegiance. Robert Ruhlmann, Traditional Heroes in Chinese Popular Fiction, The Confucian Persuasion, ed. by Arthur F. Wright (California: Stanford University Press, 1960), p. 170.

奸、贿赂之中","活动着一群英勇的斗士"梁山好汉①。在吴杰克眼里，这群"英勇"、"忠诚"的好汉正是贪官污吏、背叛者的克星。他说："在作品描写的许多故事里，他们一直向欺骗和不忠复仇。背叛的确是小说的重大主题"②。

吴杰克提出的背叛、复仇主题在小说中确实表现得很明显，不论是英雄个人还是好汉群体，都有对背叛、不忠行为的报复。遗憾的是，吴杰克并未就此问题展开比较详细具体的分析研究。

夏志清认为，《水浒传》是一部"专注于复仇的作品"③。从小说所叙述的人物故事来说，夏志清的这个概括是很准确的。因为作者所描写的梁山好汉——无论是个人还是群体，的确都有极端渴望复仇的心理。对此，他说：

> 好汉个人与好汉群体在这一基本点上并没有多大区别，那就是都渴望复仇。个人的复仇行为虽比集体复仇更多地出于对名誉的考虑，但好汉们若不是热衷于复仇，是不会服从群体的意志，参加那些与山寨为敌的城市、乡镇的战斗的。根据英雄信条，一位好汉如果感到自己或他的亲友蒙受冤屈，必须亲手伸张正义，而不依靠那拖沓多变的法律。④

夏志清认为，武松就是这类好汉的代表，小说用了整十回的篇幅叙述他为亲友、为自己复仇的故事。尽管对武松复仇的描写充满了野蛮、残忍的血腥杀戮，作者却把他完全描绘成一位令人敬重的英雄人物。对此，夏志清说："在这部专注于复仇的作品中，武松自始至终是一位朴素的可敬人物，因为小说家并不认为有必要对他的野蛮虐杀作道德和哲学上的批评。"⑤该论者还以李逵代宋江向黄文炳复仇以及杨雄、石秀惩罚潘巧云等事件为例，说明作品中复仇行为的普遍性。

事实上，谈到《水浒传》的复仇主题，最有意义的莫过于鲁达为金

---

① Wu Jack, The Morals of "All Men are Brothers", Western Humanities Review, 17: 1 (1963: Winter), p. 87.
② Ibid. .
③ ［美］夏志清：《中国古典小说》，胡益民等译，江苏文艺出版社2008年版，第98页。
④ 同上书，第93—94页。
⑤ 同上书，第98页。

氏父女报仇的故事。在这件事上，根本无关英雄个人的声誉、利益，鲁达的复仇是以"义"来对抗"不义"。鲁达拳打镇关西，完全是出于行侠仗义、同情弱者，却根本不顾及给自己带来的严重后果。

四、治乱、空无主题

《水浒传》反映了中国儒、释、道思想的融合，表现了儒家传统的治乱兴亡论题与佛、道两家的万事俱空主题，这一观点最初是由著名汉学家浦安迪提出来的。这个观点的提出，是基于其坚持认为这部小说具有浓厚的反讽色彩。如本书第三章人物塑造研究部分所讨论的，在浦安迪看来，《水浒传》里极受读者欢迎的人物形象如武松等，小说作者对他们是进行了反讽处理的。正是在此研究视角之下，浦安迪指出：

> 根据本研究对反讽所作的详细界定，我要重申这一点，即：我们感受到的这部小说的主题，既不盲目赞许梁山精神而忽略其令人不安的言外之意，也不全盘否定梁山好汉所代表的一切，而是保持一种基本的含糊不清的态度。这是反讽叙事的反面，是对个体英雄的本性与人类行为意义的某种根深蒂固信念的质疑。[①]

浦安迪认为，小说反讽叙述中这种模棱两可的暧昧态度，有助于我们对《水浒传》文本中所蕴含的整体意义的阐释。只是在进行阐释之前，必须抛开传统戏曲、说书给我们制造的潜在的意识形态预设，也必须避开把文学虚构牵强附会地当作是对"现实生活"的鞭挞的错误看法；我们的理解和阐释，必须以作品本身的叙述和描写为基础。

通过对小说故事情节的发展与水浒英雄势力不断壮大过程的分析，浦安迪认为，当梁山好汉的势力遍布天下时，《水浒传》的主旨已超越一般的伦理、政治范畴而进入到儒家"治乱兴亡"的论题。对此，浦氏说：

---

① In the light of the definition of irony developed in this study, I might restate this thesis to say that what we have in the novel is neither a blind approval of the Liang-shan mentality in disregard of its more troubling implications, nor a bitterly cynical denunciation of all that the band stands for, but rather a manifestation of a basic uncertainty. This is the other side of ironic narrative: a questioning of some of the most deep-seated beliefs about the nature of the individual hero and the significance of human action. Andrew H. Plaks, The Four Masterworks of the Ming Novel, Princeton University Press, 1987, p. 320.

到梁山兄弟的活动范围达到全帝国时,那位16世纪的作者就已超越单纯的伦理、政治问题,而开始从"忠义"主旨推进到对儒家政治理论框架之中的一个更加抽象的概念——"治乱"主题的思考。①

浦安迪认为,小说中涉及"闹"这个主题的故事情节反复出现,其中就蕴含着作者对儒家"治乱"概念的思考和关注。在浦氏看来,像第五回写鲁达"大闹五台山",这对于既定的社会秩序还没什么危害;当描写梁山好汉"劫江州法场"、"闹西岳华山"、"兵打北京城"以及"夜闹东京"时,不仅累及无辜丧命,还威胁到整个帝国的存亡,乃至震撼皇帝治天下的根基。这就是浦氏提出的小说中有关"治乱"的主题,也是"儒家历来闹不清的争端"。

浦安迪认为,治乱兴亡只是《水浒传》主题的一个方面,小说主题的另一个方面则是文本叙述之中蕴藏在字里行间的万事俱空观念。浦氏说:

> 我相信小说中还有另一层意义,即我们同时也必须估量、探讨的小说描写的对尘世、人生的总体体验。从小说开篇诗、词引出的宏大的叙事情节,到最后梁山好汉或亡散或退隐的结局,在此背景之下,流露出万事皆空的色彩。②

浦安迪认为,小说文本会让我们进行这一方面的思考与探索,是因为作品中反复出现取自佛、道两家表达空无思想的常见意象及场景。浦氏以为,第五回写鲁达的赤身露体及后来的幡然醒悟,第53回与第85回写罗

---

① By the time the scope of action of the Liang-shan brotherhood reaches empirewide proportions, the sixteen-century author begins to press the issues of loyalty and honor beybond simple ethical or political considerations into a more abstract contemplation of order and disorder 治乱 within the framework of Confucian political theory. Andrew H. Plaks, The Four Masterworks of the Ming Novel, Princeton University Press, 1987, p. 353。

② There is one more dimension of meaning in this novel, however, against which I believe we must also weigh the entire texture of experience presented in the novel. This is the backdrop of cosmic futility or emptiness (k'ung 空) out of which it dissolves with the final dispensation of the band. Andrew H. Plaks, The Four Masterworks of the Ming Novel, Princeton University Press, 1987, p. 354。

真人的偈语，所有这些都有空无的暗示。浦安迪尤以小说最后的那几首诗及徽宗的那场梦为例指出："尘世间所有的喧嚣皆归于空的观念，回荡在小说结尾的许多诗中，而末页的那场虚无缥缈的梦正好道破了这一点。"①浦氏还说，

> 容与堂刻本的评点者在最后的评点中似乎指明了这一层含义："临了以梦结局极有深意，见得从前种种都说梦……读去认真便是痴人说梦。"无论如何，当小说叙述转向分崩离析阶段时，那些空无意象的插入就变得越来越频繁。②

的确如浦安迪所论，从笔者阅读《水浒传》的个人感受来说，作品一进入叙述梁山好汉征方腊的那些章回开始，就出现伤残、衰败的气息。及至燕青对卢俊义提起韩信、彭越、英布三人的悲惨结局时，中国历史上反复上演的"飞鸟尽，良弓藏；狡兔死，走狗烹"的英雄悲剧旋律就已经在小说中奏响。而到一直强调"忠义"、希冀博得"封妻荫子"、"青史留名"的宋江被药酒毒杀之后，"玄猿秋啸暮云稠"的诗句就把英雄末路的那种悲凉气氛渲染到了极致。

浦安迪之后，德波特也表达了类似的观点，不过他强调的主要是万事皆空、一切徒劳这一层。他认为，小说对宋江的总体描写，作者是在提醒读者，人们对功名利禄的追求不过是一场空、不过是徒劳③。

总体而言，就《水浒传》所写梁山好汉由聚而散、由兴而亡的故事

---

① The idea that all the sound and fury has come to naught reverberates in a number of poems toward the close, and is finally captured in the inconclusive dream of the final page. Andrew H. Plaks, The Four Masterworks of the Ming Novel, Princeton University Press, 1987, p. 355.

② The Jung-yü t'ang commentator seems to put his finger on this when he says in a final comment:... using a dream to tie up the plot as it approaches the end is full of deeper meaning; it is evident that all the various things that went before were like the recounting of a dream ... to read it at face value would be like a madman telling his own dream. 临了以梦结局极有深意，见得从前种种都说梦……读去认真便是痴人说梦. In any event, as the cycle of action turns toward the phase of dissolution, the interjection of images of emptiness becomes more and more insistent. Andrew H. Plaks, The Four Masterworks of the Ming Novel, Princeton University Press, 1987, p. 355。

③ Throughout the entire depiction of Sung Chiang, the author reminds the reader of the emptiness, hypocrisy, and futility of human rationalization of action with mythic values and virtues. Deborah L. Porter, The Formation of an Image: An Analysis of the Linguistic Patterns That Form the Character of Sung Chiang, Journal of the American Oriental Society, Vol. 112, No. 2 (Apr.-Jun., 1992), p. 253.

情节的发展而言，确实给人以万事皆空的感受。那些英雄们即便接受招安、忠于皇帝，最终大部分人都不免死亡，生还者中的宋江、卢俊义则被毒杀，其他的也看破功名退隐山野；而浪子燕青更是在论功行赏之前就看破了一切。从这些方面来看，《水浒传》又的确表现了佛、道两家的空无观念。

本节，笔者把英语世界《水浒传》主题研究的相应观点和看法分成四类来讨论。其中鲁尔曼提出的"维护儒家价值理想"这一点主要是以"反抗"主题为基础展开的，因其重点不在讨论"反抗"而在强调梁山英雄对儒家理想的维护，笔者因而把它拿出来单独论述。此外，李惠仪对"革命、反抗主题"的质疑，一个重要的理由是认为《水浒传》的关注点是"复仇"，但因其论述太过简略，所以在"背叛、复仇主题"部分没有加以讨论。特此说明。

第二节　水浒世界的道德、价值观念与"义"

《水浒传》所描绘的是一个英雄好汉的世界，这个世界有其自成一格的伦理道德和价值观念体系，它和我们生活的世界是大异其趣又格格不入的。1963年，吴杰克就曾如此评论过《水浒传》的道德、价值问题，他说："对于任何一部具有巨大影响而又与我们的世界如此格格不入的小说来说，如果没有贴上各种道德冲突的标签，那是几乎不可能的。"[1] 那么，《水浒传》所宣扬的道德、价值观念究竟是怎样的呢？关锦（据 Jin Guan 音译）在研究时指出：

> 梁山好汉的主要特征是坚守义气的规范，而这最终充当起好汉加入梁山的入场券。……《水浒传》里的好汉，或者因为遭遇腐败政府、贪官污吏的不公待遇而被迫加入梁山，或者因为不能容忍不公而加入梁山，加入梁山之后能够保持自己的本色。在社会的边缘，这些好汉仍然践行自己的价值观念，并希望通过反对不公给社会带来积极

---

[1] It is nearly impossible for a noval of any large influence to pass through this dis cordant owrld of ours wothout being variously labeled with conflicting morals. Wu, Jack, The Morals of "All Men are Brothers", Western Humanities Review, 17: 1 (1963: Winter), p. 86.

影响。①

的确,"义气"是水浒世界好汉们行动的重要标杆,也是他们身份的主要标识。所谓路见不平拔刀相助,所谓"酷吏赃官都烧尽,忠心报答赵官家",以及后来梁山竖起的"替天行道"大旗,都是由梁山好汉的以"义气"为核心形成的伦理道德与价值观念体系所决定的。

同时,关锦认为,水浒世界的伦理道德与价值观念属于儒家思想范畴,对社会起着积极作用。对此,该论者说:

> 梁山好汉的首领宋江是个儒者,他把儒家的价值观念施加给他的群体,因而这些成员成为了社会的积极力量。由于宋江强烈的儒家信念,为了封妻荫子、光耀门庭,他最终说服同伴接受招安为朝廷服务。②

单从宋江力主招安以及希冀博得封妻荫子、光耀门庭的角度来看,似乎可以认为水浒世界的道德、价值观是属于儒家思想范畴。但其实,梁山好汉的伦理道德与价值观念是否属于儒家思想范畴,梁山好汉是不是社会的积极力量,等等,所有这些涉及水浒世界道德、价值观念的问题在批评者之间都是存在很大争议的。下面,我们就来看看英语世界的批评者对这些问题的具体认识。

---

① The main characteristic of a *haohan* is adherence to a code of honor (*yiqi*, 义气), and this ultimately serves as the member's entry into the Mountain Liang. . . . *Haohans* from the *Water Margin* are able to maintain their identities after joining the Mountain Liang outlaws because either they were forced by the treatment of corrupt government officials to join, or they could not tolerate injustice. On the margin of the society, these *haohans* still practice their values and hope to have a positive influence on society by fighting against injustice. Jin Guan, The values of Mountain outlaws and of Contemporary Gangs, "Women and Men, Love and Power: Parameters of Chinese Fiction and Drama" Sino-Platonic Paper, 193 (Novermber, 2009), p. 169.

② The leader of the Mountain Liang *haohan*, Song jiang, was a Confucian who imposed those values on his group, so that the members became a positive force for society. Because of Song's strong Confucian beliefs, he eventually persuaded his fellow *haohans* to surrecder to serve the government in order to bring honor to their family names. Jin Guan, The values of Mountain outlaws and of Contemporary Gangs, "Women and Men, Love and Power: Parameters of Chinese Fiction and Drama" Sino-Platonic Paper, 193 (Novermber, 2009), pp. 169 – 170.

一、水浒世界的基本道德规范

《水浒传》描绘的是一个非常独特的英雄的世界，英雄们所信守的道德规范是与普通百姓大不相同的。只要对这部小说有所了解，就能发现这样的问题。英语世界的批评者对作品的道德规范的关注、研究，由来已久，从早期的菲茨杰拉德到晚近的康磊诸人，也取得了很多研究成果。下面，我们就来梳理、讨论他们对此问题发表的各种看法和观念。

菲茨杰拉德对《水浒传》所反映出来的道德问题所作的研究比较简单，一方面基本肯定梁山好汉的行为，另一方面指责朝廷的不公与腐败，至于英雄好汉身上的非道德因素则几乎不提及。他说：

> 每一个梁山英雄都是在朝廷的贪腐、官员的严重不公之下被逼落草为寇的；他们是诚实的人，除非遭受无法忍受的冤枉，要不然没有犯罪的念头。一旦沦为草寇，那时，他们就为自己遭受的痛苦向贪官污吏复仇，并轻而易举就把懦弱的朝廷军队给打败了。①

该论者还指出：

> 纵观整部作品，梁山好汉才是真正的英雄，他们英勇、忠诚、讲义气。宋朝的官员大臣与皇帝，则一律被描写成是卑鄙的迫害者、卑贱的恶棍与堕落的懦夫。②

很显然，菲茨杰拉德的论述是很不公允的，既片面又与小说所写很不相符。对于像《水浒传》这么一部内容非常庞杂的作品来说，简单的肯定或否定是不行的，菲茨杰拉德的讨论仅仅触及问题最表面那一层。不过，1950年时西方学者对《水浒传》的研究毕竟还不深入，该论者提出这样的看法是可以理解的。

吴杰克对《水浒传》道德的认识比菲茨杰拉德深入了很多。他对赛珍珠提出的《水浒传》表达的是"四海之内皆兄弟"的道德信仰的观点

---

① C. P. Fitzgerald, *China, A Short Cultural History*, NewYork: Praeger, Inc., 1950, p. 507.
② Ibid..

作出了挑战。吴杰克说：

> 我们只能猜想，中国学者的道德精神之外，布克夫人对人类的爱无意中可能影响到她对一部悲观厌世作品的阐释。……在杀害无辜的受害者中英雄们普遍的残忍与完全的冷漠，他们反抗的悲哀，他们复仇的彻底，这些几乎不表明可以把他们看作是"人道主义者"。相反，这是一群被他们生活的邪恶社会所放逐的人；他们是活跃的反动分子，准备把挡在他们前行路上的任何人清除掉。①

根据上述，可以发现，吴杰克对梁山好汉身上非道德因素的认识是很清楚的。只是他同时也意识到，这些好汉身上还有不少积极、正面的道德品质。吴杰克指出：

> 作者描绘的是一个腐败的社会；但在那个社会里也有至善（immense good）。在坏人的世界里，活动着一群英勇的斗士。在背叛、通奸、贿赂之中，我们看见一群英雄，他们各有不同的缺点，却也拥有忠诚、友好、慷慨的共同美德。在作品描写的许多故事里，他们一直向欺骗和不忠复仇。背叛的确是小说的重大主题；个人的忠诚可以说是重要的行为原则。②

赞美梁山好汉身上表现出来的忠诚、好义、慷慨等道德信条，这在批评者中是很常见的。而这些也是水浒英雄们给人们带来的积极、正面的精神品质。综合梁山好汉正负两方面的道德元素后，吴杰克进一步指出：

> 对个人本身的威胁，这既是激怒这些好汉的、也是激怒每个人心的原因。好汉们反抗社会，因为他们的个性被压制。他们对敌残酷，对友慷慨，这种极端态度显示出他们既不是忘我美德的信奉者，也不

---

① Wu Jack, The Morals of "All Men are Brothers", Western Humanities Review, 17: 1 (1963: Winter), p. 86.
② Ibid., p. 87.

第五章　英语世界对《水浒传》的主题思想研究

是无知邪恶的奴隶，而是任性、热情、能爱能恨的普通人。①

从上文可知，吴杰克明确认识到梁山好汉在对敌、对友上具有两种完全不同的道德标准。只是他提出："即使英雄们的双重行动标准极大地毁坏了他们的美德，至少给予我们更强烈的直面现实的态度。"他还说："为他人而牺牲自己当然不是件容易的事，这些英雄的勇气与献身精神值得我们尊敬。"②从这些论述中我们可以看到，吴杰克对梁山好汉道德准则的肯定还是多于否定的。

吴杰克的论述虽然比菲茨杰拉德更深入、更全面，但对某些问题的讨论还是过于简单。以对待朋友来说，如下文即将谈到的夏志清、康磊所指出的慷慨之外，也存在野蛮、残忍的一面，这在招罗秦明、朱仝、卢俊义等人时表现得尤其明显。

对水浒英雄信守的道德规范，夏志清认为，从表面来看，小说作者肯定了"孝道"、"忠君"与"行侠仗义"等若干好汉信条。他说："孝道在好几位英雄那里得到强调，特别是在宋江、李逵、公孙胜身上。"③但即便如此，夏志清又指出，当宋江通风报信"私放晁天王"时，"宋江的行为是欺君、犯上、不孝的（因为其父将受牵累）"④。对李逵取母一事，夏志清认为李逵虽然出于一片孝心，事实上却害死了自己的母亲。这就如浦安迪所说的，结果与愿望之间的反差实在是一种莫大的反讽（见前文水浒人物研究部分）。说到"忠君"，夏志清认为并非所有梁山好汉都有此思想。他说，在小说中，像李逵、鲁智深、武松等人是反对接受招安为朝廷服务的。这就指出了梁山好汉的"孝道"与"忠君"信念，其实是非常含混、矛盾的。至于好汉们的英雄信条，夏志清认为"英雄信条在对待其他基本的人生约束方面却与儒家观念格格不入"⑤。在夏志清看来，梁山好汉总体上不看重夫妻之间的儿女私情，绝大部分英雄都没有家室，这与儒家倡导的"不孝有三，无后为大"以及家庭天伦之乐之间完全是背道而驰的。

---

① Wu Jack, The Morals of "All Men are Brothers", Western Humanities Review, 17：1（1963：Winter），p. 87.
② Ibid., p. 88.
③ ［美］夏志清：《中国古典小说》，胡益民等译，江苏文艺出版社2008年版，第84页。
④ 同上书，第85页。
⑤ 同上书，第84页。

此外，夏志清对水浒英雄把"友情"或"义"置于一切之上的道德信念也给予了批评。他说，好汉们讲义气、行侠仗义，但"他们行侠仗义，不是通过政府，而是以自己的双手伸张正义"①，其造成的结果往往是具有破坏性的。对此，夏志清进一步指出："英雄信条中有某种利他的爱，但由于无视法律和社会规范，它又鼓励了一种与利他主义相反的行帮道德。"② 在夏志清看来，"行帮道德"只是对"英雄信条"的"拙劣模仿"，而在"行帮道德"的驱使下，欺骗、狡诈、贪财与争权，野蛮残忍的复仇与非理性的杀戮，以及为了梁山内部个别兄弟的权利而对无辜的平民百姓带来巨大的伤害，诸般"不义行为"都会获得认可和肯定。从作品的具体内容来看，夏志清之论不虚。

上述诸人外，研究过《水浒传》中道德规范的批评者还有不少。但据笔者目前掌握的资料来看，英语世界的批评者对《水浒传》道德规范的研究，相对来说，康磊（Lei Kang）做得最系统、最深入。该论者吸收、借鉴夏志清、刘若愚、柳存仁、浦安迪等学界前辈的研究成果，对水浒世界的道德规范进行了更加全面、翔实的分析讨论，给出了更加合理、到位的分类，从而使我们对梁山好汉奉行的道德信条有了一个更加可行的认识和理解。鉴于此种情况，在下面的讨论中，笔者将会在相应的地方插入不同研究者的观点。具体见下文。

康磊从三个层面来研究《水浒传》的道德问题，一是梁山好汉内部处理相互之间关系的道德规范，二是水浒英雄处理与朝廷之间关系的道德规范，三是梁山好汉处理与普通百姓之间关系的道德规范。③

首先，我们来讨论梁山好汉内部处理相互之间关系的道德规范问题。就梁山好汉内部处理相互之间关系的道德规范，康磊说：

> 乍看起来，主宰梁山好汉处理内部相互之间关系的道德规范，似乎是明确、积极的，反映了通行的认识，即他们是组织严密的兄弟群体。他们把友谊置于一切之上，相互保护、打击敌人，通过努力支持

---

① ［美］夏志清：《中国古典小说》，胡益民等译，江苏文艺出版社2008年版，第84页。
② 同上书，第84—85页。
③ Lei Kang, The Dichotomy between Popular Opinion and the Novel: Morality in Water Margin, "Women and Men, Love and Power: Parameters of Chinese Fiction and Drama" Sino-Platonic Paper, 193 (Novermber, 2009), pp. 145 – 157.

第五章　英语世界对《水浒传》的主题思想研究　　283

彼此。①

该论者以"宋公明私放晁天王"为例说，当宋江知晓晁盖抢劫了送给蔡京的"生辰纲"将要被逮捕时，他就给晁盖通风报信，从而让晁盖逃走了。对这一事件，康磊指出：

> 然而，这里对兄弟情谊的强调存在一个显而易见的问题：自然地，把友谊置于一切之上就意味着必须忽视其他的关系。宋江维护他的朋友之情，但他背叛了上司。而且当追捕的军队被大批杀害时，他的行为也间接地造成了成百上千人的死亡。即便忽略其他的关系并未直接否认对他们友谊的通行看法，但确实淡化了对"认为他们的兄弟情谊是高尚的"的盲目信仰。这里，根据生命的价值，宋江犯下了更大的罪过：他可以挽救个别兄弟的生命，但这样做却剥夺了上百条其他人的性命。尽管他的行为有讲义气的动机，因此也不完全是不道德的，但结果却并非不容争辩地就意味着是好的。②

从生命价值的角度来说，"宋公明私放晁天王"所带来的后果不只是"不好"所能概括的，更意味着一扇"罪恶"之门——血腥杀戮的开启。从宋江个人来说，他是豪情仗义、为朋友两肋插刀，实在是英雄的楷模。但如果从晁盖一行人的行动所造成的严重后果来看，又可谓罪恶滔天。这正如夏志清所指出的那样，我们必须把好汉个人与梁山好汉群体区分开来。他说："在好汉个人的行动与好汉整体的行动之间有一个重要的区别。单个的好汉恪守英雄信条，整个梁山好汉群体则奉行一种行帮

---

① At first glance, the moral code governing the Liang-shan bandit's interactions with one another seems to be a positive one, reflenting the popular idea that they were a close-knit band of brothers. They hold the bonds of friendship above all else, protecting each other from enemies, supporting one another in their labors. Lei Kang, The Dichotomy between Popular Opinion and the Novel: Morality in Water Margin. , "Women and Men, Love and Power: Parameters of Chinese Fiction and Drama" Sino-Platonic Paper, 193 (Novermber, 2009), p. 147.

② Lei Kang, The Dichotomy between Popular Opinion and the Novel: Morality in Water Margin. , "Women and Men, Love and Power: Parameters of Chinese Fiction and Drama" Sino-Platonic Paper, 193 (Novermber, 2009), p. 148.

道德。"①

对梁山好汉内部的结义兄弟关系，康磊指出，虽然梁山好汉似乎没什么野心和权力欲望，只是一旦宋江加入、并在后来成为山寨的首领，好汉们之间存在的问题与缺陷就被揭示出来了。在康磊看来，这些问题中首先就是晁盖与宋江之间对领导权的争夺。晁盖坚持维护自己首领的地位，但宋江在好汉中的威望，以及他处理各种事情的本事远超过他，这就形成了一种无形的威胁。宋江与晁盖也就视对方为自己的竞争对手。对此，康磊说：

> 这样，好汉们之间的关系就最为脆弱。一旦为了权力，他们相互之间开始视对方为敌手，那么，他们相互支持、拥护的誓言就崩溃了。因为他们两人都没有采取任何手段维护权力，我们不能评判宋江和晁盖行为的道德问题，只是他们声称的兄弟情谊、大家认同的信任和尊重，在此听起来并不诚恳。②

关于宋江和晁盖争夺领导权的问题，浦安迪也认为他们两人是水浒世界最高权力的"竞争者"（contender）。浦安迪认为，宋江收买梁山好汉同时剥夺了晁盖的实权。当他听到晁盖最终死亡的消息时，像丧父一般嚎哭。据此，浦安迪援引金圣叹的观点说宋江是晁盖之死的"共谋"（complicity），用儒家最严厉的词来说是宋江"弑"晁盖③。当然，浦安迪等人的观点也只是一家之言。

康磊认为，梁山好汉对自己结义兄弟道德规范的违反，不只表现在宋江与晁盖之间的争权上。他说："梁山好汉对兄弟情谊规范的最显著的亵渎，发生在企图招募新成员时。"④ 对此，该论者进一步分析道：

---

① Hsia, Chih-tsing, Classical Chinese Novel: A Critical Introduction, Ner York: Columbia University Press, 1968, p. 93.
② Lei Kang, The Dichotomy between Popular Opinion and the Novel: Morality in Water Margin. , "Women and Men, Love and Power: Parameters of Chinese Fiction and Drama" Sino-Platonic Paper, 193 (Novermber, 2009), pp. 148 – 149.
③ Andrew H. Plaks, The Four Masterworks of the Ming Novel, Princeton University Press, 1987, p. 341.
④ Lei Kang, The Dichotomy between Popular Opinion and the Novel: Morality in Water Margin. , "Women and Men, Love and Power: Parameters of Chinese Fiction and Drama" Sino-Platonic Paper, 193 (Novermber, 2009), p. 149.

在这些事件里,最十恶不赦的是招募秦明和朱仝。为了招募来秦明,宋江命令一个士兵乔装成秦明,并假托秦明的名义攻打青州城。结果,秦明被斥为叛徒,他的妻小也被处死。作者声称秦明的加入是契合上界星辰,就把其中的不公搪塞过去了……然而,这样的结盟特别脆弱;他一家被屠杀的事实不可能那么轻易忘却。让秦明如此快就默认天意,作者是无视对他的不公。如果这些好汉把友谊置于一切之上,如果他们如公众认为的那样崇高,他们就不应该以如此低劣的手段来招募一名英雄。[1]

对招募朱仝的事件,康磊说:

像这种不忠的另一个事例是好汉们招募朱仝。这里,宋江指示李逵谋杀了朱仝监护下知府四岁大的儿子,以迫使他加入梁山。朱仝对这种做法怒不可遏,他要求和李逵来场决斗,这反映出对他的不公平。再一次,小说仅用兄弟情谊的漂亮话就掩饰过去了:朱仝遭受的可能不是肉体的伤害,但只有真正的友谊和一个恰当的道德规范能让他得到平静,而不是强迫他加入梁山集团。[2]

通过上面的分析和讨论,康磊的结论是:

因此,我们发现,支配梁山好汉处理相互之间关系的道德规范,远不如人们曾期望的那样正直。首先,他们把兄弟情谊置于一切之上的做法造成了无意识的灾难性后果:以数百条生命的代价换取一个兄弟,这不是最崇高的行为。在单个好汉处理相互关系时有正面的表现,其中有很多相互帮助的事例。只是一旦好汉们开始以行帮的形式行动时,当为了权力个人之间开始视对方为敌手而不是盟友时,他们宣称的兄弟情谊就开始瓦解。

对好汉们宣称的兄弟情谊最致命的打击出现在他们的招募方式

---

[1] Lei Kang, The Dichotomy between Popular Opinion and the Novel: Morality in Water Margin., "Women and Men, Love and Power: Parameters of Chinese Fiction and Drama" Sino-Platonic Paper, 193 (Novermber, 2009), p. 149.

[2] Ibid..

上：强迫"盟友"加入梁山集团所表现出来的野蛮、残忍，是无法对其进行辩护的。由此，我们可以推知支配梁山好汉处理相互关系的道德规范是什么样的。表面上，他们声称相互尊重，互为支持者。当好汉们独立、自由地活动时，他们的行为恪守这个信条。然而，一旦他们之间需要某种表面的秩序，这个信条就变质了；当好汉们抑制的嫉妒、傲慢情绪被派系冲突、被野蛮的招募方式泄露出来时，好汉就会把自己放在首位，而不是"兄弟"。这里，我们不仅看到作为道德高尚的梁山好汉个人之间最初的裂隙，也看到了把这些好汉维系在一起的极端空洞的标签。①

夏志清、浦安迪等人对梁山好汉罗致英雄的野蛮、残忍也有过研究②。而在这些受害的英雄里，浦安迪尤其对梁山好汉陷害卢俊义，使得他家破人亡的行为进行了批判③。事实上，康磊对上述这些问题的讨论，就是以他们的研究成果为基础的。康磊的研究吸收了他们的基本观点，并且把它们系统化了，因此笔者就不再一一细述了。

其次，我们开始讨论康磊对水浒英雄处理与朝廷之间关系道德规范的研究情况。在这一方面，康磊认为梁山好汉的道德规范更为明确，也更少表现出傲慢、嫉妒的情绪。对此，该论者认为，"支配梁山好汉反对当权者的道德规范，看起来更为明确：在这，总体来看，他们的行为更加高尚，同时更少染上傲慢、嫉妒的色彩"。④ 康磊说，作品最后40回左右（该论者以袁无涯刻120回本为依据）描写梁山好汉接受招安，为朝廷服务，参与征四寇保卫宋王朝，展现出爱国精神。而这正是对梁山好汉在处理与朝廷之间关系时呈现出来的积极、明确的道德规范的最好证明。康磊说："在此关系中爱国的好汉们表现出来的明确的道德规范，反映了把他

---

① Lei Kang, The Dichotomy between Popular Opinion and the Novel: Morality in Water Margin., "Women and Men, Love and Power: Parameters of Chinese Fiction and Drama" Sino-Platonic Paper, 193 (Novermber, 2009), pp. 149 – 150.
② 具体见夏志清著《中国古典小说》，胡益民等译，江苏文艺出版社2008年版，第91—92页。
③ Andrew H. Plaks, The Four Masterworks of the Ming Novel, Princeton University Press, 1987, p. 341, 345.
④ Lei Kang, The Dichotomy between Popular Opinion and the Novel: Morality in Water Margin., "Women and Men, Love and Power: Parameters of Chinese Fiction and Drama" Sino-Platonic Paper, 193 (Novermber, 2009), p. 150.

们看作好人的通行观点。"①

在该论者看来，宋江领导之下，梁山好汉接受招安、忠心为朝廷效力，展现出来的是儒家的伦理道德观念与要求。这就如夏志清所认为的那样，宋江是"深谙孔孟之道的精神首领"，是"儒家忠于皇帝的主要标志"②。从服务朝廷、忠于皇帝的层面来说，梁山好汉奉行的的确是儒家的道德信条。但这不是水浒英雄处理与朝廷之间关系道德规范的全部内容。因为小说除了描写梁山好汉对朝廷忠诚的一面之外，还写了不少两者之间对立的事件。

就梁山好汉与朝廷之间的对立，康磊说：

> 这并不意味着就没有和朝廷对立的事情。小说中出现的一个更令人不安的施虐事件，是对俘虏黄文炳——一个之前告发宋江的官员——的处理。复仇行为不只局限于黄文炳自身，这帮人还杀死了他的全家："一门内外大小四五十口，尽皆杀了。"而黄文炳一旦被俘，李逵立即对他给予惩罚。这个惩罚是那么的残忍、野蛮：黄文炳当面被李逵脔割，炙来下酒。李逵还把黄文炳的心肝与众头领做醒酒汤。③

对梁山好汉向黄文炳如此非理性的复仇行为，夏志清指出这种惩罚残酷得令人毛骨悚然，即使为宋江报了仇，却完全无法博得读者的同情和怜悯；而小说家又明显袒护英雄们的虐杀行为和嗜食人肉的做法，这显然是与文明行为相对立的④。事实的确如此，而这一点体现出来的却并不是儒家的道德观念。

就梁山好汉的复仇欲望，康磊认为，他们不仅对黄文炳这样的官员如

---

① Lei Kang, The Dichotomy between Popular Opinion and the Novel: Morality in Water Margin. , "Women and Men, Love and Power: Parameters of Chinese Fiction and Drama" Sino-Platonic Paper, 193 (Novermber, 2009), p. 151.

② Hsia, Chih-tsing, Classical Chinese Novel: *A Critical Introduction*, Ner York: Columbia University Press, 1968, p. 107.

③ Lei Kang, The Dichotomy between Popular Opinion and the Novel: Morality in Water Margin. , "Women and Men, Love and Power: Parameters of Chinese Fiction and Drama" Sino-Platonic Paper, 193 (Novermber, 2009), p. 151.

④ Hsia, Chih-tsing, Classical Chinese Novel: *A Critical Introduction*, Ner York: Columbia University Press, 1968, p. 97.

此，就是对待普通百姓、无辜者时亦具有决定性的影响。该论者说，无罪者理应不被残杀，像黄文炳的家人，尤其是孩子，不应该为他的罪负责，但结果却同样遭到残酷的惩罚。这样的行为是无法让人接受的。与之相反，康磊说："对腐败、暴政之下遭受的苦难而对那些恶贯满盈的成员加以残酷的惩罚，那一定会让人接受，甚至令人深感欣慰。"[①] 他以林冲被逼上梁山为例说，林冲是朝廷腐败的牺牲品，正是官场的不公使他沦为草寇，而非他自愿加入。正因为如此，所以当我们看到林冲手刃陆谦等恶徒时，就能得到阅读的快感，同时为林冲的遭遇深表不平，并对他流露出同情。

对康磊的观点，笔者深表赞同。但对《水浒传》来说，正是小说作者对好汉们野蛮行径的这种暧昧、含糊的态度，从而令现代读者对作品中的道德问题深感困惑。不过从总体上来看，梁山好汉处理与朝廷之间关系的道德规范，积极、明确的方面要多于矛盾、冲突的一面。

最后，我们来讨论梁山好汉处理与普通百姓之间关系的道德规范问题。就梁山好汉与普通百姓之间的关系，康磊认为：

> 虽然在政府腐败的描写上，大众的看法与小说一致，但视梁山好汉为平民百姓对抗朝廷的保护者的观点，实在难以与小说实际相符合。他们不是保护人，这实在是被夸大了，因为他们造成的伤害经常超过他们带来的好处。[②]

同时，康磊也指出，小说里面也有典型的锄强扶弱的人物故事，如鲁达。对此，该论者说：

> 当然，也有个体英雄保护平民百姓的事情。举例说，鲁达杀死郑屠——因他压迫金氏父女、强迫金翠莲做他的妾并勒索他们的钱财，鲁达就是锄强扶弱（这个屠户号称"镇关西"）。鲁达保护弱小的故事还在继续，他挽救刘太公的女儿使其避免与强人首领成亲；他也营

[①] Lei Kang, The Dichotomy between Popular Opinion and the Novel: Morality in Water Margin. , "Women and Men, Love and Power: Parameters of Chinese Fiction and Drama" Sino-Platonic Paper, 193 (Novermber, 2009), pp. 151 – 152.

[②] Ibid. , p. 153.

救了林冲，使他在流放途中免遭两个解差的谋杀。①

康磊对鲁达的这些行为给予了非常高的评价，说鲁达是一个道德高尚的人。就鲁达个人来说，毫无疑问他是真正意义上的仗义之人，是顶天立地的英雄好汉。刘若愚根据上述故事也对鲁达表达了高度的赞美之情，称其是中国之侠的标准，当人们需要帮助时他就出现了②。不过，正如夏志清、李惠仪等人所指出的那样，《水浒传》中这种锄强扶弱、济困扶危的事例实在太少了。相反，就是对待平民百姓，小说作者描写的更多的也还是好汉们的复仇行为。

在前面的讨论中，康磊曾说梁山好汉给平民百姓"造成的伤害经常超过他们带来的好处"，从作品本身来看，确实可以这么说。如夏志清所指出的那样，好汉们的道德信条主要是由复仇的欲望所驱使的，是严苛的以牙还牙③。夏志清说，武松就是这类好汉的代表性人物。对武松的复仇，不管是夏志清还是康磊等其他研究者都认为，如果杀死潘金莲、西门庆为兄弟报仇是有正当理由的话，如果在鸳鸯楼上杀死张都监、张团练与蒋门神三人还可理解的话，那么，就像众好汉杀死黄文炳的家小一样，武松血洗张都监一家是完全不可理喻的。因为那些仆妇、孩子是完全无辜的，他们不应该为其他人的罪承担任何责任。对"血溅鸳鸯楼"，浦安迪则说，武松的血腥屠杀反映了他内心极端不健康，他无视那些可怜的仆妇、佣人的恳求，展现出他人格中极卑劣的一面④。而在康磊看来，宋江杀死阎婆惜、雷横杀死歌女白秀英两事件中，宋、雷二人"施行的复仇与崇高差之太远"⑤。

上述只是好汉个体向平民百姓的复仇。按夏志清之论，单个的好汉基

---

① Lei Kang, The Dichotomy between Popular Opinion and the Novel: Morality in Water Margin., "Women and Men, Love and Power: Parameters of Chinese Fiction and Drama" Sino-Platonic Paper, 193 (Novermber, 2009), p. 153.

② Liu, James J. Y. The Chinese Knight-Errant. Chicago: The University of Chicago Press, 1967, p. 113.

③ Hsia, Chih-tsing, Classical Chinese Novel: A Critical Introduction, Ner York: Columbia University Press, 1968, p. 97.

④ Andrew H. Plaks, The Four Masterworks of the Ming Novel, Princeton University Press, 1987, p. 322.

⑤ Lei Kang, The Dichotomy between Popular Opinion and the Novel: Morality in Water Margin., "Women and Men, Love and Power: Parameters of Chinese Fiction and Drama" Sino-Platonic Paper, 193 (Novermber, 2009), p. 154.

本上能恪守英雄信条，但整个梁山好汉群奉行的却是行帮道德，当他们集体行动时，对平民百姓造成的往往是灾难性后果。康磊以"三打祝家庄"、攻打曾头市为例说：

> 在这些事件中，好汉的行动毫无疑问是错误的。这两个村庄并没有犯错：事实上，正如梁山好汉一样，他们居住在那里同样是出于个人的自主意愿。他们被消灭，仅仅因为他们不友好的自立对梁山是一个威胁。①

从现代人的角度来看，在这两个事件中，引起冲突的原因的确是无关生死命脉的小事情，梁山好汉的行为也确实有掠夺的成分。但即便如此，他们还是能够找到在他们自己看来是正当的理由，那就是为梁山好汉的荣誉和尊严而战。

根据上面的讨论，从总体上来看，梁山好汉所信守的道德规范的确如吴杰克所说的那样，是充满矛盾、冲突的。虽然康磊把它分为三个层面，但就是在同一层面内，好汉个人与梁山好汉群体之间在道德规范的遵循上也会出现很大的差异；有时，好汉们的行为甚至会出现如康磊所指出的那样，完全是对自己倡导的道德信条的"亵渎"。

夏志清等人认为，水浒世界的道德规范之所以会出现如此混乱、冲突的情形，这可能与小说作者对待梁山好汉的各种行为时保持一种暧昧、含糊的态度有关。而笔者以为，如果批评者能够站在漂浮无根的社会流民的角度，来理解梁山好汉极度缺乏安全感的生存处境的话，就能比较好地理解他们所做的各种事情。因为不论他们做了什么，他们的根本目的首先就是争得生存。而为了消除对自己的各种威胁，好汉们就会不惜铤而走险，甚至为自己的血腥杀戮找到各种借口和理由。而这些借口和理由在旁人看来根本就不成立。

此外，在梁山好汉处理内部关系的道德规范上，在招募秦明、朱仝、卢俊义等人时，会出现那种非常野蛮、残酷的方式，这一方面与小说的主题有关，另一方面则与作者要达成完整的叙事有关。小说开篇讲述了"洪太尉误走妖魔"的故事，而这个故事恰好为整部作品的神话象征结构埋下

---

① Lei Kang, The Dichotomy between Popular Opinion and the Novel: Morality in Water Margin., "Women and Men, Love and Power: Parameters of Chinese Fiction and Drama" Sino-Platonic Paper, 193 (November, 2009), p.155.

了伏笔。所谓"宛子城中藏虎豹,蓼儿洼内聚神蛟",这就决定了梁山一百零八好汉必然聚首的情节。作者为了达成这个叙事结果,自然就会搬出所谓的"上界星辰契合"等诸如此类的话来,从而对其中出现的种种野蛮、残酷与血腥杀戮抱以视而不见的态度。当然,在现代人看来所谓"上界星辰契合"自然是骗人的鬼话。但小说的叙事却正是这样一步步发展而成的。不过,这只是一家之言,不足为据。

二、水浒世界的基本价值观念

在《水浒传》研究中,夏志清把梁山好汉的信条与好汉们的特点概括为三个方面,即"讲义气,爱武艺;疏财仗义,慷慨大方;不贪女色而嗜食贪杯"①。其中"讲义气"、"疏财仗义,慷慨大方"与"不贪女色",都与水浒世界的价值观念密切相关。事实上,在《水浒传》的研究中,人们一般都能注意到上述这几点。像柳存仁、浦安迪、李惠仪等人都讨论过梁山好汉的"讲义气""仗义疏财""不好女色"等价值认同。不过,上述诸人的讨论比较零散、细琐,也并不全面。相对来说,在英语世界批评者对此问题的研究中,关锦做得是比较系统的。

对梁山好汉所认同的价值观念,在夏志清等人的研究基础上,关锦认为可以把它们分成荣誉感、慷慨大方、不好女色、正义感以及强健的体魄与武艺超群的本领五个方面。对此,该论者指出:

> 我们可以把好汉的价值观界定成五个不同的类别:荣誉感,慷慨大方,不好女色,正义感,以及体魄强健、武艺超群。根据进入梁山社会的条件来看,在这里面,荣誉感、慷慨大方与正义感是最关键的。为什么不好女色与武艺超群没有那么重要呢?因为好汉的对手与他们自己一样,通常也有好武艺,能够使用各种武器。②

---

① [美]夏志清:《中国古典小说》,胡益民等译,江苏文艺出版社2008年版,第90页。
② The *haohan* values are defined in five different categories: sense of honor, generosity, sexual abstinence, sense of justice, and outstanding physical ability. Among these categories, honor, generosity, and justice are the most crucial in terms of the qualifications for being accepted into Mountain Liang society. Why are sexual abstinence and outstanding physical skill not as important? Because the men that *haohan* oppose usually also possess good skill in the martial arts and can use various weapons as well as they. Jin Guan, The values of Mountain outlaws and of Contemporary Gangs, "Women and Men, Love and Power: Parameters of Chinese Fiction and Drama" Sino-Platonic Paper, 193 (Novermber, 2009), p.170.

笔者以为，该论者的概括是比较到位的，从内在的精神价值认同到外在的本领、特长的赞赏都点明了。梁山好汉能走在一起，首先当然是志趣相投，而首当其冲的又的确是荣誉感、慷慨大方与正义感三个方面。像鲁达不喜李忠，就与其在对金氏父女时很小气有关。不过，像林冲与鲁智深的结义，一开始还是出于对对方本领的赞赏的。

对梁山好汉的不好女色，关锦说：

> 好汉认为房事会削弱一个人的健康和战斗本领。他们视不好女色为对好汉精神力量的一个考验（夏志清）。大部分好汉把女人看作是麻烦之源或者是一种累赘。①

对这一点，夏志清是这样说的：

> 对好汉更重要的考验是他必须不好色。梁山英雄大都是单身汉。至于已婚英雄，他们婚姻生活方面的事书中很少提及，除非他们因妻子遇到什么麻烦。据称杨雄和卢俊义一心习武，根本不管妻子，宋江出于怜悯而买阎婆惜为侍妾，却极不愿去她身边。即便如此，李逵这位鲁莽而又出色的英雄也仍然将宋与阎的瓜葛视作宋江的一个污点，并认为宋江秘密进京会见名妓李师师也是不光彩的。对习武者来说，禁欲大概首先被认为是一项保健措施。但到梁山泊传奇形成的时候，禁欲已成了英雄信条的主要一项。②

夏志清还指出，对于像梁山好汉中唯一一位贪恋女色的矮脚虎王英，他是受到同伴们嘲笑的。总的来说，对梁山好汉不好女色的认识，上述两人的观点是一样的。

对梁山好汉的正义感问题，关锦指出：

---

① *Haohans* believe sexual activities weaken one's health and fighting skills. They perceive sexual abstinence as a test of the haohan's spiritual strength (Hsia 1996, 88). Most *haohans* consider women either a source pf trouble or a burden. Jin Guan, The values of Mountain outlaws and of Contemporary Gangs, "Women and Men, Love and Power: Parameters of Chinese Fiction and Drama" Sino-Platonic Paper, 193 (Novermber, 2009), p.170.

② ［美］夏志清：《中国古典小说》，胡益民等译，江苏文艺出版社2008年版，第86页。

每一个梁山好汉都拥有正义感。梁山好汉没有谁会容忍不公平的事情,无论是谁经历了那样的遭遇。一看到不公道的事情,他们就会毫不犹豫地涉身其中,打抱不平。①

该论者以《水浒传》中的重要好汉鲁达为例说,他之所以会成为和尚,并在不久后落草为寇,就是因为他对不公道事情的零容忍。鲁达一听见说郑屠欺骗、迫害金氏父女,他就和他们父女站在一起,并给予他们物质上的帮助。在帮助金氏父女逃走之后,鲁达还不忘教训那个恶霸,并因此丢了官职,开始了逃亡的生活。②

对梁山好汉路见不平拔刀相助的价值信念,关锦进一步指出:

像鲁达一样,大部分梁山好汉反抗不公,根本不会考虑哪怕是出现最严重的后果。当他们遭受不公道的对待时,为了复仇好汉们将不惜采取非常残暴的手段。③

对这一点,如夏志清、李惠仪等人指出的那样,英雄们在维护正义的名义下,往往会出现血腥屠杀,这就走向了正义的反面,同时也给作品带来了阴暗的一面。像夏志清讨论过的,李逵对黄文炳的折磨、虐杀,杨雄对潘巧云的报复杀害,凡此种种,皆是非理性的杀戮行为,而作者的描写却那样津津乐道,毫无道德上的批判意味。从这方面来说,我们就可以理解为什么刘再复会把《水浒传》视为"地狱之门"、"黑暗王国"了。

谈到梁山好汉的慷慨大方,关锦说:"好汉的慷慨大方,不仅在钱物

---

① Every *haohan* of Mountain Liang possesses a sense of justice. None would ever tolerate unfairness regardless of who is experiencing it. They would not hesitate to involve themselves at the first sight of injustice. Jin Guan, The values of Mountain outlaws and of Contemporary Gangs, "Women and Men, Love and Power: Parameters of Chinese Fiction and Drama" Sino-Platonic Paper, 193 (Novermber, 2009), p. 170.

② Jin Guan, The values of Mountain outlaws and of Contemporary Gangs, "Women and Men, Love and Power: Parameters of Chinese Fiction and Drama" Sino-Platonic Paper, 193 (Novermber, 2009), pp. 170–171.

③ Most *haohans* of Mountain Liang, like Lu Da, fight injustice without considering even the most severe consquences. The *haohans* go to an even greater length for revenge when thay themselves suffer injustice. Jin Guan, The values of Mountain outlaws and of Contemporary Gangs, "Women and Men, Love and Power: Parameters of Chinese Fiction and Drama" Sino-Platonic Paper, 193 (Novermber, 2009), p. 171.

上，也包括他们自愿牺牲自己的差事、家庭、社会地位乃至生命本身。"①该论者认为，宋江是这一方面的最好代表，"他获得及时雨的绰号，是因为任何处于困境中的人都能得到他的支助"。该论者指出，宋江不仅给他人银子，如在揭阳镇时对待病大虫薛永那样，他还担着"血海般干系"给心腹兄弟晁盖通风报信。对此，该论者指出："宋江丢掉自己的差役被迫离家出逃，全都是为了帮助自己的朋友。"②就宋江来说，该论者的说法是合乎作品的描写的。

对梁山好汉的慷慨信条，夏志清有不同的看法，他指出："由于绝大部分好汉都并不富有，因而不可能太慷慨。"③如果从总体上来分析梁山好汉的行事，夏志清的看法更符合作品本身。就作者对水浒英雄的描写来看，以慷慨闻名的主要还是宋江、柴进以及很晚才出场的卢俊义等家底比较殷实的几个人。

对上述五种水浒世界信守的价值观念，关锦认为其中核心的"正义感"和"慷慨大方"皆来自"义气"的规范。该论者说："好汉的正义感和慷慨，两者都是由义气的规范所驱动的。"④

那么，《水浒传》中梁山好汉所宣扬的"义气"或者说"义"是什么呢？下面我们就来讨论英语世界对这个问题的研究。

三、研究者对"义"的辨识

在历来的研究中，梁山好汉所信守的"义气"，或者说"义"，是一个很难对其进行清晰、明确界定的概念。中国学者王学泰认为，《水浒传》描绘的是一个游民的世界，"义"与"义气"是游民集聚的心理、文

---

① The haohans are generous not just with money and possessions but also with their willingness to sacrifice jobs, families, social status, and life itself. Jin Guan, The values of Mountain outlaws and of Contemporary Gangs, "Women and Men, Love and Power: Parameters of Chinese Fiction and Drama" Sino-Platonic Paper, 193 (Novermber, 2009), p. 171.

② He acquires the nickname Opportune Rain, hecause anyone in trouble can rely on his support.... Song Jiang loses his job and is forced to leave his familiy, all in order to help his friends. Jin Guan, The values of Mountain outlaws and of Contemporary Gangs, "Women and Men, Love and Power: Parameters of Chinese Fiction and Drama" Sino-Platonic Paper, 193 (Novermber, 2009), p. 172.

③ [美] 夏志清:《中国古典小说》, 胡益民等译, 江苏文艺出版社2008年版, 第86页。

④ The *haohan*'s sense of justice and his generosity are both driven by the code of honor (*yiqi*). Jin Guan, The values of Mountain outlaws and of Contemporary Gangs, "Women and Men, Love and Power: Parameters of Chinese Fiction and Drama" Sino-Platonic Paper, 193 (Novermber, 2009), p. 172.

化纽带，是"义"让那些英雄好汉奔向一处。在中国思想文化中，儒家倡导"义"，墨家也倡导"义"，但细究起来，水浒世界所说的"义"属于墨家的范畴。他说：

> 儒家把"义"看成是做人的义务与原则，孟子说："善恶之心，义之端也。"这种义务与原则，是和他们所主张的仁爱、忠恕之道的伦理基础与"克己复礼"的社会主张联系在一起的。他们强调"义利之辨"，认为两者往往不能兼而得之。有"君子喻于义，小人喻于利"之说；又有"见利思义"之戒。总之，"义"和"利"是对立的。利益当前，首先要看它是否妨碍"义"，不要见利忘义。墨家则与儒家相反，他们把"义"、"利"打成一片。墨子说："义"是"有力以劳人，有财以分人"。又说，"举义"是"不辟贫贱"、"不辟亲疏"、"不辟近"也"不辟远"的。由此可见，墨子主张的"义"是以"兼相爱"、"交相利"为基础的。因此，墨子在《贵义》篇中明确地说："义可以利人。"这与儒家明辨义利是大异其趣的。后世的士大夫讲的"义"多属于儒家，指本着儒家观念应该尽的义务；而游民所说的"义"和"义气"则接近墨子的主张，他们把"义"看作利，而且是赤裸裸的个人利益，在《水浒传》中的"义气"就是指白花花的银子。[①]

对王学泰之观点，笔者并不完全赞同。在《水浒传》中，虽然存在"义可以利人"的现象，但并不能把作者所描写的"义"完全等同于"利"，更不能把梁山好汉践行的"义气"等同于白花花的银子。事实上，当鲁达救助金氏父女时，在他身上所表现出来的"义"很显然是对弱势群体的人性关怀，也是对社会公平正义的维护。类似的情节在小说中还有不少。

王学泰在此提出的水浒世界的"义"属于墨家范畴的观点，与本节开篇谈到的关锦提出的梁山好汉以"义"为核心的道德、价值观念属于儒家思想范畴的认识，此两者显然是相左的。那么，其他人是如何看待这

[①] 王学泰：《游民文化与中国社会》（增订版，上），同心出版社2007年版，第330—331页。

一问题的呢？下面，我们就来讨论英语世界的批评者对"义"这一观念的具体研究情况。

夏志清较早就对梁山好汉所讲的"义"进行了研究。夏志清认为，水浒世界宣扬的"义"或"义气"是"由友谊所支配的"（dictates of friendship），梁山好汉讲"义气"就是"把对朋友的责任置于一切之上"①。对此，夏志清说：

> 他们分外看重友情，互相视若兄弟骨肉。这不仅是赞同书中常常提到的儒家格言"四海之内皆兄弟"，也是鼓励他们行侠仗义，不是通过政府，而是以自己的双手伸张正义。②

夏志清同时也指出：

> 然而，尽管这一英雄信条并不违背孔子的仁义道德，但实际上，这些信条强调"友情"或曰"义"高于一切，从而否定了更高的伦理规范，《水浒》中的英雄们在夺取豪门的财物时是从不犹豫的。……英雄信条中有某种利他的爱，但由于无视法律和社会规范，它又鼓励了一种与利他主义相反的行帮道德。③

夏志清还指出："虽然《水浒》肯定了英雄们的豪情壮举，但它同时对野蛮虐杀事实上的赞同，使得中国文化学者对这一重要作品莫知所从。"④ 在夏志清看来，水浒英雄之中有一些人是恶魔的象征，像嗜杀的李逵、武松就是如此。夏志清在分析"《水浒》的所谓反政府主题"时曾经指出，梁山好汉虽然标举"义"的大旗，反对贪官，仇恨不公与不义，但他们为了维护个人声誉和团体权益而不惜血腥杀戮，表现出完全非理性的残暴，施行的却是不义之举。对此，夏志清说：

---

① C. T. Hsia defined *yiqi* as "dictates of friendship", in which a haohan would put his duty to frieddship above everything. Hsia, Chih-tsing, Classical Chinese Novel: *A Critical Introduction*, Ner York: Columbia University Press, 1968, p. 86.
② [美] 夏志清：《中国古典小说》，胡益民等译，江苏文艺出版社2008年版，第84页。
③ 同上书，第84—85页。
④ 同上书，第99页。

要讨论《水浒传》的所谓反政府主题,就必须把好汉个人与梁山好汉整体区分开来。这一区分极端重要。单个的好汉恪守英雄信条,然而整个梁山好汉群,则奉行一种行帮道德。这种道德只是英雄信条的拙劣模仿而已。单个传奇英雄如鲁智深、武松、林冲,甚至宋江等人都是堂堂男子。如果横遭迫害,他们必定奋起反抗,充分显示出他们的英雄气概。但是,小说在讲了王进、史进、鲁智深及林冲的英雄故事后,写了一大段智取生辰纲的故事,肯定了欺骗和狡诈。……诚然,蔡京是朝廷四大奸臣之一,这些生日礼物全是民脂民膏;可是要在鲁、林、史、武等英雄,就肯定不会因此而采取这种劫夺的做法,因为这样做有贪财之嫌。吴用、晁盖、阮氏兄弟等却不因此而感到不妥。①

很显然,夏志清在此是用接近儒家的思想观念以及现代意义上的"正义"观来评论梁山好汉的行为的,并且是在一种比较高的层次上来谈论的。笔者以为这与作品宗旨的主导方面是不一致的。因为从根本上来说,水浒英雄的"义"是相对狭隘的,有其特定的适用范围。

与夏志清的观点不完全相同,詹纳尔(Jenner W. J. F)是这样界定《水浒传》中的"义气"观念的,该论者指出:"'义气'的完美表达是自愿作出个人的全部牺牲,而对其没有任何正常的义务要求。"②詹纳尔以史进为例说:

当少华山上三个头领中的朱武、杨春两人愿意献出自己的性命践行他们"不求同日生,只愿同日死"的誓言时,史进被三人表现出来的"义气"感动了。史进释放被俘的陈达,并与他们三人结成好朋友,这纯粹是出于"义气"。③

---

① [美]夏志清:《中国古典小说》,胡益民等译,江苏文艺出版社2008年版,第91页。
② The ideal expressions of yiqi is the willingness to make a complete sacrifice of oneself when no normal obligation repuires it. Jenner, "Tough Guys, Mateship and Honour: Another Chinese Tradition." East Asia History [1996], p. 11.
③ Shi Jin was toughed by sense of honor shown by the trio of minor bandits when two of them were willing to give up their lives for the third, in order to fulfill their oath of dying on the same day. Shi Jin returns the captured bandit and becomes good friends with the trio merely out of *yiqi*. Jenner, "Tough Guys, Mateship and Honour: Another Chinese Tradition." East Asia History [1996], p. 11.

就詹纳尔对"义气"的理解与认识，用关锦的话来说就是：

> 詹纳尔认为，"义气"不只是友谊；可以把它界定为这样的原则，即为了帮助朋友或是萍水相逢的陌生人摆脱困境或为他报仇，好汉将竭尽全力、不惜采取任何手段。①

关锦以林冲火并王伦为例说，当晁盖等人上梁山寻求庇护、王伦却想用希图拒绝林冲的相同的借口把他们赶下山去时，林冲无法容忍王伦不仗义的行为从而火并杀死了他，并把晁盖等人留在山寨。在这件事中，林冲虽然功不可没，但他却推举晁盖为头领，自己只坐了第四把交椅。由此，关锦认为，林冲没有从杀王伦中得到任何东西，他这样做只是出于"义气"。

詹纳尔对《水浒传》所表现的"义气"观念的认识与理解，比夏志清更全面。的确，《水浒传》中不少好汉不止对朋友讲义气，对陌生人也同样讲义气。最典型的莫过于鲁达。在渭州做提辖时，偶遇被郑屠欺凌的金氏父女，他就义愤填膺。不仅给金氏父女银子，为了他们能安全逃出郑屠的魔爪，鲁达还坐守客栈以防小儿通风报信去追赶。小说中能证实詹纳尔观点的事例尚有不少，在此不一一列举。但要指出的是，詹纳尔提到的那些展现梁山好汉"没有任何正常的义务要求"的故事，只是小说所展现出来的"义气"的一个方面。

李惠仪对《水浒传》所宣扬的"义"进行的更多是现代意义上的思辨和阐释，尤其是以西方的"正义"观念为参照系。在李惠仪看来，梁山好汉讲的"义"，形式多样，意义含混不清，而从根本上来说又与"正义"没多大关系。对此，她说：

> 一个反复出现而又意义含糊的字——"义"（有各式各样的翻译，如"righteousness"，"honor"，"valor"，"solidarity"），用它来界

---

① However, W. J. F. Jenner argues that *yiqi* is more than friendship; it is defined as the principle on which a *haohan* would go to any length to get a friend or complete stranger out of trouble or avenge him. Jin Guan, The values of Mountain outlaws and of Contemporary Gangs, "Women and Men, Love and Power: Parameters of Chinese Fiction and Drama" Sino-Platonic Paper, 193 (Novermber, 2009), pp. 169 – 170.

定梁山世界的价值观。这些好汉,当他们宣誓成为兄弟时,叫"结义";当他们认可自己联合团结的协定,或准备掠夺、发动战争,或为抢劫、战争的胜利庆祝时,叫"聚义";为荣耀结义兄弟关系而采取的行动叫"义举"。然而,把"义"翻译成"righteousness"是很成问题的。因为"righteousness"是"礼节"("仪")和"正义"的结合。而在《水浒传》里,"义"则是指好汉们维持生存和繁荣的思想观念,却很少关注"正义"本身。①

梁山好汉讲的"义"确实和我们现在所说的"正义"不一样。正如夏志清、孙述宇、浦安迪诸人所指出的那样,梁山好汉一面标榜"义",一面却又在血腥杀戮、野蛮劫掠,甚至像李逵等人在杀戮中获得快感;而且梁山好汉的很多行为都只是为了维护自己集团的利益。这些都与"义"背道而驰,同时也给梁山世界蒙上了黑暗的阴影,从而使作品缺乏温暖人心的一面。而作品阴暗、混乱的方面也为阐释研究提出了很多棘手的问题。李惠仪指出,像小说中表现出来的崇高的修辞风格与暴力现实之间的不协调是最典型的。

对作品演绎的"义气"主题,李惠仪如此说:"即使反复出现表现强烈的个人义气的主题,但朋友与敌人的界线有时正如公道与公道之曲解一样模糊、空洞。"② 以"义夺快活林"为例,李惠仪进一步指出:

> 与《水浒传》的"行帮道德"一致,个人和团体的忠诚掩盖了道德评判。以施恩和蒋门神之间的地盘之争为例,他们都试图霸占快

---

① A recurrent but nebulous word, *yi* (variously translated as "righteousness," "honor," "valor," "solidarity"), defines the values of the Liang-shan world. Bandit-rebels "form bonds of righteousness" (*chieh-yi*) when they become sworn brothers, "gather in righteousness" (*chü-yi*) when they confirm their pact of solidarity, and prepare for or celebrate robbery, raid, and battle. Actions undertaken to honor the ties of sworn brotherhood are "righteous deeds" (*yi-chü*). However, the very translation of the word *yi* as "righteous" is problematic, based as it is on the association with propriety (*yi*) and the compound "upright and righteous" (*cheng-yi*). In *Water Margin*, *yi* refers to the ethos that sustains the survival and prosperity of the bandit-rebels as a group, but often there is scant regard for "righteousness" as such. The Columbia History of Chinese Literature, Victor H. Mair editor. New York: Columbia University Press, 2001, p. 629.

② Despite the recurrent theme of fierce personal loyalty (*yi-ch'i*), the line betwween friend and foe is sometimes as tenuous as that between justice and its perversion. The Columbia History of Chinese Literature, Victor H. Mair editor. New York: Columbia University Press, 2001, p. 631.

活林,从弱小者那里收取"闲钱"。人们谈论的是施恩收买武松的忠诚,在武松的帮助下"义夺快活林",而义气与公道则似乎没有问题。施恩的名字意味着"施与恩惠",他和武松的关系,说明了个人之间的忠诚烙上了慷慨相待、大方礼赠的印痕。在《水浒传》里,这是一个常见的交换方式。①

从李惠仪的分析我们可以看到,水浒世界的"义"和"利"是紧密联系在一起的,而"义"时常又是以"利"为基础的。这就基本接近王学泰提出的"游民所说的'义'和'义气'则接近墨子的主张,他们把'义'看作利,而且是赤裸裸的个人利益,在《水浒传》中的'义气'就是指白花花的银子"。事实上,在梁山好汉内部,相互的"忠义"和对本集团利益的维护,是评判好坏、善恶的最高标准。而在小说中,相互之间的"忠义"又确实有依靠"银子"结成的因素在内。正因为如此,就出现如李惠仪所说的那样,"义气"成为了模糊、空洞的东西而失去了正义层面上的道德评判意义。这就难怪李惠仪会说:

> 梁山的口号是"替天行道","济生民"也偶尔会提及。然而,进一步考察这个世界则会发现这里没有更高的道义评判。作品开篇,鲁达杀死迫害金翠莲和其父亲的地方恶霸郑屠,但这种"锄强扶弱"的事例相对来说实在罕有。②

---

① According to the "gang morality" (C. T. Hsia's term) of *Water Margin*, personal and group loyalty overrides moral judgment. In the territorial disputes between Shih En and Doorgod Chiang, for example, each is trying to be the reigning local bully collecting dues from the weak. Shih En buys Wu Sung's loyalty and with his help "honorably take over" (yi-to) the coveted woods in question, although honor or justice hardly seems the issue. Shih En's name means literally "conferring beneficence," and his relationship with Wu Sung exemplifies personal loyalty sealed by generous treatment or liberal gifts, a common mode of exchange in the book. The Columbia History of Chinese Literature, Victor H. Mair editor. New York: Columbia University Press, 2001, pp. 630 – 631.

② The slogan of Liang-shan is "to realize the Way on behalf of heaven" (t'i-t'ien hsing-tao), and "succor for the people" is intermittently mentioned. However, closer inspection of this world reveals no higher justice. Early on in the book, Lu Ta kills the local bully who persecutes Chin Ts'ui-lien and her father, but such instances of "fighting the powerful to defend the weak" are relatively rare. The Columbia History of Chinese Literature, Victor H. Mair editor. New York: Columbia University Press, 2001, pp. 629 – 630.

综合上述英语学术界的批评者对水浒世界道德与价值观念核心的"义"与"义气"的分析、研究，我们可以得出这样的认识：

梁山好汉的"义"虽然有不求回报的一面，但它和"利"密切相关。此其一；其二，梁山好汉的"义"比较狭隘，虽然他们会帮助陌生人，但主要还是通行于好汉内部；其三，与我们常说的"正义"不同，水浒世界的"义"不完全具有道德评判的意义，换句话说就是它不具备普适性。

第三节 "厌女症"与水浒世界的女性观

不仅在中国古典小说中，就是放眼整个世界小说丛林，《水浒传》对女性的描写都可谓与众不同。而这种与众不同所包含的就是对待女性的极端态度。如在"男权社会中的水浒女性形象塑造"部分谈到的，水浒世界的女子，要么是不异于男性的女英雄，用时兴的话来说就是女汉子，要么是贞节娘子，再就是受人唾弃的所谓"淫娃荡妇"（事实上，若潘金莲诸人生活在今世，那肯定是经常要上各种媒体的头条的）。而小说会把女性描写成这些极端的人物形象，很显然是由作者的女性观所决定的。而作者女性观的形成，显然是由当时社会的文化、思想观念以及政治制度塑造而成的。

那么，小说作者的女性观究竟是怎样的呢？下面我们就来聆听英语世界的批评者夏志清、孙述宇、吴燕娜等人的论述。

一、夏志清与"厌女症"的提出

在1968年出版的论著《中国古典小说》第三章《水浒传》部分，夏志清就小说对待女性的态度提出"厌女症"（misogyny）一说。夏志清此观点的提出是以《冰岛传奇》为参照视点的。在比较论述了《水浒传》与《冰岛传奇》对待正义与暴力截然不同的态度之后，夏志清进一步指出：

《水浒传》和《冰岛传奇》还有一个基本区别：它们对处于以男性为中心的社会中的妇女们所起的作用采取了全然不同的态度。在《恩加尔传奇》的流血械斗背后的是一些灰心丧气的妇女，她们提出各种似是而非的理由，恳求男人们顾全颜面，驱使他们投入仇杀。她们被描绘成诡计多端、心狠手辣、傲慢自负的人，容不得丝毫侮慢。恩加尔，这位一心维护和平的人，对妻子煽动两个儿子不服管束的做法无能为力。加纳不幸爱上了哈尔格德。哈尔格德是一个危险的悍妇，已经导致两个前夫的死亡，加纳和她结婚后，碰到没完没了的麻烦。当加纳最后在自己家中遭到埋伏，请求她帮忙时，她却记起有一次他打了她的嘴巴，因此在人命关天的时刻，竟然拒绝给予帮助。然而，《冰岛传奇》的作者们却把妇女的这种反叛性与复仇心认作是人类生活中不可避免的一部分，甚至对她们的泼辣和任性表示尊重。他们没有表现出任何厌恶女性、决心与女人对抗的迹象。但在《水浒传》中，虽然女人惹事的范围实际上要小得多，读者却反而注意到突出的厌恶女性的倾向。①

夏志清通过比较的方法，让我们直接感受到《水浒传》与冰岛传奇两者之间对待女性态度的天壤之别。很明显，在对待女性上，前者持敌视、对抗的极端化态度，后者则表现出尊敬的一面，这在《水浒传》中基本上不存在。

夏志清认为，《水浒传》所表现出来的这种对待女性的仇视、对抗的极端化态度，首先是由水浒世界的男人即通常所说的英雄好汉对女性性别差异与社会地位的理解与认识决定的。古代中国，是绝对的男人中心社会，男性是主、女性为奴，女性只是他们的所有物，对女性的"三从"规定已经决定了她们的命运。而决定这种理解与认识的更深一层的则是水浒世界的这些英雄们所坚守的禁欲主义，而禁欲主义思想的来源则是中国文化传统中世界阴、阳二分的观念。男性为阳，女性为阴，耽于阴则损阳。在此种思想观念的影响或者可以说是束缚之下，水浒世界的英雄好汉以不近女色为对自己意志的一大考验。即使那些已有家室的好汉们，如卢俊义，为了习练武艺、打熬筋骨，根本不会顾及贾氏的心理感受与需要。其结果，这些好汉们与那些妇女们就成了无法沟通的异类。对此，夏志清说：

《水浒传》中的妇女并不仅仅是因为心毒和不贞而遭严惩，归根

---

① [美]夏志清：《中国古典小说》，胡益民等译，江苏文艺出版社2008年版，第101页。

到底，她们受难受罚就因为她们是女人，是供人泄欲的冤屈无告的生灵。心理上的隔阂使严于律己的好汉们与她们格格不入。正是由于他们的禁欲主义，这些英雄下意识地仇视女性，视女性为大敌，是对他们那违反自然的英雄式自我满足的嘲笑。①

而当那些女性僭越英雄们的信条，或为了自己的生理需要而偷夫养汉从而对这些英雄好汉的声誉造成不良影响时，她们的下场是非常悲惨的。夏志清说：

> 欺骗和残忍成了她们满足性要求的手段。她们的克星——正直可敬的英雄好汉们，都仇恨她们那种对欢乐的渴望和对生活的追求。他们把她们处死，以使英雄的信条的履行得到保证。②

在夏志清看来，像杨雄对潘巧云的残忍报复，显然是一种非理性的行为。

从现代人的视角来看，尤其是站在西方文化与文学传统来看，水浒世界这种在禁欲主义观念操控之下的对待女性的敌视态度，的确是一种非理性行为，也有对"英雄式自我满足"的嘲讽意味。

二、孙述宇从"厌女症"到"红颜祸水"论

在夏志清提出"厌女症"后不久，孙述宇对水浒世界的女性观也作了一番研究。1973年，他发表了一篇题为《水浒传的煽动艺术——厌女症者抑或亡命之徒？》的英文文章。孙氏在该文章中指出：

> 《水浒传》这部非常特殊的作品烙上了显著的阳性创作印痕。这不仅是以男性为中心的所谓"男性沙文主义"，更是对女性极端的残忍。其他著作可能集中描写男人的事务，只关注男性美德，或者描绘一系列没有女人的男性形象，却极少表现出如此极端的敌视女性的态度。因为流淌着男性的血液，这部作品对女性甚至有更高的死亡率。

---

① ［美］夏志清：《中国古典小说》，胡益民等译，江苏文艺出版社2008年版，第101页。
② 同上。

这些女性大都淫荡、低劣，她们传递出的这种基调在侮辱与痛斥之间变动。大部分读者可能赞同夏志清教授用"厌女症"一词来描绘这种态度。……然而，"厌女症"有不同的含义。说小说不描写对妇女的同情是一个方面，坚持认为小说作者与读者表现出变态的性心理征兆是另一个方面。毫无疑问，《水浒传》对女性是不友好的，但如果我们想要理解小说的艺术，就应该对这个不友好的态度进行分析和研究，而不是草率地贴个标签。这种态度的形成归因于当时的中国社会与文化，这是值得我们关注的课题。①

从这个论述中可以看出，孙述宇认为在对待女性的态度上，我们不能草率地给《水浒传》贴上"厌女症"的标签，而应该深入分析、研究作品中仇视女性态度的形成原因。在他看来，这是一个历史问题，有其特定的社会、文化语境。对此，孙述宇指出："由于旧中国是一个男权中心社会，《水浒传》反映这样的现实，自然就把女性降格到次要的位置。"②

但即便如此，水浒世界却并不完全厌恶女性、女色。孙述宇指出："仔细考察，水浒世界并不久完全憎恶女色，作品中也有个别获得赞美的女子。"③ 孙氏说："小说虽然降低她们的社会地位，却让她们享受到很好

---

① *Shui Hu Chuan (The Water Margin)* strikes one as a very peculiar book of masculine creation. It not only is centered about men and may deservedly be called "male-chauvinistic", but also is exceedingly cruel to women. Other books may focus on men's business, take note of only manly virtues, or present a cast of men without women, yet few appear to be so hostile to the other sex. Dripping as it is with men's blood, this book has an even higher mortality rate for female. These females are mostly lewd or mean, and the tone in which they are presented alternated between the abusive and the derisive. Most readers will agree with Professor C. T. Hsia's use of the term of *misogyny* in characterizing this attitude.... However, *misogyny* has different meanings. To say descriptively that the novel is not sympathetic to women is one thing, to assert interpretatively that its authors and their audiences show symptoms of abnormal sexual psychology is quite another. Beyond question, *The Water Margin* is not friendly toward women, but this unfriendliness should be analysed and studied rather than branded summarily if we want to understand the art of the novel. What this attitude owes to the society and culture of China of those days is a subject that merits our attention. Phillip S. Y. Sun, The Sedtitious Art of The Water Margin-Misogynists or Desperadoes?, Renditions Autumn (1973), p. 99.

② Since the old Chinese society was man-centered, *The Water Margin*, reflecting this reality, naturally relegates women to an inferior position. Phillip S. Y. Sun, The Sedtitious Art of The Water Margin-Misogynists or Desperadoes?, Renditions Autumn (1973), p. 99.

③ To be accurate, the world of *The Water Margin* does not hate the female sex as a whole. There are individual good women commended in the book. Phillip S. Y. Sun, The Sedtitious Art of The Water Margin-Misogynists or Desperadoes?, Renditions Autumn (1973), p. 102.

第五章 英语世界对《水浒传》的主题思想研究　　305

的艺术待遇。"只是由于敌视女性的心理与思想观念作祟,小说在描写、塑造女性形象时的确常常进行极端化的处理。这在上文"男权社会中的水浒女性形象塑造"部分已经讨论过。那么,为什么旧中国这个男权中心社会会形成对女性的仇视态度呢?为什么水浒世界的英雄们不可能像《冰岛传奇》中的那些男人一样展现出对女性尊敬的一面呢?究竟水浒世界的英雄视女人为何物?我们且来看孙述宇的进一步分析。

孙述宇认为,水浒世界女性观的形成,首先源于对男女柔情的不认可,其次是视女人为不祥之物(inauspicious)。孙氏说:

> 《水浒传》对妇女的仇视源于对男女柔情的不认可态度。因为男女柔情是不好的,漂亮的女子遭受猜疑,总体上也被视为不祥之物。由此我们可以宣告,真正的英雄是用不着女色的。即使和其他地方的人一样,中国人也认为缺少漂亮女伴的英雄不是完美的英雄,梁山好汉却远离女性,他们比许多和尚、道士更加虔诚地信守独身生活的誓言。第32回,宋江催促矮脚虎王英释放刘高妻子时,曾如此说:欲成为真正的英雄,必须内心纯净,不受女色的诱惑①。小说对待肉体欲望的态度,渲染上了宗教迷信的色彩;在这方面,梁山英雄比现实主义作品具有更多虚构、杜撰的成分。②

的确,水浒世界的英雄们是不认可男女柔情的。没有家室的那些好汉自不必说,就是曾经有过妻室的——如宋江与阎婆惜、杨雄与潘巧云、卢俊义与贾氏,他们也根本不在意或者说不懂得男女之间的鱼水之情。如第

---

① 小说中宋江原话是这样的:"原来王英兄弟,要贪女色,不是好汉的勾当。""但凡好汉犯了'溜骨髓'三个字的,好生惹人耻笑。"(明)施耐庵:《水浒传》(120回本),上海古籍出版社2009年版,第291、2292页。

② The hostility against women in *The Water Margin* stens from a basic attitude that frowns upon amorous passion. Since passion is not good, charming women are received with suspicion and generally regarded as inauspicious. From this we have the pronouncement that true heroes have no use for feminine beauty. Despite the fact that in China as elsewhere people consider a hero's image incomplete without an attractive lady companion, the Liangshan heroes stay away from women, keeping the vow of celibacy. In chapter 32, Sung Chiang, urging Wang Ying the short-legged Tiger to foreswear Liu Kao's wife, states so many words that to be a true hero one must be pure in mind and impregnable to lust and temptation. The attitude toward physical desire in the novel is coloured by religion and superstition; the Liangshan heroes are more mythical than realistic creations in this respect. Phillip S. Y. Sun, The Sedtitious Art of The Water Margin-Misogynists or Desperadoes?, Renditions Autumn (1973), p. 101.

24回写宋江纳阎婆惜为外室的那段：

> 初时宋江夜夜与婆惜一处歇卧，向后渐渐来得慢了。却是为何？原来宋江是个好汉，只爱学枪使棒，于女色上不十分要紧。这阎婆惜水也似后生，况兼十八九岁，正在妙龄之际，因此宋江不中那婆娘意。①

此话告诉我们的，一方面是梁山好汉的不近女色，另一方面是这些好汉对女性的不理解。或者如下文即将讨论到的吴燕娜提出的"恐女症"那样，其实是女性的性能力威胁到了好汉们的自尊和声誉。此问题留待下文再论。

由于水浒世界的英雄们不认可男女柔情，再加上当时男权社会盛行的男尊女卑观念，很自然地，女人只是好汉们生活中的某种工具——因为好汉不近女色，当然就不是如上文夏志清说的"是供人泄欲的冤屈无告的生灵"（女人可能是如西门庆一类人泄欲的工具，但不是水浒英雄泄欲的工具）。那么，在水浒世界的英雄们眼里，那些女性究竟是什么呢？孙述宇说，《水浒传》对阎婆惜、潘金莲、潘巧云以及贾氏等人的男欢女爱的要求是持谴责态度的，从作品的描写来看，那些女性应该抑制自己的欲望，像女舍监（matron）一样操持家务，从而让她们的丈夫能够整天耍枪弄棒、打熬筋骨②。的确，在那些已成家室的梁山好汉心里，他们的妻子在日常生活中就应该是操持家务的女舍监，而在性需求上则应该是被阉割的女太监。

而说到女人是不祥之物，这更是中国几千年来根深蒂固的观念。对《水浒传》反映出来的"女人祸水"、"红颜祸水"的思想，孙述宇说，在作品中，不仅坏女人害男人，就是好女人也害男人。他指出：

---

① （明）施耐庵：《水浒传》（120回本），上海古籍出版社2009年版，第174—175页。
② The world of *The Water Margin*, needless to say, condemns these wives unreservedly, for in its view they should bave suppressed their ungratified desire and managed the home like a good matron, so that their husbands could spend allthier time defriending like-minded heroes, exercising their bodies and practising weapons together This is the way of life of the married Liangshan heroes, who all prefer the battlefield to the bed. Phillip S. Y. Sun, The Sedtitious Art of The Water Margin-Misogynists or Desperadoes?, Renditions Autumn (1973), p. 101.

读者老是听见男人吃了女人亏的故事：潘金莲和王婆害武松兄弟；潘巧云害石秀、杨雄；阎婆惜害宋江；卢俊义的妻子害卢俊义；白秀英害雷横。……林冲的故事更是惊人。上面的例子还都是坏女人害男人，林冲的事却表示好女人也害男人。①

作品中类似的故事还有不少，不一一列举。综合小说所描写的这些人物故事，确实可以得出女人是不吉的看法。

通过考察中国文学的发展历史，孙述宇说："除了水浒文学这小小的一支外，都没有敌视妇女。"② 那为什么《水浒传》会表现出如此不可理喻的对女性的仇视态度呢？除上面提到的大的社会历史文化语境之外，孙氏还给出下面的解释。他说：

依我们看，像水浒文学所表现的对于女性的猜疑，用法外强徒的亡命心态来解释最妥当。厌弃女色的倾向，在为了一己生命而焦虑的人当中是很常见的，渴望永生的僧侣修士如此，与死亡为邻的草泽崔苻亦如此。过去的强盗有"阴人不吉"的迷信，又有"劫财不劫色"的道德戒条，并不是没来由的。（当然，盗匪与士兵都会强暴妇女，但那种事情总是发生在他们的安全得到保障之后）我们相信水浒故事是法外强徒所作，他们创作的目的，既为娱乐，也为教育。任何战斗队伍都希望成员远离妇女的，因为妇女会销蚀他们的作战意志，延误行动，增加泄露秘密的危险；反之，不接近妇女的队伍，作战效率高，与地方民众的关系也容易好。因此，《水浒》对于女性不仅流露出厌恶之情，而且着意攻击。③

从《水浒传》展现法外强徒的亡命心态的角度来解释作品中仇视女性态度的形成来源，有一定的道理。毕竟水浒世界确实是一个草莽英雄亡命天涯的世界。

---

① 孙述宇：《水浒传：怎样的强盗书》，上海古籍出版社2011年版，第27页。
② 同上书，第239页。
③ 同上。

三、吴燕娜论水浒世界的"厌女症"与"恐女症"

就水浒世界的女性观,吴燕娜则认为,在"厌女症"之下人们对所谓的"荡妇"加以无情的痛斥和责骂,而在这种痛斥与责骂声中,恰好表现出他们对女性的恐惧感。该论者说:

> 在痛斥荡妇时,《水浒传》——不论是精英分子抑或普通大众——潜在地表达了对女性破坏力的恐惧。与之相关,为了强调结义兄弟的伦理道德,小说中只出现了极少的几个女性。而在这些女性中,形成相对的两种类型,一是体格健壮的女英雄,一是妖魅的荡妇,两者构成有趣的对比。这部小说的主题,倾向于排斥家庭要求,尤其是女性。因此,它所展现出来的为团体利益而战的女英雄富有生命力,而自私自利的荡妇则必然遭遇可怕的死亡。①

而这些"荡妇"的自私自利是为了什么呢?按夏志清之论就是"满足性要求"。像宋江、卢俊义、杨雄这些英雄们,他们恰恰视"性"、"房事"为侵蚀他们筋骨、耗损他们元气的洪水猛兽。而在男人之外,"性"与"房事"直接指向的则是女性。很显然,在这些英雄们的眼中,女性就是那洪水猛兽的根源,也就是危险的根源。自然而然,女性就成为英雄恐惧的对象。对此,吴燕娜指出:

> 小说中,禁欲主义是由那些疏远女性的男性强人凸显出来的。对缺乏安全感的这些人来说,女人的危险之处正是因为她们的性能力。妖魅的女子会消耗男人的精力,男女之间的床笫之欢会耗费、耽误他们的习武时间。女人,尤其是那些给她们丈夫戴绿帽子的女人,因为

---

① In excoriating the femme fatale, *The Water Margin* (*Shuihu zhuan*) expresses the fear of potentionally destructive women by both the elite and the populace. Relatively few women appear in the novel that stresses the ethic of sworn brotherhood. Among them, two contrasting types, the physically strong, martial women and the seductive adulteresses, offer an interesting comparison. The novel's theme tends to exclude the claims of family, especially those of women, and so it shows martial women (who fight for the interest of the group) prospering, and seductresses (who act for self-interest) meeting ghastly deaths. Yenna Wu, Condemnation: Other Fiction, The Chinese Virago: A Literary Theme. Literature Criticism from 1400 to 1800. Ed. Lynn M. Zott. Vol. 76. Cambridge: Harvard University Press, 1995, p. 106.

她们是"性欲强烈的动物"而遭受惩罚。①

从小说对宋江与阎婆惜、杨雄与潘巧云、卢俊义与贾氏的描写，以及对晁盖等人"不娶妻室，终日只是打熬筋骨"的描写来看，甚至如果撇开伦理道德因素，武松对待潘金莲的描写也可包括在内，这些水浒英雄的确视女性为危险之物。

只不过，在吴燕娜看来，小说中女性的威胁不仅因为她们的"性能力"，更在于她们对男性的大胆背叛，而在这背叛背后则是对男权中心的威胁。对此，她说：

> 然而，性能力仅仅构成女性威胁的一部分。正是她们对自己男人的大胆反叛，让她们成为男性憎恨的对象。荡妇潘金莲、阎婆惜、潘巧云遭受可怕的死亡，并非主要因为她们的性欲，而是她们威胁到男性的团结和家长制的秩序。金莲的危险，是因为她侮辱并最终杀害了自己那长相粗陋的丈夫。而且，她还试图在武大与武松之间制造不和。引诱武松失败后，她还诽谤说武松调戏了她。
>
> 宋江尚能容忍姘妇阎婆惜的通奸。但当她敲诈、威胁说要揭发宋江与梁山之间的关系时，宋江就被激怒了。②

在吴燕娜看来，潘巧云的惨死虽与前两者有所不同，但根本原因还是

---

① In the novel sexual puritanism is emphasized by the male outlaws' alienation from women. To the insecure outlaws, women are dangerous because of their sexual power. Temptresses sap a man's power, and sexual dalliance takes time away from martial training. Women, particularly those who cuckold their husbands, are punished for being "creatures of lust." Yenna Wu, Condemnation: Other Fiction, The Chinese Virago: A Literary Theme. Literature Criticism from 1400 to 1800. Ed. Lynn M. Zott. Vol. 76. Cambridge: Harvard University Press, 1995, p. 107.

② Yet sexual power constitutes only one part of the women's threat. It is their daring to rebel against men that makes them the object of male hatred. The adulteresses Pan Jinlian, Yan Poxi, and Pan Qiaoyun deserve gruesome deaths not so much because of their sexuality, but because they threaten male solidarity and the patriarchal order. Jinlian is dangerous because she bullies, and finally poisons, her weakling of a husband. Moreover, she attempts to sow discord between him and his brother. 4 Having failed to seduce her brother, she slanders him by claiming that he has made sexual advances toward her.
Song Jiang would have tolerated the adultery of his mistress Yan Poxi. But when she blackmails him by threatening to disclose his connection with the outlaws, he is provoked into violence. Yenna Wu, Condemnation: Other Fiction, The Chinese Virago: A Literary Theme. Literature Criticism from 1400 to 1800. Ed. Lynn M. Zott. Vol. 76. Cambridge: Harvard University Press, 1995, p. 107.

在对男性团结与家长制秩序的威胁。吴燕娜指出：

> 与金莲、婆惜不一样，潘巧云既不侮辱也不公开刺激她的丈夫，而是假装顺从以赢得丈夫的怜悯，而后诬陷他的结义兄弟石秀，因为石秀知道她与和尚裴如海通奸的事。如果没有后来石秀杀死潘巧云的情夫裴如海，揭露出她的背叛，杨雄几乎破坏了自己与石秀之间的结义兄弟之情。①

按吴燕娜之论，水浒女性所遭受的惩罚，源于她们对水浒英雄的背叛，源于她们对以男性为中心的既定的社会秩序带来的威胁；水浒世界的男人对女性的仇视与恐惧，只是那些男人对女性带来的威胁的一种本能的回应。因为在那之前，水浒英雄都是高出女人一头的，而在女人们的背叛行为发出之后，以他们为中心的世界就面临着垮塌的危险，因而他们就会对那些背叛他们的女人采取极端残忍的手段。

从夏志清"厌女症"的提出到孙述宇法外强徒"女人祸水"论的阐释，再到吴燕娜"恐女症"的进一步挖掘，英语世界的批评者对水浒世界女性观的研究在逐渐深入。而在他们的研究视野中，男权中心社会秩序始终是讨论的核心问题。

---

① Unlike Jinlian or Poxi, Pan Qiaoyun neither bullies nor openly defies her husband. Rather, she feigns submissiveness to win her husband's pity and then slanders his sworn brother, because he knows about her adulterous affair with a monk. Her husband would have broken up with the sworn brother if the latter had not killed the wife's paramour and thus revealed her betrayal. Yenna Wu, Condemnation: Other Fiction, The Chinese Virago: A Literary Theme. Literature Criticism from 1400 to 1800. Ed. Lynn M. Zott. Vol. 76. Cambridge: Harvard University Press, 1995, p. 107.

结 语

《水浒传》不仅是中国文学的经典，也是世界文学的经典。自其诞生之日起，就为中国社会各阶层广泛接受；上至文人士大夫下至市井细民，都拥有大量的受众。《水浒传》因其蕴含如现代批评者所说的"革命造反"的思想因素，在社会动荡的时代，往往在思想乃至行军作战的战略、策略上对农民起义具有鼓动、指导的作用。因此，在明末清中前期，《水浒传》屡遭朝廷禁毁。但政治手段终究无法消灭一部文学巨著，经历上百年的风雨沧桑，《水浒传》强大的生命力并未减弱丝毫。从19世纪末20世纪初以来，因其雅俗共赏的特性，以及受政治因素的影响，《水浒传》更是在中国社会掀起一波又一波的接受、批评、研究的高潮。

在中国长篇叙事文学的发展史上，《水浒传》与《三国演义》一样都具有里程碑的意义。但与《三国演义》"按史演义"的创作方式不同，《水浒传》的创作如金圣叹所说是"因文生事"，虚构成分远超过历史事实。而且《水浒传》描写塑造的是社会中下层那些桀骜不驯、充满血性，甚至于违背当时官方主流思想——儒家的伦理道德规范的草莽英雄，这就使《水浒传》在主题思想、文化意蕴上呈现出与时代截然有别的特点。因其塑造的人物形象、表现的思想内容的别具一格，因其在文体形式上的开拓性地位，这些因素的综合，使其成为中、外学术界中国古典小说研究的典范，关注的焦点。

1840年的鸦片战争，不仅重新开启中外文化、文学传播、交流的大门，更是在极大的程度上加速了中外文化、文学传播、交流的进程。在"西学东渐"的同时，也掀起一股中国古代文化、文学典籍"西游"的潮流。而正是在此中国古代文化、文学典籍"西游"的潮流中，《水浒传》

开始了它的"西行之旅"。

　　本书以英语世界的《水浒传》研究为研究对象，属于个案研究的范畴，也是对海外汉学研究的反馈性研究。笔者选取英语世界的《水浒传》研究这一个案作为本课题的研究对象，目的在通过梳理分析《水浒传》这个在中国古代叙事文学中具有典范意义的文本在英语世界的总体研究情况，希冀从中探索海外汉学研究、即明清小说研究的基本规律，包括研究方法、研究主题、研究机制及其存在的问题。这一研究对象的选择，决定了笔者首先要解决的就是文献资料的搜索问题。历经近两年的时间，笔者通过各种途径，花费重大的经济代价，虽然未能把英语学界研究《水浒传》的所有文献一一收入囊中，但十之八九还是到了手上；特别是那些非常重要的、极具代表性的研究文章、专著与学位论文，可以说基本上都搜寻到了。只是限于笔者的学识、学力，在材料的分析处理上，难免挂一漏万、出现差池。在此，诚挚希望得到国内外专家、学者的批评、指正，并不吝提供宝贵意见。

　　《水浒传》在英语学术界的接受、研究，经历了一个不断深入发展的过程。从19世纪70年代水浒人物故事的选译到20世纪30年代赛珍珠翻译的第一个《水浒传》全译本的出现，再到杰克逊、沙博理与登特—扬父子合译的三种《水浒传》全译本的出版发行，这是《水浒传》英译走过的百年历程。从1898年出版的乔治·康德林的《中国小说·水浒传》，到1953年格雷格·欧文撰写的第一部《水浒传》英文研究专著《一部中国小说的演变：〈水浒传〉》的出版；从20世纪80年代至今，在浦安迪的带领下，以吴德安、德波特等人为核心的美国普林斯顿大学《水浒传》研究阵地的形成，再到散布在各高校与研究机构的批评者如韩南、夏志清、孙述宇、李培德、李惠仪、吴燕娜等人对《水浒传》所作的研究……所有这些，构成了百余年来英语学术界《水浒传》研究的基本框架。

　　经过一百余年的发展、锤炼，英语世界的《水浒传》研究不断成长、成熟。到目前为止，已基本形成了一套具有相当代表性的研究方法、研究范式，并形成了比较明确的研究主题。

　　从研究方法、研究范式的层面来看，由于英语世界的《水浒传》研究具有跨语言、跨文化、跨民族国家界限的特性，属于典型的比较文学学科范畴的研究论题，因而拥有非常宽广的研究视野，这也就为英语世界的

《水浒传》研究者提供了展开平行比较的天然的优越条件。比较方法的运用贯穿英语世界《水浒传》研究的全过程。这种平行比较，既有针对《水浒传》与其他中国古典小说的，也有针对《水浒传》与西方文学作品的；既有主题思想、文化意蕴方面的，也有文体形式、艺术手法方面的；还有很重要的一个方面就是人物形象塑造的比较研究。

比较研究之外，阐释研究是英语世界《水浒传》研究中另一个常见的方法。英语学界对《水浒传》的阐释研究，经历了由单向阐释到双向阐释的发展过程。不过，不论是单向阐释还是双向阐释，都存在参照系的选择问题。对那些比较纯粹的欧美文化、文学教育背景出身的研究者来说，他们基本上是以西方文化、文学的标准来批评《水浒传》。在很长一段时间里，这一部分研究者的看法与观点烙上了相当浓厚的文化帝国主义的色彩。对那些具有比较丰富的中国传统文化与文学学习、研究经历的批评者，以及那些从小享受中国传统文化与文学教育的、由中国学界进入英语学界的"脱中入英"的华裔批评者来说，他们则能够更多考虑中国的传统文学观念与批评标准，并使其与西方的文学批评思想与批评理论相结合，这一部分研究者的结论就相对更为全面、客观些。

比较研究与阐释研究之外，对原始文献进行索引、考证也是英语世界《水浒传》研究的一个重要研究方法。

从研究主题的层面来看，百余年来，英语世界的《水浒传》研究主要形成了如下几个研究主题，包括：小说作者研究，小说版本与成书研究，小说的流传接受与影响研究，小说人物形象研究，作品的主题思想与历史文化研究，作品的文体形式与艺术风格研究，等等。在这些研究主题中，又以人物形象研究、主题思想与历史文化研究以及文体形式与艺术风格研究为主。而相对来说，这几个方面也是研究的最深、最广、最成熟的；不仅涉足者多，对《水浒传》文本的挖掘也最为深入，同时批评者们提出的看法和观点也相对丰富、多元。

上述英语世界《水浒传》研究的基本方法，以及在研究过程中形成的基本主题，与中国学界的基本研究方法与研究主题是比较一致的。当然，在中国学界与英语学界的《水浒传》研究中，由于文化环境、学术背景、切入视角、知识体系构成等方面的差异性，就是面对同一问题，不同批评者提出的具体看法和观点仍然存在很大的差异，有时甚至是完全对立的。而据笔者的了解，英语世界《水浒传》研究中运用的基本方法与形成的基本主题，在海外中国明清小说研究中是具有相当代表性的。

本书的结构安排围绕着上述英语世界《水浒传》研究的基本主题展开。这种结构安排很平实，能够比较好地把握英语世界《水浒传》研究的总体状况，有助于把批评者的看法和观点非常清晰地呈现出来。不过，由于本课题关注的是英语世界《水浒传》研究过程中形成的小说作者研究，小说版本与成书研究，小说的流传接受与影响研究，小说人物形象研究，作品的主题思想与历史文化研究，作品的文体形式与艺术风格研究等基本主题，这就把"英语世界《水浒传》研究综述"部分提到的那些讨论"较小主题"的、研究内容又不足以构成相应章节的研究成果舍弃掉了。这对笔者来说是非常无奈又非常遗憾的，因为这让本书无法全面、系统地展现出英语世界《水浒传》研究的全貌。

不过从总体来看，本课题只是对英语世界《水浒传》研究状况所作的反馈性研究的开始，其中不少问题还有待进一步深入发掘。这正是笔者在此基础之上还需要完成的后续研究。而沿着像本书这样对英语世界的《水浒传》研究进行的反馈性研究的思路前进，笔者以为，我们完全可以在这种对海外汉学所作的个案研究的基础上再向前、向上迈进，从而上升到分析、总结、提炼海外汉学的总体研究范式、研究机制的层面；纵使无法混溶所有，但至少可以从文体的角度来切入、展开。这则是在海外汉学的反馈性研究中必须设立的学术目标和学术追求，也是对海外汉学反馈性研究进一步深入发展的必然要求。

在《水浒传》的基本研究方法与研究主题方面，英语学术界与中国学术界是比较一致的。然而，英语世界的批评者在小说文本细读、比照、分析论述过程中所展现出来的学术态度与学术追求，有很多是值得中国学术界的同行学习、借鉴的。在英语世界的研究者中，像赛珍珠、韩南、李培德、浦安迪、吴德安诸人，他们在《水浒传》的研究中，往往具有强烈的理论建构意识和学术目的，而非仅仅针对某一具体问题、具体现象草草了事，而是希望通过对那些具体的问题和现象的探讨，摸索出具有规律性的观点和认识。以对《水浒传》的叙事结构的研究为例，韩南提出"联合布局"与"顶层结构"的观点，李培德提出"主题单元"与"环状结构"的观点，浦安迪提出"神话框架"、"撞球式"与"聚而复散"的结构模式。吴德安则在吸收前人研究成果的基础上，通过对小说文本全面、系统的分析讨论，构建起《水浒传》的三大基本结构原则，从而有力地论证了自己提出的小说作者在创作过程中对小说叙事结构进行了精心构思的看法。在"平衡对称"结构原则的研究上，浦安迪、吴德安通过大量地分析明清时期的小说文本，并在此基础上把它提升到中国古典小说的"一般美学"特征。这样的研究态度和研究方式，这样的学术追求和学术目标，与简单地争论《水浒传》的结构是有机的还是非有机的两相比较，显然更具有学术意义和学术价值。

而且像赛珍珠、浦安迪与吴德安等人，他们的研究往往扎根于中国文化与文学的传统之中，从中国的历史、哲学与社会文化内部，来探寻像《水浒传》这样的中国古典小说在思想意蕴、文体形式、叙事艺术、人物塑造等方面的特质形成的根本原因。以浦安迪的《中国叙事学》为例，该论者深入《尚书·尧典》等中国古籍来挖掘中国文学叙述中形成的"空间化的思维方式"的古老来源。对中国学术界来说，像浦氏这样的研究，显然非常有益于我们构建中国叙事学的具体观点和理论。

"他山之石，可以攻玉。"本课题的意义和价值，如上文所论述的那样，不只是把英语世界对《水浒传》的研究资料舶回来，把那些研究者的看法和观点舶回来，而在通过反馈性的研究，通过"他者"的眼睛，让我们知晓"彼岸"的精彩及其存在的问题，并从中寻找、发现可资借鉴的方面，从而明确未来的目标和研究方向，把我们的《水浒传》研究推向一个更新、更高的层次。

附录

中英文人名、术语译名对照表（A – Z）

阿莱克斯·登特—扬　Alex Dent-Young
按史演义　romanticized history
巴赞　A. P. L. Bazin
白之（西里尔·伯奇）　Cyril Birch
比较文学与总体文学年鉴　Yearbook of Comparative and General Literature
毕晓普　John L. Bishop
词话　tz'u-hua
查尔斯·艾尔博　Charles J. Alber
丹尼斯·沃什本　Dennis Washburn
单一布局小说　unitary fiction
顶层结构　superstructure
底本　prompt-book
德波特　Deborah Lynn Porter
东方研究丛刊　Journal of Oriental Studies
东方文学杂志　Journal of Oriental Literature
反面英雄人物　negative character
菲茨杰拉德　C. P. Fitrgenald
故事环　story cycles
古德里奇（富路特）　L. C. Goodrich
哈佛亚洲研究杂志　Harvard Jounal of Asiatic-Studies
韩南　Patric Hanan
汉斯·弗兰克　Hans H. Frankle
海陶伟　J. R. Hightower
何谷理　Hegel E. Rober
合传　joined biographies
环状链　a cyclical chain
黄宗泰　Wong Timothy
话本　hua-pen
华裔学志　Monumenta Serica
昏君　hun jun, "muddle-headed"
奸相　bad minister
季节循环　seasonal cycle
杰弗里·邓洛普　Geoffrey Dunlop
杰克逊　J. N. Jackson
柯文　C. A. Curwen
空间安排模式　patterns of spatial arrangement

赖明　Ming Lai
联合布局作品　linked works
联合布局　linked-plot
李惠仪　Wai-yee Li
李培德　Peter li
理查德·G. 欧文　Richard Gregg Irwin
列传形式　biographical form
罗伯特·鲁尔曼　Robert Ruhlmann
卢庆滨　Andrew Hing-bun Lo
龙安妮　Anne Farrer
陆大卫　Rolston David Lee
吕立亭　Tina Lu
刘若愚　James J. Y. Liu
马克林　Colin Patrick Mackerras
美国亚洲评论　The American Asian Rewiew
美国东方社会杂志　Journal of the American Oriental Society
梅维恒　Victor H. Mair
末代昏君　bad last ruler
内部结构　internal structure
浦安迪　Adrew H. plaks
旁观者　Spectator
乔什·维托　Josh Vittor
清华学报（台湾）　Tsing Hua Journal of Chinese Studies
邱贵芬　Chiu Kuei-fen
日月演进　the progression of months and days
人物配对原则　the principle of paired characters

人物拆分原则　the principle of refraction of characters
沙博理（西德尼·夏皮罗）　Sidey Shapiro
赛珍珠　Pearl S. Buck
神话框架　supernatural framework
四大奇书　Ssu ta ch'i-shu
沈静　Jing Shen
商伟　Shang Wei
施友忠　Vincent Shih
书生型英雄　the scholar-heroes
松科尔　B. Csongon
孙康宜　Kang-i Sun Chang
孙述宇　Sun Phillip S. Y
太平洋事务　Pacific Affairs
天书　heavenly book
通报　T'ong pao
外部结构模型　external pattern
王德威　David Der-wei Wang
王靖宇　Wang John C. Y
魏爱莲（艾伦·魏德玛）　Widmer Ellen
武士型英雄　the swordsman-hero
吴杰克　Wu Jack
吴德安　Swihart De-an Wu
吴燕娜　Yenna Wu
西方人文评论　Western Humanities Review
侠　hsia
夏志清　Hsia C. T.
小川环树　Ogawa Tamaki
谢诺　Jean-Chesneauz

新亚学院学报　New Asia Academic Bulletin
形象叠用原则　the principle of figural recurrence
星主　Star Lord
胥吏　hsü-li
亚洲专刊　Asia Major
亚瑟·赖特　Arthur Wright
厌女症　misogyny
伊爱莲　Irene Eber
义气　yiqi
于鸿远　HongyuanYu
雨月物语　Ugetsu Monogatari
约翰·登特—扬　John Dent-Young
杂剧　tsa-chü
翟理思　H. A. Giles
翟楚　Chuchai
翟文伯　Wingberg Chai
詹姆斯·克伦普　James I. Crump
詹姆斯·欧文　James Irving
詹纳尔　Jenner W. J. F
正面英雄人物　positive heroes
整体结构模型　overall pattern
至善　immense good
芝加哥评论　Chicago Review
中国文学：论文、文章、评论　Chinese Literature：Essays, Articles, Reviews
"撞球式"　the "billiard ball"
主题单元　unity of theme
朱迪思·T. 蔡特林　Judith T. Zeitlin

参考文献

中文文献

（一）作品类

（清）陈忱：《水浒后传》，凤凰出版社2008年版。

（明）兰陵笑笑生：《金瓶梅词话》，人民文学出版社2000年版。

（明）罗贯中：《水浒志传评林》（上、下卷，影印120回简本），余象斗评，沈阳出版社2012年版。

（明）青莲室主人辑：《后水浒传》，中国经济出版社2012年版。

［日］上田秋成：《雨月物语》，王新禧译，新世界出版社2010年版。

《水浒传会评本》（上、下卷），陈曦钟、侯忠义、鲁玉川辑校，北京大学出版社1981年版。

《水浒传名家汇平本》（上、下卷），宋杰辑，北京图书馆出版社2008年版。

（明）施耐庵、罗贯中：《水浒传》（百回本，上、下卷），（明）李贽评，上海古籍出版社1988年版。

（明）施耐庵、罗贯中：《水浒传》（上、下卷，亚东图书馆藏本），汪元放校点，北岳文艺出版社2013年版。

（明）施耐庵：《古本水浒传》（一百二十回本，上、下卷），蒋祖钢校勘，中央民族大学出版社1996年版。

（明）施耐庵：《水浒传》（七十回本），（清）《金圣叹评》，凤凰出版社2010年版。

（明）施耐庵：《水浒传》（一百二十回本），上海古籍出版社2009

年版。

（清）俞万春：《荡寇志》（上、下卷），人民文学出版社2006年版。

《古本小说集成》编委会编：《宣和遗事·插增田虎王庆忠义水浒全传》，上海古籍出版社1992年版。

（二）著作类

［美］爱德华·萨义德：《文化与帝国主义》，李琨译，生活·读书·新知三联书店2003年版。

［美］爱德华·萨义德：《东方学》，王宇根译，生活·读书·新知三联书店1999年版。

［奥］彼得·V.齐马：《比较文学导论》，范劲、高晓倩译，安徽教育出版社2009年版。

［法］布吕奈尔、比叔瓦、卢梭：《什么是比较文学》，葛雷、张连奎译，北京大学出版社1988年版。

曹顺庆主编：《东方文论选》，四川人民出版社1996年版。

曹顺庆主编：《比较文学新开拓》，重庆大学出版社2000年版。

曹顺庆等著：《比较文学学科理论研究》，巴蜀书社2001年版。

曹顺庆主编：《比较文学教程》，高等教育出版社2006年版。

曹顺庆主编：《比较文学学科史》，巴蜀书社2010年版。

陈敬：《赛珍珠与中国——中西文化冲突与共融》，南开大学出版社2006年版。

陈建功主编：插图本品读《水浒传》，山东画报出版社2005年版。

［法］梵第根：《比较文学论》，戴望舒译，吉林出版社2010年版。

陈松柏：《水浒传源流考证》，人民文学出版社2006年版。

陈友冰主编、吴薇编著：《新时期中国古典文学研究述论》（第四卷）《元明清近代》，商务印书馆2006年版。

陈文新、鲁小俊、王同舟：《明清章回小说流派研究》，武汉大学出版社2003年版。

戴不凡：《小说见闻录》，浙江人民出版社1980年版。

方正耀：《中国古典小说理论史》，郭豫适审定，华东师范大学出版社2005年版。

冯文楼：《四大奇书的文本文化学诠释》，中国社会科学出版社2003

年版。

高明阁：《〈水浒传〉论稿》，辽宁大学出版社1987年版。

高日晖、洪雁：《水浒传接受史》，齐鲁书社2006年版。

［日］宫崎市定：《宫崎市定说水浒——虚构的好汉与掩藏的历史》，赵翻、杨晓钟译，陕西人民出版社2008年版。

郭英德：《四大名著讲演录》，广西师范大学出版社2006年版。

顾钧：《卫三畏与美国早期汉学》，外语教学与研究出版社2009年版。

顾伟列主编：《20世纪中国古代文学国外传播与研究》，华东师范大学出版社2011年版。

［美］海陶伟编：《英美学人论中国古典文学》，香港中文大学出版社1973年版。

［美］韩南：《韩南中国小说论集》，王秋桂等译，北京大学出版社2008年版。

［德］汉斯—格奥尔格·加达默尔：《真理与方法》（上、下卷），洪汉鼎译，上海译文出版社2004年版。

何心：《水浒研究》，上海文艺联合出版社1954年版。

胡士莹：《话本小说概论》，商务印书馆2011年版。

侯会：《水浒》与《西游》探源，学苑出版社2009年版。

黄鸣奋：《英语世界中国古典文学之传播》，学林出版社1997年版。

黄霖主编：《20世纪中国古代文学研究史（总论卷）》，东方出版中心2006年版。

黄霖主编：《20世纪中国古代文学研究史（小说卷）》，东方出版中心2006年版。

［德］胡戈·狄泽林克：《比较文学导论》，方维规译，北京师范大学出版社2009年版。

胡适：《中国古代章回小说考证》，实业印书馆1934年版。

纪德君：《中国古代小说文体及其他》，商务印书馆2012年版。

纪德君：《正说〈水浒传〉》，团结出版社2007年版。

［法］基亚：《比较文学》，颜保译，北京大学出版社1983年版。

金鑫荣：《明清讽刺小说研究》，凤凰出版社2007年版。

［丹麦］克尔凯郭尔：《论反讽概念——以苏格拉底为主线》，汤晨溪

译，中国社会科学出版社 2005 年版。

［美］勒内·韦勒克、奥斯丁·沃伦：《文学理论（修订版）》，刘象愚、邢培明、陈圣生、李哲明译，江苏教育出版社 2005 年版。

李辰冬：《〈三国〉、〈水浒〉与〈西游〉》，中国三峡出版社 2011 年版。

李桂奎：《元明小说叙事形态与物欲世态》，上海古籍出版社 2008 年版。

李希凡：《论中国古典小说的艺术形象》，上海文艺出版社 1961 年版。

李舜华：《明代章回小说的兴起》，上海古籍出版社 2012 年版。

［加］琳达·哈琴：《反讽之锋芒：反讽的理论与政见》，徐晓雯译，河南大学出版社 2010 年版。

林岗：《明清小说评点》，北京大学出版社 2012 年版。

刘仁圣等：《〈水浒〉文化大观》，百花洲文艺出版社 1997 年版。

刘世德编：《中国古代小说研究：台湾香港论文选集》，上海古籍出版社 1983 年版。

刘世德：《水浒论集》，社会科学文献出版社 2014 年版。

刘再复：《双典批判：对〈水浒传〉和〈三国演义〉的文化批判》，生活·读书·新知三联书店 2010 年版。

刘晓军：《章回小说文体研究》，华东师范大学出版社 2011 年版。

［美］鲁晓鹏：《从史实性到虚构性：中国叙事诗学》，王玮译、冯雪峰校，北京大学出版社 2012 年版。

鲁迅：《中国小说史略》，岳麓书社 2010 年版。

罗宗强：《明代文学思想史（上、下卷）》，中华书局 2013 年版。

［英］玛格丽特·A. 罗斯：《戏仿：古代、现代与后现代》，王海萌译，南京大学出版社 2013 年版。

马成生：《〈水浒〉通论》，浙江古籍出版社 1994 年版。

马蹄疾编：《水浒资料汇编》，中华书局 1977 年版。

马幼垣：《水浒人物之最》，生活·读书·新知三联书店 2006 年版。

马幼垣：《水浒论衡》，生活·读书·新知三联书店 2007 年版。

马幼垣：《水浒二论》，生活·读书·新知三联书店 2007 年版。

孟超：《水泊梁山英雄谱》，北京出版社 2013 年版。

聂绀弩：《中国古典小说论集》，复旦大学出版社 2006 年版。

聂绀弩：《〈水浒〉四议》，北京大学出版社 2010 年版。

宁稼雨：《〈水浒〉闲谈》，中国文史出版社 2009 年版。

欧阳代发：《话本小说史》，武汉出版社 1994 年版。

欧阳健、萧相恺：《水浒新议》，重庆出版社 1983 年版。

钱林森：《法国汉学家论中国文学——古典戏剧和小说》，外语教学与研究出版社 2007 年版。

［美］浦安迪：《明代小说四大奇书》，沈亨寿译，中国和平出版社 1993 年版。

［美］浦安迪：《中国叙事学》，北京大学出版社 1996 年版。

［美］浦安迪：《浦安迪自选集》，刘倩等译，生活·读书·新知三联书店 2011 年版。

齐裕焜、冯汝常等编著：《水浒学史》，上海三联书店 2015 年版。

曲家源：《水浒传新论》，中国和平出版社 1995 年版。

饶芃子等：《中西小说比较》，安徽教育出版社 1994 年版。

萨孟武：《水浒传与中国社会》，北京出版社 2005 年版。

邵子华：《〈水浒传〉人学研究》，齐鲁书社 2013 年版。

佘大平：《草莽英雄的悲壮人生〈水浒传〉》，云南人民出版社 1999 年版。

沈伯俊主编：《水浒研究论文集》，中华书局。

［美］孙康宜、宇文所安主编：《剑桥中国文学史（上、下卷）》，刘倩等译，生活·读书·新知三联书店 2013 年版。

孙述宇：《水浒传——怎样的强盗书》，上海古籍出版社 2011 年版。

孙建成：《〈水浒传〉英译的语言与文化》，复旦大学出版社 2008 年版。

孙一珍：《明代小说史》，中国社会科学出版社 2012 年版。

宋柏年主编：《中国古典文学在国外》，北京语言学院出版社 1994 年版。

水浒研究会编：《水浒争鸣》第 1 辑，长江文艺出版社 1982 年版。

水浒研究会编：《水浒争鸣》第 2 辑，长江文艺出版社 1983 年版。

水浒研究会编：《水浒争鸣》第 3 辑，长江文艺出版社 1984 年版。

水浒研究会编：《水浒争鸣》第 4 辑，长江文艺出版社 1985 年版。

水浒研究会编：《水浒争鸣》第 5 辑，武汉大学出版社 1987 年版。
水浒研究会编：《水浒争鸣》第 6 辑，光明日报出版社 2001 年版。
水浒研究会编：《水浒争鸣》第 7 辑，武汉出版社 2003 年版。
水浒研究会编：《水浒争鸣》第 8 辑，崇文书局 2006 年版。
水浒研究会编：《水浒争鸣》第 9 辑，青海人民出版社 2006 年版。
水浒研究会编：《水浒争鸣》第 10 辑，崇文书局 2008 年版。
水浒研究会编：《水浒争鸣》第 11 辑，中央文献出版社 2009 年版。
水浒研究会编：《水浒争鸣》第 12 辑，团结出版社 2011 年版。
水浒研究会编：《水浒争鸣》第 13 辑，团结出版社 2012 年版。

唐艳芳、赛珍珠：《〈水浒传〉翻译研究：后殖民理论的视角》，复旦大学出版社 2010 年版。

厦门大学历史系编：《李贽研究参考资料——李贽与〈水浒传〉》，福建人民出版社 1976 年版。

［美］夏志清：《中国古典小说史论》，胡益民等译，江西人民出版社 2001 年版。

王丽娜：《中国古代小说戏曲名著在国外》，学林出版社 1988 年版。

王逢振选编：《疆界 2——国际文学与文化》，人民文学出版社 2003 年版。

［美］王靖宇：《金圣叹的生平及其文学批评》，谈蓓芳译，上海古籍出版社 2004 年版。

王平：《中国古代小说叙事研究》，河北人民出版社 2001 年版。

王同舟、陈文新：《〈水浒传〉豪侠人生》，武汉大学出版社 2002 年版。

王晓路主编：《北美汉学界的中国文学思想研究》，巴蜀书社 2008 年版。

王学泰：《游民文化与中国社会（上、下卷，增修版）》，同心出版社 2007 年版。

王学泰：《中国游民文化小史》，学习出版社 2011 年版。

王学泰：《中国游民》，上海远东出版社 2012 年版。

王学泰：《〈水浒〉识小录》，广西师范大学出版社 2012 年版。

王学泰、李新宇：《〈水浒传〉与〈三国演义〉批判》，天津古籍出版社 2004 年版。

[美]乌尔里希·韦斯坦因：《比较文学与文学理论》，刘象愚译，辽宁人民出版社1987年版。

魏崇新：《比较文学视阈中的中国古典文学》，外语教学与研究出版社2009年版。

萧相恺：《话说水浒传》，江苏人民出版社2012年版。

萧相恺：《〈水浒传〉鉴赏辞典》，上海辞书出版社2013年版。

谢天振：《译介学导论》，北京大学出版社2007年版。

许明龙：《欧洲十八世纪"中国热"》，外语教学与研究出版社2008年版。

徐志啸：《北美学者中国古代诗学研究》，上海古籍出版社2011年版。

徐志啸主编：《中国古代文学在欧洲》，河北教育出版社2013年版。

严绍璗：《日藏汉籍善本书录》，中华书局2007年版。

严绍璗：《汉籍在日本的流布研究》，江苏古籍出版社1992年版。

阎嘉主编：《文学理论精粹读本》，中国人民大学出版社2010年版。

姚君伟编：《赛珍珠论中国小说》，南京大学出版社2012年版。

[美]伊恩·P. 瓦特：《小说的兴起》，高原、董红钧译，生活·读书·新知三联书店1992年版。

袁世硕：《文学史学的明清小说研究》，天津教育出版社2008年版。

乐黛云、张铁夫主编：《多元文化语境中的文学》，湖南文艺出版社1994年版。

乐黛云：《跨文化之桥》，北京大学出版社2002年版。

乐黛云：《比较文学与比较文化十讲》，复旦大学出版社2004年版。

张锦池：《中国四大古典小说论稿》，华艺出版社1993年版。

张锦池：《〈水浒传〉考论》，人民出版社2014年版。

张少康：《中国文学理论批评史（下）》，北京大学出版社2005年版。

张同胜：《〈水浒传〉诠释史论》，齐鲁书社2009年版。

郑振铎：《中国文学论集》，岳麓书社2011年版。

郑公盾：《水浒传论文集》，宁夏人民出版社1983年版。

周发祥、李岫主编：《中外文学交流史》，湖南教育出版社1999年版。

周思源：《新解〈水浒传〉》，中华书局2007年版。

周思源等著：《名家品〈水浒〉》，过常宝、刘德广主编，李克选编，中国华侨出版社2009年版。

竺青选编：《名家解读〈水浒传〉》，山东人民出版社1998年版。

朱迪光：《信仰·母题·叙事：中国古典小说新探索》，中国社会科学出版社2007年版。

朱立元主编：《当代西方文艺理论》（增补版），华东师范大学出版社2005年版。

朱一玄编：《明清小说资料汇编》（上下卷），南开大学出版社2012年版。

朱一玄、刘毓忱编：《水浒传资料汇编》，南开大学出版社2012年版。

（三）论文类

相关重要博士论文：

白军芳：《〈水浒传〉与〈红楼梦〉的性别诗学研究》，陕西师范大学，2005年。

邓百意：《中国古代小说节奏论》，复旦大学，2007年。

丁利荣：《金圣叹美学思想研究》，武汉大学，2007年。

郭冰：《明清时期"水浒"接受研究》，浙江大学，2005年。

高日晖：《〈水浒传〉接受史研究》，复旦大学，2003年。

韩颖琦：《中国传统小说叙事模式的"红色经典"化》，苏州大学，2008年。

刘晓军：《明代章回小说文体研究》，华东师范大学，2007年。

孙建成：《〈水浒传〉英译的语言与文化》，复旦大学，2007年。

舒媛媛：《水浒故事之流变与传播研究》，苏州大学，2008年。

唐艳芳：《赛珍珠〈水浒传〉翻译研究：后殖民理论的视角》，华东师范大学，2009年。

张曙光：《中国古代叙事文本评点理论研究：以金圣叹评点为中心的现代阐释》，山东师范大学，2008年。

张同胜：《〈水浒传〉诠释史论》，山东大学，2007年。

张扬：《胡适与古典小说研究》，山东师范大学，2012年。

相关重要期刊论文：

爱伦·魏德玛博士：《谈美国的明、清小说研究》，蔡宇知整理，《安徽教育学院学报》，1986年第3期。

顾廷龙、沈津：《关于新发现的〈京本忠义传〉残页》，《学习与批判》1975年第12期。

郭振勤：《从生成史略论〈水浒传〉的主题》，《汕头大学学报》1993年第3期。

韩晓谅：《〈水浒〉主题新解》，《明清小说研究》1994年第2期。

何满子：《从宋元说话家数探索〈水浒〉繁简本渊源及其作者问题》，《中华文史论丛》1982年第4辑。

黄卫总：《明清小说研究在美国》，明清小说研究，1995年第2期。

黄霖、陈荣：《论〈水浒〉研究中的"市民说"》，《水浒争鸣》第二辑，长江文艺出版社1983年版。

黄霖：《一种值得注目的〈水浒〉古本》，《复旦学报》1980年第4期。

李萍：《中华文化海外传播的策略性思考——基于"四大名著"海外传播的分析》，《现代传媒》2012年第1期。

李希凡：《〈水浒〉的作者和〈水浒〉的长篇结构》，《文艺月报》1956年第1期。

李永祜：《评〈水浒〉招安结局的思想倾向》，《水浒争鸣》第二辑，长江文艺出版社1983年版。

刘占勋、张同胜：《〈水浒传〉文学意义的海外阐释》，《哈尔滨工业大学学报》（社会科学版）2008年第3期。

茅盾：《谈〈水浒〉的人物和结构》，《文艺报》二卷二期，1950年。

倪长康：《封建长夜中的一个理想国梦——〈水浒〉主题之我见》，《明清小说研究》1991年第1期。

欧恢章：《〈水浒传〉主题的多元与主元》，《重庆师范学院学报》1997年第4期。

宋克夫：《乱世忠义的悲歌——论〈水浒传〉的主题及思维方式》，《湖北大学学报》1993年第6期。

佘树声：《论〈水浒传〉的悲剧意义》，《齐鲁学刊》1999年第3期。

孙一珍：《〈水浒传〉主题辨》，《文艺研究》1979年第3期。

谭汝谦：《中日之间翻译事业的几个问题》，《日本研究》1985 年第 3 期。

唐富龄：《宋江形象的分裂性、统一性及其他》，《水浒争鸣》第一辑，长江文艺出版社 1982 年。

唐艳芳：《时代背景与译者主体的互动——论赛珍珠〈水浒传〉英译选材的主体性》，《浙江师范大学学报》（社会科学版）2007 年第 5 期。

王丽娜：《〈水浒传〉外文论著简介》，《湖北大学学报》（哲学社会科学版）1985 年第 3 期。

王丽娜：《〈水浒传〉在国外（上）》，《天津外国语学院学报》1998 年第 1 期。

王丽娜：《〈水浒传〉在国外（下）》，《天津外国语学院学报》1998 年第 2 期。

王俊年、裴效维、金宁芬：《〈水浒传〉是一部什么样的作品》，《文学评论》1978 年第 4 期。

王开富：《〈水浒传〉是写农民起义的吗?》，《重庆师院学报》1980 年第 3 期。

王利器：《〈水浒〉与农民革命》，1953 年 5 月 27 日《光明日报》。

王利器：《〈水浒全传〉是怎样纂修的?》，《文学评论》1982 年第 3 期。

王齐洲：《〈水浒传〉的结构"不是有机的"吗?》，《水浒争鸣》第四辑，长江文艺出版社 1985 年。

王齐洲：《〈水浒传〉是描写农民起义的作品吗?》，《水浒争鸣》第一辑，长江文艺出版社 1982 年。

文军、罗张：《国内〈水浒传〉英译研究三十年》，《民族研究》2011 年第 1 期。

温秀颖、孙建成：《〈水浒传〉英译七十年》，见 2008 年世界翻译大会论文集。

杨光宗、李春梅、龙亚莉：《试论〈水浒传〉的文本演变及文学经典的建构》，《北方民族大学学报》（哲学社会科学版）2012 年第 4 期。

叶朝承、文燎原：《翻译目的论视角之〈水浒传〉习语英译对比研究》，《湖北工业大学学报》2012 年第 3 期。

徐剑平、梁金花：《文学翻译中审美的"陌生化"取向——以赛珍珠英译〈水浒传〉为例》，江苏大学学报（社会科学版）2009年第4期。

伊永文：《〈水浒传〉是反映市民阶层利益的作品》，《天津师院学报》1975年第4期。

伊永文：《再论〈水浒传〉是反映市民阶层利益的作品》，《河北大学学报》1980年第4期。

俞平伯：《论〈水浒传〉七十回古本的有无》，《小说月报》十九卷四号。

赵苗：《〈水浒传〉与江湖日本》，《文史知识》2010年第4期。

张锦池：《"乱世忠义"的颂歌——论〈水浒〉故事的思想倾向》，《社会科学战线》1983年第4期。

周维衍：《〈水浒传〉的成书年代和作者问题——从历史地理方面考证》，《学术月刊》1984年第7期。

庄华萍：《赛珍珠的〈水浒传〉翻译及其对西方的叛逆》，《浙江大学学报》（人文社会科学版）2010年第9期。

外文文献

（一）《水浒传》英译版本

全译本

Pearl S. Buck, trans. *All Men Are Brothers* (*The Water Margin*; *Shui-hu chuan*). 2 vols. New York：John Day, 1933; reprint, New York：Grove, 1957. New York：Moyer Bell Ltd, U.S, 2004.

Sidney Shapiro, trans. *Outlaws of the Marsh*. 3 vols. Peking：Foreign Language Press, 1980.

J. H. Jackson, trans. *The Water Margin*. Shang hai：The Commercial Press, Limited, 1937.

John and Alex Dent-Young., trans. *The Marshes of Mount Liang*. Hong Kong：The Chinese University Press, 1994-2002.

选译本

Crump James Irving. Selections from the *Shui-hu chuan*. New Haven：Far Eastern Publications, Yale University, 1947.

Zhao Ji'nan, adapt. The rescue in wild boar forest. Beijing：Zhaohua Publ. House, 1982.

（二）研究论著、文集

Albert Chan. The glory and fall of the Ming dynasty. Norman: University of Oklahoma Press, 1982.

Albert E Dien. Glossary for the *Shui-hu chuan*. Taipei: [Rev. ed.] [Preliminary version]. 1963.

Birch Cyril. Ed., Studies in Chinese Literary Genres, Berkeley: University of California Press, 1974.

Chang, Shelley Hsueh-lun. History and legend: ideas and images in the Ming historical novels. Ann Arbor University of Michigan Press, 1990.

David L. Rolston, Reading and Writing Between the Lines: Traditional Chinese Fiction and Fiction Commentary, Stanford: Stanford University Press, 1997.

David Rolston Edited. How to Read the Chinese Novel, Princeton: Princeton University Press, 1990.

David T. Roy. Chang Chu-p'o's Commentary on the *Chin p'ing mei*, Chinese Narrative: Critical and Theoretical Essays. Ed. Andrew H. Plaks. Princeton, N. J.: Princeton University Press, 1977.

David Rolston. Ed., How to Read the Chinese Novel, Princeton: Princeton University Press, 1980.

David Rolston, Traditional Chinese Fiction and Fiction Commentary: Reading and Writing Between the Lines, Stanford: Stanford University Press, 1997.

Frederick Paul Brandauer; Junjie Huang. Imperial rulership and cultural change in traditional China. Seattle: University of Washington Press, 1994.

Hanan Patrick. Chinese Fiction of the Nineteen and Early Twentieth Centuries. New York: Columbia University Press, 2004.

Hsia. C. T., On Chinese Literature. New York: Columbia University Press, 2004.

Hsia. C. T., The Military Romance: A Genre of Chinese Fiction. Studies in Chinese Literary Genres. E d. Cyril Birch. Berkeley, Calif.: University of California Press, 1974.

Idema W. L, Chinese Vernacular Fiction: The Formative Period, Leiden:

E. J. Brill, 1974.

James J. Y. Liu, The Chinese Knight-Errant, Chicago: University of Chicago Press, 1967.

Judith T. Zeitlin, Historian of the Strange: Pu Songling and the Chinese Classical Tale (Stanford: Stanford University Press, 1993).

Judith T. Zeitlin & Lydia H. Liu, with Ellen Widmer. Ed. Writing and materiality in China: essays in honor of Patrick Hanan. Cambridge, Mass. : Published by Harvard University Asia Center for Harvard-Yenching Institute: distributed by Harvard University Press, 2003.

Lai Ming, A History of Chinese Literature, New York: John Day & Co., 1964.

Leon M Zolbrod. Tigers, boars and severed heads: parallel series of episodes in *Eight "dogs"* and *Men of the marshes*. Vancouver: University of British Columbia, Dept. of Asian Studies, 1967.

Liu Chun-jo, "People, Places, and Times in Five Modern Chinese Novels," Conference on Oriental-Western Literary and Cultural Relations. Asia and the Humanities Series, ed. by Horst Frenz; Indiana University, 1959.

Liu Wu-chi, An Introduction to Chinese Literature, Bloomington: Indiana University Press, 1966.

Margaret Berry. The Chinese Classic Novels (Routledge Revivals): An Annotated Bibliography of Chiefly English-language Studies. Hoboken: Taylor & Francis, 2010.

Lu Sheldon Hsiao-peng, From Historicity to Fictionality: The Chinese Poetics of Narrative, Stanford: Stanford University Press, 1994.

Mair Victor H.. Ed. The Columbia history of Chinese literature. New York: Columbia University Press, 2001.

Mair Victor H.. Ed. Women and men, Love and Power: Parameters of Chinese Fiction and Drama, SINO-PLATONIC PAERS, (Novermber, 2009).

Minds and mentalities in traditional Chinese literature. edited by Halvor Eifring. Beijing: Culture and Art Pub. House, 1999.

Plaks Andrew. The Four Masterworks of the Ming Novel. Princeton: Princeton University Press, 1987.

Plaks Andrew. Ed. Chinese narrative: critical and theoretical essays. Princeton, N. J.: Princeton University Press, 1977.

Raymond Dawson. Ed. The legacy of China. London: Oxford University Press, 1971.

Richard Gregg. Irwin, The evolution of a Chinese novel: *Shui-hu-chuan*. Cambridge, Mass. : Harvard University Press, 1953.

Robert E. Hegel. Man as Responsible Being: The Individual, Social Role, and Heaven. The Novel in Seventeenth-Century China. New York: Columbia University Press, 1981.

Robert Ruhlmann, Traditional Heroes in Chinese Popular Fiction, The Confucian Persuasion, ed. by Arthur F. Wright, California: Stanford University Press, 1960.

Robert Hegel E. . Maturation and Conflicting Values: Two Novelists' Portraits of the Chinese Hero Ch'in Shu-pao. Critical Essays on Chinese Fiction. Ed. Winston L. Y. Yang and Curtis P. Adkins. Hong Kong: Chinese University Press, 1980.

Rosa Covarrubias; Adriana Williams; Miguel Covarrubias; Terry Horrigan. The China I knew. San Francisco: Protean Press, 2005.

Shan Te-hsing, The AestheticResponse in Chin-p'i shui-hu: An Iserian Reading of Chin Sheng- t'an's Commentary Edition of The Shui-hu chuan, In John C. Y. Wang, ed. Chinese Literary Criticism of the Ch'ing Period (1644 – 1911), Hong Kong: Hong Kong University Press, 1993.

Sidney Shapiro, translator's Note, *Outlaws of the Marsh*. 3 vols. Peking: Foreign Language Press, 1980.

Wang Tai Jane. The comparison of Dostoevsky's Notes from underground and the Chinese novel *Shui hu chuan*: a Chinese predecessor of Dostoevsky's anti-hero. Monterey, Calif. : Monterey Institute of International Studies, 1985.

Wang Ching [Jing] . The story of the stone: intertextuality, ancient Chinese stone love, and the stone symbolism in *Dream of the red chamber* [Hung-lou meng], *Water margin* [Shui-hu chuan] and *The Journey to the West* [Hsi-yu chi] Durham: Duke University Press, 1992.

Wang John C. Y. , Chin Sheng-t'an, N. Y. : Twayne, 1972.

Wider Ellen, The Margins of Utopia, Cambridge: Harvard University Press, 1987.

Wong siu-kit, Early Chinese Literary Criticism. Hong Kong: Joint Publishing Co., 1983.

Yang Lo-sa. The works of Defoe in comparison with *Shui hu chuan*. Taibei: Zhuan xian wen hua shi ye gong si, 1984.

(三) 期刊论文

B. Csongon. On the Prehistory of *Shui-hu Chuan*. Acta Orienta'lia. Vol. 25 (1972).

B. Csongon. On the Popularity of the *Shui-hu Chuan*. Acta Orienta'lia. Vol. 28 (1974).

B. Csongon. A Comparative Analysis of *Shui-hu Chuan* and *His yu Chi*: The bounds of the Classic Chinese Novel. Acta Orienta'lia. Vol. 29 (1975).

Bruno Lasker, Interrelations of Cultures: Their Contribution to International Understanding; The Evolution of a Chinese Novel: *Shui-hu-chuan*. by Richard Gregg Irwin (Book Review). Pacific Affairs, Vol. 28, No. 2 (Jun., 1955).

Charles J, Alber. A Survey of English language Criticism of the *Shui-hu Chuan*. Tsing Hua Journal of Chinese studies. Vol. 2 (1969).

Ch'en Shou-Yi, Hua-Pen to Novel. Chinese Literature: A Historical Introduction. New York: The Ronald Press Company, 1961.

Chuang H. C. Chang, "Chinese Literature: Popular Fiction and Drama" (Book Review), Jounal of Asian Studies, 34: 2 (1975: Feb).

C. P. Fitrgenald, Chinese novel as a Subversive Force. Meanjin Quaterly, Vol. 10 (951: Spring1).

Deborah Porter. Setting the Tone: Aesthetic Implications of Linguistic Patterns in the Opening Section of *Shui-hu chuan*. Chinese Literature: Essays, Articles, Reviews (CLEAR), Vol. 14 (1992: Dec.).

Deborah Porter. Toward an Aesthetic of Chinese Vernacular Fiction: Style and the Colloquial Medium of*Shui-hu chuan*. T'oung Pao, Second Series, Vol. 79, Fasc. 1/3 (1993).

Deborah L. Porter. The Formation of an Image: An Analysis of the Linguistic Patterns That Form the Character of Sung Chiang. Journal of the American Oriental Society, Vol. 112, No. 2 (Apr. - Jun., 1992).

Frederick Paul Brandauer. The emperor and the star spirits: a mythological reading of the *Shui-hu chuan*. In: Brandauer Huang (Ed.), Imperial rulership and cultural change in traditional China (1994).

Ge Liangyan. The writer learns to babble: the textualization of the *Shui-hu chuan*. In Tamkang Review. Vol. 25 (1994).

Ge Liangyan. Authoring "Authorial Intention": Jin Shengtan as Creative Critic. Chinese Literature: Essays, Articles, Reviews (CLEAR), Vol. 25 (Dec., 2003).

Hans H. Frankel, "The Chinese Novel: a Confrontation Of Critical Approaches to Chinese and Western Novels," Literature East and West, VIII, No. 1, Winter, 1964.

Hayden George. A Skeptical Note on the early history of *Shui-hu Chuan*. Monumenta Serica, Vol. 32 (1976).

Hanan Patrick. Sources of The *Chin P'ing Mei*. Asia Major N. S. (10: 1), 1963.

Hegel Roberte., Widmer, The Margins of Utopia: *Shui-hu hou-chuan* and the Literature of Ming Loyalism (Book Review), Jounal of Asian Studies, 47: 1 (1988: Feb).

Huang Martin W, Author (ity) and Reader in Traditional Chinese Xiaoshuo Commentary, Chinese Literature: Essays, Articles, Reviews 16 (1994).

Hsia. C. T. Comparative Approaches to *Water Margin*. Yearbook of Comparative and General Literature. Vol. 11 (1962).

James I. Crump, A Sherwood in Kiangsu (Book Review), Chicago Review, 12: 1 (1958: Spring).

James Robert Hightower, Topics in Chinese Literature, outlines and Bibliographies, Harvard- Yenching Institute Studies, Vol. III, Cambridge, Mass.: Harvard University Press, 1962.

J. I. Crump, The Evolution of a Chinese Novel: *Shui-hu-chuan* by Richard Gregg Irwin. (Book Review) Journal of the American Oriental Society,

Vol. 74, No. 2 (Apr. - Jun., 1954).

Jean Chesneaux. The modern relevance of *Shui-hu Chuan*: its influence on rebel movements in nineteenth-and twentieth-century China. Papers on Far Eastern history-Canberra. Vol. 3 (1971 Mar).

Jenner, Tough Guys, Mateship and Honour: Another Chinese Tradition. East Asia History, 1996.

Jonker D. R., Cyril Birch (ed.), "Anthology of Chinese Literature, from early times to the fourteenth century" (Book Review), T'oung pao, 53 (1967).

John Fitzgerald, Continuity within Discontinuity: The Case of *Water Margin* Mythology. Modern China, Vol. 12, No. 3 (Jul., 1986).

Johnl Bishop. Some Limitations of Chinese Fiction. Far Eastern Quarterly, 15: 2 (1956: Feb).

J. R. Hightower. Individualism in Chinese Literature. Journal of the History of Ideas. Vol. 22 (1961).

Ma. Y. W., The Chinese Historical Novel: An Outline of Themes and Contexts. Journal of Asian Studies, 34.2 (1975: Feb).

Ma. Y. W., PLAKS (ed), "Chinese narrative: Critical and Theoretical and Theoretical Essays" (Book Review), Journal of Asian Studies, 38: 12 (1978: Nov).

Ogawa Tamaki. The Author of the *Shui-hu chuan*. Monumenta Serica, Vol. 17 (1958).

Paul Jakov Smith. "*Shuihu zhuan*" and the Military Subculture of the Northern Song, 960 – 1127. Harvard Journal of Asiatic Studies, Vol. 66, No. 2 (2006 Dec.).

Paize Keulemans, Cha zeng ben jianben *shuihu zhuan* cunwen jijiao 插增本簡本水滸傳存文輯較 (A Compilation of the Extant jianben editions of "The Expanded *Outlaws of the Marsh*"), 2 vols by Y. W. Ma 馬幼垣. (Book Review) Chinese Literature: Essays, Articles, Reviews (CLEAR), Vol. 28 (Dec., 2006)。

Paize Keulemans, *Shuihu* er lun 水滸二論 (A second Discussion of the Outlaws) by Y. W. Ma 馬幼垣; *Shuihu* renwu zhi zui 水滸人物之最 (The

Outlaws' Most Characters) by Y. W. Ma 馬幼垣. （Book Review）Chinese Literature: Essays, Articles, Reviews（CLEAR）, Vol. 30（Dec. , 2008）。

Pearl S. Buck, China in the Mirror of her Fiction. Pacific Affairs, Vol. 3, No. 2（Feb. , 1930）.

Pearl S. Buck, East and West and the Novel, Bulletin of The American University Women Association, 1931.

Pearl S. Buck, The Early Chinese Novel, The Saturday Review of Literature, No. 46, Vol. 7, 1931.

Pearl S. Buck, *Introduction of Shui Hu Chuan*, *All Men Are Brothers*, NewYork: The John Day Company, 1933.

Pearl S. Buck, The Chinese Novel, NewYork: The John Day Company, 1939.

Plaks Andrew. *Shui-hu Chua*n and the Sixteenth-Century Novel Form: An Interpretive Reappraisal. Chinese Literature: Essays, Articles, Reviews（CLEAR）, Vol. 2, No. 1（1980: Jan. ）.

R. G. Irwin. *Water Margin* Revisited. T'oung Pao, Vol. 48（1960）.

Shadick Harold, Cyril Birch（ed. ）,"Anthology of Chinese Literature, from early times to the fourteenth century"（Book Review）, Journal of Asian Studies, 26: 1（1966: Nov）.

Shen Jing, Re-Visions of *Shuihu* Women in Chinese Theatre and Cinema. China Review; Spring 2007; 7, 1; Asian Business & Reference.

Sun Phillip. The Seditions Art of The *Water Margin*: Misogynists or Desperadoes? . Renditions. Vol. 1（Autumn, 1973）.

Shih Vincent Y. C, Richard Gregg Irwin, The Evolution of a Chinese Novel: *Shui-hu chuan*. Edited by Paul H. Vlyde and Donald Shively（Book Review）, Far Eastern Quarterly, 14: 1（1954: Nov. ）.

Sprenkel O. B. Vander, My several worlds. By Pearl Buck. Mandarin Red. By James Cameron. China Phoenix: The Revolution in China. By Peter Townsend（Book Review）, Spectator, 195: 6627（1955: July 1）.

Ts'un-yan Lui, C. T. HISA,"The Classic Chinese Novel: A Cricital Introduction,"（Book Review）, T'oung pao, 55（1969）.

Vincent Y. C. Shih, The Evolution of a Chinese Novel: *Shui-hu-chuan*. by

Richard Gregg Irwin. (Book Review) The Far Eastern Quarterly, Vol. 14, No. 1 (Nov., 1954).

Vibeke Bordahl. The man-hunting tiger: from "Wu Song Fights the Tiger" in Chinese traditions. Asian Folklore Studies. 66. 1 – 2 (2007: April-October).

Vibeke Bordahl. The storyteller's manner in Chinese storytelling. Asian Folklore Studies. 62. 1 (2003: Oct.).

Wang John C. Y., Yu (trans. and ed.), *The Journey to the West.* Vol. I (Book Review), Journal of Asian Studies, 37: 4 (1978: Aug.).

Wivell Charles. Wang, "Chin Sheng T'an" (Book Review), Journal of Asian Studies, 32 (1972: Nov. -1973: Aug.).

Winston L. Y. Yang, Nathan K. Mao and Peter Li, "*Romance of the Three Kingdoms* and *The Water Margin*," and "*Journey to the West* and *Flowers in the Mirror.*" Classical Chinese Fiction: A Guide to Its Study and Appreciation. London: George Prior Publishers, 1978.

Wu Yenna. Condemnation: Other Fiction. The Chinese Virago: A Literary Theme. Cambridge: Harvard University Press, 1995. Literature Criticism from 1400 to 1800. Ed. Lynn M. Zott. Vol. 76. Detroit: Gale, 2002. From Literature Resource Center.

Wu Yenna. "Outlaws' Dreams of Power and Position in *Shui hu zhuan.*" Chinese Literature: Essays, Articles, Reviews 18 (1996).

Wu Jack. The Morals of *All Men are Brothers.* Western Humanities Review. Vol. 17 (1963: Winter).

Wong Timothy. The Virtue of Yi in *Water Margin.* Journal of Oriental Literature. Vol. 7 (1966).

(四) 学位论文

Anne Farrer. The *Shui-hu chuan*: a study in the development of late Ming woodblock illustration. Thesis Ph. D. -University of London, 1984.

Chiu, Kuei-fen. Spatial form and the Chinese long vernacular "hsiaoshuo". Thesis (Ph. D.) -University of Washington, 1990.

De-an Wu Swihart. The Evolution of Chinese Novel form. Thesis Ph. D. -The Department of East Asian Studies of Princeton University, June 1990.

Deborah Lynn Porter. The style of *Shui – hu chuan*. Thesis Ph. D. -Princeton University, 1989.

Kathleen M. Tomlonovic. The function of the narrative frame in three classic Chinese novels: *Shui-hu chuan*, *Hsi-yu chi* and *Hung-lou meng*. Thesis M. A. -University of Iowa, 1977.

Lo Andrew Hing-bun. "*San-kuo chih yen-i* and *Shui-hu chuan* in the Context of Historiography. " Thesis Ph. D. diss. , Princeton University, 1981.

Mei Chun. Playful theatricals: performativity and theatricality in late Imperial Chinese narrative (Nai'an Shi, Guanzhong Luo, Cheng'en Wu). Thesis Ph. D. -Washington University, 2005.

Phyllis Carr. *San kuo yen i* and *Shui hu ch'uan*: a study of traditional patterns in the rise of Chinese Communism. Thesis A. B. , Honors in East Asian Studies-Harvard University, 1973.

Rolston David Lee. Theory and practice: fiction, fiction criticism, and the writing of the *Ju-lin wai-shih* (Volumes I-IV) Thesis Ph. D-The University of Chicago, 1988.

Talbott W Huey. Anti-orthodox styles and the charismatic tradition in China as revealed in three popular novels. ThesiPh. D-Massachusetts Institute of Technology, 1973.

Ted Chi-ssu Chen. Galloping mind, free-playing eyes: a Derridean re/ adding of mobile perspective in Chinese scroll painting and the Chinese classical novel: *Shui-Hu Chuan*. Thesis M. A-Tamkang University, 1989.

Yu Hong yuan. *Shuihu Zhuan* (*Water Margin*) as elite cultural discourse: reading, writing and the making of meaning. Thesis Ph. D-Ohio State University, 2000.

Yu-ting Jin. The formation and decay of Liang-shan-po: heroic destiny in-*Shui-hu chuan*. Thesis M. A. -University of Iowa, 1982.

Widmer Ellen. *Shui-hu hou-chuan* in the context of seventeenth century Chinese fiction criticism. Thesis Ph. D-Harvard University, 1981.

Wu Hua Laura, Jin Shengtan (1608 – 1661): Founder of a Chinese Theory of the Novel. Thesis Ph. D-University of Toronto, 1993.

致　　谢

本书是在本人博士学位论文的基础上修改而成的，是对英语世界《水浒传》研究所作的反馈性研究。能踏上此研究道路，得感谢我的恩师曹顺庆先生。

2011年9月，我来到四川大学，进入曹门攻读比较文学与世界文学博士学位。读博，选择博士毕业课题是最考量人智慧学识的事情。先后考虑了好几个论题，结果总不如意。迟迟不能定下博士毕业课题，心中万分焦虑。2012年7月27日下午3时许，其时已是假期，恩师给我来电，专门指导我毕业选题。通话中，曹师顺庆先生问我选题有无新进展，我说没有。恩师于是对我说，《水浒传》在英语国家（特别是英美两国）研究得比较充分，而且很多研究者的研究视角新颖、方法独特、观点让人耳目一新，要是能对他们的研究成果展开系统的研究引入国内，为国内的研究者提供外来的参照，其意义当为重大。在此次通话的最后，恩师建议我去做"英语世界的《水浒传》研究"这一课题。当时虽然说好，心中仍然犹豫。《水浒传》，贯华堂刻本，容与堂刻本，袁无涯刻本，都阅读过。阅读后两种刻本的《水浒传》，对我来说是比较悲伤的事情：伤心宋江的接受招安，伤心梁山众好汉的死伤离散，伤心水浒英雄的悲剧命运。悲伤归悲伤，选题既定，就得日夜兼程搜集英语世界批评者的《水浒传》研究资料，研读具体的研究文献。在曹师顺庆先生的悉心指导之下，历经18个月，博士研究课题"英语世界的《水浒传》研究"终于完成，并顺利通过专家审查和答辩。感谢曹师顺庆先生对我学业的悉心指导，引领我踏上科研之路。正是先生的指引、鼓励，让我有勇气在后来的日子里在科研的道路上继续拼搏前行。

博士科研课题"英语世界的《水浒传》研究"能够顺利完成，还得感谢中国社会科学院的张中良教授，湘潭大学的何云波教授，四川大学的赵毅衡教授、唐小林教授和阎嘉教授，四川师范大学的杨颖育教授……正是他们提出的宝贵意见和建议，让拙著能付梓刊行。

一路走来，能够十年坚持求学的梦想，还得感谢父母家人的理解和支持。十年求学路，风雨兼程，磕磕绊绊，挫折不少。每当心无所依，是父母，是家人，让我获得灵魂停靠的港湾。从而在休整之后，又有了重新上路的勇气和力量，终于走到现在。我要感谢我那双鬓斑白、年近古稀的父母，感谢我那在黄土地上挥洒汗水劳动的诚实本分的兄弟，以及姐姐一家。

在四川大学求学期间，在博士论文的撰写过程中，得到很多同学、朋友的支持和帮助。我诚挚感谢你们。亦师亦友的北大博士胡根法，竭尽所能帮我复印英文文献，并在第一时间把这些资料邮寄给我；师兄李伟荣，远在美国为我搜集英文研究文献，并在翻译文献过程中多次为我排解疑难，还为我校对了"中英文人名、术语译名对照表"；在厦门且工且学的小友（钟）秀珍，不仅帮助我制作论文中的多幅图表，还在我为毕业论文焦虑不安之际为我排解心结；四川大学外国语学院的杨司桂博士，也为我的文献翻译出谋划策；师兄张盛强，师弟林何，也为我毕业论文的顺利完成出力颇多。真诚感谢你们。

要感谢的人还有很多。同窗（王）永祥、张艮、（王）树文、（薛）宝生、（郭）明浩等一众好友的关心和帮助，为孤寂单调的学习生活增添了许多快乐。要感谢的人还有很多，谢意也非言语所能达。只能就此作罢。

人生如斯，感谢生我者父母，教我者师友。

做学问，搞研究，是必须严肃认真谨慎的。限于本人的学识水平，拙著中错误之处在所难免，恳请方家不吝批评指正。

谢春平

2015年5月于宋城赣南师范学院寓所